NO STAR IS LOST

James T. Farrell

with an Introduction by
Charles Fanning

D1449295

University of Illinois Press
Urbana and Chicago

Library of Congress Cataloging-in-Publication Data
Farrell, James T. (James Thomas), 1904–1979.
No star is lost / James Farrell ; with an introduction
by Charles Fanning.
p.   cm.
Includes bibliographical references.
ISBN-13: 978-0-252-03174-8 (acid-free paper)
ISBN-10: 0-252-03174-1 (acid-free paper)
ISBN-13: 978-0-252-07422-6 (pbk. : acid-free paper)
ISBN-10: 0-252-07422-x (pbk. : acid-free paper)
1. Irish Americans—Fiction.
2. South Chicago (Chicago, Ill.)—Fiction.
I. Title.
PS3511.A738N62   2007
813'.52—dc22   2006030908

NO STAR
IS LOST

James T. Farrell's O'Neill-O'Flaherty Novels: An Introduction

Charles Fanning

Background

James T. Farrell's 1935 story, "The Oratory Contest," presents George O'Dell, a middle-aged Chicago streetcar driver, and his sixteen-year-old son Gerry, who is about to compete in the senior oratorical contest at Mary Our Mother School on the city's South Side. This story opens with Gerry practicing before the bathroom mirror, "imagining the thunder of applause that would greet him at the conclusion of his oration." The scene recalls the opening of Farrell's first novel, *Young Lonigan*, published three years earlier, where Studs Lonigan strikes hard-boiled poses before his mirror on the night of graduation from eighth grade at St. Patrick's School. I believe that this is a deliberate echo, and that Farrell is making the point that two boys from the same neighborhood and Catholic school system can go in very different directions. That point would have been sharp in 1935, for the third Lonigan novel, *Judgment Day*, in which the hapless Studs dies at twenty-nine, had appeared in April, and the trilogy was published in one volume in November. The contrast is pronounced, for Gerry O'Dell is a successful student, encouraged by his teachers and considering college, although he can't afford to go unless, as his father suggests, he can "get a job and study law in the evenings downtown at St. Vincent's."

As he and his other son Michael approach the high school, George feels "increasingly timid," and realizes "that Gerry, instead of waiting for him and Michael, had gone ahead. Gerry, he suddenly felt, was ashamed of him. He argued with himself that the boy had had to get there early, and that, anyway, he had been nervous about the contest and restless, like a colt before the start of a race. But still, no, he could not rid his mind of that thought." In the ensuing competition, Gerry speaks eloquently and wins the gold medal. George O'Dell is moved to tears and "a simple and childlike joy" by his son's victory. After rushing out to a drugstore to telephone the news to his wife, he returns to congratulate his son, only to find the stage empty: "Gerry must have gone. He told himself that Gerry had known that his father would wait to see him, congratulate him, buy him a treat, and that then they would go home together. And Gerry had not waited." George O'Dell searches the few remaining faces, asks a crowd of boys if anyone has seen his son, and then the story ends: "He stood with Michael. Only a few scattered groups remained in front of the hall. Feeling blank, he told himself, yes, Gerry had gone. He solemnly led Michael away, both of them silent. He asked himself why Gerry hadn't waited, and he knew the answer to his question."[1]

When I first read this story in the late 1970s, I felt the shock of recognition, because it's my story too. My father was a school custodian, and on the night when I competed in the local high school essay contest, he was not seated in the audience, but on duty in the building, standing at the back of the auditorium. When I emerged from the hall clutching the first-prize check for $25, he was in the foyer leaning on a push broom. I remember always having been proud of how hard he worked, especially in winter when he'd have to get up at four in the morning to shovel snow. And my memory of that evening is that I went right over and shook his hand. But I could so easily have been Gerry O'Dell, and I'm sure that sometimes I was. There is no more effective rendering in American fiction of the gulf that can develop between working-class parents and their better-educated children than "The Oratory Contest." The story exemplifies the great strengths of James T. Farrell's fiction: plain-style austerity in the telling, realistic presentation of pain that can be understood but not alleviated, and a mutually reinforcing combination of clarity and compassion—the whole rendered without a scrap of condescension toward the characters and situations.

"The Oratory Contest" points straight toward the second phase of Farrell's achievement, his five O'Neill-O'Flaherty novels: *A World I Never Made* (1936), *No Star Is Lost* (1938), *Father and Son* (1940), *My Days of Anger* (1943), and *The Face of Time* (1953). His first two major cycles, the *Studs Lonigan* trilogy (published in 1932, 1934, and 1935) and the O'Neill-O'Flaherty pentalogy, share a setting (the South Side neighborhood around Washington Park where Farrell himself grew up), a time frame (roughly 1890 to 1930), and many characters. Farrell's own childhood around Fifty-eighth Street had much more in common with the experience of young Danny O'Neill in the second series than with that of Studs Lonigan. However, with a wisdom unusual in young writers, Farrell knew that in order to deal in a balanced way with his own emotionally laden personal experience, he ought to tell Studs's story first. But Farrell's eight Washington Park novels actually comprise one coherent grand design with two contrasting movements: the downward, negative alternative embodied in the passive, doomed Studs, and the upward, positive possibility embodied in Danny, who grows up to become a writer.

In June 1929 Farrell had written a publisher that he was "working on two novels. One is a realistic story of a corner gang at Fifty Eighth and Prairie Avenue of this city. . . . The other novel is a tale of a boy in a Catholic high school of this city during the early part of the jazz age." After finishing *The Young Manhood of Studs Lonigan* in 1934, Farrell reported to Ezra Pound: "one more Lonigan book to come, and I'm writing it, . . . and also am working on a long story of a family, Irish American, with a lot of autobiography, that extends from 1911 to 1933, and intends to shoot the works, and include a number of things I've held back in my other books. It may be anywhere from one to five volumes." Farrell published the first O'Neill novel, *A World I Never Made*, in October 1936. Shortly thereafter, he explained to a friend that the new series "is conceived as a complementary study to 'Studs Lonigan.' One [of] the main characters, Danny O'Neill, is planned as a character whose life experience is to be precisely the opposite of Studs." Farrell held to this conception through the writing of the remaining volumes. While finishing up the final draft of *My Days of Anger*, he wrote his publisher that "I think now, it'll come out right, and be a fitting end to the series—and a fitting companion series to *Studs Lonigan*—and that Danny and Studs will stand as I conceived them—dialectical opposites in their destinies—one goes up, the other goes down."[2] The two sequences and the many short stories that share the same South Side setting (there are at least fifty stories about Danny O'Neill) constitute a full-scale fictional chronicle of three generations of urban Americans, from nineteenth-century immigrant laborers to Depression-era intellectuals, grounded in a specific place with clear reference points like the markings on a compass. Farrell's sense of the scope and the integrity of his Chicago fiction was already clear by August 1934 when he wrote to a friend: "I hope to run to at least twenty volumes of novels and short stories attempting to describe, represent, analyze and portray connected social areas of Chicago that I have lived in, and that I have more or less assimilated. In these terms, then, the various books and stories are all panels of one work."[3]

The grandson of Irish immigrants and the son of a teamster and a former domestic servant, Farrell was born on February 27, 1904, raised in South Side Chicago neighborhoods near Washington Park, and educated at Corpus Christi and St. Anselm's Catholic grammar schools and St. Cyril's Carmelite High School, graduating in 1923. Because his parents had many children and little money, he lived from age two with his maternal grandparents and his unmarried uncles and aunts who were better off, and this double perspective of belonging to two families both enriched and complicated his youth. Farrell was first encouraged to write by his eighth-grade teacher at St. Anselm's, Sister Magdalen. He recalls sitting at the parlor window of his grandmother's apartment on South Park Avenue overlooking Washington Park on a rainy Saturday in autumn. Planning out an essay on Andrew Jackson and the United States Bank, "for the first time in my life I experienced that absorption, that exhilaration, and that compulsion which drives you to sit alone and write with the immediate world about you walled out of your consciousness and with your impulses to have fun in the present put to sleep." At St. Cyril's, which is still open at the same location at Sixty-fourth Street and Dante Avenue as Mount Carmel High School, he was further encouraged by two of the Carmelite fathers who were his English teachers, Father Leo J. Walter and Father Albert Dolan. He remembers that in his first year he wrote "an essay of two pages about two boys who didn't want to fight and who talked toughly to one another. Here was a dim forecast of my future writing." This piece became "Helen, I Love You," the first Farrell story to appear in a national publication—H. L. Mencken's *American Mercury* in July 1932. He wrote "out of passion and interest," often about baseball and the White Sox, including a long piece about the Black Sox scandal, which broke during his second year of high school, and the school magazine published his first piece of fiction, "Danny's Uncle," a vignette of the street encounter of young "Danny O'Neil" with his wealthy uncle. "We boys were naive," Farrell remembered. "We did not come from cultivated households. We did not live in a cultural milieu." And yet, under the tutelage of the Carmelites, he took his first "slow step" toward "self-expression and self-consciousness."[4]

Over the next five years, Farrell worked for an express company and as a gas station attendant, took a semester of prelaw courses at De Paul University night school, and enrolled for several quarters at the University of Chicago. In March 1927 he had resolved to be a writer, and embarked on a fierce regimen of reading and writing, in and out of schools, from which he never subsequently deviated. On February 27, 1929, he turned twenty-five. Soon after, he enrolled for what would turn out to be his last quarter at the University of Chicago, taking one course, Advanced Composition, from a favorite professor, James Weber Linn. This year also saw the first commercial publication of a Farrell story, the writing of a second and crucially important story, and the conception of the Lonigan and O'Neill fictional cycles. In June 1929, in the first number of a local little magazine, appeared the story "Slob," which describes an unnamed young man struggling with his drunken aunt in an apartment on Chicago's South Side. And a month or so previously, Farrell had written for Professor Linn's course another South Side Irish story, in which a thoughtful young man attends the wake of a former acquaintance who has died of dissolute living. Its title was "Studs." The narrating consciousness in these two stories is the precursor of Danny O'Neill.[5]

Farrell took the chance of a creative life by quitting the University of Chicago after the spring quarter of 1929. He later wrote of this "drastic step" that "there was a cost to success, and I would not pay that cost. I could not pay it, because, if I did, then I could not write." Over the next two years, unfazed by the stock-market crash (except as it would provide a certain dénouement for his novel in progress), he traveled to New York City twice, did odd jobs while living at home or flopping on couches in his friends' Hyde Park apartments, and read and wrote feverishly, day in and day out. He recalled of these years that in order to give "as much of my time as I could to study and writing, . . . in a sense, the Depression caught up with me. By early 1928, I had brought on my own Depression. I got myself jobless, not through inability to hold a job, but because I did not want one."[6] The result was, as Edgar Branch has said, that the young Farrell had, like the young Herman Melville, "swum through libraries." Among the writers he had read in depth by 1930 were "William James, Dewey, and George H. Mead, Nietzsche, Max Stirner, Bertrand Russell, Thorstein Veblen, R. H. Tawney, Sigmund Freud, Walter Pater, Ibsen, Chekhov, H. L. Mencken, Theodore Dreiser, Sherwood Anderson, Carl Sandburg, Sinclair Lewis, Ernest Hemingway, and James Joyce."[7] "There were ways," recalls Murray Kempton in his memoir of the thirties, "in which [Farrell] was the best-educated young writer of his time. He had read philosophers well outside the realm of discourse of conventional critics; he was a deep, though perhaps narrow, student of history; he had great resources in the European tradition. He was a perceptive enough critic to argue for William Faulkner in the early thirties, when Faulkner was at his peak of creation and his nadir of reputation. He was certainly better educated than Hemingway and Fitzgerald, who in many areas were not educated at all."[8]

By early 1931, Farrell had written thousands of manuscript pages of fiction, including much that would be incorporated into the *Studs Lonigan* trilogy and the O'Neill-O'Flaherty series. He got almost none of it published. In April 1931, dead broke and still without a publisher except for the smallest of the Midwest's little magazines, Farrell did the next logical thing—he got married, to Dorothy Butler, and the newlyweds sailed off to Paris for a year. There he expanded his reading by absorbing great amounts of Balzac, Proust, Henry James, Spinoza, and Trotsky. Then came his breakthrough. Shortly after arriving in Paris, Farrell learned that his first novel, *Young Lonigan: A Boyhood in Chicago Streets*, had been accepted by the Vanguard Press in New York. In April 1932, the novel was published and James T. Farrell was off and running.

What followed was one of the most extraordinary creative flowerings in the history of American letters. One thinks of Herman Melville's eight novels and several stories between 1846 and 1857, his entire fictional corpus but for *Billy Budd*, and William Faulkner's eleven books, including his masterworks, between 1929 and 1942. When he finished writing *My Days of Anger*, the fourth O'Neill-O'Flaherty novel, in February 1943, Farrell wrote a friend that "I have accomplished what I set out to. Shortly after I will have reached thirty nine, I will have accomplished my two major literary objectives—not of course that I haven't more that I want to write. But this much I have done. I have now written the books I said I would write a little over ten years ago when this seemed like a wild prediction."[9] In eleven years he had published eleven novels, four collections of short fiction, one book of literary criticism, and over 300 essays and reviews. The *New York Times* had hailed the *Studs Lonigan* trilogy as "one of the most powerful pieces of American fiction," and its inclusion in the Random House Modern Library in 1938 ensured a continuing audience of intelligent readers. As both an artist and an intellectual, James T. Farrell was a force to be reckoned with in American letters.

Farrell was far from alone in having made this sort of journey at this time in American cultural life. Although his output was uniquely prodigious, he was but one of many children and grandchildren of immigrants and the working class who made up a chorus of new voices starting out in the 1930s to expand the boundaries of American literature. Indeed, Michael Denning has argued that the extraordinary artistic and intellectual energies unleashed in that decade consti-tuted "a birthing of a new American culture, a second American Renaissance," when "for the first time in the history of the United States, a working-class culture had made a significant imprint on the dominant cultural institutions."[10] Among the new "proletarian" writers bent on bringing their experiences and those of their parents' generation to fiction were (with some of their books): Mike Gold (*Jews without Money*, 1930); Edward Dahlberg (*Bottom Dogs*, 1930); Langston Hughes (*Not without Laughter*, 1930); Catherine Brody (*Nobody Starves*, 1932); Grace Lumpkin (*To Make My Bread*, 1932); Jack Conroy (*The Disinherited*, 1933); Marita Bonner (*The Black Map*, 1933); Daniel Fuchs (*Summer in Williamsburg*, 1934); Albert Halper (*On the Shore*, 1934); Henry Roth (*Call It Sleep*, 1934); Tillie Olsen, "The Iron Throat" (1934); Nelson Algren (*Somebody in Boots*, 1935); Clara Weatherwax (*Marching, Marching*, 1935); Thomas Bell (*All Brides Are Beautiful*, 1936); Meyer Levin (*The Old Bunch*, 1937); John Fante (*Wait until Spring, Bandini*, 1938); Pietro Di Donato (*Christ in Concrete*, 1939); and Richard Wright (*Uncle Tom's Children*, 1938, and *Native Son*, 1940). These were writers who shared a faith in literature as an uncondescending chronicle of working-class and under-class lives and, at its best, a potential vehicle for social change.[11]

Farrell marked his own consciousness of this community in his April 1935 speech before the First American Writers' Congress in New York, a widely publi-cized, Communist-led event. He took as his ambitious subject "the development of literary traditions" in "a succession of patterns," using as his main illustration an inclusive look at the new African American literature and an insightful anal-ogy with the Irish tradition. The first pattern of "Negro literature" that he sees is "the Uncle Remus story of the dark-skinned Southern Handy Andy." The reference is to the stereotyped Irish peasantry in books such as Samuel Lover's *Handy Andy* of 1842, in which there is also implied "a condition of master and slave, oppressor and oppressed." The "Uncle Remus" pattern "presents a vaudevilized conception of the Negro, portray[ing] him as obsequious, shiftless, child-ishly humorous and simple, . . . the subject of comedy which, as we know, slurs and distorts the story of the tragic history of the Negro in capitalist America." Farrell sees this conception as still very much abroad in the land in 1935. He cites the *Saturday Evening Post*, the movies, and the Amos and Andy radio show, and he analyzes this pattern as "a combination of the conventions forced upon the Negro to permit, on one hand, some harmonious interaction between the Negro and the privileged class of whites living on his back, and, on the other, a wish fulfillment of what that privileged class desires the Negro to be."

Farrell goes on to connect the "literature of realism and social protest which has come to be the dominant literary tradition in twentieth-century American writing" with "an increasingly apparent contradiction between the hopes of the American dream and the manner in which human destinies unraveled in actual life." In this movement, contemporary American writers have "been introducing us to a new kind of American life, to the life of poor farmers and sharecroppers in backward rural areas, to the scenes, sights, and dialects of the urban streets, to the feelings of Slavic immigrants, the problems and discontents of sweat-shop workers, the resentments and oppressions of the factory proletariat. . . . In brief, it has been dipping us down toward the bottom of the so-called American melt-ing pot." Farrell goes on to criticize the lack of "internal conviction" in "many of the new revolutionary short stories." Authors "seek[ing] to express a revo-lutionary point of view, . . . instead of making their aim functional within the story so that the aim impresses the reader as a natural and integral aspect of the story, it seems to be glued on," in the worst cases, "as a slogan or revolutionary direction sign that possesses no coherent and vital or necessary relation to the body of the story."[12]

One conference participant who paid close attention to Farrell's speech was Richard Wright, who had come east from Chicago, where his family was living on the South Side at 3743 Indiana Avenue, ten blocks north of Farrell's childhood home on the same street and twenty blocks north of the Studs Lonigan/Danny O'Neill neighborhood. A few years earlier, Wright had lived even closer, at 4831 Vincennes. In fact, the Chicago South Side neighborhoods around Washington Park constitute an outstanding example of the resilience of urban communities as genius loci for artistic expression in the earlier twentieth century. Much has been made of the disruption to patterns of living in the wake of the great mi-gration of African Americans from the rural South to northern cities between the two world wars. And yet, where the arts were concerned, there was signifi-cant continuity as well. It was just that the dominant art form changed from literature to music. Among the jazz greats who came of age in the 1930s on the same streets where Farrell and Wright had matured in the 1920s were Doro-thy Donegan, Joe Williams, Johnny Board, Viola Jefferson, Milt Hinton, John

Young, Johnny Hartman, and Nat "King" Cole. Most attended DuSable High School at Forty-ninth and Wabash, where they were trained by the legendary bandmaster, Captain Walter Dyett.[13]

When he arrived in New York for the American Writers' Congress, Richard Wright was twenty-six, four years younger than Farrell, and had published a few poems and stories in little magazines. He also spoke at the conference—on "The Isolation of the Negro Writer." Michel Fabre has said that Wright "was enthralled to hear James T. Farrell speak on the revolutionary story," particularly Farrell's "true defense of art against propaganda and political tyranny." As Wright was just then becoming interested in short fiction, "Farrell's vigorous observations could not help but influence him, especially because he had his own reservations about the political demands of the Party. This was the beginning of a literary friendship that benefitted Wright enormously."[14]

Farrell spent impressive critical energies in the 1930s warning artists against the contaminating influence of politics on literature and distancing himself from those who would judge books ideologically. In 1936 he published *A Note on Literary Criticism*, his book-length analysis of the relationship between literature and Marxist cultural criticism. There, with detailed discussion of sources as varied as the Japanese *Tale of Genji*, Spinoza, Thomas Aquinas, Dickens, Proust, Dostoyevsky, and Joyce, he defended the integrity of art against the corruption of political propaganda, which he saw as an urgent threat from the intellectual left.[15] In this campaign, Farrell's was an early and very strong voice. Similarly, in his preface to the 1937 single-volume edition of his first three story collections, Farrell discussed the most conspicuous example of his era's blind faith in content: the demand in left-wing magazines such as *The Anvil* for didactic, so-called proletarian fiction featuring "a purely conceptualized, hypothetical, and non-existent worker [as] the hero. The stories produced in this movement were bad, lifeless, wooden. In place of the happy ending of *The Saturday Evening Post* variety, they had an 'uplifting' conclusion based on a sudden conversion to the sole correct faith in progress and the future of humanity." Thus, Farrell attacked distortions of content in the name of form in the mechanical "plot story" of popular magazines and college writing courses, and distortions of form in the name of content in "local color" and "proletarian" stories about minorities and the working class. There is little to choose, he declared, between fiction produced and endorsed by political standards or by short-fiction handbooks: "The former hypostasizes, narrows, and freezes content; the latter achieves a similar effect with form."[16]

Farrell's candid critique made him several enemies, and, as luck would have it, some of these people (among them Malcolm Cowley, Granville Hicks, and Alfred Kazin) went on to become influential shapers of literary reputation in the 1940s and 1950s. These New York–based critics utilized an embrace of high modernism and a "new critical" aesthetic to try to blackball Farrell from consideration as a serious writer. This vindictive crusade began with the publication of the first O'Neill-O'Flaherty novels, *A World I Never Made* in 1936 and *No Star Is Lost* in 1938. A good example of the level of much of this was the dismissal of the third novel in the series, *Father and Son*, by Edmund Wilson in *The New Republic* in October 1940. After confessing that he hadn't read Farrell's "last two or three novels," Wilson had the gall to declare that Farrell was "writing book after book about Irish boys growing up in Chicago," and "continuing to tell the same story." Instead of reviewing this new one, Wilson says, "I should like to ask you to state yourself why you expect people to go on reading your books. . . . Why do you keep on with this interminable record?" The magazine did allow Farrell to respond: "As for Studs Lonigan and Danny O'Neill," he says, "they can be pronounced alike only by a critic who could confuse Becky Sharp and Mrs. Wiggs of the Cabbage Patch." And as for Wilson's disingenuous questions: "I answer, because I have an unshakeable conviction that I have a true and representative story to tell of how people have lived, suffered and enjoyed, striven and forged ideals, loved and hated, died in my time. . . . When I began writing, I determined not to compromise with passing fads that come and go. I have rigidly tried to adhere to this intention. I have always been prepared to breast every hostile current that my books required and I am still prepared to do this. I make these statements not with any arrogance, but rather out of a full realization that each writer must find his own way in accordance with his temperament and his talents."[17]

Actually, the O'Neill-O'Flaherty novels were greeted in many of the most respected journals and newspapers as major literary events. For example, in his review of the first volume for the *Nation*, Carl Van Doren pointed out that the characters' "consciences make up nearly as much of the story as their acts. This helps to give to *A World I Never Made* that habitual tenderness which is quite as characteristic of Mr. Farrell's novels as their toughness." Further, Van Doren's sense of the overall effect of the style is fully congruent with Farrell's own aims: "He has an extraordinarily capacious mind which holds the persons and events of a novel as if they were, somehow, in solution, to be poured out in a full stream in which his own share as narrator may be lost sight of. You forget that you are seeing this life through the eyes of a selecting novelist. It seems merely to be there before you." As to subject matter, he went on to praise Farrell as the American city's "truest historian." Indeed, "Mr. Farrell seems to me to go beyond any other American novelist in his knowledge of the common life of an American city and his understanding of the city culture."[18] The novel sold over 5,000 copies in its first year, making it Farrell's most successful book up to that point.

When the fourth volume, *My Days of Anger*, appeared in 1943, Carlos Baker said in the *New York Times Book Review* that it "reveals in the author a heartening accession of philosophical gentleness and narrative power. It is in many ways a better book than Farrell has done before," and "if there is an accession of tenderness and even a kind of optimism in the present novel, there is also a gain in narrative power and incisiveness." The critics who praised the books of the O'Neill-O'Flaherty series as they appeared also included Bernard De Voto, Harold Strauss, Lewis Corey, Weldon Kees, Diana Trilling, and H. L. Mencken. In February 1937, Van Doren, De Voto, and Heywood Broun also testified in the successful court action against the New York Society for the Suppression of Vice, which had petitioned that *A World I Never Made* be banned as "obscene, lewd, and lascivious."[19]

What was missing from the criticism, however, was a developed sense of the projected scope and ultimate achievement of the O'Neill-O'Flaherty series as a whole. Had this been registered strongly in either 1943 with *My Days of Anger* or 1953, when the fifth volume, *The Face of Time*, appeared, then all of these books would be much better known. Militating against the articulation of full perspective on the series was everything that constituted the uniqueness of Farrell's accomplishment—the setting, characters, and style of his portrait of the artist in Washington Park on the South Side of Chicago. These all ran counter to the ultimately elitist hegemony of the "New Criticism" in the late 1940s and 1950s, which favored and praised high style, the veins of irony and allusion that cry out for exegesis, and an erudite controlling narrative consciousness, as in iconic works such as *Ulysses*, *The Waste Land*, and *To the Lighthouse*.

A clarifying visual analogy to both Farrell's achievement in the O'Neill-O'Flaherty series and the lack of critical recognition thereof is Peter Brooks's discussion of Gustave Courbet's revolutionary "Burial at Ornans" of 1849, a huge painting (ten by twenty-two feet) of a "humble" subject (an ordinary funeral in his own home village). This was the first volley in the campaign for *réalisme* in which Courbet was the salient standard-bearer. Brooks asserts that Parisian critics were scandalized both by the "heroic scale usually reserved for the grandeur of history painting" and the spectacle of a straggling parade of "low, vulgar" villagers, "in fact, portraits done by Courbet from his fellow townspeople," ranged around the "gaping hole" of a grave.[20] Similarly, Farrell chose to work on the largest literary canvas, a sequence of related novels that would reach 2,500 pages, and to take as his subject the works and days, lives and deaths of the ordinary people among whom he had grown up.

Contexts: Joyce, Proust, Chekhov, the Pragmatists

The O'Neill-O'Flaherty series is, among other things, a portrait of the growth of an artist, and in the design and ambition of his own project, Farrell's great tutelary spirits were James Joyce and Marcel Proust. With his own Irish American

Catholic background, he could hardly have failed to be affected by Joyce. After reading the galleys of *Young Lonigan* in February 1932, Ezra Pound had jibed to Farrell, "Effect a bit too much Joyce of the Portrait," to which Farrell replied, "As to the Irishness of it. I generally feel that I'm an Irishman rather than an American, and [*Young Lonigan*] was recommended at the nrf [Nouvelle Review Française, its French publishing house] as being practically an Irish novel. I had read Joyce [meaning *Ulysses*] and pretty well forgotten him in all details at least a year, and the Portrait a year and a half before even starting the book, and any similarity was all unconscious." However, upon rereading "most of the Portrait a month or so ago," Farrell continued, "I did feel that, with differences of time, climate, and country, there were certain similarities to the exterior conditions and experiences and even the personal ones portrayed there and the ones I bumped into in the course of growing up as a Catholic young man, attending a Catholic high school taught by Carmelites rather than Jesuits etc."[21]

In *My Days of Anger*, in which Danny O'Neill reaches maturity, he discusses *A Portrait* and *Ulysses* with friends at the University of Chicago. Shortly after completing that novel, Farrell wrote two essays on Joyce for the *New York Times Book Review* that were later expanded and published separately, in which he located the *Portrait* firmly in its innovative contexts. First, he insists that nineteenth-century Irish political history is necessary to understanding the book, for "Joyce was a kind of inverted nationalist," for whom "the nationalism he rejects runs . . . like a central thread." Second, he asserts that "it was Joyce who introduced the city realistically into modern Irish writing. The city—Dublin—is the focus of Ireland in his work, and in his life. We see that this is the case with Stephen [Dedalus], the genius son of a declassed family. Stephen lives, grows up in a Dublin that is a center of paralysis. Is he to have a future in such a center? Is he to prevent himself from suffering paralysis, spiritual paralysis? Stephen's painful burden of reality can be interpreted as a reality that derives from the history of Ireland's defeats and that is focused, concretized, in the very quality of the men of Dublin." Third, Farrell emphasizes Stephen's Catholicism as crucially formative: "From his considerable reading in the literature of the church the boy gained not only a sense of the past but also a sense of an ordered inner world and of a systematized *other* world. Eternity has filled his imagination." Furthermore, "his greatest sufferings are not imposed by the Dublin reality which disturbs him so much but by images of inferno as terrifying as that of Dante. He quivers and cowers before the vision of an other world which must make that of the Irish legends seem the most pale of mists. His spiritual struggle is one involving acceptance or rejection of this ordered other world."

Farrell goes on to place Joyce in the context of the European tradition of the bildungsroman, which he charts as a three-part progression through the nineteenth century. "Early in the century we see the young man—for instance Julien Sorel of *The Red and the Black*, or Balzac's Lucien and Rastignac—seeking glory and fame. Their aim is success, and the plane of action is the objective one of society." At mid-century, "in the Russian novel—Pierre of *War and Peace*, Levin of *Anna Karenina*, Bazarov of *Fathers and Sons*, and Dostoyevsky's Raskolnikov and Ivan Karamazov—there is a shift of emphasis. These young men probe for the meaning of life; they seek to harmonize their words and their deeds." Toward the century's end, "we see the young man seeking freedom in the realm of feeling. This is the object of Frederic Moreau in *A Sentimental Education*—and of Des Esseintes (in a purely decadent fashion) in Huysmans's *Against the Grain*. Marius [Pater's Epicurean] and Stephen are both of this line; they, too, seek freedom in the realm of feeling and of culture." Farrell sees this substitution of artistic for worldly or ontological goals by fiction's protagonists as a reflection of "the evolving conditions of life in the nineteenth century. The character of public life changes and decreases the opportunities to be free. The idea of culture (as the realm of freedom) begins to grow. Thus, the logic of art for art's sake. The artist, crushed by the weight of contemporary culture, adopts the attitude that art is its own end, becomes the rebel artist." Stephen Dedalus fits here. He is "the artist as rebel, questioning the whole moral sensibility of his age."

Having recently finished his fourth and, at that point, the final O'Neill-O'Flaherty novel, Farrell must also have been locating his own bildungsroman as an advance into twentieth-century America of this venerable Old World tradition. Moreover, it is clear from Farrell's description that Stephen Dedalus and Danny O'Neill are as different as their differing places, times, gifts, and limitations dictate. Farrell notes that "almost from childhood, Stephen is an exceptional character. He is separated from others. He is aloof, lonely, different. His childhood is not a normal one in which he shares the common experiences of give-and-take between boys. He seldom participates in games; he is bookish, introspective. By the time he becomes a university student his mind is monkish, cloistered, and he regards it as such." Danny O'Neill hasn't the precocity, arrogance, or self-confidence of Stephen Dedalus. Though they are about the same age at the conclusions of *My Days of Anger* and *Ulysses*, Stephen is much further along on the road toward conviction and self-sufficiency in his vocation of artist.[22]

This distinction between the two protagonists relates to Farrell's lifelong ambivalence about Joyce, which had mostly to do with aspects of literary style. In his Joyce essay, Farrell explains Joyce's brilliant melding of style and theme in *A Portrait* by observing that "Joyce's realism is a realism of the mind, of the consciousness. Stephen's life is described in a highly concentrated and selective manner, deriving from this point of view. His own mind serves as the frame of reference for the story." Thus, "in many parts of the narrative the very style in which it is written has direct bearing on the theme." Because "the inner life of the artist is what is significant in [Stephen's] life, . . . the style, the perspective, the organization of the novel all seem to harmonize beautifully with its content." That is, Joyce makes his protagonist's exceptionalism clear by making the dominant style in the last chapter of *A Portrait* and in *Ulysses* a reflection of Stephen's brilliance, isolation, and self-absorption. In Farrell's view, this was a double-edged sword. As early as 1934, he had written that "parts of *Ulysses* seem like stunt performances to permit the author the luxury of showing off. I feel that the question and answer chapter is of such a nature. But such performances remain the privilege of genius." Farrell went even further a few years later in writing a friend that *Finnegans Wake* was "a signal of a man of genius with colossal egotism," which ultimately failed to meet John Dewey's "only demand" of an artist: "that his product be communicable in some sense to someone."[23]

Dennis Flynn has pointed out that a measure of Farrell's fluctuating opinion about Joyce is his "repeated comparison of Joyce and Proust. Early in his career, he favored Joyce's 'rigorousness, restraint, and stern dignity' as opposed to Proust's 'narrowness of range' and 'repetitive succession of agonies of heart.' Later he wrote that, though Joyce was a great genius, his work no longer seemed as stimulating. He came to reconsider his earlier estimate: 'Among writers of the twentieth century, the one whom I love the most is Marcel Proust.'"[24] Farrell had read Proust's first volume, *Swann's Way*, in Chicago in about 1927, and he went on to read all seven volumes of *In Search of Lost Time* while in Paris in 1931. The many references to Proust in *A Note on Literary Criticism*, Farrell's 1936 defense of literature against propaganda, demonstrate the strong connection between them at this early stage of Farrell's career. Farrell first mentions Proust in his summary dismissal of the extraliterary critique of literature coming from the cultural left, citing the "usual Marxmanship" of Mike Gold, Granville Hicks, and others. Class and politics be damned, is Farrell's message, for a "proletarian writer" (whatever that may mean) will be influenced by all sorts of art, by the fiction of James Joyce, bizarrely condemned by D. S. Mirsky as "inseparably connected with the specifically decadent phase of the bourgeois culture," and "by literature that is unqualifiedly non-proletarian, like Proust's works, or unqualifiedly non-revolutionary, in the political sense, like T. S. Eliot's."[25]

Overall, there are at least four areas of fruitful connection between Proust and Farrell. First is their shared focus on consciousness, especially in their shared sense of the pernicious effects on consciousness of habit. Here Proust's fiction reinforced Farrell's own philosophic roots in American pragmatism, which will also be discussed a bit later in this essay. Second, there is a clarifying similarity between Proust's concept of involuntary memory and the use of daydream and reverie in Farrell's fiction. Third is the primacy of place for both writers as the object of cathexis (the objective locus for concentration of emotional energy) through which the artist realizes his overarching aim of defeating time. Fourth is the way that Proust's narrator serves as a model for Farrell's portrait of the artist.

In *A Note on Literary Criticism*, Farrell emphasizes the centrality of Proust's view of habit in an extended analysis of a passage from Proust's second volume, *Within a Budding Grove*. Farrell cites "a most excitingly exact description of certain impressions of a railroad journey taken by the 'I' of the novels," which is followed by a passage where the narrator stresses the uniqueness of the impressions of the outside world registered by each individual consciousness and the aesthetic (and moral) falseness of generalization. Here Farrell quotes Proust at length:

> We invariably forget that these [qualities that we perceive through the senses] are individual qualities, and, substituting for them in our mind a conventional type at which we arrive by striking a sort of mean amongst the different faces that have taken our fancy, the pleasures we have known, we are left with mere abstract images which are lifeless and dull because they are lacking in precisely that element of novelty, different from anything we have known, that element which is proper to beauty and happiness. And we deliver on life a pessimistic judgment which we suppose to be fair, for we believed that we were taking into account when we formed it happiness and beauty, whereas in fact we left them out and replaced them by syntheses in which there is not a single atom of either.

By extension, Farrell asserts, "so it is with a character in a novel, no matter what class he belongs to. He is not just a copy of all the other members of his class. He is a person with resemblances to all the other members of his class, and with a difference from all the other members of that class." To explain further, Farrell again quotes Proust: "As a rule it is with our being reduced to a minimum that we live, most of our faculties lie dormant because they can rely upon Habit, which knows what there is to be done and has no need of their services." And yet, the railroad journey stimulated the narrator to use more of his faculties because, Proust explains, the sights and sounds presented "a project which would have the further advantage of providing with subject matter the selfish, active, practical, mechanical, indolent, centrifugal tendency which is that of the human mind."[26]

Here Proust supports Farrell's argument in *A Note on Literary Criticism* that politics is irrelevant or worse as motivation or measuring stick for art. I also believe that this is the heart of Farrell's own design for fiction, toward which Proust's masterpiece is a model of belief in the validity for extended artistic rendering of individual consciousness. The result is the O'Neill-O'Flaherty series—*In Search of Lost Time* in Washington Park. Farrell had no illusions, by the way, as to the potential receptiveness of an American literary audience to his emphasis on the interior life. He pointed out in a lecture that "perhaps the greatest literary tradition in modern times is that of France. . . . When the novel developed in

France, there was already a very highly developed culture." He cites *La Princess de Cleves* (1678), *Adolphe* (1815), and *Les Liaisons Dangereuses* (1880s) as examples of novels in which "the characters understand a great deal about their own emotions. There is a high level of sophistication, of sophistication in a good sense, and there was an audience that could understand it." In contrast, America has been "a crude and primitive" place ("except in New England"), where "it was impossible for us to have a developed awareness, a developed consciousness of self, such as the French had, because we didn't have stabilized classes, a stabilized culture or even a stabilized language."[27]

The second link between Proust and Farrell is their shared understanding of how the mind can find release from the enslaving ballast of habit. For Proust, liberation comes only in the fresh, unbidden visitations of "involuntary memory," the most famous of which is the first—when a tea-soaked biscuit brings the narrator's entire childhood world vividly into his adult mind.[28] In Farrell's fiction, the unbidden epiphanies of involuntary memory come in experiences of daydream and reverie, and these contribute to his pioneering expansion of the possibilities for literature of the consciousness of so-called ordinary people. In his first two fictional cycles, the *Studs Lonigan* trilogy and the O'Neill-O'Flaherty pentalogy, examples include Studs Lonigan's recurrent dream of perching in a tree with Lucy Scanlan, Mrs. Mary O'Flaherty at her husband's grave, Old Tom O'Flaherty on his deathbed, Jim O'Neill dozing over Shakespeare after having suffered three strokes, and the boy Danny O'Neill drifting aimlessly through Washington Park at all seasons of the year.

The third element, place, is pervasive for both writers. When he first read *Swann's Way* in 1927, Farrell was surely struck by renderings of and attitudes toward important locations that echoed his own experience. One such is the depiction of Proust's narrator's sickly Aunt Léonie, whose "bed lay by the window, she had the street there before her eyes and on it from morning to night, to divert her melancholy, like the Persian princes, would read the daily but immemorial chronicle of Combray, which she would afterward comment upon with [her maid] Françoise." Another is the narrator's remembered perception that the steeple of the Catholic church organized the entire country town of Combray: "It was the steeple of Saint-Hilaire that gave all the occupations, all the hours, all the viewpoints of the town their shape, their crown, their consecration." Reading these passages, Farrell would have seen his own grandmother, Julia Daly, sitting at her window "reading the daily but immemorial chronicle" of Washington Park, and he would have felt the echo of his own childhood neighborhood, in which Corpus Christi and St. Anselm's churches focused everyone's works and days.

Swann's Way ends with the section titled "Place-Names: The Name," and more than half of *Within a Budding Grove* is the section called "Place-Names: The

Place." In both books and throughout Proust's entire sequence of seven novels, evocations abound of place as catalyst for remembered experience. As it happens, two more of the earliest and most important also involve church steeples. Early in the "Combray" section of *Swann* comes the lovely passage in which the narrator confesses: "And even today," if someone answers his question for directions in a strange town by pointing to a steeple, he finds himself "forgetting the walk I had begun or the necessary errand," and "remain[ing] there in front of the steeple for hours, motionless, trying to remember, feeling deep in myself lands recovered from oblivion draining and rebuilding themselves. . . . I am still seeking my path, I am turning a corner . . . but . . . I am doing so in my heart." And at the climax of "Combray," the narrator recalls one of his earliest experiences of the mystery and the power of place. While out walking, "suddenly a roof, a glimmer of sun on a stone, the smell of the road would stop me because of a particular pleasure they gave me, and also because they seemed to be concealing, beyond what I could see, something which they were inviting me to come take and which despite my efforts I could not manage to discover." And then, one day,

> At the bend of a road I suddenly experienced that special pleasure which was unlike any other, when I saw the two steeples of Martinville, shining in the setting sun and appearing to change position with the motion of our carriage and the windings of the road. As I noted the shape of their spires, the shifting of their lines, the sunlight on their surfaces, I felt that I was not reaching the full depth of my impression, that something was behind that motion, that brightness, something which they seemed at once to contain and conceal.

This time he asks the family friend who is driving the carriage for a pencil and paper, and he writes out his impressions of the steeples. The result is the narrator's first attempt to make art, and although the result is clumsy and tentative, he nonetheless recognizes immediately that the act of writing will be his weapon against time.[29]

From the outset of his writing life, place was equally important in Farrell's fiction. "Helen, I Love You," the first story, dated 1930, in his first collection of short fiction opens with "two boys . . . in front of one of the small gray-stone houses in the 5700 block of Indiana Avenue, glaring at each other." And he begins his first novel, *Young Lonigan: A Boyhood in Chicago Streets*, published in 1932, with an abundance of detailed place lore. About to graduate from eighth grade, the young protagonist Studs Lonigan defines himself in terms of "St. Patrick's" church and parochial school at Michigan Avenue and Sixty-first Street, Indiana Avenue where he walked his first girlfriend home, the "corner of Sixtieth" where he broke some basement windows, the Carter Playground where he had his first fight, and the elevated railroad structure at Fifty-ninth Street, the site of his brave acceptance of a challenge to climb a girder. This boy's reverie is followed by the stock-taking daydream of Studs's father, Paddy Lonigan, who recalls his own childhood as the son of a "pauperized greenhorn," with a wider-ranging litany of place names: Blue Island, St. Ignatius church, dances at Hull-House, "back of the yards," Canaryville, "Luke O'Toole's place on Halsted." Place is similarly paramount from the opening pages of the first O'Neill-O'Flaherty novel, *A World I Never Made*, as six-year-old Danny O'Neill stands looking "wistfully out the parlor window. He saw the vacant lot at the corner of Fiftieth and Calumet Avenue with the elevated tracks in the alley behind the lot and the advertising signboards running all around the front of the lot." He notes "an elevated train" going north, and thinks that "he rode on that train when Uncle Al took him to see the White Sox play." And when "an electric" passes, "headed for Fifty-first Street," he looks down "at the moving black roof" and "wished that he was riding in it," instead of having to get ready to go to Sunday Mass.

Indeed, the connectedness of mind and milieu infuses every page of Farrell's fiction. "No ideas but in things," as William Carlos Williams puts it, and Farrell once wrote (in an unpublished essay) that the world of Washington Park "was tremendously and vividly real to me. It was as real to me as I was to myself," and that "Santa Claus and God were real to me as a child—'There's nothing either good or bad but thinking makes it so'—as real, as true as the building off of the alley between Calumet Avenue and Grand Boulevard and set back from a gravelly, rectangular-shaped little school yard: the building was Corpus Christi School." Here, Farrell continues, "I played, and grew, and dreamed."

Thoughts such as these do not appear as often in Farrell's art as in Proust's because of the radically different narrative positions of each novelist. Proust's aim is recovery of the past from the doubled, reflexive perspective of the consciousness of one highly sophisticated narrator in full adulthood. Farrell's aim is the recovery of the past from the single perspective of the consciousness of a character living a life moment by moment—that is, recovery of the past by imagining it as the present. As Farrell put it in that same unpublished piece, "a novelist, of course, must have knowledge of many details." This is especially true of his fiction, because story, happenings, characters "are all presented from the standpoint of immediate experience."[30] In addition, even when the character is Danny O'Neill, the future artist, the insights day by day are less startling, incisive, lyrical—whatever can be said about Proust—because Danny is not looking back, but registering the moments as he lives them. Furthermore, Danny and his family are not French aristocrats and aesthetes, but working-class and lower-middle-class Irish immigrants and second-generation Americans.

And yet, despite the obvious distances between them, Proust's narrator and Danny O'Neill have much more in common with each other as portraits of the artist than either has, for example, with Stephen Dedalus. Here is the fourth way in which Proust served as a crucial, directing model for Farrell. To be sure, Proust's, Joyce's, and Farrell's large fictional projects all conclude in similar anticlimax. At the end of the seventh volume of *In Search of Lost Time*, of *Ulysses*, and of Farrell's *My Days of Anger*, none of the three protagonists has written anything of consequence. All artistic achievement lies beyond the pages with which these sequences end. This makes practical sense because the novelists would have realized that, after the artist has committed to his vocation, he's not so interesting to the prospective reader. Better grist for fiction's mill is the fits and false starts, the hard slog through the tangle of unmediated experience through which Proust's narrator, Stephen Dedalus, and Danny O'Neill fight their way toward enlightenment. The end of this inward journey marks the outer limit of the portrait in each case. But young Stephen Hero is much farther along the road than either of the other two. He knows, and thus we know, that he's definitely going to get there. In contrast, Proust's narrator is a dismayingly unprecocious seeker, stumbling, vulnerable, and maddeningly tentative in his development. So is Danny O'Neill, and Farrell got from Proust the courage of his conviction to give extended narrative treatment to so slow and painful a pilgrim's progress toward a life in art.

Thus, encouraged in so many ways by the example of Marcel Proust, James T. Farrell began fashioning a body of fiction in which the relentless, deadening force of habit faces off against the fitful, countervailing blessings of daydream and reverie. The great enemy is time, but in these novels, the characters in whose minds this war plays out are fixed in the writer's amber of fully realized place. Much in Walter Benjamin's succinct elucidation of Proust also illuminates Farrell. Benjamin declares that Proust's "true interest is in the passage of time in its most real—that is, space-bound—form." Although "there has never been anyone else with Proust's ability to show us things," he uses experience "not to drink from it, but to dream to its heartbeat," and his bass note is a "hopeless sadness" that springs from acknowledgment of "the incurable imperfection in . . . the present moment." Add to this Benjamin's assertion that "Proust approaches experience without the slightest metaphysical interest, . . . without the slightest tendency to console," and you have much of the truth about Farrell as well.[31]

Farrell's investigation of consciousness in the O'Neill-O'Flaherty novels is especially inclusive and challenging. In addition to the development of the artist's mind, he also sets out to render the inner lives of some half-dozen members of the two families from which Danny O'Neill springs, most of whom have not had the luxury of advanced education and circumstances that allow for or encourage reflection. Even in *My Days of Anger*, which focuses on the young artist's coming of age, Farrell does not abandon Danny's parents, grandmother, brothers, and sisters. All continue to contribute their individual thoughts to the interwoven pattern. It is here that the example of a third writer was crucially reinforcing for Farrell's project, an artist without either the stylistic egotism of Joyce or the focus on characters from the cultured elite of Proust. This was Anton Chekhov, whom Farrell had first read seriously in 1927 while beginning work on his own fiction. Farrell's 1942 essay on Chekhov elucidates the connection between them. He describes Chekhov's characters as "idle dreamers who live sunk in the commonplace; men and women who cannot react to cruelty, who cannot be free, who cannot lift themselves above the terrible plain of stagnation—people in whom human dignity is dissolving." Farrell emphasizes two characteristics of Chekhov's work, both noted by Maxim Gorky, which were central to Farrell's own aims. The first was Gorky's assessment that "banality always found in him a discerning and merciless judge," to which Farrell adds, "Chekhov raised the portrayal of banality to the level of world literature." The second was Gorky's statement of Chekhov's essential message: "You live badly, my friends. It is shameful to live like that." Farrell goes on to indicate the motive behind that portrayal by quoting a Chekhov letter that articulates the faith of the literary realist: "The best of [writers] are realists and paint life as it is, but, through every line's being soaked in the consciousness of an object, you feel, besides life as it is, the life that ought to be, and that captivates you. . . . Man will only become better when you make him see what he is like." Farrell underscores his sense of this passage, which also expresses his own goal for fiction: "great and good writers saturate us with a consciousness of life, and, by achieving this effect, endow us with a sense not only of what life is but also of what it ought to be."[32]

Elsewhere, in a piece on "Nonsense and the Short Story," Farrell cites a number of spurious opinions about the genre, then asks, "Which of these definitions is best suited to the stories of Chekhov?—in my opinion the greatest short-story writer who ever lived. Or which one is most applicable to the stories in Joyce's *Dubliners*? To *Winesburg, Ohio*?" Rejecting the formulaic criterion that a story should create a "*single* or a *unified* impression," he described Chekhov's "A Woman's Kingdom," as "literally, a cross section of many phases of life [in czarist Russia]. One gets from it impressions of class relationships, of characters, of moods. What, then, of the singleness of impression? In fact, Chekhov's stories are an excellent refutation of all these definitions. His stories are, in my opinion, like doors of understanding and awareness opening outward into an entire world."[33]

The idea of grafting Chekhovian concern for inclusion of the mundane on Joycean and Proustian attention to consciousness involved a dramatic change of narrative orientation for Farrell. He recalled later that his first stories came easily—too easily, and when he had first tried to write an autobiographical novel about "my boyhood and high school days" in April 1927, he had failed utterly: "I went back to my short-pants days, and attempted to create a character who had been much like myself, and who would reveal himself, and tell a story of others around him and of himself; this would be done in a stream-of-consciousness flow. In a Standard Oil filling station at Thirty-fifth and Morgan, the last of the stations in which I worked, I stood at the desk and wrote in pencil. It was a sunny afternoon in April and I thought that I had found a way of writing, one that I could do easily, rolling it off, in a swift succession of pages. But it was not that easy; it wasn't that way. I came to a dead halt."[34] Two years later, shortly after conceiving the character of Studs Lonigan, he recognized the major flaw in his early fiction to be lack of objectivity: "I analyzed my character as I considered him in his relations to his own world, his own background. I set as my aim that of unfolding the destiny of Studs Lonigan in his own words, his own actions, his own patterns of thought and feeling. I decided that my task was not to state formally what life meant to me, but to try and re-create a sense of what life meant to Studs Lonigan. I worked on with this project, setting up as an ideal the strictest possible objectivity."[35]

The result of Farrell's thinking was the reinvention of his style. Most of the proletarian realists of the 1930s had as one of their aims speaking for people for whom self-expression comes hard. This theme of tragic inarticulateness suggests a stylistic challenge, a problem of narrative voice: how to speak for people who cannot easily speak for themselves. Farrell's solution was to create a third-person-limited point of view that shifts from character to character. The result is a kind of omniscience—but with a difference. It is an omniscience of which one key aim is exclusion of the consciousness of the author. Except, of course, for the selection and organization of incidents, events, and the consciousness on which these register, this is the meaning of Farrell's often quoted goal of writing "so that life may speak for itself." This is Flaubert's "free indirect discourse," but without the irony that signals authorial control and judgment. The medium that Farrell fashioned is an austere style of scrupulous plainness that effectively renders the thoughts and speech of ordinary people. For this prodigiously gifted intellectual, encyclopedically well read and fiercely committed to the life of the mind, the forging of this style was likely a heroic effort of will. Taken in 1929, Farrell's hard decision to displace the central narrative consciousness from the sophisticated, autobiographical self to the limited other resulted in the creation of an urban plain style that is one of his great gifts to American literature. Analogues for this achievement include Mark Twain's decision to let Huck Finn tell his own story, Robert Frost's incorporation of New England idiom and rhythms into lyric poetry, and William Carlos Williams's determination to use East Coast city colloquialism in verse, including the epic.

The Farrell style can be understood in a larger literary context. Farrell has said that "I was decidedly formed and ready before the Thirties started. And I had read and been influenced by many, Ben Hecht, Maxwell Bodenheim, George Moore, James Joyce, Hemingway, Sherwood Anderson, Nietzsche, Red Lewis, etc., and not solely and simply by Teddy Dreiser." Farrell's position as a stylistic innovator with modernist roots in the twenties has been established by Donald Pizer, who credits Farrell's use of epiphany and development of stream-of-consciousness writing and links him particularly with Joyce and Anderson. Pizer identifies Farrell's stream-of-consciousness technique as a form of "indirect discourse," a third-person voice wherein "the narrator is present as reporter, structurer, and summarizer of the character's frame of mind but . . . [in which] he presents this material in the language and grammatical form habitually used by the character." And he sees *Studs Lonigan* as "a novel of the 1920s in Farrell's exploration of the inarticulate felt life of a character by means of indirect discourse."[36] Farrell's technique is notably effective in the many examples of daydream and reverie in his fiction, and his rendering of the dream life of ordinary people is part of his expansion of the literary possibilities of the consciousness of Americans. The climax of this effect in the *Studs Lonigan* trilogy is Studs's fevered death fantasy, a distorted montage of the people who have influenced his life that flickers through his failing consciousness near the end of the trilogy's 1935 final volume, *Judgment Day*. Surreal dream materials are even more prominent in *Gas-House McGinty*, his novel of 1933 set in the bustling "Wagon Call Department" of an express company, an unlikely place, before Farrell, for such literary experimentation. By the inception of the O'Neill-O'Flaherty series, these techniques were fully at his command. The result is several examples over the five novels of a hard-won, minimal eloquence that embodies Farrell's faith in the ability of relatively unreflective and uneducated people to clarify and bless their own lives, even if only in their own minds.

A final overarching influence for Farrell's fiction was the philosophy of pragmatism. In several essays and lectures in the mid-1960s, he asserted that the writings of the pragmatists William James, George Herbert Mead, and, especially, John Dewey had been the most important influence on the development of his own art. He recalls that beginning in 1929, he filled notebook after notebook with quotations and comments based on his first, excited engagement with these philosophers: "When I read book after book of John Dewey in the fall of 1929 and in 1930, I was permanently influenced. . . . John Dewey and Mead had a tremendous influence on me in the writing of *Studs Lonigan*. . . . I was concerned with how to conceive character, and I was concerned with certain general problems, both for themselves and in relationship to the writing. I was just two years a writer by then, and James on habit and John Dewey on habit in *Human Nature and Conduct* influenced me, and Mead and Dewey and the social conception of self and the personality—the social conception of individuality—and Dewey in his approach to a problem in terms of the situation rather than in an individualized way or in an abstracted generalized way."

At that time, Farrell continues, "The whole cast of my thought was really fixed and this has never changed." He recalls how much clicked into place when he read the passage from Dewey that became an epigraph for his first novel, *Young Lonigan: A Boyhood in Chicago Streets:* "While I was working on the book about a character called Studs Lonigan, I came across the following, which I quote from *Human Nature and Conduct*, which crystallized much of my thinking in reference to the book, and thinking of mine in general. 'The poignancy of situations that evoke reflection lies in the fact that we really do not know the meaning of the tendencies that are pressing for action.' And I had begun *Studs Lonigan* from the end—that is, he was going to die as a young man in his young manhood. There was actually a situation that called for reflection, I felt." He explains that Dewey, James, and Mead "saved and short-circuited" him into "a clearer conception of naturalism," a "philosophical" naturalism that differs fundamentally from that of Emile Zola, who "took two very generalized railroad-train conceptions of heredity and environment, and counterposed them to each other and said that heredity was stronger. That was the generalization of what he thought was science, and he dismissed individual opinions and impressions as lies."[37] Harry Smith has succinctly summarized the crucial distinction that Farrell makes here and at many other places in his critical writing: "Farrell was not the last great exponent of American Naturalism. Rather, he achieved the first great synthesis of realist tradition and the newer subjectivist fiction, bringing psychological exploration to social forces and the facts of ordinary life. Farrell was more concerned with consciousness, attitudes, personality, subjective time, dream and the irrational than was any 'realist' or 'Naturalist.'"[38]

In a 1966 essay, Farrell highlights what was for him Dewey's key idea of growth as a social phenomenon, which became the grounding for Farrell's own passionate commitment to fiction that locates character in its deepest social context:

> The pragmatists in philosophy are concerned with process and particularly with growth. The living organism must function in society. A child, for example, has inner impulses and a child has to grow, intellectually as well as physically. Growth springs from those inner impulses. Because the mind is an organ, developed in society—not set apart—knowledge is essentially cooperative in character. How an individual functions is to be tested by consequences, but, in Dewey's view, this is not the same as simple success. The fulfillments of functioning are in "shared experiences." He believed that certainties do not exist. Man, in a universe of peril, can reduce uncertainties that threaten him by the cooperative acquisition of knowledge and by cooperative action. In this world void of certainty, categorical imperatives are arbitrary. The only imperative, if there be one, Dewey held, was that of growth.[39]

Robert Butler has explained most usefully how the pragmatists' conceptions of time and habit also guided Farrell's fiction from the start:

> [The pragmatists] developed an idea that is crucial to Farrell's vision, that time is an organic continuum centered in human consciousness. The mind reconstructs

a past to stabilize action in the present and it simultaneously imagines a future to serve as a directive for such action. This is what Mead understands as "temporal perspective" and what James describes as temporal "equilibrium." For current action to be useful in the growth of individuals and the progress of society, it must be harmonized with the other two levels of time. Otherwise, time becomes fragmented and a fundamental loss of control over experience results. . . . Such a fragmentary experience of moments is what the pragmatists referred to as a 'specious' present—an assortment of isolated events which either drift into nothingness or eventually form a chain of repetition. But, as Dewey points out, the self can be whole and effective only if the consciousness which directs action is artfully balanced in all three levels of time.[40]

Here are the psychosocial models for Studs Lonigan and Danny O'Neill, the one caught in centrifugal drift and deadening habit, the other struggling to develop a secular, "temporal perspective" on which to ground a significant life.

Butler further explains that "both Farrell and the pragmatists saw entrenched habit as a serious human problem. Allowing the past to dominate the present rather than inviting the present to 'organize' the past for its own needs, habit makes time a rigid circle of necessity, stripping the here and now of novelty and making the future a dreary set of mindless repetitions." As Butler summarizes, "These theories of time helped Farrell to imagine human experience in coherently structured terms and were, therefore, immensely useful in the formal shaping of his fiction. . . . Seen in this light, . . . his fictive world is remarkable not only for its often acknowledged power but also for its little-recognized depth of vision and formal control."[41]

In a 1965 lecture, Farrell paid homage to Mead on aesthetics, and then described how his own thinking went beyond Mead in a more positive, humanistic direction. The result is one of his most moving defenses of the artist's endeavor: "[Mead] treated aesthetics as serial processes leading to an end or a culmination. He made a distinction between the functional and the aesthetic. The functional was what you wanted in order to get on to the next step. . . . But when you pause and contemplate the pleasure and the joy and the satisfaction you will get or gain at the end of this serial process, that is aesthetic experience." And yet, while appreciating Mead's systematic approach, Farrell disagrees, especially for the artist: "I would say that all experience is both aesthetic *and* functional—or should be. . . . It is not for [the artist] to work only for himself; rather it is for him to render multiple experience as best he can—to render it with the hope that he will leave some of it to the memory of mankind, because in the first, in the last and in every analysis the memory of mankind is what sustains us. In it is the source of all belief and of all faith."[42]

I agree with Dennis Flynn, who declares that "I can think of no American novelist who begins to approach Farrell in the degree to which his work is rooted in a philosophical world view. Farrell's roots in the philosophy of pragmatism help account not only for his being realistic and dispassionate about the Catholic Church, but also for the generally experimental and innovative nature of his writing. He was able to put into fiction . . . thoughts and feelings many people have had but which had never been held worthy of inclusion in serious literature."[43] Farrell began with a solid, philosophical basis for both style and subject matter of what he wanted to write. From the outset, he committed to fiction that emphasizes consciousness as active, seeing the mind as in process, buffeted by experience, searching for "Truth" or "truths," often unaware of that distinction, often blocked by habit—the result of laziness among the comfortable or exhaustion among the underprivileged. In my view, this is most important in the O'Neill-O'Flaherty series, where the novelist's challenge is rendering the variously damaging or fruitful applications of consciousness to the placement of the self in time by a large number of characters. This philosophical justification also explains the conviction and energy with which Farrell attempted so detailed a scrutiny of the interior lives of his characters. In this deep and thoughtful context, no mind is more or less "ordinary" than any other. Novelist Thomas F. Curley put it well when he praised Farrell's "steady attempt to make art of an experience that is at once common and significant."[44]

Neighborhood, Catholicism, Childhood

Farrell's fiction is also important to American literature from the 1930s onward in its delivery of fresh and corrective perspectives in three thematic areas: city life as actually lived, the religion of ethnic Americans as actually practiced, and the nature of experience as perceived by children. Farrell recalled that the first profound catalyst for his decision to become a writer was Sherwood Anderson—in particular, *Tar, A Midwestern Childhood*, which he read early in 1927. His excited reaction mirrors that of many subsequent writers to his own work: "If the inner life of a boy in an Ohio country town of the nineteenth century was meaningful enough to be the material for a book like *Tar*, then perhaps my own feelings and emotions and the feelings and emotions of those with whom I had grown up were important. . . . I thought of writing a novel about my own boyhood, about the neighborhood in which I had grown up. Here was one of the seeds that led to *Studs Lonigan*." He goes on to explain that "the neighborhoods of Chicago in which I grew up possessed something of the character of a small town. They were little worlds of their own. Many of the people living in them knew one another. There was a certain amount of gossip of the character that one finds in small towns. One of the largest nationality and religious groups in these neighborhoods was Irish American and Catholic. I attended a parochial school. Through the school and Sunday mass, the life of these neighborhoods was rendered somewhat more cohesive. My grandmother was always a neighborhood character, well known. I became known, too, the way a boy would be in a small town."[45]

Before Farrell wrote, few American writers had presented city neighborhoods in this way. Finley Peter Dunne's "Mr. Dooley" columns about Chicago and Abraham Cahan's stories of Jewish New York in the 1890s were among the few notable exceptions. Farrell's perspective, pioneering in its balance as well as in its accurate detail, revises a number of distorted views: Stephen Crane's vision of the city as a threatening, impressionist theater set, Theodore Dreiser's view of the city as an exciting but alien destination for immigrant and rural seekers, and the local-color journalists' (Richard Harding Davis, Brander Mathews, and others) portraits of the city as a tourist stop wherein to find the quaint and picturesque. Unlike these others, the city in Farrell's fiction is a real place where daily life is presented with fullness and fairness. Crucial to that presentation is the creation of urban neighborhoods that are as richly realized as any in fiction. Farrell knew instinctively what Eudora Welty has put so memorably: "The truth is, fiction depends for its life on place. Location is the crossroads of circumstance, the proving ground of 'What happened? Who's here? Who's coming?'—and that is the heart's field."[46]

The O'Neill-O'Flaherty novels show us what it looked, sounded, smelled, tasted, and felt like to live in South Side Chicago neighborhoods, what areas such as Washington Park provided and lacked for working- and middle-class urban Americans, and how these places changed over time, specifically from the 1890s through the 1920s. Like many immigrant couples, Tom and Mary O'Flaherty begin their Chicago life in one of the city's oldest places, Blue Island Avenue, where many generations of settlers have already come and gone. In their story of internal migration to better neighborhoods, the O'Flahertys exemplify the process by which many marginally middle-class, ethnic families got ahead—young adults lived at home until they married and contributed their earnings to the family. Thus, by the time Old Tom retires from his teamster's job, his children Al, Ned, Margaret, and Louise earn enough to allow the family to move from a crowded flat on Twelfth Street to larger apartments further south. The culminating change of location in the O'Neill-O'Flaherty series puts the family in a spacious apartment overlooking Washington Park. Similarly, Farrell documents Jim and Lizz O'Neill's laborious movement toward a better life for their large family in terms of their three homes over the course of the five novels: a cold-water tenement flat, a ramshackle cottage with outhouse behind, and, finally, a comfortable apartment with indoor plumbing, gas, and electricity. The map accompanying this introduction demonstrates the congruence between these places and the homes of Farrell's parents, James Francis and Mary Daly Farrell, and maternal grandparents, John and Julia Brown Daly.[47]

The depth of neighborhood place lore in the O'Neill-O'Flaherty novels is partly because they were very much a family affair. On February 2, 1934, begins the remarkable group of letters in which, like Joyce writing back to his relatives in Dublin, Farrell asks his brothers and sisters for help. The first is to his sister Mary: "I've started the family saga, and maybe you could help me, by, without making it apparent that you're doing it, picking up whatever you can about LaSalle Street, and Mrs. Butcher, Mrs. Meyers, etc. I'd appreciate anything you can send me, and as you can get it, and so on." These letters go back and forth for the entire writing life of the series, and include questions and answers about street addresses and neighborhood characters, racing forms and "linguistic habits," and the mechanics of various jobs. "No details will be negligible, I'm sure," Farrell writes early on, "so don't hesitate any time you feel so inclined to write more."[48] It is possible that Farrell's powerful evocation of the few square blocks that make up a city neighborhood is a vestigial link with his family's Irish heritage. After all, the literature of Ireland is remarkable in this same way, and its origins are in the ancient Irish poetic tradition of *dindshenchas*, which means a poetry explanatory of place and place lore. Whatever its roots, the South Side Chicago world that emerges in Farrell's fiction is as complete and coherent as Proust's Combray, Joyce's Dublin, and Faulkner's Yoknapatawpha County.

Farrell's rendering of Catholicism is another of his pioneering contributions to American fiction. For his Irish characters, a second familiar charted boundary, at least as vital and defining as the neighborhood, is the immigrant/ethnic Catholic parish, which provided both continuity with Ireland and help toward adjustment in America, as well as religion's traditional gifts of meaning and solace. In nineteenth-century urban America, the Irish found more negative echoes of the old country than one might have assumed. Here again, they were renters—apartment dwellers to be sure, but renters nonetheless. Here again, they were living in the worst available housing—flimsy, fire-prone, overcrowded, disease-ridden tenements. (Mr. Dooley tells us that "th' Hogan flats on Halsted Sthreet" was "wan iv thim big, fine-lookin' buildings that pious men built out iv celluloid an' plasther iv Paris.") Here again, they were at the bottom of the economic ladder in terms of remuneration for labor, with destitution and beggary looming just below the surface of daily life. Here again, as Catholics, they faced prejudice and discrimination from a Protestant governing class—with the difference being that this time the Protestants were in the majority, constituting a true demographic establishment. And here again, their religion provided both spiritual comfort and social adhesive. However, in the New World, there were formidable counterweights to second-class citizenship. The Irish in America were able to practice their religion freely, they could earn wages that increased over time, and they had the opportunity to rise in the world. As a result, they soon had the economic wherewithal—albeit often by accretion of nickels and dimes—to progress from frame and basement churches to that wonder of the late-nineteenth-century American religious world, the urban Catholic parish—a strong and vibrant complex of church, school, public meeting hall, rectory, and convent, with significant outlying institutions—Catholic hospitals, orphanages, and social settlement facilities.

Farrell's Washington Park novels describe this sophisticated cultural milieu in full swing, and they also illustrate the various attitudes toward the Church among three generations of Irish Americans. Like no other American writing when he was starting out, Farrell's fiction is bursting with descriptions of what went on in Catholic schoolrooms and schoolyards, at populous Sunday masses and quotidian visits to the peaceful, empty church, at the administration of the sacraments of penance and extreme unction, and at all sizes and manners of wakes. Notable in this vivid rendering is Farrell's balanced presentation of opposing aspects of American Catholic culture. True to his realist aesthetic, these contrasts are also a significant part of the dialectical opposition in the two fictional cycles. In the *Studs Lonigan* trilogy, St. Patrick's church and its pompous and hypocritical pastor, Father Gilhooley, fail everyone. Despite his flirtations with street life, Studs remains a conventional Catholic, never questioning the teachings of the Church, and reacting typically right up to his last illness. Although he tries to save his sinking life by joining parish groups and making countless acts of contrition, nothing avails. As a child, Danny O'Neill is terrorized by the fear of everlasting perdition instilled by the nuns at Crucifixion School, and yet, Catholic education also provides him with models of spiritual, educated, and ideologically dedicated men and women who eventually inspire the boy to translate his imaginative life into words. In addition, the Church exposes Danny to positive attributes unavailable elsewhere on the South Side of Chicago: a sense of order and ritual, historical continuity, and mystery. Although far from being the only writer in the thirties raised as a Catholic, Farrell was unique in the fullness of his exploration of Catholicism as a shaping institutional force in American life, from the graduation ceremony at St. Patrick's grammar school at the beginning of *Young Lonigan* to Danny's grandmother Mary O'Flaherty's black rosary beads at the end of her life in *My Days of Anger.* In the next decade, many would follow his lead, but it is important to understand just how innovative Farrell's fiction was in this regard. He brought Catholicism into the mainstream of American literature.[49]

The consciousness observing Washington Park and its Catholic parishes in Farrell's novels is often that of a child, for whom perceptions of urban life are fresh and formative. Here Farrell is also innovative. In his critique of the sorry state of American fiction at the First American Writers' Congress in 1935, he declared that much of "the writing about children by adults" was "of the same nature" as Harris's Uncle Remus stories and Lover's Handy Andy stage Irish stereotype: "Booth Tarkington's *Penrod,* for instance, is put into the same kind of mold, and it is a combination of certain conventions necessary for the intercourse between children and certain types of parents, on one hand, and, on the other hand, of a wish fulfillment or an adult fantasy about childhood." With his deep grounding in the works of John Dewey, Farrell saw education as the central issue. He wrote of his first novels that "the story of Studs Lonigan was conceived as the story of the education of a normal American boy in this period. The important institutions in the education of Studs Lonigan were the home and the family, the church, the school, and the playground. These institutions broke down and did not serve their desired function." In their place, "the streets became a potent educative factor in the boy's life."[50] Conversely, the path of Danny O'Neill makes it clear that education broadly defined in the Deweyan sense can have opposite, positive results for a city boy from a background much less stable than Studs's. This is another contribution to the dialectical force field that connects the two series of novels.

The Five Novels

The O'Neill-O'Flaherty series is sweeping and symphonic in structure. *A World I Never Made* is the prelude in which major themes are introduced. *No Star Is Lost* is a dark movement in a shattering, minor key. *Father and Son* consists of contrapuntal variations between the two title figures. *My Days of Anger* contains a large, focused statement of the major theme of the entire series. *The Face of Time* is a lyrical coda recapitulating the opening themes. Two streams of experience mingle in these pages: the outer stream of social life, a chronicle of the works and days of three generations of Chicagoans, and the inner stream of consciousness, the perceptions of that chronicle and of themselves in the minds of several individuals living it. Throughout the series, the same two watershed experiences recur—death and illuminating reverie. Deaths in the family constitute the central events of the outer stream and emphasize the social themes of alienation and failed community in urban America in the 1910s and 1920s. Solitary reveries are the central events of the inner streams of consciousness, and these emphasize the psychological theme of individual isolation. Clarifications of life and honest self-assessment come only in dreams and daydreams, and they are almost never shared. This theme gathers force in the last three volumes of the series, in which major characters die without having spoken their minds to anyone else. Against this choking tide, the young protagonist Danny O'Neill moves toward understanding of the social and psychological tragedies of his family's thwarted lives. His growth toward the resolution to use art as his weapon against these dual tragedies is the binding theme of the whole project. Through the first four books, Danny experiences the start of formal schooling, early adolescence, high school, and college. In the fifth novel, he comes around again to early childhood when home is the whole world. The slow and painful nature of his intellectual journey enforces another continuing motif—how hard we must work for enlightenment in this tough world. Here Farrell's love of the poetry of W. B. Yeats, from "Adam's Curse" to "The Circus Animals' Desertion," stood him in good stead. In the series overall, Farrell achieves a balance between the bump and flow of experience, both inner and outer, and a structural ordering into large thematic blocks and recurrent motifs. The mixture that results comes as close as fiction can to the rag and bone of reality. Most of the characters in these novels are caught in the flow and catch only brief glimpses of larger meanings. The Deweyan "poignancy of situations that evoke reflection" comes only to the reader, who is the one abiding witness to both confusing detail and clarifying pattern. The reader's perspective generates the sole, yet great and governing, irony that Farrell the author allows between his epigraphs and the last page of fictive text. And this whole consort makes for a powerful, compelling, and memorable reading experience.

The O'Neill-O'Flaherty series is autobiographical in obvious ways. Places and times often correlate with James T. Farrell's own facts of life. These include the ages and abodes of Danny O'Neill's grandparents and parents in the years covered in the novels, the number of his siblings and their approximate dates of birth (and death, in one case), and Danny's own formal markers of development: the start of elementary school (1911), graduation from high school (1923), and attendance at the University of Chicago (from 1925). But this is really neither here nor there for the novels. Here, once again, the example of Proust is useful. In the introduction to her translation of *Swann's Way*, Lydia Davis describes Proust's narrative in terms that also apply to Farrell's series: "The book is filled with events and characters closely resembling those of Proust's own life, yet this novel is not autobiography wearing a thin disguise of fiction but, rather, something more complex—fiction created out of real life, based on the experiences and beliefs of its author, and presented in the guise of autobiography."[51]

A World I Never Made takes place over five months, opening in August 1911 when Danny O'Neill is seven years old, and closing at Christmastime. *No Star Is Lost* covers two years, late 1914 (World War I is on in Europe) and 1915, when Danny is ten and eleven. *Father and Son* begins in 1918 with Danny fourteen and in eighth grade, and ends after his high school graduation in June 1923. *My Days of Anger* spans four years, 1924 through 1927, which include Danny's unfulfilling and abortive experiences of higher education at St. Vincent's night law school and the University of Chicago. The novel ends in the summer of 1927 when he is twenty-three. The fifth O'Neill-O'Flaherty book, *The Face of Time*, brings the series full circle, opening in the summer of 1909, when Danny O'Neill is five years old, and ending in December 1910.

In 1947, the World Publishing Company (Cleveland and New York) reprinted the four volumes of the O'Neill-O'Flaherty series that had appeared so far. The occasion prompted Farrell to write short introductions to the novels in which he outlines his aims with clarity and conciseness. He begins the first of these with a crucial distinction. Unlike *Studs Lonigan*, "which is mainly concerned with one central character," in this second series, "there are a number of major protagonists. . . . Each of them exists in his or her own right. Attention shifts from one to another of these characters. With this shift of attention the novel is unfolded in terms of a complicated series of contrasts. This story deals with two branches of one family, the O'Neills and the O'Flahertys. The former is a working class family; the latter is lower middle class. Three generations of this family appear in the work. There are contrasts in age, contrasts which have a class character and which are mirrored in different social attitudes, and, further, contrasts among the individual characters." And yet, Farrell continued, the lines from Housman that provide the first novel's epigraph and title—"I, a stranger and afraid, / In a world I never made"—indicate that "the central aim of this whole series has been that of portraying the emergence of Danny O'Neill." "An anxious little boy who has many fears," Danny "seen here first at the age of seven, is being prepared, educated in the day by day patterns of urban life." Thus, this bildungsroman begins.

In the World reprint introduction, Farrell stresses seven-year-old Danny's anxieties and alienation: "living with his grandmother, he is something of a stranger. . . . He is not in his own home." Furthermore, "it can equally be said that all of the characters here live in a world they never really made. All of them carry in their very consciousness the values of their past, of their *milieu*." Indeed, the "feeling of homelessness" experienced by Danny O'Neill and his two families is "noticeable in our whole modern period." Here, Farrell's deep reading of Dewey, Mead, and the pragmatists comes to bear. This vexed pervasive condition provoked Farrell's consideration of "one of the problems with which I was concerned in this novel. . . . What is the precise content of life of people in environments such as the environments described in this work? What does poverty mean in the intimate daily lives of those who must live in deprivation? Needless to say," he continues, "the novel does not seek to answer such questions in any formal and sociological manner. It seeks to describe, to recreate, to present in terms of immediate characterization." Not that these questions have no ramifications off the page. In the World reprint introduction, thirty-five years and one great international depression after 1911, the year in which *A World I Never Made* has its setting, Farrell declares that the "conditions of life under which the characters of this story live" and remain "strangers and afraid," still persist. Hence, the cultural relevance of the 1947 editions of the O'Neill-O'Flaherty series: "Before a world can be changed, it is necessary to know what the *nature of experience* [italics in text] is like in that world. This novel is one of the efforts I have made to go as deeply as possible into the nature of experience during the period of my own lifetime."[52] In my view, the stunning accomplishment in the O'Neill-O'Flaherty series of Farrell's dual purposes, aesthetic and cultural, justifies the present new editions from the University of Illinois Press. We are another sixty years down the road, and the value of such books is no less urgently evident. As William Carlos Williams so memorably said:

> It is difficult
> to get the news from poems
>   yet men die miserably every day
>   for lack
> of what is found there.

A World I Never Made begins in August 1911 with emphasis on the central characterization of seven-year-old Danny O'Neill as defined by his anxious, conflicted interactions with the other members of the two families between which he feels himself torn. In the first fifty pages Farrell introduces the essential dramatis personae of the entire series. First come the lower-middle-class O'Flahertys. Danny's grandmother, Mary O'Flaherty, is an aging immigrant matriarch. Recently widowed, she is devoted to her grandson but combative and cantankerous toward everyone else. Danny's Aunt Margaret O'Flaherty ("Peg") is twenty-four, a cashier in a Loop hotel, attractive but unstable. Resentful of the demands of her family and unhappy as the mistress of a married businessman whose promise of marriage she distrusts, Peg is drifting toward alcoholism. Danny's Uncle Al O'Flaherty, thirty-eight, is a fairly successful traveling shoe salesman and the main family breadwinner. Poignantly earnest, he reads Emerson and Lord Chesterfield for "self-improvement," and works hard to sustain a positive outlook in the face of the increased responsibilities and expenses of "two deaths in the family this year"—his father, Old Tom O'Flaherty, of stomach cancer, and his twenty-one-year-old sister Louise, of consumption. This is a household reeling from recently inflicted, deep dynastic wounds. In it, to young Danny's great confusion (and sometimes dread), brief periods of calm, often elicited by soothing music on the gramophone, alternate with fights that can escalate into vicious verbal and even physical pummeling, as when Mrs. O'Flaherty excoriates Peg for being an adulterous "chippy," who "goes out with the Devil," and Peg responds by accusing her mother ("you Irish whoremonger!") of nagging Old Tom into his grave.

Danny's "real" family, the impoverished O'Neills, live twenty-five blocks north in a much worse neighborhood. Lizz is an O'Flaherty, the hard-luck sister of Peg and Al. Now in her mid-thirties, she has already borne eight children. Three have died at birth, and the five surviving are Bill, eleven; Danny, seven; "Little

Margaret," five; Dennis, four; and Bob, eighteen months. Small wonder, given what she has already endured, that Lizz is old-country superstitious, fiercely pious, and sometimes hysterical. She is, when the novel opens, suffering the throes of yet another pregnancy approaching term. This new baby will be born healthy and named Catherine. Lizz's husband, Jim O'Neill, is forty years old. An overworked teamster, he is trapped in a physically punishing job, ashamed of how poorly he provides for his family, and apprehensive about the future with another child on the way. It especially bothers him that he has been forced to send his second son away to be raised by his wife's parents, and that the boy is happy with the O'Flahertys: Danny calls his grandmother "Mother." Prone to violence when drinking, Jim is nonetheless a decent, thoughtful man who still loves his wife and kids and hopes against hope for better days. The O'Neills also fight, mostly when Jim's practicality clashes with his wife's escapist otherworldliness. For example, when they come into some money, he urges Lizz to get her teeth fixed, rather than buying "high masses for all your dead relations."

Farrell begins *A World I Never Made* by placing Danny O'Neill in the four milieus from which his character will emerge: at home (chapter 1, in his grandmother O'Flaherty's apartment), at play (chapter 3, at a White Sox game), and at school (in chapter 4, his first day at Corpus Christi school). Chapter 2 introduces the contrasting world from which Danny has been removed, that of his parents, Jim and Lizz O'Neill. Throughout this novel, Danny's mind swings between fear (of the consequences of missing Mass on Sunday morning, of the recent deaths of his grandfather and Aunt Louise, of the violent fights among the adults in his two households, of the strange new world of school) and escape into daydreams of mastery. Constant throughout this novel and those that follow, Danny's reveries also point, however tentatively, toward an artist's vocation. At the beginning of *A World I Never Made*, he sees himself as Buffalo Bill saving his Aunt Louise from the Indians, "Danny Dreamer in the funny papers," and the White Sox catcher, Billy Sullivan, warming up for a big game. Later, he pretends to be a laundryman, a butcher, and an artist selling his drawings. At the end of the novel, the boy has two related imaginative experiences at Christmas of 1911—a daydream of art and a nightmare of death. The first occurs on his way to the Loop with his Aunt Margaret to see Santa Claus: "He saw himself as two Danny O'Neills. One of him was sitting in the elevated train that was going along, swish, zish. The other of him was outside, running, going just as fast as the train was, jumping from roof to roof." Here is the artist's dream of doubleness and control—to step outside the self and walk easily through a recognizable world. The second experience occurs on Christmas Eve, when Danny dreams of hissing snakes and "a boy as big as Mother, with a beard like a dwarf and a black suit like the Devil," come to carry him off and kill him. These two daydreams connect in the fourth volume of the series, *My Days of Anger*, when the use of art to answer the finality of death becomes an article of faith at the start of Danny's life as a writer.

For the second O'Neill-O'Flaherty novel, *No Star Is Lost*, once again Farrell takes both title and epigraph from Housman. Here the second reverses the charge of the first. The title could be mistakenly read as supporting divine intentionality—until the epigraph provides the bleak context of philosophical naturalism (any man's death does *not* diminish the universe) combined with the irremediable human stain:

> Stars, I have seen them fall,
>   But when they drop and die
> No star is lost at all
>   From all the star-sown sky,
> The toil of all that be
>   Helps not the primal fault;
> It rains into the sea
>   And still the sea is salt.

In his introduction to the World reprint edition, Farrell indicates that "the note of Christmas quiet" at the end of *A World I Never Made* "carried, also, a note of foreboding," for "nothing truly tragic had happened to any of the characters." In this new novel, "the treatment of poverty" represented by the O'Neill family "is extended, further developed. The tragic consequences of poverty on the lives of the children are shown in what happens to the child, Little Arty, at the end of this novel." Overall, *No Star Is Lost* "deals more with the life of the children than did its predecessor. This is especially the case with the treatment of the boy, Danny O'Neill. Here we see Danny living more completely in the public world of a boy as well as in the private world of the home, the family." The clash and contrast thus evidenced, "creat[es] in Danny a tension and bewilderment which, I trust, suggests what will be the character of the problems and the resolution of these problems that he will face in the future, when he is seen at an older age."[53]

No Star Is Lost is a lacerating novel to read, especially in its advancement of two of Farrell's strongest themes with harrowing verisimilitude: the rendering of alcoholism and the use of children as witnesses to disaster. In its tracing of the O'Neill family's painful and failing struggle toward a decent life, the book focuses Farrell's central theme of social injustice. In 1914 and 1915, the O'Neills are living in a small, cramped cottage at Forty-fifth and Wells, and on cold days the children "take turns sticking their feet in the oven." Jim O'Neill is working a backbreaking six-day week as a poorly paid teamster for Continental Express. Again, Danny is spared the physical discomfort because he continues to live at the O'Flahertys. And yet, he experiences humiliation on the streets and playgrounds, where kids make fun of his grandmother's clay pipe and other Irish ways and his Aunt Margaret's drinking. Because he is more and more interested in baseball, Danny, now ten, is outside a lot, but he wishes he could move to a new neighborhood to escape the embarrassment of his family's worsening reputation. Farrell establishes the child's perspective by presenting the first seventy-five pages from Danny's point of view, the longest such stretch in the series. His dreams of guilt and dominance continue. In one, black and white angels vie for the boy's soul and he hears the latter ordered to "Go back and be a guardian angel to the White Sox." In another, he is grown up, "a man so big he could almost touch the ceiling," walking fearlessly through the neighborhood, past the convent of the Little Sisters of the Good Shepherd on Prairie Avenue and the Willard Theater on Fifty-first and Calumet.

Jilted by her married lover and frightened by the erosion of her good looks, Peg O'Flaherty goes on a terrifying, extended self-destructive binge of several weeks that nearly tears her family apart. All through this period, she and her mother engage in verbal and sometimes physical battles of epic ferocity, many of them observed by Danny. Night after night, Peg reels home comatose, incontinent, and hounded with delirium tremens so horrifying that she attempts suicide by turning on the gas. Her Hieronymus Bosch hallucinations feature snakes and devils, waiters pouring gin from bottles shaped like phalluses, hideous animals, mud, slime, and excrement. These nightmare visions stand in stark contrast to Danny's recurrent creative daydreaming.

There is a third type of vision here as well. An effective technique of Farrell's for revealing his characters, so many of whom have trouble expressing their deepest affections and motives aloud, is a kind of daydream-soliloquy, the first of which appears in *No Star Is Lost* when Mary O'Flaherty goes out to Calvary Cemetery and has a fine long chat with her husband Tom, who has been dead for five years. Recalling Ireland, the Mullingar Fair where they met, their first hard years in America, and the death of their first son, Mary realizes that this grave site is "the only plot of ground that they had ever owned in America." Suddenly, Tom O'Flaherty is standing there beside her, "a small old man in a white nightgown, with a slightly drooping gray mustache." Not fazed in the least, Mary reverts to her everyday self by administering a typical scolding to poor Tom, for whom even the grave is no protection. Having been annoyed several times by Lizz O'Neill's reports that her dead father has been speaking to her, Mary tells her husband to stop visiting Lizz: "If you have messages, you give them to me. It's me that should get them, and not her. . . . I'm a hard woman when I'm crossed, Tom, a hard woman, and I'll make you toe the mark, dead or alive."

The death of the youngest O'Neill child, two-year-old Arty, of diphtheria in 1915 is the climactic event of *No Star Is Lost*. All the O'Neill children come down with the disease, and Lizz is about to deliver another child as well. With his brothers and sisters falling down around him, Arty dies unattended by either the doctor or the priest. Neither will risk contagion by entering the O'Neill cottage. As the delirious Lizz attempts to feed her own mother's milk to Arty, it is five-year-old Bob who realizes that his brother is dead. "There's only one crime in this world, Lizz," says the heartsick Jim: "to be a poor man." Returning on a streetcar from his son's burial in Calvary Cemetery, Jim sees middle-class homes and says to himself: "In these homes the kids were happy and well-fed and had the care of a doctor when they were sick. And in these homes, the kids were alive." That same day, the rest of the O'Neill children are packed off to a public hospital in the police wagon and Lizz bears a stillborn son. This is not melodrama, but one of the places in the O'Neill-O'Flaherty series where Farrell's own family life matches that of his characters most closely. His baby brother Frankie had died of diphtheria, similarly unattended, in the Farrell cottage at Forty-fifth and Wells on June 21, 1918. That same afternoon, Mary Daly Farrell was delivered of a stillborn son. She was to have in all fifteen pregnancies, including eight stillbirths. So much, in this far from uncommon situation, for the "wages of whiteness," the heavily theorized and poorly evidenced idea that great numbers of Irish ethnics opted for the benefits of an improved quality of life by "becoming white" at the expense of people of color.

No Star Is Lost ends with a detailed example of neighborhood placement that is also a reminder that Danny O'Neill has been spared all this suffering. The boy gets his wish of a fresh start as the O'Flahertys move further south to a new apartment at Fifty-seventh and Indiana. This also means that Danny will attend a new school, St. Patrick's, at Sixty-first and Michigan. On his first day in the new neighborhood, he meets two older kids—Johnny O'Brien and Studs Lonigan.

Father and Son, the third novel, has a span of six years, the longest in the series. The two families have moved again, but most characters continue in established patterns. The marriage of Jim and Lizz O'Neill bumps along with fights, reconciliations, thwarted resolutions for change, and increasing anxieties related to Jim's health. Promoted to night dispatcher at the express company, Jim is able proudly to move his family south to Fifty-eighth and Calumet in Washington Park into an apartment with "a bathroom inside, running hot and cold water, steam heat, gas and electricity." The O'Flahertys have also moved further south—to 5816–1/2 South Park Avenue overlooking the park. Their home life is still a buzzing hive of contentious personalities: Peg drinks to excess, though less often; Al becomes more frustrated with his job and his autodidactic optimism takes on a willed, cast-iron aspect; and their mother continues to stir the pot of controversy. If anything, the tensions in this family are greater now, because second son Ned O'Flaherty has moved back home from Madison after the death of his wife. A preening narcissist and sometime soap-box speaker at the Washington Park "Bug Club," Ned has embraced the cockeyed spirituality of "New Thought," whose main tenet is the "power of the wish." He's no help to anyone.

The great theme of *Father and Son* is the struggle of Jim and Danny O'Neill to understand one another in the context of Jim's downward spiral to unemployment and helplessness because of three crippling strokes and Danny's painful stumbling through high school toward emotional and intellectual maturity. Theirs is the story of George and Gerry O'Dell writ large, and few readers will not recognize and be moved by the fully elaborated drama of this largely failed attempt at communication. In the World reprint introduction, Farrell explains that "the effect of the years of separation from [Danny's] father begin to tell. The misunderstanding between the father and the callow boy deepens. In difficult moments, Jim can only become angry with his son. Danny can only feel guilty towards his father, and, at the same time, sorry for him."

There is epiphany for both father and son, but, in keeping with Farrell's realist aesthetic, it is muted, inconclusive, and far from clearly revealed to the characters themselves. Heartbreakingly, Jim O'Neill in his last illness sees himself as having failed his family. And yet, in this novel he faces progressive debilitation and boredom with courage, dignity, and deepening compassion. Sitting alone by the apartment window, Jim meditates on the mystery of having children, the unreflective profligacy of youth, the solace of Catholicism (and its limits, for he rejects the view that contraception is sinful), the lack of justice in the world. Shakespeare is Jim's companion and consolation, as he often sits up at night reading *Julius Caesar* and *Hamlet*. His insights include a doubleness that, unbeknownst to either, echoes his son's artistic perspective: "Lying alone in bed, as he began coming back to himself, lying there so much alone, he had felt half in this world and half not in it, watching it. Yes, men tried and fought and raised hell and wanted all kinds of things, and yes, yes, *vanity, all is vanity*." In his finest hour, Jim hears that the doctor who refused to attend his dying child Arty has himself died suddenly, and Jim forgives him his trespass. Farrell's depiction of Jim O'Neill's lonely struggle to understand his life and approaching death is one of the great achievements of modern fiction.

Jim's final weeks are filled with petty indignities. Another of his children is farmed out to the O'Flahertys, and Lizz suggests that he check into a public hospital. He is shamed by having to accept a Christmas basket from a Protestant charity. He has to make an X to get money at the bank, and he loses a five-dollar bill in the street. People on the El think he's drunk, kids mock and mimic his limp, and an apartment-house janitor accuses him of loitering. On Jim's last day, it is once again the children who register the tragic. Twelve-year-old Catherine sees that her father has wet his pants, and it is Bob, a year older, who discovers that his father has died. The social and economic dimension of this novel published in 1940 is also clear. Farrell declares in the World introduction that "the tragedy of the worker is the central social tragedy of our times. Jim's life is but one illustration of this tragedy." Furthermore, "it could well pose for the reader the question—is this a fair and open fight?"

As for Danny, "Now, on the threshold of manhood, he must find a place and a career in that world. He is still afraid, and he remains something of a stranger. But he has, among the other lessons he has learned, the example of his father's life. He gains the conviction that his father never had a chance. His father's death meant something, but he doesn't know exactly what."[54] Farrell describes Danny's abortive diary keeping and other failed writing projects, his clumsy attempts at male and female friendships, the superficial compensation of success in high school athletics, the persistent angst of his situation vis-à-vis his two families. And yet, despite the blunders and embarrassments of what Yeats called "the ignominy of boyhood; the distress / Of boyhood changing into man," *Father and Son* also contains an artistic breakthrough for Danny O'Neill. With a family fight raging around him, he is able to finish a story that he knows is good enough for the St. Stanislaus literary magazine. Here, life and art intersect again, because this turns out to be the same story, a romantic tale of a priest's martyrdom in Elizabethan Ireland, that Farrell wrote in 1922 for his high school magazine, the St. Cyril *Oriflamme*. In one sense, appropriating here his own adolescent version of sentimental Catholic fiction is Farrell's way of saying that, as a mature writer, he will not contribute to this genre of literature as propaganda. But in another sense, the story documents the milieu of the Catholic high school in the 1920s as an environment somewhat encouraging to the imagination.

Here again, Farrell's epigraphs speak volumes. For Jim O'Neill, he quotes Tolstoy: "Ivan Ilych's life had been most simple and most ordinary and therefore most terrible." For Danny, there is the Baudelaire of *Les Fleurs du Mal:* "—Ah! Seigneur! Donnez moi la force et le courage / De contempler mon coeur et mon corps sans dégoût!" And for himself, Farrell provides a credo of Bertrand Russell, who counters man's brief, powerless, suffering condition with an admonition "to cherish, ere yet the blow falls, the lofty thoughts that ennoble his little day; disdaining the coward terrors of the slave of Fate, to worship at the shrine that his own hands have built; undismayed by the empire of chance, to preserve a mind free from the wanton tyranny that rules his outward life."

As Farrell points out in his World introduction, *My Days of Anger* "differs in method of presentation from its three predecessors. . . . Here, the story is told with auctorial concentration on one central character, Danny O'Neill." Farrell will do this by limiting twenty-eight of the twenty-nine arabic-numbered chapters of the book to the consciousness of this protagonist. The thoughts of everyone else are relegated to brief, italicized interchapters. His aim is "to present the way in which the disposition of an American artist is forged." This word naturally echoes Joyce's *Portrait of the Artist*, where Stephen Dedalus sets out

for Paris "to forge the uncreated conscience of my race." Because of the challenges of his background and upbringing, Farrell explains, Danny's "disposition
as an artist is forged in bewilderment and anxiety, in confusion and insecurity."
However, along his difficult way, he makes "small decisions and resolutions [that]
suggest a tension within him, a tension which is symptomatic of his need for
change, for escape from the circumstances of his life." And when he prepares to
leave for New York at the novel's end, "his mood is one of determination. He
asks no quarter. He looks forward to struggle. In this sense, *My Days of Anger* is
an optimistic book." Further, Danny "rejects the values of his past, but he does
not completely destroy his sense of identification with his own people. He feels
that he is going forth to fight not only war but their war. His conception of art,
of writing, is a militant one." Again, as a realist, Farrell knows that anger is a
limited and, ultimately, a distorting tool for the artist, and so this novel will end
with Danny not quite launched into the concerted action of a life committed to
writing. The novel's first epigraph, from Baudelaire's *Intimate Journals*, makes
this proviso clear: "Nevertheless, I will let these pages stand—since I wish to
record my days of anger."

In the World introduction, Farrell refutes the idea that his book is in any way
a pastiche of Joyce by pointing out that his aspiring artist/protagonist "emerges
from a background which is common rather than special; it is the background
known to millions of Americans. Here, in short, I feel, is a detailed story of the
American Way of Life."[55] At the same time, that *My Days of Anger* is Farrell's
"common," "American" *Portrait* is clear from its second epigraph, an homage
that takes the form of a poetic fragment by Joyce:

> Ah star of evil! star of pain!
> Highhearted youth comes not again
>
> Nor old heart's wisdom yet to know
> The signs that mock me as I go.

The poem is dated "*Bahnhofstrasse*, Zurich, 1918," when Joyce was thirty-six.
Farrell had turned thirty-nine in February 1943, the year he completed and
published *My Days of Anger*.

This novel's great emphasis on Danny is the capstone of Farrell's pioneering
presentation of the growth of an American artist from working-class, urban,
ethnic, and Catholic backgrounds. Again, scrupulous detail is all. In the outside
world, Farrell continues to describe Danny's home life among the O'Flahertys
and O'Neills, who appear in the counterpointing interchapters as stuck in familiar troubles. Peg steals at work, is fired, and gets drunk for a week. Al's shoe
company fails and he has to go back out on the road in a lesser position. The
aging Mary O'Flaherty becomes ill. Danny's brothers and sisters are growing
up aware of their social and economic limits and restless for change. When *My*

Days of Anger opens, Danny is a year out of high school and still working at the Continental Express Company. He goes on to a South Side gas station, where he has more time to read and also learns about American capitalism firsthand. Farrell also breaks new ground for American fictional milieus by detailing Danny's "pre-legal" night-school classes at "St. Vincent's" in the Loop, and then taking us into his economics, history, and writing classes at the University of Chicago and the lunchroom dialectic among his fellow students. Emotionally, although he is now out of high school, Danny still suffers the tortures of the damned in his relationships with the opposite sex. He cannot find a steady girlfriend, he loses his virginity in a casual encounter on his twenty-first birthday in February 1925, and he picks up the habit of going to whorehouses with friends from the neighborhood. Intellectually, Danny's continuing fascination with words evolves at last into his first honest "Thought Diary" entries, and then into a torrent of fiction produced for his creative-writing teacher at the university, Professor Saxon. He loses his faith, at first in a dream, and wakes up a nonbeliever, "free of lies." (Studs Lonigan brings the news of Danny's atheism to the pool hall, diagnosing the cause as "too many books.") Other liberating rejections follow: of his pseudo-Nietzschean friend Ed Lanson, of the University of Chicago, and of Chicago as a place to live. At the same time, Danny's days of anger and confusion slowly give way to understanding of and sympathy for his family, friends, and other exploited Chicagoans, especially African Americans. In this process, the crucial experience is his grandmother's death in the spring of 1927.

A classic immigrant matriarch who has held her family together by sheer force of often vituperative will, Mary O'Flaherty, a self-described "hard woman from a hard country," has never been able to express love or compassion for her family—with the single exception of her grandson. As she nears death at eighty-six, a last extended daydream-soliloquy—the only full chapter in this novel from inside a mind other than Danny O'Neill's—provides a summary of her character and concerns. Farrell had been planning Mrs. O'Flaherty's reverie at least since 1938, when he traveled to Ireland for the first time to verify the immigrants' background. Upon completing *My Days of Anger* in 1943, he wrote a friend announcing the conclusion of this phase of his writing life, the "years of driving work, years of eight to fourteen hour days concentrating on these connected books." He was especially proud of the "long chapter, in Anglo-Irish, when Grandmother O'Flaherty sits by the window in a wheel chair, hip broken, slowly fading out of this life; it is a long reverie, more or less Joycean, in which past and present jumble, time loses significance, she dreams and she awakes." The writing here "is something fresh—the fading consciousness of an old woman, further, an old Irish immigrant woman, illiterate, who came out to America, raised her family here, [has] seen them grow up, and sits doing this while her grandson sits preparing to write, even about her own life."[56] As with

Jim O'Neill's lonely meditations, Farrell here solves the problem of speaking for those for whom self-expression comes hard with a restrained eloquence that is a hallmark of his achievement as a novelist.

When his grandmother dies, Danny finds his rejection of Catholicism tempered by understanding that "the sorrows of death remained, remained in the hearts of the living. . . . He understood now why people did what he could not do, what he could never do—pray." In an earlier conversation with friends at the university, Danny had agreed with Stephen Dedalus's refusing to pray at his dying mother's bedside in *Ulysses:* "What has kindness got to do with conviction? I won't bend my knees." And yet, on the morning of his grandmother's death, Danny kneels down, blesses himself, and pretends to pray with his family. A month later, as he prepares to leave Chicago for New York and a new life as a writer, Danny walks home down Fifty-eighth Street from the El, and feels the weight of the Washington Park neighborhood as "a world in itself . . . a world in which another Danny O'Neill had lived." Realizing that he has "finally taken off a way of life . . . as if it were a worn-out suit of clothes," he now has confidence in the "weapons" of his writer's trade: "now he was leaving and he was fully armed." In this, he echoes Stephen Dedalus leaving Dublin for Paris in 1902 with his own weapons of "silence, exile, and cunning." Danny also has a mature understanding of his position as an artist in relation to his family: "His people had not been fulfilled. He had not understood them all these years. He would do no penance now for these; he would do something surpassing penance. There was a loyalty to the dead, a loyalty beyond penance and regret. He would do battle so that others did not remain unfulfilled as he and his family had been." Rather than ending the novel here, Farrell goes on to create one final contrast between honest and false consciousness in the form of an overheard conversation back at the Continental Express Company, where the bosses who used to ridicule Danny look back with distorting nostalgia at his time with them, declaring that he was "a crackerjack clerk" and "one of the best kids I ever had."

Ten years after finishing *My Days of Anger,* Farrell published the fifth and final O'Neill-O'Flaherty novel. Although not part of his original plan, *The Face of Time* is an appropriate coda for the series. Opening in the summer of 1909, this book brings the design full circle to the final illnesses of Old Tom O'Flaherty and his youngest daughter Louise, the memory of which hangs over the first volume, *A World I Never Made.* Farrell also renders the elder O'Flahertys' memories of Ireland, the journey to America, and their early years in Brooklyn, Green Bay, and Chicago, thus returning his narrative to the beginning of this family's story. The result is one of the finest American fictional treatments of the felt experience of immigration.

For most of this novel, the focus alternates between the minds of the aging Irish immigrant, Old Tom O'Flaherty, and his five-year-old American grandson,

Danny O'Neill. Again, the child is witness to pain and conflict. The family fights among Mary O'Flaherty and her children are well under way, and Danny is also precociously aware that living with his grandparents has wounded his parents, especially his father. In addition, he is the terrified observer of his favorite aunt's worsening health and his beloved grandfather's decline and death. Old Tom lives out a restless retirement, bored or harassed within the family, and dies of a painful stomach cancer. In his characterization, Farrell's theme of thwarted communication of the heart's urgent concerns has a last statement here as well. Only in the unshared daydream-soliloquies of his final illness does Tom reveal his sad secrets: the "greenhorn" humiliations of his first displacements in the New World still disturb the old man; he has never felt at home in America; he is puzzled and embittered by having worked so hard and ended up with so little; and he wishes he could go back to die in Ireland. Tom's closest bond is not with his wife Mary, who tends to ignore him, but with his son-in-law, Jim O'Neill, representative of a new generation of hardworking, ill-rewarded laborers, people for whom the American dream remains unfulfilled. In turning over the insults and injustices to which the working man is prone and the compensating mysteries of marriage and children, these two share the closest moments in this novel.

The Face of Time is most moving in the variations—sometimes harsh, sometimes lyrical—that Farrell plays on the theme of elemental loneliness. In his fiction, immigration is but the prototype and metaphor for what he sees as an inevitable condition of humanity. The other most important voice here is the consciousness of Louise O'Flaherty, dying of consumption at twenty-one and holding terror at bay with dreams of the arrival of "Prince Charming," marriage, and children of her own. It is she who asks the big question, though only to herself: "And was this the end of love, one going, dying, the way her father was dying? Must you, in the end, always be alone?" Farrell's answer pervades this novel's conclusion. On his way to the hospital, Old Tom's voice breaks and he is unable to say good-bye to Danny. During the family's last visit to his bedside, Tom can hear his wife and daughter discussing his imminent death, but he cannot speak to them. When the hospital calls with the news of Tom's passing, Mary O'Flaherty shuts the bedroom door to grieve alone. Standing in front of his grandfather's casket, six-year-old Danny thinks, "There was Father. He couldn't talk. He was Father all right, and he wasn't Father." Underscored by the deaths of Old Tom and Louise, the inability of the O'Neill and O'Flaherty families to articulate the heart's speech of love and compassion brings *The Face of Time* around again to the initial provocations for Danny O'Neill's hard journey through the course of the other four novels of the series out of this stalemate and toward the solution of art.

In Farrell's materialist/pragmatist universe, time is the archenemy of all such solutions, a point underscored by this novel's title and epigraph from Yeats's

"Lamentation of the Old Pensioner." Relegated to "shelter from the rain / Under a broken tree," the speaker in the poem recalls his youthful participation in talk of love, politics, and revolution. Now, "My contemplations are of Time / That has transfigured me." And yet, he continues to affirm the storyteller's power of memory and to defy the changes rung by Time:

> There's not a woman turns her face
> Upon a broken tree,
> And yet the beauties that I loved
> Are in my memory;
> I spit into the face of Time
> That has transfigured me.

This is also the novel in which Farrell provides his most positive rendering of place. Grandfather and grandson walk abroad in their neighborhood world thoroughly at ease. Because they are absolved by age and youth from the crises and challenges faced by the other family members who are in the responsible middle way of their lives, Old Tom and Danny encounter fewer obstacles. Through them, Farrell presents Washington Park as home on a human scale. The two companions take great pleasure in the daily round: feeding the ducks on the pond in Washington Park, talking to the cop on the beat and the clerk at the corner grocery, checking in with a sympathetic priest who knows their story, watching Ty Cobb in town against the White Sox at Comiskey, and "rushing the can" for beer at the saloon. Given the fullness and fairness of his presentation throughout the series, Farrell is entitled to the lyrical backward glance at his native city in *The Face of Time*. In fact, it's part of the novel's overall elegiac tone. But he nonetheless avoids distorting nostalgia by keeping illness and isolation as the grounding bass notes.

Shortly after publishing the last O'Neill-O'Flaherty novel, Farrell wrote an essay, "How *The Face of Time* Was Written," that speaks tellingly of his method, themes, aims, and a crucial influence. He recalls the origin of this unplanned fifth volume on "a raw and sunless September afternoon in 1951" in the Chelsea Hotel in New York, just eight days after he had completed *Yet Other Waters*, the final volume of his Bernard Carr trilogy of novels: "Then suddenly . . . I had an impulse to write a short story which would tell of the death of Old Tom. I sat down and began it in longhand. Immediately, I thought of the old man and his grandson Danny. I began by putting them together on Forty-ninth Street in Chicago." Again, the imagination's catalyst is place. As he worked on, day by day, the conception blossomed into "a long story or novelette," and then into a novel. "When a story or book evolves in this manner," Farrell continues, "I know that I have a clear path from my unconscious. I have always believed that one must trust the unconscious and write out of it."

While completing the first draft in Paris in August 1952, "I thought of Proust, to me the greatest writer of the twentieth century. *Remembrance of Things Past* ended in that deeply tragic death mask scene and in Proust's mystical sense of time and existence in two times at once. I was living in two times at once. I had no mystical sense of time, but I felt, too, the dual sense of time." His working title, "to me very exact," was *A Legacy of Fear,* but to avoid mislabeling ("It could seem like a detective story"), he searched for another and found it in Yeats's poem. Farrell concludes this essay by generalizing from the completion of *The Face of Time* to the central goal that drove his working life: "In that novel I tried to achieve what is my constant and major aim as a writer—to write so that life may speak for itself. And life, speaking for itself, tells us again and again of the transfiguration of time. Joy and sadness, growth and decay, life and death are all part of the transfiguration of time. To look into the Face of Time, and to master its threat to us—this is one of the basic themes and purposes of art and literature."[57]

An appropriate gloss for James T. Farrell's commitment and career is the last poem, "Epilogue," in Robert Lowell's last book, *Day by Day.* What Lowell comes around to after his circus animals have deserted is what Farrell's life of unremitting literary labor represents and accomplishes:

> Yet why not say what happened?
> Pray for the grace of accuracy
> Vermeer gave to the sun's illumination
> stealing like the tide across a map
> to his girl solid with yearning.
> We are poor passing facts,
> warned by that to give
> each figure in the photograph
> his living name.

Notes

1. James T. Farrell, *Chicago Stories*, ed. Charles Fanning (Urbana and Chicago: University of Illinois Press, 1998), 106–15.

2. Letters to Clifton Fadiman, 24 June 1929; Ezra Pound, 14 February 1934; Ernest W. Burgess, 9 January 1937; James Henle, 12 February 1943; James T. Farrell Archives, University of Pennsylvania (hereafter, Farrell Archives).

3. Letter to Jack Kunitz, 7 August 1934, Farrell Archives.

4. "My Beginnings as a Writer," in *Reflections at Fifty and Other Essays* (New York: Vanguard Press, 1954), 157–63.

5. Farrell recalled that he made "the decision to write" on "a March morning in 1927." It was spring, and he was looking for a metaphor "to make new the miraculous unity of life. . . . I know that my sentimentalities were just that, and no more." Unpublished

manuscript, Box 495, Farrell Archives. See also "Beginnings," unpublished manuscript, 1961, Box 494, Farrell Archives.

6. "Beginnings," Box 494, Farrell Archives; "The World Is Today," *Park East* (New York), 8 May 1975.

7. Edgar M. Branch, *James T. Farrell* (New York: Twayne Publishers, 1971), 23. See also Branch's elegant short book, *A Paris Year, Dorothy and James T. Farrell, 1931–1932* (Athens: Ohio University Press, 1998), and Robert K. Landers, *An Honest Writer, the Life and Times of James T. Farrell* (San Francisco: Encounter Books, 2004). Wholly inadequate as criticism, Landers's biography is useful for details of Farrell's life.

8. Murray Kempton, *Part of Our Time: Some Ruins and Monuments of the Thirties* (New York: Simon and Schuster, 1955), 128–29.

9. Letter to James J. Geller, 16 February 1943, Farrell Archives.

10. Michael Denning, *The Cultural Front: The Laboring of American Culture in the Twentieth Century* (New York: Verso, 1997), xvii, xx.

11. Farrell preferred the term "bottom-dog literature," which he borrowed from the title of Edward Dahlberg's novel: "If we use 'proletarian' in the strictly Marxist sense, many of these works cannot be said to deal with the proletariat but rather with the lower middle class, the urban lumpen proletariat, the poor farmer." "Social Themes in American Realism," in *Literature and Morality* (New York: Vanguard Press, 1947), 21. See also Douglas Wixson, *Worker-Writer in America* (Urbana: University of Illinois Press, 1999), passim.

12. "The Short Story" [Speech before the First American Writers' Congress], in *The League of Frightened Philistines and Other Papers* (New York: Vanguard Press, 1945), 136–48.

13. Dempsey J. Travis, *An Autobiography of Black Jazz* (Chicago: Urban Research Institute, 1983), passim.

14. Michel Fabre, *The Unfinished Quest of Richard Wright*, 2nd ed. (Urbana: University of Illinois Press, 1993), 118–19.

15. *A Note on Literary Criticism* (1936; repr., New York: Columbia University Press, 1992).

16. Preface to *The Short Stories of James T. Farrell* (New York: Vanguard Press, 1937), l–li.

17. "James Farrell on James Farrell," *The New Republic*, 28 October 1940, 595–96. Murray Kempton recognized the class divide between Farrell and some, like Wilson, who opposed him: "Farrell once said that a writer's style is his childhood; in middle age, he chose to put on the title page of his *Bernard Carr* a terrible reflection of Anton Chekhov's: 'What writers belonging to the upper class have received from nature for nothing, plebeians acquire at the cost of their youth.' . . . Farrell's world, like Dreiser's, was one whose inhabitants understood the price the artist pays. They looked at the New York literary world and thought it commercial, supercilious, log-rolling, and absolutely alien." *Part of Our Time*, 128–29.

18. Carl Van Doren, "The City Culture," *Nation* 143 (24 October 1936): 483.

19. Carlos Baker, "Another Milestone in the Long Saga of Danny O'Neill," *New York Times Book Review*, 24 October 1943, BR 3; *New York Times*, 4 February 1937, 19; 12 February 1937, 21.

20. Peter Brooks, *Realist Vision* (New Haven and London: Yale University Press, 2005), 71–75.

21. Letters, Ezra Pound to James T. Farrell, 3 February 1932; James T. Farrell to Ezra Pound, 17 February 1932; Farrell Archives.

22. "Joyce's *A Portrait of the Artist as a Young Man*," in *League of Frightened Philistines*, 45–59.

23. "A Note on Ulysses" (1934); letter to Meyer Schapiro, 6 August 1938, both quoted in Dennis Flynn, ed., James T. Farrell, *On Irish Themes* (Philadelphia: University of Pennsylvania Press, 1982), 86, 169. Flynn's book is the invaluable guide to Farrell's engagement with all things Irish.

24. Flynn, introduction to Farrell, *On Irish Themes*, 4.

25. *Note on Literary Criticism*, 78, 83, 88.

26. *Note on Literary Criticism*, 118–23. Another writer who grasped fully and early on the importance of this concept in Proust was Samuel Beckett, whose brilliant little book, *Proust* (New York: New Directions), appeared in 1931. Here is Beckett:

> Memory and Habit are attributes of the Time cancer. They control the most simple Proustian episode, and an understanding of their mechanism must precede any particular analysis of their application. . . .
> The laws of memory are subject to the more general laws of habit. Habit is a compromise effected between the individual and his environment, or between the individual and his own organic eccentricities, the guarantee of a dull inviolability, the lightning-conductor of his existence. Habit is the ballast that chains the dog to his vomit. (7–8)

27. "The Writer and His Audience," Indiana, Pennsylvania, 12 June 1958, in Donald Phelps, ed., *Hearing Out James T. Farrell, Selected Lectures* (New York: The Smith, 1985), 108–10.

28. Here again, Beckett understood this fully in 1931: "Involuntary memory is explosive, 'an immediate, total and delicious deflagration.' It restores . . . the past object. . . . Because in its flame it has consumed Habit and all its works, and in its brightness revealed what the mock reality of experience never can and never will reveal—the real. But involuntary memory is an unruly magician and will not be importuned. It chooses its own time and place for the performance of its miracle." In all of Proust, Beckett counts "twelve or thirteen" of these miracle moments, "but the first—the famous episode of the madeleine steeped in tea—would justify the assertion that his entire book is a monument to involuntary memory and the epic of its action. The whole of Proust's world comes out of a teacup, and not merely Combray and his childhood. For Combray brings us to the two 'ways' and to Swann, and to Swann may be related every element of the Proustian experience and consequently its climax in revelation" (19–23).

29. Marcel Proust, *Swann's Way*, trans. and ed. Lydia Davis (New York: Viking Press, 2003), 53, 68, 182, 184–85.

30. "Beginnings," unpublished manuscript, Box 494, Farrell Archives.

31. Walter Benjamin, *Illuminations* (New York: Knopf, 1969): 203–13.

32. "On the Letters of Anton Chekhov," in *League of Frightened Philistines*, 60–71. Farrell returned to this idea in judging John O'Hara to be a gifted short-story writer but a failure as a novelist, except for *Appointment in Samarra:* "In this novel, O'Hara attained what Henry James called 'saturation.' I interpret this word to mean that the characters and their environment, including their cultural, social, and moral background, became a world, or a segment of a world, with a past and a present, and an assumable future, and with a play of meanings." "The Eternal Question of John O'Hara," in Jack Alan Robbins, ed., *Literary Essays 1954–1974* (Port Washington, N.Y.: Kennikat Press, 1976), 90–92.

33. "Nonsense and the Short Story," in *League of Frightened Philistines*, 81.

34. Unpublished manuscript, Box 495, Farrell Archives.

35. "How *Studs Lonigan* Was Written," in *League of Frightened Philistines*, 86.

36. Farrell, quoted in the introduction to Ralph F. Bogardus and Fred Hobson, eds., *Literature at the Barricades: The American Writer in the 1930s* (Tuscaloosa: University of Alabama Press, 1982), 3–4; Donald Pizer, "James T. Farrell and the 1930s," in *Literature at the Barricades*, 75, 81.

37. Unpublished manuscript, "Memories of John Dewey by James T. Farrell," 5 November 1965, Newberry Library, Gift of Cleo Paturis. Farrell registered the excitement of first absorbing the pragmatists in a June 1930 essay published in *Earth*, a little magazine out of Wheaton, Illinois. The piece, "Half Way from the Cradle," is a concise anatomy of the serial engagement with and rejection of belief systems among adolescents and young adults in Jazz Age America: from athletics, sex, and rote education to the ideals of success, family life, and organized religion (for the less adventurous), and to Bohemianism, "art for art's sake," and engagement with "the twin [philosophical] problems of duality and certainty" (for the more thoughtful). His own resolution, a young man's bold declaration, is straight out of William James, Mead, and Dewey: "Only by eliminating certainties that are not referable to human experience can we be men—human beings—rather than parasites on an extra-experiential source of immutable Being." *Earth* (Wheaton, Illinois) 1, no. 3 (June 1930): 1–3, 14.

38. Harry Smith, "Defictionalizing Farrell," *The Smith* 22: 8.

39. "Topics: The Democratic Faith of John Dewey," *New York Times*, 22 October 1966, 25. See also James T. Farrell, "Reflections on John Dewey," *Thought* (New Delhi, India) 19 (27 May 1967): 14–16.

40. Robert James Butler, "Parks, Parties, and Pragmatism: Time and Setting in James T. Farrell's Major Novels," *Essays in Literature* 10, no. 2 (Fall 1983): 242.

41. Robert James Butler, "Christian and Pragmatic Visions of Time in the Lonigan Trilogy," *Thought* 55, no. 219 (December 1980): 465, 475. Butler points out that Farrell cogently reviewed G. H. Mead's *The Philosophy of the Present* in 1930 while he was working on the Lonigan material. The review demonstrates the importance for the beginning novelist's plan for fiction of the pragmatists' ideas on the consciousness of time as a three-part exercise in integration. Farrell explains that in Mead's thought, "the locus of both consciousness and value is the present, and it is in terms of this present that the past and the future are organized"; "Christian and Pragmatic Visions," 464.

42. "Continuity and Change" (2 July 1965, Austin, Tex.), in Phelps, *Hearing Out James T. Farrell*, 136–37.

43. Dennis Flynn, "James T. Farrell and His Catholics," *America*, 15 September 1975, 111–13.

44. Thomas F. Curley, "Catholic Novels and American Culture," *Commentary* 36 (July 1963): 34–42. Curley's essay remains one of the most insightful analyses of Catholic literary culture in the middle of the twentieth century.

45. "A Note on Sherwood Anderson," in *Reflections at Fifty*, 164–68.

46. Eudora Welty, "Place in Fiction," *South Atlantic Quarterly* 55 (January 1956): 57–72.

47. See also Charles Fanning and Ellen Skerrett, "James T. Farrell and Washington Park: The Novel as Social History," *Chicago History* 8, no. 2 (Summer 1979): 80–91.

48. Letters to Mary Farrell, 2 February 1934; 6 March 1934; 21 March 1935; 12 April 1935; 26 August 1935; 12 July 1937; Farrell Archives.

49. Farrell's example was followed by many Irish American writers of the 1940s, among them Thomas Sugrue, Leo R. Ward, Jack Dunphy, Harry Sylvester, Mary Deasy, Mary Doyle Curran, Betty Smith, Edward McSorley, and J. F. Powers. See Charles Fanning, *The Irish Voice in America*, *250 Years of Irish-American Fiction*, 2nd ed. (Lexington: University Press of Kentucky, 2000), 292–312.

In an unpublished manuscript, "The Church in My Fiction," Farrell rejected the term "Catholic novelist" as inappropriate (given his unbelief) and limiting (given his wider aims). He continues: "However, my fiction is saturated with Catholicism. Many of my characters are Catholics. They are from cradle to the grave Catholics, and I bury a number of them in Calvary Cemetery, in Evanston, Illinois. The fundamental point to be made concerning my fiction is that being a Catholic in the world of my expressed imagination is a normal experience that need not be explained and defended. The Church is in their lives. It is part of their lives. Their reactions are those of persons who have lived in relationship with and to the Church. Their thoughts, emotions, actions are wound through the body of belief, ritual and practice of the Catholic Church"; Box 640, Farrell Archives.

50. "The Short Story," in *League of Frightened Philistines*, 137–38; "How *Studs Lonigan* Was Written," in *League of Frightened Philistines*, 87–88.

51. Lydia Davis, introduction to *Swann's Way* by Marcel Proust (New York: Viking Press, 2003), ix. Davis goes on to assert Proust's great theme—"how time will be transcended through art"—in terms that also describe Farrell's artistic faith: "For only in recollection does an experience become fully significant, as we arrange it in a meaningful pattern, and thus the crucial role of our intellect, our imagination, in our perception of the world and our re-creation of it to suit our desires; thus the importance of the role of the artist in transforming reality according to a particular inner vision: the artist escapes the tyranny of time through art"; *Swann's Way*, xi.

Interestingly, the French publisher of *Young Lonigan*, Nouvelle Revue Française, was the second of three houses to reject *Swann's Way*. André Gide was in charge at the time, and he later said this decision was one of the greatest mistakes of his life. With its name changed to Gallimard, the house did publish later editions of Proust. Gallimard has continued to publish Farrell as well.

52. Introduction to *A World I Never Made* (Cleveland and New York: World Publishing, 1947), ix–xii.

53. Introduction to *No Star Is Lost* (Cleveland and New York: World Publishing, 1947), ix–x.

54. Introduction to *Father and Son* (Cleveland and New York: World Publishing, 1947), xi–xii.

55. Introduction to *My Days of Anger* (Cleveland and New York: World Publishing, 1947), xi–xii.

56. Letter to Jim Putnam, 18 February 1943, Farrell Archives.

57. "How *The Face of Time* Was Written," in *Reflections at Fifty*, 35–41.

Selected Bibliography

Works by James T. Farrell

Novels and Novellas

Studs Lonigan: A Trilogy. New York: Vanguard Press, 1935. Comprised of *Young Lonigan: A Boyhood in Chicago Streets* (New York: Vanguard Press, 1932); *The Young Manhood of Studs Lonigan* (New York: Vanguard Press, 1934); and *Judgment Day* (New York: Vanguard Press, 1935). There have been many reprints since, including in the Library of America in 2004.

Gas-House McGinty. New York: Vanguard Press, 1933; London: United Anglo-American Book Company, 1948; revised edition, New York: Avon, 1950.

Tommy Gallagher's Crusade. New York: Vanguard Press, 1939.

Ellen Rogers. New York: Vanguard Press, 1941; London: Routledge, 1942.

O'NEILL-O'FLAHERTY PENTALOGY:

A World I Never Made. New York: Vanguard Press, 1936; London: Constable, 1938.

No Star Is Lost. New York: Vanguard Press, 1938; London: Constable, 1939.

Father and Son. New York: Vanguard Press, 1940; [as *A Father and His Son* (London: Routledge, 1943)].

My Days of Anger. New York: Vanguard Press, 1943; London: Routledge, 1945.

The Face of Time. New York: Vanguard Press, 1953; London: Spearman and Calder, 1954.

BERNARD CARR TRILOGY:

Bernard Clare. New York: Vanguard Press, 1946 [as *Bernard Clayre* (London: Routledge, 1948); as *Bernard Carr* (New York: New American Library, 1952)].

The Road Between. New York: Vanguard Press, and London: Routledge, 1949.

Yet Other Waters. New York: Vanguard Press, 1952; London: Panther, 1960.

This Man and This Woman. New York: Vanguard Press, 1951.
Boarding House Blues. New York: Paperback Library, 1961; London: Panther, 1962.

UNIVERSE OF TIME SEQUENCE:

The Silence of History. New York: Doubleday, 1963; London: W. H. Allen, 1964.
What Time Collects. New York: Doubleday, 1964; London: W. H. Allen, 1965.
When Time Was Born. New York: The Smith-Horizon Press, 1966.
Lonely for the Future. New York: Doubleday, 1966; London: W. H. Allen, 1966.
New Year's Eve/1929. New York: Smith-Horizon Press, 1967.
A Brand New Life. New York: Doubleday, 1968.
Judith. Athens, Ohio: Duane Schneider Press, 1969.
Invisible Swords. New York: Doubleday, 1971.
The Dunne Family. New York: Doubleday, 1976.
The Death of Nora Ryan. New York: Doubleday, 1978.
Sam Holman. Buffalo, N.Y.: Prometheus Books, 1983.

Short Fiction Collections

Calico Shoes and Other Stories. New York: Vanguard Press, 1934 [as *Seventeen and Other Stories* (London: Panther, 1959)].
Guillotine Party and Other Stories. New York: Vanguard Press, 1935.
Can All This Grandeur Perish? and Other Stories. New York: Vanguard Press, 1937.
The Short Stories of James T. Farrell. New York: Vanguard Press, 1937 [as *Fellow Countrymen: Collected Stories* (London: Constable, 1937)]. Reprints the preceding three volumes.
$1,000 a Week and Other Stories. New York: Vanguard Press, 1942.
Fifteen Selected Stories. Avon Modern Short Story Monthly, No. 10. New York: Avon Book, 1943. Reprints stories from several volumes.
To Whom It May Concern and Other Stories. New York: Vanguard Press, 1944.
Twelve Great Stories. Avon Modern Short Story Monthly, No. 21. New York: Avon Book, 1945. Reprints stories from several volumes.
When Boyhood Dreams Come True. New York: Vanguard Press, 1946.
More Fellow Countrymen. London: Routledge, 1946. Reprints stories from several volumes.
The Life Adventurous and Other Stories. New York: Vanguard Press, 1947.
Yesterday's Love and Eleven Other Stories. New York: Avon Book, 1948. Reprints stories from several volumes.
A Misunderstanding. New York: House of Books, 1949. Small-press printing of a single story.
An American Dream Girl. New York: Vanguard Press, 1950.
French Girls Are Vicious and Other Stories. New York: Vanguard Press, 1955; London: Panther, 1958.
An Omnibus of Short Stories. New York: Vanguard Press, 1957. Reprints *$1,000 a Week and Other Stories, To Whom It May Concern and Other Stories,* and *The Life Adventurous and Other Stories.*

A Dangerous Woman and Other Stories. New York: New American Library, 1957; London: Panther, 1959.

Saturday Night and Other Stories. London: Panther, 1958. Reprints stories from several volumes.

The Girls at the Sphinx. London: Panther, 1959. Reprints stories from several volumes.

Looking 'Em Over. London: Panther, 1960. Reprints stories from several volumes.

Side Street and Other Stories. New York: Paperback Library, 1961.

Sound of a City. New York: Paperback Library, 1962.

Childhood Is Not Forever and Other Stories. New York: Doubleday, 1969.

Judith and Other Stories. New York: Doubleday, 1973.

Olive and Mary Anne. New York: Stonehill, 1977.

Eight Short Short Stories and Sketches. Ed. Marshall Brooks. Newton, Mass.: Arts End Books, 1981.

Chicago Stories of James T. Farrell. Ed. Charles Fanning. Urbana: University of Illinois Press, 1998.

Literary Criticism and Other Publications

A Note on Literary Criticism. New York: Vanguard Press, 1936; London: Constable, 1937.

The League of Frightened Philistines and Other Papers. New York: Vanguard Press, 1945; London: Routledge, 1947.

The Fate of Writing in America. New York: New Directions, 1946; London: Grey Walls Press, 1947.

Literature and Morality. New York: Vanguard Press, 1947.

[Jonathan Titulescu Fogarty, Esq., pseud.] *The Name Is Fogarty: Private Papers on Public Matters.* New York: Vanguard Press, 1950.

[with Jeannette Covert Nolan and Horace Gregory] *Poet of the People: An Evaluation of James Whitcomb Riley.* Bloomington: Indiana University Press, 1951.

Reflections at Fifty and Other Essays. New York: Vanguard Press, 1954; London: Spearman, 1956.

My Baseball Diary: A Famed Author Recalls the Wonderful World of Baseball, Yesterday and Today. New York: A. S. Barnes, 1957.

It Has Come to Pass. New York: Herzl Press, 1958.

[edited] *Prejudices,* by H. L. Mencken. New York: Knopf, 1958.

[edited] *A Dreiser Reader.* New York: Dell, 1962.

Selected Essays. New York: McGraw-Hill, 1964.

The Collected Poems of James T. Farrell. New York: Fleet, 1965.

Literary Essays 1954–74. Port Washington, N.Y.: Kennikat Press, 1976.

On Irish Themes. Ed. Dennis Flynn. Philadelphia: University of Pennsylvania Press, 1982.

Hearing Out James T. Farrell: Selected Lectures. New York: The Smith, 1985.

Secondary Sources

Our understanding of the writings of James T. Farrell springs from the work of Edgar M. Branch, whose essays, books, and bibliographies have created Farrell criticism and made further work possible. See his *James T. Farrell* (New York: Twayne Publishers, 1971), and *A Bibliography of James T. Farrell's Writings 1921–1957* (Philadelphia: University of Pennsylvania Press, 1959). Branch has published bibliographical supplements as follows: "A Supplement to the Bibliography of James T. Farrell's Writings," *American Book Collector* 11 (Summer 1961): 42–48; "Bibliography of James T. Farrell: A Supplement," *American Book Collector* 17 (May 1967): 9–19; "Bibliography of James T. Farrell: January 1967–August 1970," *American Book Collector* 21 (March–April 1971): 13–18; "Bibliography of James T. Farrell, September 1970–February 1975," *American Book Collector* 26, no 3: 17–22; and "Bibliography of James T. Farrell's Writings: Supplement Five, 1975–1981," *Bulletin of Bibliography* 39, no. 4 (December 1982): 201–6. Branch has also published the beautifully illustrated *Studs Lonigan's Neighborhood and the Making of James T. Farrell* (Newton, Mass.: Arts End Books, 1996), and an elegant short study of *A Paris Year: Dorothy and James T. Farrell, 1931–1932* (Athens: Ohio University Press, 1998).

Corroborating Branch, other critics have placed Farrell firmly in the context of American realism. See Horace Gregory, "James T. Farrell: Beyond the Provinces of Art," *New World Writing: Fifth Mentor Selection* (New York: New American Library, 1954), 52–64; Blanche Gelfant, *The American City Novel* (Norman: University of Oklahoma Press, 1954), 175–227; Charles C. Walcutt, *American Literary Naturalism, A Divided Stream* (Minneapolis: University of Minnesota Press, 1956), 240–57; Charles C. Walcutt, *Seven Novelists in the American Naturalist Tradition* (Minneapolis: University of Minnesota Press, 1974), 245–89; Nelson M. Blake, *Novelists' America, Fiction as History, 1910–1940* (Syracuse, N.Y.: Syracuse University Press, 1969), 195–225; Richard Mitchell, "*Studs Lonigan:* Research in Morality," *Centennial Review* 6 (Spring 1962): 202–14; Barbara Foley, *Telling the Truth: The Theory and Practice of Documentary Fiction* (Ithaca, N.Y.: Cornell University Press, 1986); and Barbara Foley, *Radical Representations: Politics and Form in U.S. Proletarian Fiction, 1929–1941* (Durham, N.C.: Duke University Press, 1993).

William V. Shannon began the consideration of Farrell's ethnic dimension with a section in *The American Irish: A Political and Social Portrait* (New York: Macmillan, 1966), 249–58. On Farrell and Irish America, see also Charles Fanning, *The Irish Voice in America: 250 Years of Irish-American Fiction*, 2nd ed. (Lexington: University Press of Kentucky, 2000), 257–91; Fanning, "Death and Revery in Farrell's O'Neill-O'Flaherty Novels," *MELUS* 13, nos. 1 and 2 (Spring–Summer 1986): 97–114; and Fanning and Ellen Skerrett, "James T. Farrell and Washington Park," *Chicago History* 7 (Summer 1979): 80–91; Ron Ebest, "The Irish Catholic Schooling of James T. Ferrell, 1914–23," *Eire-Ireland* 30, no. 4 (Winter 1996): 18–32; Patricia J. Fanning, "'Maybe They'd Call the Doctor': Illness Behavior in the Novels of James T. Farrell," *New Hibernia Review* I, no. 4 (Winter 1997): 81–92. A breakthrough book for placement of Farrell in the larger context of American ethnicity is Ron Ebest, *Private Histories: The Writings of Irish Americans, 1900–1935* (Notre Dame: University of Notre Dame Press, 2005).

Other useful criticism of many aspects of Farrell's work includes: Jack Salzman and

Dennis Flynn, eds., Special Issue: "Essays on James T. Farrell," *Twentieth Century Literature* 22, no. 1 (February 1976); Leonard Kriegel, "Homage to Mr. Farrell," *Nation* 223 (16 October 1976): 373–75; Celeste Loughman, "'Old Now, and Good to Her': J. T. Farrell's Last Novels," *Eire-Ireland* 20, no. 3 (Fall 1985): 43–55; Shaun O'Connell, "His Kind: James T. Farrell's Last Word on the Irish," *Recorder* 1, no. 1 (Winter 1985): 41–50; Bette Howland, "James T. Farrell's Studs Lonigan," *Literary Review* 27 (Fall 1983): 22–5; Blanche Gelfant, "*Studs Lonigan* and Popular Art," *Raritan* 8 (Spring 1989): 111–20; Donald Pizer, "James T. Farrell and the 1930s," in Ralph F. Bogardus and Fred Hobson, ed., *Literature at the Barricades: The American Writer in the 1930s* (Tuscaloosa: University of Alabama Press, 1982), 69–81; Marcus Klein, *Foreigners: The Making of American Literature 1900–1940* (Chicago: University of Chicago Press, 1981), 206–15; Lewis F. Fried, *Makers of the City* (Amherst: University of Massachusetts Press, 1990), 119–58; Arnold L. Goldsmith, *The Modern American Urban Novel* (Detroit: Wayne State University Press, 1991), 39–58; Charles Fanning, ed., Special Issue: "Irish-American Literature," *MELUS* 18, no. 1 (Spring 1993), which contains essays on "Farrell and Richard Wright" by Robert Butler (pp. 103–11) and "Farrell and Dostoevsky" by Dennis Flynn (pp. 113–25), as well as a recently discovered 1931 essay by Farrell on "The Dance Marathons," edited by Ellen Skerrett (pp. 127–43).

Explorations of Farrell's relevance as a social critic include: Ann Douglas, "Studs Lonigan and the Failure of History in Mass Society: A Study in Claustrophobia," *American Quarterly* 26 (Winter 1977): 487–505; Alan M. Wald, *James T. Farrell: The Revolutionary Socialist Years* (New York: New York University Press, 1978); Alan M. Wald, *The New York Intellectuals* (Chapel Hill: University of North Carolina Press, 1987): 83–5, 249–63; Douglas Wixson, *Worker-Writer in America: Jack Conroy and the Tradition of Midwestern Literary Radicalism, 1898–1990* (Urbana and Chicago: University of Illinois Press, 1994); Daniel Shiffman, "Ethnic Competitors in *Studs Lonigan*," *MELUS* 24, no. 3 (Fall 1999): 67–79; Kathleen Farrell, *Literary Integrity and Political Action: The Public Argument of James T. Farrell* (Boulder, Colo.: Westview Press, 2000); and Lauren Onkey, "James Farrell's *Studs Lonigan* Trilogy and the Anxieties of Race," *Eire-Ireland* 40, nos. 3 and 4 (Fall/Winter 2005): 104–18.

Robert James Butler has established both the philosophical underpinnings and the subtle architectonics of Farrell's fiction in these essays: "Christian and Pragmatic Visions of Time in the Lonigan Trilogy," *Thought* 55 (December 1980): 461–75; "The Christian Roots of Farrell's O'Neill and Carr Novels," *Renascence* 34 (1982): 81–97; "Parks, Parties, and Pragmatism: Time and Setting in James T. Farrell's Major Novels," *Essays in Literature* 10 (Fall 1983): 241–54; and "Scenic Structure in Farrell's *Studs Lonigan*," *Essays in Literature* 14 (Spring 1987): 93–103.

Dennis Flynn was the first to open the rich Farrell Archive at the University of Pennsylvania, a voluminous collection of letters, diaries, and manuscripts that constitutes one of the great personal records available to us of the social and intellectual history of America in the earlier twentieth century. See James T. Farrell, *On Irish Themes* (Philadelphia: University of Pennsylvania Press, 1982), edited by Dennis Flynn. Flynn's work in progress is an edition of Farrell's selected letters and diary notes, which will open up the possibilities of the collection for other scholars to follow. Much remains to be done to elucidate the full range and accomplishment of James T. Farrell as a writer. His work and influence in short fiction needs to be further explored. His last, unfinished sequence, *A Universe of Time*, has only just begun to be considered critically. In his later fiction he often left Chicago and the Irish to continue his explorations of time, death, and the possibilities in modern life for self-knowledge, growth, and creativity. Recent evidence of renewed interest in Farrell studies includes the completion since 1978 of at least twenty-five doctoral dissertations in which Farrell is a major figure.

Farrell's first posthumously published work, *Sam Holman* (Buffalo, N.Y.: Prometheus Books, 1983), is a novel of New York intellectual life in the 1930s, and there are other valuable works in manuscript form that have yet to be made generally available. One story published since Farrell's death is "Cigarette Card Baseball Pictures," in *Crab Orchard Review* 1, no. 2 (Spring/Summer 1996): 3–12. His novel of the 1919 Chicago "Black Sox" scandal, *Dreaming Baseball*, appears in 2007 in the Kent State University Press Writing Sports Series.

☙ ☙ ☙

In Farrell's centennial year of 2004, a new hardbound edition of *Studs Lonigan: A Trilogy* was published by the Library of America. This was followed by several new paperback editions of *Studs*. The publication of the five O'Neill-O'Flaherty novels by the University of Illinois Press guarantees that Farrell's grand design of the eight Washington Park novels will again be accessible to the American audience. Also in 2004, Robert K. Landers's biography of Farrell appeared. *An Honest Writer: The Life and Times of James T. Farrell* (San Francisco: Encounter Books) is useful for its collection and organization of the facts of Farrell's life, especially the early years. It is, however, inadequate as literary criticism. The integrated critical biography that Farrell deserves remains to be written.

From Rand McNally *Atlas of Chicago* for 1913

1. 4816 S. Indiana, Daly ("O'Flaherty") home, 1906-1910
2. 4953 S. Calumet, Daly ("O'Flaherty") home, 1910-1911
3. 5131 S. Prairie, Daly ("O'Flaherty") home, 1911-1915
4. 5704 S. Indiana, Daly ("O'Flaherty") home, 1915-1916
5. 5816 S. Park, Daly ("O'Flaherty") home, 1917-1928
6. 5939 S. Calumet, Farrell ("O'Neill") home, 1918-1923
7. 4831 S. Vincennes, Richard Wright home, 1929
8. 5730 S. Michigan, "Studs Lonigan" home
9. Corpus Christi ("Crucifixion") church and school, 49th and Grand
10. St. Anselm ("St.Patrick") church and school, 61st and Michigan
11. St. Cyril College ("St. Stanislaus High School"), 6410 S. Dante: one block south and five blocks east of this marker
12. University of Chicago

NO STAR
IS LOST

James T. Farrell

Stars, I have seen them fall,
　　But when they drop and die
No star is lost at all
　　From all the star-sown sky,
The toil of all that be
　　Helps not the primal fault;
It rains into the sea
　　And still the sea is salt.

— *"More Poems" By A. E. Housman*
　(By kind permission of the Housman Trustees
　and Messrs Jonathan Cape Ltd.)

To
Evelyn Shrifte
and Eva Ginn

SECTION ONE

1914

1

I

Bill and Danny O'Neill idled in front of the small confectionery store on Prairie Avenue, their pockets full of money and their bellies full of ice cream. Danny was ten, going on eleven, and small for his age. He had curly brown hair, blue-gray eyes, and wore gold-rimmed glasses. Bill was fourteen, long-legged, and skinny, with a sallow face, sunken cheeks, and irregular teeth. The ornate façade of the new neighborhood theater was to their right, and a square of cement sidewalk stretched from it to the curb. Almost at their feet were their own initials, traced into the cement when it had been laid at the time the theater was being built. A few yards to their left was an alley exit, and down farther was Fifty-first Street, with its street-car tracks and stores. Across the sidewalk small girls were playing hopscotch, and a nine-year-old boy to whom they paid no heed was patiently circling around and around on roller skates. Bill jangled the small change in his pocket.

"If the Sox were home we could go to the game today," Bill said.

"Yeah," Danny wistfully exclaimed.

"The Cubs' Park and the Feds' out on the North Side are too far away for us to make it this afternoon," Bill said.

They drifted over to the curb.

"Want another soda?" Bill asked.

"I couldn't eat one if I tried," Danny said.

"Me neither. Three in a row's my limit today," Bill said.

"I got a bellyache from all I ate yesterday," Danny said.

"Well, Dan, we sure been having a swell time with this dough," Bill said, jingling his silver.

Danny watched the boy on roller skates cross the street. The boy patiently skated along the opposite sidewalk past the row of identical three-story, red-brick apartment buildings which included the one in which he lived. Bill lit a cork-tipped cigarette, inhaled, gazed up at the sunny blue August sky as he let the smoke escape from his nostrils.

"Bill, you weren't afraid when you copped the money, were you?" Danny asked.

"Why should I have been? There wasn't any chance of me gettin' caught. I knew that Robinson guy sometimes sends money to Aunt Peg. So every time I came up to Mother's to see you, I looked in the mailbox. And I found it. I thought there was dough in the letter and I held it up to the light to make sure. Then I knew there was. So I opened it and found a fifty-dollar bill in a sheet of paper with no writing on it. I never thought I'd get such a big haul," Bill said.

"Aunt Peg's been lookin' for a letter. She keeps runnin' down to the mailbox to see if it's there, and she's nervous about it."

"Listen, you see this?" Bill said, unexpectedly shoving his right fist under Danny's nose.

Danny drew back a pace, directing a wounded and frightened expression at his brother.

"If you let 'em know, you're gonna get so much of this that you'll never forget it!" Bill said, continuing to menace Danny with his fist.

"Bill, I cross my heart I won't," Danny said with the utmost sincerity, simultaneously tracing a cross on his chest.

Bill unclenched his fist. He took a last drag from his cigarette and shot the butt onto the street. He grinned at Danny. He strolled over to the billboard in front of the theater to look at the photographs advertising the evening's features. Danny tagged after him.

"Dan, you seen any of the installments of this one, *The Million Dollar Mystery?* Tonight's the seventh one," Bill said.

"No, I ain't. But I bet it's a good one," Danny said.

"Serials are swell. Maybe we'll go tonight and see this one. Dan, remember when we saw *The Adventures of Kathleen?* Boy, Kathleen Williams, and Bruce, wasn't that the hero's name, they had plenty of adventures, didn't they?"

"I'd hate to be in some of the tough spots they were in in the jungle, not knowing when they might be eaten up by lions and tigers or leopards or killed by the Hindus," Danny said.

"It'd be a lot of fun," Bill said with bravado.

Bill studied the picture display. Danny stood beside him, toying with the money in his pocket, a dreamy expression clouding his face.

"What yuh thinkin' about, Dan?" Bill asked, glancing away from the billboard to face Danny and, as he did so, observing the faraway look in Danny's eyes.

"Oh, nothin'," Danny answered casually.

"You're afraid," Bill said.

"I ain't," Danny protested.

Bill wandered back to the curb and stood there jangling the money in his pocket. Danny scampered after him.

"Boy, I like bein' rich," Bill said, continuing to play with the silver.

Danny didn't answer. He gazed up Prairie Avenue. Almost a block down on his right, the yellow bricks of the rambling convent of the Sisters of the Good Shepherd glittered in the hot sun. From its belfry came the toll of a bell, filling the street with mournful, plaintive echoes.

"Three o'clock," Danny said.

Bill lit another cigarette. Again he jangled the coins in his pocket. Danny imitated him.

Suddenly they heard the raucous shouts of newsboys selling extra papers.

"Something musta happened," Bill said.

"Uh huh! Extras," Danny said.

A newsboy of about Danny's size, wearing dirty khaki trousers, black stockings, and a black waist, tore around the corner of Fifty-first and Prairie and came up the center of the street with a bundle of papers under his left arm. He yelled in such a mumbled jargon that none of his cries made sense.

"It's Marty Hogan," Danny said.

The newsboy came nearer.

"Extry Paper! Kaiser Invades France! Extry Paper! Czar Strikes!" the newsboy bellowed, his words suddenly more audible.

"We shoulda known it was about the war," Bill said.

"We might be fightin' a war with Mexico, too," Danny said.

"This war's in Europe," Bill said.

"Extry Paper! Read About the War!"

"I wanna see France lick the Germans because Lafayette came over here to help us lick the British and the Hessians in the American Revolution," Bill said.

"Hey, Marty!" Danny called.

"Whatcha want?" Marty answered impatiently as he ran toward Bill and Danny; he was olive-skinned, with jet-black hair, dark, shifty eyes, a dirty face, and holes in his stockings.

"What yuh doin', kid?" Bill asked.

"Sellin' war extras, what yuh think I'm doin'?" Marty said.

"Here's a good cigarette," Bill said, handing him a cork-tipped cigarette.

"Thanks. Where'd yuh get it?" Marty asked, examining the cigarette closely and carefully putting it in his waist pocket.

"Sellin' many papers?" Bill asked.

"There's dough in this war, Skinny. I get 'em for two cents and sell 'em for a jit. Made nearly half a buck yesterday," Marty said.

"How many yuh got there?" Bill said, pointing to the bundle under Marty's arm.

"Ten! But, say, I gotta skiddoo. Lots of kids sellin' 'em. Here, look at this prick comin' to beat me out," Marty said.

A boy of Marty's size came running up Prairie, bellowing out his extras.

"Hey, get off my street, you mutt!" Marty yelled at the kid threateningly.

"You don't own it," the kid yelled back.

Bill grabbed Marty as he was about to go for the rival.

"Let 'im go, Marty. I'll buy your papers," Bill said.

"Take your hooks off me, you big bastard, or I'll get my brother Fag after yuh," Marty yelled at Bill.

"I'm gonna buy your papers and save you the work," Bill said.

Marty looked suspiciously at Bill.

"Sell 'em to me," Bill said.

"I ain't got no time for your horse turds," Marty said.

Bill pulled a handful of change from his pocket and held it out. Marty stared at the money.

"Gimme your papers," Bill said.

"A jit apiece for 'em?" Marty asked.

"No, a dime apiece," Bill said.

"It's a bargain," Marty said.

Bill gave Marty a half dollar and two quarters. Marty handed the papers to Bill, not knowing what to make of the transaction. He tried to bite one of the quarters to see if it was lead.

"Say, you nuts?" he asked.

Bill nonchalantly looked at one of the papers, reading the headline of an article:

BRITAIN TO KEEP ALOOF FROM WAR

"It's a war, ain't it?" Bill said with a grin.

"Say, you must be goofy givin' me all this dough for my extras," Marty said.

"I felt like it. Wouldn't you rather bum with us than sell extras? Get your brother Fag and we'll all go downtown to a penny arcade," Bill said.

"Sure, I'll be meetin' him by the el station. But where did yuh get your dough?" Marty asked.

"What difference does it make so long as it's good?" Bill replied.

"I never counted on luck like this. Skinny, you're a swell guy," Marty said.

"You kids watch me," Bill said.

They were surprised as he began tearing one of the papers into ribbons and tossing them in the air, grinning as he did this. He laughed, watching the ribbons come down.

"Here, tear 'em up with me," Bill said, handing some of the papers to Danny and Marty.

In an exuberant mood, the three kids tore up the papers and flung them in the air, littering the sidewalk with scraps and shreds. The girls who had been playing hopscotch began picking up the papers and throwing them up a second time.

"Boy, this is more fun than sellin' papers, runnin' your can off and yellin' your lungs out," Marty said; then he tore more shreds and tossed them in the air.

"Whoops!" Bill yelled, doing likewise.

"Boy!" Marty yelled, continuing the sport, letting some scraps fall on his hair and shoulders. He laughed. "Say, this war's a whizz. I'm gettin' rich sellin' papers. Hurray for the Kaiser!"

"Wahoo!" Bill loudly yelled.

"Whee!" Danny yelled, flinging paper scraps at Marty.

"Yip!" Bill shouted, letting go the last shreds of his papers.

"Jiggers!" Marty cried.

The three of them looked. They saw a man hurtling out from the theater. They ran across the street and down an alley which led them eastward to the elevated structure half a block away.

II

"Here we are," Bill said, turning into the open front of a penny arcade.

He walked over to a cashier, a bleached and dissipated-looking blonde who sat in an open booth on the left, next to a hot-dog stand.

"Pennies and nickels, dollar of each," Bill said, giving her two one-dollar bills.

She pushed out the change in small stacks, and Bill pocketed it. He rejoined the others, who had been gazing about in wide-eyed expectation of enjoyment.

"Let's try the shootin' gallery first," Fag said.

"All right with me," Bill said.

He and Fag walked to the shooting gallery in the back. Marty and Danny stopped to watch a muscular six-foot man slam a punching bag so hard that he drove the connected scale indicator to the top, ringing a bell.

"That takes muscle," Marty said in gaping admiration.

"Yeah," Danny exclaimed.

They heard the crack of rifle shots. They went back to the shooting gallery. Bill and Fag stood at a counter which stretched across the entire width of the arcade, aiming their rifles at the targets which were set about twenty yards back. The targets were of clay and wood, a sundry assortment of circles, moving birds and ducks, concentric circles ranged about small red eyes, balls held aloft by jets of water, and clay pipes.

"I was hittin' at the end there, Fag," Bill said after both of them had emptied their rifles.

"So was I," Fag said.

"Another time?" Bill asked.

Fag nodded.

"You kids try shootin', too," Bill said to Marty and Danny.

He laid forty cents on the counter, and the attendant loaded four rifles.

"Now, you boys be careful and keep the guns pointed at them targets," he said.

They shot. The rifles were too unwieldy for Marty and Danny. They could not hold their guns steadily nor sight properly. They fired away.

"I guess I'm not hitting anything," Danny said.

"Hey, Skinny, your brother can't hit the blind side of a barn," Marty shouted.

Danny fired again, his bullet landing below the targets.

"Let's try the revolvers now," Bill finally said.

"You kids be careful with these," the man said, handing them loaded revolvers after Bill had paid him.

"Hit one of the moving ducks," Bill said to Fag.

"I'll try," Fag said, aiming his gun.

Fag fired, missed. Danny aimed carefully at the red center of a series of concentric circles. He slightly bruised his finger in firing and missed. He didn't even see where the bullet had landed.

"Boy, wouldn't I like to be a cowboy with this here six-shooter! Boy, you could just watch me knocking Indians off their barebacked ponies," Marty said, holding his finger to the trigger of a revolver which he waved carelessly.

"Aim that gun at them targets and quit wavin' it that way, you!" the man said.

"Huh?" Marty exclaimed, still holding his finger to the trigger and unwittingly letting the gun point at Danny.

"Aim that gun at the targets or put it down!" the man yelled.

"Oh, me!" Marty exclaimed; he looked down the nozzle of his revolver, with his finger still to the trigger.

"Stop that! Put that gun down!" the man said excitedly.

Marty looked at him, surprised.

"What's the matter, mister?"

"You're liable to kill somebody waving that gun like that. It's loaded," the man said.

"I didn't shoot it at anybody," said Marty.

"It might go off on you. Put it down! You can't shoot here any more," the man said.

"Why?" Marty asked.

"You're liable to kill yourself, you goddam little fool!"

"Lay that gun down on the counter, Marty, or I'll slam yuh one!" Fag yelled at Marty.

Marty obeyed his brother.

Danny tried to aim carefully and hit something. It was no use. He lost interest in shooting because he wasn't good enough at it. He closed his eyes and emptied the chambers.

"I'll finish your shots in this gun. You're liable to kill yourself, yuh damn fool!" Fag said to Marty.

"That ain't fair," Marty said.

"You two little kids get away from here before you're hurt," the man said.

Fag shot off the remaining bullets in Marty's revolver while Marty and Danny moved off a few feet. Fag then turned to Marty and frowned.

"You goddam little fool, you coulda killed somebody. Get away from here like the guy told yuh to!"

Marty sulked off. Danny followed him. Bill and Fag continued shooting, the noise from their guns echoing through the arcade.

III

Danny and Marty wandered by the picture machines which were ranged along the two side walls of the arcade. Danny paused before one which advertised *The Oriental Harem*.

"Hey, I'll bet these pictures'll show you an eyeful," Marty said.

Not answering, Danny moved on to stand before one called *Beauty Goes to Bed*.

"These movin' pictures?" Marty asked, joining Danny.

"The ones with the little handles on the side are," Danny said, pointing to a small crank handle at the side of a machine which featured the title, *Pretty Dimples*.

Bill and Fag joined them.

"Here's somethin' to see, Skinny," Fag said.

"Uh huh!" Bill said.

They each went to a picture machine. Danny and Marty, by standing on tip-toe and straining themselves in an uncomfortable position, could just manage to see down inside the machine. Danny dropped into a slot a penny Bill had given him. He looked down through the glass. He saw nothing but blackness. He guessed that it was out of order, but he kept on turning the handle. He heard a click. Inside, the machine lighted up, and he saw a shelf of pictures set up vertically. He turned the handle, and they began falling forward one by one in such rapid succession that the illusion of motion was created. It was hard for him to make out everything that was happening in the picture. There was a buxom, dark-haired girl in a bedroom with a large bed in one corner. She wore a long, flowing, satin gown. She sat down on a chair. She leaned forward and daintily took off one slipper. He couldn't make out clearly what she was doing next. The picture blurred. She seemed too small. He turned the handle more slowly, but the picture blurred more. He stopped turning the handle and looked intently at a picture which revealed her leaning forward to touch her other slipper. But the picture was even more blurred, and she seemed very small. He turned the handle fast again. She yawned. He was able to make it out a little better again. She walked around the room and started taking her dress off, pulling it over her head. She stood before a mirror in her petticoat, corset, and underwear. Maybe she was going to take off all her clothes. He was going to get a real eyeful. If the picture was only bigger so he could see her better and she'd seem to be closer to him. She was getting her petticoat off. He wanted to see a picture of a naked woman. Gee, if it would only be bigger so he could see more. She had her petticoat off. He could see part of her leg, bare above her knees. He wanted to see more. She was facing him, and he could make out where her breasts started. She sat down and slowly unhooked the garter on one stocking. She pulled off the stocking. She stood up and daintily held the stocking by the toe. She let it drop beside the bed. She took off the other stocking, got up and looked at it before she dropped it beside the first one. She stood near the dresser and began unhooking her corset. Now it was going to get good. Maybe this picture was going to show everything. He wanted to see the hair. Now she had her corset off and he got a side shot of her. Her breasts stood up. She only had on what Aunt Peg called a shimmy. If she'd only turn around to let him see her in front. He stopped cranking to get a better look and see everything the picture showed. But it blurred and seemed smaller. He could see less that way. He turned the handle again. The woman went into a closet. She came out right away wearing a nightgown. The last picture fell downward, there was a click, and he saw only darkness. He turned away, disappointed, and for a brief moment, while the light struck his eyes, he blinked and wasn't sure where he was.

Bill and Fag finished the pictures they'd been watching. Marty stood on tiptoe, his eyes glued on one called *Nude Bathing*. Fag goosed him. Marty let out a yell as he jumped and twisted himself into an awkward position.

"Cut it out!" Marty cried.

"See anything?" Fag asked while Marty looked at him sulkily.

"I seen a dame swimmin' without a stitch on," Marty said.

"See the hair?"

"Naw. Most of the time I saw her from the side, and she was far away," Marty said.

"Skinny, I saw a dame with swell boobs," Fag said.

"There was lots to see in *The Oriental Harem*," Bill said.

"I expected I was gonna see more than I did," Danny said.

"What the hell you wanna see things for?" Fag said, giving Danny a patronizing look.

"Let's look at more pictures of naked women," Marty said.

"Sure. Lemme see what one I wanna see this time," Fag said, walking slowly along to study the titles.

"Look, *Garter Girls*," Marty said enthusiastically.

"I wanna see that one," Fag said, shoving Marty aside.

The others found pictures to look at also.

IV

"Skinny, I'm hungry. How about treatin' us to eats?" Fag asked after they had all tried the punching bag; Fag had registered a higher score than Bill, and Marty had outpunched Danny.

"Come on," Bill said.

"Skinny, you're a swell guy. I know lots of guys who wouldn't do this if they found money. They wouldn't treat the way you are," Fag said, walking beside Bill as they went over to the hot-dog stand.

A greasy, unshaven fellow in a dirty apron stood behind the counter and silently waited for their order.

"Two red-hots and root beer for me," Bill said.

"Same again," Fag said.

"Ditto, fellow," Marty said.

"Me, too," Danny said.

"I always wanted to come to one of these joints. Of course, I been in 'em before, but I mean I always wanted to come to one of 'em when I had more than a jit to spend," Fag said.

"Dan and I been in 'em before," Bill said.

The orders were set before them. Fag began eating voraciously.

"Bill, can't we all get our pictures taken in cowboy suits?" Danny asked.

"I'm game on that," Marty said, his mouth packed.

"All right, after we eat," Bill said.

"I wanna see some of them dirty pictures again, too," Fag said.

"Boy, I saw some boobs," Marty said.

"Yeah, only they ought to give more," Bill said.

"I seen postcard pictures that did," Fag said.

"Two more and another root beer for me," Bill said after finishing his order.

"How about me gettin' more, too, Skinny?" Fag asked.

"Me, too?" asked Marty.

"Go ahead."

"You're a swell kid, Skinny. You and me are pals," Fag said. He turned to the counterman who was filling Bill's order. "Same for me, mister."

They received more red-hots and went on eating. Danny also got two more sandwiches.

"Boy, am I glad I met you today!" Fag exclaimed.

"We had fun. Gettin' shagged by the guy for throwin' papers in front of the theater, meetin' you, and comin' down here," Bill said.

"I can't eat any more," Danny said after having consumed his third red-hot.

"Gimme your last one there," Fag said, and Danny pushed his remaining sandwich along to Fag.

"I wanna shoot some more," Bill said.

"Me, too," Fag said, biting into Danny's sandwich.

"We ought to try that electric machine that gives a shock," Bill said.

Gorging away, Fag nodded his head in agreement with Bill.

"Let's do it now," Bill said, turning away from the counter.

V

They went to the photograph booth which was screened off near the hot-dog stand. Inside, a man drowsed in a chair beside a camera set on a tripod, and to his right was a large dresser, with hats set on hooks above it. On the right of the camera was a piece of scenery on which a park setting was painted, and facing the camera was a view of a calm lagoon with trees in the background. The other side of the room was filled with additional pieces of scenery turned to the wall.

"What do you kids want?" the man asked.

"We wanna get our pictures taken in cowboy suits," Marty said.

"Got any money?" the man asked.

"We can pay for it," Bill said.

"Pictures'll cost you a dime. Three for a dime."

"All right. Got cowboy suits?" asked Bill.

The man opened a bureau drawer and pulled out chaps and sheepskin cowboy pants. Then he handed them colored handkerchiefs. He took cowboy hats from the hooks over the dresser. They pushed and shoved, taking their choice, and hastily put on what they had selected.

"Do we get guns?" Danny asked.

"Sure. All you want," the photographer answered.

He took out belted holsters containing guns. They grabbed these and tied them around their waists. They examined their guns, fondled them, aimed them, and kept pulling them out and putting them back into the holsters.

"This shoot?" Fag asked, holding up a heavy silver-handled revolver.

"Sure, if there was bullets in it."

"No bullets in it?" Fag said, pulling the trigger.

"Nope. You don't think I'd be lettin' you kids monkey with them guns if they was loaded, do you?"

Danny was outfitted with sheepskin pants, a checkered handkerchief, and a wide-brimmed cowboy hat which was too big for him. He strapped on two belts, enabling him to wear a gun on either side. He slung two more belts with guns across his chest.

"I'm ready for the picture," he said.

"Take your glasses off, boy, if you wanna look like a real desperate character," the man said, smiling at Danny.

Danny smiled back shyly. He removed his glasses and glanced about for a place where he might put them.

"Here, I'll take care of 'em," the man said.

Danny handed him the glasses and the man laid them on the top of the bureau.

"Well, I'm ready," Fag said, hitching up his holster belts and slapping his leather chaps; he stood waiting, fingering his revolvers.

"You kids got enough cannons to rout the whole Mexican army," the photographer said, joking with them.

"We could, too," Fag said, drawing one of his guns.

"Fag, watch! Tell me if I'm good on the draw," Marty said; he snapped out a revolver, but he was slow and clumsy getting it pointed and putting his hand on the trigger. "Pling!" he exclaimed, pulling the trigger.

He glanced at Fag for comment, but Fag hadn't watched him. Fag stood with hands on hips, making fierce faces.

"Fag, how'd I do?" Marty asked.

"I'm busy," Fag said.

"All right, you Bronco Billies, let's get the picture taken," the photographer said.

He placed Danny and Marty on a chair, and stood the older boys behind them. They moved and twisted about nervously. Fag and Bill shuffled their feet, and Fag screwed his face into a scowl. Danny tried to think of himself looking like Bronco Billy.

"Now, look this way," the man said.

They obeyed. Covering his head with a black cloth, he sighted them through the camera.

"You're all set. Now, don't move and don't blink your eyes," the man called.

He lifted the black cloth and grabbed a plate.

"Hold it, now," he said.

He inserted the plate in the camera. Then he stood on one side of the camera, holding the bulb.

"Good! Hold it, now! Don't move! Keep looking to the right, there!" he said while they sat tense and waiting, their faces set so that they seemed almost in pain.

"All right," he said.

"Over?" asked Fag.

The man nodded that it was. They relaxed.

"Try a couple more, too," Bill said.

Four more pictures were taken.

"You kids wait a few minutes now and I'll have these ready for you," the man said after the pictures had all been taken and Bill had paid him.

"Let's go shoot while we're waitin'," Fag said.

They ran out of the booth and back to the shooting gallery.

VI

The sun was going down and the sky above the buildings on the west side of Prairie Avenue was flushed with pink. Bill and Danny turned the corner of Fifty-first and Prairie and walked along beside the long, low, yellow-brick wall which formed the side of the corner cigar-store building.

"Gee, it's too bad about Ed Walsh," Danny said.

"He's through," Bill said.

"He went good for three innings today and then wobbled," Danny said.

"He's through," Bill said.

"Gee, I'm glad that Uncle Al ain't home," Danny said, dragging his feet.

"He'd give us hell for gettin' in so late for supper," Bill said.

"I can't eat supper after all the hot dogs and root beer I had downtown," Danny said.

"We had lots of fun, didn't we?" Bill said.

"Uh huh!" Danny exclaimed dejectedly.

"Even with all the money I spent downtown with you and the Hogan kids today, I got a lot left," Bill said.

They passed the closed entrance to the nickel show that had gone out of business after the new theater had opened. They stepped off the sidewalk and crossed the entrance to the alley which ran in back of the Fifty-first Street stores to the elevated tracks. Bill pulled out a handful of coins and studied them in the palm of his hand.

"I got so much money it's like lead in my pants," Bill said.

Danny glanced away, up at the pink-flushed darkening sky.

"I never knew money could be so much bother. When you got your pants full of it, it's trouble runnin', and if you get shags, it slows you up," Bill said.

"We got to do something about the change we have or it'll make noise in our pockets and they'll find out about it at home," Danny said.

"Yeah, we gotta," Bill said.

"I'm gonna hide the cowboy pictures we had taken, too, so they don't know about them," Danny said.

"Now you're really gettin' smart. Gee, I wonder how far I can throw a penny," Bill said.

He dumped the change back into his pocket and held a penny between his right thumb and index finger. He wound up like a baseball pitcher and threw the coin overhanded. He watched it skim through the air and heard it land on the street some distance away. He threw away another penny, listening as it hit the paved street.

"Say, they travel," Bill said.

Danny nodded. Bill flung a third penny. He walked to the curb edge. Danny followed. Bill threw again, and Danny imitated him. Bill repeated. Danny scaled another penny, but it didn't have Bill's distance. They stood at the curb, throwing away pennies. A band of little kids who had been playing in front of the theater scrambled to recover the pennies, fighting, pushing, shoving one another to get each one. Bill and Danny laughed as they watched the kids go for the money. They began tricking the kids, bluffing a throw in one direction and then wheeling about to fling the penny the opposite way. It was fun. They each took a final handful of pennies and tossed them underhanded in the air. The coins bounced and rolled in all directions. The kids yelled and lunged for them. Bill and Danny laughed again. They turned on their heels and went back to the sidewalk. They walked on in front of the row of apartment buildings which included the one in which Danny lived. These buildings were divided into two groups by an open gangway which led to the back yards.

"Here's the gangway, Dan. Let's bury our change under the back porch and go up the back way. It'll be safe, and we won't be taking a chance of having them find out about it," Bill said.

The two boys turned into the gangway.

2

I

Danny lagged behind the kids as they trooped noisily past the Fifty-first Street elevated station. They'd been going around getting shags, and each of them but him, Bill, Fag, Marty, Mush Jones and Tony Angela, had gone into a soda fountain alone and pulled off this stunt. Now it was his turn. He had to go into Dunne's confectionery store right ahead of them and do this trick. He wanted to be brave like Bill and Fag and the other kids. He wanted to do this, run away, and then laugh with them at the fun it all was. But suppose he got caught?

He ran to catch up with them.

"Bill, don't you think we done enough of this?" he said.

"What's the matter? Yellow?" Bill answered.

"Skinny, the kid brother ain't crapping in his pants, is he?" Fag asked, sneering.

"Yeah, he is," Bill said in scorn.

"No, I ain't," Danny said.

"Well, then, do it! It's your turn," Bill said.

"I didn't say I wouldn't do it," Danny said with a whine in his voice.

"Then go ahead," Tony Angela, a twelve-year-old kid, said.

"We'll walk down to the corner and wait for you," Fag said.

Dunne's confectionery store was between the elevated station and Prairie Avenue. Danny halted in front of a delicatessen a few doors east of Dunne's. He watched his companions stroll on ahead. They stopped in front of the cigar store at Prairie Avenue. Bill motioned for him to go ahead. The others began waving their arms, signaling to him. He stood close to the delicatessen-store window, wistful-eyed, indecisive. A sweat was breaking out on his forehead. He told himself to go ahead and do it and not be a baby and a yellowbelly. He motioned to them, trying to tell them with waving arms that he couldn't and didn't want to do it. They waved back at him. Bill suddenly started running toward him. Trembling, he waited for Bill.

"I ought to drive that yellow streak out of you with a sock on the nose," Bill said, coming up to Danny.

"Bill, I don't want to do it," Danny said.

"They're all laughing at you, that's what they're doing," Bill said.

"I don't care," Danny said feebly.

"Well, if that's what you are, all right," Bill said, turning away in disgust.

"Bill, if you'll come in with me, I'll do it," Danny called after him.

"All right, you yellow little punk," Bill said.

They entered the cool, shadowed ice-cream parlor and walked up to the soda fountain on the left. Danny turned pale, colorless. Bill leaned against the marble fountain as if there were no danger in sight. Mr. Dunne, a large plump man in shirt sleeves, came from the rear and went behind the fountain.

"Well, boys, what can I do for you?" he asked, smiling cordially.

"Two banana splits with double chocolate ice cream," Bill calmly ordered.

"All right," Mr. Dunne said, but he raised his brows knowingly.

Bill waited, unruffled. Danny felt that his brother was brave, all right, and he wished that he was as brave as Bill. But he just wasn't. Danny nudged Bill while Mr. Dunne started peeling a banana. Bill sideswiped Danny with a kick, warning him to cut it out. Danny wished that he and Bill hadn't spent all that money already. Coming in and buying banana splits would be much more fun. But Bill's money was all gone now.

Placing the sliced bananas on the sides of the elongated dishes, Mr. Dunne watched the boys from the corner of his eye. Taking the scoop, he dug down into the ice-cream container. Danny wished that Bill would hurry up, say something, and run out now while Mr. Dunne was bent down to get the ice cream. Then they'd be safe. And there weren't any more stores around to do this in. If this was only over! But Bill waited as if there were no need to worry. He was going to let the man make the banana splits before doing it.

"Here you are, boys. Forty cents," Mr. Dunne said, setting the banana splits on the counter.

"Stick 'em up your ass!" Bill yelled, turning away from the fountain and running toward the door.

Danny followed on Bill's heels, squealing. Mr. Dunne, fast on his feet, quickly swept from inside the fountain to pursue them. Bill bolted headlong through the screen door. Danny stumbled, and as the door slammed back after Bill had pushed it, Danny fell. Trying to get up, he felt himself pinioned by strong arms.

"You damn little mischief-maker!" Mr. Dunne said angrily.

Mr. Dunne pulled Danny to his feet. Danny quailed before the man whose face was flaming and bloated with anger. Danny started bawling.

"Please let me go, mister! I'll never do it again," Danny begged between sobs.

Mr. Dunne gave Danny a shove toward the rear of the store. Then he took him by the ear and led him along. Danny suddenly broke away and started for the door, but Mr. Dunne pounced on him before he had gone more than a few feet. Mr. Dunne picked him up and half carried him to the back. Danny strained and squirmed in the man's arms. He let out a piercing yell.

"Shut up!"

"Don't hurt me," Danny cried.

"Shut up!" Mr. Dunne repeated.

Danny whimpered.

II

"I got one of them this time," Mr. Dunne said to his wife in the rear room.

"Thrash him!" she said, glancing up from her sewing.

She was a big woman in her late thirties. Her face was fat and her features had a strained expression. She had brown hair and wore a blue skirt and a fluffy tan shirtwaist.

"Sit down!" Mr. Dunne said curtly to Danny, pointing to an empty chair by the table in the center of the room.

Sniffling, Danny obeyed. Mrs. Dunne stared at him with stern and unrelenting brown eyes. He couldn't look straight at either of them. He sniffled. He sobbed, wiping his eyes with the back of his hands and streaking his face. He looked around the small room. It was crowded, and there were boxes, old ice-cream cans, glasses, rags, aprons, all sorts of odds and ends scattered about. There were a sink and faucet in one corner and a small gas stove in another. A coat and some old shirts were hung on hooks over the sink.

"Go ahead and cry, you little gutter rat!" the woman said.

"I ain't a gutter rat," he haltingly protested. He sniffled again. He glanced around the room. It smelled of candy. She set her sewing aside and glued her eyes on him. He felt as if her eyes were needles being stuck into him.

"What's your name?" Mr. Dunne asked.

"If he's got any money, take it away from him," she said.

"I ain't got no money," Danny sobbed.

"Well, I was laying for them this time. These damn kids have been doing this to me, on and off, all summer. They won't play their game on me any more, though," Mr. Dunne said.

"I didn't ever do it before," Danny said sulkily.

"Shut up!" Mr. Dunne said.

"Turn him over to the police, Mr. D. Brats like him will end up on the gallows. They shouldn't be allowed to run the streets, molesting business people, doing destructive things," she said in mounting indignation.

"What's your name?" Mr. Dunne asked.

Danny sat in grim silence. He sniffled again.

"You can't talk now. You could, though, when you were trying to make mischief for me," Mr. Dunne said.

Danny continued to sniffle.

"Gutter rats! They belong in the reform school," she said with a frown.

Danny sat frightened, his lips clenched tightly. He looked yearningly at the bolted rear door.

"What kind of parents must such brats have?" she asked.

"My grandmother's better than you are," Danny said in a shrieking, high-pitched voice.

"Listen, you, answer our questions! For the rest, you'd better be seen and not heard!" Mr. Dunne said.

"If he was mine, I'd whale him," she said.

Suddenly, with these words, Mr. Dunne gazed sadly at his wife. She frowned at him. His expression became a hurt, wounded one. He shrugged his shoulders wearily. She sneered at him. Then both of them simultaneously turned fierce and angry countenances upon Danny. He cowered and wished he wasn't there with them, and that someone would come and rescue him from these awful people. He wondered where Bill was.

"If you don't tell me your name, maybe the police will!" Mr. Dunne said. He lit a cigarette, puffed it nervously, and stood threateningly over Danny. "Are you tongue-tied?" he asked sharply.

"Don't hurt me," Danny said, his body shaking with fright.

"You ought to be hurt—belted," she said.

They heard a customer enter the store. Mr. Dunne hastened out to the front. Danny lowered his eyes to avoid the woman's steady gaze. He wished he could just shrivel up into nothing and disappear. If he could disappear and not be seen, he'd be able to stand up and run out of here, and they wouldn't know where he was or what had happened to him. To be able to walk and have nobody see him. What wouldn't he do then to these mean, awful people? He didn't like her. She was mean and awful, worse than Mr. Dunne was.

"Aren't you ashamed of yourself?" she asked in a nagging voice.

He didn't want to answer her. He didn't want to speak to her or to that man. He just wanted to be able to get out of here and never come back or see them ever again. And he was afraid that they were going to have him arrested and put in reform school. But Mother wouldn't let them do that to him.

"Any business?" she asked when Mr. Dunne returned after waiting on the customer.

"Only a dime," he answered glumly.

"Maybe business'll pick up soon," she said.

Mr. Dunne's brows clouded. He shrugged his shoulders.

"Well, did he tell you his name yet?" Mr. Dunne asked.

"He's tongue-tied," she said sarcastically.

"He is, is he?" Mr. Dunne said.

Danny again cowered.

"All right, talk or I'll call the police! Then you'll talk!" Mr. Dunne said with a clenched fist raised over Danny's head. Danny ducked in fear of a blow. "I'll give you until I count five to talk, and if you don't I'll call the police on you!"

"Hit him, Mr. D. He deserves it," she said.

Danny sobbed again.

"One . . . two . . . three . . ."

"My name's Daniel O'Neill."

"Where do you live?"

"5137½ Prairie Avenue."

"What school do you go to?"

"Crucifixion."

"Aren't you ashamed of yourself? A Catholic boy, too! What would the Sisters and Father Mulligan say about you if they knew that you were going around marauding this way on your summer vacation?" she said, clucking with disgust.

"Why did you come in here, bothering me, losing money for me?" Mr. Dunne asked.

"They made me do it. I didn't want to, honest, I didn't. I'll never do it again. Honest, I won't! They made me," Danny said, shaking his head in naïve sincerity, as tears slid down his dirty cheeks.

"I suppose if they, whoever they are, went and jumped in the lake and drowned, you'd do it, too," she said.

"Honest, Mr. Dunne, I'll never do it again," Danny said.

"I know damn well you won't," Mr. Dunne said.

"Get the names of the others, Mr. D.," she said.

"Who made you do it?" Mr. Dunne asked.

"We'll round up the whole dirty gang of them and have them put away in reform school," she said.

"Who was the older kid who came in with you and did the talking?" Mr. Dunne asked.

"My brother," Danny said, nervous and trembling.

"Must be a fine family, a fine family, Mr. D.," she said.

"How old is your brother?"

"He's . . . he's fourteen."

"You'll both have to pay for those banana splits you wasted on me," he said.

"You bet they will!" she said.

"Does your mother and father know you do things like this?" Mr. Dunne asked.

"I don't live with them. I live with my grandmother," Danny said.

"What's she doing that she lets you run the streets like a gutter rat?" Mrs. Dunne asked.

"She went to the cemetery today to the grave of my dead Aunt Louise and my grandfather."

"And you kids doing this? Shame on you! You ought to be ashamed of yourself. If someone in your family doesn't whale your dirty little bottom for you for what you did, I'm going to see that the reform school people do," he said.

"We ought to tell the Sisters at Crucifixion on him," she said.

"Your brother ran away and let you get caught, didn't he?" Mr. Dunne said.

"I fell down going out the door," Danny said.

"I got an idea," Mr. Dunne said.

Alert and fearful, Danny eyed him, waiting for the next move, thinking maybe if he answered questions, he might be let go. She was worse than Mr. Dunne. He had to be careful about her.

"Please, let me go, Mr. Dunne. I won't never do it again," he said.

"I know you won't."

"You're not going to get out of this so easy, you nasty little mischief-maker," she said.

"What's your brother's name?" he asked.

"Bill."

"Dear, you watch the store, and don't let him get away. I'm going to get some kids and give them a nickel and some candy to get this lad's brother and bring him here. That fellow is the one to get. He must be the ringleader of the gang."

Danny watched Mr. Dunne put on a straw hat and go out. He sat trembling. It was awful to be kept a prisoner, alone with her!

III

Bill walked along Calumet Avenue, past the vacant lot near Fifty-third Street. He guessed that they'd given up hunting for him. But he'd had a pretty close shave. It had looked like he was caught, but he'd given them the slip by ducking through a trick passageway in a basement. And he'd hidden himself under a back porch. They'd gone right by, not even guessing how close he was to them. Boy, his heart had been in his mouth for a minute. Fag and his gang had a job on their hands trying to get him. He was a good runner and he knew all kinds of gangways and hiding places all over the neighborhood. He was proud of the way he'd given them the slip.

But Fag had played a dirty trick on him. Fag and his gang were a bunch of bastards. They'd all been together getting shags. Then after Dan had been caught, they'd split up. Dunne had gotten Fag to look for him. That was a dirty trick. He and Dan had always done favors for Fag and Marty. Look at all the times he'd given Fag cigarettes, treated him to sodas, taken him to nickel shows! Look at all the dough he'd spent on Fag taking him down to the penny arcade. Gee, that fifty bucks had gone fast. He wished he hadn't wasted so much of it. And now Fag was doing this to him. Fag and his gang were a bunch of bastards. He wished he was a better scrapper than Fag. Even so, he'd get even with him.

He walked on, proud of the way he'd ditched them. But he was in a hell of a hole. Dan was caught. He'd be blamed for it because he always got the blame when he and Dan got in any kind of trouble. He passed an apartment building and walked on by another vacant lot. He wondered where he'd go. He better not go down to Fifty-first Street. There was more chance of the gang being there than here on Calumet. He wondered what he'd do. What was going to happen to Dan? And what would he get for this? If the damn little fool hadn't let himself get caught. It proved to you that you couldn't let littler kids go around with you when you were getting shags. He'd learned a lesson, all right.

"There he is!" a kid yelled from in front of the orphan asylum playground on the other side of the street.

Bill shot into the vacant lot toward the elevated tracks, running like a frightened animal. The gang of yelling kids followed him, pausing to pick up rocks and fling them as they ran. A stone whizzed by his left ear. He ran as fast as he could, breathing out of his nose because he thought that would help him save his wind. As he ran, a plan formed in his mind. He'd go up the alley under the elevated tracks to the schoolyard across from the convent. He'd cut through it and get onto Prairie. There he might get a hitch on a passing truck. If not, he'd go up Prairie Avenue to Fifty-third Street and then dash over to Washington Park. He ran on. They were after him, throwing rocks, shouting, yelling to get him, kill him, get the lanky sonofabitch. He ran on, forcing himself. He could outrun all of them except maybe Fag.

"Stop, you skinny bastard!" Fag yelled, leading the pack.

Fag bent down, picked up a rock, let it go. Bill ran on under the elevated tracks, their cries drowned out momentarily by a passing train. He felt a stitch in his side. He was tempted to give up. Holding his side, he struggled on, losing ground. They'd have to catch him. If he could only get his second wind. He could hear them. They were getting closer. No, he wouldn't give up. They'd have to catch him. He turned into the schoolyard. Small children playing there stopped their games to watch the chase. He floundered on, hoping for his second wind, the pain knifing his side. And on they came, yelling like a pack of wolves. He made Prairie Avenue. Gasping, he turned south. He knew that he was a goner. Another rock whizzed by his head. His legs were heavy. His arms ached. He panted. He ran on with a staggering gait. Turning to get off the sidewalk and onto the street, he fell. Before he could get up, Fag was on top of him. They wrestled, both boys panting. Fag pinioned Bill's arms. The gang caught up to them.

"Now we got you!" Fag said, still breathing heavily.

"All right," Bill said.

Fag let Bill up. The gang shouted as they formed a group around him.

Bill couldn't get his breath. He looked Fag in the eye. Fag turned his eyes away.

"You're not gonna give me over to Dunne?" Bill asked.

"You're wanted," Fag said, not looking at Bill.

"Sock 'im in the nose, Fag!" Marty yelled, and others repeated the cry.

"Shut up, you punks!" Fag snarled at them.

Bill made a break to get away, but he was blocked by the circle of kids, and Fag grabbed him.

"No you don't!" Fag said, again pinioning Bill's arms.

"All right, I'll go," Bill said, docile.

They formed a group around him, with Fag and Marty holding his arms. They marched him down Prairie Avenue.

"What yuh want for lettin' me go, Fag?" Bill asked after having walked along several paces in silence.

"What yuh got?"

"I'm broke, but I'll cancel what you owe me for all my treats," said Bill.

"I didn't ask yuh to treat me," said Fag.

"Well, what yuh want? I'll get it and promise to pay it to you," Bill said.

"We're collecting from Dunne," Marty said.

"Come on along," Fag said curtly.

Fag still didn't look Bill in the eye. Bill was marched on and the kids yelled and shouted. Fag didn't say anything. They led him into Dunne's.

The kids guarded Bill while Mr. Dunne went behind the counter. He came out and handed Fag a handful of pennies and several bags of candy. Bill watched them go out. Mush Jones turned and wiggled his ears at Bill. They left. Mr. Dunne shoved Bill toward the rear. Bill saw Danny sitting red-eyed by a table.

"You weren't as smart as I was," Mr. Dunne said, pushing Bill into a chair.

"Call their home up," Mrs. Dunne said.

"I'll call again. And they'll pay for the call," Mr. Dunne said.

Bill and Danny faced each other with pain and fear in their eyes.

IV

It was getting dark outside. Bill and Danny sat worried and concerned but saying nothing. Danny knew that Mother and Aunt Peg had been sent for, but they hadn't gotten here yet. When would they come? He wanted them to come but he was afraid of what might happen when they did. They'd get sore at him and Bill. And these people here were still talking about the police and the reform school. He sat waiting, and he could almost hear his own heart beating. And Bill didn't look like he was going to be brave now. He guessed that Bill was afraid, too. Suddenly he heard someone entering in the front. Mr. Dunne went out. He sat on the edge of his chair, hoping that it was Mother and Aunt Peg. He had a feeling that it was.

"Where is my grandson?"

Bill and Danny both recognized the voice. Their faces lighted up.

"Are you Mrs. O'Flaherty?" Mr. Dunne asked the beak-faced little old lady, meeting her near the door.

"Let my grandson go or I'll break every window in your store," Mrs. O'Flaherty shouted.

Mrs. Dunne, in the rear, stiffened up and raised her eyebrows.

"Just a minute, Mother, let me talk to the man," said Margaret, a handsome woman in her late twenties.

Danny bolted off his chair, burst through the door, and ran straight to his grandmother.

"Mother!" he exclaimed frantically.

"Son, what happened?" she asked, bending down to kiss his dirty forehead.

"I'm very sorry, Mr. Dunne. Please tell me what happened," Margaret said ingratiatingly.

"These kids have been coming in here regularly, there's a whole gang of them, and they've been ordering expensive dishes, and after I get the order made up they run out, yelling and laughing and cursing at me. You know that isn't right, and it costs me money," Mr. Dunne said, his manner self-righteous, his voice complaining.

"Oh, I'm so sorry. I'm the aunt, Miss O'Flaherty. They aren't bad boys. This boy is very sweet, and I'm very sorry that this has happened," Margaret said.

"I got the brother in the back," Mr. Dunne said.

"I'll pay you. How much? Tell me, and I'll pay," Mrs. O'Flaherty said, gesticulating wildly.

"I should think you would. You can thank me that I didn't call the police and put them in their hands," Mr. Dunne said, leading the way to the back of the store.

"Just try! My cousin is a police sergeant, and my first cousin is Alderman Paddy Slattery," Mrs. O'Flaherty said rambunctiously.

"Mr. Dunne, you must excuse my mother. She's excited and she really doesn't mean all that she says. Here, let me pay you for the damage they've done, and I promise you that they won't do it again and that they'll be properly punished," Margaret said as she walked beside him.

They entered the back room, and Mrs. Dunne frowned triumphantly at the two women.

"This is Mrs. Dunne, Mrs. O'Flaherty, and the aunt, Miss O'Flaherty," Mr. Dunne said.

Mrs. Dunne said nothing, but she bowed stiffly. Mrs. O'Flaherty acknowledged the introduction with a curt nod.

"How do you do, Mrs. Dunne. I'm so sorry this happened," Margaret said.

"These boys will come to a bad end," Mrs. Dunne said.

"William!" Mrs. O'Flaherty cried.

Bill was silent. He looked at his grandmother.

"I'll tear the eyes out of your head for doing this to me little grandson," Mrs. O'Flaherty said violently, shaking her fist at Bill.

"No use locking the barn door after the horse is gone," Mrs. Dunne said dryly; her husband cast a cautioning glance at her.

"What did they cost you?" Margaret asked.

"Forty cents, and five cents for the telephone call," Mr. Dunne said.

Margaret dug into her pocketbook and handed him forty-five cents.

"I'm so sorry. I promise you that this will never happen again. It's a shame, and I'll see that they are punished," she said while Mr. Dunne self-consciously accepted the money and pocketed it.

"I'll think over what I want to do about it. You bring them back to see me tomorrow. I don't know but what it would be a good idea to put the fear of the Lord into them by turning them over to the police," Mr. Dunne said.

"It's a disgrace that such things should happen in a neighborhood of decent people like this," Mrs. Dunne said.

"Their mother and father are very poor, and we keep the young one for them. It would be a terrible thing for their poor parents if the older boy got in trouble over this, Mrs. Dunne. I promise you that we'll not let it happen again," Margaret said.

"Well, you know, ladies, it costs business people money and they can't be tolerating things like this," Mr. Dunne said.

"I should say not!" Mrs. Dunne said.

"You should be ashamed to have the name of me Uncle William in the old country," Mrs. O'Flaherty said, jabbing an accusing finger at Bill.

"Well, I'll think it over whether or not I want to let it go this time or prefer charges against them for doing such rascally things to business people," Mr. Dunne said.

"Mr. Dunne, I understand perfectly just how you feel. I promise you it won't happen again. I'm a business woman myself, and I understand exactly how you and Mrs. Dunne must have felt. I'm so sorry. It was kind of you to send for us instead of calling the police. I'm very grateful to you," Margaret said, her manner still ingratiating.

"Come on home, Son, and I'll give you some supper, but the Lord knows you should be put to bed on bread and water," Mrs. O'Flaherty said.

The boys timidly followed their aunt and grandmother out of the store.

"Look at him, Peg! He's just like his buck-tooth father, the buck-tooth!" Mrs. O'Flaherty said, pointing at Bill.

"Wait until we get home, Mother," Margaret said, annoyed.

"Ah!" Mrs. O'Flaherty exclaimed disgruntledly.

"Gee, Mother, we were only having a little fun," Danny said apologetically.

"Peg! Peg!" Mrs. O'Flaherty said.

"What's it now, Mother?" Margaret asked.

"Peg, I didn't like that one in the store. The next time I meet her, I'll have a stone in me glove," Mrs. O'Flaherty said.

They walked on home.

3

I

After eating his noonday dinner, Danny sat on the parlor floor with the Steel's baseball game that Uncle Al had bought him. Steel's was better than any other baseball game he knew about. The other ones he had or had played weren't any fun. There was too much hitting in them, too many extra base hits. You couldn't play them and pretend you were seeing a regular big-league game because the scores were always so big. But Steel's was different. Often Steel's would go play-by-play just like a big-league game. Many games you played would be tight, with shutouts, one and two and three hit games. And then sometimes there would be hitting splurges. It was a swell game.

Steel's was played with three dice and a folding board. The dice were read from the lowest number upward. Thus, if a one, two, and three were rolled, it was to be read one twenty-three. On the board there were columns of numbers, each one listing every possible combination of the dice in serial order. Beside each combination was the interpretation of the combination, whether or not it was a hit, an out, a base on error, or the like. There were eight such columns, one for when the bases were empty and the other seven for every possible position of base runners.

Most of the time when he was blue or worrying, he found he could forget everything by playing Steel's. He could imagine that instead of playing he was really watching a regular big-league game. He decided to pretend that the White Sox and the Cubs won the pennant and to play the world series between them. He ruled off a score card on a blank sheet of paper and wrote in the starting lineups of both teams. He started playing the game and keeping score. The Cubs got five runs in the first inning and three in the third. For the first five innings, the White Sox made only one hit. He suddenly lost interest in the game. He sat on the floor.

He wondered what he'd do. He was afraid to go back to play in the prairie because he might be laughed at. It was Mother's doing. She'd been sore at him ever since the trouble at Dunne's. Aunt Peg had fixed it up with Mr. Dunne so that nothing would be done to him and Bill. But Mother still wouldn't forgive him. She'd nagged him ever since. She'd gotten a police whistle to blow every time she wanted to call him home when he was out playing. The kids laughed at him because his grandmother used a whistle to call him home. Monk said why didn't she get him a dog collar and license, too, and put them around his neck. This morning he'd been watching the Wolfe's ball team play a game of indoor with a team from Fifty-third and Cal. He liked to watch the Wolfes and always rooted for them. It had been a pretty good game, and with the score ten to ten in the last of the seventh, the Wolfes had started a rally. Just then she'd started blowing the whistle. And that hadn't been enough. She'd come all the way down to the alley and stood under the elevated tracks blowing it. The kids had stopped the game and laughed at him. He'd had to get up and leave. He'd run across the prairie yelling to her that he heard her and was coming. And she'd seen him coming, too. But think that was enough for her? No, she'd blown the whistle until he ran all the way across the lot to her. She did that because she was sore at him. Aunt Peg was sore, too, but more at Bill than at him. Aunt Peg had told Mama that Bill couldn't come up here any more. He didn't know how Uncle Al might punish him. He hadn't seen Fag or Marty since that day. But he didn't care about that. He'd been playing with the Prairie Avenue kids over in the lot. They didn't get shags and get you in trouble like Fag and Marty. But now Mother had them all teasing him and laughing at him.

He started playing the game again, but lost interest in it. He sat, his face pensive, the board spread before him, the dice-cup in his hand. Mother came to the parlor entrance, puffing on a clay pipe.

"So there you are!" she said.

"Don't nag me," he said in a sulk.

"Well, isn't he the one! Don't nag him! No, I won't nag you. I'll not nag you. I'll just tell you what's right and·what's not right, what's decent and what's not decent," she said.

"Gee, didn't I tell you I was sorry?"

"Go on out and run the streets with the Devil again," she said.

"Mother, I'm sorry. Won't you please forgive me and stop nagging?" he begged.

"Indeed I won't!"

"All right, then, don't," he said in a pout; he set down the dicecup and held his hands to his ears.

"He can't hear me now! Look at him sit there, look at the crust of him, will you?" she said.

"I don't hear you," he yelled.

"But you heard them that led you into wrong. Tell me who your companions are and I'll tell you who you are," she said.

"I don't hear you!"

"Well, the crust of one his size! Merciful God, look at him!" she said, lifting her arms to the ceiling, the pipe in her right hand.

"I don't hear you!" he repeated.

"You little devil!" she said, and then she turned and went back through the hallway to the kitchen.

He sat alone, a brooding expression clouding his face. He thought that he might run away from home. He couldn't stand it here any more, being nagged, treated like a baby, made into a laughingstock before all the kids in the neighborhood.

He had a good mind to run away. He didn't see why he had to stand for being nagged. And she hadn't stopped it ever since he'd been caught in Dunne's. Hadn't he told her enough times he was sorry? What more could he do? What more did she want?

And with Uncle Al coming home from Madison any day now, there was much more in store for him, maybe a licking, maybe not getting permission to go to the show or the ball games or something like that. Well, just wait until he grew up! That was all!

He sat, thinking that maybe if he went over to the prairie they mightn't laugh at him. Maybe they'd forget it. But they wouldn't! They'd all kid him because of that darn old whistle, call him his grandma's boy, kid him. He didn't want to stay here in this old house, and he didn't want to hang around here. He wanted to go out and play in the prairie. Yep, he guessed, too, that he'd be glad when school started, even if he didn't like school any too much. Then he'd be seeing and playing with different kids than he was this summer. But he wouldn't have anything to do with Marty Hogan.

"So there you are!" Mrs. O'Flaherty said, reappearing at the parlor entrance but this time without her pipe.

"I can't hear you!"

"The impertinence of him! If you was living with your long-legged father, you wouldn't be doing that!" she said.

"I'm going out to play," he said, getting up from the floor.

"Go and the Devil take you, to be running in the prairie with Protestants. That I should have lived to see the day when you'd be disgracing me before that man on Fifty-first Street, a man that's not worth the spittle one would waste spittin' in his face."

"Goodbye!" he said, brushing past her.

"It's a queer one, that one is," she exclaimed aloud, watching him run toward the kitchen.

II

"Hello, Four Eyes," Moe Freeman said.

"Where's the whistle?" Louie Bergen asked.

Danny knew that he shouldn't have come over here to the prairie. Well, most of the kids here weren't Catholics anyway. Some of them were Jews. Maybe that's what you'd expect from Jews and Protestants, he guessed.

"How's your aunt?" Tommy Moriarty asked knowingly as he tripped and staggered into a boy's burlesque of a drunken adult.

"How's your aunt?" they all said, joining in Tommy's clownlike imitation.

Danny didn't know what to do or say. He felt like turning and running, but if he did, he knew they'd laugh at him even more than they were doing now.

"Say, kids, let's play ball," he suggested.

"We can't play with you. If we do, your grandmother's liable to get out the whistle and call you home so she can help you pee, and that'll break up the ball game," Stewie O'Leary said.

"Come on, we got enough for a little game. Who's going to choose up sides?" Danny asked while they laughed at him.

"Hey, Stewie, did your aunt have her whiskey last night?" Tommy asked.

"No, but my grandmother smoked her pipe," Stewie answered, and again they laughed at Danny.

Danny stood impotent in the face of their jeers and jibes. He didn't seem to have a friend among them. He wished the summer vacation were over and that he was back in school with the kids he knew and played with there, Perc Dineen, Albert Throckwaite, Jimmy Keogh, Tom Cantwell. They wouldn't kid him this way. But Tommy and Stewie went to Crucifixion, too, and they'd soon tell all the kids.

"His grandmother smokes a pipe, his aunt gets drunk, hey, guys, get the whistle," Moe Freeman said, and the kids took up this cry and circled around Danny, shouting it as a refrain.

"You guys shut up and let me alone," Danny said.

"Make us," yelled Louie Bergen, and Danny knew that he couldn't, because Louie was a better fighter than he was. And Moe and Tommy and some of the others were bigger than he.

"He's his grandmother's baby," said Moe Freeman.

"Goofy Four Eyes, get the whistle," Stewie said.

He'd beaten up Stewie in a fight at noon hour one day at school in the third grade. But Stewie had the gang with him, and that was why Stewie was kidding him, too.

"Better be careful, now, guys, so's he don't get his grandmother after us," Tommy said.

"Yeah, you guys watch your step or his aunt might bean you with one of her old gin bottles," Moe said, and they laughed.

"His aunt smokes cigarettes," said Dominic, who was wearing a black waist.

"Boy, you should hear the word my mother uses when she talks about any woman who drinks whiskey or smokes cigarettes," Moe Freeman said.

"What?" asked Danny, on the verge of tears.

"I couldn't even say it. When you say such words you feel like you got dirt in your mouth," Moe Freeman said.

"Say, Four Eyes, who you gonna get after us now?" jeered Ken Olson.

"Your big brother, I suppose. That skinny sonofabitch!" said Monk Malone, a kid as big as Bill who was Catholic but went to a public school.

"Naw, he always gets his grandmother after a guy," Moe said.

"Sure, he hides behind his grandmother's skirts," Stewie said.

"You sonofabitch!" Danny screamed at Stewie.

"Who's a sonofabitch?" Stewie asked, stepping up to Danny.

"You stop picking on me," said Danny.

"Who's a sonofabitch?" Stewie repeated.

"Why don't you guys pick on somebody else?" Danny asked.

Tommy placed a stick on Stewie's left shoulder.

"Knock it off!" Tommy told Danny, pointing at the stick.

"He won't. He's a yellowbelly," Monk said.

"Look out, Stewie, or he'll get his grandmother to knock that stick off your shoulder," said Louie Bergen.

"If anybody called me a sonofabitch, boy, but I wouldn't let him get away with it. That's an awful name to call anybody's mother," Tommy said.

"Well, I'm tellin' him to take it back or I'll fight 'im," Stewie said.

"What the hell are you, Stewie? A guy that's afraid to fight a goof like him?" Monk said, tossing a contemptuous glance at Danny.

"He's afraid of me. Last year one day at noon at school I licked him," Danny said, sensing that they might all suddenly turn against Stewie and let him alone.

"Did he? Don't speak to me if you let that Four Eyes clean on you, O'Leary," said Monk.

"I did," said Danny.

"You're yellow, O'Leary," said Ken Olson.

"Sure, he's a scared cat," said Danny.

"I'm tellin' yuh, Four Eyes! Do you take back what you called me or doncha?" Stewie demanded with bravado, seeking to keep the upper hand.

The stick fell off his shoulder. He bent down, picked it up, and set it back in a balanced position.

"See, he's a scared cat," said Danny, facing the others, trying to turn their contempt from him to Stewie.

"I'm tellin' yuh for the last time!" said Stewie.

"What did I call you?" Danny asked with sudden boldness; he was beginning to suspect that Stewie might be afraid and that the kids were ready to side with him against Stewie.

"I donno, what?" Ken Olson asked.

"O'Leary, I think you're yellow," Dominic said.

"I'm not yellow," Stewie said.

"Then prove it!" Monk challenged.

"Call him that name again! Dare yuh to, O'Neill!" Dominic said.

"Yeah, he's a sonofabitch!" Danny said, sneering at Stewie.

Danny now strutted, his self-confidence completely regained. The tortured animal that had been chased now became one of the chasers. Danny glared melodramatically, enjoying his new status and his sudden advantage. With slow deliberation he took the stick from Stewie's shoulder and placed it on his own.

"What yuh gonna do, huh?" he challenged.

"Well, I never thought that Stewie O'Leary was a yellow-belly," Monk said.

Tommy got behind Stewie and shoved him into Danny. The stick fell to the ground. Danny took his glasses off and handed them to Tommy, who dropped them in the grass on the side. With clenched fists, both boys circled warily around one another. Dominic and Monk exchanged meaningful glances and got behind the two antagonists. They shoved them into each other, and the kids formed a noisy and exuberant circle. Danny rushed Stewie, punching wildly. They clinched. Tommy separated them. Stewie, with his head down, went in, and one of his unaimed blows caught Danny in the left ear.

"Sock him, Irish!" yelled Moe.

"Come on, O'Neill, don't let him think you're a grandma's boy," said Monk.

They squared off. They grimaced. Danny was in a state of internal tension and confusion. His hands, his entire body, were suddenly beyond the control of his will power. He did not know precisely what he was doing. The yelling kids seemed vague to him, and the fight was almost like a fight in a dream. There seemed to be a fog in his brain.

"What the hell's the use of their pretending to fight if they won't fight?" said Tommy.

"Ask me another," said Louie in answer to Tommy.

"Fight, you guys!" yelled Monk.

"Sock him!" yelled Moe.

"Slap the piss out of the little baby," said Monk.

"Come on, Stewie, give it to him!" yelled Tommy.

Encouraged, with the shouts of the kids music to his ears, Stewie ran head down into Danny and slugged without aim. Some of his blows landed. Danny was helpless before Stewie's punching, more confused than hurt. He didn't seem to be able to see straight. His ear stung from another punch. The kids were now against him, all of them yelling for Stewie.

"That a boy, Stewie!"

"Keep it up, hit 'im again!"

"Sock him another, Stewie!"

"Smash him in the eye!"

"Kill him!"

"Enough?" Stewie asked, winded, but standing triumphantly in front of Danny, who was almost in tears, an expression of pain on his face as he stood with his tired arms raised.

Danny did not answer. He began to cry. He tried to defend himself as Stewie came in again, head lowered, throwing wild overhand punches at Danny. Danny was helpless. He was punched again. He could not make himself punch and fight back and he could not ward off the blows directed at him. All he felt was the pain of the blows, a sickening headache, stinging in the face and ears. His nose started bleeding, and the blood trickled over his lip, drops falling onto his waist.

"That's enough now," said Monk, stepping between the two.

"Good stuff, Stewie!" said Louie Bergen.

"Better run along home to grandmother now," jeered Monk.

"He's had enough. We ought to let the poor kid alone now," Tommy said.

Danny stood helpless and humiliated. He cried, holding a dirty handkerchief to his bleeding nose.

"I want my glasses," he whined, still sobbing.

"They're by the rock in the grass there," Tommy said, pointing.

"Get them yourself, yellowbelly," said Moe.

"Where are they?" asked Danny.

"Can't you see?" sneered Moe.

"Of course he can't. If he could, he wouldn't be four-eyed, would he?" said Ken Olson, and they laughed.

They laughed at Danny while he looked for his glasses. He found them and put them on. His nose was still bleeding, and he held his head back. He continued sobbing. He wanted to stop crying. He couldn't make himself do it. Tears came against his will.

"Well, what'll we do now, guys?" asked Monk.

"I wish there was a couple of more four-eyed goofs like that around to fight. I like fighting such goofs," said Stewie.

"Go on home, you, and have your grandmother wash your face. We don't want you hanging around with us," Monk said.

"Aw, Monk, let the kid alone. He got licked, didn't he? That's enough to do to him in one day," said Tommy.

"I ain't doin' nothin' to 'im. We don't have to have him around here if we don't want to, do we? We don't have to play with him when we don't want to, that's all," said Monk.

Tommy seemed to think for a moment. He screwed up his face in contemplation, and a kind of dreamy look came into his blue eyes. He nodded his head from side to side, and then he said slowly,

"Well, no, we don't have to do that."

"That's all I'm sayin'," said Monk.

Monk suddenly whistled, loudly and shrilly. Danny was taken by surprise and jumped backward. It was a shock which paralyzed him for a few seconds. They laughed at him.

"Your grandmother's whistlin'. Go home to her! Go on! Have her tie a bow ribbon on your ears, put a Buster Brown collar on you and put you in a dog show," said Monk.

"You don't own the prairie," Danny said, trembling as he spoke.

"We don't want you around, see!" said Moe.

"And when you go, don't trip over your own feet," said Monk.

"Skiddoo!" said Ken Olson.

"I can stay here if I want to. You guys don't own the whole prairie," Danny said, still shaking and nervous.

"Listen, I'll give you ten to beat it while the beatin's good," said Monk.

"You better blow, O'Neill," said Tommy, his tone milder than that of the others.

"One, two, three . . ."

Danny stood undecided while Monk counted. He still held his handkerchief to his nose. His left ear was red. His waist was dirty and spattered with blood. His hands were slightly caked with coagulated blood and were also dirty. His face was partly hidden by his handkerchief, but the visible parts were smeared. He stood, tense, unable to move, and he breathed rapidly. He was afraid, and he felt, gee, why should they want to chase him? Monk and the rest of the gang didn't own the prairie.

"Eight, nine, ten!"

Danny stood his ground, as much out of bewilderment and indecisiveness as out of courage. Monk gave him a shove. He tumbled backward and then fell.

"Quit picking on me! Let me alone!" he screamed at them while sitting in a pile of sand.

"Aw, let him go, Monk," Ken Olson said.

"Didn't I tell you to get the hell out of here? Well, go ahead! Don't yuh understand English? What are you, a greenhorn?" Monk shouted, looking at him with hatred.

Danny screamed, his hands over his face, his nose no longer bleeding, a patch of coagulated blood on his upper lip.

"Come on, Monk, we're gonna choose up sides," said Tommy.

"Yeah, you must be dumber than a greenhorn. Well!" Monk said; he bent down and tried to grasp Danny under the armpits.

Danny shrieked.

"Jiggers, Monk!" yelled Tommy.

"Jigs, guys, the old lady!" yelled Moe.

Mrs. O'Flaherty came running and stumbling across the prairie, a switch in her hand, holding her dress and apron with her left hand as she moved.

Danny wriggled, squirmed, yelled while Monk tugged with him. Louie Bergen poked Monk in warning. Monk looked up in surprise. Louie pointed at the old lady as she came nearer. Monk laughed, gave Danny a quick boot in the thigh, laughed again, and followed the others who ran off, jeering, out of the prairie. They stood on the sidewalk of Calumet Avenue.

"Son! Son! Son!" Mrs. O'Flaherty cried as she hastened forward.

Danny sprang to his feet. He took off his glasses and wiped his eyes with his right sleeve.

"Jesus Mary and Joseph, who was hittin' you, Son?" she asked in excitement as she came up to him.

"I'm all right. I was only playing," he said.

"There they are! They were picking on you, the Jews!" she said, pointing her switch at the kids, who had moved out past the curb onto the street.

"I'm all right. Gee, can't I even go out to play without you chasing me?" he complained.

"Look at the blood on you! Merciful God, who hit you? What did they do to you? Are you hurt? Tell me the names of them that hurt you and I'll skin them alive! I won't leave a pinch of flesh on their hides! Tell me the names!" she said, brandishing her switch.

"Nobody hit me," Danny said weakly.

The kids, over on the street, still stood together and watched. People passing along the sidewalk had stopped to look at the strange spectacle of an old lady with a switch; some of them were curious, others laughing. Several men began to approach Mrs. O'Flaherty and Danny. She looked down at him and said tenderly,

"Son, wipe your face, you poor thing."

He didn't answer her or wipe his face. He stood sniffling, wishing that he was just far away from all this trouble. Besides being beaten up by Stewie and picked on by the kids, his grandmother had come out to stick up for him. He felt that he would never again be able to show his face around in the prairie and play with the gang. He would always be teased and kidded as the guy who was beaten up by Stewie O'Leary and had to have his grandmother come out to stick up for him.

"Mother, let me alone," he protested.

She waved her switch and glared at the kids on the street. They laughed back at her, and Monk lip-farted.

"Come here and I'll skin you alive!" she shouted, waving her switch energetically.

The men came closer. The kids stood their ground, laughing but alert, waiting for the fun of being shagged by the old lady. Holding her skirt and apron with her left hand and swinging the switch with the other, she took several steps toward the gang.

"You limbs of Satan, if I lay these hands on you, I'll switch the hide off you," she yelled at them.

"Aw, go on home and smoke your pipe," Moe yelled back at her, and all the kids laughed.

She strode on toward them.

"Sons of the devils! Go on about your business before I tear you limb from limb!" she shrieked.

The spectators on the sidewalk drew closer. The kids saw what was likely to happen. The men might chase them. They turned and ran away in the direction of Fifty-first Street, passing out of sight. Danny was unable to utter a word. He just wanted to disappear. That's all he wished, that he just had the power to disappear so that nobody could see him, and they wouldn't even know where he was to laugh at him. If he'd had that power, he could have beaten them all up, Stewie and all of them, because he would have disappeared, hit them, appeared, disappeared, and hit one of them when they wouldn't have known where he was to hit him back.

"What's the matter, lady?" a man asked; he was tall, thin, dark, and he seemed curious.

"The ragamuffins!" she exclaimed.

"Did anything happen, lady?" another man asked.

"Come on, Mother, let's go home," Danny said, blushing in shame.

"Just let me lay these hands on them. I'll tear the eyes out of their heads. I'll break their bones. I'll pull the hair out of their heads. Ah, but I'll put the switch to them," she said, dramatically holding her switch aloft.

"What happened, Son?" the tall, thin man asked.

"Nothing," Danny mumbled.

"Are you hurt, boy?" a second man asked.

"I'm all right," Danny said, still ashamed; he pulled at his grandmother's apron to get her to go home with him.

"They beat my grandson. If I ever see them again, I'll get them arrested. The ragamuffins! The whores' sons! The horns of the Devil!" she said, her actions drawing a group of spectators about her.

"Mother, let's go home," Danny said, tugging at her apron, only wanting to be out of this, thinking again that if he only had the power to disappear he wouldn't have to go through what he was going through now.

"But the lad isn't seriously hurt, are you, Sonny?" the tall, thin man said.

"What are you talking about?" she said, turning sharply on him. "Go on about your business, the whole pack of you."

"But, lady!" exclaimed the tall, thin man.

"None of you can lady me. I'll have you know I don't address strangers. Be gone about your business and stop talking to me," she said.

The tall, thin man turned to the group, smiled knowingly, shrugged his shoulders, walked off.

"Come home, Son! Turn your back on the whole pack of them," she said, turning up her nose while some of the spectators laughed uproariously.

She started moving away but, hearing their laughter, turned and called back at them.

"Laugh and be damned!"

"Mother," Danny pleaded.

"Go on, scat, all of you, or I'll put the switch to you," she said, and then she turned, took his hand, led him across the prairie. The crowd watched her and laughed.

"Why did you come out? I didn't ask you to. You made a fool out of me," Danny said.

"So your grandmother made a fool out of you, did she!" she said. She stopped and blessed herself, muttering simultaneously, "Glory be to God! Holy Mary! So I made a fool out of you, did I? There I was, working in the kitchen, and all the way from over here I hear screams as if somebody is being killed, murdered. I say to meself, 'Glory be, is that me grandson? Are they killing him?' And I come over to see if it is me grandson, and what do I find but a big lummox on top of him, pounding the daylights out of him, beating him, and him screaming for mercy, and I chase them, and find my grandson, white as a sheet, and bleeding, beat up, and so I made a fool out of you, did I?" She blessed herself a second time. "Good Mary, Mother of the Infant Jesus, so I made a fool out of you, did I? Go on, get along with you," she said, cracking him on the legs with her switch.

"Ouch, let me alone!" he complained, and again he felt the stinging switch on his legs.

"Go home with you and wash your face! Go ahead, be home with you," she said, following him with the switch until he ran ahead of her so that she couldn't reach him. For self-protection, he walked faster than she, and she hastened along, wielding the switch in her right hand, holding up her dress with the other. "Ah, if I was a man! If you were like me, ah, but you'd have their skulls lying over the prairie, you would have."

He hurried along with her chasing him.

III

Danny sat alone in the parlor. If he had licked Stewie O'Leary, it all would have been different. He'd be out playing with them right now instead of Stewie. But now, suppose he'd licked Stewie. Danny saw himself standing toe to toe with Stewie, punching. Instead of being hit all the time, as he'd been in the fight, he saw himself tearing into Stewie, hitting him, socking him, slamming away, slamming the living crap out of Stewie. He saw himself giving Stewie a bloody nose and a black eye. He saw Stewie on the ground and himself saying:

You had enough now?

And he saw Stewie crying, saying he was licked. And he imagined all the kids praising him, telling him he was swell, and they were glad he licked Stewie.

But he hadn't won the fight. And one of the things he hated the most was to be called Four Eyes. Why was it that he had to wear glasses when other kids didn't have to? Well, he was going to get even for everything.

But he hadn't licked Stewie O'Leary.

Suppose that the next time Stewie saw him, Stewie should start picking on him. What would he do? He guessed that now he would just be made the butt of all kinds of jokes. A guy like Stewie was a bad guy to be beat up by. Most kids could lick Stewie. When Stewie found some guy he could lick, then Stewie wouldn't let up on that guy and he'd do the same things to him that so many kids did to Stewie. That was just the trouble with being beat up by a kid like Stewie. Yes, he was afraid that when Stewie saw him again Stewie would pick on him. He would have to do something to stop Stewie from doing that. If that damn thing hadn't happened at Dunne's, he could get Marty Hogan to stick up for him against Stewie. He had used to buy Marty candy or divvy candy with him sometimes at school, if he had any, and Marty had always stuck up for him. But now maybe it wouldn't be that way any more. He couldn't really count on Marty any more.

And, gee, he hadn't licked Stewie O'Leary.

Well, when he grew up to be a man, wouldn't he make everybody pay for what they did to him. Maybe he'd be a cop, and maybe Stewie would grow up to be a burglar. He'd catch Stewie cracking a safe like Alias Jimmy Valentine, or robbing a house, and he'd run Stewie in and have Stewie sent to jail in Joliet. Then Stewie would be sorry about this very afternoon, all right. And if he grew up and became a cop, he'd run in every kid who'd been in the prairie this afternoon, if he got the least chance to. They would all go down the road to Joliet, and, like Bill said, make little ones out of big ones. Or he would become a big-league star like Ty Cobb or Heinie Zimmermann or Hal Chase, and then they would all be proud to say they grew up with him, and some day at the game they'd come and want him to shake hands with them, and he wouldn't let them.

And, yes, it seemed to him that they ought to be getting out of this house and moving to another one in another neighborhood. But they wouldn't now, until next May at the very earliest, because that was when the lease ran out. That was a long time to live here and go on being the goof on the block, the goof in school, being known everywhere as the kid who was licked by Stewie O'Leary and had to have his grandmother come out and stick up for him. But if they moved to a new neighborhood, maybe he wouldn't be called Four Eyes, maybe he wouldn't be thought a bum fighter, maybe he wouldn't nearly always be the kid who was picked on and teased and kidded. There, they wouldn't know he'd been licked by Stewie, and about his grandmother and her smoking a pipe and all those things. Everything would be different. There, the first kid who picked on him, he'd clean that kid up, because by then he'd have learned how to fight better than he did now. He was going to learn how to fight until there wasn't a kid his size that he couldn't lick. And he'd live in a new neighborhood, go to a different school, not be called Four Eyes. Maybe even by then he wouldn't have to wear glasses, and then they wouldn't have any chance to call him Four Eyes. He wanted next May to come in a hurry, and he wanted them to move away when it did come. Look, they had only moved from Fiftieth and Calumet, where they had been put out because of the noise Aunt Peg made when she got drunk, and he hardly ever saw the kids from around Fiftieth and Cal. any more. If they moved not very far even, that was what would happen again. Darn it, they had to move, even if they were disgraced again by being asked to get out. He'd run and make noise here just so they would be put out. He'd shout and scream at the top of his voice so the neighbors would demand that the agent kick them out. He didn't care, he'd do it.

He got up and started running up and down the hallway, stamping his feet as heavily as he could. He was sure he would almost knock down the gas jets in the apartment under them.

"What in the name of Mary are you doing now?" his grandmother asked, watching him.

"I'm just running," he said, a trifle breathless.

"Bless me heart, you'll be tearin' down the house. Go down in the yard if you want to run," she said.

He went back to the parlor and sat moodily looking out on Prairie Avenue. It was sunny. Georgie Doolin was riding up and down the sidewalk on his three-wheeled bicycle.

4

I

Danny's fielder's glove hung from his left wrist and he wore the shirt to the blue baseball suit that Uncle Al had bought him a year ago. He walked slowly across an empty space in the Washington Park baseball field. He could see men playing on a diamond ahead of him, and in the distance there were other games in progress. But he didn't see any games of kids his own size that he could get into, and that was what he wanted. He rambled on toward the nearest game. He stopped to watch the men play. But it didn't interest him. It was a scrub game, with easy pitching, and he didn't know who any of the men playing were. He walked on. He wished he belonged to a team of kids, and that they played every day. Wouldn't it be fun if there was a league of them, and they played a regular schedule in Washington Park for a championship, and the scores of the games were all kept so that the batting and fielding and pitching averages could be figured out! He could figure out batting and fielding averages, pitching averages, and team percentages now. You only had to know long division to do that. It was decimals, too, Bill said, and he hadn't come to decimals yet in arithmetic. But all you did here was put zeros after what you were dividing into and divide by long division until you got three figures, and that was the average. He sat down under a tree and looked south across the large athletic field, the green of it dazzling in the summer sun. He pulled out blades of grass and chewed them. Hughie Jennings, manager of the Detroit Tigers, always chewed grass when he coached at third base.

Danny wanted to be on a team. Well, in a year or two, he'd be older and bigger, and then he was sure he'd be on some team. But that was a year or two ahead. He was thinking of right now. A year was a long ways off. It was next summer. Before that, there was the rest of this summer. There was going back to school. And the fall when they played football. He didn't understand football. And Christmas. And long months when it was winter. He wanted to get ice skates next winter and learn how to ice skate. Albert and Hortense Audrey and a lot of the kids went ice skating on the duck pond in winter. He wanted to ice skate with them, too. There was February. His birthday. Aunty Margaret said she was going to let him have a birthday party for the kids at school this year. And March. Waiting in March for it to become spring and for the ground to be all right so you could play ball. Reading about the White Sox in spring training, waiting for each day to go by so that it would get closer to the opening of the baseball season. That was the time he hated the most. Waiting for the snow to melt and the ground to harden so you could play ball. A year was that much off, that far away, and two years was just twice that much. He pulled out a long, slender blade of grass and chewed it. He spat out, pretending that he was chewing tobacco and spitting out the juice the way Papa did, and the way a lot of baseball players did. He spat out the chewed blade of grass and pulled up fresh ones to chew. He listened, hearing the noise of an automobile on the park driveway behind him which ran out onto Cottage Grove just where Fifty-first Street became Hyde Park Boulevard. Before Uncle Al had gone away, he had taken him to the beach. They had walked there, through the park, out onto Cottage Grove, across it, along Hyde Park Boulevard where people who had a lot of money lived. Uncle Al had pointed out a big house, and he remembered Uncle Al saying to him:

"Sport, some day, if I make enough money, you and I, and all of us are going to live in a house like that."

Uncle Al was coming home soon. He had gone up to Madison to see Uncle Ned and Aunt Mildred, and he was going to bring Little Margaret home with him and she was going to live with them and sleep with Aunty Margaret. Uncle Al was coming home any day. He was awful afraid of what was going to happen when Uncle Al came home. They'd tell Uncle Al on him and Bill. Uncle Al might beat Bill up and not let Bill in the house. Bill hadn't been up to see him since then, either. And Mother or Aunty Margaret might tell Uncle Al about his fight with Stewie O'Leary. He was more worried about Uncle Al coming home this time than he was most times. And he didn't want Little Margaret coming up and living with them. Why didn't she live in Madison? He didn't care if he did or didn't have a sister around the house to play with him. What did he care? But Aunty Margaret said that if Little Margaret lived with her, she would never drink any more, and so Uncle Al had gotten Mama and Papa to let him bring Little Margaret home from Madison and have her live with them.

He looked across the park. He was lonesome. He wished it was Sunday morning. When he went to mass on Sunday mornings, he always went hoping he'd see one of the girls in his class that he liked, and he hadn't all summer. He had even walked around where they lived on the other side of Grand Boulevard, and walked by their houses, but he hadn't seen them. He liked some of them, all right, and he wished one of the girls he liked would be his girl. He wanted to have a girl. Only if he did, he wouldn't want them to know at home, because they might tease him. He didn't like to be teased. That was why he hadn't shown up where the Prairie Avenue kids were playing in the lot, because he didn't want to be teased. And that was why he hadn't tried to find Marty and Marty's gang any more. They were tough, and every one of them could clean him up, and he didn't want to go around with kids when he was the worst fighter in the gang, and when, besides poking him around, they were sure to get him in trouble getting shags.

The men were playing ball on his right on the sand diamond that was called number two. The sand diamonds were all numbered from one to nine, and they started here on the Fifty-first Street side and ran along on the left on the Cottage Grove Avenue side of the park.

But he wished that one of the girls in his class that he liked would come to him and say to him that she wanted to be his girl and wanted him to be her fellow. And then sometimes, when school was on, and after the class was let out for the day, he'd take her over to the candy store by the elevated tracks at Forty-ninth and buy her sticks of candy. One of the girls he liked was Hortense Audrey. The kids called her the Washerwoman.

He picked up another blade of grass and held it between his lips. He looked unseeing across the ball field, his eyes dreamy.

Hortense Audrey had black hair, and it was cut short. He liked her. She was the first girl in his class that he had liked, and she was one of the smartest. Helen Smith had red hair, let down her back in long curls, she lived over around Forty-eighth and Forestville, and she walked to school every day with three other girls. He liked her, too. He didn't know if he liked her as much as he liked Hortense Audrey. But maybe if she came to him and asked him to be her fellow, he might get to like her better than he liked Hortense Audrey. Sometimes he guessed he liked Helen Smith the best, and then again, some other times, he guessed he liked Hortense Audrey the best.

And then there was Virginia Doyle. She had started in school last year. Most of the time he thought he liked her the best of the three of them. She had blond hair that was almost white, and it fell down her back in curls. Many times he wished that she'd come to him and ask him to be her fellow. He guessed that most of the time he liked her best, Hortense Audrey next best, and Helen Smith next best after her. And then there was Jennie Conlan, and she had short blond hair, and she liked him the best, and after his birthday party last year she'd stayed when all the other kids left and talked to him about the presents, but he didn't like her so much. Her cousin, Joe Conlan, was, next to Albert, the smartest boy in the class.

There were two more sisters and three more brothers in Virginia Doyle's family, and they lived at Forty-ninth and Forestville, and once he had gone roller skating by her house, just hoping to see her, but when he had seen her jumping rope she had hardly said hello, and he had skated by as fast as he could, hoping she would like the way he skated. Hortense lived on Langley and Forty-eighth. She didn't have any brothers and sisters. He guessed he had more chance to get her to be his girl than Virginia, because Albert nearly always walked home from school with Virginia, and he didn't have much chance because of Albert. Girls liked Albert better than they liked him. But he had real tough luck because all the girls he liked lived on the other side of Grand Boulevard, and he didn't ever get any chance to walk home from school with them. The best chance he had to see them outside of school was in winter ice skating at the duck pond, and that's why he wanted to get ice skates. Only girls that he wouldn't give half a whoop or two cents' worth for lived where he could walk home with them, and he didn't want to walk home with Maggie Grady who lived at Forty-eighth and Prairie.

Gee, now if they would get put out of the place they lived, maybe Aunt Peg would find a place over around Langley or Forestville, or one of the streets there, and if they did he could see lots more of Virginia Doyle and Hortense Audrey and Helen Smith than he saw now. But then, suppose they did that, suppose they should move right next door to Virginia Doyle's house, and Aunty Margaret should get drunk and Virginia's brothers and sisters and mother and father should know all about it, and hear Aunty Margaret cursing in the house. Then, maybe her mother and father wouldn't even let her talk to him. That would be bigger than any disgrace he had ever had. It would be so much worse than the kids on Prairie Avenue knowing that his grandmother smoked a pipe and Aunt Margaret got drunk drinking gin. If any of these girls knew this, then he would never have any chance at all to get them to be his girl. And then if they moved there and Mama came up to see them when her face wasn't washed and, just like Aunt Margaret said, she looked like somebody's scrubwoman, and Virginia Doyle would see his mother, he'd be disgraced that way, too.

He spat out a wad of chewed grass, and lay, hands under his neck, looking up at the sky.

II

With a blade of grass sticking out of his mouth, Danny got up and started wandering about the ball field in his lazy, droopy manner. His eyes were far away, and he walked along lackadaisically, his course a zigzag one. He wished he was playing ball. He wished he was older, and he didn't at all like the idea of having to wait so long until he would get older. Gosh, look at Uncle Al. Uncle Al must be somewheres around forty. Now, Uncle Al had lived a long time. He wished

Uncle Al would stay up at Uncle Ned's longer. If you were a man, you didn't have an old man, an old lady, a grandmother, an aunt, an uncle, a teacher all over you, and you didn't get into pickles with them any more. It took an awful long time to get older. But look at Mother. She was so old she was an old lady. Now, she had lived a long time. Look at all the days in the life of somebody as old as Uncle Al and as old as Mother. He'd have to wait a long time until he got as old as Uncle Al, let alone as old as Mother.

But still, it was good that he did. Because it meant that it was a long ways off before he would die. He was afraid to die and he didn't know what to do about it. Now, that was really the worst pickle he had ever been in. It was much worse to be in a pickle with God than it was to be in a pickle with Uncle Al, bad as that was. And he had been in a pickle with God ever since he had made his first Communion in first grade, and that was long enough ago. When he had made his first confession, he'd gone to Father Mulligan instead of his friend, and Father's friend, Father Hunt. Everybody in the parish was afraid of Father Mulligan, and sometimes people would say that even if he was a priest, he was an old devil. He had been afraid to go and tell his sins to Father Hunt because he knew him. And he had gone to Father Mulligan. Father Mulligan was old and gray-haired and cranky, and once he had been in the confession box, he had gotten so afraid that he had not told all his sins for fear he would be bawled out. He had made a bad confession and gone to Holy Communion, and that was a sacrilege, the worst sin you could commit. It made your soul black in the sight of God. But now, it was more than two years ago, and he had gone to confession a number of times, and he was always afraid to tell the priest that he had been making bad confessions and committing sacrileges ever since he had made his first Communion. He was afraid to even try and think what his soul was like and how black it was in the sight of God. And there was Father and Aunt Louise in Heaven, and they could look down and see and know this about him. And if he was to die now, be run over by a street car and killed or something like that, without confessing all of these black sins, he would go to Hell and burn there forever.

If he hadn't done it that time in first grade. But he had. He and Bill had stolen money from Aunty Margaret's pocketbook and used it to buy candy. When they'd been caught, he'd told them that it was Bill's fault, and that he hadn't been doing it too, and Bill had gotten beaten up and socked all over the house by Uncle Al, while he hadn't been touched. And after seeing the way Uncle Al had beaten up Bill, he'd been afraid. And he hadn't confessed it to Father Mulligan because he was afraid that if he did, Father Mulligan would have made him go and tell Aunty Margaret and Uncle Al, and then, because he lied like he did, it would have been so much worse, and he never could make himself do it because he was afraid to. Every time he went to confession he told himself that this time he would do it, and then when he got in the box and was confessing his sins, he never could do it. He wished he was some other kid. They said at school that it was so much better for them all that they were Catholics instead of Protestants or Jews. But look, a Protestant or Jew kid didn't have all these things on his mind, and he didn't have to be worrying about his sins, because he didn't know them. They said it was easier for a Catholic to go to Heaven than it was for a Protestant, but sometimes it didn't at all seem that way, because you knew what sin was, and when you sinned you had to go and confess your sins or you would be sure to burn in Hell forever. Being a Catholic seemed to get you into more trouble than being a Protestant kid, that was all. And now he'd helped Bill spend that fifty dollars and that was another sin on his soul. His soul was just black with sin.

Two kids passed him. He was always seeing them and he didn't know who they were. They always came out together and played. One was dark, and the other was light. The light kid looked like he had a father who was rich and that he might be a little bit of a sissy, and the dark kid always wore a black waist. Most kids who wore black waists were poor, and Mother would never have him wearing one. The light kid had a funny walk, stiff and straight, and he had his behind always sticking out, and when he walked, it wiggled in a funny way.

"Hey, you guys, wanna play catch or knock out grounders?" he called, hoping they would say yes, because it would be good practice and he was lonesome.

"Naw," the dark one said.

"No," the light one said, and he watched them go off toward the other end of the park.

He walked on slowly, changing his direction so as not to follow them. He was going to go to confession Saturday and he was going to tell of all his sacrileges, even if it meant being told he had to tell Uncle Al and Aunt Peg that he had been to blame, too, and had lied and let Bill get all the blame and that awful beating-up. He was. Yes, he was. He walked on. He saw kites flying in the sunny blue sky. He had never flown a kite. He wondered if he could, and if he could get one way up in the sky like some of those were, their tails moving in the wind, looking so small. He looked all around the large ball field. He didn't see one game of kids his own size. He wanted to play ball. He wanted to be older so that he could play ball with bigger kids.

He turned to the right, toward South Park Avenue. He didn't feel like hanging around here. He wished he could go and play with the Prairie Avenue kids but he was afraid to face them after his scrap with Stewie.

III

Al came home with Little Margaret, and he embraced his mother at the door.

"Al, sure I didn't expect you so soon," she said.

"Ned and Mildred decided to take a little vacation in the country so I came. I sent you a telegram," he said.

"But they're all out, and sure I couldn't read it and know what it says," she said.

"Hello, Mother," Little Margaret said.

"And bless me eyes, look what a fine big girl you are now," the grandmother said, looking at her granddaughter.

Little Margaret had grown several inches since she had gone away to live in Madison with her aunt and uncle two years before. She was a thin-faced, blue-eyed girl with lightish bobbed hair, skinny legs, and a skinny torso. She was wearing a white dress with a pink sash, white stockings, and black shoes.

"Peg ought to be home early today. She went to work early," the mother said.

"I want to put these things away, and then we'll talk, Mother," Al said. He picked up Little Margaret's suitcase and started down the hall to Margaret's bedroom off the long, narrow hallway. "Come on, Little Peggy, and I'll show you your room," he said, and the girl shyly followed him down the hall.

"You must be hungry, Al," the mother said, following them, excited and hopping as she talked.

"No, we ate on the train. Where's Danny?" Al asked.

"Yes, Mother, I want to see my brother Danny," said Little Margaret.

"He's out with the tinkers some place," she said.

"Has he been obedient?" said Al.

"Oh, Al, he's plagued the life out of me. I can't tell you how much," she said.

"Why, what's he done?" Al asked, going back to put his own grips away, his mother following him, while the girl sat on the bed in her new bedroom, shy, and unadjusted to her new surroundings.

"He's run with the tinkers," she said.

"What do you mean?" Al asked, beginning to take ties and clothes out of a grip.

"Al, I can't show my face on the street after what he and that buck-toothed tinker of a brother did," said the mother, raising her hands to the ceiling in added emphasis of her words.

Al stopped in the center of the bedroom with a handful of ties.

"What was it, Mother?"

"Al, his buck-toothed brother hasn't set foot inside of this door since it happened," she said.

"What was it, Mother?" he asked, nervously and sharply.

"Merciful God, I was disgraced," she said.

"But tell me what it was, Mother," Al said, dropping the ties on the bed and looking at her.

"Peg was off early one day, and she and me hied out to the cemetery, and we didn't get back till late. And, Mother of Jesus, we no sooner were in the door than the telephone rings. The two of them are being held in a candy store owned by the son of an informer named Dunne on Fifty-first Street."

"But what was it, Mother?" Al asked.

"Peg and me, we whists up there, and there the two of them are and the man won't let them out and he's saying he's going to turn them over to the police," she said.

"Did they steal? Wait till I get my hands on that goddamn dirty little Bill," Al said.

"Sure they were running in stores and telling the man to make them sodas and then running out again. The man caught them, and Al, Peg had to pay forty-five cents, forty-five hard-earned cents for the waste they caused. Al, I told the man I'd break every window in his store if they didn't leave my grandson go," she said.

"Where's Danny at now?" Al asked, still nervous and angrily excited.

"Running the bush with the tinkers. Sure, I haven't been able to do a thing with him. He no sooner gets out of that, than one day I am in me kitchen and I hear screaming and killing the like of which makes me think that someone is being murdered. And I go out to the prairie, and there are the tinkers, all of them leppin' and jumpin' on top of him, beating him within an inch of his life. I chased them. I chased them good with me switch, and I told the tinkers where to get off at, and there he was, his nose was bleeding, and he would make your heart bleed to see him the way they lepped on him and beat him up, and he, poor boy, down beneath them all, crying and screaming," she said.

"Has that bastard Bill been here since?" he asked.

"Oh, but he knows better after what he did to the little fellow. If it wasn't for me and Peg, the two of them would have been in the police station," she said.

"Goddamn it, I told Lizz to keep him away from here," he said, pacing back and forth across the room, slapping his left fist into his right palm.

"I ain't seen sight or light of him since, and, ah, but it's good that I ain't. Trying to make a tinker out of that innocent little fellow. I ain't seen sight or light of the buck-toothed one from that day to this," she said.

"Goddamn his dirty little neck, he better not let me see him," Al said, and he went back to his unpacking.

"I'm going to see how the girl is, Al," she said, leaving the room.

Little Margaret sat on the bed, kicking her legs out and swinging them back and forth.

"You poor little one, you must be hungry after your long ride on the train," she said.

"No, Mother, I'm not," she said.

"How did they treat you up there?" she asked.

"Nice. I had a room to myself to play in and sleep in," she said.

"Ah, but you became the pretty little thing, you did," she said to Little Margaret.

"Mother, where is my brother Danny?"

"Out running the bush. Sure and your mother and father won't be knowing you when they see you," she said.

"I liked my Uncle Ned and my Aunt Mildred," she said.

"You went to school and were a scholar, weren't you?" the grandmother said.

"I did," Little Margaret said.

"Come on out to the kitchen and let me give you a glass of milk," Mrs. O'Flaherty said.

Little Margaret followed her grandmother to the kitchen.

IV

Danny wandered idly along Fifty-first Street, not knowing what he was going to do, still lonesome, feeling disappointed because he hadn't found a ball game to play in over in the park. And he missed Bill these days, all right. He wondered when Bill would be coming up again, and he wondered, too, if Bill was sore at him after what had happened at Dunne's that day. He walked on. The street was busy and rather crowded, noisy because of the traffic, the street cars, the elevated trains passing into and out of the station overhead. He hardly saw anything. The noise, the people, the familiar sights and store-fronts, all were vague. His eyes expressed the inward direction of his thoughts. He slouched along, his body loose and ungainly, his nervousness given free play. He walked on, not seeing.

"Hey, for Christ sake, watch where you're going, you mutt!"

Danny looked up, vacant-eyed for a moment. He had been jerked away from his thoughts, and before he oriented himself to the scene about him there was a moment of vagueness. His face was blank for a second or two, and then it lit up with recognition.

"Bill!" he said in a sudden rush of happiness.

"Who the hell did you think it was?" Bill said.

"I didn't know. Gee, I'm glad you came up today," he said.

"Were you playing ball over in the park?" Bill asked.

"I went over there, but there wasn't any games for me to get into," he said.

"We ought to have more teams around here," Bill said.

"Yes, I wish we did. When did you come up?" Danny asked, standing under the elevated station with Bill.

"I just got off the street car," Bill said.

"Gee, I'm glad you came," Danny said.

"Who's at Mother's?" Bill asked.

"Just Mother. But Aunt Peg went to work at the hotel early this morning. She'll be home for supper," Danny said.

"How is she these days?"

"She's all right. She ain't been saying she's nervous or having the blues the last couple of days. But she keeps looking for mail," Danny said.

"She doesn't suspect anything?"

"No."

"Uncle Al ain't come home yet?"

"No, he ain't," Danny said, following as Bill started walking westward toward Prairie Avenue.

"When's he coming home?" asked Bill.

"They ain't said, and I don't know," said Danny.

"They said much about Dunne's?" asked Bill.

"Mother's chewed the rag a lot, but she isn't as bad as she was right after it happened," Danny said.

"Pa got sore, and I was beat up. He used his razor strap on me, and he sure hurt," Bill said.

"Gee, I'm sorry," Danny said.

"Hey, Dan, we can't go this way. We almost walked by Dunne's," said Bill, and he about-faced and started going back toward the elevated station.

They walked rapidly. They went through the passageway on the right of the station and came out in the alley behind it.

"This is a good short cut to home anyway," Bill said.

"Bill, you ain't sore at me, are you?" asked Danny.

"For what?"

"Dunne's. They made me tell them who I was," he said.

"It was Fag and the gang. And I'll get even with them, too. Ain't seen them, have you?"

"No, I ain't," Danny said, unconsciously kicking and spreading dust as they turned into the side alley which ran behind the Fifty-first Street stores.

"Say, Dan, I got enough cigar-store coupons now to get us two BB guns, and I'm goin' downtown after them tomorrow," Bill said.

"Maybe I can go with you," Danny said.

"Sure. We ought to have a lot of fun with the guns," Bill said.

"But, gee, maybe Uncle Al won't let us have 'em?" Danny said.

"He ain't my boss. Ma doesn't care," Bill said.

Danny led the way through a narrow passageway between the side of a greenhouse and a high fence, and they came into the back yard next to and identical with Danny's back yard. Both back yards were rectangular in shape, and each of them served two apartment buildings. They were divided by a low fence. Opposite the back porches there were hothouses forming a boundary to the yards. These were divided into two groups and separated by a fenced-off open garden. Behind the greenhouses towered the elevated girders.

"We'd have more fun downtown tomorrow if we had some of our dough left. I was a damn fool wasting it on Fag and his brother," Bill said regretfully.

"And we'll have to watch our step with the guns," Danny said, walking along a narrow sidewalk by the porches.

"After Dunne's, I'm always gonna watch my step," Bill said.

They walked on along the narrow sidewalk, skirting the dividing fence to enter Danny's yard.

"Let's play ball," Danny said.

"All right. You be the White Sox and I'll be the Boston Red Sox," Bill said.

"Say, Mother must have gone to the store," Danny said, looking up and seeing that the dining-room windows on the second floor were closed, with the shades drawn. "Mother sometimes does that when she goes out," he added, pointing. "She says that she won't let tinkers riding on the elevated look in her house, but, gee, the elevated trains are too far away and go too fast to let anyone on them see over into our windows," Danny said.

"We got to wait till she gets back then?" asked Bill.

"I got the balls and bat on the back porch," Danny said.

He ran upstairs. The porch door was locked. He climbed over the banister. Mother always told him not to, because she said he might fall and break his neck and get killed. But he liked to do it. Sometimes he'd start at the bottom, climb up outside the stairs and railings, and go all the way up to the third-floor porch. It was fun. But they always yelled at him if they caught him, and they said stairs were made to walk up and down on, and if you walked on them you couldn't fall and break your neck and get killed. He flung his baseball glove in a corner and got two small ten-cent soft balls and a light indoor bat.

"Bill!" he called, leaning over the railing.

Danny dropped the balls one by one and Bill caught them easily. He motioned Bill to get out of the way and he threw down the bat, aiming so that it landed on the grass instead of the sidewalk. He could unlock the door and go out that way and down the steps but he wanted to climb down. He climbed over the porch railing and stood with his feet on the porch edge, holding the porch railing with one hand and the stairway railing with the other. He cautiously let down one foot onto a beam and worked himself down to the first-floor porch. He jumped from there, landing in the dirt.

Bill threw him the bat and he caught it in his right fist. They placed fists, one on top of the other, choosing for ins and outs. Bill lost and Danny chose outs.

V

Danny liked playing different kinds of ball games with Bill and pretending that these were big-league games. When they played them, each of them would represent a team and they'd talk about the players they supposed in the game. Sometimes, they'd pitch balls and strikes for nine innings this way. Sometimes, one of them would be a first baseman and the other an infielder or outfielder. The first baseman would throw flies and grounders to the other one and these had to be fielded cleanly to be outs. They'd go on that way for nine innings, too. But the game Danny liked best, except Steel's, was the one they played in the back yard with a ten-cent soft ball. They each represented a big-league team and batted according to that team's lineup, hitting right-handed or left-handed just as the real players in the lineup did. They played swift pitching and called balls and strikes. The home base was near the back fence so they didn't have to chase pitched balls that weren't batted at. The whole yard was plotted out and the game was played according to a complicated set of rules devised to make hits hard to get and to keep the score tight. Foul balls that went over the back fence or up on the greenhouses to the right were outs. Over the whole yard, there were only certain places where batted balls were scored as base hits. Over the back fence was a home run.

But Danny wasn't good enough to beat Bill at this game because Bill was bigger and could hit harder, and he could hit better left-handed. Danny wasn't so good yet batting left-handed. But he gave Bill good games and he was getting better all the time, so that their games were getting tighter. Now he warmed up before starting, and this time he wanted to win. He was going to play carefully, wait out Bill's pitches, place his hits carefully. He wanted to win one of these games.

VI

In the last of the eighth inning, the score was four to four, and this was his chance. He was on edge to win, and he had right-handed batters coming up in his lineup. He caught Bill's warm-up pitches, nervous, anxious to get going and score some runs this inning. He had a good chance of holding Bill down for one inning because there were many innings in these games when Bill couldn't score.

"Who's up, Dan?" Bill called.

"Schalk, Tom Daly, my third baseman in this game, and Jim Scott," Danny said.

Danny stood waiting, batting in Ray Schalk's stance and prepared to imitate that player's choppy swing at the plate. He waited Bill out to the count of two and three. Then Bill tried to fool him with a slow ball. Danny caught it squarely and slammed it onto the first porch below his. That was a two-base hit. Here was his chance. He stood ready to bat again, his face determined, his lips clenched, his eyes alert.

"You outguessed me that time. This time you won't," Bill said confidently; he wound up and pitched one in swift, cutting the heart of the plate.

"Strike," Danny said.

He picked up the ball and flung it back to Bill.

He bunted the next pitch for a sacrifice hit. That made one out and a runner on third. He had two chances, and Scott and Buck Weaver, his batters, were right-handed.

"Letting Scott, your pitcher, bat, or putting in a pinch hitter?" Bill asked.

"He's batting," Danny said grimly.

He waited. Instead of using the stance and swing of the players he was representing, he was going to swing as hard as he could to get a run in.

"Come on, pitch," Danny said while Bill dallied, pulling at his belt, looking at the ball.

"My catcher's coming out to have a conference with me," Bill said.

Danny liked going through all these pretendings, as if there were talks of players on the field and all that. But Bill was doing it now to get his goat. Bill always took a lot of time if Danny looked as if he might start a hitting rally.

"Come on, pitch!" Danny said impatiently while Bill continued to stall.

Bill walked away from the pitching box.

"I'm talking about what I'm gonna do with my infield," Bill yelled, grinning at Danny, knowing that he was making Danny nervous.

Danny stood swinging his bat, stamping his feet, asking himself if he could slam a couple of hits out now, anxious to have the game go on, losing his nerve and his confidence with every second Bill delayed.

Bill went back to the pitching box. He started winding up slowly. Now he had to hit.

"Come on, hurrish! Come up here!"

Bill pitched a wide one.

"Ball," Danny called, and he bent down to pick the ball up.

"Come upstairs, Son!" Mrs. O'Flaherty called.

"Mother, I'll be right up as soon as we finish our game," Danny called to her.

She took the whistle out of her apron pocket and blew it loudly.

"We better go, Dan, and we can come down and finish the game afterward," Bill said when they both realized that she wouldn't stop blowing that whistle until they went upstairs.

Danny dropped the bat, and Bill left the ball in the pitcher's box. Danny followed Bill upstairs, disappointed and sulky. He had just that kind of luck. Darn it! Now, maybe when they came down again to finish the game he'd be jinxed. Darn it! Just his luck!

"Hurrish, come inside," she said as he opened the porch door.

"Gee whiz, you could have let us finish the game before you called us and started blowing that old whistle. It's too early for supper anyway," said Danny sulkily as they trooped into the kitchen.

"Hello, Danny, and hello, Brother Bill," Little Margaret said.

She stopped and stood shyly before them. Danny's sulkiness changed to fright. Uncle Al! And with Bill here!

"Mother, I got to go home right away," Bill said, seeing that he had unwittingly fallen into a trap and was in the hands of Uncle Al.

At this moment Uncle Al came into the kitchen.

"Hello, Uncle Al," Danny said in fear.

"Hello, Uncle Al," said Bill, also in fear.

"I want to see you two," said Al, and they knew they were in for it from the tone of his voice.

"There he is, Al. He came here straight from the mouth of Hell," the grandmother said, pointing at Bill.

"Go on in the parlor, both of you," Al ordered, and they obeyed, knowing they were in for something pretty awful.

VII

"Sit down, both of you!" Uncle Al said, following them into the parlor.

They sat down, Bill dropping on the edge of a chair, his lips compressed. Danny's face was white.

"What did you come here for?" he asked Bill.

"I came up to see Dan and play ball with him," Bill answered, his voice tense, almost throbbing.

"I don't want you coming to see Dan any more," Al said, pacing nervously to and fro.

"All right, I won't," Bill said.

"And I didn't ask you to give me any of your saucy lip, either! Get me?" Al said in rising anger.

Bill didn't answer.

"Why did you get him into trouble? What kind of an example is that to set for him? You're older than he is, and you ought to know better," Al said.

"What?" Bill asked.

"You know goddamn well what! The dirty nerve of you! What? Why, you little bastard, the candy-store business, what the hell do you think I'm talking about, the moon?" Al said, rushing over to Bill, standing over him, clenching and unclenching his fists, breathing asthmatically.

Danny sat, and all he could do was to mumble silently over and over again, God, please! God, please! God, please!

"The other kids made us do it," Bill said.

"Don't give me any of that!"

"I'm not. They made us," said Bill.

Al drove a curving left punch at Bill. Bill ducked, but not quickly enough, and the blow landed on his jaw, knocking him against a side of the chair.

"Please, please, Uncle Al, don't hit me! I won't do it again," Bill cried, trying to cover his face with his hands and arms.

Al punched again with his left.

"Please, let me alone!" Bill begged, crying, still vainly trying to protect himself.

"I'll let you alone, doing such things to your little brother! Goddamn you, I'll let you alone!" Al said rapidly, punching as he spoke.

Bill lunged out of the chair, trying to get free and run to the front door. Al grabbed him by the collar, dragged him back, and faced him, blocking all exit.

"You pup! What did you do it for? Answer me! You dirty pup!" Al said.

Bill stood silent, tears streaming down his face. Danny sat, unable to do anything but keep murmuring to himself, Please, God! Please, God! Please, God! Little Margaret came to the door, but stood there, speechless. She began quietly to cry.

Al swung again, and Bill went down under the blow.

"Please, let me alone! Ouch!"

"Get up!" Al commanded, standing over Bill with clenched fists, still breathing asthmatically.

Bill curled up on the floor and cowered.

Al bent down and punched Bill in the ear. Bill screamed. Mrs. O'Flaherty rushed into the room.

"He's a devil out of hell, Al, give it to him good! Strike a blow against the Devil, Al!" she said.

"Mother, please make him let my brother alone," Little Margaret begged in tears.

"Go on, get out of here and don't bother me. Go on back to Wisconsin!" Mrs. O'Flaherty said.

Al pulled Bill to his feet.

"What did you want to do, make a criminal out of your brother, you deceitful little sonofabitch?" Al said, his temper now completely beyond control.

"I'll never do it again! Uncle Al, honest, I won't," Bill said.

"You're goddamn right you won't!" Al said.

"Fist him, Al! Doing such things to my little grandson! Brain him! He's no good! Brain him, he's like his long-jawed pauper father," the grandmother said.

Little Margaret grabbed her grandmother's skirt.

"Go on, and stop pulling at me skirt," the grandmother said.

Little Margaret ran to her aunt's bedroom, flung herself on the bed and sobbed.

"You're never coming to this house again! Do you hear?" Al said, his voice raised.

Bill sniffled, cried, stood silent before his uncle, watching him closely in order to try and duck the next punch.

"Answer me when I speak to you!" Al said, giving Bill a quick and ringing slap in the face.

Bill cried.

"Answer me!"

"I understand," Bill said in tears.

"I'm damn glad you do, you dirty little liar!" Al said, pounding Bill until he again fell onto the carpet and curled up there, screaming for mercy.

Danny began screaming.

"Shut up, you, or I'll pinch your ear," the grandmother said, turning to her grandson.

"Goddamn you! After all our kindness and generosity to you, doing that to your brother!"

"Please don't hit me any more," Bill begged abjectly.

"Goddamn you!"

Al kicked Bill in the ribs. He still breathed heavily. He relaxed and stood about five feet away from the boy.

"It serves you right, you spawn of the Devil," Mrs. O'Flaherty said, looking at Bill, who was on the floor, shaking, quivering, sobbing.

Danny sat on his chair, frozen quiet, pale, his lips trembling.

"Now, get out! Don't let me catch you around here again, and let this be a lesson to you," Al said, speaking more slowly, his voice tense, his words coming irregularly because he was short of breath.

Bill got up slowly. He wiped his eyes with his shirt sleeve. He walked out of the room, casting a quick, hurt, frightened glance at Danny.

"Hurry up and get out of the house, and tell your father and mother to keep you away from here," Al said, his anger almost choking him.

Bill left, shutting the door quietly behind him. Danny jumped off his chair and ran to the window.

"Get away from there! And don't run! We were put out of the flat on Calumet because of noise. No running!" Al said, and Danny turned back from the window, walked past Al, with his head lowered.

"Come back here," Al said as Danny started to leave the room.

Pale, Danny turned around. Al pointed to the chair. Danny timidly took it.

"You're going to be punished, too. No more ball games. And you go to bed tonight without supper," Al said.

Danny trembled, hoping he wouldn't get a beating like Bill.

"Hear me?"

"Yes."

"Say yes, sir!"

"All right."

"Al, you did right," Mrs. O'Flaherty said; she went back to the kitchen.

VIII

Al went to his room. He sat on the bed. He got up and closed the door. He sat on the bed again and sank his head in his hands. He got up again, looked out the window. He took his mouth organ from a dresser drawer and stood by the bed playing *Bell Brandon*.

IX

Danny sat in the hammock on the back porch.

"Now you'll toe the mark!" Mrs. O'Flaherty said to Danny, looking at him through the screen door.

Not answering, he swung slowly back and forth.

"Ah, there's right and wrong and them that's wrong will toe the mark!" she said, turning away from the door.

Little Margaret came out on the porch.

"Hello," she said.

"Hello," Danny said.

She was his sister and he didn't seem to know her well.

"What did you and Bill do?" she asked.

"Something that doesn't concern girls," he said.

"I'll bet it's no worse than what we did in Madison," she said.

"Little Margaret! Little Margaret, go to your aunt, she's just come in the door," Mrs. O'Flaherty called excitedly, and Little Margaret bolted through the door to run to her aunt.

Danny sat moodily rocking in the hammock.

5

I

When Aunt Margaret had come home, she'd told Uncle Al to give him supper. And after cleaning Bill up and chasing him home, Uncle Al hadn't been cranky any more. He always acted that way. When he lost his temper, then soon afterward he was very quiet and sorry, and not cranky. Uncle Al had gone out after supper, and Mother and Aunt Peg were in the back talking to Little Margaret.

He sat on the parlor floor. Spread before him were sheets of paper, a pencil, enough playing cards to make up five or six decks, and an atlas opened at the map of Mexico. He was playing a war game that he had made up with cards and tracing the course of the armies on the map with a pencil. Every time there was a battle, he marked the battle down on a sheet of paper, and figured the killed, wounded, and captured. The United States was invading Mexico, and he was imagining himself an American general like Major General Wood. When he'd started playing this war game, the United States Army had lost battles at the Rio Grande. He'd had to do something about it, so he'd found more old cards around the house and had divided them up, giving most of the aces and picture cards to the American Army, and the rest to the Mexicans. But the Mexicans still had a chance, because it was sometimes easy to take an ace with a small card. He'd made up this game all by himself. He stacked up two piles of cards, and set them face downward. He'd drawn one from each pile, and the higher card took the other one. The ace was highest, with the king, queen, and jack in order, and then the numbered ones. There was a battle every time matching cards were drawn from the two packs. Then he laid the next cards face down on the ones he'd just drawn. Then he drew again, laying the newly drawn cards face upward, and whichever was the higher won, taking the two previously drawn cards. In the long run, by giving the United States Army a higher proportion of the big cards, it ought to win the war.

He liked playing this game. He had an atlas with the map of every country in the world, and he was going to go on playing wars until the American Army conquered every country in the world. Dreamy-faced, he played, trying to imagine scenes of war and battle as he drew the cards, and seeing himself a general in these scenes. The next big battle would be at Monterey. And after each battle, he figured out the casualties. All black cards taken by one side were killed. All diamonds were wounded. All hearts were captured. Sometimes he'd figure these by the numbers of the card, counting jacks eleven, queens twelve, kings thirteen, and aces fifteen. And sometimes he'd add ten to each number to make it more, because in real battles there were sometimes a lot killed and wounded and captured. Look at the war in Europe with the Germans going through Belgium. He didn't want the Germans to win. In his war game, after the American Army had captured all of Mexico, Central America, and South America, he'd play out a war with the Americans invading Europe. He'd only just figured out his war game in the last couple of weeks after seeing about trouble between the United States and Mexico and the war in Europe on the front pages of the newspapers. He sat on the floor, absorbed in his cards and map, playing his war game, figuring the lists of the killed, wounded, and captured after each battle, and listing them on a sheet of paper.

II

"Are you glad to be back here and to live with your Aunty Margaret?" Margaret asked her niece as she, Mrs. O'Flaherty, and the little girl sat around the dining-room table.

Little Margaret nodded her head decidedly, and the aunt smiled.

"Peg, they fed her well in Madison," the grandmother said, looking at her granddaughter.

"We always had better things to eat than I used to get to eat with Mama and Papa on La Salle Street," Little Margaret said.

"Did you have children to play with, too?" asked Mrs. O'Flaherty.

"Uh huh! I used to play with Bob and Heinz. They are Aunt Mildred's nephews, and we used to play a lot and do things," Little Margaret said.

"What games did you play with them?" Margaret asked.

"Sometimes we played tag, and hide and seek, and sometimes we used to do things to play jokes on people," Little Margaret answered.

"That wasn't nice, was it?" said Aunt Margaret.

"We had lots of fun," Little Margaret said.

"What would you do?" asked Margaret.

"Sometimes we'd get an old pocketbook, and tie it with a black thread that was hard to see at night, and we'd leave it on the sidewalk. Then somebody would come by and see it and think maybe they were finding a pocketbook full of money, and they'd go to pick it up, and when they did we'd pull it back and laugh. We'd have lots of fun," she said.

"But little ladies don't do that," Margaret said.

"Ah, sure they were just playing and the little ones meant no harm," the grandmother said.

"Did you like school?" asked Margaret.

Little Margaret bobbed her head affirmatively.

"She's a scholar, and she can read and write, can't you, you little darling?" Mrs. O'Flaherty asked.

"I know my ABC's, and I can write my own name," Little Margaret said.

"Uncle Ned and Aunt Mildred were good to you, weren't they?" Aunt Margaret asked.

"Yes, but Uncle Ned was away a lot of the time on the road, and Aunt Mildred when she wasn't sick used to have to be in the store on State Street. Sometimes she used to take me riding in her electric. I liked to ride in it. Aunty Margaret, I wish you had an electric," Little Margaret said.

"Maybe I will some day," Margaret said.

"Sure, I wouldn't be seen in one," Mrs. O'Flaherty said.

"Why, Mother?"

"I want a horse and carriage like the people of quality used to own in the old country," Mrs. O'Flaherty said.

"But, Mother, they're out of date in this day and age," Margaret said.

"Sometimes we went riding around the lakes in a horse and buggy. Uncle Ned would hire it, and sometimes he would let me drive the horse," said Little Margaret.

"See! See! See, Peg! They had a horse and buggy," the grandmother said.

"I like to drive a horse," said Little Margaret.

"Some day we'll all be rich and we can have lots of fine things," said Margaret.

"Sure, it's a waste of money," the grandmother said.

"Am I going to go to school here?" asked Little Margaret.

"Yes, your brother can take you," said Margaret.

"Peg," said the mother.

"Yes, Mother," said Margaret.

"Read me what's in the paper. I want to know if they got that man who killed the woman in Wisconsin. And what does it say about the President, that poor man losing his wife only the other day," Mrs. O'Flaherty said.

"You love to hear about murders, don't you, Mother?"

"Sure, and don't I want to find out if they got that heathen that murdered the poor woman in cold blood," the grandmother said.

"All right, I'll get it. I left it in my room," Margaret said.

"Why don't you play with your brother?" the grandmother asked Little Margaret.

She jumped off her chair and ran into the parlor.

III

"What are you doing?" Little Margaret asked.

"Nothing," Danny said, closing his atlas and quickly shoving his sheets of paper with his casualty lists and record of battles under the book. The American Army had just captured Monterey, and he had been studying the map to figure out where the next battle ought to be.

"You were playing cards. That's not doing nothing, that's doing something," she said.

He looked at her, annoyed, and didn't answer.

"You don't act like you're glad I came here to live with you," she said.

"Sure I am," he said to be saying something, and, still looking at her, he decided that she wasn't as pretty as girls like Virginia Doyle and Hortense Audrey and Helen Smith.

"Why don't you play cards with me?" she said.

"You probably ain't any good," he said.

"How do you know I ain't, if you never played with me to find out?" she said.

"Well, you probably ain't," he said.

"I can play casino," she said.

"I don't like casino," he said.

"Uncle Ned taught me how to play casino," she said.

"He did?"

"Yes, and sometimes I beat him," she said.

"That's because he must have let you win," Danny said.

"No, it wasn't. Danny, why did Uncle Al lick Bill like he did today?" Little Margaret asked.

"Because of what we did," said Danny.

"What did you do?" she asked.

"We ran into Dunne's on Fifty-first Street and ordered banana splits and ran out, and I got caught, and then the kids caught Bill, and they found out about it," he said.

"Let's us do it some time," she said.

"Oh, no, I won't," said Danny.

"Are you afraid? Bob and Heinz in Madison wouldn't be," she said.

"I got caught. I won't try that again. No, sir," he said.

"You're afraid," she said.

"I got into too much trouble already over it. We were almost sent to reform school," he said.

"You were?"

"Uh huh!"

"I'm afraid. I don't want to stay here with Uncle Al. He's got a temper. Uncle Ned's different. He hasn't got a temper like that. He never got mad at me and Bob and Heinz for what we ever did having fun," Little Margaret said.

"Uncle Al goes off the handle sometimes. I was afraid today," said Danny.

"So was I. I went and cried and wished I was back in Madison," said Little Margaret.

She sat down on the floor beside him.

"What grade are you in?" she asked.

"I'm going in fourth," he said.

"I guess I'll be in third grade," she said.

"Where'll you go to school?"

"I don't know. I guess where you go to school," she said.

"That'll cost a dollar a month," he said.

"Aunt Margaret will pay for it. Play casino with me," she said.

Danny had to sort out a deck from his stack of cards. He shuffled them and dealt. They played casino, Danny winning the first game.

"Gee, it's easy to skunk you at casino," he said.

"Well, I used to win from Uncle Ned," she said.

IV

"Well, Al, you don't need to worry about your heart. Take that digitalis, and keep on as you have been doing. It's nothing serious," Doctor Mike Geraghty said.

"I thought you might as well look me over while I was coming to see you," Al said, he leaned back in his chair in his friend's office, pulled out cigars, gave one to the doctor, and took one himself, cutting off the end with his pocket-knife.

Mike Geraghty was about forty, a heavy-set, gruff-looking man who was just starting to become soft and plump.

"I'm sorry that Nora isn't home," Al said.

"She went down to her sister's," said Mike.

"Well, I'll see her the next time I come over," Al said.

"How long before you go on the road, Al?" Mike asked.

"After Labor Day," Al said.

"Everything at home fine?" he asked.

"Yes. My sister's herself again," Al said.

"That's good. She's a good, fine girl. It was too bad she took to that habit of hitting the bottle, but maybe she's going to settle down now," Mike said, drawing on his cigar.

"Holy smokes, Mike, I hope so," Al said.

"Mother all right?" asked Mike.

"Ah, she certainly is. Say, but she's alive and kicking," Al said proudly.

"She's a great old gal," Mike said.

"I didn't tell you what she pulled at the ball game this summer, did I?" Al asked.

"Don't tell me she goes to the ball game?" Mike asked in surprise.

"Sure, she sometimes goes with my nephew on ladies' day," Al said.

"Does she understand the game?"

"No, but she loves to go. Well, this time the man at the gate wouldn't let Dan in free. Holy sailor, she stormed at him and said she'd never come to the games again. She raised such a fuss the man let my nephew in free with her. And she never goes except on ladies' day, that's the joke of it," Al said.

"A great old woman, a great old woman," Mike said as both of them laughed.

"How's your other sister?"

"Cripes, Mike, I better knock on wood. I haven't seen her yet. She's sometimes like a real tornado, all right," said Al.

"Every time I meet her she tells me of a new saint to pray to," Mike said, smiling.

"She has all the saints right down pat. You can't trip her up on a saint, Mike," Al said.

"That's one thing you can't do," Mike said.

"Poor thing, she's had a hard time, but God, Mike, she's a corker. She's usually ready to fight at the drop of the hat. You have to kid her a little to keep her in good humor. But that oldest boy of hers has me worried," Al said.

"He's not a bad kid, what's the matter with him, Al?" asked Mike.

"Well, when I was away on my vacation, he pulled something and got Sport in trouble," said Al.

"How come?"

"He induced Dan to go into soda stores and order sodas and then run out without paying. They were caught at it," Al said.

"What happened?" asked Mike.

"Oh, Peg paid for the wastage, and that was all. But it's bad business for kids to be doing that," Al said.

"Al, don't take it so seriously. Hell, kids are kids. Every kid worth his salt does something like that, and if he doesn't, that's when you better begin worrying about him," Mike said, laughing.

"But, Mike, starting his younger brother doing that, look at what it might lead to," Al said.

"I wouldn't worry, Al," Mike said, and Mike's lightmindedness toward this incident caused Al to be all the more regretful of what he had done to Bill.

"Well, maybe," Al said reflectively.

"How does business look for the fall?" Mike asked.

"I can't say. It might be up, and it might be down. Every shoe man I talked to in the Loop is in the same uncertain state of mind. Of course, some factories will make something selling shoes to the armies, but that's not our line. You can't tell. This war has made everything uncertain. You saw from the papers how the stock market went all to hell. And then, with the high cost of living these days, well, you just can't prophesy," Al said.

"I noticed it, but didn't read much about it. Too damn many of the Irish have been having kids, Al, and they kept me busy."

"Well, it's hard to say what business is going to be like. Prospects are not too good, though," said Al.

"This war took me on the jump. I never expected it," said Mike.

"Mike, you always want to remember this. The Germans are a thick-headed lot, and they like to dominate and tell the other fellow," said Al.

"Well, Al, I guess if you come down to it, the German, he isn't like the Irishman," said Mike.

"But then, Mike, this war isn't our business. If they want to shoot each other on the other side of the ocean, it's more their business than it is ours. All I have to say is that I hope that because they do that, the shoe business doesn't suffer over here," Al said.

"Al, no matter what happens, I don't have that worry," Mike said.

"What do you mean, Mike?" Al said.

"You were talking about business. Well, maybe business is not the exact word for it in the case of my patients, but when it comes down to it, that is what it amounts to. My patients are my business. And a doctor doesn't ever have to worry about there being no business for him. If there is or if there isn't a war in France and Belgium and Europe, well, the doctor always has business. Of course, sometimes he doesn't get paid for it, but that's another matter. You might have shoe buyers afraid or hesitant to buy your goods. But I'll never find myself without enough sick people to keep me busy. But then, as I said, when it comes to paying, that's another matter. There's two sides to it, Al. Whatever you sell, you can feel pretty sure it's going to be paid for. With me, well, it's another matter. I'm always busy, but a lot of it isn't paid for," Mike said, smiling ironically.

"I never thought of it in that light, Mike, but it's so," said Al.

"Want a drink, Al?" asked Mike.

"No, thanks, Mike," said Al.

"I always ask you that, Al, and I know you damn near never take a drink. The reason I do is that I'm announcing that I think I'll have one myself," said Mike.

"Sure, go ahead, Mike," said Al.

Mike went to a cupboard to fix himself a drink. Al sat back in his chair and drew contentedly on his cigar. He liked to visit Mike. Whenever the cares of the world were pretty heavy on his shoulders, whenever he just wanted to forget something, whenever he just wanted to see a friend, he came over to Mike. Mike was his best friend. It was not what they talked about. He didn't tell Mike everything that went on in his head. He had worries and fears and anxieties that he didn't broach to Mike. It was just that he liked to be with Mike. There was rapport between them. Now, there was a word, *rapport*, that he'd have to spring some time on some of these wise-aleck salesmen.

Mike came back with his drink and sat down.

"I don't believe in getting drunk, but now and then a drink is a damn good thing for a man," said Mike.

Al sat with his head back, blowing smoke rings from his cigar.

"What you tell me about your nephews makes me think, Al, that, golly, when I was a kid I did some things myself. I broke down fences, and copped candy out of stores, and raised some hell in my own right. It's nothing to worry about if it doesn't get too serious," Mike said.

"The point is, when does it get too serious? Whenever a habit is getting serious, you don't know it. It's only after it's too late, Mike, that you know if it's too serious or if it isn't," said Al.

"You're right there, Al," said Mike, taking a sip from his glass.

"The idea in life, Mike, is to be a wise guy, not a fool or a sucker. Now, why be a sucker even to your own habits? The idea is to instill the correct habits in a young boy when there's time, and then, when he grows up, dangers have already been eliminated," Al explained.

The doctor took another sip.

"But, Mike, I'm hoping that everything is going to be better on Prairie Avenue now. With my little niece home, I think that my sister is going to behave herself better than she did. I guess that she just let herself become unbalanced because of that man, but now that she's recuperated, she'll forget him. The sooner she does, the better," Al said.

"Yes. Of course, I don't know him, but from the newspapers it seems to me he was a little rat. He tried to be something he wasn't, and this lumber man, Brophy, he showed him up," said Mike.

"That's all finished now. And she'll forget him," Al said.

"I hope so for your sake, Al. You deserve it. Al, I don't know why in the name of God you've never gotten married."

Al seemed embarrassed.

"I know what you're going to say about responsibilities to your mother, but you could manage that and have your own life. You should get married, Al," Mike said.

"Well, Mike, Ned ran out. I never would say this to anyone but you, but it was really that. He ran out and married, so what was I going to do? The old fellow couldn't take all the responsibility on his shoulders, and neither could Peg. And we had the little fellow, Danny, with us. My mother thinks the world of him, and so do I. I want to see him make his name in the world. So what was there to do?" said Al.

"Of course, Al, my people made it easier for me. I had a tough enough time studying medicine. But then it wasn't a tough time in the sense that I was poor. They had enough to educate me," said Mike.

"I never went to college," Al said wistfully.

"I know it, but, Al, you've already outdistanced many a fellow who did," said Mike, taking another sip.

"You think so?" Al said, leaning forward.

"You know it. And you're coming along, Al. There's no question about that," Mike said.

"I want the young fellow to have a better start than I had, so that he can go so much farther," Al said.

"What do you want him to become?" Mike asked.

"A lawyer," Al answered.

"You don't want him to be a doctor?" Mike asked.

"Well, I set my mind on making him a lawyer, but I wouldn't object to his becoming a doctor if he has his mind set on that when he grows up," Al said.

"If you had a nephew who studied medicine, why, when he's finished, I could take him under my wing. I'll be an old man by the time a nephew of yours is in his prime and I could give him my practice and, you know, coach him along," said Mike.

"Maybe we can do that with Bill. I wish I could do something about the rest of my sister's kids, and, God willing, I might. Maybe we can save the older boy that way, and make him come out all right," said Al.

Mike took another sip of his drink.

"Yes, and I can help him a lot," said Mike.

"That's damn nice of you," said Al.

"You know, Al, you're my best friend. What the hell, we can't have any kids ourselves, and a man wants to leave something behind him, doesn't he?"

"Yes," Al said reflectively.

They were silent and thoughtful.

"My brother-in-law, he's all right, but he doesn't have any refinement, and he has his hands full making a living for his family. So he can't give any genuine direction to his kids. And Lizz, poor thing, I can't make her out. Always belligerency. She is the most belligerent woman I ever saw," said Al.

"Al, you're the best of your family. And remember my words! It's a noble thing that you're so concerned about them and are taking care of them. But you should look out for yourself, too. You owe that to yourself. You're too good a man, and you're making your way on your own merits. You must always see to it that you decently provide for yourself," Mike said; he took another sip of his drink.

"Well, Mike, prospects aren't bad for me. I'm confident that I'll always make a living for myself," Al said.

"Living be damned! I make that. You've got in you the stuff that should bring a man to the top. You must see that your future is provided for," Mike said.

"God willing, Mike, we'll all be better off and happier and prosper in the years to come," said Al.

"I hope so. I get along and find myself building up a better practice as the years go on," said Mike, and he took another sip.

"Well, Mike, I hope for the best," Al said, knocking ashes into a tray beside him.

"No law against hoping," said Mike.

They heard the outside door opening.

"Here's the girl now," said Mike.

Suddenly Mike's office door opened and Mrs. Geraghty came in. She was a plump but pretty woman in her thirties.

Al stood up and smiled. Mike turned in his chair and smiled, too, as she came toward him.

"Hello, dear!" he said.

"Hello, dear!" she said, and she smiled at Al and said, "Why, hello, Al. How are you?" She came toward Al and offered her hand, and he shook hands with her.

"I'm feeling greater than great, and how are you feeling? You're looking six degrees better than most wonderful."

"Al, you're a great kidder, and that's one of the reasons I like you," she said.

She went to her husband, bent down, and kissed his forehead perfunctorily.

"No calls tonight, dear?" she asked.

"Thank God, no," he said.

"Well, the evening isn't over," she said.

"Don't remind me of that," said Mike.

"Al, how was your vacation?" she asked, sitting down near her husband and facing Al.

"Fine! Fine! Never had a better time," he said.

"Al, did you get any fishing in?" asked Mike.

"Some. Of course, you don't catch big fish where I was. The best I could do was a bass weighing two and a half pounds. That was a pretty good catch. And I went out one evening and caught a number of bullheads. They're good eating," Al said.

"Some time, Al, you and I will have to get off for a week or so in the summertime on a vacation and do some fishing," Mike said.

"That'll be great! Great," Al said.

"How's your family, Al?" Mrs. Geraghty asked.

"Good, thank you, good, Nora," Al said.

"I'm glad to hear it. And your little nephew?"

"He's all right. He'll be going back to school. These days, of course, he has nothing on his mind but baseball. He's a real fan," said Al.

"Well, it won't do him any harm," Nora said.

"He's a fine lad," Al said proudly.

"You're so good to raise him, too," said Nora.

"But say, Al, maybe we can get away together next summer, and we'll go up somewhere, maybe to northern Wisconsin, and fish for two weeks," Mike said.

"Fine, I'm agreed," said Al.

"That would be something good," said Mike.

"It would be so good for Mike, Al. He has a pretty hard time of it, don't you, you old darling," said Nora.

"Well, I could tell you that there are plenty of other lines and professions that give you an easier life than being a doctor does," Mike said.

"Say, Al, wouldn't you like a cup of tea or coffee?" she said.

"Don't bother, Nora," Al said.

"Sure you would. You and Mike always like it when you're together of an evening like this. Tea, that's what you like. I'll make some for you," she said.

"You're a real sport, Nora," Al said as she left the room.

"Nora's as fine a wife as they come, Al," Mike said.

"No gainsaying that," said Al.

"But, Al, I'm all for our vacation, fishing next summer," said Mike.

"So am I, Mike," said Al.

V

"Where's my daughter? Where's my little baby girl?" Lizz O'Neill said in a loud voice when Margaret let her in. Lizz wore a soiled black dress which hung on her fat body like a sack, and she had an old rag tied under her chin.

"The darling dolly's here, Lizz," Margaret answered, and just as she did, Little Margaret ran down the hall.

"Oh, but here's my wandering little baby girl," Lizz said, and she bent down, kissed Little Margaret, and petted the girl's head.

"Let's go out in the back," Margaret said.

"Peg! Peg! Is that Lizz?" Mrs. O'Flaherty called from the rear end of the hall.

"I want to see my darling mother," Lizz said, rushing to embrace Mrs. O'Flaherty.

"Don't kiss me. I don't know but what you'll give me something," her mother said, freeing herself from Lizz.

"Hello, Mama," Danny said, and Lizz kissed him.

They went into the dining room.

"You've grown, you little angel, since you left your mother and father," said Lizz to Little Margaret.

"They fed her better than you did, Lizz," said Mrs. O'Flaherty.

"Were they good to you?" asked Lizz, looking at Little Margaret.

"Lizz, how's Jim?" asked Mrs. O'Flaherty.

"Say, I got a bone to pick! I got a bone to pick!" Lizz said, getting to her feet energetically.

"Lizz!" Margaret exclaimed in surprise.

"Where is he? Where is that tyrant, that Kaiser?" Lizz asked.

"Don't be speaking disrespectful of my son, Al. Show me a better boy than him. He never got married so he could take care of his mother," Mrs. O'Flaherty said.

"He hit my first-born," said Lizz.

"Sure, and I would have if he hadn't," said Mrs. O'Flaherty.

"Oh, Lizz, I was so sorry. But it's done with, and please don't aggravate Al if he comes in. I'll make it up to poor Willie-boy. My heart bled for him when I heard of what Al did. And Al was so sorry he did it," Margaret said.

"I couldn't dare to let Jim come. My Jim was raving when he heard it. If he came, say, he would have made mincemeat out of that Kaiser, Kaiser Al," Lizz said, raising her voice.

"What will the neighbors think if they hear you talking so loud? Sure, they'll think we're greenhorn Irish. Don't be talking so loud. And if your teamster ever tries to touch my son, I'll sic the janitor on him and have the janitor turn the hose on him," Mrs. O'Flaherty said.

"Lizz, let me make you a cup of tea," Margaret said, gently leading Lizz back to her chair.

"But, Mother, Jim was fit to be tied," said Lizz.

"Sure, and didn't he almost get my little grandson arrested?" said Mrs. O'Flaherty.

"Oh, but Jim gave him a licking. But Jim says no one is going to hit his children but himself," Lizz said, suddenly more quiet and tractable.

"Ah, sure, he shouldn't have hit the poor boy so hard, but he is a one to lose his temper," said Mrs. O'Flaherty.

"Did he touch my lovely little curly-haired Danny?" Lizz asked, looking at Danny.

"No, he didn't," said Mrs. O'Flaherty.

"He's too hot-tempered. He means well but he can't control his temper, and he's terribly sorry the minute afterward. I never saw a man feeling so badly as Al did at supper. Lizz, it's best to forget it, and we'll make it up to the poor boy. Al really likes Bill," Margaret said.

"Sure, and didn't me mother always tell me to let sleeping dogs lie," said Mrs. O'Flaherty.

"I have to get your tea," said Margaret.

"Peg, bring me a cup, too," said Mrs. O'Flaherty.

"But, Mother, look at my darling daughter. Did you ever see a sweeter little girl? Oh, your mother is glad you are back," Lizz said, going to Little Margaret and kissing her.

"I got a lot more dresses than I had when I went away, too, Mama," said Little Margaret.

"She's the dearest thing. I think she looks like you, Mother," Lizz said, walking toward a chair.

"She does not. She takes after you," said Mrs. O'Flaherty.

"You do, too, don't you, little darling, look like your grandmother?" Lizz said, turning to her daughter.

"I don't know," the girl said.

"Maybe she looks like Peg," said the grandmother.

"Oh, but, Mother, wait until I tell you. Old Connerty got drunk the other night. He was rolling drunk, Mother, and he didn't have a leg to stand on."

"You don't say, Lizz?" the grandmother exclaimed.

"She, with her airs, too. And she's always talking about her man and how he doesn't take a drop. The liar! What does she think I am, a sucker?" Lizz said.

"Sure, what do I be caring about what the tinkers and the beggars are doing? I got better things to be thinking of," Mrs. O'Flaherty said.

Danny left the room and went to the parlor to play his war game. He wanted to get the invasion of Mexico over in a hurry and have the American Army go all the way down the map to Panama.

"Lizz, why do you bother with such common talk?" Margaret asked, annoyed.

"Lizz, wasn't it a shame, the poor President's wife dying the other day," Mrs. O'Flaherty remarked.

"Mother, I knew that was going to happen," Lizz said.

"How did you?" Margaret asked.

"Pa came to me and told me that Mrs. Wilson was going to die two days before she died," Lizz said.

"Little enough he had to do," Mrs. O'Flaherty remarked sourly.

"Lizz, you don't mean it?" Margaret said.

"Just as sure as I'm sitting here seeing you, I saw my dead father, and he told me that Mrs. Woodrow Wilson would die," Lizz said.

"It's funny that you're always seeing him instead of me," Mrs. O'Flaherty said.

Margaret brought in tea, sugar, and milk. Mrs. O'Flaherty and Lizz sat close to the table and sipped tea as they continued talking.

"Oh, Mother, do you know what?" Lizz said.

"What?" the old lady eagerly asked.

"That nigger woman that lives next door to me and is married to the white man, do you know what she does?"

"What?"

"She lets her dog eat with her at the table," said Lizz.

"Glory be! Is she a washwoman?" asked Mrs. O'Flaherty.

"She doesn't work at all. She has a damn fool of a white man who married her working for her. She work? Not on your life," said Lizz.

"Well, never trust a black washwoman," said the grandmother.

"Never trust a nigger, Mother," said Lizz.

"A black washwoman eats too much food," said Mrs. O'Flaherty, sipping her tea.

Margaret left the room frowning, and Little Margaret followed her. Lizz and Mrs. O'Flaherty were alone together.

VI

Al was surprised when he found Lizz and his mother in the dining room.

"My brother, my mother's board and keep," Lizz said, smiling.

"Hello, Lizz. How are you?" Al said abruptly.

"Al! Al, how is Nora?" said Mrs. O'Flaherty.

"She's fine," said Al.

"Sure, she's a good woman," said Mrs. O'Flaherty.

"She comes from a nice family, a good family," said Lizz.

"Indeed she does," said the mother.

"How's Jim?" asked Al.

"He's home, watching the children. I came to see my mother and my two little ones," Lizz said.

"Well, haven't you seen them now?" said Al.

"Say, but that's a how-do-you-do. Hello, here's your hat, what's your hurry," Lizz said.

"But, Lizz, it is getting late," Al said.

"Sure, she's going to have another cup of tea with me and she'll be going home then," Mrs. O'Flaherty said.

Al left and went to Margaret, who sat reading a newspaper in her bedroom.

"I couldn't stand her common talk. She'll drive a person insane," Margaret said.

"What's she want to be staying up here now for? And if she feeds Mother some of that blood-and-thunder talk of hers, then Mother will be getting up in arms," Al said, and as they talked they both could hear the murmur of conversation from the dining room.

"I tell you, Al, I never saw the beat of her, and I never heard talk like she gives to Mother. Goodness, it's all about the shanty Irish, and the nigger woman next door to her having her dog eat at the table. I simply couldn't stand it," Margaret said.

"Well, maybe she'll go soon. She's a troublemaker, she is, and her talk is never elevating. She always talks about fights, and gossip, and backbiting. I tell you, Peg, she's a lulu," Al said.

He went to the front and saw Danny on the floor with his map and his cards.

"Better go to bed, Sport," Al said.

"All right," Danny said, and reluctantly he picked up his cards, closed his book, and left the parlor, yawning.

"Peg, better have the girl go to bed," Al called.

VII

Al was reading a popular magazine. They were still out there talking. And it was eleven o'clock. She ought to be home now. It was too late for her to be out. He dropped his magazine on the parlor floor and rushed to the kitchen.

"Don't you think you better be going home?" he said.

"I am, right away. I want to finish telling something to Mother," Lizz said.

"It'll keep until you see her again," Al said.

"That's a fine way to treat a sister and a daughter in the house of her own people," said Lizz.

"We're not mistreating you. We want to go to bed ourselves and want to see that you get home to your family at a respectable hour," Al said.

"Say, I ain't a drunkard," said Lizz.

"Who said you were?" asked Al.

"Well, you should worry. I'll get home all right," said Lizz.

"Well, you better be going now," said Al.

"Mother, are you going to let him put me out of your house? Mother, who's boss here, you or him?" Lizz asked, standing up and gesturing dramatically.

"Come on, now, cut it out," Al said.

"I didn't come here to see my mother for you to insult me," Lizz said.

"Oh, for Christ sake, shut up and go on home to your family!" Al said impatiently.

"Mother, are you going to sit there and let him say that to me?" Lizz asked, turning to her mother.

"Lizz, don't be talking so loud. The neighbors'll be hearing you," Mrs. O'Flaherty said.

"The neighbors be damned!" Lizz shouted.

"Go on, get on home and cut it out. When you're in our home you'll observe the rules of conduct we have here. Now, I asked you nicely to go home. Please go," Al said.

"You better go, Lizz. He doesn't want you," Mrs. O'Flaherty said.

"Doesn't want his own flesh and blood! All right, I'm going. But wait till I tell my Jim how I was insulted," Lizz said.

"Oh, Jesus Christ, shut up! You come up here without even washing your face, and want to stay all night yelling like a fishwife. Now, goddamn it, get the hell out of here before I throw you out," said Al.

"Threatening me! Say, you, just try and lift a finger to me," said Lizz.

"Lizz, what'll the neighbors think?" Mrs. O'Flaherty said.

"Throw me out! Throw me out!" Lizz challenged.

Al grabbed Lizz.

"Take your hands off of me! Let me alone! Murder! Call the police! Police!" she screamed while Al grappled with her to get her toward the front door.

"Glory be, stop them, Peg, before the neighbors come," the mother cried melodramatically, standing by her chair as Margaret came into the room.

"Al! Al, please!" Margaret said nervously, clutching at her brother's arm.

Margaret seemed to check Al's temper. He let go of Lizz.

"Sister, protect me. The brute! The bully!" Lizz shouted.

"Now, please go home like a lady, won't you?" Al asked.

"I'm a lady. But you're no gentleman! You're no gentleman!" Lizz said, standing between Al and Margaret.

"Al, please let me handle this," Margaret said.

"No gentleman would touch a lady! No gentleman would throw his sister out of her mother's home," Lizz said.

"Come on, Lizz. It's getting late. You better go. Forget it, and the next time we won't have any trouble," Margaret coaxed.

"I'll never come back here. Mother, if you want to see your favorite daughter, you got to come to her," said Lizz.

"You're welcome here, but you have to go home at a proper hour," said Al, calmer now.

"Welcome, yes, to get beat up. I'll never come back. And wait until I tell my Jim. You hit my oldest son today, and then his mother. Jim will beat the hell out of you, by Christ, or I ain't his wife," said Lizz.

"Goddamn you, don't be swearing and using vulgarities in this house," Al said, rushing toward Lizz.

"Please, Al! Control your temper and let me handle this," Margaret said, blocking Al.

"Jesus Mary and Joseph!" Mrs. O'Flaherty exclaimed, lifting her hands toward the ceiling as if in entreaty to the Almighty.

"Don't worry, I'm going, and I'm not coming back to a house full of barbarians. I'm going. But my man is coming back to settle with you, though," said Lizz, pointing at Al.

"All right, let him, but you get the hell out of here," said Al.

"Lizz, let me talk to you," Margaret said, taking Lizz by the arm and leading her out of the room.

"I'm a lady, and that little runt in there hitting me is a little Kaiser," Lizz said.

"Please, Lizz. We've had trouble enough, and you know what a temper Al has," said Peg in the hallway.

"I'm poor, honorably poor, and he hit me and threw me out of my mother's house," said Lizz.

"He's hotheaded. He hit me, too, like that when I was a little girl. When he loses his temper, it's best to let him alone," said Peg.

"I'll dare him to lose his temper with my Jim," Lizz said.

"Lizz, please go. Do it for me. I have to get up early and be at the hotel," Margaret said.

"Honest, I swear by God and the Blessed Virgin, I wasn't saying a word when he comes in and lets go at me like a lion," said Lizz.

"I know, Lizz, dearie. He has that godawful temper," said Margaret.

"Go on home!" Al yelled from the entrance to the dining room.

"I am, and goddamn any man that hits a lady," Lizz shouted.

Margaret motioned Al to stop and not say anything. He stood in the hallway. She led Lizz toward the front door.

"Please, Lizz!" she coaxed.

"I was insulted like a nigger. I'll never forget this," Lizz said.

"Lizz, I'll do something nice for you next payday. Please, now, go before we have any trouble. You know Al's temper," said Peg.

Lizz allowed Margaret to lead her to the front door.

"I was insulted!" she said, holding the doorknob.

"Please, go, Lizz, for my sake," Margaret said.

Lizz opened the front door. She looked down the hall at Al, who stood, hands in his pockets, watching her.

"Go on home, now, in a nice quiet way," he said.

"You bastard!" she shrieked. She lifted her dress, turned her bare buttocks on him, and yelled, "Six pounds of bacon for you, you sonofabitch!" She slammed the door as Al ran after her. From the outside hallway she yelled, "Six pounds of bacon for you!" She went down the steps, hearing Al within talking loudly to Peg. A door in the Doolin apartment on the first floor closed as she came down to the first landing. Frowning, she went out the doorway and looked up to see if they were looking at her from the O'Flaherty window. She thought she saw Al, and again turned around and lifted her skirts to show her buttocks to him. She walked toward Fifty-first Street.

6

I

"Al, she's not working today. She was calling up someone at seven o'clock this morning, getting them out of bed to work for her at the hotel," Mrs. O'Flaherty said to Al in the kitchen, her manner that of a person conveying secretive and mysterious information.

"I know it. It's that goddamn Lizz. I don't know why she wants to be coming up here making trouble, upsetting Peg with her Irish gossip and her damn-fool talk," Al said.

"Ah, Al, don't believe a word of it. It's that man again," said the mother.

"What do you mean?" Al asked, showing sudden worry.

"She's waiting to hear from him. She's waiting for a letter with money in it from him and it didn't come yet," Mrs. O'Flaherty said.

"Are you sure of that?" Al asked.

"I'm as sure as the day is long. She hasn't heard from him in months, and she was in there in her room one night a while ago writing him and asking him for money," said the mother.

"Goddamn it!" Al exclaimed; he walked to the kitchen door and stood there looking out, clenching and unclenching his hands. The summer morning played on his senses. He could see spots of grass still glistening with dew. The hothouses were shimmering. The sun was high and golden above the elevated tracks. The smell of the morning was fresh and new.

"Good morning, Uncle Al," Little Margaret said.

"Hello, there," Al said, turning around and seeing his niece, dressed in a clean wash-dress.

"I came out to have breakfast with you," she said, and Al smiled at her; she seemed sweet and innocent. And he did hope that her presence in the house would be instrumental in aiding Peg to settle down. If the little girl would only make her forget Robinson! It was because of Robinson that she drank, smoked, became nervous and ran around with good-for-nothing people whom she should hold beneath her.

Danny came into the kitchen, sleepy-eyed and in his pyjamas.

"Son, sit down and get a cup of coffee into your little stomach," Mrs. O'Flaherty said to her grandson.

"Here, you, go and wash and dress before you come to the breakfast table. And when you wash, use cold water on your face, and sprinkle and rub your chest with it, too," Al said.

Danny turned, said nothing, and left the kitchen.

"Little Margaret, we always dress before we eat here. You'll remember that," Al told his niece, and she nodded her head affirmatively.

"Here, Al, have your breakfast," Mrs. O'Flaherty said.

She put fried eggs and coffee before him.

"You want coffee, little one?" Mrs. O'Flaherty asked her granddaughter.

"I always drink milk. Uncle Ned and Aunt Mildred wanted me to drink milk instead of coffee," said Little Margaret.

"Milk costs money," the grandmother said.

"Give her milk, Mother," Al said.

Al began eating. He saw his sister coming to the kitchen, wearing a pink kimono. He looked up at her and smiled.

"Say 'good morning, Queen of the House' to your aunt when she comes in here," Al whispered to his niece.

"Good morning, Queen of the House," Little Margaret parroted as her aunt entered the kitchen.

Aunt Margaret turned a forced smile on her niece.

"Hah, she knows her aunt right off, doesn't she?" Al said, his effort to be jolly sounding artificial.

"I couldn't sleep, so I thought I'd have some coffee," Margaret said.

"Here, you sit down and let me get it for you," Al said, jumping up.

"Go ahead and eat your breakfast and I'll take care of myself," Margaret said. Her voice suddenly changed as she added, "I'm used to taking care of myself and depending on myself."

Al looked anxious, but when Margaret sat down at the kitchen table he forced a smile.

"It's good you can stay home and rest today. Is there anything you want me to get you?" he said.

"Don't worry about me. I'm all right," she said; she turned and gazed at the clock.

"It's a bright and sunny day. Maybe you'd like to take a refreshing walk with Little Margaret," Al said.

"I want to do some things around the house," said Margaret.

"Forget it! Forget it! We'll have a woman in to do it. We'll get the whole place cleaned spick and span," said Al.

"A woman will never clean a house the way it should be cleaned. Not those niggers. They're lazy, and they never go into the corners," Margaret said while she reached for the sugar and cream.

"Al, a nigger's no good," Mrs. O'Flaherty said.

"Oh, forget that talk," Al said to his mother.

"It's the effect of Lizz. I told you, whenever Lizz is here, I get all of that old Irish talk the next day," said Peg.

"I ain't Irish. I'm English," Mrs. O'Flaherty said.

"Mother, you're a lady, aren't you?" Al said.

"Indeed, I am," Mrs. O'Flaherty said.

"Well, a lady never says *ain't*. She says *I'm not*."

"Oh, for God's sake, Al!" Margaret exclaimed.

"I was only seeking to improve Mother's diction," Al said.

"Please drop it! I'm nervous," Peg said.

"Aunt Mildred always says ain't," said Little Margaret.

"We don't care. Eat your breakfast," Al said curtly to Little Margaret.

"Yes, little girls should be seen and not heard," Mrs. O'Flaherty said, sitting down at a corner of the table with a cup of coffee.

"Mother, are you going to start picking on her the first day she's here?" Margaret asked peevishly.

"Mother, can't you talk about nice things like the beautiful morning and the sunshine?" Al said.

"Sure, I wasn't saying anything," the old lady said.

They ate on. A tense silence reigned over the breakfast table. Danny came in, dressed, wearing his blue baseball shirt.

"I must get my grandson's breakfast. Sit down, Son!" Mrs. O'Flaherty said with bustling enthusiasm.

Danny squeezed in at the table and waited while his grandmother boiled eggs for him.

Margaret gazed at the clock. It was now a quarter to nine.

"Mother, what time does the mailman come?" Margaret asked.

"Sure, I don't know. Nine o'clock," Mrs. O'Flaherty said.

"You could at least give me a civil answer," Margaret retorted.

"I don't know. I don't want to be bothered. I'm cooking me grandson's breakfast," Mrs. O'Flaherty said.

"Mother, why don't you be nice, and not so belligerent?" Al asked.

"She was born that way," Margaret said, sipping coffee.

"We all have to be happy here and stop wrangling and having difficulties," Al said.

"Yes!" Margaret said heavily.

"Son, here is your eggs. Do you want coffee?" the grandmother asked.

"Yes," Danny said.

Margaret looked at the clock again, and they continued with breakfast, the atmosphere at the table still strained.

II

"Peg, I won't go out to the park with Danny. I'll stay home here with you," Al told Margaret in the parlor.

"What for? Al, I'm all right. I'm just nervous and tired. After Lizz coming here yesterday, I couldn't get any sleep last night," Margaret said.

Al got up from his chair and paced back and forth, his hands behind his back.

"Oh, Al, don't worry about Lizz so much. She was always that way," Margaret said.

"Why does she have to come here?" Al asked.

"That's the way she is," Margaret said.

"Goddamn it! Most of the trouble we have is because of her fighting and belligerence and because of her goddamn son, Bill," Al said.

"Forget it, Al," Peg said.

"Now, you take it easy this morning and don't worry about anything. Relax and give yourself a good rest," Al said.

"I will. There's nothing wrong except my nerves were bad, that's all, so I took the day off," Peg said.

"Slip us a kiss and tell us you're going to rest this morning," Al said.

She went to him and kissed him perfunctorily.

"Hey, Sport, let's go," Al called from the hallway.

Al went to his room, got out a baseball, his left-handed pitcher's glove, and a willow fungo bat. He was wearing old blue trousers, a white shirt turned in at the neck, tennis shoes and a gray cap. He went out to Danny, who was waiting for him in the kitchen.

"Your aunt's nervous, so you go out and play in the yard and don't bother her," Al said to Little Margaret, who was still seated at the table.

"Ah, it's that devil not sending her a letter. Nerves be damned!" the old lady said without turning from the kitchen sink where she was washing the dishes.

"Mother, didn't I ask you to stop it? We don't want any flare-ups," Al said curtly.

"Al, I'll have a nice dinner for you," she said.

"Please, now, Mother, no nagging or anything so that she doesn't go off the handle," said Al.

"Sure, I won't even pass the time of day with her. I'm busy," Mrs. O'Flaherty said.

Al and Danny went out the back door.

III

Carrying the ball in his fielder's glove, Danny scooted along rapidly to keep up with his uncle because Uncle Al always walked pretty fast. Uncle Al owned a pair of spiked baseball shoes but he wasn't wearing them. Danny wished that Uncle Al would buy him spiked baseball shoes. He knew that he would own a pair some day, only he wished that that some day was now. There were heavy nails in his shoes because they had just been half-soled, and Danny dragged his feet a little over the sidewalk, because sometimes when he did that the nails would scratch on the pavement and make a sound something like the sound made when a person walked on stone with spiked baseball shoes. He and Uncle Al walked along Fifty-first Street, eastward toward Washington Park.

"Well, Sport, summer is soon going to be over and there won't be any more baseball," Al said.

It was the first time he'd said anything to Danny since they had left home, and Danny knew that Uncle Al was worried; he was pretty sure that Uncle Al was worried because of Aunt Peg, but Aunty Peg hadn't drunk anything since she had come home after going away to take that Keeley cure.

"Yes," Danny said, moody and thoughtful.

"Will you be glad to be going back to school?" Uncle Al asked.

"Yes," Danny said, knowing that he wasn't telling the truth.

"That's the fellow! You want to be a real wise guy, you know, Dan, and a real wise guy studies. Get all you can out of school. And this year when you get back in school and are studying, there's a book I'm going to have you read. It's called *Lord Chesterfield's Letters to His Son* and it will teach you how to be a real gentleman. And don't forget it, Sport, the gentleman's the real wise guy," Al said.

"All right," Danny said, half mumbling; most of the time when he was with Uncle Al alone like this, going out to the ball field in Washington Park, or going to big-league games, there wasn't much that he could think of to talk about.

"Yes, Sport, get all you can out of school," Al said.

"Uh huh," Danny mumbled.

"And you'll have to keep your eye on your little sister and see that she gets to school. Watch her crossing the streets, and help her with her studies. Will you do that?" Uncle Al asked.

"Yes, I will," Danny said.

"That's the Sport. And you won't be getting into any more scrapes like that candy-store one?" Uncle Al said, patting Danny on the shoulder in a friendly, intimate manner.

"No, I won't," Danny said, trying to put genuine determination and conviction into his words.

They walked on. Uncle Al didn't speak for a few paces. Danny could see, all right, that there was something that was worrying his uncle, and he guessed it must be because of Aunt Peg, who'd said she was nervous this morning. He looked sidewise at his uncle from the corner of his eye, and he could tell that Uncle Al was thinking. He felt sorry for Uncle Al. They crossed the driveways and entered Washington Park at Fifty-first Street.

"If we had managed to get out a little earlier, we could have gone barefooted in the dew. But there isn't much dew left on the grass," Uncle Al said.

"It's fun going barefooted," Danny said.

"It's good for your feet," Uncle Al said.

"I like to go barefooted, all right," Danny said.

"Sport, how do you walk?" Uncle Al suddenly asked.

Danny halted and glanced perplexedly at his uncle, not knowing what had been meant by the question.

"Go ahead, let me see you walk ahead of me," Al said, but Danny was not afraid, because Uncle Al wasn't talking the way he did when he was sore or crabby and going to criticize.

Danny obeyed.

"That's the way. You walk the right way, with your toes pointed straight. You know, you don't want to walk with your toes pointed out like this," Uncle Al said, illustrating by taking several steps with toes pointed outward at angles instead of straight ahead. "That's the way the Jews walk," he added.

"Yes, I always walk straight," Danny said, knowing that before this minute he'd never even thought about the way he pointed his toes when he walked. He beamed. He liked to do things right when he was with Uncle Al, so that he wouldn't be bawled out.

"Yes, Sport, it's better for your feet if you walk with your toes pointed straight ahead. That's the way the Indians have always walked, and they have very good feet," Al said.

"I guess I always walk the right way," Danny said.

"Well, it is the right way," Uncle Al said positively.

Striding beside Uncle Al, and suddenly not knowing what more to say, Danny tossed the ball a few feet in the air and caught it with both hands.

"If everything is well at home when we get back, maybe we'll go to the ball game this afternoon," Al said, and Danny again beamed.

Suddenly his face clouded. Even though she hadn't drunk in the last few weeks, he'd learned to know that you could never be sure when she'd start drinking gin again.

"Gee, I hope she doesn't go and get drunk again," Danny said.

"Don't say drunk. Say sick."

"Well, sick," Danny said, but he knew it wasn't sick, it was drunk.

"How's she been? And how have affairs been going at home while I was away?" asked Uncle Al.

"She hasn't been dr . . . sick. She hasn't fought much or been so nervous, either," Danny said.

"Good. Make a wish right now with me and ask the Lord that affairs will be happy at home from now on," Uncle Al said, stopping in his tracks, his face revealing a sudden concentration.

Danny stopped and wished with his uncle, asking God to give them both their wish.

"Have you heard her say anything to Mother about Mr. Robinson?" Uncle Al asked as they walked on across the grass toward the ball field.

"I heard her telephoning the Shrifton Hotel and asking was he registered, and she asked me to telephone once and ask if Mr. Robinson was registered," Danny said.

"And what happened?" Uncle Al asked.

"The clerk said he wasn't registered," Danny said.

"Is that all?"

"Uh huh," Danny mumbled.

"Your aunt isn't always happy, and you should pray for her. Do you say your prayers?" Uncle Al asked.

"Yes, every morning, and when I go to bed at night, and of course when I go to mass on Sunday," Danny said.

"That's good. And you always want to include a prayer for your aunt, and one that business will be good for me," said Uncle Al.

"I will," said Danny.

"Your friend Bill Murphy won't be out here now," said Uncle Al as they walked on.

"He won't?"

"He's a race-track man. He's in a place called Saratoga Springs, where big races are run this month. Some time when you're bigger, if business is good for me, I'll take you to Saratoga Springs and you can see the horse races. We'll do lots of things, and we'll live over near the lake in a large house of our own, too, and own it some day if business is good enough for me. And then maybe your aunt won't be so nervous as she sometimes is at the present. We both want to hope for good things like that, Dan, and pray for them every day, and then maybe, some day, we'll have them," Uncle Al said.

"Yes," said Danny.

"And you want to be careful about your aunt and what you say when she's nervous. Try not to make any noise or do anything that will make her go off the handle. She goes off the handle easily sometimes," Uncle Al said.

"I do try not to make her go off the handle," said Danny.

"That's the Sport. And now, with your sister living with us, you don't want to be quarreling with her. You're the oldest, and shouldn't quarrel with a girl," Uncle Al said, smiling.

"I won't," Danny said; he could hear the crack of a bat and he was anxious to get where the men would be knocking out flies. It was just beyond the bushes now, too. He only wished that he was bigger, because if he was, then he'd be able really to play with men, and have them hit out long flies to him that he'd be able to catch. Some day, all right, he would.

IV

"Mother, I can't understand why no money came. I was sure that he'd send it, and it should have come a couple of weeks ago. And it isn't here yet," Margaret said.

"Sure, I don't know what's keeping it from coming. Maybe if you said a prayer it might come faster," said the mother.

"It would be so nice to get some money now and buy things for my lovely little niece," said Margaret.

"Ah, Ned and Mildred bought her enough clothes," Mrs. O'Flaherty said.

"I know, but with her coming, and soon she'll be going to school, if that money I'm expecting from Lorry would come, it would be such a help," said Peg.

"Sure, with the girl here and having another mouth to feed and schooling for her, it is going to be an expense," said the mother.

"You needn't nag me. I'll pay for her keep, just as I have always done for myself. I'm nervous today and I don't want to be nagged," Margaret said.

"Glory be! I'm only after saying that it will cost us more money to live with the girl here and she says I'm nagging her," Mrs. O'Flaherty said.

"Oh God, I wonder why Lorry hasn't sent it to me! What time is the next mail delivery, Mother?" Margaret asked.

"Twelve o'clock," said the mother.

Margaret looked at the clock. It wasn't ten yet. She got up and walked down the hall. She turned at the end and came back.

"Oh God, why must I have such nerves!" she exclaimed.

She walked broodingly up and down the hall.

V

"Hello, Al," a lanky fellow said as Danny and Al came upon the group of men who were sitting on the grass, while others were catching flies which a fellow was fungoing out to them. The lanky fellow was standing up watching the ball as it was batted out, caught, thrown back to the hitter. He had a cigarette between his lips, and his shirt was off, showing the top of his B.V.D.'s and a sun-tanned pair of arms and shoulders.

"Hello, Joe," Al said.

"Glad to see you again, Al," said Joe.

"Ditto, Joe, old man," Al said.

"How was business this trip?" Joe asked.

"I was away on a vacation this time. But I'll know about business soon, because I'll start on the road for my fall trip after Labor Day," Al said.

"Think it's going to be good?" asked Joe.

"I don't know. This war in Europe makes everything uncertain," said Al.

"Say, wasn't that a damn crazy stunt for them Europeans to pull off, starting that war. It looks like the Germans are going to bounce the French around, too, and maybe take Belgium and France like Jack Johnson took Jim Jeffries," said Joe.

"The Germans like to dominate, that's the trouble with them," said Al.

"You know, that's a fact, Al. Now, down in my office there's a German. Do you know, he doesn't only like to run his own department. He likes to run the whole office. He comes in to see me and says that I ain't attended to some damn thing or other, and that I ought to do everything more orderly. That's a fact. They want to dominate," said Joe.

"Of course, this war can't go on a very long time. Wilson and the Pope will probably stop it the way Teddy Roosevelt stopped that war between Japan and Russia," Al said.

"I guess so, but you know what I'm more interested in than this war on the other side of the ocean? I'm more interested in who's going to win that world series," said Joe.

"Who do you think will win the National League pennant first?" Al asked.

"I don't know. Those Braves have spurted into second place, but then I think Muggsy McGraw is going to bring the Giants down the home stretch," said Joe.

"I think so. Boston hasn't much of a team. They have Johnny Evers, but Evers can't win it alone, smart as he is," Al said.

"Looks like Connie Mack's just about cleaned up his league again with that hundred-thousand-dollar infield of his," Joe said.

VI

Margaret telephoned the Shrifton Hotel.

"Desk clerk, please," she said; her left hand, holding the receiver, shook; her heart began to palpitate.

She waited, sending a wish to God to help her and to have Lorry there, and, if Lorry was there, to make him come to the telephone and speak to her.

"Is Mr. L. R. Robinson registered?"

Oh God! Please, God! Her heart, beating so! Her hand, look at it shake! Oh, please, God!

"He isn't?" she said forlornly as if hoping that after she'd said these words, the clerk would tell her that she'd misunderstood him, and that Mr. Robinson was registered.

"Would you please leave a message in case he checks in? Ask him to telephone Mr. Olson immediately. Mark it important."

She hung up. She paced the hall, back and forth, back and forth. Why must she be treated this way?

VII

"Out for a workout, huh, O'Flaherty?" the man hitting out flies yelled.

"Yes," Al called over to him.

"Well, go on out and I'll give you some to shag," he called.

"I want to warm the old soupbone up first," Al called back.

"Going to warm up first, huh, Al?" Joe said.

"Yes. You always have to do that or else you're liable to throw your arm out," Al said.

"We're all getting old and got to watch out for our wings now, don't we?" a stout fellow on the grass said.

Danny watched the man with the bat lift one way out, watched a fellow out there judge it, draw the ball down with both hands. He wished he could catch long flies now like that man did.

"Let's warm up, Dan," Al said.

They played catch in a corner by the gravel walk which ran through the park at this edge of the athletic field. There were two old men on a bench near them, talking Yiddish. Danny thought that it was funny, all right, old men talking Yiddish. They were Abie Kabbibles, that's what they were. Al threw the ball with an easy and unstrained overhanded motion. He was a southpaw, and after tossing the ball he spit into the glove on his right hand. Danny caught the throw, returned it. Al continued tossing them easy. Danny wished that he was a little bigger and that Uncle Al was a pitcher on a team, and that when Uncle Al pitched, he would catch him. He wished that he could catch everything Uncle Al threw just as Bill did. Uncle Al could pitch pretty good. He had a fast ball, and a curve. Bill thought so, too, and Bill often caught Uncle Al, warming him up in the back yard. He guessed that when Uncle Al was younger and played ball a lot, he must have been a pretty good pitcher.

"I'm going to throw them faster now, Dan," Uncle Al said.

"All right. I can catch them," Danny called back; he spat into his glove, wished that he had a catcher's glove on. But then, by catching hard ones with a fielder's glove, he would toughen his hands, and it would be good for him to learn how to catch them fast with a fielder's glove.

Uncle Al wound up like a pitcher, swinging his left arm around in a circle twice, raising his right foot, and then he zoomed the ball at Danny straight and fast. His windup and motion were graceful. Danny caught the ball, returned it to him.

"Good work, Dan," Uncle Al said.

Danny set himself as Uncle Al wound up. He hoped that Uncle Al wouldn't toss them in too fast, and he hoped that he would. He hoped that he'd catch everything that Uncle Al threw at him, and he hoped that Uncle Al would burn them in, and he was a little bit worried because he only had a fielder's glove on, and he was worried anyway because maybe Uncle Al would pitch them too fast. He tried to imagine himself a big-league catcher warming up somebody like Red Russell or Eddie Plank just before a game. He missed a pitch.

"You didn't watch. I signaled to you that I would pitch a drop that time," Uncle Al said.

"I missed it," Danny said; he turned and trotted to retrieve the ball.

He tried to wing it all the way on the fly to Uncle Al, but he didn't have enough power in his arm. The ball rolled to Uncle Al. Danny trotted back to where he had been standing, to continue warming up his uncle.

VIII

"You're eight years old?" Anna Hamilton said to Little Margaret, the two of them seated on the steps in front of one of the buildings just down the street from where the O'Flahertys lived.

"I'm eight years old," replied Little Margaret.

"I'm seven years old," Anna Hamilton said; she was a plump, chubby little light-haired girl, and she wore white socks and a pink wash-dress.

"Then I'm older than you are," Little Margaret said.

"And you just come from Madison?"

"Yes, I lived with my uncle and aunt in Madison," Little Margaret said.

"Where is Madison?" asked Anna.

"Madison is in Wisconsin," said Little Margaret.

"Where is Wisconsin?" asked Anna.

"Wisconsin is in Wisconsin. You go to it by train," said Little Margaret.

"We came in a train, too, from Grand Rapids, Michigan," Anna said.

"I like to ride on trains," Little Margaret said.

"I like your doll," said Anna, pointing to the bisque doll with a blue dress which Margaret held in her arms.

"Her name is Mary," Little Margaret said.

"Why did you name her Mary?" Anna asked.

"Because that's the name of the Blessed Virgin," said Little Margaret.

"And you got a brother?"

"I got lots of brothers. One of them lives with me at my grandmother's, but I got lots more with my Mama and Papa," said Little Margaret.

"Does your mama go out with men?" asked Anna.

"No, she goes to church, and sometimes she comes to see my grandmother, and she sees cousins, and likes to go to wakes and funerals," said Little Margaret.

"My mother goes with men, and my aunt who lives right upstairs, Aunt Hilda, she says to my mother not to do that, and my mother does, but my father doesn't know it. He isn't with us because he couldn't come," said Anna.

"What does she do when she goes out?" asked Little Margaret.

"She goes out. Sometimes she brings back candy and things. But, oh, if we told my father she did, she'd spank us."

"Why?"

"Because she doesn't want him to know," Anna said.

"Let's play something," Little Margaret said.

"What?"

"Let's play millinery store," said Little Margaret.

"What's that?" asked Anna.

"That's a store where you buy hats. My Aunt Mildred in Madison owns a millinery store with all kinds of hats in it," said Little Margaret.

"How do we play millinery store?" asked Anna.

"Now I own the store, and you come in to see me and buy a hat," said Little Margaret.

"And what will Mary, your doll, be?" asked Anna.

"Here, she's your baby, and while you try to buy a hat she cries and you got to tell her to be good," said Little Margaret.

"I'd like to play millinery store if I can hold your doll," said Anna.

"Here, but don't you break it," Little Margaret said, handing the doll to her newly found friend and standing up to play millinery store.

IX

Margaret paced the floor, back and forth, back and forth, wringing her hands, asking herself questions. Why did she see so little of Lorry? The trouble with Brophy and the Graham scandal couldn't be an excuse any more. That was over and done with for over two years now. Ever since then, she'd seen less and less of Lorry. She heard from him most infrequently. She had received no money from him since June. Some should have come. Why hadn't it? What was she going to do? What was she going to do with herself? She didn't know and she had to ask herself this question and answer it.

She got a cigarette from her bedroom and continued walking up and down. What she needed was a drink, just one, to quiet her nerves, to make her feel better. She couldn't go on all day like this, walking up and down with her nerves jumping, her heart suddenly palpitating so that it seemed as if it would jump right out of her and through her dress. Oh God, what was she going to do? Could she go on as she had? Of course, she loved Mother, and wanted to see that Mother had a comfortable home as long as she lived. And Al was good, and she loved to be able to do things for him, cook meals, help to see that he had a home. And her niece and nephew were the darlingest children, and she'd do anything that she could for them. But that was not all of life for a young girl like herself. Well, yes, she was still a young girl, going on twenty-eight.

She walked up and down. She wrung her hands. Oh, God! Oh, God be with her and give her help and strength! Oh, God, what was behind Lorry's acting this way? Oh, God, please make him let her know and come back to her!

She couldn't stand it any more. She had to have a drink. She wasn't going to get drunk. She wasn't. She was just going to get one drink of gin at the saloon to quiet her nerves. That was all.

"Mother, I'm going to take a little walk. I'm nervous, and a walk will be good for me," she said to her mother in the kitchen.

"My son and grandson will be home soon, and they have to have their dinner," Mrs. O'Flaherty said.

"I'll be back and help," said Peg.

"And it's getting late in the summer, and soon I can't be going out to Pa and Louise. I'm going to hie out there this afternoon," Mrs. O'Flaherty said.

"I'm just going to take a little walk, and I'll be back and help with the dinner," Peg said.

She went to her room and dressed hurriedly, putting on a blue suit and shirtwaist. There was a desperation about the way she dressed. She looked at herself in the mirror when she was ready. She was a handsome girl, even if she did say so herself. And she had a good figure, too. She was not the kind of a girl that men would run away from. She had real possibilities, and why must she be living and suffering this way . . . why? Why must she live so unhappy and miserable a life? She turned from the mirror and walked out of her bedroom.

"Goodbye, Mother," she called.

No answer. Mother was mad at her because she was going out for a walk. A harmless walk. Well, that showed just what kind of a mother she had. Mother didn't understand. Al didn't. No one did. She went to the front door, walked out and quietly closed the door.

In the front hallway she paused by the O'Flaherty mailbox. She'd already looked for the morning mail and knew that there was nothing in it. She looked again and turned away, disappointed.

In front of the building she met Mrs. Doolin, a neighbor who lived downstairs. She observed the woman closely. Mrs. Doolin was carrying an armful of groceries. She was getting fat. She had a cowlike face, and it was getting fat. Her breasts were big and her hips were wide. She had a kid, had her man, and she was settled down, living like a cow.

None of that for me, Margaret thought to herself.

"Hello, Miss O'Flaherty! Are you off today?" Mrs. Doolin said with a smile.

"Hello, Mrs. Doolin. How are you?" Margaret said cordially.

Just like Lizz, a bird of the same feather, only her husband was better off, Margaret thought to herself.

"I see you have a niece with you," said Mrs. Doolin.

"She's going to stay with us. She was with my brother and sister-in-law in Madison, but she's going to live with us now," said Margaret.

"I saw her. She's a very sweet little girl. I guess girls are not as hard to raise as boys. I sometimes wish that I had a girl instead of my Georgie. Of course, Mr. Doolin is glad to have a boy. But then, it isn't the father that does the work of raising the children, it's the mother. And sometimes a boy is fierce to raise. I'm wore out doing it, and I get pains in my stomach all of the time and have to sit down and rest. It's fierce sometimes, my Georgie's so active, and needs so much care, and washing for him, and cooking, and watching. Yes, it is," Mrs. Doolin said.

"But your boy is such a lovely child. And he's so well-mannered," Margaret said.

"Yes, he is a good boy," Mrs. Doolin said.

"Well, I must go. You must come and see us some time," Margaret said.

"I will, thank you. Or you come down to see me. But I never get a minute to turn around in with a husband and a boy to raise, both of them needing so much tending. Sometimes, you know, the father is more care than the child. Wait until you get married, Miss O'Flaherty, and you'll know what I mean. But I have to go in and tend to my housework," Mrs. Doolin said.

"Goodbye," Margaret said sweetly.

She walked slowly toward Fifty-first Street. No, one drink wouldn't hurt her. It would help her. She would pull herself together and quiet her nerves. That Doolin woman, a cowlike wife! She never wanted to be that, a slave to a man like that woman's husband.

And the world said women like that were good. The ignorant cows! And the world, if it knew, would condemn her. No, it wouldn't, it would be sorry for her. Men didn't love wives like Mrs. Doolin. How could a man love the likes of that, fat, and with no interest in life but raising kids and cooking a meal, living almost like a cabbage in the ground? But there was Little Margaret ahead of her with another little girl. The little darling! Little Margaret was going to be brought up right, given good care and every chance in life.

Little Margaret yelled with glee as she ran to her aunt. Anna Hamilton followed her.

"Aunty Margaret, where you going?" Little Margaret said, trying to grasp her aunt around the legs.

"I'm just going to the store," said Aunt Margaret.

"I want to go with you," said Little Margaret.

"No, you stay and play with your little friend. What is her name? What is your name, dearie?"

"Anna Hamilton."

"We were playing millinery store," said Little Margaret.

"You sweet things. And where do you live, you little darling?"

"I'm staying with my aunt. I live in Michigan. We came on the train to stay with my aunt," said Anna.

"Please, take us with you," Little Margaret begged.

"I can't now, darling. I will some other time. Here, you buy candy for the two of you," Margaret said, handing her niece a nickel.

She walked on, trailed by their goodbyes. Such lovely and innocent little girls. Ah, she had been innocent once. No, she was born sad and knowing too much, and she had learned the hard facts of life too young. Well, she'd take care of her niece, give her what she had never been given.

She oughtn't to take any drink. Maybe it would start her off. The curse of drink was in her blood. She inherited it from Father. She shouldn't take a drink now. But how would she quiet her nerves? She could take one and let it alone, conquer the curse of drink in her blood. She'd prove it to herself that she could take one and quit. No, she shouldn't do it. She'd had her lovely, innocent niece brought from Madison and had said she wouldn't drink if she had Little Margaret with her. She had Little Margaret now. Was she going to drink the first day? Once wasn't drinking. One drink of gin wouldn't make her drunk, and since her cure, she had conquered the curse in her blood. She'd have one to quiet her nerves. Her heart was beating so fast right now. Her poor heart! She extended her hand and looked at it. It was shaky. She had to have one. No, she shouldn't have it. She should have will power.

Slowly, Margaret walked on and turned the corner of Fifty-first and Prairie, debating with herself about the question of that one drink.

X

Uncle Al was out farther with the men, catching long flies that were being fungoed out there. Danny wished that he could go out farther and catch flies with them, but Uncle Al had told him to stay in closer, and to catch the throws as they came in and then to relay them to the fungo hitter. He had to stand in close, and every so often the man hitting out the flies and using the fungo bat Uncle Al had brought with them would bat him an easy fly or grounder. That wasn't so much fun. He was hardly able to wait until he could hurry up and get bigger so that he could play ball with bigger guys and men and catch flies with the men instead of being made to stay in here close. The man with the fungo bat was signaling to him that he was going to hit an easy one now. Danny set himself, his hands on his knees, waiting, watching the man with the fungo bat. The man slapped an easy grounder to Danny. Danny moved in on the ball to field it as if he were in infielder who was going to get off a quick throw and nail a man on a slow infield roller. The ball came bobbing along the grass. Danny grasped it. It dropped out of his hands. Just is if he'd made an error. Danny threw it underhanded along the ground. He was disappointed in himself. He stood now, hands on hips, and watched the man hit out a long fly, watched the ball sail outward in a curving arc, a small white pellet outlined against the enormous blue sky.

"I have it," he heard Uncle Al cry.

He watched his uncle back up a few feet, wait, make an easy cupped catch. Uncle Al caught flies nicely. Uncle Al threw the ball to him, rolling it along the ground, his throw overhanded and without strain. The ball just rolled to Danny. He picked it up and flung it sidearm to the man batting them out.

But this wasn't any fun for him.

XI

Margaret stood in front of O'Callahan's saloon at Fifty-first and Calumet. She remembered her niece and that other little girl running up to her, the innocence of their voices, the sweetness and purity in their faces. And to think that she was once like that! Should she or shouldn't she take just one drink? These people on the street must think that she was a funny sight, the way she stood here in front of the saloon. Well, let them! They didn't know the sorrow that was throbbing in her heart. If she was only an innocent little girl again! She took several steps to go around the corner to the family entrance. She stopped. She stood looking down Calumet Avenue, seeing nothing because of her inner state. She walked back to the corner. She would take a little walk. Maybe she could walk off her state of nerves. Maybe she could do that and not need that one glass of gin. She would do it! She would conquer herself. Even if Lorry deserted her, even if everything turned to bitter ashes in her mouth, she would conquer herself, and she would go on and live, live, if for nothing else, then for that sweet and pure and innocent little girl. She would! She walked on in the direction of Washington Park.

XII

Danny and Uncle Al sat with some of the men on the grass near the gravel path. He liked this. He might have liked it even better if he was with these men and Uncle Al wasn't around, because then he wouldn't have to watch what he said as he had to do now. And if his uncle wasn't one of the men, the others would let go in their talk, even if he was with them and was only a kid. But even so, he still liked it.

"Well, O'Flaherty, it wasn't a bad workout this morning, was it?" Joe said.

"It was good, good exercise," Al said.

"The kid here looks to me like he ought to be a ballplayer some day," Joe said, pointing at Danny. Danny beamed; he liked this fellow Joe, and he hoped that Joe was right in what he said.

"He has to learn a little yet," Al said.

"Sure he does. Everybody's got to learn. But he looks like he's got the makings of a ballplayer," Joe said.

"Want to be a ballplayer, Son?" a fellow named Jake asked Danny.

Danny nodded his head in the affirmative.

"Answer the gentleman, Sport," Al said, glancing proudly at his nephew.

"Yes, yes sir," Danny said.

"That's the Sport," Al said.

"Well, we won't have many more of these days," a fellow named Guy said.

"Nope, we won't," said Joe.

"Another summer come and gone. Pretty soon, you know, I'm going to be giving up this sort of thing. I was forty-three years old last week," Guy said.

"You want to say forty-three years young, not forty-three years old," Al said.

"It's all right to say that. But many a time I feel like it's old, not young," Guy said.

"Guy, remember this. Tuck it away in your bonnet and keep it there. A man is as old as he feels, or as young as he feels. You know this thing in the air that they call psychology. Well, a man ought to use that. It'll work wonders for him, personally and in his business," Joe explained.

"That's the ticket, Joe," Al said.

"Psychology won't do a damn thing for an old soupbone. Ask Ed Walsh about that if you don't believe me," said Guy.

"Well, I don't know, now," Joe said, puffing on a pipe.

"If you have the right slant on something, that doesn't do you any harm or impede your progress. And psychology, now, I have gone into it and studied it some in the last couple of years. Psychology amounts pretty much to having the right slant on something," Al said.

"Well, that much might be true, come to think of it," Guy said.

"Who's playing out to the Federal League ball game today?" a fellow named Jack asked.

"The Buffeds," Danny answered promptly.

"Rankin Johnson pitching?"

"He ain't due today. But he's started off good with the Chifeds," Danny said.

"That kid knows his game. Well, it's a good thing to keep a growing boy's mind occupied. Keeps them from asking too many questions," a fellow named Mike said, getting his words in before Al could speak. Al had opened his mouth to say something, and Danny knew what it was going to be. Uncle Al was going to call him down for using the word *ain't*.

"The kid is up on the game," Joe said.

"Yes, he is," Uncle Al said, and Danny was grateful for the men talking just then because they had saved him from a call-down on that use of *ain't* which he hadn't intended at all.

"Well, it's a great game, for men as well as kids. You know, I was thinking, if those Europeans that are at each other's throats now in this war had a national sport like baseball, they wouldn't be having this war. You got to have something that lets the steam off, and baseball does that. Yes, sir, if they had baseball, the French would be playing a series in Berlin now, and the Germans would be yelling kill the ump instead of trying to kill the Frog-eaters," Guy said.

"There's something to what you say there," said Jake.

"Why did we have a war with Spain and why have we got trouble with the greasers in Mexico if that's so?" asked Mike.

"That was different. They sunk the *Maine* on us. And anyway, we had our rights to protect in Cuba, we had to make the Cubans free," Guy said.

"Well, I tell you fellows, it's pretty hard to say what's what these days," Joe said reflectively, tossing a ball up and catching it.

Joe tossed the ball in the air again but missed the catch. The ball glanced off a bat and popped away. Danny got up to retrieve it.

"Well, anyway, whatever you say, this war in Europe's gonna make American business as busy as a whore with two beds," Joe said.

"Watch the step, the kid," Al said.

"Oh, sorry! But he didn't hear me," Joe said.

Danny came back and dropped the ball beside Joe.

"Anyway, you guys can go ahead and jaw. I got to get home, see what the missus has put on the table and then hop down to work. See you boys tomorrow," Jack said, rising.

"I have to be going, too. Come on, Sport," Al said.

Danny jumped up, and after saying so long, he and his uncle left.

XIII

"Sport, you want to watch the words you use. You never want to say *ain't*. A regular guy doesn't say *ain't*, because it's bad usage," Al said, walking beside Danny, carrying his glove and the willow fungo bat.

"I didn't mean to. I forgot," Danny said.

"Well, watch yourself on that after this. You want to be a wise guy and a regular guy," said Al.

"I will," said Danny.

"Well, now, Sport, send out a thought of hope that your aunt will be in good spirits and happy when we get home," Al said.

They walked in silence. Uncle Al seemed to have something on his mind again. It must be Aunt Peg. Gee, wouldn't it be awful if Aunt Peg had gone and gotten drunk again? Then there'd be yelling and fighting and trouble, and he wouldn't be taken to the ball game today, either. Oh God, have Aunty Peg sober and not nervous when he got home. Oh God, please do that.

If only God would, he'd make the nine first Fridays beginning next month, and he'd make a general confession tomorrow to receive absolution for the sacrileges that were on his soul. He promised God he would.

They came out of the park and walked along Fifty-first Street, still silent. Danny could see that Uncle Al was really worried. Danny swung along at his side, thinking of the game this afternoon, hoping that it would be a good one. Hal Chase was with the Buffalo Feds and he'd see Hal play. They walked on in silence, taking a short cut by going under the elevated station and on to the back yards. They both became anxious and increased their pace, quickly reaching the back stairs.

"Well, Sport, let's hope everything upstairs is fine and dandy," Uncle Al said, his voice sad and gentle.

7

I

"Have mercy on our souls!" Mrs. O'Flaherty exclaimed melodramatically when Al and Danny entered the kitchen.

"What's the matter, Mother?" Al asked, worried by the greeting.

Danny's mood became suddenly one of despair. It wasn't because he mightn't now be taken to the ball game today. It was what might be happening in the house until she sobered up again. Because he knew just what it was that Mother was going to tell them when she acted this way.

"Where is she, Mother?" Al asked.

"She's been out all morning, drinking some place," Mrs. O'Flaherty said.

"Why did you let her?" asked Al.

"And how in the name of mercy could I stop her? There she was, walking up and down the hall, walking up and down, saying she was nervous, filling her mind with thoughts of that black Protestant devil. And she says to me that she's only going out for a little walk because she has nerves. Nerves in a pig's back door, if you ask me," said Mrs. O'Flaherty.

"Jesus Christ! Are we never going to have any peace and quiet and comfort in our home?" Al exclaimed.

"Not so long as that one has her mind filled with thoughts of that Protestant devil," the mother said.

"Goddamn it! She promised me. She said to me that she was through drinking forever after she came home from taking the Keeley cure. It cost me two hundred and fifty dollars, and here she is not out a month before she's starting again," Al said in disappointment as he sank into a chair by the kitchen table.

"I tell you, Al, there's no good in that one," Mrs. O'Flaherty said.

"I don't know what to think, Mother," Al said. He turned to Danny and said, "Here, Sport, will you put the baseball things away for me?"

Danny took the bat, gloves, and ball and went to the front of the house with them.

"I'm going to the cemetery today to Pa and Louise. I'm going if she's drunk or sober. So you and the little fellow have your dinner. I have to hie out of here if I want to get back by supper. I don't care if she's out sinning. She's not going to deprive me of a visit to the cemetery to see me own dead ones. The summer is drawing nigh onto its end, and soon, with the snow on the ground, I won't be seeing their graves for a long time," Mrs. O'Flaherty said.

"Mother, you hadn't better go that far alone," Al said.

"Ah, sure, I know my way out there alone. Let the little fellow run the prairie. Soon he'll be in the classroom again," Mrs. O'Flaherty said.

"Where's the little girl?" Al asked.

"How would I be knowing? I called her, but I got no answer," said the mother.

"Sport! Sport!" Al called.

Danny hastened into the kitchen.

"Go out and see if you can find your sister and have her come home to her lunch," said Al.

"Ah, Al, let the boy eat his dinner."

"Go ahead, Sport," Al said.

Danny rushed out of the kitchen.

II

"Mother, I don't know why so many things have to happen in our home when they don't in others," Al said, eating his lunch.

"And, sure, hasn't she put a curse on this house?" Mrs. O'Flaherty said.

"Mother, don't say that," said Al.

"I only speak the truth," the old lady said.

"Maybe she just took a walk and will be back," Al said.

"I tell you, she's out with the Devil, drinking," Mrs. O'Flaherty said.

"Mother, we mustn't prejudge. Maybe she's just taking a long walk," Al said.

"Ah, I tell you, she's out drinking because of that Protestant. The Lord has put a curse on her," Mrs. O'Flaherty said.

"Mother, don't be saying such things. You don't know what you're saying," Al said.

"Indeed I do," said the old lady.

"If you did, you wouldn't say such things, talking that way about curses," Al said.

"Ah, but I know what I'm saying. If that one keeps on the way she's going, she'll end up in Hell. I tell you, and I'll bet you, I'll bet you the price of five bars of soap that if she keeps on, the Lord will curse her and hers," said the old lady.

"Goddamn it, Mother! Please, please, in the name of God, don't be voicing such thoughts!" Al said.

"But eat your dinner, Al, my son, before it gets cold," the old lady said.

"I don't care about dinner. I haven't any appetite," Al said.

"Eat your dinner. I have to get out to go to the grave of your father," the old lady said.

"Poor Pa," Al said sentimentally.

"You were a good son to him, and you made his end as easy as you could. He was a good man," Mrs. O'Flaherty said.

"I couldn't find her," Danny said, letting the screen door bang as he came in.

"Goddamn her! She's old enough to know that we have rules and regulations in this household," Al said.

"Let her aunt take care of her," Mrs. O'Flaherty said. She turned to her grandson and said, "Son, sit down and eat your dinner. Your grandmother is going out to Calvary and has to hurry."

"Go ahead and get ready. We'll take care of Danny's dinner ourselves," Al said.

"It'll only take me a jiffy, and then I'll go," she said.

"Mother, when you pray at Father's grave, say a prayer that things will go smoothly in the house here," Al said.

III

Danny sat by the window looking down at the back yard. Georgie Doolin was riding up and down on his tricycle. Danny didn't like him or his father. He and Bill and the kids sometimes played ball with Mr. Doolin in the back yard. He turned back and sat brooding. He was mad at Aunt Margaret. Because of her he wasn't likely to see the ball game today. He watched his uncle who sat at the dining-room table playing solitaire. He could see that Uncle Al was worried and feeling terrible. He had a cigar butt in his mouth but it wasn't lit now, and he was keeping his mind on the game. He played one game after another. Again he didn't win. He was shuffling the cards. He took a long time to shuffle, and he was very careful to mix the cards a lot. He shuffled and shuffled, and he didn't seem interested in the cards as he shuffled them.

"Sport, see what time it is," Al said.

Danny was glad to do something, anything. He went to the kitchen.

"It's two o'clock," Danny said, coming back from the kitchen and noticing that Uncle Al was still shuffling.

Danny sat down beside his uncle and watched him lay out the cards.

"This is called Canfield. In gambling houses, a man pays fifty-two dollars to play it, and he gets five dollars for every card he puts up here," Al said, pointing to where he had just placed an ace above the arrangement of cards.

"You can make money playing it," said Danny.

"You usually lose if you try. You're only allowed to go through the deck once, pulling up one card at a time, that's all," Al said.

"Oh, that's different," Danny said, and just as he spoke the screen door banged.

"Hello!" Aunt Margaret called, and they both jumped up and went to the kitchen.

"Hello, Al! Where's Mother?" Margaret said, her niece with her.

"Mother went to the cemetery," said Al.

"Oh, that's right, she said she was going to go this afternoon."

"How are you?" Al said, and Danny was glad, because she didn't act at all like she was drunk.

"I feel all right. I was nervous and took a long walk over in the park," she said.

"Good," said Al.

"And coming back, I met this little darling. She was playing with the sweetest little girl, and I met her mother, Mrs. Hamilton. She's the loveliest woman, and she's so pretty. I was talking to her. I meant to telephone you, but I was so interested in talking to her."

"I was worried about you, Princess," Al said.

"Oh, Al, you're a darling, but you needn't have. I was nervous, but, Al, I wouldn't take a drink if it would save my life. I'm through with doing anything like that. I was nervous and took a walk. And I took Little Margaret home with me to wash her up. I'm going over to the Poor Clares and going to take her with me," Margaret said.

"That's fine. And when you do, Peg, say a prayer that business is good when I go on the road this fall," Al said.

"Of course I will," said Peg.

"I think that Sport and I will go to the ball game. We've just about time to make it," Al said.

"Do, Al. And I'll be home in time to shop and cook you a lovely supper," Margaret said.

"Have you enough money to shop with? Here, you better take this," Al said, drawing a five-dollar bill out of his wallet and handing it to her.

"I'll give a dollar of it to the Poor Clares to pray for special intentions," Peg said.

"Come on, Dan, we better hurry," Al said.

Danny, all smiles, followed his uncle to the front.

"Goodbye, Peg," Al called after he and his nephew had put on their coats.

"Goodbye, Al, and have a good time. And don't worry. I'll have the loveliest supper for you when you come home," said Peg.

"Don't do too much. Anything will do," said Al.

"Now, you go ahead and enjoy yourselves," Margaret said, and Al and Danny, both of them joyous and relieved, went to the ball game.

8

I

    Mrs. O'Flaherty knelt beside the grave of her dead son, John. John had died when he was a year old. She stopped praying to think to herself that, ah, John had been a good son. She prayed again.

    At the head of the sunken grave there was a small and weather-beaten headstone, also sunken. On it were engraved the still legible words:

JOHN O'FLAHERTY

BELOVED SON OF THOMAS AND

MARY O'FLAHERTY

BORN 1870   DIED 1871

REST IN PEACE

She looked at the headstone with pride. She and Tom had sacrificed the cost of many a loaf of bread for this headstone to their little John. She looked at it with pride, even though she could not read the words. She knew that the stone had her name, her husband's, and that of the dead son. It was a good deed they had done, putting up this stone, and the Lord would repay her.

    And she was proud also of the plot of burial ground here that she and Tom had bought out of their hard-earned savings when Tom had worked with the horses on the wagon. Ah, she and Tom had had a hard life since they had come out from the old country, and this was the only plot of ground that they had ever owned in America. Well, thanks be to God, Tom had had a decent burial, and he was resting here in peace. And when she was called away, her own weary bones would be placed out here. She would have a decent burial, too.

    The graves in her little square plot were untended, sunken, with weeds growing over them. She had to see to it that they were given more care. The least that she could do for her own dead was to see to it that they had decent graves.

She moved over to the grave of her dead husband. Like the grave of her dead Louise, it was beginning to sink and to show signs of being uncared for. Tom and Louise had been a long time in the ground, since before her little grandson had started to school, and now he was growing up to be a fine big scholar, able to do his sums and read the newspapers. Grass and weeds were growing over all of her graves, and it made her feel ashamed. She had brought roses and laid one at the head of each grave, the only flowers on them. Ah, poor Pa, Lord have mercy on his soul, he was a good man, and he worked hard in his life.

"You were a good man, Pa," she said, half aloud, kneeling at her husband's grave.

She blessed herself, lowered her veiled head, and prayed, saying five Our Fathers and five Hail Marys. She moved over to the grave of her Louise and again prayed.

There was a small bench on the well-tended plot to the left of her ground, and she went to it to rest. Whoever owned this plot, she thought, they were good people. They kept up the last resting place of their dead. She sat down, and sighed. She saw before her endless plots of graves, some well-tended, others uncared for, and here and there were tombs, marble mausoleums, and many, many more tombstones. The lake was some distance behind her. Gentle breezes wafted from it, murmuring in the trees, playing softly on her back. It was very quiet here, as quiet as it had been when she ran the brush, barefoot, a girl in the old country. It was so quiet here, quiet as it was in Heaven, the home of the good Lord God Himself. She sat, looking over the silent cemetery. All these poor people sleeping out here, lying in cold graves, they were good people. They were good Catholics and they had been given a decent Christian burial. Many of them had come out from the old country, like she and Pa had, and they had been out at sea for five or six weeks in the rolling ship. Ah, well may they rest in peace. Good, hard-working people they must have been, and may the Lord have mercy on their souls.

She untied the small bundle of sandwiches she had brought with her for lunch, and she slowly bit into one. She was wearing her false teeth and she could chew a little with them. She sat nibbling at her sandwich, and the gentle lake wind lapped and stirred the grass and weeds on her plot of ground. Ah, yes, she and Pa had worked hard for this little plot of earth. And now look at it! It looked like a bush or a prairie, a place fit only for the burial of Orangemen and heathens. It did not look fit to be the burial ground for the graves of her own dear dead ones. Yes, it was a crying shame! Sure, and hadn't Pa worked hard to earn the money they had paid, the good hard-earned cash they had paid for this plot of ground. And after his getting up early in the morning in the freezing weather, to be laid away in such a place, with no nice grass, no flowers growing on the graves. Sure, a stranger seeing it would think that the O'Flahertys were heathens.

And look at poor John's headstone, sinking away into the cold earth. Glory be to God, the least her children could do was to tend the graves of her dead. And sure, wouldn't her poor old bones be resting out here soon enough.

She nibbled at her sandwich. She saw people moving over the cemetery, quiet, silent, kneeling at graves and before tombs and vaults, sitting on benches, walking about, crunching gravel under their feet. Sure, they respected their Christian dead. Over to her right, along the road, she saw a funeral procession led by a black hearse and followed by black automobiles. She blessed herself as the hearse passed, muttered a prayer to God for the repose of the soul of the dead one.

"Pa," she said, half aloud, looking toward her husband's weedy, sandy grave. "Pa, 'tis well you left us when you did, before you could get to know the likes of the daughter you left behind. 'Tis well, you poor man, that you left when you did, that you didn't live to see your daughter runnin' around like a high-lifer and a chippy with a black devil of a Protestant."

The cemetery was silent, save for a diminishing sound from the funeral procession and the softly lapping wind. She was attracted by a marble tomb some distance off to her right, and she looked at it gleaming in the sunlight. Ah, that must be for a fine man, to have a resting place like that for his bones. Ah, if the Lord let her live until her grandson became a fine upstanding man, he would give her a marble resting place as fine as that one. But she wouldn't live that long. She was coming onto the latter end of her days. Her man had been departed these last three years. She had only a little while more.

"Pa, sure, I'll be coming here soon to have me bones laid beside you," she said, addressing the grave.

She chewed on her sandwich, a little, sharp-faced woman in a black dress, wearing a black hat with a veil over her face.

Suddenly Pa seemed to be talking to her. She felt as if she had seen him rising out of his grave, standing there, a small old man in a white nightgown, with a slightly drooping gray mustache.

—Ah, Mary, he seemed to say.

"Pa, I knew that I'd be seeing you if I came out here today," she said.

—Mary, how does it be these days with our family? Are you happy, Mary, me one? he seemed to say.

"Pa, me days are bitter, and I'll be better off when I'm dead and gone. Sure, Pa, but your own daughter, Margaret, she's not me own flesh and blood. She's a child of Satan himself, she is. I never knew that I would live to see the day when me own daughter would be runnin' after a black devil of a Protestant, and a married man, at that. And he seems to be after giving her the gate. There she is, walking up and down the house, telephoning, wasting good hard-earned nickels to see if he is in the hotel, chasing after him. Ah, Pa, me days are bitter, and I do be thinking what a shame it is, what a pity, that she is the flesh and blood of that poor dead man lying out there in Calvary cemetery, and his grave not cared for with weeds growing over it, and, by the looks of it, it not fit to be the grave of a pagan," she said dolorously.

Pa was gone. She looked at the grave. He was not there. She saw the grass and weeds, stirred slightly by the lake wind. She watched a yellow butterfly floating over the grave, arching away to her right.

And he wasn't gone. There he was.

—Goodbye, Mary, he seemed to say.

"Goodbye, Pa. You were a good man," she said.

She sat crying. What a disgrace! Her own children, and they would not see to it that their own father had a better grave, and they would not have the graves of their own brothers and sisters fixed up. The lot now, sure, it didn't even look like it was fit to be the burying ground for pigs. She got up and went over again to her lot. She bent down and slowly pulled out weeds one by one, the tears in her eyes as she worked. She dropped the weeds on the narrow gravel path beside the lot, pulled more out, and dropped them also on the path. She worked slowly and steadily, pulling up weeds, throwing them away. When her back began to ache, she returned to sit on the bench again.

And look at the ground on this lot. Nice, well-cared-for grass and flowers. There should be flowers, a garden on Pa's land there. She took another sandwich out of her bundle. She breathed heavily from her exertions.

Again she seemed to see her dead husband arising out of his grave, standing before her, brick-faced, sad, with that slightly drooping mustache.

"You come back to see me, Pa?" she said.

—And that I did, Mary, he seemed to say.

"Ah, you poor man, having to rest in such a grave. It's a disgrace and a crying shame to the Lord. Ah, after working hard all these years for your children, the least they could do is see that you have a decent grave," she lamented.

—Do you be missing me, Mary? he seemed to ask.

"Indeed, I do. You were a good man, but I had to make you toe the mark," she said.

—Indeed, you did, he seemed to say.

"I did the right thing. Indeed, I did. And I would be making you toe the mark again, if you was me man and me the young girl fresh out of the old country. Tom, ah, I'll never be seeing the fields again, and the steeple of Athlone, and the church where I made me first Communion, and the brush we ran in before we came out. And, Pa, me aunt, Nellie Gannon, she's a hundred and eight years old now, a hundred and eight years old, and I'll never see the old soul again on this earth. Sure, and I'll never be seein' the old country and me people again," she said.

—It was a poor country and a hard country, Mary, me darlin', he seemed to say.

"But the people were good people, and they always gave their own a decent wake and burial," she said.

—Indeed, you're right, he seemed to say.

"I say the truth," she said.

—Louise, our angel in Heaven, is happy. She is, the little lamb, he seemed to say.

"Well should that angel in Heaven be happy. Ah, that the Lord Almighty should have spared her, and taken her sister, Peg, and left the lamb to me. Pa, it was that typewritin' she was learning to do with that machine of the Devil that sent her into the consumption. Ah, you would be home of an evening and I would see that poor sick girl learning at that machine when the strength wasn't in her, and me heart would bleed for her. It was that typewritin' machine that sent her into the consumption," she said.

—You say the truth, Mary. There I would be of an evening, taking it easy with me pipe in me mouth, and the cancer tearing at me vitals like a snake, and I would see the poor girl working, and I would tell meself that the Devil had put a curse on that typewritin', he seemed to say.

"You say the truth, Tom," she said.

—The truth, indeed, he seemed to say.

"Sure, Pa, all that I have to comfort me in the latter end of me days is the little grandson and me son, Al. Ah, but he's a good boy, and there he is home now with that drunken one. Jesus Mary and Joseph, the poor boy," she said.

—Our Al is a good boy, indeed, Mary, he seemed to say.

"Pa, I say to you, it was the mercy of God that took you off of this earth before you would live to see the day that I have. The mercy of God spared you, and you a sick man, in the latter end of your days. There she is, me own flesh and blood, high-lifing with tramps and tinkers and beggars, running with sinners and a Protestant married man that will have none of her, drinking, smoking with the very limbs of the Devil. It was the mercy of God," she said bitterly.

—I was the sick man, I was, he seemed to say.

"Pa, and how is me poor old mother in Heaven?" she asked.

—Sure, but aren't you the spittin' image of her, Mary? She was a good woman and she had a hard life, he seemed to say.

"She made me toe the mark. Ah, but she was a woman after me own heart," she said.

—You're a good woman yourself, Mary, but, ah, you're a hard woman, you are, he seemed to say.

"Hard it is that I am," she said spiritedly.

—Hard, indeed, he seemed to say.

"Hard I am, and hard I'll be until they'll be carrying me sorry old bones out here to be laid at rest beside you, Tom," she said.

—Mary, make them all toe the mark, he seemed to say.

"Oh, but I'll wager you, I'll wager you they will! I'm not me mother's daughter for nothing," she said.

—Make our Peg go to mass on Sunday, he seemed to say.

"The Lord Himself couldn't get that one into a church of a Sunday morning. The Lord Himself couldn't," she said.

—Mary, indeed it's a sad world, and it's glad I am to be out of it, he seemed to say.

"You good man, you say the truth," she said.

—'Tis a sad world, indeed, he seemed to say.

"Yes, indeed," she said sadly.

—Oh, but, Mary, it's well that I remember you as a girl running the bush in the old country. Well do I remember you at the Mullingar Fair. It's pretty you were, with the light shining in your eyes, and you that could run with the swiftness of a deer, he seemed to say.

"You always said that to me, Tom," she said.

—Mary, the longest life is short and it's soon that you'll be coming out to me and to your well-earned rest, he seemed to say.

"And that I will. There's not much strength left in me bones," she said.

The ghost of her dead husband seemed to stand there before her, silent. He seemed to look at her, sad-eyed. She began to cry quietly. She cried and looked at what seemed to her to be the vision of him.

"I must be whisting home to tend to me grandson," she said.

—Indeed, you must, he seemed to say.

"Goodbye, Pa," she said.

—Goodbye, Mary, me darlin' girl, he seemed to say.

"Goodbye, Pa," she said, her voice breaking with sadness.

—Be hard on them, Mary, he seemed to say.

"That I will. And, Tom, don't you be going and giving all these visions to me daughter, Lizz, that she does tell me about. If you have messages, you give them to me. It's me that should get them, and not her. Don't you be giving your visions to her. If you acted like that when you were here with me on earth, I would have skinned you alive. I'm a hard woman when I'm crossed, Tom, a hard woman, and I'll make you toe the mark, dead or alive. You be comin' to me with your words and your messages. You're my man. When Lizz's man dies, let him come to her. That will be time enough, time enough for her to be having visions. You be comin' to me," she scolded.

—Yes, Mary, I will, he seemed to say.

"Goodbye, Tom," she said.

—Goodbye, me darlin' Mary, he seemed to say, and then he seemed to disappear into his weedy, sunken grave.

She sat alone, quiet and uplifted in the still cemetery, nibbling at the remains of her last sandwich. The wind rustled softly off the lake, through the weeds and the grass and the surrounding trees. From some distance off, she heard the echoing sounds of an automobile motor, and then the rumble of a train outside the cemetery gates. She went over to the graves of her dead, knelt, and prayed. Tears welled in her eyes and she prayed for the repose of the souls of all her departed. Her tears dripped onto her husband's grave. She blessed herself, stood up, and wiped her eyes. She looked lingeringly at the sunken gravestone of her long-dead infant son. She wiped her eyes again. She blew her nose. She walked slowly down the path to the main road. She increased her gait.

"Goodbye, Tom. You were a good man," she said, half aloud, her voice throbbing as she looked back.

She turned again, hurried on, half running.

9

I

It was hot in the kitchen on a hot day, even with the door open. Well, it was getting on to the end of summer, and soon there would be cooler weather. She liked the fall. The fall was sad and she liked it. Some people would say that you should not be sad, even in the fall, but they didn't understand. If you were sad inside, you were sad. She had been so sad this morning, but after having gone to the Poor Clares, she was not so sad. She felt better. Those good and lovely Sisters would pray to the Lord for her and the Lord would not refuse them the intention of their prayers.

Margaret jumped up from the kitchen table where she was peeling potatoes, grabbed a dishcloth from a hook by the sink, wiped her hands, went to the oven, opened it, and looked at the cake she was baking. She smiled with a pride which suffused her whole being. The cake was rising just right. Not too fast, but just right. She had the oven at the right temperature. It looked so lovely, so golden, too. She was going to give them a layer cake that would melt in their mouths, one that they couldn't buy for love or money in even the best bakery in the city. If she was only Lorry's wife and could cook lovely meals for Lorry like this. She closed the oven door and returned to her potatoes.

Should she make cooked or uncooked frosting for it? She looked at the clock. Four o'clock. She decided to make uncooked frosting. She wished she'd thought of making the cake this morning. But it hadn't occurred to her until she'd come home from the Poor Clares. Well, it was too late for worrying about that now. The cake would be cooled by supper time. Al liked to eat a nice meal, but he didn't know the difference between just a nice meal and a meal that she cooked when she really wanted to cook. Men generally didn't appreciate all that a woman did in cooking. They sat down and ate, and if you asked them if they liked it, they just said oh, yes, it's all right. They took it for granted. She'd like to see them cook a meal, that is, men like Al. Of course, the cooks in the hotel, they were wonderful. Ah, but she could teach Lorry to appreciate good cooking. This gang expected its meal at six o'clock, and if it wasn't ready they wanted to know why. They had no appreciation of what it took to bake a cake. She had to peel the potatoes, peel the carrots, shell the peas, put the frosting on the cake, broil the steak, fix the salad.

She went on peeling the potatoes. She liked it. To be all alone by herself in the kitchen, attending to everything herself, thinking her own thoughts. She liked every little thing that she did in the kitchen when she had no interference, no one to get in her way. She liked to do it, and she would have to see that she did it more often, even if she was always busy at the hotel. She even liked the dirt she got on her hands from the potatoes. It was clean dirt. Ah, but Little Brother would be happy tonight. The little darling, he loved his mashed potatoes so. But it was bad for him that he didn't like other vegetables. When he grew up, if he didn't eat green vegetables he wouldn't be healthy. Poor Mother, she didn't know how to feed a child.

She went on peeling potatoes, cutting them very close to the skins because the best part of the potatoes was close to the skins, and she did not like to lose that. And those other poor children of Lizz's, and poor Jim. They didn't get the right food. It wasn't just because they were poor. Poor Lizz didn't know any better. She always fried something for them, bought soggy cakes and buns, gave them anything. The poor thing, she would never learn how to cook. She never gave her family good soups, broiled meats. Always fried things. That wasn't good for their stomachs. That poor man, Jim O'Neill. He never had the proper food.

"Aunty Margaret, can I help you?" Little Margaret asked, suddenly appearing at the kitchen door.

"Oh, you little darling, your aunt loves you, but she's busy. You run out and play and don't bother her now, and you'll get a nice supper. I'm baking a lovely cake for all of you," Margaret said.

"All right. I like cake," she said.

She skipped away, followed by the fond eyes of her aunt.

When the potatoes were peeled, Margaret washed them, covered them well with water, and set the pot on top of the stove. She'd peel the carrots now.

Another thing about so many women. They were so sloppy in the kitchen. God, she almost went crazy whenever she watched her sister cook. And some of the girls in the hotel. When she told girls like Susie Jacks that she cooked meals for her family, Susie would look at her with such eyes of pity. Susie thought that she was too good to cook, and that she would demean herself and spoil her hands in a kitchen. Well, she loved to cook if her cooking was only appreciated.

Margaret took the carrots, sat down to peel them. She liked their earthy vegetable aroma. She liked to peel carrots and smell them. She took a long carrot, held it to her nose, and sniffed it. If she was married to Lorry, she'd have him buy a farm and live in the country all summer. She would raise all her own vegetables and attend to them herself. She would be so happy. Sometimes you could almost cry. You could be so happy with just such a few little things, and you were so unhappy. People could be so happy, and they were so unhappy, always insulting each other, backbiting, cursing and fighting. If she was married to Lorry and had a farm, she'd be in the kitchen now, peeling carrots just as she was doing, cooking a fine supper, baking a cake like the one now in the oven—for Lorry. She could be so happy with so few little things. She went on peeling carrots, enjoying the mechanical labor of it, the smell, the thoughts she let run through her mind.

II

Her vegetables were all prepared. Some women made so much fuss about cooking. It could be done so systematically. She didn't make it hard, slop all over the kitchen, and spread everything all over the place. She sat down and did it and liked it, and that was all there was to it. Not like Mrs. Doolin downstairs. She was the sloppy Irish type, like Lizz. Margaret wiped her hands, opened the oven door with the dish towel, smiled at the sight of the golden layers. It was going to be one of the best she'd ever baked. She took a straw from the kitchen broom, wiped it carefully, stuck it into one of the layers. She pulled it out and looked at it with gratification.

"It's done," she told herself.

She'd start making the frosting now and leave the cake in the oven just a minute more. She got a box of powdered sugar and a can of cocoa from the pantry. She took the butter dish out of the icebox, and bringing it in she thought of her mother and smiled. Mother had the butter divided up, and part of it she called the help's butter. She wondered if she was using Mother's help's butter, or the butter for Mother's grandson and son. She took the pans out of the oven and set them on top of the stove to let them cool off a bit.

She knew the recipe for the frosting and didn't have to look it up in the cookbook. It was two cups of powdered sugar, a large chunk of butter, and three or four tablespoons of cocoa. She poured the powdered sugar into a bowl, and cut a large slice of butter which she put in with the sugar. She began creaming it with a fork, thinking how the gang was going to get the surprise of its life with this cake. She mashed the butter and sugar around slowly, her face beaming. Then she stopped and went to the stove. She looked a moment at the golden brown, perfectly baked and rounded layers. She smiled. Taking two clean towels, she took the layers out of the pans and placed them face down on large plates. She put the plates on the table and returned to cream the powdered sugar and butter.

She then poured in what was approximately four tablespoons of cocoa, and again creamed it, stirring the mixture around with her fork, humming a love song to herself as she worked. Next, she turned the cold-water faucet on in order to let the water run cold enough before putting in a few drops to give her frosting the right consistency. When she had creamed the frosting for another brief period, she tasted it and was satisfied. She took the bowl over to the table and began to spread on the frosting. She continued humming a love song.

III

Margaret had just put the steak in the oven to broil and she was almost finished setting the table when her mother came in.

"Sure, Peg, have you fixed supper?" Mrs. O'Flaherty asked.

"I thought that I'd surprise all of you. I baked a cake, and I was at the Poor Clares this afternoon," Margaret said.

"I was out at the cemetery," the mother said.

"Al told me. I took a long walk this morning and got back just after you had gone," Margaret said.

"Where's Al and my grandson?"

"They went to the ball game. I am expecting them home any minute," Margaret said, and her mother went to her small bedroom off the kitchen.

"I have just about gotten everything ready," said Margaret.

"I'll be there in a jiffy to help you, Peg," Mrs. O'Flaherty said.

"It's all done now, Mother, except that I have to mash the potatoes," Margaret said.

"Peg, I saw Pa," said Mrs. O'Flaherty from her room.

"Poor Pa!" Margaret exclaimed dolorously, going to the pantry, returning into the kitchen with a potato-masher.

"Peg, what can I do to help you? Al and the boy will be in now and wanting their meal," the mother said, now wearing a gingham apron.

"You can finish setting the table, Mother," said Margaret.

"Sure, I got to see that they get fed," said Mrs. O'Flaherty.

IV

"Hello," Al called, letting himself in.

"Al, is that you?" Mrs. O'Flaherty shouted.

"I'll be right out. Is supper ready?" he called back.

"I knew it. The only thing on their minds," Margaret said, half aloud.

Al came out, followed by Danny and Bill.

"Why, Willie-boy!" Margaret exclaimed.

"Hello, Aunt Peg," Bill said shyly.

"I met him on the street just now and took him home. Have we enough for supper for him?" Al asked.

"We have plenty. I cooked a nice supper, and I baked a cake. Brother, wait until you and Willie-boy see my cake. You boys have never eaten a better one," Margaret said.

"Fine! Fine! Peacherinoes, Peg," Al said.

"Ah, Al, I tell you we worked hard getting your supper ready. Peg and me, we worked hard," Mrs. O'Flaherty said.

"Fine, Mother! Thanks. We're going to have a nice happy supper now, a lovely last rose of a summer evening," said Al.

"I'm all right, Al. I'm going to be all right now," said Margaret.

"You went to the Poor Clares?" Al asked.

"Oh, Al, they're such a consolation," said Margaret.

"Those nuns are the holy virgins of the Lord," said Mrs. O'Flaherty.

"And, Peg, Bill here is going to turn over a new leaf. Aren't you, Bill?" Al said.

"Yes, sir," said Bill.

"Hello," Little Margaret said, coming into the kitchen.

"Oh, you little darling!" Margaret exclaimed.

"Come on, we got to have supper," said Mrs. O'Flaherty, bustling about.

V

"So you didn't think that the Federal League is as good as the American League," Bill said to Danny.

"Naw," said Danny.

"Hell, compared to fellows like Cobb and Collins and those fellows, the Federal Leaguers are a bunch of bush leaguers," said Al.

"Well, they have Hal Chase," said Bill.

"Sure. He's good, but they have a lot of bush leaguers," Al said.

"Like your supper, Brother?" asked Margaret, smiling over at her nephew.

"Uh huh!" said Danny.

"That's because I didn't let him overeat at the ball game," Al said.

"No one makes mashed potatoes for her little brother like Aunt Peg, do they, Brother?" Margaret said.

"No," said Danny.

"And I'm so glad that you brought Willie-boy home to supper. He can have a nice supper. Like your supper, Willie-boy?" asked Peg.

"Yes, it's good," said Bill.

"Aunt Margaret!" said Little Margaret.

"Yes, you little darling," said Margaret.

"I like what you give me to eat here better than what I got at Uncle Ned's in Madison," she said.

"Al! Al!" the mother said.

"Your aunt is going to take good care of her niece," said Margaret.

"Al, what are they doing in that war?" asked the mother.

"Oh, the Germans are causing a lot of trouble," Al said.

"All the men I hear talking about the war, you know, the business men and men of affairs at the hotel, say that the war ought to mean a lot of money to this country," said Peg.

"I guess it ought to, but that's no piker's war. Lots of men are getting killed," Al said.

"Al, what do they let the Germans do that for? I don't know why they don't stop the Germans," Mrs. O'Flaherty said.

"Well, Mother, I guess that they can't stop them. If they could, they would," said Al.

"Ah, they're no good," said Mrs. O'Flaherty.

"Come on, finish up, everyone, and I'll bring in the cake," said Margaret.

"I tell you, Al, they're no good, or they wouldn't be letting the Germans walk all over them," Mrs. O'Flaherty said.

"Here, Peg, let me help you get the tea and cake," Al said.

"No, I can do it better myself. Stay where you are, Al," Margaret said, getting up.

VI

"Mother, our sister certainly knows the gentle art of cake-making," Al said as Margaret brought the cake in, all the children looking at it avidly.

"Isn't it nice-looking?" Margaret said.

"You bet it is," Bill said.

"Now I'll bring in the tea," said Margaret.

"Let me help you, Peg," Mrs. O'Flaherty said, following her daughter to the kitchen.

"Listen, you kids, when your aunt comes back, you all say, now get this straight, you all say, 'Aunt Margaret, eating your cake is going to be a gorgeous adventure.' Got that, all of you?" Al said in a low voice, and the children all nodded.

They waited, struggling to keep the words in mind, and when their aunt came back to the dining room carrying cups of tea, they said self-consciously and in unison, the end of their sentences trailing off:

"Aunt Margaret, eating your cake is going to be a gorgeous adventure."

"I hope you darlings like it," she said, smiling.

Margaret and Mrs. O'Flaherty finished bringing in the tea.

"Now I'll cut the cake," Margaret said.

She cut large slices and passed them around.

"Al, it would cost a dollar apiece to get a supper as nice as this in a good restaurant or hotel."

"Hell, more," said Al.

"Sure, prices are a fright," Mrs. O'Flaherty said.

"They are. I was reading in the paper where the government is going to do something. Ever since the war, the price of food has kept going up and up. It's frightful, Al. I don't understand why it's allowed," Margaret said.

"I guess it's because a lot of food is being shipped to Europe," Al said.

"Well, it's a shame," Margaret said.

She watched the children concentrate on their cake.

"You darlings like your aunt's cake, don't you?" she asked, and they all nodded their heads.

"Sure they do. It's a wonderful cake," said Al.

There was a brief silence at the table. Suddenly Al looked up at Peg and said:

"The little girl going to the Sisters' school, too?"

"Al, you know I was thinking about it, and wanted to talk to you. There's a public school down the block here, and she's so small, it might be better to send her there. She wouldn't have to cross any streets. Of course, Danny could take her to school, but then in the cold winter she wouldn't have as far to walk, and she's so thin," said Margaret.

"I like it cold out," said Little Margaret.

"Sure, girls don't need to go to the Sisters' school, and it costs a dollar a month, a dollar a month," Mrs. O'Flaherty said.

"Nix on that, Mother," said Al.

"Well, I was only telling you the truth, Al," Mrs. O'Flaherty said.

"Whatever you think, Peg," said Al.

"It's not the dollar a month I begrudge. She's just small, and the wind'll blow her over on some of these cold winter days. Next year she will be bigger, and then we can let her go to the Sisters' school along with Brother," Margaret said.

"We'll see that she's taken to school the first day. Sport, there, doesn't need to have anyone take him," said Al.

"Naw," said Danny.

"Hey! Where do you get off at? You're getting old enough to use some diction. Say no, not naw," Al said.

"No," said Danny.

"Bill will soon be big enough to work and help his poor father," said Mrs. O'Flaherty.

"Maybe, with the Lord helping, he won't have to. Perhaps we can have Mike Geraghty help him to become a doctor. His brother can be a lawyer and he a doctor," said Al.

"Would you like to be a doctor, Willie-boy?" asked Peg.

Bill nodded affirmatively.

"I know something they'd all like better than anything right now," Al said.

"What, Al?" asked Margaret.

"Some more of their beautiful aunt's sumptuous cake. I think that since it's around the end of vacation time for all of them, we might let them have it, don't you, Peg?" Al said.

"I think so. You darlings want some more cake?" she asked.

"I do," said Little Margaret.

"Me, too," said Danny.

"I like it," said Bill, and their aunt was already cutting slices of cake.

"Al, you have some more cake," said the mother.

"No, thanks, Mother, but I'll have another cup of tea, if you please," Al said.

She took his cup and went to the kitchen.

Margaret passed back the children's plates with the cake on it.

"Well, Peg, we're coming now to the mellow season of the year. Let's hope there'll be good business," Al said.

"There will be, Al. I know it," said Peg.

"Here, Son," Mrs. O'Flaherty said, setting a cup of tea in front of Al.

"Peg, why don't you and Mother see a moving picture down the street to-night?" said Al.

"I was thinking of doing that and getting Mrs. Hamilton to go with us. She's a lovely woman," said Margaret.

"And if it's a proper picture, take the little girl. I'm going to play catch with these two big leaguers here while there's a little light left," said Al.

"Swell," Bill said.

"But here, let's help you with the dishes first," Al said.

"Don't you bother. I'll get them done in no time, and have time for the show," said Margaret.

"We'll do them, Al," said Mrs. O'Flaherty.

"Al, I'll never forget the time I took Little Brother to the moving pictures, and he saw an actress in the show. He stood up right in the crowded theater and said about the actress, 'Why, that lady looks like my Aunt Louise.' And I could have died, because then he said, 'My Aunt Louise was beautiful, and everybody says I looked just like her.' The whole show roared," Margaret said.

Al laughed heartily.

"Lord have mercy on Louise. Sure, her grave and Pa's grave is a disgrace.

I was ashamed of myself today seeing the condition they're in," said Mrs. O'Flaherty.

"Yes, Al, next year we must try and have them attended to," said Margaret.

"With the help of God and some luck, we'll be in shape to," said Al.

"I'm going to call up Mrs. Hamilton and ask her to go to the show with me," said Margaret, going to the phone in the front of the house.

"Dan, think Joe Tinker's slowing up?" Bill asked.

"I guess he is. He's only hitting around .240," Danny said.

"Who's Joe Tinker, Danny?" asked Little Margaret.

"You wouldn't know if I told you," said Danny.

Al got up from the table.

"We'll rest a few minutes and then play catch," Al said.

"Al, wouldn't you like to go with us?" asked Margaret, coming back from the phone.

"I have a good book to read. Say, Peg, ever read any books by Winston Churchill?" asked Al.

"No, gee, I never have time to read," she said.

"When I go away I'll leave it. Try and read it. It's a fine story," Al said.

"I know it, Al, and I must read it. I'm one, you know, Al, who believes that women should think and learn," said Margaret.

"Slip us a kiss on that, Peg," said Al.

She gave her brother a chaste, perfunctory hug and kiss.

"Everything is going to be fine and dandy now, Peg, isn't it?" he said.

"Yes, Al, it is," she said.

"Have a good time at the show tonight," he said.

"I want you to meet Mrs. Hamilton. She's a lovely woman and she's going home Sunday. Maybe I'll bring some ice cream home after the show and have her in for a dish," Margaret said.

"Sure, do, Peg, and have a good time, Princess," Al said.

While the women were washing dishes, he sat in the front, smoking a cigar, looking out on the street contentedly. In about fifteen minutes he got up and went for his ball and glove to go downstairs and throw a few pitches to Bill. He could let go more with Bill than with Danny, try out curves and put smoke on the ball because Bill was bigger. He was glad he had found Bill on the street. Bill would turn over a new leaf, maybe, and be all right. Everything was going to be all right. He felt it in his bones that life was turning over a new leaf for all of them, and it was going to be shinier and prettier than the old leaf.

SECTION TWO

1914

10

I

Lizz O'Neill bent over the washtub in the kitchen. She had the tub propped up on boxes between the stove and the sink. The sink was behind her and she faced the stove. On either side of it were windows through which she could catch glimpses of her children playing in the back yard. She liked having a back yard where the children could play because it gave her a chance to keep an eye on them. And through the other window on her right she could see the side of Saint Martha's, the parish church the front entrance of which was only a short block away from her corner cottage. She bent over the washtub, working slowly with a weariness in her body. Always washing. Washing diapers, washing for the kids, washing Jim's shirts, and socks, and woolen underclothes. She hummed brief snatches of song and continued, tiredly rubbing clothes on the washboard. It was a dark October afternoon outside, but there was some wind and it ought to dry the clothes quickly. She caught a sudden flash of Catherine as she ran yelling in pursuit of her brother Bob, a lad who was going on five.

It seemed as if it was only yesterday in the old place on La Salle Street where Catherine was born. And she was already three years old. There was a younger brother, Arty, over two. And another boy born dead. And now she was about three months gone again. She rubbed out a pair of Arty's diapers. Three months gone again. Oh, good Jesus Mary and Joseph, would it never end? Children coming all the time, coming too soon, coming dead, almost never coming in easy births. The doctor had to use instruments to bring out her precious little angel Arty. And the new one. Oh, good Mary, Mother of the Crucified Saviour! She wearily rubbed away on the washboard. Outside, the little ones were playing, running, and shouting. Well, thank the Lord that Dennis was old enough for school. And it was so nice that he could go to school so near home, right across the street. Past the picket fence and withered grass of the parish grounds across the street she could see the tan brick side of Saint Martha's school with its evenly arranged rows of windows. She rubbed away at the last article of clothing, a pair of Jim's red flannel drawers. She poured the soapy, dirty water down the tin-plated sink, groaning as she lifted the heavy tub. She set the tub back on the boxes. It was so heavy, and she with another one growing inside of her, her sore feet, her aching teeth, her neuralgia, she couldn't be lifting heavy tubs of water. Laboriously she began drawing pots of water from the single faucet at the sink and dumping them into the tub, and as she did so she sang over and over again:

> Holy God, we praise Thy name!
> Lord of all, we bow before Thee.

When she had the tub almost filled, she took a kettle of boiling water from the stove and poured it into the tub. Her hands were red and chapped. She filled the emptied kettle and set it again on the stove, took a second one, emptied it, refilled it and set it, too, back on the stove. She told herself that she was lucky, getting this much done while her little Arty was taking his nap. He would be up crying soon. She rinsed the clothes, again singing in a monotonous singsong:

> Holy God, we praise Thy name.

Lizz rinsed out the wash and dropped each piece into a large basket. When she had finished, she picked up the basket and plodded out and down the back stairs to hang up the clothes. She left the kitchen door open so that she could hear Arty if he began crying. Bob and Catherine clambered around her.

"Mama, I don't wanna play tag with him," Catherine said.

"Why?" asked Lizz.

"He runs too fast for me," Catherine said.

"You two play something. Your Mama's busy," Lizz said.

They dogged her steps. She went past the privy to a post on the left which stood near the fence which separated her yard from that of the Negro woman who was married to a white man. The line stretched diagonally across to another post by the street fence, and then down to a hook on the tumble-down old barn in a back corner. North of the yard stood the two-story clapboard Connerty house. She and Jim had never had a yard as good as this one since they had been married. And it was all her own, not a yard to be shared with niggers like the one at Twenty-fifth and La Salle. She hung up the clothing, shirts, socks, stockings, underwears, torn sheets, diapers, a faded pink petticoat, and the boys' waists. Her back ached. One whole side of her face was in pain because of her neuralgia. She sighed. The wind slapped the clothes as they were hung out; the larger pieces bellied, while the smaller ones swayed in the wind. When she had hung up the clothes, she sighed and picked up her basket to return to the house.

"I know what you want, you little shysters," she said to her two children who still followed her.

"Mama, can I have a piece of bread and butter and sugar?" Bob asked.

"You ones would wear out an elephant if you had one for a mother," she said, sighing.

They tracked her into the kitchen.

Taking half a loaf of bread from the battered breadbox, she cut two thick slices with the saw-edged bread knife. She spread oleomargarine on the bread and then sprinkled sugar on top. She gave a slice to each of them. They ran out again, and soon she could hear them shouting in play. She sat down to have a cup of tea, but she was no sooner about to drink it than she heard little Arty crying.

The dining room and parlor of the O'Neill cottage were connected by a doorless opening in which there stood a fat-bellied stove. It usurped almost half the space of this opening. Both rooms smelled musty and were disorderly and strewn with papers. There were two windows on the street side of the dining room, and one window in the front wall of the parlor. There was also an entranceway by the front door. There were dark bedrooms off each room.

Lizz hastened to Arty in the front bedroom.

"Oh, you noisy fellow. You want your mother and you'll raise the roof for her, won't you?" she said in a cooing voice as she entered the dark bedroom.

The baby continued to cry. She picked him up, but he kept up his petulant, angry cries. Holding him, she felt his behind. Thank God, he hadn't wet himself. That was one job not to be done for a little while. She kissed him several times.

"He wants his Mama to give him a piece of bread, Mama's grown-up baby does," she said.

She carried him out to the kitchen, and he stopped crying. He was getting heavy, though. The angel, he was growing.

"Mither," Arty said.

"Yes, my angel," she said.

"Arty hungry," he said.

II

Arty had been two years old in July. He was a thin, sickly-looking, undernourished baby. He had white curly hair that was gradually darkening. His cheeks were sallow and sunken, and his face seemed set in a prematurely old expression. His glowing brown eyes dominated his appearance. They seemed liquid, sad, as if filled with tragic memories far beyond his capacities for experience. No one failed to observe his eyes.

Lizz carried him to the kitchen.

"Here, sit on a chair and I'll give you a piece of bread," she said.

She set him in a chair, and gave him a chunk of bread. Arty gazed at her. He looked at the bread. He smiled. Lizz pointed her right index finger at him and smiled. He uttered wordless sounds as she slowly twisted her finger close to his face. He laughed. He threw the bread on the floor and watched and waited. She gently poked the dimple on his chin, and he laughed again.

"Mither! Mither!" Arty exclaimed.

"Yes, you angel, won't you let your Mama have a cup of tea?" she said.

"Mither, Mither, where fither?" he asked.

"Your father's gone to work," she said, her decayed teeth showing as she smiled.

"Fither gone work," Arty said, laughing.

He saw the chunk of bread on the floor. He climbed off the chair. He grabbed it. He carried it to Lizz.

"Oh, he's going to be kind to his Mama when he grows up and give her things," she said, and Arty looked questioningly at his mother, not understanding her words.

He reached out his dirty right hand for the bread, and she gave it to him. He walked bowleggedly away. He sat down on the floor. He watched his mother, and chewed the bread.

"Fither gone work. Fither gone work. Fither gone work," he said.

Lizz sipped tea. Arty held the bread aloft in his hand and watched her attentively. Outside in the yard, Bob and Catherine were playing, and their shouts could be heard in the kitchen.

III

When school let out, Dennis ran across the street, climbed over his side fence, ran into the house and threw his books on a chair. He dashed out to Bob and Catherine in the yard. Dennis was a thin boy of seven, pale, and beginning to look like his father.

"You out of school?" Bob asked him.

"Uh huh. Let's play cowboy," he said.

"You got to be the Indian this time and get shot dead," said Bob.

"I wanna play cowboy with my brothers," Catherine said.

"You're too little," said Dennis.

"I don't care. I wanna play cowboy and Indian," said Catherine.

"I'm the Indian. You two are chasing me," Dennis said, galloping away from them. Pretending that he was on horseback, he turned and pointed his finger at them.

"Bang! Bang! Bang!" he yelled.

They chased him, Catherine trailing behind Bob. They pointed their fingers and pretended to be shooting Dennis. Catherine fell down. She got up and ran. Dennis circled the yard, with Bob unable to catch him. Catherine still trailed in the rear, striving with all the might of her skinny little body to catch up with her older brothers and pulling up her falling underpants as she ran.

"You're dead. I shot you," Bob said, coming up to Dennis who had paused to catch his breath.

"You didn't catch me," Dennis said.

"When I'm the Indian, you always make me fall down dead," Bob said.

"But you got to catch me," said Dennis.

"But when you play cowboy and Indian, the Indian always gets killed," Bob said.

"Why? Who told you that?" Dennis asked, sneering at Bob with his two years' superiority.

"Because the Indian is always killed by a cowboy. When Papa took me to the nickel show and I saw the cowboys and Indians, the cowboys killed the Indians," Bob said.

"You run too fast when you play cowboy and Indian with me," Catherine said.

"A girl can't be a cowboy. Go on and play with your dolls," said Dennis.

"I'll tell Papa," Catherine said.

"Tattletale! Tattletale! Tattletale!" Dennis yelled, and he started running toward the far end of the yard.

"Bang! Bang! Bang!" Catherine yelled, her voice sad and hopeless as she started after them.

Trying to pull up her underdrawers as she ran, she fell. She let out a shriek.

"I told you you shouldn't play with us," Dennis yelled at her angrily.

"You made me fall down," she sobbed, the tears streaming down her face.

"I wasn't near you," he shouted.

She noticed the blood on her finger. She let out a loud yell.

"Cut it out, you cry baby," Dennis said.

"Ooo, I cut my finger. Mama! Mama! Mama!" she yelled, running into the house.

"In the name of Jesus Mary and Joseph, what's happened to you now?" Lizz said sharply, meeting her daughter just inside the kitchen door.

"I cut my finger," Catherine said.

"You little shyster, you're always doing something to yourself," Lizz said.

"I fell down and cut my finger," Catherine said, still crying.

"What did you do it for?" Lizz said angrily.

"I fell down," Catherine answered, holding up her bleeding finger.

"You little pisspots are always falling and cutting yourselves," Lizz said.

"Dennis did it. He tripped me," Catherine sobbed.

"Here, come on over to the sink and I'll wash it," Lizz said, grabbing her daughter by the arm and dragging her over to the sink while the child cried.

Lizz took the finger and let cold water run on it.

"All that trouble and it's only a scratch. I'll put a rag on it," Lizz said.

She went to the front bedroom and came back with a rag which she hastily tied on Catherine's finger.

"Now, go out and play, and don't cut yourself again if you know what's good for you," Lizz said.

Lizz had no sooner uttered these words than Arty began crying.

"Now that one has done something," she said, and went into the parlor.

She found Arty sitting in a pool.

"Oh, you pisspot!" she exclaimed, picking him up while he still bawled.

The other children in the yard could be heard loudly yelling:

"Bang! Bang! Bang!"

IV

"I thought it was the insurance man, and I haven't the money to pay him," Lizz said, letting Bill in at the front door.

"Well, it's only me, Ma," he said.

"Bill, you got to go down to the store at Twenty-fifth for the groceries," she said.

"Aw, gee, I wanted to go over to Fuller Park and play football," Bill said.

"Well, go ahead, and there won't be a thing on the table for your father when he comes home tonight," she said.

"All right, I'll go. Gee, I wish we could get credit around here, and I could go here instead of way down there," he said.

"Well, I owe every storekeeper money around here and they won't give me any credit," she said.

"All right, what do you want?" he said.

"Take your time. For Christ sake, hold your horses! I'm your mother, and you won't talk to me that way," she said.

"Well, gee, Ma, I didn't mean to. Only if I'm going, I want to get started. It wastes the rest of the afternoon, going and coming," he said.

"So it does, does it? Well, what about your mother? It wastes the whole day taking care of this gang of pisspots here," she said.

"Where are the kids?" he asked.

"They're out in the yard yelling and playing. I want you to stay here and mind the house and watch your baby brother for a minute while I run across the street to church," she said.

"Aw, gee, Ma, I'll never get started, and I'll get caught in the crowd coming home," he complained.

"Say, you, I'll put the stove poker on your back if you talk back to me! I'm your mother, and you're not going to give your mother any lip. When I'm dead and gone you'll wish you had a mother like me. I'm only going to be gone a minute. I want to pay a visit to the Blessed Sacrament," she said.

Bill slumped in his chair and sulked. Lizz went to her room, and came out wearing a man's tattered coat. She was dirty, and there was a soiled rag tied under her chin. She wore an old, crushed hat, and her uncombed hair straggled from under it. Her face needed washing. Her dress was stained. She was wearing men's shoes, and the uneven laces were knotted together in several places.

"Now, if the insurance man comes, tell him your mother isn't home and for him to come back next Wednesday," she said.

"All right, Ma. And you won't be gone long?" he said.

"I'll be back before you can say Jack Robinson," she said.

"Mither! Mither! Take Arty bye-bye, Mither," Arty said plaintively, tagging after her.

"No, I won't. You stay here with your big brother and show him what kind of a big little man you're becoming," she said.

"Mither! Mither!" Arty sadly exclaimed.

At the door, she removed his hand from her coat, gently pushed him back. She went out and closed the door. Arty screamed. He stood against the door and cried loudly, sadly.

"Aw, shut up and give your ears a rest," Bill yelled at Arty as the baby continued crying.

Arty stumbled to the window, looked out on the empty street of old wooden cottages, narrow sidewalks, dirt, garbage, wooden paving blocks.

"Mither! Mither! Mither! Mither! Mither!" he kept repeating with the seeming infinite sadness of a baby whose wishes are blocked and frustrated.

He turned from the window, sat down, rubbed his dirty face and eyes, and cried. Bill sat slumped. Arty looked at Bill. He smiled.

"You quit crying, huh, kid?" Bill said, smiling back at Arty.

Arty laughed. He stood up. He wavered, his right hand extended in Bill's direction. He tottered to Bill.

"You're too big a guy to cry like a bawling girl, ain't yuh, kid?" Bill said.

"Kid," Arty said, and he laughed.

"Come, we fight," Bill said.

He sat on the floor with Arty, extended his fists, gently tapped his baby brother's cheek. Arty laughed and giggled. He clumsily slapped at Bill, laughed. Bill shook his fists at Arty and gently touched the baby's nose. Arty laughed.

"You're going to grow up and lick Freddy Welsh, huh, kid?" Bill said.

Arty suddenly tottered away and knelt beside the couch.

"Nobody see Arty. Nobody see Arty," he called.

Bill crawled on his hands and knees, pretending to look for Arty and not to find him. Arty stood quiet, smiling, tense, waiting.

"There you are!" Bill exclaimed, and Arty laughed happily.

V

Lizz reluctantly left the church. She had stayed only about ten minutes. She would have liked to stay longer and have said the Stations of the Cross. But Bill had to go down and get the groceries. Children were playing on the broad sidewalk in front of the church, a group of boys were lagging buttons and some girls were playing hopscotch. She smiled on seeing them. She sighed, realizing that she had to go home now. There was the washing to be taken off the line. And she hadn't gotten time to clean up the house. Jim didn't like it, coming home to a house all messed up. Well, she couldn't help it. Here she was, going to have another baby, and still with so much to do. He should be thankful that she did as much as she did.

"Oh, Mrs. O'Neill, Mrs. O'Neill!"

It was her neighbor, Mrs. Connerty. Mrs. Connerty was a meaty, ruddy woman. She was dressed up this afternoon. Her coat was open, revealing a white blouse and a kelly green skirt which had huge pink roses on it and a ruffle at the bottom. It looked like an underskirt. She had on a wide straw hat with velvet ribbons and flowers around the crown.

"I'm so glad to see you. I see you're dressed up. I was just paying a visit to the Blessed Sacrament. I try never to let a day go by without paying a visit to church," Lizz said, covertly eying her neighbor, her mind working as she tried to think of things to say which would dig into this tub of meat.

"Sure, the Lord bless you, Mrs. O'Neill, how are you? I'm on my way to have a cup of tea with my friend, Mrs. McGahan, down on Root Street," Mrs. Connerty said.

"Oh, I know her. I know her family," Lizz said.

"You do? I never heard her speak of you," said Mrs. Connerty.

"Oh, yes. Her family is a fine family, fine people. They have an uncle named Pat McGahan. You ask her about her uncle Pat McGahan," Lizz said.

"What is he?"

"He's dead now, poor man, Lord have mercy on his soul. He was stabbed in the back. He was a good man, a fine decent man. But one night he stopped in a saloon to have just a glass of beer, and there was a fight and some bum stabbed him in the back. But they're fine people," said Lizz.

"It must be another family. She never told me of her uncle, and the men in her family are not drinking men," said Mrs. Connerty.

"Neither was Pat McGahan. He just stopped for a glass of beer," Lizz said.

"No, it must be some other family. The McGahans are fine people, the salt of the earth, and not the like of some of the shanty Irish in this neighborhood here," said Mrs. Connerty.

"But you're dressed up so nice. Why, you look so grand," said Lizz, eying her neighbor up and down.

"My man bought me this," said Mrs. Connerty.

"It's a lovely dress. It makes you look so young. Lovely," said Lizz.

"I never have a minute's peace with my boys, so today I said to myself, I'm going to let them play in the park, and I'll put my Sunday clothes on and go and see my lovely friend, Mrs. McGahan, for a cup of tea," Mrs. Connerty said.

"It's good to get away," Lizz said, and while she spoke Mrs. Connerty kept looking at the dirty rag tied under Lizz's chin. "Your neuralgia isn't bothering you still, is it, Mrs. O'Neill?" Mrs. Connerty added.

"It is. I have an ache on this side of my face," said Lizz, touching her left cheek as she spoke.

"'Tis a pity. My sister, the one that lives in the fine big house with radiators on Paulina Avenue, sure, she had the neuralgia for years until she got holy water from the shrine of Saint Jude, and would you believe it, it cured her," said Mrs. Connerty.

"Saint Jude is a powerful saint," Lizz said.

"He is that," said Mrs. Connerty.

"If I didn't have to stay home and take care of my little ones, I could make a novena to the shrine of Saint Jude and be cured of my neuralgia through his intercession," Lizz said.

"And don't I know that children are the most trouble when they're wee ones," said Mrs. Connerty.

"Yes, they need watching all the time or they'll tear the house down," said Lizz.

"Mine were well-behaved, but well-behaved or not, they're a bother when they're little. But maybe your mother could come down and watch them for a day while you go to the shrine of Saint Jude," said Mrs. Connerty.

"Oh, my mother's a lady. She's a lady. Her family owns acres in the old country," Lizz said.

"My mother was, too. Her father owned acres and acres, and they were the largest landowners in the whole of County Clare," said Mrs. Connerty.

"And my father, Lord have mercy on his soul, if he was alive today, he could go back to Ireland and he would own more land than there is in a city block," Lizz said.

"My man's family owned land, but he wasn't the oldest son, and he had to come out to America," Mrs. Connerty said.

"It's too bad you couldn't come and have a cup of tea with me, Mrs. Connerty," Lizz said.

"I'd love to, but I have a previous engagement with my friend, Mrs. McGahan. Fine people, and her man has a good job and makes a good living for her and hers," Mrs. Connerty said.

"You must drop in some other day," Lizz said.

"I'd love to. Sure, the first chance I get, I'll be coming in and seeing you," said Mrs. Connerty.

"I have to be getting home now, but you must come and see me for a cup of tea," said Lizz.

"Oh, my body and soul, but I'll be late for my engagement with Mrs. McGahan. But I'll see you soon. Good day, Mrs. O'Neill," said Mrs. Connerty.

"Goodbye, Mrs. Connerty. But I can't get over how grand you look. Why, say, your clothes make you look like a spring chicken," Lizz said.

"Sure, and you're just giving me the blarney. A fat thing like me," Mrs. Connerty said modestly.

"Well, have a good time, Mrs. Connerty, and come in for a cup of tea with me," Lizz said.

They parted. Lizz looked after her. The ass on her, and the getup of her, and the nerve of that tub of beef. And her skirt looked like an underskirt worn by a chippy. Shanty Irish! But she had dug some things into her, telling her she looked like a spring chicken. Shanty Irish! And wait until she had a chance to tell Mother about Mrs. Connerty.

She went on home.

VI

Catherine eyed her brother Bill jealously as he sat by the cluttered dining-room table with a sheet of yellow paper before him. Arty sat on the floor, playing with old pieces of cardboard. The dining-room table was by the side wall, with a narrow window on either side of it. Lizz sat on the couch which stood against the wall off the entrance to the kitchen.

"And let's see, three cans of condensed milk," she said.

"I got that," he said.

"And a pound of American cheese," she said.

"Yeah," he said.

"And two Ward's cakes," she said.

"Got it," he said.

"Mama! Mama!" Catherine interrupted.

"Shut up, you shitpot! Your mother's busy," Lizz said.

Catherine glared at her mother.

"Ma, can't we get some meat?" Bill asked.

"Meat costs money and your father is a poor man," Lizz said.

"Well, we could get some bologna sausage or liver sausage," he said.

"All right, get twenty cents' worth of bologna and ten cents' worth of liver-wurst," she said.

"I want my animal crackers," Catherine said determinedly.

"Oh, yes, a package of animal crackers," Lizz said.

"No, two," Catherine interrupted.

"Say, who the hell do you think you are, Beverly Bayne?" Lizz said, turning an angered glance on her daughter.

"You got to get two, one for me, and one for everybody else," said Catherine, pouting.

"You can divide one up for all of you. Your father's a poor man," Lizz said.

Catherine let out a loud shriek, turned her face down on the couch, kicked her legs, sobbed and yelled.

"Well, glory be to God!" Lizz exclaimed.

"I'm going to run away," Catherine said, looking up with tear-filled eyes, and again she sank her head on the couch, kicked and yelled.

"Cat-rine! Cat-rine! Cat-rine!" Arty called, rising and running over to his sister.

She cried.

"Don't cry, Cat-rine!" he exclaimed, standing beside her and petting her.

"Oh, Lord love him, look at him," Lizz said, suddenly smiling.

"Ma, I always get Dolly a box of animal crackers for herself," said Bill.

"All right, two. Hear that, you'll get your animal crackers," said Lizz.

Catherine sat up and wiped her eyes.

"Here," Arty said, handing her a torn piece of cardboard.

"I always get my animal crackers," Catherine said determinedly.

"Yes, Dolly, I'll bring you back your own box," Bill said.

She smiled.

"And Son, a pound of oleomargarine," Lizz said.

"Yes, Ma," he said.

"Wait until I get your carfare. I'm lucky. I just got it. I hope your father was able to borrow something from one of the men today," she said, going to her bedroom.

"Dolly has to get her animal crackers, doesn't she?" Bill said to Catherine.

"Animal cackers," Arty said, and he smiled.

"Say crackers," Catherine said to him.

"Cackers," he said, laughing.

"Here, Son, now hurry up back. I have to make supper for your father and the regiment here," she said, handing him pennies.

"All right, Ma," he said, going to get his hat and then leaving.

"Say Mother," Catherine said to Arty.

"Mither," Arty said.

"Dolly, you watch your little brother, like a good girl, while I take down the clothes, and you'll get your animal crackers," Lizz said, going to get the basket in the kitchen for the clothes she had on the line.

"Say Catherine," Catherine said to Arty.

"Cat-rine," Arty said.

Catherine and Arty laughed.

VII

Lizz was at the stove and the kids were in the dining room when Jim came home. After leaving his coat and cap in the closet of the front room, he came out to the kitchen, followed by all of the children except Bill. Bill had gotten his father's newspaper and was seated with it by the lamp in the dining room.

"Well, Lizz, how did everything go today?" he asked.

"Oh, Jim, I had so much washing to do, and my neuralgia bothered me. I ran over to church for a minute and I met that tub of beef, Mrs. Connerty," Lizz said.

"The hell with her," Jim said.

"Oh, but, Jim, you should have seen the getup on her," Lizz said enthusiastically, turning from the stove. "She was going to see her friend, Mrs. McGahan, you know, the one whose uncle was a bum and was killed in a saloon fighting with other bums. And she was wearing a dress like an underskirt. You should have seen her. Say, she looked like a circus," Lizz said.

"I don't give two whoops in hell what that cow wears," Jim said.

"Well, neither do I. She gives me a pain," Lizz said.

"What do you see her for, then?" Jim said, a twinkle in his eyes.

"I met her in front of church. And you know the shanty Irish, Jim. She loves to chew the rag," Lizz said.

"She's a troublemaker, Lizz, and, mark my words, the less you have to do with her the better off you'll be. Mark my words," Jim said.

"Don't I know it? Because her man is janitor of the church she thinks she's the cock of the walk. And, Jim, I'll bet my right arm that they talk against us to Father Corbett across the street," Lizz said.

"He's too smart a man to listen. And anyway, he doesn't care a lot for us. We don't have enough nickels to put on his collection plate to have him care about us," said Jim.

"Why, Jim, he's a good kind man, and he gives the kids pennies, and doesn't he let Dennis go to school free?"

"He ought to. He's a priest, and doesn't Christ stand for charity?" said Jim.

"Fither! Fither!" Arty said, pulling at his daddy's pants legs.

"Jim, did you borrow that money?" she asked.

"Yeah, Ambrose McGinty loaned me a dollar. You know, a lot of the fellows on the wagons always kid Mac. But he has a good heart," said Jim.

"He must have. He hasn't gotten a girl and gotten married yet, has he?" asked Lizz.

"No. Porky was kidding him about it today. And Mac, he's a funny bird, he said give him single blessedness to double wretchedness any day in the week. But here's the castor oil I got for you, Lizz," Jim said.

"I'll take some now, and then finish getting supper. You must be starved, you poor man," she said, going to the sink.

"Well, here's praying, Lizz," said Jim.

"If it's the will of God to have another, it's the will of God. And when we're old, we'll have them to take care of us," she said.

"Papa, swing me over your head," Catherine said, looking up with loving eyes at her tall, leathery-faced father.

"Fither! Fither!" Arty said, holding up his hands.

"Arty O'Neill, you'll be a man before your mother," Jim said, bending down to pick up his two youngest children.

11

I

Dennis O'Neill didn't like school. This morning, every morning, he went from home across the street to school, afraid. He was afraid of Sister Gloria up there at her desk. He was afraid of the girls on the other side of the big classroom, and he was afraid of some of the boys on his own side near the blackboard. He wished that he was sitting on the other side of the room near the windows, because he could sometimes look out of the window, and he could see home, and maybe see Catherine and Bob and Little Arty and Mama in the back yard. He wished that he didn't have to go to school. If he was littler he wouldn't have to. Like the others at home, except Bill, who were littler than he and didn't have to go to school yet. If he was bigger he wouldn't care because he'd be in one of the grades ahead. Maybe his brother Danny didn't care because he was bigger. Bigger kids acted like they were used to going to school. He wanted to be bigger or he wanted to be littler, but he didn't want to be a kid in the first grade. He didn't really want to be littler. He wanted to be bigger. When you were littler you were picked on. If he was bigger, and Bill was littler, Bill couldn't pick on him. He could pick on Bill. And he should be listening now while they were having catechism.

School was the same every morning, like now. They had come into the room, marching in line, and the first thing they did was say prayers after Sister Gloria. And now it was catechism. Catechism was about God. God made the world. God was bigger and stronger than Papa. Just like Papa could whip them all and beat up Mama and make everybody in the house do what he told them to, so could God do that with everybody in the world. God could lick Papa. He could wrap Papa around His little finger and beat him up. That's what God could do. God was bigger and stronger than Papa. And God never did some of the things that Papa did sometimes. God never got drunk. Catechism was about God and that's what they were having now, and he should listen while they had it. Sister Gloria always told them that every boy and girl should pay attention to the lesson all of the time they were in school. He had come to school every morning now since school started, and they had had catechism every morning, but he didn't know a lot about it. Sister asked questions like she was doing now, and told them the answers, and they had to say it all, and here he was in the back of the room, supposed to be doing that, and he couldn't always keep paying attention like Sister Gloria wanted him to. After they could all read better, and when they got bigger and went into second and third grades, they'd have to study the lessons and learn them themselves, and answer the questions. But now Sister Gloria asked catechism questions and they were all answering. She'd gone back to the first catechism lesson because she said she wanted them to learn it good.

"Dennis O'Neill," Sister Gloria called.

Hearing his name called, he stood up.

"Yes, Sister," he said shyly, the eyes of many of his classmates turned on him, boys and girls of his own age and size, many of them roughly dressed, some not clean, some with torn dresses and ripped waists and coats.

"Who made you?" she asked.

He knew the answer, and he couldn't speak. He told himself that God made him. He blushed, nervously shifted his feet, looked helplessly at the nun.

"Don't you know the answer?"

"Yes, Sister," he said.

She smiled at him, and he noticed her white teeth.

"Tell me the answer, Dennis," she said in a gentle, coaxing voice.

"God made me," he said.

"Good, Dennis. Don't be afraid to answer me when I call on you. I won't bite you," she said.

"Yes, Sister," he said.

"You may sit down now, Dennis," she said.

Relieved, his face red, he sat down.

"Gerald Connerty," she called, using his real name instead of Buddy, his nickname.

Buddy, a chubby boy who looked like his mother, stood up; he was in the seat directly in front of Dennis.

"Why did God make you, Buddy?" she asked.

"No, Sister," Buddy said, and Dennis laughed because of Buddy's answer.

"Gerald, don't you know the answer?" she asked.

"Yes, Sister."

"Gerald, my question is, 'Why did God make you?' I will give you the answer. And all of you children stop looking around the room and listen to what I say. The question is, 'Why did God make you?' The answer is, 'God made me to know Him, to love Him, and to serve Him in this world, and to be happy with Him for ever in the next.' Now, Gerald, you tell me and all of the children here why God made you," she said patiently.

"God made me to go to Heaven," Buddy said.

"Yes, but, Gerald, give me the whole answer I just told to you," she said.

"What answer, Sister?" Buddy said, and Dennis smiled; he knew the answer, and he could give it better than Buddy; he liked to be able to give answers in school better than Buddy could.

"The answer I just gave you. Listen now, Gerald. The question is, 'Why did God make you?' The answer is, 'God made me to know Him, to love Him, and to serve Him in this world, and to be happy with Him for ever in the next.' Gerald, now tell us all why God made you."

"God made me to love Him and be happy with Him in Heaven," Buddy said.

"Listen again, and get the whole answer, and you say it after me. God made me to know Him . . . say that after me, Gerald."

"God made me to know Him," Buddy repeated.

"To love Him."

"To love Him."

"And to serve Him in this world."

"And to serve Him in this world."

"And to be happy with Him for ever in the next."

"And to be happy with Him for ever in the next."

"Now, try not to forget that, Gerald," she said.

"Sister?" Buddy said, raising his hand as he stood in the aisle.

"Yes, Buddy?"

"The next world, that's Heaven, ain't it, Sister?"

"Yes, Buddy."

"I thought so," he said, his face lighting up with sudden understanding.

The catechism lesson went on. Dennis told himself that he should pay attention like Sister Gloria wanted everyone to. She told them they all had to know catechism so they could all make their first Communion next spring. Catechism was first, and then every day they had other lessons. They had reading in the afternoon. He couldn't do a lot of reading yet. Almost none of the kids could. Buddy Connerty couldn't, either. To read you had to know your ABC's, and you had to know words, and how they were spelled. Like his name. He could spell it. He knew most of his ABC's. A B C D E F G H I J K L M N O . . . what next? Let's see. But he ought to wait. It wasn't that lesson now. Sister was talking to the girls, making them answer questions. The girls were smarter than the boys, and Sister said she could teach them easier than she could a lot of the boys. He wanted to know how to read. There was a library in Fuller Park. When he knew how to read he'd go there and get books and read them, and he'd read the funnies in the papers. Maybe when he learned to read better, he'd like to go to school better. He'd like it here in school better if Bill went to school here, but Bill was going to high school now. If he had a big brother in the same school to stick up for him, older kids would be afraid to monkey with him. When he got bigger, he would be the big brother of Bob and Catherine when they went to school.

He wanted to be home now for dinner. And the next lesson was arithmetic after the ten o'clock bell rang. He could add. How much is one and one. One and one makes two. How much is two and one. Two and one makes three. And two and two makes four. And he could count. One, two, three, four, five, six, seven, eight, nine, ten. He could subtract. How much is three less one. Three less one is two. But he should pay attention to the catechism lesson going on. And he didn't like school. And he wished the bell would ring so they could go home to dinner.

II

Dennis was glad it was time to go down to the toilet. He had to pee, and he had begun to be afraid that if the time to go didn't hurry up, he wouldn't be able to hold it. And he had not raised his two fingers to ask to be excused because he knew that it was getting time for them to go. He walked in the double line along the corridor with Buddy Connerty beside him, and Billy Collins and Eddie Mooney behind him. The boys' toilet was just at the end of the hall ahead of them. Sister stood near the middle of the hall, because she had to watch both the boys and the girls, and the boys went to one end and the girls to the other. But she had to watch the boys more because they made more noise than the girls did. As the boys filed into the toilet, they crowded and rushed forward in a jam to get to the urinal stalls. Dennis was toward the end of the line, and he couldn't get there as quickly as those in the front. Nearly everyone began to shove, and push, and yell. Dennis couldn't push much because he could hardly move, he had to pee so badly. After he had, he felt much better. The kids were pushing and shouting. He didn't. Sister didn't want them to, and he was doing what Sister Gloria said he should. Near the window there was a scramble. He liked to make noise, too, but he would do what Sister Gloria said he should do.

"Hey," Buddy Connerty said, coming up to him.

"What?" Dennis answered.

"You ain't got your house painted," Buddy said.

"We don't paint our house," Dennis said.

"My mother and my old man were talking about your family, and I heard my ma say to the old man that if the O'Neill's painted their house outside, the street would look better. And my old man said your old man doesn't own his own house. My old man owns his own house," Buddy said.

"We don't paint our house," said Dennis.

"Hey, Billy," Buddy said to Billy Collins, a dumpy-faced kid.

"What yuh want now?" Billy answered.

"O'Neill's old man don't paint the outside of his house," Buddy said.

"Your old man don't paint the outside of your house?" said Billy.

"No, he don't," said Dennis.

"What's that mean?" asked Billy.

"Know what I just did?" asked Mickey Dolan, a skinny boy taller than the others.

"What yuh done?" asked Buddy.

"I pissed on the floor," said Mickey.

"Sister'll sock you if she knows it," said Buddy.

"You done something else," said Billy.

"What?" asked Mickey.

"Swore," said Billy.

"I can swear, too," said Buddy.

"Let's hear yuh," said Eddie Mooney.

"It's not right to swear. But, say, my old man and old lady swear, too," said Buddy.

"Dare yuh to swear," said Dennis.

"Bastard," said Buddy.

"You got to swear, O'Neill," said Billy.

"No, I don't," said Dennis.

"Go ahead. You're afraid to," said Eddie.

"Then swear," said Billy.

"Bastard," said Dennis.

"Hey, let's all swear," said Eddie.

"Come on, guys," said Billy.

"Bastard," a number of them said.

"Hey, Kenny O'Donnell, does your old man paint his house outside?" asked Billy.

"Huh? Why?"

"I donno," said Billy.

"Hey, guys, Sister says everybody's to come out and get in line," yelled Jackie Smith, the boy Sister Gloria always asked to deliver this message when they went to the toilet.

They rushed out, but once outside and under the nun's eye, they were quiet. They formed in line.

"Hey, if my brother, Albie, was as big as your brother, Bill, he could lick 'im," Buddy said as they began to march back to their classroom.

"No, he couldn't," said Dennis.

"Betcha two buttons," said Buddy.

"I ain't got any buttons," said Dennis.

"Silence," Sister Gloria called firmly.

III

Dennis couldn't wait to get outside of the fenced-in schoolyard. They had to stay in line until they got to the gate. Then they could run. If they ran before that, Sister might punish them.

"The niggers are coming," a big kid whose name Dennis didn't know yelled just as Dennis reached the gate.

Dennis saw lots of kids running toward Wentworth Avenue. Buddy's brother, Albie, ran by him with a rock in his hand.

"The niggers!" Buddy yelled.

Buddy ran. Confused, Dennis followed him. All around him, boys of all ages were running. There was a crowd of kids down near Wentworth Avenue, and they were shouting, cursing, screaming, bawling. He saw white and black boys fighting. A kid in the sixth grade, whom he knew only by the name of Snotty, ran past him, carrying an opened pocketknife, and his stockings kept falling down as he ran.

"Get the black sonofabitches!" a kid yelled just ahead of him. The kid knelt down and aimed a slingshot at a colored boy ahead. Getting closer, Dennis saw the fighting more clearly. A gang of colored and white boys were mixing, some with their fists, some with sticks and stones. He heard all kinds of cries, shouts, and curses.

"Kick 'im in the shins," he heard someone yell loudly.

"You go 'way, white boy, or Ah'll cut your gizzards out," he heard a Negro boy yell.

They were fighting all around him. He was afraid and he didn't know what to do. A white boy in front of him slashed a Negro boy with a knife. He ran a few yards away. He stopped again and stood watching as another Negro boy was cut on the cheek; blood poured from the wound. A screaming black boy ran, chased by three fifth-grade Saint Martha kids. Not even thinking what he was doing, Dennis stuck out his foot. The black boy sprawled on the street, and his pursuers pounced on him.

"Atta boy, O'Neill," Albie Connerty said, running up to Dennis.

A colored boy rushed at them. He and Albie began slugging.

Still bewildered, Dennis stood in the street while there was vicious fighting on all sides of him. A black boy came toward him. He turned and ran off. When he looked around he saw the black boy hit a white one, giving him a bloody nose.

Two others wrestled in front of him and tumbled to the street. The white boy bit the Negro's ear. A colored boy with a stick ran up and smashed the white boy between the shoulders.

The fighting continued, accompanied by screams, shouts, curses, shrieks, cries of pain.

Suddenly a cry arose on many sides.

"Jiggers, the cops!"

The fighting suddenly stopped. The Negro boys ran madly across Wentworth Avenue, and the white boys ran in the opposite direction or across the vacant lot facing the school. Police swarmed out of a patrol wagon. Dennis ran. He bumped into a large red-faced policeman. The cop caught him as he fell.

"Hurry on home, sonny!" the cop said.

Dennis ran away. He saw Father Corbett and the nuns rushing out and people streaming by him from all over the neighborhood. Mama suddenly grabbed him.

"You little pisspot, fighting!" she said, giving him a slap.

"I was only watching," he said.

She grabbed his hand and looked at him.

"Are you hurt?" she asked.

"No," he said, shaking.

"All those niggers carry razors," she said.

"Glory be to God, did you ever see the like of it?" said a stout woman in a dirty apron, coming up to Lizz, holding the hand of a dumpy boy of fourteen.

"Oh, Mrs. Roonan, is your boy hurt?" asked Lizz.

"Naw," the Roonan kid said.

"You keep your trap shut. When himself is home from the stockyards tonight, himself will attend to you, fighting in the streets, bringing the police down on you," Mrs. Roonan said.

"Well, the shines came over here," he said.

"Not a word out of you, you and your hooligans going over to plague them the other day on the other side of the tracks," said Mrs. Roonan.

"I was so afraid my little one here would be hurt. My heart was in my mouth," Lizz said.

"Sure, and isn't it a shame? Poor Mrs. Coakley! Her boy has his wrist cut with a razor," said Mrs. Roonan.

"Did they arrest any of the niggers?" asked Lizz.

"Sure, they are after taking five of them in the paddy wagon, but nary a white lad," said Mrs. Roonan.

"Move on! Break it up!" said a policeman with a brogue; he was followed by several other bluecoats who were pushing back crowds of boys.

"Indeed, and I am," said Mrs. Roonan.

"Sure, move on. We don't want any more throuble," the cop said.

"Officer, what county in Ireland do you come from?" Lizz asked.

"Move on, lady. Sure, it's no time for jawing. We don't want any throuble," said the cop.

"Say, don't tell me to move on! I'm a freeborn woman, and you don't own the sidewalk. If you arrest me, I'll take that star off your coat," said Lizz.

"Move on, lady, please. We don't want any throuble," said the cop.

"Say, why don't you go after the niggers who cut decent white boys with razors, instead of telling a mother of seven children to get off the earth," said Lizz.

"Lady, please go on home," a cop said, coming up to join the one with the brogue.

"I don't need to be ordered. I will. Come home, you, and if I ever catch you fighting again, Denny O'Neill, I'll have your father put the razor strap to you," Lizz said, and she dragged Dennis on toward home.

The cops looked at her as if she were crazy.

"Oh, Mrs. Connerty, are your boys all right?" Lizz asked, meeting her neighbor at the corner just outside the cottage.

"That they are, and my oldest gave some of the black ones some good whalings, he did," said Mrs. Connerty.

"I was so worried for my little one here," said Lizz.

"I tell you, Mrs. O'Neill, those black ones are a plague," said Mrs. Connerty.

"Say, that one living next to me didn't dare show her face when this happened," Lizz said.

"And it's well for her that she didn't," said Mrs. Connerty.

"They're heathens and savages," said Lizz.

"That and worse, Mrs. O'Neill. Well, it's a sad day when the black move into decent neighborhoods where self-respecting white folks live," said Mrs. Connerty.

"A pity," said Lizz.

"I must be getting home to give my family its dinner," said Mrs. Connerty.

"Goodbye, Mrs. Connerty, and I'm so glad your boys didn't get hurt," said Lizz.

"And I'm so glad your little one hasn't any scratches on him," said Mrs. Connerty, walking down toward her house.

"Don't ever let me catch you fighting those niggers again. They got razors, and they'll cut you," Lizz said, taking Dennis by the hand and leading him through the cottage gate and up to the front door.

"Mither! Mither!" Arty exclaimed, running to her as she came in the door.

"Come on, you kids, and eat your dinner," Lizz said, brushing into the house.

12

Lizz looked out the window. It was raining. Dennis ought to be out of school now, and he'd have to run home in the rain. She didn't want him to be catching cold. And because of the rain she had to keep all the children in the house. When they stayed in the house, you'd think a hurricane hit it. The way they could throw paper around and wreck a house. They were house wreckers, that's what they were. Well, it was better to have them in the house and healthy, than not healthy, even if they did throw a little bit of paper on the floor. If they were healthy, that was good enough. She would rather have them healthy and dirty than not healthy. And the young ones had been lucky. Catherine had had the measles, and so had Bob and Dennis, but that's about all they'd had. The last one that had the whooping cough was Catherine. Well, she prayed to God that they wouldn't, any of them, catch anything more. It was trouble enough watching them and taking care of them when they were well, let alone when they were sick. And with winter coming on, it was the time when they would be catching colds and bronchitis. In winter the cold and wind came right through the boards and windows. The two stoves weren't enough to keep them all warm. Well, winter would soon be here. She looked out the window, watching the slanting rain. Behind her on the floor Arty, Catherine, and Bob were playing, scattering paper all over the room.

School was out. She saw girls emerging from the building and running in all directions. The girls were of all ages from about six to thirteen and fourteen, and they ran, laughing, calling to each other, hunching themselves up because of the steady rain. But there were no boys. The Sisters must be keeping the boys after school because of the fight with the niggers. She knew it. That Connerty boy in Denny's room must have gone and told on her Denny, and that was why Denny was being kept in. She knew what the Connertys were like, and, oh, but she'd fix them some day. From the father and the mother to the children, they were all one and the same, cut from the same piece of cloth. She knew the father went and told Father Corbett lying things about her and her family because that Connerty one wanted to turn the priest against the O'Neills, and she had her boys do the same with the Sisters to turn them against Dennis. Oh, but wouldn't she fix that Connerty one some day!

Lizz went to the door and called out to a passing girl.

"Little girl! Little girl!"

A youngster of about nine, in a shabby brown coat, stopped, looked up suspiciously at Lizz standing in the cottage doorway.

"Aren't the boys out of school yet?" Lizz asked.

"No, mam. All the boys in the whole school were kept after school because they fought with the niggers," the little girl said, and then she ran on in the rain.

Lizz closed the door. She would fix that one of hers for disgracing himself before the Sisters and priests and the whole neighborhood, she would.

"Mama, is school out?" Catherine asked.

"Uh huh, it is," Lizz said.

"Where's my brother, Dennis, then?" she asked.

"He was bad and the Sister is keeping him after school for fighting with the niggers," Lizz said.

"Was he fighting the niggers?" said Bob.

"Yes," said Lizz.

"Why?"

"Go on and play and don't bother me. You ask too many questions, the whole shooting match of you," Lizz said impatiently.

"Mither, nidders! Nidders!" Arty said, laughing up at his mother, his big brown eyes shining as he spoke the word he had just learned.

II

Mama was in the kitchen doing something, and little Catherine sat on the couch by the dining-room wall, cutting paper dolls out of old newspapers. Arty sat on the floor near her, with a small stack of old newspapers beside him. He was slowly tearing them up, laughing, gurgling, talking to himself as he threw around scraps of paper, retrieved them, and threw them again. He tore off half of a sheet of paper, crumpled it into a ball, put it in his mouth, looked up shyly at his sister, took the paper out of his mouth, and threw it toward the table by the east wall of the room.

"Bad boy," Catherine said, seeing him do this.

"Bad boy," Arty parroted, looking at Catherine, a wide smile breaking over his pale, dirty face.

He laughed babyishly. He put a scrap of paper in his mouth and watched his sister. She snatched it out. He looked at her in a moment of doubt. His little left hand reached upward for the scrap of paper she had taken out of his mouth. His face became tense with babyish uncertainty. He looked up at his sister, begging with those brown eyes of his. He was suddenly on the verge of tears.

"Bad boy, then take it and eat it," she said, handing him back the paper.

"Bad boy," he said, starting to coo at her.

Catherine continued cutting out dolls, the scraps falling to the floor. Arty stood up and began flinging pieces of paper to all sides. Tearing the scraps up smaller, he tossed these in the air, and stood while they fell, several landing on his curly hair.

"Mama?" Catherine called.

"Mither!" Arty called.

"Yes, my little precious angels," Lizz responded, coming to the doorway which connected dining room and kitchen.

"Arty is bad," Catherine said.

"What's he doing?"

"He tears the paper up and he throws it all over the floor," Catherine said.

"Let him, precious, as long as he doesn't do anything worse," Lizz said.

"But Papa don't want papers all over the carpet when he comes home from work," Catherine said.

"We'll sweep them up before Papa gets home," Lizz said.

"Well, I don't see why Bob has to stay in the parlor drawing all by himself and not watch Arty," said Catherine.

"I ain't doin' nothin', Mama," Bob called from the parlor where he lay on the torn old carpet, drawing pictures with his left hand.

"Your little brother is just a baby. Let him play, and just keep your eye on him so he doesn't hurt himself," Lizz said, casting a smile on her young ones.

"Mither, paper! Paper!" Arty said, pointing to the paper strewn all over the floor.

"Yes, paper," Lizz said.

"Sisser, paper," Arty said, starting to laugh as he ran to her.

"Kiss your baby brother, Catherine," Lizz said.

Catherine kissed Arty on the forehead.

"You baby," Catherine said.

"Baby," Arty said.

"Oh, but he's going to be the smart boy, and the way he's learning to talk. Come to Mama, you angel," Lizz said, stooping and holding her arms out for him.

Arty ran to Lizz. She gathered him up and kissed him. She looked into his big brown eyes.

"Ah, you smart little sugarplum, your mother's beautiful wise old little baby," she said, and she planted a wet kiss on his cheek.

Arty strained in his mother's arms, and she let him down. He ran to the table by the wall, pointed, said:

"Table."

"Yes, table," Lizz said, smiling, and the baby laughed back at his mother, waiting expectantly as he watched her.

"Sisser," he said, pointing to Catherine.

"And where's mither?" Lizz asked.

Arty ran toward his mother, pointing his finger as he ran to her.

"There mither!"

"Ah, you precious angel food cake," Lizz said, kissing him again.

She turned back to the kitchen.

"Mama?" Catherine called.

"What do you want now? Your mother's busy here in the kitchen," Lizz said, reappearing in the kitchen doorway.

"See my dollies?" Catherine said.

"All right, let me see them quick. I'm busy," Lizz said.

Catherine took an awkwardly cut figure from the top of a pile of cutout dolls, and handed it to her mother.

"My, my, but that's pretty!" Lizz said, holding the figure in her hand and gazing at it as if she were meditatively studying it. "Who is it?" Lizz asked.

"That's my Papa," Catherine said.

"Fither," Arty exclaimed, and he laughed.

"It's nice. And it looks like your father, too," Lizz said.

"And here's Mama," Catherine said, handing her mother another cutting that was similar to the previous one, but larger.

"My! My! They're very nice, my precious," Lizz said.

"And here's Arty. See, I cut him out crawling," Catherine said, handing still another to her mother.

"You make more like this, Mama's precious," Lizz said.

"Mama?" Catherine said.

"What now?" Lizz asked.

"I want to go to the pot and make number one," Catherine said.

"You're a big enough girl to do that yourself," Lizz said.

"I want you to put me on the pot to make number one," Catherine said, a childlike imperiousness and insistence in her voice.

"Come on, then, and hurry. Your mother has a lot to do still today," Lizz said.

She led her daughter by the hand to the kitchen. Arty toddled to the stove, and stood looking at it, screwing up his face as he contemplated it.

"Oooh, hot!" he exclaimed, and he continued looking at it with eagerness and curiosity.

"Hey, get away from the stove, you," Bob called from the parlor.

"Ba-Ba," Arty called, running to his brother.

III

Googooing, Arty ran from the parlor straight to the couch by the dining-room wall. He stood against it, uttering wordless syllables. He turned around and dug into the pile of old newspapers on the floor.

"Fither!" he exclaimed, and held a crumpled sheet of paper in his hand, as if reading it as his father did at night.

He threw the paper on the floor. He stood looking at it. He fell down onto the floor and sat laughing. His eyes wandered around the room.

"Table," he exclaimed, his roving eyes catching the table.

He flung a crumpled scrap of paper away and crawled to it on the dirty carpet, a distance of three feet. He picked up the paper he had just thrown and put it in his mouth, holding it there with his right hand. He took it out, and clutched it tightly. He laughed, a sunny, happy baby laugh. He laughed as he did when one of his parents or brothers was watching him play. He played with his paper. He stopped every so often to look around with the same expression as when he was being watched and would suddenly turn on his spectators to laugh and hear them say something to him. He crawled into the stack of papers and lay with his face down on them.

"Where Arty?" he said aloud.

He gazed around the room expressively. He again put his head down in the papers.

"Nobody see Arty," he said, and he lay very still for several seconds. He sat up and began tearing paper again. He got to his feet, half toddled and half ran to the couch, grabbed his sister's paper dolls, and began tearing them up.

"Sisser," he exclaimed as he continued tearing up the figures Catherine had just cut.

IV

"You bad boy!" Catherine shouted at her brother as she returned to the dining room and saw what he was doing to her paper dolls.

Arty looked blankly at his sister. He smiled sunnily and exclaimed:

"Sisser!"

He held up to her a scrap of paper from one of her torn dolls. She pulled it out of his hand and slapped him. Arty broke into tears. Rubbing his eyes with one hand, he stood crying, reaching for the torn paper with the other.

"Bad boy!" she yelled.

He bawled. She slapped him again. He yelled. Lizz rushed into the room and found Catherine slapping Arty, both children screaming.

"Stop hitting your little brother, you dirty thing," Lizz shouted, pulling Catherine away and slapping her in the mouth.

Arty sat on the floor, continuing to bawl. Lizz slapped Catherine again. The little girl whimpered, drew away from her mother, let out a long and plaintive cry. Bob stood by the stove between the parlor and dining room, pale, watching the spectacle.

"You little pisspot, you ought to be ashamed of yourself, hitting your little baby brother," Lizz shrieked at her daughter.

"Well, he tore up my pretty dollies," Catherine sobbed.

Arty continued to bawl. He crawled to his mother and pulled at her dress.

"You shouldn't hit him, even if he did," Lizz said loudly.

"He don't have to tear my dollies," Catherine said sulkily.

"Oh, you children will be the death of your poor sick mother," Lizz said, sighing, looking down at the little baby at her feet, then at the sulky, sobbing daughter on the couch.

She picked up Arty, sat down with him on the couch, kissed and caressed him. He stopped crying.

"You always stick up for him against me," Catherine pouted.

"He's a baby and you're growing up into a big girl. You got to take care of your brother and not be hitting him," Lizz said.

"I don't care. He tore up the pretty dollies I cut out to show Papa," Catherine protested.

Lizz set Arty down on the floor and handed him a torn piece of newspaper. Arty looked at it with curiosity. He went into the pile of papers and began scattering them.

"You can cut out some more of them, and watch your little brother in here," Lizz said.

"I don't care. I wanted my paper dollies for Papa," Catherine said.

"You got time to make more before he gets home from work," Lizz said.

"Mither! Mither!" Arty said, pulling at his mother's dress.

She looked down and saw him offering her a handful of paper scraps. She bent down and accepted them.

"Mama's precious gave her a present, you darling boy, you pretty angel," Lizz said, smiling, her decayed teeth showing.

She kissed Arty. She stood up again, and Arty sat watching her.

"He only gave you torn papers," said Catherine jealously.

"You go cut your dolls and tend your own business, my smart lady," Lizz said to her.

Catherine didn't answer. She cast a sullen, sulky expression at her mother. Lizz went back to the kitchen. Catherine glared at Arty.

"Copy cat! Copy cat! Copy cat!" she said, sticking out her tongue.

"Dollies," Arty exclaimed, holding up a piece of paper.

He went into the papers again, tearing them up, sticking scraps in his mouth, chewing them, throwing them around the room, talking to himself, sometimes articulating words, sometimes syllables which had meaning only for himself. Catherine started all over again to cut out paper dolls.

V

"You got kept after school," Bob said when Dennis came home.

"They kept us all for fighting niggers," Dennis said.

"Were you fighting niggers?"

"You bet I was," said Dennis proudly.

"Say, you, it's about time you came home from school," Lizz yelled at Dennis.

"Sister kept in all the kids. The boys in every grade in the school had to stay in after school because they were fighting niggers," Dennis said.

"It's a scandal. You ought to be whipped," Lizz said.

"I couldn't help it," he said.

"I bet the Sisters didn't keep those dirty Connerty boys after school," Lizz said.

"Yes, they were kept, too. All the boys in school," Dennis said.

"You listen to me. I'm your mother, and you listen to me. You keep away from those niggers. They'll just as soon slash your throat with a razor as look at you," Lizz said.

"We licked 'em," Dennis said.

"You shut up. You keep away from the niggers. Your father can't be affording bills to bury you if you get killed," Lizz said.

"Sister says anybody caught fighting 'em again gets put out of school. And they got cops at school now. They're right in front of school," Dennis said.

"You stay away from the cops, too," said Lizz.

"I couldn't help it, Ma," Dennis said.

"Don't be giving me lip. You stay away. And don't let me see you with those Connertys. They're bad actors, and I don't want you going with them," said Lizz.

"Ma, you know what Buddy Connerty said to me today?" Dennis said.

"What?" Lizz asked explosively.

"He said my father don't paint our house outside. He said his father said that," Dennis said.

"Jesus Mary and Joseph!" Lizz said, striding across the room frowning angrily and making belligerent gestures.

"Yes, Ma, he said that. And he said that my father didn't own his own house like his father did," Dennis said.

"The next time he says anything to you, you tell him that your mother is going to spit in his mother's eye when she sees her, and that your father will make mincemeat of his father," Lizz said.

All the children, including Arty, looked curiously and a little fearfully at their mother. She walked back and forth across the dining room.

"God will forgive me if I take a stove poker to that fat cow!" Lizz said.

"Ma, who's a cow?" asked Bob.

"Buddy Connerty's mother. Oh, but wait till I see her, wearing her green underskirt and calling herself dressed up! Oh, but wait until I lay my tongue on her! Oh, Blessed Mary, give me the words to make her crawl on the sidewalk before me like a worm! Give me the strength to give her the trimming she's got coming to her! Dennis, what else did Buddy Connerty say?"

"He said his father and mother said the neighborhood would look better if we painted our house," Dennis answered.

"Sanctified Mother of Jesus! He said that! The crust of those Connertys! Oh, wait until I lay eyes on that one again! Just wait! And wait until my own mother hears what those ones are saying about her daughter!" Lizz exclaimed.

She went to the side window as if to see if Mrs. Connerty were passing outside. The street was deserted, and the rain beat down on it steadily and dismally. She again paced back and forth, watched by her silent children.

"When your father comes home tonight, he doesn't sit down to a bite to eat until he goes in there and drags that man of hers out and wipes the street with him. The low shanty Irish with their lace curtains on the windows! She and her gadding about in a getup to have tea with shanty Irish relatives of booze fighters! Sacred Heart of Mercy! Denny, if that Buddy Connerty ever talks against your mother to you again, poke your finger in his eyes."

There was a rapping at the door.

"That must be the insurance man. Tell him I'm not in," said Lizz.

She went to the kitchen. Dennis went to the door, and Arty toddled after him.

"Your mother in? I'm the insurance man," a tall, fat-faced man asked.

"No, she's not in," Dennis answered.

"Mither say not in," Arty said, the longest sentence he had ever uttered.

"I want to see your mother. She's 'way behind in her policies," the man said.

"She's not in," Dennis said.

"Well, I don't believe you, but tell her if she doesn't want to lose these policies, I'll be back the day after tomorrow and she better pay something on them," the man said, and turned away from the door.

Dennis closed the door.

"What did you let the baby give me away for?" Lizz asked Dennis.

"I couldn't help it," said Dennis.

"Mercy of God on me, but I don't know what nuthouse I'll end up in with you kids and the insurance collectors and that cow of a Connerty woman. God have mercy on me!" Lizz said, raising her hands toward the ceiling.

They watched her, silent and puzzled.

"Get me the clock in the front bedroom, Dennis," she said.

Dennis ran for the clock. She took it from him, looked at it.

"Twenty minutes after four and Bill isn't home to go to the store for me. Jesus have mercy on me!" she exclaimed.

"Tick-tick," Arty exclaimed, pointing at the clock.

"You children play now and be quiet. Catherine, don't let the baby hurt himself," Lizz said, and she went back to the kitchen.

VI

Arty was again at papers in the dining room, and Catherine hummed to herself as she cut out paper dolls. Bob and Dennis were in the parlor.

"What did you do when you fought the niggers?" Bob asked.

"We fought 'em," said Dennis.

"You hit 'em?" asked Bob.

"Sure we did," said Dennis.

"What else did you do?"

"I'll show you," Dennis said.

"It won't hurt?" asked Bob suspiciously.

"No," said Dennis.

"Well, what?"

"You run by me here," said Dennis.

"Why?"

"You want me to show you, doncha?"

"Uh huh!"

"Well, just run by me here. Get over there by the stove and run by me," said Dennis.

Bob went back by the stove and ran forward. Dennis put out his foot. Bob was spilled on the floor, landing on his face. He cried.

"That's a dirty trick," he said, getting up, still crying.

Dennis laughed. Bob went out to the kitchen, crying and rubbing his eyes with his sleeve.

"Ma, Denny tripped me and hurt me," he said to his mother.

"Shut up and stop bawling," Lizz said.

"He tripped me," Bob sobbed.

Lizz glared at him and grabbed the stove poker. Bob dodged past her and got between the kitchen stove and the wall. Lizz was too fat to get in at him.

"Get out of there, you shyster!"

"Well, I didn't do nothing," said Bob.

"Get out of there and let me get at you, falling and crying like a bunch of pisspots!" Lizz screamed.

Bob didn't answer. He stood there, alert and watchful. His mother shook the poker at him.

"Come here to me or I'll lay the poker over your head!"

"I didn't do nothing. It was Denny," Bob said.

"Get the hell out of here and stop bothering me so I can do some work around this dirty kitchen. If any more of you come crying to me, I'll split your heads with the poker. Get out of here before I lose my patience," Lizz yelled at him.

Bob ran out of the kitchen. She sighed, and went to the dirty dishes in the sink.

13

Danny and Bill lay on the parlor floor of the cottage, the soles of their feet touching the wallpaper right under the front window. They had a clear aim at the back wall in the dining room and they were shooting at a tin plate which they had placed on the couch by that wall. The little kids were out playing in the back yard, and Mama was in the kitchen. Danny and Bill were pretending that they were with the American Army in Mexico, fighting the Mexicans. They were somewhere in a desert, and the army was advancing, to go all the way to Mexico City, and then the Mexicans would all be conquered. They were a company of American infantry, but they were outnumbered five to one by greaser soldiers and bandits. They were being attacked and fighting for their lives, and if they were beaten it would be bad for the whole American Army. And if they were captured, they'd be tortured, because Mexicans were bandits, and they weren't civilized, and they'd torture American soldiers. Danny cocked his BB gun and pulled the trigger. He didn't hit the pan. Every time the pan was hit, they pretended a Mexican was killed. Bill shot. They heard the resounding note as the BB smacked the tin.

"One less greaser. Another Mexican hit the dust, Dan," Bill said, smiling.

"Yeah, but you're not supposed to call me Dan. I'm Buck," said Danny.

"That's right, Buck," Bill said.

"Now watch them, Snake. They're creeping along on the desert, and there's some of the greasers behind that mound of sand there. Watch out for 'em. Tricky bastards, they are," Danny said.

They pumped BB's into the wall without a hit.

"We're losing our aim. Better shoot straight, watch 'em close. Can't waste our ammunition, Buck," Bill said.

"We got to hold out. I hope Crabeye Pete got through to the colonel and brings us reinforcements and more bullets," said Dan.

"The Crabeye always gets through. He'll save us. We got to stick here and watch 'em close, and when you shoot, Buck, shoot straight," said Bill.

Bill looked through the sight on his gun, aimed very carefully, held his gun steadily and pulled the trigger. They heard the resounding ring of the BB's striking the target.

"That dirty Mexican'll never kill another American soldier, Buck," Bill said.

"That's the way to shoot, Snake," said Danny, wishing that he could do as well as Bill.

Danny looked carefully through the sight on his gun. He tried to make himself hold his gun unwaveringly. He aimed. He had it this time. His hands wavered and he lost the target. He aimed again. While he tried to get his aim straight, Bill made another hit. Four for Bill. None for him. Danny quickly pulled the trigger, hoping for a chance hit. He missed.

"I got four notches more in my belt now, Buck. You got to get your aim. You ain't shootin' like you did when we was in the Philippines, fighting them damn greasy Filipinos," Bill said.

Danny aimed.

"That's the stuff, Buck," said Bill, hearing Danny's next shot resound against the target.

"That greaser's dead as a doornail. I hit him square," said Danny proudly.

He sat up, his pocketful of BB's rattling. Bill grabbed his arm.

"Those bastards are all around, Buck, and they play music with their Mausers, if they get a shot at you. Lay low there, Buck," Bill said.

Danny ducked down and stretched out on the dirty carpet again. He aimed and missed another shot. Bill and he kept on shooting steadily. There were two more hits, making seven in all. Danny's mind was full of a vision of Mexico. He had seen things about Mexico in the movies, and pictures in the papers and in a copy of the *National Geographic* magazine that Uncle Al often bought. He imagined a desert all around him, full of Mexicans with big hats, greasy, cruel faces and mustaches, and himself with this small company of American soldiers in khaki that had to fight against odds like Custer for Uncle Sam and Old Glory that had never fallen in defeat. He liked this game; he aimed again, hitting the pan for the second time. If he shot the BB gun long enough, he'd learn how to aim and shoot. But he couldn't shoot as well as Bill. He couldn't do anything, it seemed, as well as Bill could. They shot. Bill was shooting a lot of Mexicans in this game. Another one for him.

"I hope the rescuers come before it gets dark. We'll have a hell of a time at night here, Buck, in the desert with greasers all around us," Bill said as they reloaded their guns.

Lying on the carpet and again shooting, Danny seemed to freeze with fright. He was not Danny O'Neill in Mama's house, shooting BB's into the wall, and trying to hit a tin plate. He was an American soldier in the Mexican sands, and the afternoon was passing, and he and the soldiers with him were fighting for their lives, and if reinforcements didn't come by night, they might all be massacred like Custer's soldiers in Custer's Last Stand. But if a soldier died for his country, he wouldn't go to Hell. He'd been told that in a catechism lesson. That was martyrdom. He shot, trembling. He was going to be killed by the Mexicans.

Bill yawned and suddenly stood up.

"Hey, they'll get you," Danny said.

"I'm tired of this. I done enough of it. Let's quit. It's more fun shootin' pigeons with the guns," Bill said.

Danny relaxed from his fright and got up.

"But say, Dan, it would be fun, wouldn't it, if it was real instead of playing like we done," said Bill.

"Gee, wouldn't it?" said Danny.

"Well, maybe we'll go to war to fight the Germans or the French in this war in Europe, and I'll be big enough to go," Bill said.

"But you might get killed," said Danny.

"I'm always lucky," said Bill.

Danny sat down on the couch, holding his BB gun between his legs.

"You know, Dan, this is good practice. I never thought about it before, but this gives me an eye, and the next time there's a fight with the niggers I'll drag this out if I'm around. It'll be handy, and the target practice don't hurt me none," said Bill.

"And maybe if I'm here, I'll have my gun and shoot the niggers, too," said Danny.

"There was a fight this week. Our kid brother Denny was in it, and Mama raised hell, and so did Pa. Pa said for him not to be starting that way or he'd kick hell out of him," said Bill.

"But we might knock their eyes out with BB's," said Danny.

"They all carry razors. If they got a white kid alone in a dark alley in their neighborhood, think they'd care if they slit his throat? Remember the time when we was still living down at Twenty-fifth and La Salle, and we was going to Mother's, and walked over to take the el at Twenty-sixth Street? The gang of nigger kids tried to get you just as you was walking up the elevated steps after me," Bill said.

"And the nigger kid that grabbed me, he grabbed my wrist and told me to come along with him," said Danny.

"Anything might've happened to us, only for that white telephone man standing there that told them to cut it out," said Bill.

"That was a close shave," said Danny.

"None of the kids around here think much of the niggers. They say a nigger ain't like he was part of the human race. That's why they always go over and fight them by the viaduct. But now they aren't fighting them. There's lots of cops in the neighborhood because of the fight with the Saint Martha kids. But there's gonna be more fights, don't worry," Bill said.

"Jesus Mary and Joseph!" Lizz suddenly exclaimed from the dining room.

"What's the matter, Mama?" Danny asked, surprised both by her sudden exclamation and the tone of voice in which she had uttered it.

They saw their mother examining the wall against which they had just been shooting.

"We shouldn't have shot in the wall," said Danny.

"Mama'll get over it. She goes up in the air and then gets over it," Bill said.

"What were you two doing?"

"We were playing with our BB guns," said Danny.

"We didn't think we were doin' anything wrong," Bill said.

"Look at what you did to the wall. You shot it all over, and the wallpaper was bad enough without your having to rip it worse," Lizz said.

"Gee, I didn't think of that, did you, Dan?" Bill said.

"Me, no," said Danny earnestly.

Carrying their guns, they went to examine the wall. They saw that BB's were lodged in the wall quite thickly near the pan, and that the wallpaper was torn in many spots.

"I don't care so much. It ain't my house. But maybe your father won't like it. He takes a pride in his home, your father does," Lizz said.

"Gee, we didn't think we were doing anything wrong, did we, Bill?" Danny said.

"No! You know, Ma, it just never came to us that we'd hurt the wall," Bill said.

"Well, I'll tell Pa I just made you stay in and play, because I didn't want you gettin' into trouble on the street with your guns for fear a cop would grab you," said Lizz.

They examined the dented wall with continued amazement.

"These guns got power, ain't they?" Bill exclaimed.

"They'll hurt if they hit you," said Danny.

"You be careful with them guns. They'll put somebody's eye out if you ain't," said Lizz.

They still looked amazed at what they had done to the wall.

"Come out and have a sandwich before you go to the ball game. It was nice of your uncle to send you the money for it, too," Lizz said, going back to the kitchen. They followed her.

II

"The Cubs got the Sox going, two games to one," said Bill as he and Danny sat at the kitchen table with raisin-bread cheese sandwiches and cups of tea before them, the tea whitened by thick, condensed milk.

"The Sox'll even it up today," said Danny.

"We'll see about that. And the Braves are three to nothing. Nobody but a real National League fan ever expected that," said Bill.

"The Athletics might come back," said Danny.

"Bushwah," said Bill.

"Son, why didn't you bring your little sister Margaret down with you?" asked Lizz.

"Aunty Margaret was home this morning, and Little Margaret wanted to stay with her," said Danny.

"She did? Why? What's your aunt saying to her to turn her against your mother?" asked Lizz.

"Nothing. Little Margaret wanted to stay, and Aunty Margaret said she didn't trust me taking her on the street car," said Danny.

"She did, did she?" Lizz said, frowning.

"But, Ma, if Dan's going to stay all night, there wouldn't be room for her to stay, too, would there?" Bill said.

"There's always room in my house for my children," Lizz said.

"Little Margaret likes school, she says," said Danny.

"Girls always like school better than guys do," said Bill.

"I don't see why they didn't send her to the Sisters' school," Lizz said.

"They were afraid that it was too far and would be too far for her to go in winter when it's cold. They said next year when she's bigger they would," said Danny.

Lizz poured herself a cup of tea and sat down at the table with her two boys.

"Your father would have liked it if your sister was here tonight, too. He gets paid and he's bringing home a nice supper," Lizz said.

The three of them sat at the table in silence. Lizz looked at her boys, her eyes going from one face to the other and back again.

"Your aunt ain't drinking again then, is she, Son?" Lizz asked Danny, and Danny shook his head negatively from side to side.

Again there was silence.

"Where's Uncle Al now?" asked Lizz.

"I don't know. He's away, but I don't know where."

"They didn't tell you not to tell me where he is, did they?" she asked, watching his face closely as she spoke.

"No. I don't know, Mama," said Danny.

"When you go home, if I call you up, will you find out and tell me, and not tell your grandmother and aunt?" asked Lizz.

"No, I won't tell them," Danny said.

"I want to write and ask him to help me. Those ones up there guard him and won't let him give me anything," Lizz said.

Again there was silence. Lizz saw that they had finished their tea and sandwiches.

"Here, let me get you more," she said, getting up.

"We'll have to be going soon," Danny said while their mother was making them more sandwiches.

"Yeah. But we'll get seats, all right," said Bill.

"Gee, I'm sorry the season's over," said Danny.

"Next year's another year, and the Cubs'll cop it," said Bill.

They sat waiting for the food. Lizz served them, and again sat down to her tea. Bill and Danny poured several full spoons of condensed milk into the tea.

"What time will you boys be home?" asked Lizz.

"We'll be home early. The game starts earlier than in summer," said Bill.

"Be home before your father is here," said Lizz, taking a sip of tea.

"We will," they said together.

"If you get back in time, I want to run across the street to confession this afternoon," Lizz said.

"We'll try, Ma," said Bill.

After finishing, they got up in silence.

"We're going to go now," Bill said.

"Kiss your mother goodbye," she said.

They both kissed her casually and left, happy at the prospect of seeing the city series game between the Cubs and White Sox.

14

I

It was Saturday. There was no school on Saturday, and all the kids liked Saturday because there wasn't. On Friday, kids would tell each other that to-morrow was Saturday and they'd all be glad about it. They liked that because they could play all day. His brother Danny had come down to see them, and was going to stay all night. Bill and Danny had gone to the baseball game. Uncle Al took care of Danny, and Danny wore clean waists, and Mama always said that her son Daniel had the best of care at the O'Flaherty's. Dennis wanted to go to the ball game with them, but they wouldn't take him. It was no fun having big brothers. It was only fun having little brothers. You could tell them what to do, and if they didn't do it, give them a sock or a kick in the pants and make them do it. You could treat your little brothers the way your big brothers treated you. Dennis and Bob left the yard to go out. Arty followed them, but they shagged him back.

"Go on, get back. You're too small," Dennis said to Arty.

"Arty go bye-bye," Arty yelled, following them through the front gate.

Dennis got sore. He told Catherine to take care of Arty and keep him from following them.

They led Arty by the hand back into the yard.

"Take Arty bye-bye," Arty exclaimed.

"Where you going?" Catherine asked them while sitting in the dirt in the yard and digging with an old fork.

"Mind your own business," Dennis said, acting important.

"I'll tell Papa," said Catherine.

"Go ahead and see what you get," Dennis said to her, thinking she was just a little tattletale anyway.

They left, went over to Wentworth Avenue, and walked along it. Dennis liked to do this, to go away from home and the yard, and walk and play around the neighborhood.

"Denny, buy some candy," Bob said, tagging along beside him.

"I ain't got no money," Dennis said.

"I want some candy," Bob said.

"So do I," Dennis said.

Walking along, they saw all different kinds of people on Wentworth Avenue, and there were lots of stores. Bill went to the store for Mama. Dennis did too, sometimes, but not so much. He didn't like to be made to go to the store. When he got bigger, he'd be made go to the store a lot. Bill went down to the store at Twenty-fifth Street twice a week and came back with a box of groceries. He brought home animal crackers. Catherine always got a box of animal crackers for herself. If Bill got only one box of animal crackers, she took them and hid them, and wouldn't give any to anybody.

"Look, Denny," Bob said, running to a bakery window.

They looked at a luscious chocolate cake in the window, and then at a cocoanut cake beside it. Near the cakes were charlotte russes and sugar buns. Their eyes roved back and forth and then were fastened on cupcakes, rich with vanilla and chocolate frosting.

"Gee!" Bob wistfully exclaimed.

"When I'm a man, I'll be rich and buy windows full of cakes like that every day," Dennis said.

With wanting eyes still riveted on the contents of the window, they stood there. Bob suddenly looked up at Dennis.

"Will I get some of 'em?" he asked.

"Maybe I'll give you some, and maybe I won't," Dennis said.

Bob's face grew sad. He gazed at his bigger brother, his eyes seeming almost to expand. He could say nothing. He could do nothing but look up sadly.

"Yes, maybe I will. And maybe I won't. It depends on what you do."

"What?" Bob asked hopefully.

"I'll see. If you do what I want, when I grow up and become rich and buy cakes every day maybe I'll give you some," Dennis said.

"I will," said Bob.

"Promise," Dennis commanded.

"Uh huh!"

"You'll do anything I tell you to?" asked Dennis.

Bob shook his head up and down.

"You'll do anything I say?" Dennis asked.

"Honest, I will," Bob said, meaning it.

"Now, don't forget. You promised me. Once you don't, you're gonna be out of luck. You get that?"

"What you want?" Bob asked.

"Come on, let's get a move on," Dennis said, turning from the window and grabbing Bob's arm.

Bob pulled back. Dennis walked on a few feet, turned around, and noticed Bob still gazing into the bakery window.

"Hey, you said you'd do what I said," Dennis said curtly.

"Yeah," Bob said, turning from the window.

"I told you to come on," Dennis said.

"Yes," Bob said.

"Well, come on," Dennis said.

Bob followed his brother along the sidewalk.

"Whenever I tell you to do something, you gotta do it. Don't look in windows," Dennis said.

II

"Let's play I'm Papa," Dennis said.

"And whom am I? Bill?" asked Bob.

"No, you're my horse," Dennis said.

"What do I do?" asked Bob.

"I'm driving you and you pull my wagon. When I say giddyap, you run. When I say whoa, you stop," Dennis said.

"Then if I do, can we play I'm Papa and you're my horse?" Bob asked.

"You're the horse, and you gotta do what I tell you to do. I'm Papa. You say I'm Papa," Dennis said.

"I'm Papa," Bob said obediently.

"You ain't. I'm Papa. Tell me I'm Papa," Dennis said.

"You're Papa."

"And who are you?"

"I'm your horse."

"Who am I?" asked Dennis.

"Papa."

"Who are you?"

"You're Papa's horse," said Bob.

"Who's Papa's horse?" Dennis quickly asked.

"I'm Papa's horse."

"You said I was. Don't do it again. Now, who are you?"

"I'm Papa's horse."

"All right, get ahead of me and stand there," said Dennis.

Bob obeyed.

"Giddyap!" Dennis called.

Bob ran and Dennis ran behind him, pretending he was holding a driver's reins and that he was using a whip every few feet. He was Papa on the seat of an express wagon, and he was driving it just like a man, just like Papa.

"Whoa!" Dennis yelled.

Bob halted.

"Now, let's play something else," Bob said.

"Shut up! You're a horse. Horses can't talk," Dennis said.

Bob stood facing his brother, waiting for him to say something.

"Turn around and wait like you was a horse," Dennis said.

Bob obeyed. Dennis pretended that he was delivering a package. He ran up to a dry-goods-store window, stood there a minute, looking into the window but not observing the miscellaneous contents. He turned around, came back to where he pretended the express wagon was and went through the motions of climbing up onto the seat. There he was now, seated on the seat, snapping his whip, just like Papa would do.

"Giddyap!" he called.

Bob ran. Dennis, older and with longer legs, kept right behind him, egging him on, slapping his buttocks as Bob zigzagged in and out and around the groups of people walking along.

"Run straight!" Dennis commanded.

Bob tried to run straight, except when he had to dodge around somebody.

"Giddyap!"

Bob tried to run faster, still trailed by his brother.

"Whoa!"

Bob ran on over four sidewalk squares.

"Whoa!" Dennis said angrily.

"I'm stopping to play I'm going into a saloon to get a glass of beer. A horse just waits, stands still. Don't you move a speck, now," Dennis said.

Bob stood in the center of the dusty sidewalk. Dennis went over close to the dirty window of an unlet store with iron fronting below the window. He made believe he was in a saloon, and went through the motions of drinking a glass of beer. He stood there and pretended he was drinking another and talking with a man beside him.

"Denny," Bob called.

"Shut up. Horses don't talk."

Dennis pretended to finish his glass of beer. Then he pretended to wipe his lips. He ran a few steps and imagined again that he was climbing up onto the wagon.

"Giddyap!"

Bob ran along the sidewalk. Dennis followed, slapping Bob's buttocks continually.

III

"You can't do this," Dennis said, and he showed what he meant by holding air in his mouth until his cheeks were blown and puffed out; then he let the air out, making a slight blowing noise.

"Do it again," Bob said.

Dennis did, deliberately making more noise as he let out his breath this time.

"I can too do it," Bob said.

"You can't, either," Dennis said.

"I can too."

Bob imitated Dennis.

"There," he said.

"That wasn't right," Dennis said.

"It was too."

"Was not."

"Why?" asked Bob.

"Don't ask me questions all the time. It wasn't what I did, because you're too young and don't know how it was," Dennis said.

"I'll show you," Bob said.

"Go ahead," Dennis said.

Bob repeated, imitating Dennis more obviously, making more noise with the emission of air.

"I told you you couldn't do it," Dennis said.

"I did too do it," Bob said.

"When you're old enough to go to school and fight niggers, you won't be so dumb like you are now," Dennis said.

"I ain't that."

"What?"

"Dumb."

"You are."

"I'm not."

"You can't catch me," said Dennis.

"You got longer legs than I got," said Bob.

"Catch me. Dare you," Dennis said.

"I can't. I ain't got long legs like you got."

"Try it and see if you can," Dennis said.

He and Bob stood facing each other for a moment. Dennis dodged beside Bob and ran about six yards away. Bob looked at him. Dennis faced Bob, jumping up and down, ready to dodge and spring away again if Bob came after him.

"Come on, you baby, catch me," Dennis challenged.

"Catch me," Bob said, suddenly running in the opposite direction, pumping his legs as he ran, trying to make himself go as fast as he could, determined not to be caught. Bob lost his balance. He staggered. Just as he did, Dennis came upon him with a shriek. Bob fell. He started to bawl.

"Aw, what's the matter now?" Dennis asked.

Bob still bawled.

"What yuh cryin' for, yuh baby? You ain't hurt," Dennis said, standing over Bob.

"I ain't cryin'," Bob sobbed.

"You're bawling like you was Arty," Dennis said.

Holding his hand to his right knee, and still crying, Bob got up.

"If you fell and hurt your knee, you'd cry, too. I seen you cry when you fell down," Bob said, the tears streaming down his dirty face.

"You're a liar," Dennis said.

Bob looked at his knee. His black stocking was torn and the flesh was bruised, with blood and dirt in the cut.

"Come on. The next time you'll know better not to fall down," Dennis said, walking ahead.

Bob sniffled, wiped his eyes, and walked on after Dennis.

IV

"Where we going?" Bob asked, walking northward along Wentworth Avenue with Dennis.

"This way," Dennis said.

"Why?"

"If we're gonna walk, we got to go some way," Dennis said.

"Why don't we walk that way?" Bob asked, turning to point his left arm in the other direction.

"Because we're walking this way," Dennis answered.

They walked along without talking. Wentworth Avenue was filled with a Saturday afternoon crowd. The green-painted street cars clanged by, and there was a steady flow of horse-drawn vehicles and automobiles. Dennis and Bob wove zigzag through workingmen going to the stores or standing in front of and emerging from saloons, drunken men, kids like themselves, girls with doll buggies and real baby buggies, women marketing, fat women, women in shabby clothes carrying bundles, carrying babies, dragging along young children who were just able to walk, women standing on street corners gossiping, old peasant mothers and grandmothers with shawls covering their gray heads. A drunk almost fell in front of them. Dennis began staggering, and Bob imitated him, Dennis' actions a burlesque of the drunken man's, Bob's a burlesque of Dennis'.

"Hey, you!" a man called, running out of a store.

The two boys stopped and gaped at a fat man in a dirty white apron, thinking he was talking to someone else. He walked over to them.

Bob drew back several paces.

"Your mother owes me a dollar and forty-three cents," the man said in self-righteous anger.

Both boys looked at the man.

"I want my money from your mother," the man said, and passers-by stopped to watch him. He began waving his arms and talking to strangers. "She sends this one and I give her credit. She never pays me."

"Now you said a mouthful, Smitty," a young fellow in the crowd said.

"That's not honest. I give credit, I don't get my money. How am I going to run my business?" the storekeeper asked.

"Are you going to wait on me or not?" a stout woman in a frayed brown over-coat said, coming up to the man.

"Huh?" he asked, and the crowd laughed.

Dennis and Bob stood in the center of the group, bewildered, a lost look on their faces.

"His mother sends him to get credit. They owe me a dollar forty-three for two months. I want my money," he said.

The woman in the brown coat folded her arms and frowned at him.

"Look!" she said, taking a crumpled dollar bill out of a small pocketbook. "Do you want to wait on me, or do you want to yell at little babies?"

"Yes, Mrs. Black. I wanted to ask this boy for my dollar and forty-three cents. Ah, these Irish," he said. He turned to Dennis. "Tell your mama to pay me or I'll get the police after you."

"Hey, get a soapbox," a wit in the crowd said, drawing laughter.

"Come, Mrs. Black. You're good, you pay your bills," the man said, going back to his store.

Dennis slipped through the crowd, and Bob followed him.

"What was the matter?"

"Mama owes him money," said Dennis.

"Will he arrest us?" asked Bob.

"I'm gonna get Papa after him," Dennis said.

"Can Papa lick him?"

"Papa can lick everybody but God," Dennis said.

"Why can he?"

"Don't ask me questions," said Dennis.

Dennis held his right foot in his hand, and hopped. Bob did also and lost his balance. He fell down. He jumped up. He followed Dennis. He strolled over to a dry-goods-store window. Dennis followed him.

"You don't want to look in here," Dennis said, standing beside Bob while Bob continued to stare at the array of cheap goods, yards and bolts of bright calico and other stuff, handkerchiefs, baby things, overalls, blue and black men's shirts, pins and needles, buttons, hooks and eyes, lacy stuff of various sorts, all of it crowded into the window.

"I wanna look at it," said Bob.

"That's funny. There ain't nothin' in it you can eat," said Dennis.

"I can look at it, can't I?" Bob asked, screwing up his face.

"Sure. But I won't. I'm goin'. I ain't lookin' at windows unless I can eat something or see toys," Dennis said, moving on.

Bob still stared in the window. He turned away and saw Dennis ahead.

"Denny?" he called.

Dennis strolled on.

"Denny?" Bob called.

"Hurry up!" Dennis yelled back, his voice shrill, its echo suddenly drowned out by the rumbling of a passing street car.

"I'm coming," Bob called.

"Did you get your eyes full?" Dennis asked.

"I wanted to look at the window," Bob said.

"What'd you see?"

"Things," said Bob.

"What things?"

"Lots of things," said Bob.

"Funny. Lookin' at a window like that," Dennis said.

"I was lookin'," Bob said.

"Why?" Dennis asked.

"I was lookin' at pins and needles. Denny, what would happen if Arty swallowed all the pins and needles in the window?"

"He would if he got a hold of 'em. Arty'd swallow anything if he could," Dennis said.

"He's goofy," said Bob.

"You used to swallow, too," said Dennis.

"I didn't," said Bob.

"Oh, you bet your boots you did," said Dennis.

"Denny?" Bob said.

"What do yuh want now?"

"What would happen if Arty swallowed all the pins and needles I saw in the window?"

Denny didn't answer. He put his feet together and jumped, landing within one of the sidewalk squares.

"What'd happen?"

"He'd die," Dennis said.

"Then what?"

"You wouldn't see him any more," Dennis said.

"Why?"

"Because when you die, you die," said Dennis.

"Where do you go?"

"To Heaven if you're good."

"Will I?"

"If you're good," Dennis said.

"Gee, that's funny."

"Hey," said Dennis.

"What?"

"Mama said Papa gets paid today and we get meat for supper," Dennis said.

"Gee!" exclaimed Bob.

"When Papa gets paid, we get meat to eat," said Dennis.

"I like meat," said Bob.

"Who don't?"

"I do," said Bob.

"I heard Mama tell Papa to bring meat home for supper and he said he would. I heard them talking about meat this morning," Dennis said.

"Goody," Bob said.

"I wish Papa got paid every day," said Dennis.

"Why?"

"Because if he did, we'd get meat for supper every night," Dennis said.

"Why?"

"There you go askin' questions again," Dennis said.

"Well, why?" asked Bob.

"Because Papa brings home meat when he gets paid," Dennis said.

"Gee!" exclaimed Bob.

"Listen!" said Dennis.

"What?" asked Bob.

"You watch yourself. Don't grab too much meat. Pa gets sore if you grab too much meat and don't let everybody else get any. He beat me up with his razor strap because I did it last time he brought meat home on payday," said Dennis.

"Why?"

"Because he wants everybody to eat meat, and not you, you hog, to eat all of it. He gets sore. Once he beat Bill because Bill ate too much meat. Papa said he'd show Bill doing that, not leavin' any meat for anybody else. So you just don't grab all the meat Pa brings home tonight. It hurts when Pa gives you a licking with his razor strap," Dennis said.

"I won't," Bob said.

"If you do, don't say I didn't tell you," Dennis said.

They walked on in silence. Each seemed to have become suddenly absorbed in his own boy's thoughts, and there was a faraway expression on both of their dirty faces. Dennis began to walk pigeon-toed. Bob imitated him. Dennis then made himself walk bowlegged, and so did Bob. They laughed, and started wiggling from side to side as they walked on, liking it when people on the street looked at them. Bob picked up a piece of tin foil and put it in his pocket.

"Gimme half," said Dennis.

"No. Because I'll have to tear it if I do, and it won't be so big," said Bob.

"All right! Keep it!" Dennis said.

"It's the same color as money," Bob said, feeling the tin foil in his pocket.

"If it was money, what'd you do with it?" Dennis asked.

"Buy candy and cakes. What else could you do?" Bob asked.

"I don't know, maybe see a nickel show," said Dennis.

"Why ain't it money?" Bob asked.

"'Cause it ain't," Dennis said.

"If it ain't money, what is it?" asked Bob.

"It ain't money," said Dennis.

"What is it?"

"Silver that comes with candy and tobacco like the tobacco Pa gets to chew and smokes sometimes," said Dennis.

"I wish it was money," said Bob.

"Me, too."

"We could buy lots of cakes and candy then," said Bob.

They walked on, Bob holding the tin foil in his pocket. He suddenly walked outside of a lamppost at the edge of the curb. Dennis went over near the stores and began touching store windows. Bob did likewise. They walked for a block, touching and running their fingers along every store window. They passed a group of girls who were playing hopscotch on marked-off squares on the sidewalk. They stopped touching windows, and Bob walked on, dragging his feet, making a scraping sound with each step.

"Bum! Bum! Bum! Bumb!" Dennis began muttering over and over again.

Still dragging his feet, Bob imitated him.

"You got to do everything I do?" Dennis asked.

Bob didn't answer. But he ceased making bum-bum sounds. He darted ahead of Dennis, turned around, walked backward until he bumped into a lamppost.

"Thought you were smart," Dennis said, laughing.

"It didn't hurt me," Bob said.

Bob pointed his finger at Dennis and yelled, "Bang! Bang!"

"Bang! Bang! Bang!" Dennis yelled, pointing his finger at Bob.

Dennis chased Bob, and both of them kept yelling, "Bang, Bang."

V

"Is this the nickel show that Bill and Danny sometimes go to?" Bob asked.

"Uh huh!" Dennis muttered.

They stood in front of a motion-picture theater on Wentworth near Forty-third Street. There was a ticket booth, and a narrow stretch of tile behind the booth. There were several doors. On either side of the booth there were photographs advertising the features for the day. They went to one of the boards to look at the pictures.

"What does it say?" Bob asked.

"I can't read all the words," Dennis said.

"I know what it is," Bob said, pointing to a picture of a United States marine who stood before a petty officer on board a warship with the sea in the background.

"What?" asked Dennis.

"He's a sailor," Bob said proudly.

"The pictures must be about ships and sailors," Dennis said.

"Denny, why do moving pictures move?" asked Bob.

"I donno. They move," Dennis said, looking wistfully at the pictures as he spoke.

"Funny," Bob said.

"I can spell out all these letters," Dennis said, pointing at the board.

"Do it," Bob said.

"All right. T H E, The M A R I N E. I don't know what that means but it must be some kind of a sailor," Dennis said.

"I want to see the nickel show," Bob said.

"Ask the man to let us in," Dennis said.

"You ask him. You're bigger," Bob said.

"You do it. You're littler than me. Maybe he'll let us in if the littler one of us asks him," Dennis said.

Bob went to the ticket booth and reached his hand up, trying to look over the counter.

"Tickets, Sonny?" asked the man in the booth.

"I want two tickets," Bob said.

"That's a dime, Sonny," the man said, handing out two tickets.

Bob grabbed the tickets, ran to Dennis, and handed them to him.

"I told you you'd get 'em," Dennis said.

"What's the idea?" the man from the ticket booth asked, suddenly standing over them and grabbing both boys by the scruffs of their necks.

"I wanted tickets to see the nickel show," Bob said.

"Where's your money?"

"Here," Bob said, digging into his pocket and handing the man his tin foil.

"You kids better run along. You got to have a nickel each to see the show," he said.

They looked at him, scared. He released them. They walked away.

"I had the tickets," Bob said.

"We didn't see no show," Dennis said.

"If we got in the nickel show we'd a seen ships and sailors," Bob said as they walked along slowly.

"Uh huh!" Dennis said wistfully.

"I like to see cowboys and Indians, too, more than I would ships and sailors."

"I like to see moving pictures," Dennis said.

"Papa gets paid tonight. Maybe he'll give us nickels to see the nickel show," Bob said.

"You ask him," Dennis said.

"I asked for the tickets. Your turn now," Bob said.

"If you ask, I'll let you go with me," Dennis said.

"You always make me do things," Bob said.

"I'm gonna take you, ain't I?"

"I ain't no baby. I know my way here alone," Bob said.

"All right. If that's the way you feel about it, I should worry. Only don't ask me to let you play with me any more," Dennis said.

"Let's play cowboy and Indian, Denny," Bob said.

He ran down the street and bang-banged as he pointed his finger. Dennis followed him in a galloping trot, caught him, and said as he bang-banged:

"Fall down, you're dead."

Bob fell down. Dennis stood over him with his finger pointed at Bob.

"You're dead now."

Bob got up. He stared at a passing horse and wagon.

"If that was Papa, we'd get a ride," Dennis said.

"It ain't Papa," Bob said.

"I wish it was. Maybe he'd let me drive his horse," Dennis said.

"I'm going to be like Papa and drive a horse when I'm a man," said Bob.

"Me, too," Dennis said.

They walked on. It was getting toward dusk, and the street was noisy with the sounds of traffic. They walked on, touching windows, Dennis first and Bob behind him.

15

I

The kerosene lamps were lit, and their odor pervaded the entire house.

"Jim, we have our whole family here except my Little Margaret," Lizz said with joy while Jim stood over a pan of frying hamburger.

"Is Dan staying all night with us?" Jim asked.

"Of course he is. He's my son, he came to see his mother and father today, he did," Lizz said.

"I'm glad he did," Jim said.

"He'll never forget who his mother and father are," Lizz said.

"I hope to God not. Not if I got any say in it," Jim said.

Jim seemed preoccupied. He bent over the stove and turned over the hamburger balls. He suddenly jerked his head back so as not to get hit by the flying grease which began popping out of the pan.

"They went to the ball game today, and when they came home I sent them to confession. They can watch the little ones while you and I go tonight," Lizz said.

"You didn't give them any money, did you?" Jim asked.

"Poor as we are, where in the name of God would I be getting the money to give them for ball games, treating them like the sons of a rich man? My brother sent his nephew the money," Lizz said.

"It's not that I begrudge them anything. There's too many things we need now for us to be letting them waste money, what with another mouth we'll have to be feeding next spring," Jim said.

"We know that somehow our Daddy Long Legs will provide, and God will help him," Lizz said.

"It seems a long time ago, don't it, Lizz, old girl, since we got that money when Bill broke his leg. But it didn't last long. Damn it, I'd wanted to get your teeth fixed with that money, and we never managed it," Jim said.

"The time will come for that," Lizz said.

"Well, we got to save our nickels now. We got to pinch 'em," Jim said.

"Say you, I'll have you know that I ain't extravagant," Lizz said.

"I didn't say you were," Jim said.

"Ah well, Daddy, the Lord always provides for His own," Lizz said.

"Yeh," Jim said wearily.

He watched the frying hamburgers, and Lizz set the table. The kids in the other rooms were noisy.

II

"Hey, you kids, come on and eat," Jim called from the kitchen doorway.

"Papa, we got meat tonight?" Dennis asked, coming in first.

"Yeah, come and eat. Your mother and I can't wait all night for you. We got to go over to church," Jim said.

The others followed, Arty tagging after Catherine. Danny came in after Bill, shy.

"You came down to see your folks, didn't you?" Jim said to Danny.

"Yes, Papa," Danny said, still shy.

"Well, you're always welcome at your father and mother's. After all, we're your parents, and we're always glad to see you," Jim said, noticing that Danny was so much better dressed than any of the other children.

Jim glanced at the table. The kids were all seating themselves, and Lizz was putting the little fellow in his high chair. He saw that Danny hadn't sat down yet.

"Sit down. Make yourself at home. Don't act like a stranger at your father's table," Jim said.

"I am," Danny said meekly.

He sat down beside Bill. Jim saw how all of his kids except Danny were so eager to eat, sniffing the smell of the meat. His eyes fell on Catherine. Her face was dirty and she sat looking intently at Bill and Danny, shifting her attention from one to the other. He saw that she was tightly clenching her fork. It was always hard for a father to know what was inside the heads of his kids, and particularly of a girl. He watched Bill. Bill was leaning slightly forward, holding his knife and fork prepared. Jim went to the table and sat down opposite Lizz, with the kids lined up on either side, Little Arty in the high chair on Lizz's left.

"Listen, you kids. There isn't too much to go around here. Don't be grabbing more than your share. If I catch any one of you doing that, cheating a brother or sister, I'll tend to the one that does," Jim said.

Lizz got up and went to the stove to serve, Jim reaching over to hand her the plates one by one. She gave him the first plate of hamburger, putting two balls and several large spoonfuls of carrots on it. She began serving the kids. She put two meat balls on Danny's plate, and gave the others only one. She took half a hamburger for herself and put a few bites of it on Arty's plate.

"Why do you give him more than his brothers and sister? They don't get meat every day," Jim said.

"He's our guest," Lizz said.

"Guest, hell, he's our kid," Jim said.

"I got too much to eat. I don't want two of these," Danny said quickly, with a defensive note of apology in his voice.

"Yes, you do," Lizz said.

The other children already were eating voraciously, except for Arty, who was struggling with his food.

"Take one back. If there's any left, they'll divide it equal and equal," Jim said.

"Please, Mama, take one back. I can't eat this much," Danny said, handing his plate down to his mother.

She reluctantly took it and pushed one meat ball back into the frying pan. Then she handed the plate back to Danny, who was pale and nervous. He began eating slowly. They were all silent, as they ate ravenously. In no time the kids had cleaned their plates. Bob picked his plate up to lick it.

"Don't act like you were born in a barn. Put your plate down," Lizz said sharply.

He set down his plate, passed an anxious glance at his mother and then at his father. Jim's lips compressed for a moment.

"Ma, I want more meat," Dennis said.

"We're going to have meat tomorrow, and more of it than tonight. Fill up on bread and carrots for tonight and be thankful for what you got," Jim said.

Dennis looked disappointed. He ate the carrots his mother had given him, and a large slice of bread that was spread thickly with oleomargarine. He reached for another slice of bread, while Lizz was dishing second helpings of carrots to the other children. He began smearing oleomargarine all over the bread.

"Don't take it all. You got others here waiting for some of it," Jim said with authority.

His voice produced a sudden state of tension at the table, and it was manifested by the silence and the concerned expressions on the faces of the children, all except Arty, who dug away at his food, pushing and fighting it, spilling bits over the board, getting his face greasy. The kids sat waiting, even breathing with a slight irregularity.

"Jim, the Lord will always provide," Lizz said.

"I know, Lizz. And, God, I'm not begrudging. But when there's only so much food and so many mouths to feed, one can't let one have it all. They're the same flesh and blood here and they got to be one for all and all for one. This is a family, and it's got to learn to stick together now," Jim said.

"The poor children are hungry. Here, Dennis, let Mama butter your bread for you," she said.

Jim's face sank. He shrugged his shoulders in a gesture of helplessness as he watched Lizz coating Dennis' bread with chunks of oleomargarine and then covering the oleomargarine with sugar.

"I want to have the kids eat and not go hungry, but I don't want one to get too much and the others nothing," Jim said.

"This is our family, not the war in Europe," Lizz said.

"When you got only so much, one can't have everything," Jim said.

They continued eating. Lizz gave Jim another meat ball, which he guiltily and shyly ate.

"Papa, can Denny and I go to the nickel show tomorrow?" Bob suddenly asked.

"No!" Jim said, flaring into sudden anger.

"I don't want to go. I didn't tell you to ask Papa. Pa, I don't wanna go to the nickel show," Dennis said.

"You do too. You told me to ask Papa," Bob said.

"I didn't!" Dennis said.

"I don't care who wants to. There isn't the money for you kids to be going to shows. You ought to be glad to get something to eat. And I brought you home candy. That should satisfy you. Your mother here never gets to go anywhere," Jim said.

"Danny and Bill went to the ball game," Bob said.

"Your uncle gave them the money, that's why they went, my Bobby-boy," Lizz said.

"Why doesn't Uncle Al give some money to me?" Bob asked.

"If you don't ask too many questions, you won't get yourself in trouble," Jim said, looking at Bob.

"Why?" asked Bob, and again the children were thrown into a tense state of fear and apprehension.

"Because your father told you that if you don't ask too damn many questions, you won't get into trouble. Now, keep still and finish your supper!" Jim said as he dug his fork into what remained of his meat ball, conveyed it to his mouth, and chewed grimly.

They finished supper in silence, eating Ward's cake and drinking tea. Jim got up from the table and walked to the front of the cottage. He looked out the window on the street, the houses, sidewalk, paving blocks, all flooded with moonlight.

"Your father is in a temper tonight and you kids mustn't make him angry or he might put the razor strap to you," Lizz said.

"I didn't say nothin'. It was them," Catherine said.

"I didn't do nothin'," Dennis said.

"You kids keep your mouths shut and stop scrapping or we'll all get it in the neck. Shut up!" Bill said.

"Mither! Fither! Down, Mither!" Arty exclaimed.

"Catherine, let your brother down," Lizz said.

"Oh gee!" Catherine said.

"Do what you're told," Lizz said sternly.

Catherine took Arty from his high chair, sighing because he was heavy. Arty ran bowleggedly to his father in the front, exclaiming:

"Fither! Fither! Fither!"

"Now, you kids be good and quiet tonight. I got to get the dishes washed and go over to church," Lizz said, starting to carry the supper dishes to the sink.

III

Bill and Danny sat close to the lamp at the dining-room table, playing the world series between the Braves and Athletics with the Steel's game. Arty yawned on the floor, holding a piece of cardboard. Catherine sat next to Bob on the couch with her chin cupped in her hands. Both of them were silent. Dennis sat at the table, removed from his older brothers, doing simple examples in arithmetic. Jim and Lizz were in the darkened parlor, talking in low voices.

"But what do you do with the money?" Jim said, a puzzled quality in his voice.

"Merciful God!" Lizz exclaimed.

"Never mind that. Can't you answer a simple question?" Jim asked.

"With all these little mouths to feed! Merciful God, what do I do with what he brings home?" Lizz exclaimed, flinging her arms above her head in an extravagant gesture.

Jim rose and paced silently and brooding back and forth across the parlor.

"We got to live within our means," Jim said.

"We do," Lizz said.

"Then why do we owe bills to every damn storekeeper in the hull neighborhood? I was coming home tonight and a Jew on Wentworth Avenue ran out of a store and collared me. He said, 'Mr. O'Neill!' I looks at him, wondering what the hell does he want? I felt like taking a punch at him. And he says to me that my wife owes him three dollars. For Christ sake, I want to know where the money goes! Down a sewer? Where? We don't have meat hardly twice a week. Where in the name of Jumping Jupiter does the money go?" Jim said.

Lizz sighed. Jim stood in the center of the room, his long arms hanging at his sides.

"Ah!" she exclaimed. She sighed again. "I only wish to God I could go out and work and be the breadwinner and let you stay home and take care of this regiment and make ends meet on a pauper's wages."

"I guess if it was that way we wouldn't be any better off, or any worse off, either," Jim said gloomily.

"We got to pray and ask the Lord for everything to get better and our cross to be lightened," Lizz said.

"Pray, hell! We need money. A man's pocketbook is his best friend," Jim said.

"Oh, don't I know it!" Lizz said.

"Well, old girl, our pocketbooks aren't such good friends," Jim said.

He pulled a plug of tobacco out of his pocket, bit into it, chewed with his cheek puffed out. Little Arty came into the parlor.

Jim turned and picked up his youngest child.

"Ah, you little beggar," Jim said tenderly.

"He's Mama's Angel Child," Lizz said.

Jim walked silently back and forth, the child on his shoulder. Bob and Catherine came to the stove dividing the two rooms and watched.

"When they all grow up, we'll be better off," Lizz said.

"Sure, and when we're dead we'll be better off," Jim said.

"Look at them watch their daddy," Lizz said, pointing at Bob and Catherine; they smiled.

"Lizz, the little beggar is asleep. Come on, put him to bed, and I'll get the others in bed and we'll go," Jim said.

Lizz arose.

"Give him to me. He sleeps like an angel, Jim," Lizz said, and Jim gently gave Arty to the mother.

"Papa, rock me to sleep tonight?" Catherine said.

"Come on," Jim said.

He picked up Catherine, carried her with him to the rocking chair, and rocked slowly, while the dice rattled on the Steel's board.

"I love my Papa," Catherine said.

"You're his girl," Jim said.

"I am," Catherine said.

"What are you going to be when you're a big girl?" Jim asked her.

"Papa's girl. Papa's big girl," Catherine said.

"Ah, you're a deep little one," Jim said; he kissed her on the forehead. She snuggled against him, and he stroked her hair.

"Jim, come on. Let's get ready to go," Lizz said.

"She's asleep, too," Jim said.

"No, I'm not," Catherine said.

"Well, you ought to be. Come on and go to bed. Your father's going to church. Come on, Bobby, you too," said Jim.

"We ought to hurry, Jim," said Lizz.

"All right," said Jim.

"You should go to confession more often. You haven't gone since you made your Easter Duty," Lizz said.

"Well, I'm going now, ain't I?" said Jim, carrying Catherine to the bedroom.

16

I

Danny and Bill lay at the head of the bed, and Bob was at the foot. Dennis was sleeping on the dining-room couch, with a blanket and an old coat thrown over him. There wasn't much room in the bed. Bill tossed a lot in his sleep and kept pulling the covers off everyone without knowing what he was doing. If you pulled them back, you might wake him up, and he would be sort of half asleep and half awake, and when he was woke up and got like that, he was just as liable as not to swing on you, and you might get cracked in the jaw. Bob was tossing and moving around at the foot of the bed, too. Danny wasn't used to sleeping like this.

He didn't like it, sleeping here all night at Mama's and Papa's. There was no room in the bed. He didn't like the darkness. He didn't like the smell of the room. The smell of the room was very different from the smell of the bedroom where he slept at home. The smell here was musty, and it made him feel dirty. He didn't know what made the smell except the bed and the dirty sheets and blankets, and it was musty. The sheets were stiff, and he didn't like the blankets touching him. He didn't get the same feeling out of the sheets and the bed that he got at home. He always liked the clean sheets, with the bed made, sinking in, the soft feeling of the mattress, the clean sheets over him and the warm blanket. And no smells in the bedroom. Here, the smell and the bed and everything made him feel dirty. And he was itching.

He reached down and scratched his knees. There was no light in the house and everyone else was asleep. He wanted to go to sleep and he couldn't. He didn't want to be here. Why was he? Itchy again. His ankle. He pulled his ankle up and scratched it. He hated to be itchy this way. He wanted to go home to Mother's and stay there, and he belonged there and didn't belong here. You were supposed to belong where your mother and father were, but he just didn't feel that way.

Papa had got mad at supper, too. He was afraid of Papa. He'd been afraid that Papa was going to sock him. Papa hurt a kid when he took a poke at him, and he hurt, too, when he beat your can off with his razor strap. Uncle Al didn't use a razor strap to sharpen his razor. He used what was called a safety razor. A safety razor cost more money. But Papa was poor and Uncle Al wasn't. He just couldn't think of Uncle Al being as poor as Papa was.

Why was he so itchy? He was getting itchy all over, and bites like mosquito bites were coming up on his legs, all up and down the right one. Maybe he was catching something. Mother was always afraid of letting him come down to Mama's because she was afraid he was going to catch something. When he left the house this morning, Mother had said to him:

"Son, be careful. Be careful you don't catch anything. You never got the whooping cough because I took good care of you, and don't catch anything down there."

Once Mother had told Mama she didn't want him going to Mama's because she didn't want her grandson catching things at Mama's and Mama got sore as blazes and raised hell and shouted. He remembered that Mama said to Mother:

"Say you, my house is clean and we're clean. I'll have you know that."

Wouldn't he ever stop itching and getting these bites, and wouldn't he ever get to sleep tonight? He never knew what to say when he was talking to Papa. He never knew but what Papa might get sore any minute. It was harder for him to talk to Papa than it was to talk to Uncle Al, even though it was sometimes hard to talk to Uncle Al. One of the differences between talking with Papa and talking with Uncle Al was that he knew some of the things, at least more of the things, that would make Uncle Al sore than he did the things that would make Papa sore. And why couldn't he go to sleep?

He scratched his legs again, and it felt as if he had scratched a bite until it was bleeding. In summer at home, mosquitoes did that, but never in winter. It must be bedbugs they had. Mother never had bedbugs. Sometimes she and Aunty Margaret got afraid about bedbugs and they looked at the mattress or they called a man in and he shot funny-smelling poison on the mattress.

Danny turned to the wall. He wished that it was morning. He wished that it was tomorrow and he was back home. He would have to go home tomorrow because he had to be at school on Monday. They couldn't make him stay to-morrow night because of school. Why was he here? He didn't want to be here, sleeping in this old bed, in this room full of smells, with bedbugs or something biting him, with it being so dark, with everything smelling a way he didn't like it to smell.

He scratched his legs again. He twisted, and wanted to yell out because of all the bites on his legs. And now his left wrist. He scratched it. He wanted to twist and yell about it, and he didn't dare. Bill had gone to sleep a long time

ago, and everybody else in the house was asleep, and if he yelled out he'd wake
the house up, and if he twisted and moved around too much in bed, he'd wake
Bill. He couldn't sleep in this bed, with all the bites he got. Bill didn't seem to
get bites. So here he was, still awake in the dark house. He smothered a groan
and scratched his left thigh. He was afraid. He didn't know what mightn't happen. But he didn't think anything was going to happen. Like once when he was
here, he heard Mama and Papa talking about robbers, and he remembered that
Papa said that they need never fear or worry about a burglar breaking into their
house, because burglars didn't go breaking into poor men's houses. He didn't like
it here, that was all, and he wanted to get out of here as fast as he could. They
had all told him how when he was little, after staying at Mother's when Little
Margaret was born, he was brought back home to Papa and Mama, and in the
middle of the night he cried like bloody murder and Papa had had to take him
back to Mother's. But he didn't remember much about it, only himself being
carried on a street car by Papa, with lights in the street car and people whose
faces he couldn't remember, and himself crying and crying and afraid. It made
him feel like he felt sometimes at night alone in the dark when he was dreaming and he suddenly woke up and didn't know where he was, heard noises, was
afraid of things, and he didn't know what he was really afraid of.

He wiped a tear from his eyes. He was crying. But he couldn't let himself cry
out loud. If he did and woke Papa up, Papa would get sore as all hell at him and
maybe give him a clout, and Bill might laugh at him, and he would be showing
himself off like a bawl baby. He sniffled. He didn't know what it was that made
him cry and feel like this. He guessed it was very late. He guessed it was late, but
it wasn't late enough for him, because he wanted it to be morning, tomorrow,
and he wanted it to be later than tomorrow morning because he wanted to be
back home at Mother's.

He had been sorry to see the Sox lose, and now the Cubs were ahead of them
three to one in the city series. Gee, he hoped that they'd win tomorrow. And he
wished he could be there to see them win. And after the game, he and Bill had
gone to confession. Did Bill make bad confessions? He had gone to church today
with Bill, afraid of what kind of a priest he would get, trying to make himself
face what he had to face. He had knelt in church, examining his conscience. He
had looked at the altar, watched the altar light burning, seen the statues, but not
very clearly because of his eyes and the darkness of the church. He'd knelt there,
and Bill had been beside him, and he had asked himself was Bill afraid? Would
Bill tell about that fifty dollars? If Bill did, the priest might make Bill tell and
then they would know about him. Even if you couldn't pay back money you had
stolen, you might have to tell the person it was stolen from. He'd knelt there,
trying to make himself do it, because what was the punishment you got in this
world alongside of what you would get if you died and went to Hell and burned

there forever and forever. He had gone to confession to Father Nolan, and he had gone in there telling himself that he had to go ahead and tell it all, and tell all about the dirty sins on his soul ever since he made his First Holy Communion. Waiting for his turn, he could hardly breathe, he had been so afraid, because he had to tell that, and he had to tell that he had had dirty thoughts. But he couldn't think about dirty thoughts now because it might make him have thoughts in his mind that were sinful and he was receiving Holy Communion in the morning. And his soul was dirty with sin, worse than this bed.

Why wasn't he just a little kid like Arty, not yet reached the age of reason so he couldn't have any sins yet, and he could start all over again when he reached the age of reason? Maybe if he said some prayers, he'd go to sleep. He ought to try and say a good Act of Contrition. First, he had to be sorry. He was sorry. He gazed upward in the darkness. He closed his eyes. He lifted his hands outside the blanket which was now only half covering him because Bill had pulled it away in his sleep. He had to be sorry. He was sorry. God, please keep him to be truly and really sorry.

O my God! I am heartily sorry for having offended Thee . . .

When he prayed, he had to keep God in his mind. He tried to hold before him the picture of God on His throne in Heaven. God was sitting on His throne. There were the angels around Him, and the Blessed Virgin, and Jesus on His right, but Jesus wouldn't just be naked except for a cloth around Him and have His side and hands and feet pierced and the thorns on His head. Jesus would be like a king in robes, and there was the Holy Ghost on the other side of God, but he couldn't see the Holy Ghost in his mind because he didn't know what the Holy Ghost really looked like. Now he had to keep God in his mind, and say his Act of Contrition and be really sorry.

O my God! I am heartily sorry for having offended Thee, and I detest all my sins . . .

He did. He detested his sins. He hated his sins. He hated his sins, and what he had gotten with them, the ice-cream sodas, and, yes, even the ball games he had seen. But he had to keep God in his mind and pray.

O my God . . .

Monday at school he would see Hortense Audrey and Virginia Doyle. Every day at school he saw them. He wanted to speak to them, and he never seemed to be able to get himself to. It was going to happen. He was going to speak to them. This year, one of them was going to be his girl. But he had to say his Act of Contrition.

O my God . . .

Again he scratched himself on the legs. Bill was tossing around again. He hated to sleep with Bill in this bed, because Bill kept turning and taking up so much room all of the time. And Bob was making some sound in his sleep, as if he was talking to somebody or to himself.

He wanted to go home to Mother's. He wanted to go home to Mother's. He wanted to go home to Mother's. And he couldn't go to sleep in this darn bed. If he could go to sleep the time would go fast. Every night when he went to sleep, he seemed no sooner to have gone to bed than he was asleep and awake again and it was morning. He wanted to go to sleep to make the time pass faster, because then it wouldn't seem so long until morning, and morning was going to make it nearer the time he was going home. And he wouldn't smell the room, either, or itch.

Did Papa snore? He couldn't hear because the door of the bedroom where Papa and Mama and Catherine and Arty all slept was closed. Uncle Al snored. He didn't like the sound of snoring. And people always laughed at snoring, like in the movies when you saw a fat man snoring. It was always funny in a picture when John Bunny snored. It made everybody in the nickel show laugh.

He was never going to be caught like this again where he had to stay here all night. Every time he did, he didn't like it when he got to bed and couldn't sleep, or when he did get to sleep and woke up suddenly in the middle of the night and lay there in the darkness and couldn't get back to sleep and was afraid, and wanted to cry and was afraid to cry. He sniffled again. He scratched himself. He curled up against the wall and lay there.

II

Danny O'Neill was dead.

There was a street. It was dark, and it was a street that he had never seen before. The people who walked on it looked like undertakers in a nickel show, and they didn't say a word. They walked along, and just to see them made him afraid.

And Danny O'Neill was dead.

There was Mother. She was walking along the street, wearing a black shawl, and she stopped, and God suddenly was talking to her. God was wearing a red robe, and he had a golden crown on His head, and His beard was long and white.

Danny O'Neill is dead, God said to Mother.

Where did he go?

I sent him to Hell. Never again will he hurt My feelings by his sins.

Burn him up! Burn him within an inch of his life. I gave him clean waists every day, paid good money to the nigger washwoman to wash them, and sent him to school to the holy nuns. Burn him up, Mother said to God.

He is burning up. When I made him, I made him a Catholic, and he sinned when he reached the age of reason. I took him away.

I don't want him, Mother said, and still the men who looked like undertakers in a nickel show walked back and forth, never saying a word.

Burn him up good and plenty, Mother said to God.

God disappeared, and Mother stood on the street shaking her fist, and the men walked by and didn't look at her.

You'll rue the day you sinned now, and it serves you right, she said, still shaking her fist.

The street was getting darker like it was night coming.

You little devil, you broke the heart of God with bad confessions.

And Mother was gone and he knew it was the last time he ever would see her and he knew that Danny O'Neill was dead.

Danny O'Neill was dead, and there he was in Hell, with the red-hot flames licking and leaping all around him, and the red devils were jumping in and out of the flames at him, yelling like Indians doing a war dance, sticking him in the legs with their pitchforks, yelling like wild Indians in a nickel show.

Lemme alone, Danny whined.

Get down in the fire and use good diction, a red devil with horns and the voice of Uncle Al told him.

Danny looked over the leaping flames and he saw the bars of a cage, and he knew that the cage was the cage of Hell. He could see people looking through the bars of Hell, looking just like the people watching the animals in the Lincoln Park Zoo.

I wanna go home, Danny whined. Hell is your home, the Devil Himself said, jumping over the flames and standing in front of him.

The book of his sins, another red devil said, leaping over the flames and handing a black book to the Devil Himself.

Danny looked at them with begging eyes. The Devil Himself grinned and opened the black book. The people outside pressed closely against the bars of Hell.

A black angel suddenly stood at the left of the Devil Himself and Danny knew that he knew this black angel.

Here is the black angel I put on your left side when you were born. Here is the black book of your sins he kept when you were alive and committing sins because my black angel told you to. Because of the sins in this black book, you're mine now. You're mine now.

Red devils came out of the flames and did an Indian dance around him and the people watched from outside the bars of Hell, thinking how terrible Danny O'Neill was.

You're mine now. You'll burn here. Stick a pitchfork into him, the Devil Himself said, and a red angel came forward.

Danny felt a sting on his legs. He felt that they were swelling on him. He touched his legs and they seemed to be swelling on him so that he couldn't move them.

And the Devil Himself opened the black pages of the black book and held it before Danny's eyes, and there, in big, black letters, Danny read the word SIN on every page.

And out of the darkness above him there appeared a white angel in white robes, with golden wings and the face of a girl. He saw a white book in the hands of the white angel.

You're worse than the White Sox, Danny's black angel said, looking up at the white angel with scorn.

Danny watched the white angel fly around and around in the darkness over the flames, and he saw that the white angel was sad and crying. He knew that the white angel was his guardian angel, and that the white book was his guardian angel's book of good deeds, and there was not one good deed of his written in it.

You never listened to me when I spoke to your conscience, Danny's guardian angel said with deep regret, and the tears of the guardian angel fell like rain, dropping on him.

Let me out of here. I'll listen. I'll be good. I'll never make bad confessions, Danny yelled and pleaded, surrounded by all the fires of Hell.

And the Devil Himself laughed at Danny, like a villain in a show.

When I capture a soul, it never gets away from me, the Devil Himself said.

Go back and be a guardian angel to the White Sox, Danny's black angel yelled up to his white angel who still flew overhead, crying, shedding tears that fell like a rainfall into all the raging fires of Hell.

I wanna go home, Danny sobbed, trembling in mortal fear.

> *Oh, come all ye faithful,*
> *Danny O'Neill is dead.*
> *Oh, come all ye faithful,*
> *His soul belongs to the Devil Himself.*

All the devils in Hell sang, dancing around Danny, who looked on one side, and then another, seeing only dancing devils and the raging fires of Hell.

Take him to the oven, the Devil Himself said.

Devils marched on all sides of him like soldiers of a conquering army, and they carried pitchforks, baseball bats, and BB guns. The souls of the damned were all over Hell, and each soul looked like a skeleton. The souls of the damned were all burning in bonfires, and they were weeping the bitter tears of the damned, crying because they were burning and because they would never see the sight of Almighty God. Devils stuck pitchforks into them, and the souls cried out for mercy and there was no mercy. Danny saw them and heard them and the red devils marched him through the darkness and the red fires of Hell.

Down there is the furnace where we burn souls dirty with the sin of a sacrilege, the Devil Himself said.

Danny looked down, down, down through a funnel of darkness, and he saw the opened doors of a furnace with red-hot coals inside. He saw little red devils heaping more coals into the furnace.

A great thirst overcame him, and his lips became parched and blistered. His legs began swelling again. Somewhere beyond the flames there were voices coming out of the darkness, and he knew that he'd heard these voices before, but he didn't know whose voices they were.

Danny O'Neill is dead and burning in Hell.

He seemed like a good boy.

But he made bad confessions and received the Blessed Sacrament when he wasn't in the state of grace.

He'll never see God.

He's gone to Hell.

He's in the power of the Devil in Hell.

Danny O'Neill is dead. Danny O'Neill is burning in Hell.

His legs were swelling. He wanted a drink of water. He was falling, falling, falling, down through darkness, down into a bottomless pit of fire, sinking and falling. On all sides he saw faces like skeletons pop out of the wall of darkness to wail and shed the tears of the damned. And he was falling, falling, falling, and he knew that he was going to fall forever and forever down into the pits of the fires of Hell, and above him was only blackness, and he heard voices saying over and over again:

Danny O'Neill is dead and in the power of the Devil Himself.

It was all blackness. There were no fires. He wasn't falling, but he didn't know where he was. His tongue was parched, and he felt as if he was nowhere, facing something terrible. He remembered hearing that he was dead, and he knew that he had just had something horrible happen to him.

He scratched his legs.

It had only been a dream. He knew where he was. He was at Mama's. Bill was beside him. It was still night. He shuddered, hearing a creak in the boards. He was thirsty, but he knew it must be after twelve o'clock and he couldn't drink because he was going to Communion in the morning. He was being bitten again. He scratched some more, feeling blood on his legs. He lay against the wall, shuddering, closing his eyes to keep the blackness out. When would the morning come? When would he go home? He sobbed, while everyone else in the house slept peacefully.

17

I

"I'll fix your breakfast now, Jim," Lizz said when they both got home after having attended eight o'clock mass and received Holy Communion.

"I'll change my clothes first," Jim said; he wore a black, single-breasted suit in which he looked awkward and ungainly. With his rough, leathery face and his large and bony hands, from one of which the little finger was missing, in his Sunday best he looked as much the workman as he did in his work clothes.

"Ma, I got to go to nine o'clock mass now," Dennis said.

"Go with your brothers," Lizz said.

"They can't sit with me. I got to sit with my class," Dennis said.

Bob came out of the front bedroom. He looked nervously at Dennis.

"Say, Jim, I can't for the life of me make out why Mrs. Connerty went to eight o'clock mass this morning," Lizz said.

"Lizz, get that blatherskite out of your mind," Jim said.

"She always goes to ten o'clock mass and tries to act and cut herself out like she was one of the ladies of the parish. She, acting the lady! Jim, did you ever see the beat of that?" Lizz said, laughing.

"I believe in minding my own business. When we met her and her husband in front of church, I just said good morning," Jim said.

"William, are you and Danny ready? You know you have to receive," Lizz said.

"Uh huh," Bill answered, coming out of the bedroom in his brown Sunday suit, the sleeves a trifle too small.

"Mama, I can't receive Holy Communion this morning," Danny said.

"Why? You went to confession yesterday," Lizz said.

"When I got up this morning, I was awful thirsty. Before I remembered that I had to fast, I went to the kitchen and got some water, and I just started swallowing it when I remembered. I only swallowed one mouthful, but that's not allowed if you're to receive Holy Communion," said Danny.

Dennis and Bob seemed nervous, and Bob kept looking at Dennis. Dennis was making signs to Bob. Catherine and Arty were in the parlor, Arty running about the room, Catherine looking at her father while she sat on the floor.

"You didn't do it on purpose and the Lord will overlook it. He will today because I want all of my family who can to receive. You can receive. When you two come home, I'll give you a nice breakfast. Come, Dennis, and your mother will give you a cup of coffee to hold you until you get back from mass," Lizz said.

"I ain't hungry, Ma," Dennis said; he seemed to be getting increasingly nervous.

Bob shot a worried look at him.

"Well, old woman, you can give me some coffee. I won't refuse," Jim said.

He walked out to the kitchen. Dennis followed and stood near the back door, watching his father. Bob went to the kitchen door and stood there, pale. They saw their father going to the chair in which he always sat.

"Look out Papa, there's glue on the chair," Dennis yelled, and he darted out of the house and over the fence. Lizz saw him running across the street. Bob tried to run out but fell down. Jim saw the glue on his chair. He went after Bob quickly and grabbed him.

"You dirty little ingrates!" he said, his voice throbbing.

Bill and Danny stood surprised and petrified.

"Did you do it?" Jim asked Bob, his anger almost uncontrollable.

Bob whimpered.

"Answer me! Did you?"

"Dennis told me to," Bob whimpered.

"Why didn't you two stop them from doing that?" Jim said in rage to Bill and Danny while he held Bob, who was shuddering and trembling in his grasp.

"We didn't see them. We were in the front with Dolly and Arty, and they must have done it then," said Bill.

"Mother of God! Putting glue on their father's chair, and it would ruin the only decent suit the poor man has. I knew it, I knew it. He learned that trick from the Connertys," Lizz said.

"I'll teach you to be disrespectful of your father, I'm goddamned if I don't. You won't be able to sit on any damn chair, glue or not," Jim said.

"Papa, I won't do it again," Bob said whimperingly.

"Lizz, get me my razor strap. I'll teach these goddamn little ingrates a lesson they'll never forget," Jim said, pale with anger.

"Jim, it's not their fault. I know one of the Connerty boys put them up to it. The Connertys are wild ones," Lizz said.

"Shut up! Get me my razor strap," Jim said, still holding Bob tightly.

"I just received Our Lord," Lizz said, folding her arms.

"Bill, get me that razor strap and be damned quick," Jim said.

Bill obeyed in great haste. Jim cuffed Bob on the ear, and Bob let out a yell.

"Shut up!" Jim said.

He took the razor strap from Bill. He let down Bob's breeches, and set Bob over his knee on the dining-room couch. He used all the force of his arm in hitting, and he beat Bob's buttocks until they were red; Bob screamed loudly as he underwent the punishment. Bill and Danny watched, both of them pale, Danny's lips quivering slightly.

"Goddamn you, I don't care how old you are, you'll learn to respect your father," Jim said, raising his voice.

"Jim, for the sake of Mary, you'll kill the boy," Lizz said.

"Get the hell out of here, woman!" Jim said, and again brought down the strap forcibly on Bob's bare behind. Bob let out a heart-rending shriek.

Jim dropped the strap on the floor, pushed Bob off his lap, and frowned as he looked down at the boy sobbing on the floor.

"If I ever catch you doing anything like that to me again, you're going to get three times as much. Do you hear me?"

Bob cried, his head buried on the floor.

Jim reached down and pulled the boy around, looked at him.

"You hear me!"

"Yes, Papa," Bob said timidly, still sobbing.

"You boys better go so you're not late for mass," Lizz said, and Bill and Danny started to leave by the back door.

"Listen, you two!" Jim said.

They turned around to face their father.

"When your brother comes out of church, catch him and bring him right home to me. If he gets away from you, you'll both get what that little one got. I'm a reception committee waitin' for him, and he's not going to forget the warm reception I'll give him. You hear me!" Jim pointed the index finger of his left hand, the one on which the little finger was missing. "Get him when he comes out of church and bring him right home."

"All right, Pa," Bill said.

Bob still lay on the floor, sobbing, holding his reddened buttocks.

"Now you'll be good," Catherine said, standing over him.

Bob didn't answer. He continued sobbing.

"Don't cwy," Arty said, touching Bob's hair.

II

"It's your fault. You're their mother. What in hell do you teach them?" Jim said, gesturing dramatically before Lizz in the kitchen.

"Blessed Saint Joseph!" Lizz exclaimed.

"Oh forget the saints for once," Jim said.

"Say you, I'm a mother, and I just come from the altar rail of my God, and I won't let you talk to me like that," Lizz said.

"You're with them all day. Why in the name of God don't you teach them some manners? Trying to pull a stunt like that on their father!" Jim said.

"They don't get that from me or from my family," Lizz said.

"I don't give a good goddamn where they get it. Why don't you teach them something?" Jim said.

"Say, it ain't my fault. Don't you blame me. You can't blame me," Lizz said.

"All I ask of them is a little respect. Goddamn it, I work my ass off for you and them, and on Sunday they put glue on my chair and would ruin the only suit of clothes I got. Now isn't it one hell of a pass we're comin' to!" Jim said.

"Don't yell at me about it," Lizz said.

"You're their mother."

"And you're their father. And if it wasn't for their father, they wouldn't be here. Talking like that to me, me a sick woman with another one on the way," Lizz said with self-pity.

"Well, who the hell is going to teach them manners if their mother don't?" Jim yelled.

"Say, everything good in them comes from me. What you saw this morning is their father in them. It's from you they take it, you and the influence of the Connertys. I never did want to move in a neighborhood with neighbors like them, and you made me," Lizz said.

"Shut up, for Christ sake!"

"Goddamn you, don't you tell me to shut up after I return from the holy altar rail. Don't you say that to me! I'll not let you talk that way to me, you big bully," Lizz said.

"Look at her, talking like she's nuts," Jim said.

"I do, do I? Say you, if it wasn't for me you'd be nothing now but a damn old booze-fighter. You were a booze-fighter when I met you and you'd still be one if it wasn't for me," she said.

"I wouldn't be any worse off if I was," he said.

"What am I? A drudge, a slave. Look at me, and another coming, and not a tooth in my head that doesn't ache," Lizz said.

"Goddamn it, quit bellyaching. You don't have it any harder than I do," Jim said.

"Only for my marrying you, I'd be living the life of Riley with my mother and my family," said Lizz.

"Yes, and I'd be a free man without kids trying to turn me into a vaudeville show," Jim said.

"They're yours, and when the shoe fits, you got to wear it," Lizz said.

"I tell you, I'm givin' you fair warning to shut up!" Jim said, shaking his right index finger at Lizz.

"I ain't afraid of you! If you hit me I'll get the police after you. I'll turn you in to the Humane Society. I'll have that holy man across the street, Father Corbett, after you. Hit me, and I swear I'll go to the archbishop," Lizz said.

"I'm telling you for the last time, shut up!"

"Bully! Brute! You reformed booze-fighter!" Lizz said.

"Why, goddamn you!" Jim said, his voice tense.

He took a step toward Lizz. She picked up the bread knife and waved it.

"Doddamn!" Arty said.

Both parents looked at their little son. He looked back at them with large liquid brown eyes, smiling. He put his left thumb in his mouth. Jim relaxed.

"I'm sorry, Lizz," he said, bending down and picking up his boy.

"Sit down and I'll give you your breakfast. And don't sit on that glue. We got to take that off the chair," Lizz said, going to the stove.

Carrying Arty in his arms, he went to the kitchen table and sat down.

"We got to teach you better words than that, you cute little beggar," Jim said, and he smiled.

"Fither, shursh," Arty said, pointing through the window at Saint Martha's across the street.

Jim played with Arty, and Catherine came out, sat at the table, and watched her father intently while Lizz prepared breakfast.

III

"Jesus, we sure get paper on the floor here, don't we?" Jim said, seeing the paper stacked and piled under the dining-room table as he came into the room, wearing his work clothes.

"Well, Jim, I always think this. When the children are playing, I think to myself that if they got their health, it's good, and the paper they throw on the floor don't hurt the floor, not this floor full of slivers. You couldn't hurt a floor in this dump," Lizz said, standing in the door.

"The floor's sometimes so covered with papers that we can't even see it," Jim said.

"Our Lord was born in a stable. It isn't what the outside looks like. It's what the inside looks like. If your soul is clean, that counts more than if your house is.

Many there are in the world with clean houses and dirty souls. And this morning, the souls in this house are clean. This morning, everyone who's old enough to in my house received the Body and Blood of our Blessed Lord," Lizz said, her voice rising in pride as she drew to the end of her declamation.

"Well, it isn't necessary to have a dirty house in order to have a clean soul," Jim said.

"The children are playing in the yard now. I'm going to give them all a bath," Lizz said.

"Denny and Bob still sulking because of the whipping they got?"

"Can't you hear them yelling like wild Indians?" Lizz said.

"I didn't want to whip Denny. But after tanning his brother it wouldn't have been fair. By the time he came home from mass, I wasn't so sore as I was when I found the glue on the chair. But mind me, Lizz, if they ever pull a stunt like that again, God help them! God help them! I'm going to bring them up right, by God, if I have to put the strap to them every damn day of the year. Spare the rod and spoil the child? Not Jim O'Neill," Jim said.

Jim began sweeping the carpet.

"Mercy, the dust!" Lizz exclaimed.

"It's got to be raised a little, Lizz, if we want to get rid of it," Jim said.

"If those people of mine were any good and had any kindness in their bones, they'd hire a nigger to help me out, me with all these little ones," Lizz said.

"Lizz, there's nobody to rely on in this world but one's self. Forget the damn O'Flahertys for this Sunday at least. Let's have a happy Sunday with our family without any intrusion of the O'Flahertys. We nearly spoiled it once already this morning, and let's not go doin' it again," Jim said.

"I didn't spoil it," said Lizz.

"I know it," Jim said cursorily, still sweeping.

"I'm heating kettles of water for the children's bath," Lizz said, turning back into the kitchen.

Jim worked on, sweeping the dust into a corner, his nostrils irritated by it. He bent down and pulled papers from under the table, stacks of them torn and cut up, and dropped them into a wooden box he was using for waste. He thought that if the kids didn't tear up every newspaper he brought home, they could be saved and sold. Every little penny counted in this house, particularly when there was another mouth to come. He found an old pair of his suspenders in the papers, and held them up. He smiled. Things in this house were liable to be any place. And what was there that a regiment of kids couldn't get into? All kids were pretty much the same when they were young ones. They got into anything and everything. That was kids. But damn it, there was one thing they wouldn't do in his house. They wouldn't make a fool out of their father. They weren't going to play Katzenjammer kids on him. He swept the dust and dirt from under the table, thinking to himself that he'd bet even fellows like Al O'Flaherty and Dinny Gorman had been like other kids in their own kid days. Sure, they were. He swept under the table again. He moved the couch from the wall, and in doing it he saw the many punctures from BB's. What kids couldn't think of to do! Well, as long as they did no harm, he didn't care, and as long as they didn't do dirty things to themselves, what the hell! A few BB's shot into the wall of an old shack like this. Funny, he was calling this cottage an old shack already. When he'd found it and moved here from La Salle Street, he didn't call it an old shack. Well, it was an improvement over that other place. It was the best place they had been able to live in yet. But there were degrees in shacks and dumps as there were in everything in this world. And there sure were degrees of improvement ahead for the O'Neills. Would he ever be able to give his family a decent living, and his kids a chance to get ahead in life?

The dust almost choked him as he swept it from under the couch. Finishing his sweeping, he brushed the piles of dust into a large piece of cardboard which he used as a dustpan and dropped it on top of the newspapers in the wooden box. He put the sticks of furniture back in order, and looked at the room. It seemed a hundred per cent better, clean. Now, if the table were cleaned off and the trash on it put away, that'd be another improvement.

"Lizz," he called.

"Yes, Papa," Lizz replied.

"Bring me a damp cloth," he said.

He picked the trash off the table and dumped it on the couch.

"Here, Jim," she said, coming in with a damp rag.

"I'm gonna fix this house up spick and span for once," he said, taking the rag from her.

"Oh, Jim, you work hard and you're a ruptured man. Don't do too much on your off day. I'll fix it up next week. You need your rest," she said.

"That's all right. I'll get it in tiptop shape this morning, cook dinner, and then rest this afternoon," he said.

He wiped off the oilcloth with the rag and then went over to the kitchen doorway.

"Oh, my, it's going to look nice," Lizz said as she noticed him glancing around the room.

"Now, if we can only keep this clean and a little bit in order," Jim said.

"We're going to," she said.

She went to him, embraced and kissed him.

"My rabbit, we're going to make a home that'll make us happy, and that's more than many with plenty in their pocketbooks can say," he said with feeling, holding her in his arms.

He kissed her again.

IV

After sorting out the odds and ends on the table, Danny and Bill got out the Steel's game Danny had brought with him.

"You won as the Braves last night in our world's series, but I'm going to beat you in the city series now. The Cubs might win today and clean up, but I don't think they will, but I'm going to win our city series for the White Sox," Danny said.

"Don't count your chickens before they're hatched," Bill said.

"You boys want a cup of coffee before I give the little ones their bath?" Lizz asked.

Both of them nodded their heads affirmatively.

"Come out in the kitchen and have it there," she said.

They followed her to the kitchen and sat down, noticing that the tub, filled with cold water, was set up for the baths. And that steaming kettles of water were on the stove.

"Now, after you drink your coffee and go back to play your game, don't make any dirt. Your father is cleaning house," Lizz said, setting cups of coffee before them.

"Do we got to use the lineups that have been used in the city series or can we put in the lineups we want to?" asked Danny.

"I'm making my own lineup and pitching Jimmy Lavender in the first game," Bill said.

"Then I don't have to keep Ping Bodie on the bench but can put him in the game," Danny said.

"It don't matter what lineup you got. Watch those dice speak for me," Bill said.

"Catherine! Catherine!" Lizz called from the steps leading down to the yard.

"Yes, Mama?"

"Come on in for your bath and bring your baby brother," Lizz called.

"Can't I play a little longer?"

"I told you come on. If you don't, I'll drag you in," Lizz yelled.

"Hello, kids," Jim said, coming out to the kitchen.

"Hello, Pa," they said together, and just as they did, Arty toddled in, followed by Lizz who had Catherine's hand.

"You come when I call you," Lizz said.

"Arty splashes too much water. I don't want to get in the tub with him," Catherine said.

"Take your clothes off now and get your bath," Lizz said.

Catherine sat on a kitchen chair and began taking off her dress.

"When you kids finish your coffee, I want you to help your old man some more. You can pick things up in the bedrooms. For once, this house is gonna be clean as a whistle," Jim said.

Danny and Bill exclaimed hasty looks of disappointment.

"Jim, Danny-boy is our guest, and we can't put him to work," Lizz said, pouring kettles of hot water into the wash-tub.

Catherine stood up, pulled off her soiled underclothes, and stood naked. Danny and Bill cast sidelong glances at her. But she was too young for them to see what girls and women looked like.

"Here, let me put you in the tub," Lizz said.

She bent down and picked up Catherine.

"My, but you're getting heavy. Now, stay there and don't splash. Is the water warm enough?"

"Uh huh," Catherine exclaimed, standing in the tub, running her fingers playfully through the water.

"No, Jim, we shouldn't make our guest work," Lizz said, going over to Arty and setting him down on her lap in order to undress him.

"Mama, I can help. I help at home sometimes," Danny said to avert any anger from his father, and Jim frowned when he used the word home.

Lizz looked up while Arty squirmed in her lap.

"What? They put my son to work up there when they get a nigger woman in to wash? Oh, when I see them I'll give them a piece of my mind," Lizz said, holding Arty more firmly so that he couldn't squirm out of her lap.

"A little work won't hurt any kid. When I was Bill's age, I was doin' a damn sight harder work than I hope he'll ever have to do in his hull life," Jim said.

"I'll put a stop to them making my son work," Lizz said.

She continued undressing Arty.

"If he can do things in that place on Prairie Avenue, he can pick up a few things in his father's house," Jim said.

Lizz carried Arty to the tub and set him in it. He splashed water immediately.

"Mama, I tol' you he'd splash me," Catherine protested.

"A little water won't hurt you. Now, stand still while I put some soap on him. Oh, Mama's Angel Child gets a bath, and he likes his bath," Lizz said.

"Wawa. Wawa," Arty exclaimed, splashing his hand down in the water.

"Have a cup of coffee, Jim," Lizz said as she soaped Arty.

"I think I will," Jim said; he went to the stove and poured out a cup, carried it to the table, and sat down with Danny and Bill.

"Wawa! Wawa! Wawa!" Arty exclaimed, gay and laughing, splashing while Lizz continued to soap him.

"Water!" Catherine said.

"Wawa!" Arty said, laughing at his sister.

"Goodness, the way he can get dirt on him," said Lizz.

"Well, all kids do," Jim said absent-mindedly as he stirred his coffee.

"Jim, do you know that Gertrude O'Reilley doesn't have to lift a finger out at Joe's? Not a finger does that little girl lift. Don't be nervous. I'll soap you as soon as I finish with him. He's harder to wash than you, Catherine. No, Jim, not a finger does she lift. Now, I'll try and soap you. Here, Arty, hold this little piece of soap and don't eat it." Lizz began to soap Catherine, who stood still as the operation was performed. "They're going to make a lady out of her. But I fix them. Whenever I see Mary or Martha, I fix them. I just pitch in and tell them about what my people do for Danny and my Little Margaret. I tell them a thing or two. There, now, Catherine, you're going to be clean, you little angel."

Lizz went on washing Catherine, and then began to rinse both children, pouring water over their little shoulders.

"Bill, you can help keep the house clean from now on, can't you?" Jim said.

"Sure, Pa," Bill said.

"I got the hull place fixed up now except the bedrooms. I want to get them fixed up and I'm going over the mattresses to get some of those damn bedbugs. I want to see that papers aren't left on the floor. That's going to be your job from now on. Don't let me find papers on the floor when I come home from work," Jim said.

Bill nodded his head.

"Now, you stay there a minute, Catherine, Mama's princess, and I'll dry Arty and dress him, and then fix you up," Lizz said.

"Can I have a ribbon in my hair?" asked Catherine.

"You're not going out, and you'll get it dirty playing," Lizz said.

"I want a ribbon in my hair," Catherine said, her voice betraying deep disappointment.

"All right, then," Lizz said, drying Arty as he stood on a chair.

"Wibbon!" Arty exclaimed and laughed, and Jim looked over at him, and saw his thin little body, with the ribs noticeable, his pale face, his large, laughing brown eyes.

Jim turned to the older boys. Catherine watched her father, her hands playing in soapy water.

"Well, I suppose you heard the same sermon in church we heard," Jim said to Bill and Danny to make conversation.

"It was about the Blessed Sacrament," Danny said.

"I noticed there was no sermon about the collection plate this week," Jim said.

"Jim, that's no way to talk," Lizz said.

"I wasn't meaning any harm by it," Jim said genially.

"The Church says you must contribute to the support of your pastor," Lizz said, still rubbing Arty with the towel.

"Shursh!" Arty exclaimed.

"And that's a point of Christian Doctrine that's never neglected," Jim said with an ironic smile.

"Mama, I'm getting cold. I want to get dried," Catherine said.

"Hold your horses. I got this Indian," Lizz said as she started pinning a clean diaper on Arty.

When she had it pinned on, she looked at Jim and said:

"You shouldn't talk disrespectfully of the Church in front of your boys, and doing that right after we've all received Communion, that's not right."

"I'm as good a Catholic as the next man, Lizz. I'm just helping the Church out by telling about Christian Doctrine," Jim said.

"I never heard the like of it. A father talking that way to his boys," Lizz said.

"I was just teasing you, Lizz," Jim smiled, finishing his cup of coffee.

"That's no matter for lightness," Lizz said.

She stood Arty on the chair and put the old red dress he had been wearing back on him. She held him up.

"Look, Papa, isn't your precious clean now? He's so pretty. Look at his eyes. He has the eyes of an angel. Take him a minute," Lizz said.

Jim held out his arms.

"Fither!" Arty exclaimed as Jim took him.

Lizz took Catherine out of the water, stood her on a chair, and began to dry her.

"I'll be gettin' back to finish cleanin', and then I'm gonna cook these kids the best dinner they ever had. Today they're gonna have enough to eat," Jim said.

"I'll have this precious fixed up in a minute. Hold Arty until I do, Jim. He's so clean, I don't want him getting into things right after his bath," Lizz said.

"Fither, sisser clean," Arty said, pointing at Catherine.

She smiled as Lizz continued rubbing the towel over her.

"Pa, wanna play Steel's with us this afternoon?" Bill asked.

"Sure," Jim answered.

V

Wearing a narrow blue ribbon around her head, Catherine sat on the couch with Arty.

"You be good now and don't get dirty," Catherine said, while out in the kitchen Lizz was washing Bob, and Dennis sat on a chair awaiting his turn.

Jim took the kerosene lamp off the table and went to the front bedroom.

"The first thing we got to do is to air this room out," he said without looking behind him where Danny and Bill stood in the doorway waiting, looking in at the small stale-smelling room, with the disarranged bed, the old blankets, the large dresser with rows of drawers, its top cluttered with rags and clothes.

Lizz came to the front.

"Jim, you poor man, you did enough. Leave the bedrooms be and I'll take care of 'em. You need a little rest on your off day."

"I started it and I want to finish it," he said.

"Mama, Bob's calling. He wants his bath finished," Catherine called.

Lizz went back to the kitchen. Jim took the bedding to the parlor.

"What do you want us to do to help, Pa?" Bill asked.

"Pick the things off the floor in the closet, take everything on the floor out, and lay it in the parlor here," Jim said.

The boys obeyed, picking up old rags, shoes, odds and ends that lay on the floor and in the closet beside the dresser. Jim moved the bed, and swept energetically. The older boys sat in the parlor, waiting for further instructions, while the sound of voices, Bob's, Dennis', Lizz's, Catherine's, and Arty's, could all be heard mingling together in the kitchen.

"Bill, bring me that piece of cardboard I use for a dustpan," Jim called.

Bill obeyed. Jim swept the dirt onto the cardboard.

"Now bring me that wooden box full of dirt and papers from the dining room," he said.

Bill did, and Jim dumped the dirt and dust into the box.

"Now, you and Danny put the things back neatly, and then close the door so that there isn't a draft in the house," Jim said.

They obeyed, slowly setting back shoes and boxes. Jim went to the other bedroom, swept and aired it, and had the boys pick things up. He came out smiling when he had finished.

"Now, I'll see about bugs in the bedding and mattresses," he said.

He went to the kitchen where Lizz was giving Dennis his bath, and got a can of kerosene. He bent down over the mattress, looking slowly and carefully along a seam.

"Ah, you sonofabitch!" he said, catching a big fat bug, squeezing it between his fingers, its blood smearing them. He wiped his fingers on an old rag beside him and went on slowly looking, putting kerosene on the seams of the mattress.

"Jim! Jim!" Lizz called excitedly from the dining room.

Jim looked up, surprised, concerned because of the hurried note in her voice. He saw her by the dining-room window.

"What?" he asked.

"Come here! Quick! Hurry up, Jim," Lizz said.

Jim hastened to Lizz.

"Look!" Lizz said, pointing.

Across the street, Mrs. Connerty, in her Sunday getup, was seen passing with a large woman who wore a brown coat.

"That's why she went to early mass. She's going out some place with Father Corbett's housekeeper. They're thick as thieves, the two of them are," Lizz said.

"What the hell do I care?" Jim said.

"Well, I thought you'd be interested. I wonder who's cooking dinner for the Connertys and the poor priests. That housekeeper isn't a woman to be taking care of a saint like Father Corbett. And she thick as thieves with the Connerty one," said Lizz.

Mrs. Connerty and the other woman passed out of sight. Jim went back to look for bedbugs in the mattresses, and Lizz returned to the kitchen.

VI

Jim put the mattresses and bedding in the back yard to give them a good airing, and then came into the kitchen and put on an apron to start cooking the Sunday dinner. He whistled as he started his preparations. Dennis came out and watched him.

"Papa has an apron on," Dennis said as Jim tied up the roast.

"Yeh, the old man is housemaid today," Jim said.

Dennis, Bob and Catherine watched him with wide-eyed interest and absorption. While he prepared the meat for the oven, the dice could be heard rattling on the game board in the dining room as Bill and Danny played.

"I put the peas and potatoes on," Lizz said.

"All we got to do now is baste the roast now and then and keep our eyes on it," Jim said, after putting the roast in the oven.

"Papa, when we gonna have dinner?" asked Dennis.

"Time enough. And you're gonna have a dinner today that you won't forget. Danny, here, is gonna eat as good a dinner, too, as he ever gets at the O'Flahertys," Jim said proudly.

"All he and Bill think of is that baseball game of theirs they're playing," Lizz said.

"Yeh, it's like a bug that bit them. Well, it don't do them any harm. Keeps them from having mischievous thoughts," Jim said.

"Papa, I'm hungry, too," Catherine said.

"You're all gonna get enough to eat today," Jim said.

"Our money man is providing for all of us today," Lizz said, smiling.

"Say, damn it, Lizz, the next time we get our hands on any money, we got to get your teeth fixed," Jim said, noticing them when she smiled.

"There'll be time enough for that," Lizz said.

"I always said that we should have had it done that time when we got the money from Bill's leg," Jim said.

"Jim, the Lord has given us our health. With our health and a little food for our mouths, we shouldn't complain," Lizz said.

"Mama, will we eat now? I'm hungry," Bob said.

"You kids go and play a little bit. But keep the house clean. And I'll call you soon as your dinner is ready," Jim said, smiling.

SECTION THREE

1915

18

I

Danny awakened suddenly, and for a moment he hung between sleep and waking. He couldn't remember what he had been dreaming. All that remained from his dreams was fear, and fear seemed like a river running through the darkness of the bedroom, flowing out of him into the darkness, and back from the darkness into him. He sat up in bed. It was Aunt Peg. She was drunk again. She was screaming at the top of her lungs. There she went again, letting out another yell. He closed his eyes. It seemed as if her yelling hurt his ears. Now, after her last scream had died down, there was complete silence in the apartment. There was an elevated train, and again, nothing. Again she yelled. It was not a word, just a loud, awful noise. He was sure the police would be coming here if she kept it up.

"I don't want to live," Margaret said in a loud, drunken voice from the back of the apartment.

Mother said something to Aunt Peg, but he didn't hear what it was. Then Aunt Peg talked in a lower voice, and it sounded like she was crying and mumbling at the same time. He lay back in bed, hoping she wouldn't make any more noise. He covered his head with the sheet and blankets, but he still heard her going on in that low mumbling and crying, and now and then he heard Mother's voice, but he couldn't make out what it was she said. He wanted to get it all out of his mind and go to sleep. He had troubles enough of his own. Coming home from school today, he'd had a fight with Les Parkes, and he'd quit because Les was beating him up. Tomorrow they would say to him that he'd been licked. He had troubles enough of his own and he didn't want to stay awake until all hours of the night because of Aunt Peg. Why didn't she go to bed? He wished Uncle Al was home, but Uncle Al had gone away on the road last week after being home for Christmas and New Year's. Maybe if Uncle Al was home, she wouldn't make such a racket. But she sometimes did even with Uncle Al here. She would sometimes even curse him at the top of her voice. He tried to think of baseball to get himself to sleep. The White Sox would have Eddie Collins next year, and he was the greatest second baseman in the game. With Eddie Collins, they might win the pennant. He wished the season was already started. Gee, if Hal Chase was still with them instead of being in the Federal League! What an infield they'd have, Chase, Collins, Buck Weaver, and they could use Bobby Roth at third. He dozed off and it seemed that he had hardly been asleep for a minute or a jiffy when her loud voice woke him up again. She was yelling at Mother, and Mother was telling her to go to bed and not make such a holy show of herself.

"Ah, they wouldn't let a daughter in the old country do what you're doing. They'd flay you black and blue. They weren't the people for fooling," Mother was saying.

He was glad anyway that Mother hadn't been drinking beer, because look how much worse it always was when both of them were drunk than it was with only one of them soused.

"Don't be giving me any more of your ignorant Irish lip," Aunt Margaret said.

"Ah, but we Irish may be poor and ignorant, but I'll have you know we're decent, we're decent people."

"Yes, and your decency turns your daughters into whores. To hell with your kind of decency, you old hypocrite. Just like your filthy daughter, Lizz O'Neill. She goes to church and prays to the Lord and comes home and backbites everybody."

He was afraid that Aunt Peg might start hitting Mother. He wished he was big enough to be able to stop Aunt Peg from hitting Mother when Aunt Peg was drunk.

"Now you take your beads out and pray. Well, pray and be damned! The Lord will never hear your prayers," Aunt Margaret said.

"*Hail, Mary, full of grace, the Lord is with thee, blessed art thou among women and blessed is the fruit of Thy womb, Jesus. Holy Mary, Mother of God, pray for us sinners now and at the hour of our death. Amen!*" Mother prayed loudly.

He heard her coming down the hallway. Aunt Peg went into the parlor. She was quiet in there. Maybe she was getting tired and would go to sleep. He heard her crying. He lay in bed, hearing her sobs for a long while, and again he dozed off into sleep.

It seemed suddenly as if there were a wind that cried like somebody he knew, a wind that cried like a voice. And, gee, he was a man. He was a man so big he could almost touch the ceiling. And there was Mother, and she seemed to be so little, and she was looking up at him. To see her he had to bend down.

My grandson is bigger than Jack the Giant Killer and he will stick up for his old grandmother, Mother said, and then he saw her dancing a jig around him.

Gee, he didn't know how he grew up to be so big in such a hurry. He used to be a little kid and was licked in school by Les Parkes, and now look how big he was, and who could lick him now? And he was on this street and he didn't know how he had gotten here. It wasn't Prairie Avenue. It was a street he'd never been on before, but still in front of him was the convent of The Little Sisters of the Good Shepherd that used to be on Prairie, and right next to it was the Willard Theater that used to be on Fifty-first and Calumet. And he and Mother were walking down this street, and everybody was getting out of his way, and suddenly a mad dog was coming at them, barking wildly, and the wind that cried like a voice of somebody he knew got louder and louder, and he picked up the mad dog and threw it against a wall,

and

he saw them

dimly beside the bed, struggling in the dark.

"Take your hands off me," Aunt Peg cried.

"You won't be wakin' up me grandson, the little angel!" Mother said.

He cried. They stopped scuffling and bent over him.

"What's the matter, Son?" Mother tenderly asked him.

"Little Brother, are you sad like your poor aunty?" Aunt Margaret asked in a thick voice, and then she bent down and kissed him, her breath almost making him sick because of the bourbon odor; it was bourbon because he knew what bourbon smelled like and he hated the smell.

"Let me alone," he protested.

"Don't turn on your poor unhappy aunt like the rest of them, Little Brother," Aunt Margaret said.

He turned his head to the wall.

"Can't you see that the poor child is sleepy and wants his rest? Let him be," Mother said.

"Don't you dare turn him against his aunt. I'm good to him, and don't you dare turn him against me, you witch," Aunt Peg said.

"The shame of Mary, the Blessed Mother of God, be on you that you would do this to the child at night," Mother said.

"I want to sleep," Danny said whiningly.

"All right! Never speak to me, you little brat! Never look at me! Never ask me for nickels for candy! Never ask me again to sweat over a hot stove cooking meals for you! You little brat!" Aunt Margaret said, and then she staggered out of the room.

19

I

Margaret felt that she was going crazy. She didn't know what she was going to do. She didn't care what she did. She was turned into stone inside. She was stone. She had become stone in her heart. She had no more feeling. She had nothing to feel.

She turned over and faced the wall. The light hurt her eyes. If she stayed in bed, she didn't feel so badly. It was when she got up that she was weak. Her head ached. It was full of nerves, and it seemed that each one of the nerves ached and twitched. Her tongue felt thick and was coated as if there were an untasty foreign substance in her mouth. She would never drink again. The price she was paying this morning was too high. Never again.

Everything in life had a price. It had to be paid. And she was the best payer of prices she knew of. Thinking of this, her sleepy face broke into a wide grin. But she couldn't joke with herself now.

All she wanted to do was sleep. She tried to imagine herself as a stone dropped into the cold, icy waters of the lake. It went to the bottom and stayed there, feeling nothing. She wanted to die. She wanted to be dropped into Lake Michigan, into the cold, icy waters, like a stone that would sink and never again feel anything.

She could see herself doing it. Cold, snowy, icy out as she went to make her end. No sun out. Just an awful day this winter. With a real blizzard. She could see herself tramping through the snow. Not a soul on the streets. Walking through the snow, wet, cold, chilled, walking through the snow to the lake. Not a soul around to see her tragic, pitiful end. Jumping into the lake, drowning, alone with herself at the last miserable hour of the most miserable life that any woman ever lived.

She felt so, so, so like a stone that she didn't even care if she lived or died. Black was the world. Heavy the cross. Miserable the road. Oh, God Almighty, why did you give a poor weak woman such a cross to bear? But God would. God was a man. He made it a world for men. A man could take a woman's all, take her body and soul, and then he could walk away with a light heart. He could go and find another woman.

Why should Lorry do this to her? What did another woman have that she didn't? She had a figure. She had a body. She had a soul. She had a mind. She had experience. She knew how to take a man and make him like it, make him crazy for it. Could another do this better? What? Why? How? She was intelligent. There was not a better business woman among the cashiers at the hotel. What mistakes she made, these were made because of her sadness and her worries, the heaviness that lay on her heart. She was interesting. She was handsome. She wasn't old, only twenty-seven going on twenty-eight. That wasn't old. That was the best time of a woman's life so far as a man should be concerned. Unless a man wanted something young and dumb, a virgin who didn't know a thing! What did a man want something like that for? Oh, why had Lorry forsaken her? Why?

And he had. She lived for Lorry. She lived for him alone. He was such a man. So handsome! So upright! So fine! He was like a boy. He was not just like her lover. He was her lover, and he was like her son. She lived for him. He owned her, every inch of her, body and soul. And what did he do? Threw her away like a dishrag. It wasn't right. It wasn't fair. It wasn't decent. It wasn't the honorable thing to do. He had no right to do that. Not to her. Look what she'd done for him. Only for her, his life would have been ruined. Suppose she had told Brophy, sold information about Lorry to Brophy three years ago when Brophy and Lorry had been fighting and there had been that scandal?

What would you be today, I ask you, Lorry Robinson, if I had done that? Where would you be today, Lorry Robinson, if I had not protected you?

And this was what she got for being honorable. Oh, piss on honor! What good had it done her? It had only made her cross the heavier. She was through. She was turned into stone. Her heart was cold as ice. Ice!

Well, if that was the kind of a man he was, good riddance to bad rubbish. She had been made a fool of. Here she had been a poor, trusting girl. She had believed in him. He had told her he loved her, and ah, fool that she was, she'd believed him. Dirty lies! All the lies he had told her. When business was better, she needn't worry. When the scandal and investigation blew over, he'd divorce his wife and come to her. She would be Mrs. Robinson. He'd take her to Europe. Lies! The lies of a man. And she had been so trusting. Well, Margaret O'Flaherty had learned her lesson. No man would ever make a fool out of her again.

She wished she could sleep. And she couldn't because of the goddamn elevated trains always going by. She'd told Al they had to move. But Al didn't care. He was another man. All men were alike. They owned the world. They treated women like dogs. Al didn't care. He was away. He could go to bed early when he was home, get up early, get out. He didn't have the elevated trains and their goddamn noise making him a nervous wreck because he couldn't sleep. He didn't care. No man cared as long as he had his comfort. That was all a man wanted. Men were all alike. They were all selfish.

If she could only see Lorry, talk to him. If she could go to him and say, Lorry, why did you do this to me? If she could only put her arms around him again, kiss him, pet him, make him forget the worries of the world. If she could only be alone with him, show him again her charms, comfort him, let him see her charms and have her beautiful body, then she would keep him. He'd come back to her. He'd come to his senses. Something just must have come over him.

Oh, God, please let her sleep! Oh, why had she drunk last night? But she'd had to because she'd been so sad. There was that buzzing inside of her. She'd gone around and around and around in her head. All of her inside had throbbed. She'd had to. Hers was the penalty of a poor, trusting, unhappy girl. So now she was sick. She was sick in body, sick in heart, sick in soul. Margaret O'Flaherty was a poor, sick, useless thing, thrown away like garbage by the man she loved and adored. Ah, who would ever have dreamed that such was to be her fate, that such was to be the cross she'd carry through life? Who?

If Lorry would only come back to his senses! He'd see then and know that she was better for him than any other woman. No woman could love him the way she could. There wasn't a woman on earth who could satisfy him the way she could. There wasn't a woman on earth who could be as tender to him as she could. She'd go through Hell for him. She'd walk on the hottest coals. She'd work herself to the bone. She'd slave for him. Because she loved him as no other woman could. Why didn't he see that? What had she said? What had she done? She must see him, bring him back to his senses. She must tell him, Lorry, you're making a big mistake, a big mistake, and you'll regret it all of your living days. Lorry, just think of what you're doing. Lorry, don't think of what you're doing to me. Me, I don't count. Think what you're doing to yourself. You need me, Lorry. I know you do. Oh, Lorry, I know you so well. I know how you need me. Think! Come to your senses! If she could only see him and tell him this, then he'd come to his senses. Then he wouldn't throw her away like garbage.

Oh God! That goddamned elevated!

They'd have to move, before next May if they could break the lease, and if not, then on May first. Al should have some consideration for her. She had to work harder than he did, and he didn't have her nerves. He had no nerves. All that he had was his own selfishness and a bad temper.

She jammed her head, face down, into the pillow.

Oh God!

II

"I got a bite of lunch for the little ones and got them off back to their lessons. Do you want your breakfast, Peg?" Mrs. O'Flaherty said as Margaret, wearing an old kimono, came sleepy-eyed into the kitchen.

"Just a cup of coffee, Mother. I'll get it myself," Margaret answered dully.

"Let me get it for you. You mustn't be feeling so good today after last night," Mrs. O'Flaherty said.

"I'm sorry, Mother. Mother, you must have patience with me these days. I'm not myself," Peg said.

"Did you hear from that man?" Mrs. O'Flaherty asked, setting a cup of black coffee down before Margaret.

"Mother, I never want to speak of him again, not as long as I live, not as long as I live," Peg said bitterly.

"You don't say!" Mrs. O'Flaherty exclaimed.

Margaret put sugar in the coffee. She yawned, rubbed her forehead, and sat looking miserably into the black coffee.

"I saw him yesterday," she suddenly said.

"You don't say? Did he get you drinking?" Mrs. O'Flaherty asked.

"He didn't even see me. Mother, that's why I was the way I was last night. I saw him on the street with some whore. A whore! I know it. Some goddamn filthy whore, that's all. He was with her. And only yesterday morning, didn't I call the hotel and get the message from the desk that he wasn't registered? Oh, Mother, I didn't know what I was doing. I was on my way home from work. I was feeling good because I knew I was going to be off today and be able to get a little rest. And I saw him. Mother, you don't know what it did to me."

"The black Protestant. What kind of a hat did the chippy wear?" Mrs. O'Flaherty said.

"Oh, Mother, I don't know! I don't know! I can't talk about it," Margaret said melodramatically and with great weariness; she stirred her coffee.

"Ah, but let him come to this door. Peg, tell him to come here, and I'll have my son-in-law, Jim O'Neill, knock him down the stairs," Mrs. O'Flaherty said, gesticulating energetically as she spoke.

Margaret didn't answer. She sat brooding over her coffee.

"Ah, and well don't I know it! You can never place a word of trust in a Protestant. Isn't that what I said all me livelong days? Isn't that what me mother before me said to me in the old country when I was running the bush with the backside sticking half out of me dress?" Mrs. O'Flaherty said.

She poured herself a cup of coffee, carried it to the table, and sat down opposite her daughter.

"And so he gave you the gate, did he? I always said there was no good in that one. Peg, I once heard tell of an Orangeman named Robinson and there wasn't an honest bone in his body. Ah, yes, I said it time after time, time after time. There's no good in that devil of a Protestant," Mrs. O'Flaherty said.

"Mother, that he should have done it to me. But I'm all right now. It just struck so, just as if the sidewalk fell away from under me when I was walking on it. Mother, I could have turned into stone right there on the street," Margaret said.

"Like Lot's wife turned into a pillar of salt. Ah, Peg, you should have spit in his face and stuck your hatpin in the eyes of that chippy," Mrs. O'Flaherty said.

Remaining silent, Margaret sipped her coffee. She sat staring vacantly past her mother. She got up and went to her bedroom. Mrs. O'Flaherty sipped coffee, too, nodding her head gravely from side to side. Margaret returned with a cigarette in her mouth.

"Ah, Peg, but I'm the one to deal with the likes of a chippy and the likes of a black Protestant. Ah, but I'm the one for them, and, I tell you, I'd have fixed them! Ah, but I should have seen him with that chippy!"

"Forget it, Mother! I have enough worries now. Just forget it," Margaret said nervously.

"Forget it! In a pig's eye, I will! What? Let a chippy take a man away from you and forget it? I'm not the one for forgetting. Peg, I never forget. I never forgive one that's done something to me. Not me, me mother's daughter," Mrs. O'Flaherty said.

"You're a hard woman, aren't you, Mother?" Peg said.

"Indeed I am!" Mrs. O'Flaherty said, hastily getting to her feet. "See these veins in me arm!" she said, pulling up her sleeve and extending her right arm. "There's iron in them. I come from a hard country! Indeed I am a hard woman!" she said, standing in the center of the kitchen, her small fists upflung, her bony wrists prominent as she waved her arms.

"I guess your daughter isn't hard like you are, that's all," Margaret said, going to the stove, getting warm coffee, and then returning to the table with it.

Mrs. O'Flaherty sat down again.

"The likes of me isn't found every day. Ah, but I should have seen him. With a chippy, was he! With a chippy!"

"Please, Mother, I'm brokenhearted. You'll drive me crazy with that talk. I got to forget him. Please stop it. Don't nag me!" Margaret said.

"Sure, my angel, I'm not nagging you. Sure, and don't I know you're sad? Ah, but if your father had ever done that to me when poor Pa was alive, Lord have mercy on the poor man's soul! Ah, but he knew better. If he had looked at another woman, I'd have ripped the eyes right out of her head and stuck my thumb in his eyes. I'd have blinded him just as sure as the day is long," Mrs. O'Flaherty said.

Margaret smiled wanly at her mother. Mrs. O'Flaherty fumbled in her apron pocket and drew out her pipe and a package of Tip-Top tobacco. She filled the pipe, lit it, sat with her right hand clasping the corncob as she puffed out clouds of smoke.

"And poor Little Brother and Little Margaret. I didn't let them sleep, either. I'm so sorry," said Peg.

"He took his skates to school with him, and he's going skating. I'm going down to see Lizz and her little ones," Mrs. O'Flaherty said.

"Mother, you got to promise me, on your word of honor, that you'll not mention a word of this to her," Peg said.

"Sure, and tell me what in the name of the Holy Ghost I would be wanting to breathe a word of it to her for?"

"You won't, will you, Mother?"

"Sure, I won't breathe a word of it to a soul. Not to me daughter, Lizz. Peg, that one is a gossip," Mrs. O'Flaherty said.

Margaret sat with her chin cupped in her hands.

"Poor Brother, and poor Little Margaret. I'm so sorry I woke them up last night. But, Mother, when I came home I was out of my mind. It wasn't from liquor. It was from grief," Margaret said.

"Peg, that man will burn in the fires of Hell. May the curse of God be on him!" Mrs. O'Flaherty said.

Margaret jumped to her feet and left the kitchen. She walked up and down the hallway, wringing her hands, sighing to herself. Up and down, silent, up and down she paced.

"Well, it serves you right," Mrs. O'Flaherty said, watching her daughter.

III

Margaret went to the phone, called a number, and dropped a lead slug in the box. When there was a response from the other end of the connection, she said:

"Room clerk, please."

She waited several moments. The delay seemed longer in fact than it was in actual seconds. She heard a hello through the receiver.

"Is Mr. L. R. Robinson registered?" she asked in a formal and disguised voice.

A wave of sadness and disappointment swelled through her when she received a negative reply.

"Thank you."

She hung up the receiver. She paced back and forth along the hallway.

IV

What was she going to do to get hold of herself? She wasn't going to drink today. The more she drank, the more she postponed getting a grip on herself. It was only a way of delaying the day when she would be whole again, when her heart and soul would be healthy, recovered from the wounds they had suffered. She paced the floor of her room, the hall, the parlor, asking herself what could she do, how could she quiet the nerves that were hopping, jumping, twitching, inside of her?

Oh, God, why was she not a cow like her sister, Lizz?

And she had no one to talk to. Mother, poor dear Mother, she meant well, but she didn't understand. Poor dear Mother, she was such a darling, but she was a greenhorn. What did she know of things like these, sufferings such as these that her daughter was undergoing?

God had taken her sister Louise before Louise, poor, sick, dear, lovely girl, should know such terrible pain and sorrow. Why hadn't God also taken her? Everything in life seemed planned so that she, Margaret O'Flaherty, would know the hardest road. Ah, Christ, He was not the only one who had trodden a road of rocks with a heavy cross on His shoulders. A wooden cross on one's shoulders, that was not the heaviest cross. The heaviest cross of all was the cross of broken love that a woman carried on her heart.

Why was she living? Why did she let herself go on living? Why did she bear this sorrow? Why didn't she just end it all, once and for all? God would not punish her forever in Hell if she committed suicide. After what she had suffered in this world, God would not condemn her. God was not that kind of a God. Thinking of God just as a punisher, that was just the ignorance of a greenhorn like poor dear Mother, of a fool like foolish, dirty, ignorant Lizz. God was good, and He was all love.

What would Lorry say if he heard that she had killed herself? Would he know why? No, he couldn't. He couldn't because no man could know what a woman suffered, what price she paid in the blood of her soul and her heart. No man could know, not even Lorry. *No man!*

V

It was like a buzzing inside of her. She was going around and around inside.

Lorry, why did you do it to me? Why? Oh, why?

It must all be a misunderstanding. If only she could see him. Maybe if she saw him alone and talked turkey to him, straight, no flirting, maybe he would tell her. She would see him. He would kiss her. She would let him. She would ask him, Lorry, did you mean that kiss, or did you kiss me just because you always do when we meet and you didn't want to make me feel bad?

What would he answer? Would he say, My Peg, why do you ask me that? You know what I think of you. Would he try to wheedle her? Would he try to beguile her into smiling? No, he wouldn't succeed if that was to be his game.

Lorry, don't play with my heart, she would tell him. Don't try to fool me, Lorry. You have to tell me. I don't ask anything but the truth. I don't ask anything but to know just how you feel. Don't you love me any more? Don't you want me any more? Tell me! Tell me, Lorry! Lorry!

She wouldn't let him escape answering questions. She'd talk to him point-blank. All she wanted was the truth. Only the truth.

Lorry, I am woman enough to face the truth, she would say. Lorry, she would say, Lorry, if you're tired of me, tell me. I'll go out of your life. I'll never put myself on you. I'll never be a burden. I'll never bother you. Lorry, I live for you. I love you so much and so dearly that I only want your happiness. If I can no longer make you happy, I'll step aside and let you be free of me, from any burden of me for the woman who can make you happy.

She would talk to him like that. And she would mean every word of it. Yes, every word of it. Jesus Christ, she wouldn't for one minute be a burden to a man. She didn't want to. She just wanted to know. She just wanted to know if it was the end, or if it was some small misunderstanding between them, or what it was. Could it be that Lorry was jealous of her, and he was not seeing her and seeing other women because of jealousy?

God, there would be this buzzing, this going around and around in her head until she saw him. She had to see him. She had to talk to him. If she could only see him, talk to him, then, then if he said he was through with her, that would be all. She would brace up. He would never again have to hear from her. If she knew, then, then she'd kill herself before she'd ever burden him. The trouble was that she didn't know. She couldn't be sure. That was why she was like this, in such a state of twitching nerves.

She got up from her bed on which she'd been sitting, and again she paced the house. But the external world was almost completely out of her consciousness. She was only vaguely aware of where she was. She walked almost like one in a dream.

Yes, she had to see Lorry. She couldn't go on like this. She had to see him. She had to know. And when she did see him she'd talk to him in plain words.

Lorry, don't you want me any more? Yes, she'd talk to him like that. She'd talk to him, calling a spade a spade. She'd even say to him, point-blank, Lorry, is it that you don't think I'm any good in bed any more? If not, what is it? What does a man want, what do you want, that I can't do, that I can't give you, that I haven't got? Oh, if she could only see him alone, talk plainly to him then, and ask him.

Then, if he told her, if he said he didn't want her, was tired of her, she would be resigned. But she didn't know. She didn't even know if he was tired of her or not. She couldn't be resigned, at peace within herself, unless she knew. She had to know. She had to know what it was in her that made him tired, if he was tired of her. She'd ask him. Why? What had she said, what had she done, why? She'd make him answer her. The least that he could do, the least he owed her, was to tell her the truth.

Why didn't he?

She'd seen him on the street yesterday with a woman on his arm. And now, at every hotel where he was likely to be, the same answer—*not registered*.

When she saw him, she'd say, Lorry, you're not square with me. You're not doing the honorable thing. Why don't you be square with me? I always believed that you were a gentleman. But you're not acting the way a gentleman should.

She'd tell him things like that.

If Lorry was an honorable man, he wouldn't make her suffer this way. Ah, and she, fool that she was, she'd always thought that he was honorable, that he was a gentleman.

Well, there was a God in Heaven. There was a God in Heaven Who punished those who were mean. There was a God in Heaven Who would not stand by and see meanness go unpunished. As sure as the day was long, as true as she was Peg O'Flaherty walking back and forth in her home at this very minute, Lorry Robinson would be punished by God for what he'd made her go through. He would be repaid. A man who treated a woman badly, he needn't think that he'd go scot free. There was a God.

She went out to the kitchen and had another cup of coffee.

"Peg, are you better?" Mrs. O'Flaherty asked.

Margaret did not hear her mother. She sipped her coffee.

"Peg, do you feel any better?"

"Oh, don't bother me."

"Sure, and I wasn't. I was only asking you if you feel any better," said Mrs. O'Flaherty.

"Yes," Margaret said dully.

VI

Margaret sat down at her writing desk. She wanted to write a letter to the Poor Clares. They'd pray to God for her, and their prayers would be heard. God would have to hear their prayers. God would know what the plea of their prayers was. God would know that their prayers were the plea of a poor, stricken, sinful and unhappy girl who could not pray herself, whose heart and whose soul were too torn by the misery of life to pray herself. God would know that.

She sat at her desk. She picked up her pen and set it down. She cupped her chin in her left hand, and her eyes vacantly concentrated on the roses in the wallpaper. God would know. She could feel that God would know. God was good. God was kind. God was merciful. God didn't want people to be unhappy and in misery. God didn't punish as people said He did. That was just old greenhorn Irish superstition. She could see God in Heaven. She had a picture of Him in her mind. He was wearing robes and He was sweet and kindly. He was saying that He did not send unhappy souls to Hell for the sins that they could not help committing. He was saying it to her sister Louise. Louise was in Heaven with God and with Father. Father was there, too, her dear father. God was saying to her dear, dead father and her dear, dead sister that no, He did not send poor unfortunate sinners to Hell. He was saying sin was in yourself, in your mind. He was saying that what poor Mrs. O'Flaherty and Lizz O'Neill thought of Him was only Irish superstition. They did not know Him truly as He was. He had not made the world to be a place of misery. He had not created Hell to make those who were miserable on earth more miserable in Hell. That was God. She had a picture of Him in her mind. He was good, and He was kind, and He would not punish as the old Irish superstitiously said He would. That was God.

Her vision of God as good, and helpful, and comforting, and merciful and gentle, and full of charity, was strong and stirring in her mind as she addressed the letter.

Dear Good Pious Lovely Sisters

These Poor Clares, these kindly virginal nuns, they were the ones who were really holy. And they weren't like Lizz O'Neill. They were not *holy* like Lizz. They were holy the way God wanted some women to be holy. *Judge not and you shall not be judged!* They weren't judges. Lizz was. Her mother was. The world was. All her life she had known a world full of hypocrites and judges.

> *Please pray for my special intention. I am very sad and unhappy and please, lovely Sisters of God, pray for my special intention. Please pray. I am sending you this offering of one dollar which is all that I can possibly afford but if I could afford a larger offering I would enclose it and it would make me so happy to do it. I have so much on my poor mind and I must carry such a heavy cross through life. Please lovely good sisters, please pray for me. Ask God and my poor dear dead father and my lovely darling departed sister Louise in Heaven to join you by asking God to give me the strength to carry my load and my cross through life. My poor sister who is married she is so poor and I am so worried that I cannot give her more help and my dear mother is old and I want her last days to be happy and I have to carry so many burdens and responsibilities on my poor shoulders. Please good sisters pray for my*

special intention and as soon as I can I am going to send you a larger offering. You are so good. I don't know how I can tell you how much you are a help and a consolation to me. From the bottom of my heart I write this letter and ask you this favor and tell these things to you.

+Margaret O'Flaherty+

++

+

P.S. Thank you dear sisters from the bottom of my heart.

Peg drew a dollar bill from her large, black leather pocketbook, folded it up in the letter, placed both in an envelope, and addressed it to the Convent of the Poor Clares.

The prayers of the Poor Clares, the plight of herself, these would wring even the heart of God, she told herself with gloomy confidence. Such prayers would bring her the help of God in sending Lorry back to her and easing the buzzing buzzing buzzing that went on in her head like some awful bug or spider.

She paced her bedroom, smoking cigarette after cigarette and wringing her hands. She sat down again at the desk, a determined look on her face. She placed a clean sheet of paper before her.

Dear Al

I detest having to write this letter to you but I cannot stand conditions at home. Mother nagged and talked all morning and I was almost driven crazy. Danny of course is the loveliest boy but he is wild and careless. When he washes his hands in the bowl in the bathroom, he does not wash the bowl out. His carelessness is a bad example for Little Margaret. And sometimes it is hard to make her go to school. She does not like school. I work hard as you know at the hotel. I do not mind doing things at home, and I would willingly do anything. But it seems to me that Danny is old enough to clean out the bowl in the bathroom when he washes his hands and the very least he could do would be to wash the bowl out. When you were home for Christmas you talked to both of the children and they promised you they were going to cooperate. On Monday morning, I went in to clean up before going to work and the bathroom looked as if a cyclone had hit it. Wet towels were on the floor and the sink was filthy. I said to Danny, Brother you shouldn't be so careless and he said to me that he was not a servant or a nigger. Al you know how I love Mother and she is such a dear good lovely darling even if she does nag me until I want to scream but Al you must do something when you come home because she is responsible for spoiling the boy and she is not fair to his sister, nags her all the time. If you don't do something I will just have to leave because I cannot stand it one more day. Mother simply must stop spoiling him and stop her old gabbing old Irish nagging and talking. I am almost out of my head with nerves and I cannot go on like this. If I cannot have a little peace and comfort at home I shall have to go away and try to find it some place else. I know of no girl my age, making the money I make, doing the work

I do, holding the position of responsibility I hold down, who puts up with what I put up with. I cannot do it any more. My nerves are shattered. You must do something. If things do not change you must come home and straighten them out. If you don't, you will not find me here when you do come home. It is the breaking point. It cannot go on any longer. It is final. I will lose my head because of my nerves unless there is a change. I hate to have to write you like this but I simply cannot go on.

    Peg

She addressed and sealed the letter. Well, everything she said was so. She couldn't go on with things like this. Mother nagging and nagging and nagging. Danny spoiled, becoming a brat, dirty and noisy. Last night, look at the way he talked to her after all she'd done for him, and she with a broken heart. Little Margaret getting sassy, fighting with Danny. Mother nagging Little Margaret. She could not go on. She couldn't stand it. Her nerves!

Of course, Brother was a sweet boy. She would do everything in the world she could for him to make him happy, to see that he got a good education, to see that he could become *somebody* in this world. But there was a limit. Yes, there was a limit. And that limit had been reached.

Margaret sat down again. She was going to write to Lorry. She didn't care if he had said not to. She was going to write to him. The time was past when she cared. He had not treated her right. He had not done the right thing by her. If he was going to let her pay, she was going to make him pay, too. She sniffled. She wiped her eyes and blew her nose with the sleeve of her kimono. She was going to make him pay.

Dear Lorry

    I cannot go on any longer. My nerves are killing me. I cannot stand it. I cannot go on. Lorry, I must see you. I don't care where you are. You must come to Chicago right away and see me. Lorry, this cannot go on as it has been. I have to see you. I have to know are you through with me, don't you want me any more. I cannot stand this uncertainty. I know you warned me against writing you letters like this. But I don't care. I can't stand it. I can't help myself any more. I got to know. You have to tell me. There are things in life more important than what the world knows. I don't care any more what the world knows and thinks. I hate the world. I don't care. Let the world know. I am killing myself with worry. I don't care if I live or die. I don't care. You have to see me. I have been fair and square with you Lorry Robinson. Lorry Robinson you got to be fair and square with me.

She crumpled up the letter she was writing and threw it in the wastebasket. She got up from the chair. She lit a cigarette. She walked to and fro across the bedroom, puffing, her face cloudy, sad, absorbed. She went to the wastebasket, pulled out the crumpled sheets of paper on which she had written, went to the bathroom with them. She tore them into small pieces, slowly, carefully, and then she dropped them into the bowl. She pulled the chain, watched the rush of water, the swirl, the bits of paper curling around and around, carried down. She left the bathroom.

Oh God!

If she wrote him such a letter, he'd be more angry. She might let the cat out of the bag. Suppose she did? Would she gain? Would she lose? She didn't care. He didn't care about her nerves, her feelings, her heart, her very own life, did he? Why should she show him any consideration? Look at all she had done for him, sacrificed for him, all the love and devotion she had lavished upon him! What did he care? He asked her not to write to him, not to let the world know. But why? Why shouldn't she, when he treated her like a cur? Why shouldn't she? What gratitude did he show to her for all that she had done for him? None. Absolutely none. *None. And the blackest sin in the world was the sin of ingratitude.*

She had to see him. She had to speak to him. What would she do? She couldn't go on living like this any longer. She couldn't! Oh, God, why must such unhappiness befall her, and only her? So many others she knew, they did not have such unhappiness. She could do nothing but worry. She couldn't think. She couldn't work. She couldn't even pray. Only worry. Only nerves. Only this state she was now in. Oh, God! Oh, Jesus Christ! Jesus Christ! Jesus Christ! Oh! Oh! Oh!

Again she sat down at the desk, cupped her chin in her hands. What should she say to him? Maybe she would try one letter written like a business letter. But he was in Chicago. Would he be going back to his office? Would the letter be forwarded to him if he wasn't? When would he get it? Would he ignore it as he had ignored all the other letters she had sent him these last months? Oh, this uncertainty would kill her.

She drew out a fresh sheet of paper. She dipped her pen in the ink bottle.

> *Dear Lorry*
>
> *I know you don't want me to write to you like this and I know that I shouldn't. I know, oh Lorry dearest, I know. But I have to. If you only knew how I feel and what I am going through, you would understand. Lorry I simply must see you. As soon as you receive this letter and read it you must come to Chicago and see me. I must see you. I must hear your voice. I want to know and I must know Lorry is it all over? Is all our beautiful love dead? You must tell me. You simply must. I cannot stand this uncertainty. My nerves are killing me.*

She tore up this letter, went to the bathroom, dropped it in the bowl and pulled the chain. She paced the hall. She wouldn't write to him. She'd be proud. Never again would she see him. She'd freeze her heart to him until it was like ice. She'd go on living with a heart of ice. He didn't care. He had hurt her. She wouldn't care in time. She would become cold and hard and calculating. She'd act as other women did. What she had paid because of him, other men would pay because of her. She would be proud. She was young. Lorry wasn't the only goldfish swimming in the bowl. He wasn't the only grain of sand on the beach. He wasn't the only man in the world. She'd be proud. No, the world wouldn't be told of her sorrow and her disappointment. The world would never know. For the world, she'd laugh, she'd sing, she'd smile, she'd dance, she'd be gay and have a good time, and the world would pay. She walked up and down the hallway, trying to steel herself. Suddenly, she ran into her bedroom, closed the door after her, flung herself on the bed, and cried with her head sunk into a pillow on the unmade bed. She quivered as she sobbed.

With equal suddenness, she jumped up, went to the desk, and wrote again.

Dear Mr. Robinson

I have just had a long and confidential business talk with Mr. Olson. Conditions are worse than they were for him. If something does not happen immediately I am afraid that he will do something dangerous. His depression because of business is black. I fear that he might commit suicide. I cannot do anything for him. I advise you to try and come to Chicago immediately and have a long business talk with him. Unless you do and right away, it might be too late. I have never seen him in such a black depression in all my experience with him. I am afraid he will commit suicide. I advise you to come to Chicago and see him immediately for a long helpful business talk. He wants that and only that, he says, will save him. He says so. If you don't his death might be on your conscience. It is most urgent.

Sincerely yours

A. J. Johnson

P. S. I am writing this letter in my own hand instead of dictating it to my secretary because it is so confidential I wouldn't even allow my secretary to know about it.

With determination, she sealed the letter and addressed the envelope, marking it *personal* and *important*. She began dressing hurriedly in order to get her letters mailed. She was determined. She'd give him time to receive this letter. If he didn't come, she'd kill herself, and before she died she'd leave a letter behind to be opened after she was gone, telling everything, *everything* to the world. She would. Her mind was made up, once and for all.

20

"I'm so glad you came down today, Mother," Lizz said as the two of them sat at the kitchen table with cups of tea before them, while from the dining room, Arty, Bob, and Catherine mumbled as they played together on the floor near the stove.

"Ah, Lizz, you're a good thing, me best daughter. And today isn't so cold, so I says to meself, wait till I gee down there and tell Lizz," Mrs. O'Flaherty said, and after speaking she lifted the thick muglike teacup to her lips.

"Mother, I tell you, Peg'll rue the day she took to the scarlet road of sin," Lizz said, frowning, holding her finger steadily before her mother as she spoke.

"Lizz, they used to say in the old country, 'Sup with the Devil and you need a long spoon,'" Mrs. O'Flaherty said knowingly.

"It's the truth, Mother. There's no way out. You got to be good or bad, holy or sinful. Sin, and you're punished. If you're pure and holy and live in the fear of God, you'll have all the joys of the Kingdom of Heaven waiting for you when you die," Lizz said.

"You say the truth," Mrs. O'Flaherty said, and she took another sip of tea.

"Jim and me are poor, but we're good. We live in the fear of God. We won't be poor in the next world," Lizz said.

"You say the truth," Mrs. O'Flaherty said.

"Mother, you say he gave her the gate?" Lizz asked.

"Indeed he did. He tied a can to her," Mrs. O'Flaherty said, wagging her chin dramatically.

Lizz pursed her lips knowingly, looked squarely at her mother, raising her brows and nodding her head up and down as if in thought and realization.

"And small loss he is," Mrs. O'Flaherty said.

"Mother, I always told you that no good would come from her running after him," Lizz said.

"Didn't I once hear tell of an Orangeman named Robinson who ran out on a debt?" Mrs. O'Flaherty said.

"I dreamed it. Last night, Mother, Father came to me last night, and he told me. When you walked in the door this afternoon, I knew you were coming to tell me what Father told me last night," Lizz said.

"You saw Pa again?" Mrs. O'Flaherty asked sharply.

"Yes, Mother," Lizz said.

"The devil of a nerve he has," Mrs. O'Flaherty said acidly.

"Mother, whenever Father comes to me, he tells me to look after you," Lizz said, while from the front the children could be heard quarreling. "Hey, you in there, keep quiet and play without making so much noise," she yelled.

"I'll let you know I need no looking after," Mrs. O'Flaherty said.

"And so he tied a can to her? Well, it serves her right. She carried on like a disgrace, Mother, a disgrace," Lizz said, taking another sip of tea.

"All that I ask is that I should have seen him on the street like Peg did," Mrs. O'Flaherty said.

"Mother, no, never do that. It isn't ladylike to fight on the street," Lizz said.

"Ladylike be damned! Ladylike to spit in the eyes of a streetwalker and suck the blood out of a Protestant limb of the Devil," Mrs. O'Flaherty said.

"Mother, oh no! Oh no! You should never lower your dignity by fighting on the street," Lizz said.

"I'll fight!" Mrs. O'Flaherty said, curving her right arm upward in a demonstrative gesture. "If your Jim should run after a chippy, I'd split his head open and let the dogs drink his blood."

"Mother, my Jim is a good, hard-working man. You can't compare him with a trifler like Lorry Robinson. Mother, he's a trifler, a dirty, stinking trifler. That's all he is," Lizz said self-righteously.

"Oh, but if I ever lay the sight of day on him with these eyes!"

"Mother, if you see him on the street, don't speak to him. Don't give him the satisfaction. Here's what you do," Lizz said. She arose, and her pregnant abdomen stuck out. She walked across the kitchen in a clumsy, mincing manner, swinging her arms, swaying her buttocks, and holding her nose in the air. "Just do that. Walk by him as if you didn't know him from Adam. Pass him by like he wasn't even there. And then, after you pass him by, do this," Lizz said, illustrating what she meant by spitting on the floor.

"He'll come to a bad end," Mrs. O'Flaherty said while Lizz went to the stove for the teapot.

"You need some hot tea in that cup. It's winter and cold out," Lizz said, pouring more tea for both of them. She returned the pot to the stove, and then she sat down and said, "And so he gave her the air?"

"And she's walking the house wringing her hands, crying her eyes out, walking the house white as a sheet and saying she's nervous. Nervous in a pig's backside," Mrs. O'Flaherty said.

"Mother, when she bellyaches about nerves, don't you believe her. That's all a stall. Mother, if she worked as hard as I do, as you did, as your mother did, she wouldn't have time to bellyache about nerves. Look at me with all my little ones and another one on the way. Do I bellyache about nerves? Mother, don't you believe her. She's stalling. She heard some swell down at the hotel where she works talk about nerves, and that's the whole story."

"Lizz, and how are you?" asked Mrs. O'Flaherty.

"Oh, Mother, it's hard. I'm getting big, and it's hard moving around, and I have pains and my morning sickness. I have to get up, sick or not, and take care of this regiment," Lizz said.

"You poor thing," said Mrs. O'Flaherty.

"If I led the life of Riley like that one behind me does," said Lizz.

"Who's that?" asked Mrs. O'Flaherty.

"That Connerty one," said Lizz.

"I came over on the boat and I was out five weeks, five weeks, and there was a Connerty from Galway on the boat, and do you know, she talked the shirt off the back of every man on the boat. Pass her by, Lizz," said Mrs. O'Flaherty.

"I do. Say, but you should see the way I high-hat that one. But, Mother, she's thick with Father Corbett's housekeeper. They go out all the time. Mother, they're cronies, and the two of them talk the legs off one another, backbiting. Mother, all they do is backbite. They're trying to turn Father Corbett against me. I know they are. But they can't do it. They can't. I told Father Corbett that my mother's sister is a nun in New York, and he liked that," said Lizz.

"Have you heard from me sister?" asked Mrs. O'Flaherty.

"No, I must write to her. Have you?"

"Sure, and who would write her for me, with Al on the road, and that one at home," Mrs. O'Flaherty said.

"She and the airs she puts on! Who is she? What is she? Mother, even if she is my own sister, she's a hussy. That's what she is. A dirty hussy. Her and her nerves. When Jim hears talk of her nerves, he always says that a good swift kick in the ass would cure her of nerves."

"Lizz, she does be walking up and down the hall pale as a ghost," Mrs. O'Flaherty said, raising her hands and looking upward with a shocked expression.

"Mother, you should have married her off to a good man when she was a girl just like you married me."

"And sure, I didn't marry you off."

"Why, Mother, you did, too. Every good mother marries her daughters off," Lizz said.

"And tell me, what decent man would have her with her cigarette-smoking, and her pot under the bed too lazy to go to the bathroom, and her high-lifing out at night till all hours. What decent man would have her?"

"She never could have gotten a man as good as my Jim. Decent men want decent women," Lizz said boastingly.

"Indeed they do," Mrs. O'Flaherty said, while from the other rooms the children could be heard trying to sing.

"Mother, if you make yourself cheap and easy to get like she did, all you can get is a dirty stinking rotter like that Robinson, and then, when he gets tired of you, he throws you overboard and doesn't care if you sink or swim. But if you don't make yourself easy, you get a good, decent, dependable man like my Jim, who doesn't throw you overboard," said Lizz.

"Ah, Lizz, but I should be the girl again. The man isn't alive who would do to me what that Protestant devil did to my Peg. That married man!" Mrs. O'Flaherty said.

"The least he could have done if he was a decent man was give her five or ten thousand dollars when he threw her overboard," Lizz said.

"I wouldn't spit on his money. It's money that's come out of the mouth of Hell," Mrs. O'Flaherty said.

"I know it is, Mother, and I wouldn't touch a red cent of it, but I was saying, it's the least he could have done if he was a man and a gentleman," Lizz said.

Lizz got to her feet and spoke with many gestures, her heavy breasts wobbling.

"Mother, it's easier for a camel to go through the eye of a needle than for a rich man to enter the kingdom of Heaven. Mother, mark my words! When Robinson dies, he'll go straight to Hell on an express train with no stops on the way! Mother, when I die, if I go to Heaven, I'll look down and see him roasting and toasting, parched for a drop of water to drink, crying out to be rid of his suffering and agony, crying and bawling for the sight of God. Because, Mother, to be deprived of the sight of God for all eternity is the worst punishment of God. Mother, he'll be suffering and crying, and I'll spit on him. I'll spit on him, and I'll tell him, 'Go ahead, you devil, you're with Satan where you belong! Burn down there, you trifler! Roast and toast away, you dirty bum! You haven't a swell suit of clothes and money now to hide from the world that you're just a bum and a no-account. Burn! Toast! Go ahead, go ahead, fry away, you sonofabitch!' Mother, that's the way I'll greet him in the next world."

"I often do be thinking that the people in the old country would have run the likes of him into the sea with pitchforks," Mrs. O'Flaherty said while Lizz sat down, tired and breathless.

"Mother, he hasn't any conscience. That's why he's such a bad one," Lizz said, pointing a finger under her mother's nose to emphasize what she was saying.

"Since when did anyone hear tell that a black Protestant has a conscience?" Mrs. O'Flaherty said.

"And, Mother, it would tear your heart out. When Peg first met him years ago, she was such a lovely thing, such an innocent girl, so sweet. And now what is she? What? I'll tell you. She's damaged goods. When you go to the grocery store, do you want damaged goods, broken eggs, and stale bread, damaged goods? Do you?"

"I'd break the window of him that sold them to me."

"It's the same, the very same thing, when men go into the market and look for a wife. They don't want women to be damaged goods, either. Mother, do you think for one minute that my Jim would have wanted me if I was damaged goods? I should say not! I was a virgin, Mother, a virgin, as pure as a flower when he got me. If I wasn't, he never would have had me. No man, Mother, wants damaged goods. And Peg's damaged goods now. That dirty bum has ruined her life, ruined my lovely sister's life. Now no decent man will have her because she's damaged goods," Lizz said.

"And to think that I would see the day in the latter end of me life when me own daughter would come to this. It would make your blood run cold. Heavy is the world on me poor old heart. But, Lizz, you're a good daughter."

"I'm your favorite, ain't I, Mother?" Lizz said, her decaying teeth showing as she flashed a broad smile. "I'm my Mama's favorite child, ain't I?" she repeated, adjusting the soiled rag under her fatty chin while she talked.

"Oh, but if I was a man, I'd fist him for doin' that to me daughter. Ah, but if Pa was alive, he'd get some of the men that worked on the wagons with him, and they'd fist him, they would," Mrs. O'Flaherty said.

"I'll tell you what, Mother. Jim'll get some of the men on the express wagons after him. They'll do it. Some of them men are fighters. Oh, but they're fighters! Many a time my Jim has come home with his face all swollen up after fighting and I've had to send Bill out to get raw beefsteak to put on his face. Them men are fighters, and my Jim will get them after him," Lizz said.

"I'll give every man that punches him a quarter."

"You won't have to, Mother. They'll do it for nothing for my Jim," Lizz said.

"If they beat him within an inch of his life, God will reward them," Mrs. O'Flaherty said.

"Mother, when you told me today, I was sick. She used to be such a lovely girl," Lizz said.

"My Louise never would have become a chippy," Mrs. O'Flaherty said.

"Oh, my sister Louise was an angel. An angel, purer than the flowers, she was. An angel out of Heaven," Lizz said.

"Indeed, she was," Mrs. O'Flaherty said, beginning to cry.

The tears welled in Lizz's eyes.

"God took her because she was too pure for this earth," Lizz sobbed.

"She's with Pa and me mother now," Mrs. O'Flaherty said.

"A pity, Mother," Lizz exclaimed.

"A shame, indeed," Mrs. O'Flaherty said.

II

The four youngest O'Neill children were playing house. They halted their game when Lizz and Mrs. O'Flaherty, wearing her fur coat, stopped to look at them.

"Ah, the cute little things," Mrs. O'Flaherty said, smiling at them.

"Every one of them is their Mama's Angel Child, Mother," Lizz said.

"The little fellow is so cute, but he's pale. Sure, the poor baby is pale as a ghost," Mrs. O'Flaherty said.

"He had a cold, Mother. It was so cold here. Look, we have wrapping paper all around the windows and on the floor to keep some of the cold air out, but it doesn't help a lot. Jim, poor man, had to spend two nights, after being out all day on the wagon in the cold, laying that paper under the beds and couches, taking up rugs and putting it under them, putting it on the walls there near the window sills," Lizz said.

"Lizz, and sure he has such beautiful eyes," Mrs. O'Flaherty said.

All the children looked up at their mother and grandmother.

"Arty, precious, say hello to your grandmother," Lizz said.

"Lo," Arty said.

"Ah, the little dream. He's such a pretty baby," Mrs. O'Flaherty said.

"That's your grandmother," Lizz said to Arty, pointing to Mrs. O'Flaherty.

"Dammither," Arty said, pointing to his grandmother.

"And little Katy here. Hello, you little darling. She's a cute one, Lizz, and look at the little face of her. She looks like a deep one," Mrs. O'Flaherty said.

Catherine smiled.

"Mother," she said, addressing her grandmother.

"Yes, you little darling," Mrs. O'Flaherty said.

"We were playing house," Catherine said.

"They're such good children. They've been so good today," Lizz said.

"And little Dinny here, he's a scholar now. Do you know your letters, little Dennis?"

"Oh, Mother, the Sister thinks the world of him, and he's so smart. He reads and writes now," Lizz said.

"I know the alphabet, and I read from my reader, and I write," Dennis said.

"You little scholar," Mrs. O'Flaherty said.

"Mother, when is my sister Margaret coming to see me?" Catherine asked.

"Soon it will be. Little Pegeen is a cute little one, too, Lizz," said Mrs. O'Flaherty.

"I want to see my sister Margaret," Catherine said.

"And there's the left-handed one," Mrs. O'Flaherty said, pointing to Bob. Bob smiled up at his grandmother.

"He'll be going to school in a year or two," said Lizz.

"They're all going to be little scholars. But, Lizz, look at the face on the little one. Ah, Lizz, he has a wise face," Mrs. O'Flaherty said, pointing to the baby.

"He's wise, a wise one, Mother. He has big, wise eyes," Lizz said.

"He looks as wise as an old man. Look at the face on him," Mrs. O'Flaherty said.

"Mother, he is. And don't you think he takes after Pa?"

"Glory be, he does. He's an O'Flaherty, Lizz," said Mrs. O'Flaherty.

Arty smiled shyly at his grandmother, held her in his deep brown eyes.

"I never saw a baby with such beautiful eyes," Lizz said.

"They're brown eyes, Mama," Catherine said.

"They have the look of an old man in them. He's going to grow up to be a wise one. But he looks so pale and thin. Sure, he needs to be built up," Mrs. O'Flaherty said.

"It's always terrible for them in winter. They are so cold in the house here. The wind comes right off the corner and hits us. I'm thankful that the weather is warmer now. I hope it stays this way," Lizz said.

"Cold," Arty said; he crossed his hands, screwed up his face, pursed his little lips, blew air out of them rapidly.

"Mother, he's saying cold to you," Lizz said.

Mrs. O'Flaherty bent down and held her arms out to Arty. He looked at her suspiciously. He came to her slowly. She picked him up, kissed him. He was quiet in her arms and watched his mother closely.

"That's your grandmother, Arty," Lizz said to him.

"Dammither," Arty said, and laughed.

"Mother?" Catherine said.

"Yes, Little Katy," Mrs. O'Flaherty said.

"Arty is learning to talk good," Catherine said.

"He is, is he? Lizz, he's almost as beautiful a baby as my grandson Daniel was at his age," Mrs. O'Flaherty said.

She looked at her grandson in her arms.

"Danny was a beautiful baby with his curly hair," Lizz said.

"They're all fine children, Lizz," Mrs. O'Flaherty said.

"I wish they were bigger. They'd be less care," Lizz said.

"The time will come when they will be," Mrs. O'Flaherty said.

She put Arty down, and he ran to Lizz, clasped her dress, and pressed his curly head against her leg.

Mrs. O'Flaherty bent down and fumbled in her pocketbook. She handed each of them a penny.

"Buy yourselves some candy," she said.

"Say thank you to your grandmother," Lizz said.

"Thank you," the three oldest said in unison.

Arty studied his penny. He started to put it in his mouth.

"Arty!" Catherine said, rushing to him, taking his hand away from his mouth. "Don't you swallow that."

"He doesn't know better yet, does he, Lizz?" Mrs. O'Flaherty said.

"Gimme your penny. I'll mind it for you," said Catherine.

"Ma, can I mind Arty's penny for him?" Dennis asked.

"I will," Lizz said, bending down and taking the penny from Arty.

"Here, Lizz. Buy something for the little ones, and get the baby some milk," Mrs. O'Flaherty said, giving Lizz a dollar.

"Thanks, Mother. I will," said Lizz.

"I got to be going, Lizz," said Mrs. O'Flaherty.

"All of you kiss your grandmother goodbye," Lizz said.

Mrs. O'Flaherty bent down, let each of them kiss her cheek, kissed each one on the forehead, and patted their heads. She kissed Arty twice.

"You wise one," she said to him, giving him a pat on the head.

"Goodbye, Lizz," she said.

"Bye-bye," Arty said.

"Let me kiss you goodbye, Mother," Lizz said.

"Don't make free with me. Goodbye, and take care of the little ones," she said, and she was gone.

21

I

Some day he would be a better ice skater than he was now. He had to keep trying to learn so that he could skate better like Albert and some of the others did. And maybe some day he would have Johnson racers instead of clamp skates. Albert had Johnson racers and he could skate pretty good going around in circles.

Danny set his body, stroked with his left foot, followed with his right. He swayed awkwardly, and he lost his rhythm. His head and shoulders were jerked backward. He was afraid that he'd fall, and he struggled to regain his balance, stroking his left foot again. He just escaped a tumble. Had to try it slower.

"Getting along all right?" Albert Throckwaite, a thin, blond boy of Danny's size, called as he went by rapidly.

"Yeah," Danny yelled after him, but Albert had gone on toward the other end of the pond. Danny struggled along by himself, unable to keep a steady and rhythmic stride. He was on the verge of tumbling when he grabbed onto a branch in the small, snow-covered island in the center of the Washington Park duck pond.

He saw the half-crowded duck pond. Most of the skaters were young boys and girls. It was warm and it would be fun here today if the ice was not melting and so sloppy, and if he could skate better. He saw Jimmy Keogh trying to catch Albert. They could go so good. But they had been skating longer than he had been. He'd only gotten the skates as a Christmas present from Uncle Al. He was learning.

He saw little Hortense Audrey about fifteen yards ahead of him. She wore a green plaid skirt, a red sweater, and red mittens and stocking cap. She couldn't skate good, and she had worse form than he had. She tried, went several strokes, stopped and looked around.

"Washerwoman," Tommy Keefe yelled; he skated up to her and gave her a push.

She fell down and sat on the ice, laughing.

"You go away," she said when she got up.

Tommy laughed and skated away. He suddenly fell, but got right up.

"Serves you right," Hortense Audrey called after him, and she laughed.

Danny laughed, too. It did serve him right.

Danny shoved away from the island, struggled through the moving figures. He drew up awkwardly beside Hortense Audrey.

"Did you see Tommy fall?" she asked him.

"Yes, he took a funny spill," Danny said.

"I was glad," she said pertly.

"I didn't care," Danny said.

"You haven't fallen down?"

"No," he said.

"You're lucky. I did, three times," she said.

"The ice isn't good today," he said.

"No, it's melting," she said.

"Washerwoman," Tommy Keefe yelled at her, shooting by.

"Peddle your fish," she called after him.

"He's a good skater," Danny said.

"He's too fresh, and every time he tries to show off how fast he can skate, he falls down," she said.

"Want me to push you?" Albert asked Hortense, coming up to them.

"If you don't make me fall down," she said.

"I won't," he said.

He got behind her, skated slowly, and pushed her. Danny heard her laughing as she was pushed. Some day he would be able to skate good enough to push her. He was afraid to ask her yet because he wasn't sure of himself on the ice. And there was Jimmy Keogh, skating with crossed hands with Helen Smith. Virginia Doyle wasn't out skating. She never went skating, it seemed. But then, Hortense and Helen Smith did, and he could see them out here.

Danny took a long stroke with his left foot, followed with his right, lost his balance, heard a laugh as he tumbled, and found himself sitting on the ice. He got up and looked about, abashed.

"Now you fell down," Hortense Audrey said, coming up to him beside Albert.

"It takes time to learn how to skate," Albert said.

"Gee, I'll never learn," said Hortense Audrey.

"If you come out enough, I can teach you," Albert said to her, and Danny, hearing Albert say this, looked wistfully past them.

"My daddy is a good skater and he says he's going to teach me how to skate."

He took a stroke away from them. Tommy Keefe and Helen Smith skated by. She threw a snowball at him, and it caught him by the side of the ear. Tommy hit Hortense with a snowball. Tommy and Helen stood there, laughing, and Danny, unsteady on his skates, wiped the snow away from his cheek and neck, some of it trickling under his collar and forming a cold stream that slid down his chest.

"Can't catch me, Al," Tommy said, skating away, and Al pursued him.

He set his lips grimly and slowly took strokes, trying to keep himself going. He didn't know why he didn't learn quicker. He was a good roller skater. But it was just that way. Some things you could learn easy, like he always learned the arithmetic lessons. And some things you couldn't learn easy. Like when the school year started, he had gone with some of the other kids to study and be an altar boy. But he went twice to learn the Latin after school, and he couldn't learn the Latin. It was too hard. So he quit going. Albert learned it, and he was an altar boy now. Albert learned all kinds of things easy.

Danny went persistently ahead, going around the edge of the pond. There weren't so many skating at the edge and he could keep out of collisions. He could only learn how to skate by practicing all the time. It was just starting to get dark. They would all have to be going home soon. Would Aunt Peg be home drunk? Gee, it was going to be terrible if she fell off the water wagon and stayed off it. He didn't want to think of that now.

He went on slowly around the pond, taking awkward strides, fighting himself to keep from spilling. Uncle Al had said he would give him a dollar if he got ninety on his report card. He got ninety last month, and it was the first time since he had been in school that he'd gotten an average that high. Uncle Al would be glad of it. He bent down and made a snowball. He threw it at a small tree.

"My ankles won't hold me up good," Joe Conlan said, almost bumping into Danny.

Joe was a dark boy in fourth grade, smaller than Danny.

"Mine get weak," Danny said.

"Gee, you shoulda seen me fall," Joe said.

"I took a bad spill, too," Danny said.

"Well, the ice ain't any good today," Joe said.

"No, it's getting warm," Danny said.

"Yeah. Say, all the kids are inside the house. Let's go in," Joe said.

They struggled toward the green-painted temporary wooden house.

II

It was half dark inside, and there were benches around the side and a few rows of them in the center. There was a large stove in a corner. Joe and Danny walked on their skates along the wooden floor to a corner where the gang was. Albert, Jimmy Keogh, Tommy Keefe, Hortense Audrey, Helen Smith, and blonde-haired Jennie Conlan were there. Danny got behind Joe because he'd have to sit down beside Hortense Audrey. He wanted to, and he couldn't get up the nerve to do it. It'd look like he was sweet on her. He was sweet on her, and he knew he'd blush if they teased him.

"Everybody's here now," Hortense Audrey said.

"Yeah, and it's more fun inside than falling down on that sloppy ice," Joe said.

"Poor Joey can't skate so good, can you, Joey?" Jennie Conlan said.

"Well, what about yourself?" Joe retorted.

"I'm a girl," said Jennie.

"Danny, next month when Lent comes, what are you gonna stay away from?" Hortense Audrey asked.

"Gee, I don't know, something," said Danny.

"I guess I'll lay off school," said Tommy Keefe.

"You can't do that," Helen Smith said.

"Sure I can. You got to sacrifice something, and that's a big sacrifice for me," said Tommy, and the girls giggled.

"You fell asleep in school this afternoon, and you're lucky Miss McGinnis didn't catch you," Jennie Conlan called down to him.

"Tommy Keefe is too funny for words," Helen Smith said.

"I'd like to give up falling on the ice for Lent," Joe Conlan said.

"That's not serious. I was talking serious," Hortense Audrey said.

"I'm going to give up candy and shows," Danny said quickly, hoping to catch the attention of Hortense Audrey.

"I don't think I could give up candy," Hortense Audrey said.

"Why?" asked Danny.

"I got a sweet tooth," she said.

"Virginia Doyle is giving up candy, shows, ice cream, and cake," said Jennie Conlan.

"Well, she's awful holy. She goes to Communion every Sunday," Hortense Audrey said.

"She's as holy as holy water," Tommy Keefe said.

"That's bad to say that," Hortense Audrey said.

"What intention are you going to make, Danny, when you give something up in Lent?" asked Jennie Conlan.

"Gee, I ain't thought about it yet," said Danny.

But he knew. Only he couldn't tell them. He went off into a dreamy state, suddenly not hearing what they were saying. He was going to give up something and make a sacrifice in Lent with the special intention that his Aunt Margaret would stop drinking for good. But he couldn't say that.

He looked down the line of kids on the bench. He looked from Hortense Audrey to Helen Smith. He guessed that if Hortense Audrey would like him, he'd like her better than he would Helen Smith. And she'd spoken to him today.

"Won't it be fun to eat candy on Easter Sunday if you go without it all during Lent?" said Hortense Audrey.

"And what fun won't I have coming back to school after Easter when I sacrifice school during Lent," said Tommy Keefe.

"Go on, you," said Helen Smith, laughing.

"Red-head, gingerbread, five cents a loaf," Tommy singsonged.

"Fresh," said Helen Smith.

"Fish," said Tommy Keefe.

"For sale," Danny added, trying to be funny.

"Boys try to be funny and aren't," said Helen Smith, and the girls all giggled.

"I know a girl who's funny," said Hortense Audrey.

"Who?" asked Albert.

"Maggie Grady," said Hortense.

"She had dirty stockings on in school again today," said Jennie Conlan.

"Sourface," said Tommy.

"That's not a nice name to call even Maggie Grady," said Helen Smith.

"Maggie Grady is a baby," Tommy said.

"I don't like her," Hortense Audrey said.

"Who does?" asked Helen Smith.

"It's gonna be dark soon, and I got to go home," Hortense said.

"Let's all go out and skate once again before we go," Danny said, hoping to keep the gang together a little longer.

They crowded out of the warming house.

III

Danny felt sad when he left the kids at Fifty-first and the park. All the rest of them went down Grand Boulevard, and he had to go eastward alone on Fifty-first Street. It was dark now, and Fifty-first Street was noisy with clanging street cars; there were many people on the street, and the stores and lampposts were lighted. It was getting chillier out, too. He wished it was tomorrow afternoon, and it was colder to make the ice better, and he was at the duck pond again with the kids. He liked the gang. None of them teased him the way the Prairie Avenue kids did. Hortense Audrey had been friendly to him today, too. He felt like he could hardly wait until tomorrow.

And now he had to go home.

He walked along Fifty-first Street, dragging his feet, his books slung under one arm, his skates strapped together and slung over his shoulder. Would Aunty Margaret be drunk or sober? If she was drunk, there would be yelling and fighting in the house. None of the kids in the gang were going home now afraid that they were going to have somebody drunk in the house like he was. He envied the kids. And if she got drunk and was seen staggering on the street by a kid from school who knew her, and it was told? Tommy Moriarty and Stewie O'Leary knew it, but Tommy was a grade ahead and didn't seem to talk much with kids in his gang, and Stewie was not liked by the kids. He was one of the dunces in the room, and nobody liked him much. Stewie had never picked on him after the fight last summer and it was all forgotten. Stewie always talked to him when they met or walked to school together.

He walked on, taking his time. He didn't want to get home, and the longer it took him, the better. He kicked a piece of ice along the sidewalk and it slid around from side to side. The street cars passing and the elevated trains ahead seemed to be noises that were much farther away than they were. He didn't want to go home. And, gee, would she be drunk? And suppose, some time, Hortense Audrey and the kids in the gang and Virginia Doyle would get to know it? He wished it was tomorrow afternoon and they were all skating together again. He kicked the ice. He let it go and walked on. Why did people get drunk? Whiskey and gin had an awful smell and he once tasted beer and he didn't like it. Why did they get drunk?

He wished he could go to the moving-picture show tonight, but he didn't think Mother would let him, and he had his homework to do. It wouldn't be hard to do if Aunty Peg was sober. She'd been asleep when he got home at noon. He was glad it was getting chillier. The ice might be good again tomorrow. If the ice was good and he went skating every day, he would be learning to skate. Then, he'd say to Hortense Audrey:

Let's skate together.

Yes, she would say.

He would hold her hands crossed with his, and they would skate around the duck pond. They would skate around and around. All the kids would see they could skate good.

It's fun like this, he would say.

Yes, it's fun, she would maybe say.

Danny turned the corner past the cigar store at Fifty-first and Prairie. Oh, if she would only be sober. His heart began to beat more rapidly, and he walked on home sadly, full of fears, seeing his aunt at home, staggering and yelling and cursing at the top of her voice.

22

I

Margaret let her eyes rove about the overstuffed parlor of her friend, Myrtle Peck, admiring and envying her friend's home and her friend's private income from a divorced husband. Myrtle's home was spick and span. There was a maid to keep it up, and Myrtle didn't have to lift a hand. Sitting on a large upholstered divan, Margaret watched Myrtle, who sat in an enormous rocking chair which sprouted an abundance of strange-looking carved animals. On the wall behind Myrtle there was a dreamy Maxfield Parrish picture. A small table to her left supported a Chinese vase. Yes, Margaret thought that Myrtle had a lovely home. She fixed her eyes on the lamp placed in the center of a beautiful cherrywood table in a corner. And it was all so clean and orderly. And just think, Myrtle didn't have to lift a finger in it, not a finger.

"Peg, you mustn't worry. You must live and be gay," Myrtle said.

Margaret looked straight at her friend, a woman slightly larger than herself, but with a fine figure, a round face, blue eyes, blonde hair, a lacy, embroidered shirtwaist, and an expensive blue serge skirt.

Myrtle had money for clothes, too, and she could live just like a lady, Margaret thought to herself.

"I know it, I know it, Myrtle," Margaret said, her voice strained, as if from wearied and tired emotions.

"Life was made for joy," Myrtle said.

"You can say it, Myrtle, because you don't have the troubles I've got, my responsibilities," Margaret said.

"Peg, you got to shake them off like the dust and live your own life," Myrtle said.

"If I only could!" Margaret said heavily.

"Will you have a cup of tea, dearie?" Myrtle asked, and Margaret nodded her head affirmatively.

Myrtle rose. Margaret watched the slow, languid manner in which Myrtle walked out of the room. The life of a lady, Myrtle had. Well, she wasn't jealous of Myrtle. Myrtle was too dear and kind and understanding and lovely to be one that Peg O'Flaherty would envy and be jealous of. She heard Myrtle telling the colored maid to make tea and toast and to serve it in the parlor. Myrtle lived just like a lady.

"Yes, Peg, you got to live your own life," Myrtle said, returning to the parlor and sinking into the heavy rocking chair.

Margaret leaned back on the divan and stretched her feet out across the green carpet, wanting Myrtle to see the new buckskin laced boots Al had given her.

"Why, what lovely shoes, Peg! Where did you get them?" Myrtle asked, and at the same time she stuck out her own feet, showing off the laced tan oxford walking-shoes she was wearing.

"My brother Al got them for me," Margaret said.

"They're simply beautiful," Myrtle said.

"Al sells only the best women's footwear," Margaret said.

"He must have some good in him to sell shoes like that," said Myrtle.

"Of course, he has. It's just that he's a man and a bachelor. Myrtle, he just doesn't understand a girl like me," Margaret said, breaking into a sigh.

"Mr. Peck understood too much," Myrtle said slyly.

"Your poor heart must have been broken when you found out how he was chasing other women, you poor dear. You must have suffered so. That's why I decided it would be you I'd come to see today and talk to. I knew you'd understand," Margaret said.

"Oh, not at all! I was glad to get rid of him, so long as I got a good settlement. I get enough alimony to live on, and I live my own life. I didn't care two hoots. Love and heartbreak are sad and beautiful in storybooks and plays. But in life, I feel differently. Live your own life," Myrtle said.

"Oh, but if I was strong like you. I'm just such a weak thing," Margaret sighed.

"Peg, you're too young, too lovely, and too handsome to be talking like that," Myrtle said.

"Oh, Myrtle, I don't know what to do! I don't know what to say!" Margaret said, jumping up from the divan and striding back and forth across the room.

"Peg, the first thing to do is to control your nerves," Myrtle said.

"That's it!" Margaret said hastily, her tone one of self-laceration; she gazed tragically at her friend.

"You must take it easy, relax," said Myrtle.

"But how can I? I try to. But my nerves are killing me. They're driving me crazy. Myrtle, I wouldn't tell this to anyone else but you. But you're such a dear friend, I can say it to you. Because I have infinite trust, infinite trust in you. Sometimes I stop and ask myself, am I going insane? I feel as if I'm losing my head. I don't know what I'm doing, what I'm saying, half of the time."

"Now, Peg, you sit down there! I'm going to talk to you," Myrtle said with kind impatience.

Margaret mutely obeyed. She glanced almost worshipfully at her friend, her face alive with interest and attention.

"The first step you have to take is to stop thinking this way. You simply can't let your whole life go to pieces because of one man."

"But I love Lorry," Peg said with a throb in her voice.

"I don't care. No man, not even the richest man on earth, is worth that much. You can't ruin your life because of any man," Myrtle said firmly.

"I know it! I know it! I know it!" Margaret said.

"I don't care what you feel toward him. If he was a *man*, he wouldn't have treated you that way," Myrtle said.

"I simply cannot understand it. He was always so kind, so tender, so gentle. He seemed to love me," Peg said, her voice filled with melancholy.

The maid entered, set the tea things down for them, and retired noiselessly. Myrtle poured the tea and gave Margaret a cup and buttered toast on a plate.

"You have it so nice here. It's so lovely, so comforting," Margaret said, biting into her toast.

"I like it," Myrtle said.

"How much rent do you pay?" Margaret asked.

"Sixty-five," said Myrtle.

"We pay fifty. It seems to me that we could get something better than what we're getting for that much money. But it's that brother of mine," Margaret said.

"I liked the apartment you had at Forty-ninth and Calumet. Why did you move from it?" Myrtle asked.

"We had to get out because of my nephew. He was always running up and down the hallway, and he was rolling his baseball bats off the back porch, and the neighbors were afraid they were going to be killed by his baseball bats falling down from our third-floor porch. So we had to move. I loved that apartment, even though my sister died in it. I'm not superstitious like the old Irish," Margaret said.

"You're not superstitious?" asked Myrtle.

"No, not a bit," Margaret said.

"I'm not superstitious, either," Myrtle said.

"Of course, I believe in God," Margaret said.

"So do I," Myrtle said.

"But I don't believe that He's going to punish poor unhappy sinners in a Hell of fire," Margaret said.

"Of course not. That's a trick of the ministers to scare you. Hell is in people's hearts," said Myrtle. "But more tea, Peg?" she added, seeing Margaret put her teacup aside.

"No, dearie. Hell is this earth. Hell is being a woman like me," Margaret said.

"None of that, Peg. That's no way to be gay," Myrtle said.

"Dearie, I can't be gay. I can't be happy. I'm too sad," Margaret sighed.

"You're only making yourself feel worse by talking that way," Myrtle said.

"But I love Lorry, I'd slave the skin off my hands for him," Margaret said, beginning to sob.

"That's probably just the reason why he doesn't like you," Myrtle said.

"Myrtle, do you think so?"

"Yes," said Myrtle.

"Do you really think that he doesn't love me?"

"I don't know. I was just going on what you've told me," said Myrtle.

"If I was sure he no longer cared, I'd end it all. I couldn't live then," Margaret said in tears.

Myrtle went to Margaret and stood over her.

"Come, Peg, you mustn't carry on like that. You'll only wear your poor heart out," she said softly, patting Margaret's head, stroking her shoulders.

"I have no heart. My heart is stone. I don't care. I don't care. I can't live without Lorry," Margaret sobbed, her head still lowered.

"Peg, you gotta learn that no man is worth a fine girl like you wearing her heart out and crying her eyes out over him," Myrtle said.

"Oh, Myrtle, if you only knew him, then you'd understand," Margaret said, still in tears.

"Now, here!" Myrtle said, lifting Margaret's head. Margaret was docile. Myrtle wiped her eyes. "Now, stop cutting up like that. It doesn't make you attractive and it does you no earthly good."

"I know it! I know it! I know it! I just can't help it!" Margaret said drearily.

"You gotta brace up, Peg, dearie," Myrtle said.

"I will! You'll forgive me. I'm going to get over it. I'm going to do just what you told me. I'm going to be gay, and full of life, and have a good time. Oh, Myrtle, you're such a dear, wonderful girl, such a dear, wonderful friend," Margaret said.

"I try to be a good friend, and I can't stand to see a handsome, gifted girl like you just going to pieces. I tell you, no man is worth that price," Myrtle said.

"You're so right. You know so much more than me," Margaret said adoringly.

"We got to take life as it comes, and not give our hearts to it. If we give our hearts to it the way you've done, we'll break them. Human hearts are too tender for life," Myrtle said.

"Oh, I know it! I know it! I'm a fool because of my heart," Margaret said.

"Yes, that's just your trouble," Myrtle said.

Margaret nodded agreement with Myrtle.

"Here, have a cigarette," Myrtle said, and both women lit cigarettes.

Myrtle set an ash tray beside Margaret.

"It's always been my trouble. I've got to look out for myself instead of everybody else. All my life I've worried about others. And where did it get me? Why, it didn't even bring me gratitude!" Margaret said.

"Peg, you're too smart a girl to go on that way."

"I only wish I was."

The colored maid appeared in the doorway.

"You can take these out now, Clarisse," Myrtle said, pointing to the tea things.

They watched her as she removed the dishes from the room.

"I got to change and start looking out for A-Number-One," Margaret said as if with newborn determination.

"I tell you, Peg, dearie, that's the policy that always wins out," Myrtle said.

"All my life I've been a fool! A fool!" Margaret said melodramatically.

"Well, it's never too late to learn. You're young yet," Myrtle said.

"I've got to get out of the rut I'm in," Margaret said.

"You ought to be able to go out with lots of men and have good times and forget this man," Myrtle said.

"I will. It was just such a shock to me. I never expected it," Margaret said.

"Nothing a man ever does should shock you," Myrtle said.

"Yes, I've learned that. I thought that Lorry was different from other men. But I've learned. I've learned my lesson," Margaret said, her voice full of sobs and sighs.

"Well, I'm glad, because, Peg, I like you, and it's a shame to see you in the state you were in when you came here today," Myrtle said.

"Myrtle, I don't know what I'd've done if I hadn't seen you. I might even have gone to the lake," Margaret said, squashing her cigarette.

"Don't talk like that," Myrtle said.

"It's the truth. I might have. Myrtle, you've never had the sad life, the troubles I've had. I've never been happy," Margaret said.

"But you're going to be," Myrtle said.

"Yes, I'm going to be," Margaret said slowly, heavily, almost throbbingly.

"Now, what did I tell you? Do I have to keep telling you to brace up, or don't you want to? Sometimes, Peg, you're your own worst enemy," Myrtle said, putting out her cigarette.

"I can't help it. I have such nerves. I think I must have gotten too nervous when I was a child and had diphtheria. I almost died. I've had bad nerves ever since."

"That was a long time ago, and you're healthy now," Myrtle said.

"Oh, no, I'm not. Do you know, I should really be under a doctor's care, a nerve specialist. But I can't afford it. Every cent I earn, I give home," Margaret said.

"But, Peg!" Myrtle said, shocked and surprised.

"It's the God's truth," Margaret said.

"I thought your brother was doing well," Myrtle said.

"He isn't."

"Why, I thought he was a good business man," Myrtle exclaimed.

"Poor Al, he's saddled with expenses, too. He tries. But we have such burdens. My poor sister, Lizz, we have to give her so much help. She's so poor. All my life it's been the same. I had no schooling, no education. My lot has always been an unhappy one. I had to work as a little girl and bring home every penny I made. I've done it ever since. And now we're saddled with two of my sister's kids. We have to keep my niece who was in Madison. There's no end to it."

"That's not right, it's not fair."

"No, it isn't fair. And I can't even have a friend of mine in the house. My mother insults them. My brother is nosy and doesn't like my friends. I have no rights. When I was a girl, if I went out with a boy in the most innocent way, I was beaten. My brother would beat me black and blue."

"If a man laid his hands on me, I'd kill him. My husband once did, and I threw a hundred-dollar vase at him. He never did it again," Myrtle said spiritedly.

"All of the spirit was taken out of me when I was just an innocent little child. I was sick and almost blind, such an innocent little thing. My sister, Lizz, was always coming home and telling lies about me. If she saw me just talking to a boy on the street corner, she made mountains out of it, told Al, and he'd beat me for it. That has always been my lot."

"It's a shame. I don't know why you stay with your family. You can be independent," Myrtle said.

"It's just that I've been a fool. I've been a fool, Myrtle," Margaret said.

"Let me tell you, Peg O'Flaherty, if you have any sense you won't stick around with that family of yours," Myrtle said.

"I can't if I want any life. I can't," Margaret said.

"A girl's a fool to stay with her family," Myrtle said.

"Oh, but don't I know it!" Margaret said.

"Just a minute, I got to wee-wee," Myrtle said, rising and leaving the room.

II

Alone in the room, Margaret paced back and forth, wringing her hands. She looked out the window at the quiet street bathed in the fading light of the late afternoon. Opposite, there was a lovely home, with trees in front of it, and a wire fence surrounding a snow-covered lawn. Next to it was an apartment building that must have gone up recently. Here it was so quiet. No peddlers yelling in the alley all day long like at home. No elevated trains. No noises. Why did they have to live where they were now? They had never even lived in a decent place. Oh, God, why had she been given such a family? If Lorry had only divorced that woman, that dirty bitch of a wife, and married her, she and Lorry would have had a nice, lovely home like that one across the street, and an automobile. And children instead of that idiot son she'd had by him. It was now put away and the world didn't know. She couldn't think of that. Oh, Lorry! Well, she had written him a strong letter today. He'd understand it. He could take it or leave it. She turned from the window and paced the room again.

"Why, Peg!" Myrtle exclaimed in surprise as she returned to see her friend crying without restraint.

"I can't help it! I can't! Oh, Myrtle, you must understand."

"Peg, dearie, I do," Myrtle said, putting her arms around Margaret.

Margaret laid her head on Myrtle's shoulder.

"I got to cry. I can't help it. Oh, Myrtle, I'm such an unhappy girl. I'm so weary, so tired. I love Lorry," Margaret sobbed, her head still on her friend's shoulder.

"Peg, crying is not going to do you any good. Dry your eyes," Myrtle said, leading Margaret to the divan, sitting her down, and then seating herself beside her friend.

"I will in a minute. I just got to cry," Margaret said.

Margaret sank her head in Myrtle's lap and sobbed, her entire body shaking and quivering. Myrtle stroked her friend's head and continued to sit there, looking concerned, then bored, then perplexed. The room was quiet, the street was quiet, except for Margaret's sobbing. Gradually her sobs died down. She sniffled, sighed, cried lightly. Her sobs began to come only periodically. She sat up. Her face was distraught, the powder rubbed off by tears, her hair mussed, straggling, hairpins hanging out over her ears.

"Go to the bathroom and fix yourself up," Myrtle said.

"I will. I must stop this. I don't want to do it, but I can't help myself. Oh, Myrtle, I loved Lorry. I adore him. I'd kiss the dirt for him. I love him. I can't help myself."

"I see this must have been serious."

"And I know he loved me," Margaret said, again sniffling.

"Margaret, if he loves you, you got to make him show it to you. A woman must never let a man get the upper hand," Myrtle said.

"I know he loved me. And he was so wonderful. So handsome. He was so often like a boy, like my own son," Margaret said.

She thought of that child of his, an idiot, put away, forgotten. Should she tell Myrtle? No! She could never tell a soul about that! Never! And while this thought flashed through her head, Myrtle was talking.

"Peg, do you think you can get him back? Would he marry you?"

Margaret didn't answer.

"Do you think he'd marry you?" Myrtle repeated.

"He's married already. He used to say that as soon as his hands were free he'd get a divorce and marry me."

"Are his hands free now?"

"I don't know! I don't know. I don't know a thing!" Margaret said, shaking her head nervously from side to side.

"I didn't know he was a married man," Myrtle said.

"He married her when he was young. She's a skinny bitch. I'm better than she is. I always gave him more satisfaction. He said so. He told me so many times. He told me he'd rather sleep with me than he would with his wife. Maybe you won't like what I say, but it's the truth. And why hide the truth? Please don't think badly of the way I talk."

"Get those silly thoughts out of your head. What do you think I am?" Myrtle said.

"Lorry said to me, 'Peg, my chick, I'd rather sleep with you than with Mrs. Robinson.' Those are the very words he said to me."

"When?"

"Many many times."

"Well, then, what happened?"

"Oh, I don't know. I write letters and I get no answer. I call the hotels where he is likely to stay when he's here and I always get the same answer. 'Not registered.' 'Not registered.' I'll go crazy from those two damn words. At night in my dreams, I keep telling myself, 'Not registered!' I don't know! I don't know what happened. I told you about yesterday. Myrtle, if I could only see him. Myrtle, I want your advice. When I see him how should I act? Should I go to him and say, point-blank, 'Lorry, what's the matter? Don't you want me any more? Am I no good any more? Am I used up or what?' Should I go to him that way?"

"My God, no, Peg. No! Never!"

"What should I do?"

"It's hard to say, since I don't know him," Myrtle said.

"Well, I can make you know what he's like. He's a wonderful man. He's brainy, and he's so brilliant. So intelligent. So smart, and everything he's got in the world he's earned himself. He's a self-made man," Margaret said.

"What business is he in? I remember you once told me, but I forgot," Myrtle said.

"He's in the lumber business," Margaret said.

"Is he surly or anything like that?"

"No, he's the most wonderful man. He has the kindest, the nicest, the gentlest disposition," said Margaret.

"Here, Peg, a cigarette?" Myrtle asked, offering Margaret her box. They lit their cigarettes and inhaled. Myrtle let the smoke out of her nose.

"Yes, he has such a lovely disposition. He's so kind and so tender. The way he kisses me, and pets me, and holds my head on his shoulder and strokes it so tenderly. He is the kindest and the most tender of men," Margaret said.

"If he is, why does he treat you the way he does?" Myrtle asked.

"I can't understand it. I don't know what's come over him," Margaret said.

"He doesn't treat you kindly," Myrtle said.

"It must be that some woman has gotten to his ear and she's made him infatuated and driven him out of his senses," Margaret said.

"Does his wife know about you and him?"

"I don't think so. That's why he never wants me to write to him," Margaret said.

"But you do write to him. You said you did," Myrtle said, puffing, dumping her ashes beside her in a tray.

"Oh, yes, but I write letters like they were business letters and sign a man's name," said Margaret.

"Does he write you?"

"No. He used to send me money, just addressed to me with the money in an envelope, pinned to a sheet of paper with no writing on it," Margaret said.

"Peg, you're a goddamn fool. You ought to be spanked until you get some sense in your head," Myrtle said, getting quickly to her feet, frowning down at Margaret.

"Why?" Margaret said, looking innocently at her friend.

"That man doesn't love you," Myrtle said slowly and emphatically.

"He doesn't?" Margaret asked, looking like a person in a trance with her tear-reddened and swollen eyes, her face blotchy, her hair unkempt.

"No! Decidedly no! And you're a poor damn fool, you are. Letting yourself waste your heart on him. He protects himself in every way. He played with you. And you got to make him pay for it. You got to forget this love talk, this talk of his tenderness. It's not true. That man doesn't love you. He trifled with you. You're a damn fool if you don't make him pay now, and pay plenty. He can afford it," Myrtle said.

"I don't know. He was in difficulties for years."

"Forget that! Think of yourself. You make him pay! You make him set you up living in decent style and fixing you regularly so you can quit your job and live like I do," said Myrtle.

"Oh, I don't know what to do. I don't know what to say," Margaret said.

"If you don't take my advice, you don't deserve any sympathy," Myrtle said, sitting down beside Peg.

"I will! You're right, darling. You're so smart. Oh, what would I do if I didn't have a friend like you, Myrtle, dearie?"

"Make him feel guilty. You're the wronged one. Make him feel that you are. And you make him pay you. He wronged you. You were an innocent girl until he met you. He ruined you. He took your all," Myrtle said.

"But he didn't. I got over all my innocence with a boy. It must have been when I was fourteen. I didn't know what it was. Some boy did it to me. I didn't even know what it was," Margaret said.

"That ain't his business," Myrtle said.

"But he knows. I told him everything. I told him of all the different experiences I had with men before I met him," said Margaret.

"I told you, he ruined you. You're ready to go into court and accuse him, sue him and say he ruined you, trifled with you. You got to make him feel guilty and afraid of you," Myrtle said.

"I couldn't do that," Margaret said.

"Why?" Myrtle asked, annoyed.

"Lorry wouldn't love me then," Margaret said.

"He doesn't anyway," Myrtle said harshly.

Margaret collapsed in tears, flinging her head in Myrtle's lap.

"If Lorry doesn't love me, I'll kill myself," Margaret said hysterically.

III

"Now, I've got to get dressed. I got a date tonight," Myrtle said after they had had supper.

"Myrtle, dear, don't you want me to help you get dressed? I'll do that and then leave. I got to go home and get to bed early. Maybe I'll help my little niece with her homework to get my mind off these things," Margaret said.

"Don't bother. Clarisse helps me," Myrtle said.

"Let me help, too," Margaret said, rising.

"No, don't bother. Please, don't," Myrtle said.

Margaret rushed to Myrtle, embraced her, kissed her.

"You've helped me so much," she said, still enfolding Myrtle in her arms.

"I'm so glad," Myrtle said.

"You're such an understanding friend. You don't know it, but you've saved my life," Margaret said.

"Now, you forget all these blue thoughts you've been having. Get yourself a good night's rest, and you'll go on. We'll have parties and dates together. I'd have you come along tonight, but you know, Peg, two's a couple and three's a crowd. But some other night," Myrtle said.

"I couldn't tonight. I have to go home and sleep," Margaret said.

"Well, promise me that you'll take care of yourself and brace up," Myrtle said.

They kissed.

"Can I just fix myself up before I go? I must look a sight," said Margaret.

"Yes, do," said Myrtle.

IV

Walking away from Myrtle's in the chilly January night, the prospect of returning home seemed gloomy to Margaret.

She told herself that she was all at sixes and sevens. And Myrtle was such a nice understanding girl in her way, but there were certain things about Myrtle. Myrtle was glad to have gotten rid of her. Why? Because she was jealous. Myrtle was going out with some fellow and didn't want to take any chances. Of course, the last thing in the world that she'd want to do would be to take any fellow away from Myrtle. Gee, she was glad she hadn't mentioned that child business. She must never do that. Oh, God, why did people talk and backbite and tell lies and stories about others?

She walked on. The street was quiet and a full moon was shining, a moon which seemed cold and distant. Margaret looked at it. In songs, the moonlight stood for love and lovers. On this winter night it had nothing to do with love, not for her. It was a very cold moon. But it was a lovely night, she felt. Oh, she had always wanted to have winter nights like this, many nights like this with Lorry. Oh, she must be like one of those persons Mother and Lizz always talked about, one of those poor creatures who had had a curse put upon them. She must be. She walked along. Yes, the street was so quiet, and ahead she could see the traffic passing along Grand Boulevard, automobiles, horses and carriages. Every year there were more automobiles on the streets and fewer and fewer horses and carriages. The horse and carriage was a thing of the past. Ah, she, too, she was a thing of the past. These houses and buildings along the street. So many of them with lights in the windows. Some of the women in these homes and apartments were happy women, women who had their men. Ah, but didn't she know something about the happy women who thought they had the love of their men? Lorry, he must have a finer home than any of the people living on

Forty-ninth Street. Passing by Lorry's home and seeing lights, a stranger might feel that there was a happy home. And his bitch of a wife must think she was a happy woman possessing the love of her man.

Myrtle had such a wonderful life. Not a care, not a worry in the world. Some girls got so much of the goods of life, and look at poor, miserable Margaret O'Flaherty! Hers was a sad lot, the saddest lot of any girl in the world.

A man came toward her. He looked at her. Men nearly always did. They were that way. And why shouldn't he look at her? If he got anything out of it, let him. She walked slowly on. She wasn't interested in men any more. She knew too much about them, too much about their dirty souls. He was wearing a silk hat. He came closer. They passed, and she could see that he was young and handsome. He might look around after her. She walked on, resisting the temptation to turn and see if he had. But she was sure he'd turned around to look after her. She knew the ways of men. She drifted on, and suddenly she looked behind her. Yes, she was certain. The man in the silk hat was entering the building where Myrtle lived. He was Myrtle's date. That's why Myrtle had been afraid. But Myrtle needn't have been. Margaret turned down Grand Boulevard. Myrtle needn't worry that Peg O'Flaherty was going to cut in on her. She walked slowly on. All these people in the fine houses on Grand Boulevard, they were so goddamn happy. She could scream at them through their windows. Oh, God, what was going to become of her?

23

I

"Why, Peg O'Flaherty, hello," Jack Doolin said, almost colliding with Margaret in front of the Fifty-first Street elevated station.

"Oh, hello, Mr. Doolin, how are you?" Margaret said, smiling.

"Oh, I'm so-so. Ever feel that way, so-so?" Jack Doolin said.

He was a man in his thirties, tall, well-built, but beginning to get fat. He had an insensitive face with ruddy cheeks. The jowls were coming out. The contours were forming for middle age. He had sensual lips, blue eyes, and sandy hair.

"You just getting home?" Margaret asked.

"Yeah," he said disconsolately.

"I was out to see a girl friend and I'm on my way home, too," she said.

"Not working at the hotel today?"

"I worked Sunday so I was off today," she said.

"A fine girl like you on your off day, and where is your fellow?" he asked jovially.

"Have a heart, Mr. Doolin. Don't be sugaring me when you don't mean it," Margaret said coyly.

"But I do. And don't call me Mr. Doolin. What the heck! Here I am, a neighbor of yours for about two years. I know Al, and I have a glass of beer with Ned when he comes to town and sees you. Ah, there's a fine chap. And you and the old lady know my missus, and I play ball with your nephews in the back yard sometimes, and what does she do, calls me Mr. Doolin. I'm Jack to all my friends," Jack Doolin said.

"Well, Jack, walk home with me. It's cold and it's noisy here with the elevated and street cars," she said, smiling, showing white teeth.

"You're not doin' nothin'?" he asked.

"I was going home. I've been blue all day," she said.

"So 'm I. I'm deep in the dumps today," he said.

"I can't stand this noise here," she said.

"Say, Peg, be a sport. Come on and have a glass of beer with me, and then I'll walk you home," he said hesitantly.

"Well," she said, thrusting out her lips as if to indicate that she was thinking about his proposal.

"Come on, don't be a killjoy. We'll help each other be blue over a glass of good beer," he said.

"But would Mrs. Doolin like it?" she asked.

"Just having a glass of beer with me, what the devil!" he said.

"But in a saloon," she said.

"There's nothing wrong in it," he said.

"No, there isn't, is there?" she said.

"Of course not," he said.

They walked toward O'Callahan's saloon at Calumet.

"Why are you blue?" he asked, glancing at her.

"I'm just worried and nervous," she said.

"A girl like you shouldn't have a worry in the world. You got looks, a good job, a nice personality," he said, smiling.

"You think so?" she said.

"I know so," he said, his tone becoming more familiar, causing her to have a sudden resentment and to think that if he thought he was going to get anywhere with her, he was sadly mistaken.

They said no more, turned the corner at Calumet Avenue and walked on to the family entrance on the side of the saloon. There was a couple in a corner to the right of the door, and they took a table opposite them near the swinging doors which led into the saloon proper. He rang for a waiter, and when the waiter came Jack smiled at Margaret. She nodded curtly.

"Beer?" he asked Margaret. She nodded. "Two beers Budweiser," he said to the waiter.

II

"Peg, I'm mighty damn glad I ran into you tonight," he said.

"But what about your wife and family?" she answered.

"She's home with the kid and all right, and they had a good supper. Didn't I just call her up and tell her I was held up. And she's been having trouble with her stomach, nothing serious, just indigestion pains. She said they were better now," he said.

"I hope they are. She should watch what she eats, lots of green vegetables and things like that. She's a lovely woman," Margaret said.

"Peg, a woman doesn't come any better than my missus," he said.

"She's very lovely. My mother and I both think the world of her," Margaret said.

"The trouble is, Peg, you know, she's too good for a guy like me. She's too good for me, too damn good," Jack said.

"Why do you say that?" Margaret asked, just to be making conversation; she wasn't the least interested in this man, but she didn't want to go home to her own black, bleak home, she didn't; she wanted to have somebody to talk to, to take her mind off her sorrows.

"Well, now, you take me. I like to bum around, drink, raise a little bit of cain on the side. You know what I mean," he said, and she caught the significance of the look he gave her, but she felt like telling him that for a girl like herself there was much better pickings if pickings was what she was interested in.

She didn't answer him. She lifted her glass of beer. They were silent for some time, sitting there, quietly drinking their beer.

"When I left you to call up the missus, I said I'd be a little late. She trusts me, all right," he said with a slight snicker.

"Why shouldn't she?" Margaret asked pointedly.

"Now, that's a question," Jack said.

"Can I have one of your cigarettes, Jack?"

"Oh, you smoke, too?" he asked in surprise.

"Yes, didn't you know it?" she answered.

"Well, here, have one," he said, offering her his package of Piedmonts.

She pulled a cigarette out and set the package back near him on the table. He scratched a match on his box, and she leaned forward with the cigarette between her lips to get the light. The couple in the opposite corner looked at Margaret with curiosity when they saw her smoking.

"Not many women smoke. Women who smoke are pretty rare, as rare . . . well, as suffragettes," Jack said.

"I'm not one of these suffs. But if men smoke, why can't women?"

He seemed suddenly to think. He scratched his head and let his mouth hang agape for a moment.

"Guess you're right. Only we're not all accustomed to it. Now, I don't think I'd want my missus to smoke," he said, coming out of his philosophical trance.

All alike, Margaret thought to herself, but she didn't speak. She lapsed into moodiness. They sat. He rang for the waiter.

"One more, huh, Peg?" he asked.

She nodded affirmatively. He held up two fingers to the waiter. He leaned back in his chair. He puffed forcibly on his cigarette. He seemed to be trying to hit on a subject of conversation, and she was giving him no assistance. He puffed again, inhaled, watched the smoke he let out of his nose drift to the calcimined ceiling. He looked around the room and eyed another couple that had just entered and found a table. He inhaled again. The waiter returned with their beers and went away. Jack drank and wiped the foam from his lips with his handkerchief.

"It was nice coming here. I'm glad I met you," he said.

Margaret brooded into her beer.

"Say, Peg, you seem to have something serious on your mind," he remarked, leaning across the table.

"Oh, no, I feel all right," she said, and she took a hasty gulp of beer.

"I been watching you since we came here, and I can see. You seem blue. Don't be blue. You're too young and pretty, and let me assure you, you got too many cards in your hands for you to be blue. Just lookin' at you, I can see you have." His voice became sly and insinuating. "And you know, there are things that can take a girl's blues away."

"Not mine," she said with bitterness.

"Did something serious happen to you? What's the matter?" he asked, both curious and sympathetic.

"I don't know, Jack," she said.

"Aw, come on, take a drink and forget it. There's only one thing to do in this world with your troubles. That's forget 'em. That's the prescription of Jack Doolin, and let me tell you, it works."

"Well, you can say it. You're a happy man, with your own business and family," she said.

"My business? Yeah, it goes along just like a mule. Don't talk to me about my business," he said.

"I don't know. Sometimes I think I'm going crazy," Margaret said dully.

"I tell you, Peg, forget your troubles. Forget 'em and they aren't such a bother," Jack said.

"Yes, I have to forget. I have to forget," she said, speaking as if she were talking to herself instead of to him.

"Peg, I don't want to butt in, but tell me. Sometimes relieving your mind by telling your troubles to a friend helps. It helps to get them off your chest. And you can count on me as a friend. I like you, girl," Jack said.

"I know you're twenty karat, Jack. If I hadn't thought you were, I wouldn't have come here with you," Margaret said.

"Peg, don't cry. That never helps," he said sympathetically, seeing the tears welling in her eyes.

She quickly drew a handkerchief from her pocketbook and wiped away her tears. She smiled wanly.

"I lost the man I love," she said sadly.

"Why don't you get another?" he said.

"Oh, you don't understand. Jack, you're a man. You don't understand. A man never understands how a woman feels," she said.

"No, I guess not. Not if he's married, he doesn't," Jack said with mild irony.

"He doesn't love me," Margaret said.

"And you love him?"

"I'm going crazy. I can't think. I don't know what to do. Do you know what you just did for me, Jack?"

"What?" he asked in surprise.

"You saved my life."

"What do yuh mean, Peg?"

"When I met you I was trying to decide should I go home, or should I go to the lake?"

"You're kiddin', Peg."

"As true as there is a God, I'm not."

"It must be serious. Peg, never take anything that serious. It's bad," he said.

"I can't help it. I love Lorry. I love him, and he doesn't love me."

"Is that his name? Lorry? Lorry what?"

"Lorry Robinson. You must have read about him. He's a very well-known man and he was an important witness in the Graham case," she said.

"I don't remember it," Jack said.

"He's the most wonderful man," she said.

"What does he do? A politician?"

"He's a lumber man. He was a partner with Brophy. That's how he came to be a witness in the Graham case a few years ago."

"Is he big-league stuff?"

"He's one of the finest men that walks the earth," Margaret said.

"Anything happen between you and him? Why don't you sue him for breach of promise?" Jack said.

"He's married," Margaret said and, noticing the startled expression that popped in Jack's eyes, she added, "You think it's awful of me, don't you?"

"Why, no, not at all. I'm a broad-minded fellow. I am, Peg," he said.

"I don't care if it's good or bad. I don't care if the world does judge me. I love him. I don't care," Margaret said, her voice choked and nervous.

"I tell you, Peg, I wish I could help you. I'm awful sorry to hear it. All I can say to you is that you got to brace up, girlie. You got called out on strikes this time. Next time up, you got to make a base hit."

"I don't know what to do. I'm so unhappy," she said.

Jack drank. He seemed to be in a mood of serious cogitation. Margaret looked beyond him, at nothing, brooding, her face a picture of misery.

"Yes, you got to buck up, girlie. It's a stiff jolt, and then there's nothing much more to say than buck up. That's all," Jack said.

"I will. Forgive me, Jack, for the way I just acted," she said, trying to put on a gay smile.

"There's nothing to forgive, girlie. Forget it," Jack said, reaching across the table and squeezing her hand sympathetically.

"I'm not nice to be with. It's not fun to be with me," she said.

"I tell you, Peg, forget it," he said with husky-voiced sympathy. "And have another beer."

III

"There's nothing like good old-fashioned Budweiser to drive the blues away. You know, Peg, I got a confession to make. I was in the dumps myself when I met you. A man gets down in the mouth and his teeth drag on him sometimes. I was feelin' just that way when I met you tonight," Jack said, his voice drunken and wobbly.

"I'm all right now. I'm never going to worry about him again. I've gotten over the shock now," Margaret said.

"That's the way I like to hear you talk. You know, you always got to figure it out this way, Peg, and you'll never lose. Figure it out this way. It's the only way in the world to figure it out. There's always more than one gazabo in the world."

"Just like my girl-friend Myrtle told me. You got to be gay," Margaret said, forcing a laugh.

"Hell, yes. There's nothing else in life left except to be gay, unless you want to be a damn fool. But say, Peg, you don't object to a little cursing, do you?"

"No, not if it's just a little," she said flirtatiously.

He leaned back in his chair and laughed. She laughed with him.

"Drink on it, Peg. You're a damn swell girl. You look awful good to me, kid," Jack said.

They tipped glasses and drank.

"I feel so much better," she said.

"Sure you do. I wrote you a little ticket that puts the blues in the hock shop. Whenever you're blue, Peg, you come and see me and I'll fix you up," he said in boisterous good spirits.

"How?"

"Ask me no questions and I'll give you no answers," he said, and he laughed heartily, from his belly.

"Answers I don't know?"

"You're saying a mouthful, all right. Answers you don't know. Ha! Ha! Ha! How can I tell you answers you don't know when I ain't found out the answers or not. You got to gimme time because I can't answer that one until I know," Jack said.

Margaret leaned back and laughed. He joined her in laughing.

"But I'd like to get the chance to find out," he said with a meaningful wink.

"You're a married man," she said.

"That ain't no obstacle, is it?" he said insinuatingly.

"Go away with your flirting," she said.

"Flirting? I calls it more than flirting."

"You've got too nice a wife to be talking that way, Jack," she said.

"Sure. Nicest wife you'll ever see. A good wife is Heaven's best gift to man. That's the trouble. She's too damn nice, and I got some of Hell's gifts, too," he said.

"Which means that I'm not too damn nice," Margaret said, pouting.

"Oh, no, not at all. Don't take it that way, Peg," Jack said.

"I understand, gotcha, kid. You men are all alike," she said disgustedly.

"You don't want to go misunderstanding me, Peg, after we've gotten to be good friends like this," Jack said.

Margaret began to cry again.

"I'm awfully sorry I hurt your feelings. I am," he said with drunken awkwardness.

"I knew it! I knew it all along," she singsonged.

"What?"

"Lorry feels the same way. It's the way men feel toward a girl. A girl is a fool, a fool to let herself get put into such a position. A fool. It's the way men feel. It's the way Lorry feels. I know it."

"Not at all, not at all."

"Yes, it is," she insisted.

"You just have too much worry in that pretty head of yours. The breaks went against you and you're worried. Take this from me, Peg. I mean it. When the breaks go against you, that's the time you got to keep your hair on," he said.

"I want to go home," she said.

"It's early yet."

"Your wife must be waiting for you. And I'm so tired," she said.

"Well, all right, if you say so."

He rang for the waiter, paid the bill, and they left. They turned the corner onto Fifty-first Street and walked along. It was now clear and frosty, and the moon was pouring a fine light over the street.

"Peg, you're not sore, are you?" Jack asked after they had walked past the elevated station without talking.

"Of course not, Jack," she said.

"That's the girlie," he said, squeezing her arm.

"I was just upset," she said.

"I know how it is," he said.

They walked on, Jack holding her arm. He stopped around the corner on Prairie Avenue and said:

"Gee, must be pretty late. The old woman'll be worried."

"Will she be up?"

"I don't know," he said.

"Maybe you'd better walk on ahead of me."

"But I want to talk to you a minute, and the missus might be in the window, watching. Come on through the alley and the back yards here," he said.

"We can talk another time," she said.

"No, now! I want you to understand that I didn't mean anything personal tonight," he said.

"Jack, I know you didn't."

"Well, come on Peg. I wanna talk to you," he said.

"Oh, please, Jack," she said.

He placed his arm around her. She drew away.

"You're not afraid of me, are you, Peg?"

"Why, Jack!"

"Well, come on, then," he said.

"No, please, Jack. I don't like that. I can see you some other time," she said.

"All right, girlie. But I don't want you to be sore, and I do wanna see you again."

"You will, Jack."

"Won't you slip over a little good-night kiss on us?" he asked.

"On the street!"

"No one's around," he said.

She lifted her veil and raised her face. He kissed her.

"Good night, Peg," he said, giving her arm a squeeze and going ahead, singing.

She watched him walk ahead. She didn't want to wait too long here, and so when he got on a little way, she proceeded. She wanted to go to bed. She was sad and tired.

IV

There he was waiting for her in the hallway. She turned the lock in the inner hall door to go to the steps leading to the upper stories. He stood by the steps, and his apartment was on the first floor, to the left. He put his finger to his lips and approached her.

"The missus wasn't lookin' out the window so I waited for you," he whispered.

"But, Jack, why?"

"I wanted to talk to you. You look awful good to me."

"This is foolish, Jack."

"You like me?"

"Of course. But please, Jack, don't be foolish," she said.

"Walk up a landing with me. I wanna talk to you," he whispered.

She walked upstairs toward her floor, and he followed her quietly. She turned on the landing between the first and second floors, out of sight from the street.

"Peg," he whispered huskily.

She waited. He grabbed her clumsily, planted a thick, sensually wet kiss on her lips. She quietly struggled to free herself. His thick, wet lips and hot, wheezing, beery breath made her shudder. Moving her face as she squirmed in his arms, her cheeks, nose, and chin were brushed by his lips.

"Please, not here," she begged.

"Just a kiss. We're alone," he said.

She submitted and allowed him to have his way, her manner cold, relaxed. Suddenly his masculine nearness seemed to fire her. She wanted to forget, to let herself go. She hated this man and thought that he was crude, but she wished to lacerate herself, punish herself, humiliate herself by letting him have his complete way with her. She deserved to have such humiliation inflicted on her, she suddenly felt. She met his sensuous kisses with seeming sensuousness. Suddenly she came to her senses, realizing the dangers of being caught in the hallway, and she restrained him.

"Jack, we can't here," she said.

"We can take a chance," he said.

"No!" she said firmly.

"How about your place?"

"My mother's there, and my niece sleeps with me. It's too risky. Mother would raise the roof off," she said.

He reached for her, but she grabbed his arm firmly and shook her head.

"It's got to be some other time," she said.

"Why? Can't we sneak out and go around to the back yard or down to the basement?"

"Why, Jack! What do you think I am?"

"Forgive me, Peg," he said humbly. "I was just anxious. I got to liking you so much I couldn't control myself," he added.

"Good night," she said.

"One more kiss?" he asked.

She lifted her face. He gripped her firmly, kissed her, strained his body against hers. She remained in his arms for long kisses, and then she relaxed. Her hat was askew. Her face was smeared from her own lipstick which had gotten onto his lips and had been pressed back on her own mouth and cheeks. She saw that his face was marked with rouge. She took her handkerchief, wet it with her tongue, wiped his face.

"Good night, Jack," she said.

"When am I gonna see you again?"

"I'll see you," she said.

"But when?"

"Please, it's late. I'll see you," she said.

"Don't forget," he said.

She smiled at him, a smile that was a promise. He squeezed her hand.

"Good night, and don't forget, girlie," he said.

She turned and walked slowly upstairs. He leered after her. She stood outside her door and, with mirror in hand, made herself presentable. She heard the key turning his lock, the door closing. She hated herself. With such a man! He was a pig. Crude, no refinement. What was she coming to? She hated herself, and she began crying copiously as she let herself into her apartment.

V

"What the hell are you kids up for?" she asked angrily on finding Danny and Little Margaret at the dining-room table.

"I was doing my homework. It was hard and Danny wouldn't help me. I just got finished," Little Margaret said.

"I got my own homework to do," Danny protested.

"Quit it! Can it! I'm too nervous to listen to you brats arguing," she snapped.

"Blessed God, it's not late, only a quarter after ten," Mrs. O'Flaherty said, coming from the kitchen where she had overheard the conversation.

"God, I thought that it was midnight," Margaret said.

"Did you have your supper?" Mrs. O'Flaherty asked.

"Yes, I went to see Myrtle Peck," Margaret said.

"That one, a divorced woman!" Mrs. O'Flaherty exclaimed.

"I don't have to ask you what friends I can see. I'm of age," Margaret said.

The two children looked timidly and fearfully at their aunt.

"Birds of a feather flock together," Mrs. O'Flaherty said, going back to her bedroom.

Margaret went to her bedroom, and soon Danny and Little Margaret could hear her sobbing.

"Gee, is she drunk again?" Little Margaret asked.

"I donno. But she's sore, all right, and she's gonna make noise again. She always does, and fights when she gets crying like that," said Danny.

"I wish I was still living in Madison with Uncle Ned and Aunt Mildred. They never got drunk," Little Margaret said.

Suddenly the doorbell rang loudly. The two children looked fearfully at one another.

"Answer it!" Little Margaret said.

"Mother, the doorbell is ringing," Danny called.

"Don't let any beggars in," Mrs. O'Flaherty called.

The ringing continued. Danny waited a moment. He got off his chair and started walking shyly down the hallway. Margaret came out of her bedroom, muttering:

"Jesus Christ!"

The bell still rang.

"Who is it?" Margaret asked sharply.

"It's me, Jack Doolin. For God's sake, open the door," he said.

"I can't. I'm going to bed," Margaret said.

"For God's sake, Peg. Open the door. It's serious! My wife, they're taking her to the hospital," he said.

Margaret opened the door and saw Jack Doolin in his shirt sleeves, a crushed, harassed man with a concerned and worried look on his face.

"What's the matter, Jack?"

"I came home and found my wife in terrible pains, moaning. She had the kid call the doctor. He got there just after I did. She's got appendicitis. They're rushing her away to the hospital. Please, come and stay with the kid and put him to bed and wait until I get back or my sister-in-law comes over. I just called her," Jack said hysterically.

Mrs. O'Flaherty rushed to them.

"What's the matter?" she asked.

"My wife's going to the hospital with appendicitis. I wanted one of you to watch my boy until my sister-in-law comes," he said.

"Peg, go down. I'll get a blessed candle and bring it down. You poor man, God bless you," Mrs. O'Flaherty said.

"I'll be right down, Jack," Margaret said.

"Thanks. I got to get back. The ambulance will be here in a second," he said.

He turned and hurried downstairs.

"God forgive me!" Margaret said in the hallway.

She went to her room and fixed herself up again, powdering her swollen eyes.

She went downstairs. Mrs. O'Flaherty was digging about in her room and finally found a holy candle.

"Son! Son!" she called.

Danny went to her.

"Bring this down to the Doolins and have them light it. It'll bring good luck and the help of God," she said.

Danny took the candle downstairs. Just as he did, the door opened and two white-garbed internes carried Mrs. Doolin out on a stretcher. Her face was drawn and she was pale. She looked at Danny, smiled weakly.

"Goodbye, Danny, be a good boy," she said faintly; then she began moaning.

"Don't worry. I'll watch everything," Margaret said to Mr. Doolin as he walked out after the stretcher, biting his lips, looking very worried.

Danny gave his aunt the candle, and saw Georgie Doolin sobbing behind her.

He went back upstairs, perplexed by the suddenness and the excitement of what had just happened. He felt that Mrs. Doolin was going to die. He ought to pray for her, that she would go to Heaven. He found his grandmother sitting in the dining room, fingering her rosary beads and mumbling prayers.

24

I

Mrs. O'Flaherty rocked away in her bedroom with a can of beer beside her on the floor. She reached down, picked it up, took a swig, and wiped her lips with the sleeve of her dress. She could hear the mumble of conversation from Danny and Little Margaret in the dining room. They were good little ones, they were. She took another swig. She wiped her mouth again. Her eyes began watering and she put a handkerchief to them. She gazed up at the picture of the Sacred Heart which hung over her dresser. She cried. An elevated train passed. She took another swig of beer. She heard the front door opening.

"Peg, is that you?" she called.

She heard footsteps in the hall. It was Peg. She heard her daughter going into her bedroom. She placed the lid on the can of beer and threw a cloth over it. She got up and staggered out of the room, across the kitchen, and down the hallway to Margaret's bedroom. Margaret sat on the bed, bleary-eyed, her face dirty.

"Hello, Peg," Mrs. O'Flaherty said.

"Hello," Margaret said lifelessly.

"Ah, 'tis a shame you couldn't go to that poor woman's funeral to pay your last respects. That poor woman! Ah, she was a good neighbor woman, a good Christian soul. And that poor man with his boy left behind. Ah, Peg, it was a fine funeral, and he was so nice to me. He treated me like I was the grand lady, and after they put her away, poor Mr. Doolin took me along with them and bought me a glass of beer," she said.

Margaret did not answer.

"Ah, it would break your heart seeing the good soul laid away, leaving that man with a boy on his hands. It would make your heart bleed," Mrs. O'Flaherty said.

Margaret still sat, her eyes fixed on the radiator.

"It was sad. But I went. I'm not the one not to pay my last respects to a neighbor woman like Mrs. Doolin. May the Lord have mercy on her soul! May the Lord be good to the husband and boy she left behind!"

"My poor heart is broken," Margaret sighed.

II

"Honest, doncha like any of the girls in your class at school?" Little Margaret asked, seated across from Danny at the dining-room table, her hands on the pages of a *Billy Whiskers*, which lay open before her.

"No. I never pay no attention to them," Danny said; he wanted to tell Little Margaret that that wasn't so, and that he did, he paid attention to Virginia Doyle, Hortense Audrey, and Helen Smith, and today at school Hortense Audrey had sent him a note asking him if he was going skating. But he couldn't tell Little Margaret because she might tease him. She'd tease him in front of them all, and they would ask him questions about girls and he couldn't stand that.

"I like a boy at school," she said.

"Who?"

"I won't say."

"Do I know him?"

"No. But he's a nice boy. All the girls in my grade like him," she said.

"I don't care," he said.

"I'll bet you do have a girl," she said.

"You'll lose your money betting me that," he said.

"I didn't say I'd bet you money. I just said I'd bet you," she said.

"You're dumb. You mustn't learn anything in the public school," he said.

"You don't know. You don't go to it," she said.

"Well, if you learned anything, you'd know that if you bet you gotta bet something. You can't just bet nothin'," he said.

"Know what happened today at recess?" she said.

"What?"

"We were playing in the yard, and Aunt Margaret walked by on the sidewalk, drunk. All of the kids said, 'Oh, look at the drunken woman.' Then they all pretended they were staggering and walking just like Aunty Margaret walked. But I didn't let on she was my aunt, and I ran away so's she wouldn't see me."

"Some of the kids around here know she gets drunk. Gee, I hope the two of them don't fight," he said.

"I don't like to be alone like this when they're drunk," she said.

"Uncle Al doesn't know," he said.

"Why did Uncle Al write you the letter bawling you out, and saying you and I must be good? What did we do?" she asked.

"I don't know," he said.

"Well, why did he write?"

"Aunt Peg musta written him and said things," he said.

"That wasn't right of her," she said.

"If he knew she was drunk like this, he'd be sorer at her than he was at us. I thought we'd been pretty good," Danny said.

"It's getting dark now. I don't like it to be dark and be alone with them when they're drunk," Little Margaret said.

"Neither do I," Danny said.

III

The beer in the can had gotten warm, but Mrs. O'Flaherty sat finishing it, taking large swigs. The beer trickled down her chin and she wiped it with her sleeve. When she had emptied the can, she got up and went to the sink, washed the can out, dried it, and set it on a shelf in the pantry with the pots and pans. She staggered into the dining room and saw Danny and Little Margaret sitting opposite one another, speechless, their eyes caught in a gaze of fear.

"Ah, me darlin' grandson," she said, bending down and planting a wet, beery kiss on his cheek; he didn't like it because there was too much spit in her kiss, and her beer breath was terribly strong. "Me darlin' grandson. You'll be a fine man some day."

She swayed over him. She looked at her granddaughter.

"A pity 'tis you're not a boy," she said.

Little Margaret didn't answer. She sat, watching her grandmother, suspicious, afraid.

Margaret staggered into the room.

"Hello, Aunt Margaret," Little Margaret said timidly.

"Ah, my angel niece," Aunt Margaret said, going to Little Margaret, kissing and fondling her.

She dropped down into a chair between Danny and Little Margaret.

"Little angel niece, your aunt's gonna raise you not to be unhappy like she is," Aunt Margaret said slowly and drunkenly.

"Yes, Aunt Margaret," Little Margaret said.

Mrs. O'Flaherty floundered over to her daughter and clumsily stroked her hair. Margaret sank her head on the table and cried. The two children sat speechless, as if hunched up into themselves.

"Don't cry, Peg. Sure, it ain't worth the crying," Mrs. O'Flaherty said.

Danny watched them, sad-eyed. He wished that Bill were here with them, or his Mama, or even that Uncle Al were home. He hated for him and his sister to be left alone with them when they were like this.

Margaret looked up at her mother.

"Mother, Mother, dearie, you're all I got, you and the children here. All I got. All I got."

The tears streamed down her face. She slowly turned to her niece and said:

"Angel niece, don't you ever let yourself grow up brokenhearted."

"No, I won't, Aunty Peg," Little Margaret said.

"You and my mother, all I got in this worl'," Margaret said.

She let her head sink on the table again.

"Don't cry, Aunty Margaret," Little Margaret said.

"Please don't cry, Aunt Peg," Danny said.

Margaret sobbed loudly. Mrs. O'Flaherty staggered to the rocking chair by the window and rocked, her tears coming freely. The children sat, waiting, hopeless.

"Ah, Peg, 'twas a sad sight seeing poor Mrs. Doolin laid away leaving that poor widowed man and motherless child behind. May the Lord have mercy on the poor woman's soul, and may He be good to them she left behind," Mrs. O'Flaherty said.

IV

Danny answered the bell in fear and trembling, his sister standing behind him, pale. But when they saw it was Bill, they were both overjoyed.

"Hello, Dan. Ma got Pa to let me come and stay all night. Pa was sore about it, but Ma made him. She said I had to come up and be with you kids while things were going on here. She raised the roof about it," Bill said.

Little Margaret took Bill's hand.

"Bill, they're both stewed," said Danny.

"They do nothing but cry," Little Margaret said.

"Mother is stewed, too, huh?"

"She went to Mrs. Doolin's funeral and came home stewed. And I had to go out and get her a can of beer, and it made her cry more. But they haven't fought yet," Danny said.

"They ain't raising cain?"

"Not yet," said Danny.

"They just keep crying," Little Margaret said.

"I'm not gonna stay here if they're both drunk," Bill said.

"You got to take me with you then," Little Margaret said.

"Please don't leave us, Bill," Danny begged, almost in tears.

"No. I'll go back. Pa'll be glad because he doesn't want me around them when they're stewed," Bill said.

"Please stay. Little Margaret and me don't wanna stay alone with them like this," Danny said.

"Come home along with me," said Bill.

"I will," said Little Margaret.

"I can't. I can't leave them alone," Danny said.

"Why?"

"Suppose Aunty Margaret tries to commit suicide again, and turns on the gas? Maybe she'll kill Mother," Danny said.

"She tried to turn on the gas last night and we turned it off, and then she went out. Some man called her up and she went out with him and didn't come back until noon today. And she went out again and just came back a little while ago," Little Margaret said.

"Gee, maybe I better stay," Bill said.

"Who're you?" Aunt Margaret asked, meeting Bill in the hallway. Danny and Little Margaret had lagged behind Bill.

Margaret's kimono came open.

"It's me, Aunt Peg," Bill said.

"Willie-boy, my darling nephew," she said.

She flung her arms around him, her naked body pressed to him. It was warm and he liked that, but he couldn't stand her whiskey breath. She released him and said:

"Your aunt is sad."

She sobbed, and the three children stood there, awkward and uncomfortable.

"Where's your mother?" she asked.

"Home," he said.

"I wanna see her," Margaret said.

"She ain't well. She got neuralgia, and Catherine and Bob got colds," Bill said.

"Mother!" Margaret called, turning from them and staggering toward the back of the house.

"She's stewed to the gills," Bill said.

"Yes," Danny said sadly.

"I don' wanna stay here," Little Margaret said, crying.

<h1 style="text-align:center">V</h1>

Little Margaret sat reading the Billy Whiskers book, and Bill and Dan sat opposite her.

"Gee, that's a swell idea, all right," Danny said.

"Yeah. We each make up three teams. We each pick a team, and then take some of our favorites from other teams, and we play a regular Pacific Coast League schedule with our six teams. We'll keep averages, batting, pitching records, stolen bases, everything we can with Steel's, and play the whole schedule," Bill said.

"We can start tonight," Danny said.

"Have you got a notebook to start keeping the scores in?" Bill asked.

"Uh huh," Danny said.

"We ought to have a big-player limit, because we got to have a lot of players. We got favorites on other teams beside the ones we'll pick," Bill said.

"We'll shake the dice for first pick," Danny said.

Bill shook, and his total of the three dice added to ten.

Danny was hopeful, and shook, getting seven.

"I'll take the Cubs as my first team," Bill said.

"I'll take the White Sox," Danny said.

"Let's see, now. I'll take the Red Sox," Bill said.

"Giants," Danny said.

"I gotta think for my third team, and after we each get that, we'll pick players from other teams," Bill said.

"Gee, I hope they're asleep now," Danny said.

"Me, too. They aren't so bad this time as I seen them when they were drunk," Bill said.

"I don't like to sleep with Aunt Margaret when she's drunk," Little Margaret said.

"They didn't fight yet," Danny said.

Suddenly, Margaret let out a piercing scream which paralyzed the three children with terror. Bill put down his pencil. He and Danny looked at each other, disturbed and frightened. Little Margaret shuddered, sat with mouth agape.

VI

They heard their aunt run through the hall and close the kitchen door.

"Goodbye," she yelled.

"She's turning on the gas," Bill said in fright.

"She'll kill Mother and all of us. Mother's sleeping," Danny said while his sister cried.

Bill got to his feet. Danny followed him. There was a chair set against the kitchen door. They could hear their grandmother saying something, but they couldn't make out what it was. Bill pushed and the door gave. He and Danny entered the kitchen and saw Margaret standing naked over the kitchen stove and Mrs. O'Flaherty in her flannel nightgown standing at the entrance to her bedroom.

"She's killing me! Help!" Mrs. O'Flaherty yelled.

Bill rushed to the stove. Two gas jets were turned on. He reached in front of his aunt and turned them off. Both boys looked at the naked body of their aunt, a well-modeled body with firm and compact flesh and medium-sized breasts.

"Get out of here, you dirty little rats. I haven't any clothes on," she said.

"You can't kill us and my grandmother," Bill said.

"Don't you leave. Sure, she's scandalizing the neighborhood and trying to kill her poor old mother," Mrs. O'Flaherty said.

"I was not. I was going to make myself some coffee. I couldn't find any matches," the drunken aunt said.

"Please go to bed, Aunty Peg," Danny said almost in whispers and like a frightened puppy.

"Trying to kill your poor old mother. You ought to be ashamed of yourself. Standing before these little boys in your pelt, scandalizing them," Mrs. O'Flaherty said.

"Leave me alone! Get out of my sight! And you, you dirty little thief," she cried, pointing at Bill. "You, you dirty little thief, you get out of my home and go back to your sloppy mother and your drunkard of a father. Go on, go home before I brain you!"

Bill caught sight of an old baseball bat of Danny's under the sink. He quickly grabbed it and turned and faced his aunt, tears in his eyes.

"Don't you come near me! Don't you touch me!" he sobbed, holding the bat ready.

"Don't hurt my aunt," Little Margaret, unheard, called from the kitchen doorway.

Margaret, who had started a lunge toward Bill, halted in her tracks and looked at him in awe and surprise.

"Hit her, Bill! Hit her and I'll never let you want for a penny!" Mrs. O'Flaherty said, rolling around the kitchen.

"You'll pay for this. Taking a baseball bat to your aunt," Margaret said, dropping her head, beginning to cry.

The two boys stood before their aunt as if petrified. Little Margaret was still fixed in the kitchen doorway. Mrs. O'Flaherty spat in Margaret's face.

"Go put some clothes on your sinful body, you hussy," Mrs. O'Flaherty said.

"He won't even let me make a cup of coffee for myself in my own home. He stands there and won't leave my sight when I haven't a stitch of clothes on," Margaret said, her tears sliding off her face, some dropping onto her upright breasts.

"I don't wanna stay here," Little Margaret sobbed.

"As long as I live, I'll never forgive you, you little thief!" Margaret shouted at Bill.

Crying, he still faced her with the baseball bat held ready.

"Go home!" Margaret said to him.

"Stay here, William. It's my son's house and I'm boss in it," Mrs. O'Flaherty said.

Margaret staggered out of the kitchen and Bill put the bat down.

"William, you're a fine boy," Mrs. O'Flaherty said.

She floundered into the bedroom. Bill and Danny looked at each other, speechless. Little Margaret came and stood quietly beside them.

"Here, Son, you're a fine boy. Here, Son," Mrs. O'Flaherty said, handing each of them a quarter.

"Thanks, Mother," Bill said.

"You stay here tonight and watch her, watch her or she'll murder us," Mrs. O'Flaherty said.

Mrs. O'Flaherty went back to her room.

"Why does she wanna turn on the gas?" Little Margaret asked.

"I donno. She's been yelling she wants to commit suicide ever since she started gettin' stewed this time," Danny said.

"Danny, she'll try it again. We got to do something so she can't lock herself in here and do it," Bill said, going to the kitchen door, taking the key from the lock, and pocketing it.

"Gee, she'll kill Mother," Danny said.

"I got an idea," Bill said.

"What?" asked Danny.

"Where's the clothesline?" Bill asked.

"It's in the pantry," Little Margaret said.

Bill went to the pantry, and he rattled pots as he searched for the clothesline.

"What are you doing in my son's pantry, you whore?" Mrs. O'Flaherty yelled from the bedroom.

"It's me, Mother," Bill yelled to her.

"What does he want in there? Are you hungry, child?" Mrs. O'Flaherty called.

Bill came out of the pantry with a small piece of clothesline.

"Mother, I'm gonna tie the kitchen door to the table so she can't close it and keep us out if she tries to turn on the gas again," Bill called.

"Ah, you're a smart boy," Mrs. O'Flaherty said from the door of her bedroom.

Bill set the table sidewise against the door and tied it to both knobs, cutting off what line remained.

"The Lord will bless you and you'll never want a day for this," Mrs. O'Flaherty said.

"She can turn the gas jets on in any room," Danny said fearfully.

"We got to get the key to her bedroom," Bill said.

"I'll get it," Little Margaret said.

She tiptoed down the hall.

"Get out of here, you filthy thief. Sneaking looks at me. Dirty little pervert," Margaret yelled on hearing her niece without looking up to see who it was.

Little Margaret grabbed the door key from Margaret's door, and ran back to the kitchen with it. She handed it to Bill.

"Now we got to fix the bathroom," Bill said.

"William, you'll never want for a day as long as your grandmother lives," Mrs. O'Flaherty said, crying drunkenly.

Bill searched around the kitchen and found more rope. Danny and Little Margaret followed him to the bathroom and watched him tie the door against the faucet in the bathtub, knotting the rope many times so that it would take time to undo it.

"Now, is there any other place she can lock herself in and turn on the gas jet?" Bill asked.

"Uncle Al's and my bedroom in the front," Danny said.

Bill went and found the key in the keyhole of the front bedroom and locked the door, putting the key in his pocket. Mrs. O'Flaherty came staggering down the hallway.

"Sure, she'll never have a day's luck," she said.

"We got to stay up all night and watch her," Bill said to Danny while they could hear Margaret sobbing in her bedroom.

"Yes, Son. And I'll pay you," Mrs. O'Flaherty said.

"I'll make coffee so we can stay up. I think coffee helps to keep you awake," Bill said.

"We can get our teams all picked and set and start our Steel's League," Danny said.

"I wanna stay up with you. Tomorrow's Saturday and there ain't no school," Little Margaret said.

VII

"She didn't have a stitch of clothes on, did she, Dan?" Bill said in a low voice while both boys sat drinking coffee and eating ham sandwiches at the dining-room table; sheets of paper, a notebook, and the Steel's board were spread out before them.

"She's nice to look at. We never saw any as close as that when we went to the penny arcade, remember?" Danny said.

"Yeah. But, say, if Pa knew we were seeing her naked, he'd sure raise a lot of hell about it," Bill said.

"Uncle Al, maybe wouldn't he be mad! And he wouldn't like it if he knew she was trying to commit suicide and yelling drunk like this. I got a good mind to tell him. She wrote a letter and told him about me and Little Margaret, and he wrote me a letter and bawled us both out. I'm afraid of what'll he say to us when he comes home," Danny said.

"He'll be sore at her when he finds this out," Bill said.

"Why does she do this, Bill?" Danny asked.

"I heard Ma telling Pa about it. Mama was saying that Robinson gave her the gate, and that's why she's raising all this hell," Bill said.

"Oh!" Danny exclaimed knowingly, but he couldn't really understand it at all.

"I think she's asleep now. I don't hear her bawling," Bill said.

"I hope she don't wake up until she's sober in the morning," Danny said.

"I do, too," said Bill.

Little Margaret came into the dining room from the bathroom.

"What were you talking about?" she asked.

"Baseball," Danny said quickly.

"You wouldn't understand it," said Bill.

"Why don't you talk about things I like and play games I can play with you instead of that old baseball game?" she said.

"Why don't you go to bed? It's getting late," Bill said.

"I ain't got no place to sleep. I won't sleep with Aunty Margaret while she's drunk. She crushes me and I can't sleep," Little Margaret said.

"Read *Billy Whiskers* then. He's funny," Danny said.

"Gee, he is. I just read about how he broke up the circus. I wish I had a goat of my own," she said.

"Let's start our season, Dan," Bill said.

"You rule the book for the score, and I'll figure out my White Sox lineup," Danny said.

VIII

"I skunked you that time. Fourteen hits and a homer for Heinie Zim. Only four hits for you. Jimmy Lavender gets a good start with seven strike-outs," Bill said.

"It's only the opening game. I'll pitch Mel Wolfgang this game," Danny said.

"I'll put in Hippo Vaughan," Bill said.

"I got to figure out my lineup now," Danny said.

Bill started ruling off lines to keep an inning-by-inning score of the second game.

IX

They heard her going barefooted into the kitchen. Then they heard her at the kitchen doorknob. Bill went into the kitchen right away, and Danny followed him. Little Margaret had her head down on the pages of *Billy Whiskers* and didn't wake up.

"What do you want?" Margaret asked savagely.

"Please go to bed," Danny begged.

"Can't I even get a glass of water without you brats spying on me?" Margaret asked.

"I'll get you a glass of water, and then please go to bed, Aunty Margaret," Danny said.

Bill walked over to the stove. One gas jet was turned on, and gas was escaping from it. He turned it off.

"I was going to make coffee," she said.

"Please go to bed, Aunty Margaret," Danny said.

"A grown woman and brats spying on her," Margaret complained bitterly.

Bill sat down by the table which was still tied to the door. He yawned.

"Why don't you go to bed? It's too late for you to be up," Margaret said.

"We're playing," Danny said.

"You're keeping me awake with that goddamn dice game," Margaret said.

Bill put his finger to his lips in a signal to Danny not to talk to her and get her wound up again.

"Who asked him to stay? Who said he could stay in my house?" Margaret said.

"Mother," Danny said.

"Mother! Goddamn her greenhorn soul! Jesus Christ!" Margaret said explosively, and as she uttered the Lord's name, Danny bowed his head just as he had been taught to at Crucifixion school.

Margaret stamped out of the kitchen.

"Is she at it again?" Mrs. O'Flaherty asked, coming into the kitchen sleepy-faced and with her hair mussed, her flannel nightgown trailing on the floor. Sleepy and with her shrunken gums showing when she talked, she looked older than she normally did.

"Yes, but she's gone back. She's sore," Bill said.

"Let her be," Mrs. O'Flaherty said.

"She said she wanted coffee, but she had the gas turned on again," Bill said.

"That God may curse her soul!" Mrs. O'Flaherty exclaimed with deep bitterness.

X

"Stop that goddamn dice game and go to bed!" Margaret shouted, waking up Little Margaret, who had continued sleeping with her blonde head over the book.

Danny and Bill exchanged glances of disappointment. Margaret, wearing an old kimono, walked up and down the hall, making all three of the children nervous. They sat silent, as if waiting for something dangerous to happen. A bitter January wind could be heard from without, blowing, rattling the window-panes.

"I'm afraid," Little Margaret said.

"Sssh!" Bill exclaimed.

They sat silent, alert, their nerves so tense that they almost jerked with each sound of the wind, each creak of the boards, each of Margaret's footsteps, sighs, and sobs.

"You children are up too late. You should be in bed. It's bad for you to be up at this hour of the night, and if your uncle was home he wouldn't let you be staying up," Margaret said in the doorway.

Danny opened his mouth to say something, but Bill signaled him to be silent. Margaret turned and walked away. She came back. Up and down, she nervously paced the hallway, and the three O'Neill children sat on the edge of their chairs, waiting with palpitating hearts.

XI

Bill ran to the front of the apartment.

"Get out of here!" Margaret cried as he came into the lighted parlor.

"You got the gas on," he said.

"I haven't. You got dirt in your nose. Blow it," she said, and as she spoke Danny and Little Margaret joined Bill, both of them making faces as they smelled the gas. Bill couldn't reach the gas jet, so he started to move the piano bench to the center of the parlor to stand on it. Margaret grabbed him, and they wrestled.

"Help me, Dan," Bill called.

"Get away, you little thief!" she gasped, still struggling with Bill.

Danny grabbed at Margaret's legs, and Bill was enabled to free himself as Margaret tried to slap Danny. She caught him with a ringing crack on the cheek, and, off balance, he slipped to the floor. His face stung and he put his hand to it. He cried.

"I'll scream at the top of my voice if you don't get out of here!" Margaret threatened.

"Glory be to God!" Mrs. O'Flaherty exclaimed, coming into the parlor, smelling gas, seeing Margaret wrestling with Bill.

"She's murderin' us! Help! Murder!" Mrs. O'Flaherty exclaimed. She blessed herself. "Go get me a stick and call the neighbors," she said, turning to her terrified granddaughter, who stood in a corner, her mouth open.

Margaret struggled like a tigress with Bill. He squeezed out of her grasp. She rushed at him. He blindly punched at her, and his fist landed flush on her left breast. She held her breast and moaned.

"Give it to her! Don't leave her a leg to stand on!" Mrs. O'Flaherty encouraged.

"After all I done for you, that you should hit me like this," Margaret said, still moaning, holding her breast, her face contorted in pain.

Bill hastily shoved the piano bench under the gas and electric chandelier, stepped up, reached, turned off the gas jet. He jumped down.

"Open the window!" Mrs. O'Flaherty said while Margaret sobbed, still holding her breast.

"I want to die! They won't even let me die. I want to die. I'm through. I'll go and jump in the lake," she cried, sinking onto the bench, bending over, still holding her breast.

"She'd kill us all, the tinker! But she won't kill the tramps and beggars she runs with. She'll kill her poor old mother and me little grandchildren. Ah, the Lord will punish her for this. As true as the day is long, the Lord will punish her, and she'll never see sight nor light of Heaven. Ah, she's born of the Devil, and to the Devil she'll go," Mrs. O'Flaherty said.

"Gosh, Dan, that gas smells awful," Bill said.

"It makes me sick," Danny said.

"I wanna go to my Papa," Little Margaret sobbed.

"You poor little child," Mrs. O'Flaherty said, enfolding Danny in her arms.

"I'll get cancer of the breast," Margaret cried, almost in a state of collapse as she sat on the piano bench, still holding her breast.

"May you rot with cancer and not have anything but vinegar and gall coming out of your breasts," Mrs. O'Flaherty said, squeezing Danny tightly to her as she glared at her daughter.

Margaret went slowly out of the parlor. They heard her sobbing in her bedroom.

"Gee, that was a narrow one, Dan," Bill said.

"Glory be, but she'll make an end of me yet when I'm in me bed," Mrs. O'Flaherty said, releasing Danny and making the sign of the cross.

She knelt in the center of the parlor, blessed herself again, raised her hands as if to Heaven, prayed silently. The children stood around her, not knowing what to do.

XII

Margaret was in bed and seemed to have cried herself to sleep. Mrs. O'Flaherty, now sober, with a shawl over her shoulders, sat rocking away near the dining-room window, yawning, her rosary beads in her wrinkled fingers, mumbling prayers, sometimes whispering the words of the Hail Mary, sometimes uttering them in a low but audible voice.

"I wish it was morning," Bill said at the dining-room table.

"Me, too," Danny said.

"She's asleep," Bill said, nodding his head toward Little Margaret whose head was again on her Billy Whiskers book.

"I'll ask Mama to come up tomorrow," Bill said.

"Do you think she'll kill us with gas?" Danny asked.

"She's been trying damn hard to," Bill said.

"Maybe we better tell Uncle Al to come home," Danny said.

"I'm not going to hang around here another night," Bill said.

"What'll we do if you don't?" Danny asked.

"That ain't my lookout," Bill said.

"Gee, I can't keep her from that gas," Danny said.

"I can't stay up all night every night," Bill said, and both boys yawned.

Hail, Mary, full of grace, the Lord is with thee, and blessed art thou among women.
. . .

Danny's head dropped onto the table. Bill sat back, yawned, stretched his arms. An elevated train rumbled noisily by. The grandmother's lips moved fervently in prayer, her fingers going from bead to bead. Danny stirred slightly in his sleep. Bill yawned again. He looked at the scores of the games they'd played. He stretched again. There was a sound of floor boards stirring. He got up quickly and tiptoed down the hall past Margaret's bedroom. He heard her snoring. He returned to the table, sat, yawned. His head dropped, his chin sinking against his chest.

Hail, Mary, full of grace, the Lord is with thee . . .

Mrs. O'Flaherty continued praying. Her lips moved, but the words were only sibilant sounds. Her wrinkled finger advanced from one black bead to the next. Bill dropped his head on the table and slept. The first streaks of the winter dawn could be seen in the cracks between the window shades.

Holy Mary, Mother Of God, pray for us . . .

25

I

"You say the three kids had to stay up all night?" Jim angrily asked, striding back and forth across the kitchen. Lizz stood near the kitchen stove, swathed in sweaters. The young children sat huddled together near the stove. Bob and Dennis had their feet stuck just inside the oven. Bob and Catherine sniffled with colds, and their running noses were red and chafed. They kept blowing their noses into rags. The wind whistled and sang outside, moaned against the windows, filled the house with a steady barrage of strange sounds.

"My kids got to stay up all night and turn the gas off while that drunken sister of yours tries to kill herself and yells and curses up and down the house!" Jim said, still pacing back and forth.

"That's what Mother told me on the phone," Lizz said.

"Cold!" Arty said.

"The little fellow is cold. I'll go get an old shawl and put it around his shoulders," Lizz said.

She left the kitchen, took the kerosene lamp off the dining-room table, and went to the front bedroom. She quickly reappeared in the kitchen with an old white shawl which she pinned around Arty.

Jim paused in the center of the kitchen. He rubbed his unshaven face. He stuck his hands in his pockets and looked at Lizz.

"Don't blame me," Lizz said.

"We let them take the girl out of a decent home life in Madison to live up there with that no-good, drunken sister of yours," Jim said.

"I tell you, Jim, she's possessed," Lizz said.

"I don't care what she is. I don't want my kids seeing that kind of stuff," Jim said.

"If they hadn't stayed up, my poor mother would have been dead today," Lizz said.

"I'm going up and get them. I'll be goddamned if this monkey business can go on any longer. Danny and the girl can take pot luck with their brothers and sister. I'm not going to have my kids live in that kind of a house with that drunken sister of yours," Jim said.

"No, Jim, let me go to my mother," Lizz said.

"Over my dead body you'll go out of this house tonight in a blizzard to take care of that puking drunkard," Jim said, speaking very slowly and distinctly because of his anger, pointing his finger at Lizz as he talked.

Bob, Dennis, and Catherine, huddling together because of the cold, looked awe-stricken and curiously at their father.

"They're gonna fight," Bob whispered to Dennis.

"Shut up!" Dennis whispered back.

"Don't take all the room in the oven. My feet get cold, too," Catherine said.

"You boys let your sister keep her feet in the oven there," Jim said.

He went to the woodpile beside the stove and dumped in almost a half of a grocery box that had been broken up. They could all hear the fire roaring within the stove.

Arty tried to imitate the roaring sound of the fire.

"God Almighty, why do I have such damn problems with my kids and my in-laws?" Jim said.

"My heart goes out to my poor mother," Lizz said.

"Why doesn't Al throw that sister of yours out of the house bodily?" Jim asked.

"My poor brother is away, working hard, and he doesn't know all that goes on in that house," Lizz said.

"It's high time that somebody told him," Jim said.

"Stove. Hot!" Arty exclaimed.

"If you ask me, Lizz, that Robinson guy wasn't so dumb, dropping her down the chute. My God, I'd feel sorry for any man getting tied to such a woman," Jim said.

"Jim, the little ones!" Lizz said.

"I forgot," Jim said.

"But, Jim, she's been good to us and our kids. We can't be too hard on her," Lizz said.

"I don't give two hangs in Hell for her kind of goodness and generosity. I don't want it, and don't forget that! I don't want you to accept a penny off that, that . . ." Jim looked down at his children. "That one," he concluded.

"Well, I don't want her spoiling my sons and my daughter. They're innocent children," Lizz said.

"I'm gonna talk to Al when he gets home," Jim said.

"I am, too. I'm going to give them all a piece of my mind. Oh, but am I going to give them a piece of my mind and tell them what my Jim thinks!" Lizz said.

"It's a holy shame," Jim said.

"God won't permit her to go on like this," Lizz said.

"Leave God out of it. It's our problem," Jim said.

"That poor mother of mine, living in that house. The Lord doesn't know but when she might kill my mother. Jim, I got to go to my children and my mother," Lizz said.

"No!" Jim said emphatically.

"Jim O'Neill, I will hold you responsible before God if you don't let me go and take care of my mother. I'm a mother and she's my mother," Lizz said.

"What about these little ones?" Jim asked, pointing to the children.

"You can watch them until I get back," Lizz said.

"I'll go," Jim said.

"You can't. You've been out in the cold all day, and you aren't the one to be there, not with a drunken woman," Lizz said.

Jim walked back and forth.

"My God, with all the poor sick people in the world, and with a war and men getting killed wholesale in Europe, she, with everything in the world before her, has to make this trouble. I can't make head or tail of her. She's just no good, that's all," Jim said.

"I'm going to get ready. You can put the little ones to bed," Lizz said.

"Lizz, you're not going out on a night like this, not in your condition," Jim said.

"I got to go to my mother," Lizz said.

"No!"

"Don't put this on your conscience by keeping me here. My mother and my babies are there. That's my place," Lizz said.

"Goddamn it, I wish the O'Flahertys lived in Honolulu or Asia," Jim said.

"Jim, duty calls me to my mother and my little ones," Lizz said.

"All right, go, but don't go staying there if she's drunk. And don't coddle her. If she starts any monkey business, take a chair and brain her and let her sleep it off," Jim said.

"I'll bundle myself up warm and go to my mother and my babies," Lizz said.

"Mither go bye-bye," Arty said.

"Jim, give them their cough medicine before you put them to bed," Lizz said.

She went to the front of the house to bundle herself up warmly.

II

Lizz walked into the blizzard with her head bent to protect herself from the wind. The night was powdered with falling snow, which blurred and distorted the school building ahead of her. The sidewalk was already blanketed, and no matter how she walked, she had to go through snow and wet her feet. Snowdrifts had been piled up and the howling wind kept whirling flakes about, slapping them into her face. She wore several sweaters under her coat, and her face was bandaged under the old hat she had on. She clutched her pocketbook tightly. She walked carefully in order to keep her footing. Every time she looked ahead the brilliant whiteness blinded her. Her eyes watered, and the exposed parts of her face were becoming chafed by the raw wind. She stepped into a snowbank and had to wade on through it. Her feet were soggy. She struggled on. Her face began to burn because of the wind. She could see only a few feet in front of her. Snow crusted the lamppost near the entrance to Saint Martha's school, and its rays were dimmed. She looked up again. The flying whiteness was dazzling. Her watery eyes pained her. She plodded on, her nose running, her feet cold and soggy, her clothes feeling heavy, her coat covered with snow.

Oh, but she wished she was already at Mother's. God would punish Peg for this. But she had to go to her mother and her children. She patiently fought her way onward toward Wentworth Avenue. Suddenly, she slipped. There was no support which she could grasp. Her feet slid from under her and she fell on her buttocks. She was wet. She blessed herself. She asked God to protect her. She felt no pain. She was only getting soaked and cold. She sank her hands in the snow and tried to lift herself. She got halfway up. She breathed heavily. She could see nothing but blinding snow. She raised herself to one knee. An arm grasped her firmly.

"I'll help you, lady," a strange man said.

"Oh, thank you," she said in a terrified voice.

The man assisted her to her feet.

"Thank you. God will bless you. I'm not drunk. I fell in the snow," she said.

"I know, lady. It's an awful night to be out in," the stranger said.

"I got to go to the street-car line," she said, determining to go on despite her fall, her chill, her wetness, her physical misery.

She plodded to the car line and waited in the entrance of a closed store, shielded from the worst assaults of the wind. Wentworth Avenue was deserted. Snow was blowing along the street, and the wind rushed, whistling in eerie tones. She heard a clanging street-car bell.

"Thank God!" Lizz muttered.

She walked out, going slowly in order not to fall, wading through snowbanks, getting her feet soaked again. She stood waving her arm and yelling:

"Street car! Street car! Street car!"

The front of the car was coated with snow, and the lights from within were blunted. The car approached like a moving, yellowed fog. It stopped.

"Hold it, please! Hold it, please!"

She waddled to the entrance at the back. The conductor leaned down from the platform and helped her on.

"Oh, thank you, sir," she said.

"Not at all, lady. Sure is one terrible night. We're lucky to be running. The cars are tied up all over. It's taken us over an hour to come from downtown," the conductor said; he was a ruddy-faced man, with blue eyes and a kindly expression.

Lizz dug in her pocketbook and handed him pennies. He took her fare and rung it up. She took the proffered transfer.

"My third cousin, Patrick Fox, is on the cars. Do you know him?" she asked the conductor.

"No, lady, don't think I do," he said.

The car was going on slowly, and Lizz went inside. It was half empty. She could see the faces of some of the passengers gloomy, tired faces. Nobody liked to be out on such a night. Nobody felt good being out in this weather. She huddled into a seat by the window, suffering utter discomfort. The window was coated with snow and she couldn't see out of it. She sat, and the weight of the child within her womb seemed to drag wearisomely on her.

III

"Oh, my poor mother. I came to you," Lizz said on being let in by Mrs. O'Flaherty.

She was coated and crusted with snow, and her cheeks were stung into redness.

"God bless you, Lizz, for coming, but you shouldn't have come on a night like this."

"I would never desert my mother and my little ones in trouble," Lizz said.

"You must be wet, you poor thing. Take your wet things off and I'll make you a cup of warm tea," Mrs. O'Flaherty said.

"Where is she?" Lizz asked.

"Out. Ask the Devil where she is. And she has me head aching, she has," Mrs. O'Flaherty said.

"Out on this night?" Lizz said.

"Devil or man couldn't keep her in," Mrs. O'Flaherty said.

Lizz started taking off her things.

"You poor thing, coming out in this weather. Ah, Lizz, the Lord will repay you for it," Mrs. O'Flaherty said.

Mrs. O'Flaherty led Lizz to the rear. She saw Danny and Bill playing Steel's and Little Margaret drawing pictures with colored crayons at the dining-room table.

"Here are my brave sons, and my little girl! Here are my chicks. Mother, has any woman got chicks like mine?" Lizz said.

She extended her arms. Little Margaret ran to her, and she kissed the girl. She then kissed Danny and Bill.

"Your mother came to you," Lizz said.

"Lizz, I'll fix you a cup of warm tea," Mrs. O'Flaherty said, going into the kitchen.

"Mama, I can't stay here," Little Margaret said.

"Your mama will take care of you now, you lovely child," Lizz said.

"Ma, is Pa sore I didn't come home?" Bill asked.

"I came after you," Lizz said.

"Mama, you're not going to take Bill home and leave us here alone with Aunty Margaret while she's drunk?" Danny asked in fright.

"Your mother will never desert you," Lizz said.

Mrs. O'Flaherty came back, saying:

"The tea will be ready in a jiffy. It'll warm you up."

"Mother, your favorite daughter came to you. Mother, you can always come to me. I'll always have a home for you," Lizz said.

"Sure, this is me home, and me son pays for the sacred roof over me head."

"Mother, if she doesn't sober up, you come to me," Lizz said.

"No, take that chippy with you," Mrs. O'Flaherty said.

"I wouldn't have her," Lizz said.

"Well, she's got to get out of here," Mrs. O'Flaherty said.

"Mother, my Jim is disgusted with her," Lizz said.

"Tell him to tie a flatiron around her neck and throw her in the Chicago River," Mrs. O'Flaherty said.

"Oh, Mother, all day my heart bled for you and these poor innocent chicks," Lizz said.

"Come in the kitchen," Mrs. O'Flaherty said.

Lizz followed her mother to the kitchen. Little Margaret went also.

"How is the little fellow?" Mrs. O'Flaherty asked as she served Lizz with a hot cup of tea.

"Mother, can I have some tea?" asked Little Margaret.

"Indeed you can," said Mrs. O'Flaherty.

"Mother, do you mean my precious Little Arty?" asked Lizz.

"Yes. Ah, Lizz, he's such a beautiful one, and such a wise-looking one. Sure, it takes the heart right out of your chest to look at him," Mrs. O'Flaherty said.

"He's not sick. But my Catherine and my Bob have colds. That house, Mother, it's so cold. The poor little chicks have to sit all day shivering by the stove with their feet in the oven," Lizz said.

Lizz poured milk into her cup and then took two spoons of sugar. Mrs. O'Flaherty sat down with a cup of tea. Little Margaret sipped tea, too, listening intently to her mother and grandmother as they talked.

"Oh, Mother, I was brokenhearted when I heard that Mrs. Doolin died. I wanted to go to the wake, but I was so sick. I've had neuralgia. It was such a pity," Lizz said.

"She was a good, decent woman," Mrs. O'Flaherty said.

"Mother, he's a widower now. Why don't you try to marry Peg off to Mr. Doolin?" Lizz said.

"Blessed Mary! He's a decent man, with a boy and his wife not cold yet in the ground. Sure, what would the neighbors think if he was to be running off and marrying now? And sure, what decent man would have the likes of her, smoking cigarettes, running with beggars, and drinking the way she does be doing. Merciful God, he wouldn't have her," Mrs. O'Flaherty said.

"This tea makes me feel better," Lizz said.

"You were such a good thing to come out to us on a night like this," Mrs. O'Flaherty said.

IV

"Here she is, Mother," Lizz said in a low voice as they heard a key turning in the lock.

"You talk to her. I won't. That I may be tongue-tied if I say as much as a to-do to her," Mrs. O'Flaherty said, her right hand on her teacup.

"I won't, either," Lizz whispered.

Mrs. O'Flaherty looked dolorously at Lizz, shook her head sadly from side to side, and raised her hands above her head in a gesture of shame and shock.

"You're her mother," Lizz whispered.

Mrs. O'Flaherty picked up her cup and saucer and scooted into her bedroom, leaving Lizz and Little Margaret at the kitchen table. Danny and Bill played Steel's, their dice constantly rattling on the game board.

V

Margaret was covered with snow. She shook herself, removed her coat, and went to the bedroom. She came out and called out in a sober voice:

"Hello, Lizz."

"My sister, how is my beautiful sister?" Lizz said, rushing down the hall to meet Margaret, who was on her way to the kitchen.

"I'm glad you came, Lizz. But it was an awful night to come up in. I went out because I was nervous. The beautiful snow rested my nerves a lot."

"I came to see my children, my mother, and my beautiful sister," Lizz said.

"How are you, Lizz darling?" Margaret asked.

"Oh, Peg, it's a hard time for me. With the coming one in me, it wears me out, and the house is so cold. It's like paper in a winter like this one."

"I know. Some day, Lizz, my boat will come in and you'll be taken care of. And there's my little niece. You darling," Margaret said.

Margaret kissed Little Margaret.

"She's your namesake, Peg," Lizz said enthusiastically, showing her decayed teeth when she smiled.

"Lizz, I'm brokenhearted," Margaret said.

"You must have faith in the goodness of God, Peg," Lizz said.

"Yes, I know it," Margaret said.

"I was in church yesterday afternoon, Peg, and I said the Stations of the Cross and lit a candle for guess who? For my sister Margaret," Lizz said.

"Just a minute, Lizz," Margaret said, and she went to her room.

Lizz poured a cup of tea for Margaret. Margaret returned from her bedroom.

"Here, Lizz, you darling. Here's a two-dollar bill. You buy something for yourself and the children," Margaret said.

"Oh, thanks, Peg. I'll buy something for my little Arty. You must come and see him. He's growing so, becoming so wise, say, you would split your sides to listen to him talk. You'll fall head over heels in love with the precious chick of mine. And, Margaret, he has such lovely eyes," Lizz said.

"You have such wonderful children, Lizz," Margaret said.

"Here, Peg, sit down. I poured a cup of hot tea for you."

"I don't want it, thanks, Lizz," Margaret said as Lizz slid the two-dollar bill down her bosom.

"Where's Mother?" Margaret asked.

There was no answer.

"She hasn't gone out, has she?"

"The lady of the house is not home to some people," Mrs. O'Flaherty called angrily from her bedroom.

"Mother, she's your daughter," Lizz called in.

"And it's the curse of Almighty God that she is," Mrs. O'Flaherty called out.

"Mother, please don't abuse me when I'm so upset," Margaret pleaded.

"I have me own nerves. I'm not to be bothered," Mrs. O'Flaherty answered.

Margaret stood in the doorway of her mother's bedroom. She saw the old lady, her eyes gleaming in the darkness, the cup and saucer in her hand. Seeing Margaret, Mrs. O'Flaherty set the cup and saucer beside her, got up, and went to the holy-water font over her bed. She dipped her fingers in it and said, as she blessed herself:

"In the name of the Father, and of the Son, and of the Holy Ghost!"

"Please forgive me, Mother. I'm so sorry," Margaret said.

"Mother, a mother mustn't be so hard," Lizz said, joining Margaret in the doorway while Little Margaret silently watched and listened.

"Go to God and ask Him. I leave you in the hands of the Man Above," Mrs. O'Flaherty said.

"I'm sorry, Mother! I'm so sorry!"

"Tell your sorrow to Satan and the tinkers," Mrs. O'Flaherty said.

"Mother, she's sober and comes asking forgiveness. You must forgive her. Our Lord forgave two thieves on the cross. He will forgive even the blackest sinner if he is sorry and asks forgiveness. It is not Christian to be hard and not to forgive," Lizz said.

"I wash me hands of her," Mrs. O'Flaherty said, standing proud and erect.

Margaret turned from the door in tears.

VI

"Lizz, you're so good," Margaret said in the parlor. "I don't know how I can ever repay you for your kindness. If I hadn't had you to talk to tonight, I might have gone crazy. I don't know what I mightn't have done. I was in such a state of nerves. But now I'm myself again. I'm through. Monday morning I'm going back to work."

"It's for the best to do that. Peg, you're a good girl, and the Lord will forgive if you only ask Him," Lizz said.

"I couldn't help myself, couldn't control myself. Lorry did a terrible thing to me," Margaret said.

"God won't let him go unpunished for doing anything to one of God's own children," Lizz said.

"And, Lizz, it's such a comfort to have Little Margaret here with me. She's such a comfort. And I'm going to raise her and give her every opportunity. She'll grow up different than I did," Margaret said.

"She's a darling girl, my Peggy is," Lizz said.

"You know, Lizz, Ned wasn't fit to take care of her. He's away a lot, and he's a man. And his poor sick wife, Mildred, she didn't have the energy, and she had that millinery store of hers to take care of. She's the sweetest and loveliest of women, but Little Margaret will get better care here," Margaret said.

"I know she will, Peg," Lizz said.

"I never had a chance. But my niece will," Margaret said.

"Neither did I," Lizz said.

"You didn't have it as bad as I did," Margaret said.

"Oh, but Peg, I did," Lizz said.

"You were older than I was, and Al never beat you the way he beat me," Margaret said.

"Al is good, a good fellow, Peg. It's just that he's quick-tempered. He's quick-tempered like my Jim is," Lizz said.

"Of course, I don't hold it against him. But I suffered so as a little girl," Margaret said.

"I know, you poor thing," Lizz said.

"And I love Mother so much. I can't bear to have her cross with me the way she is now," said Margaret.

"Mother forgets and forgives," Lizz said.

"Lizz, ask the boys to be quiet so I can sleep. I don't mind their playing that game, but if I hear the dice I can't sleep. And I got to have sleep," Margaret said, her voice becoming almost tragic in tone.

"I'll see that they don't disturb you," Lizz said.

"All I ask of them is to talk low and close the door. And if you and Mother talk in the kitchen, close the door, too, so you don't wake me," Margaret said.

"Of course, sister-darling," Lizz said.

"Good night, Lizz. You've comforted me more than you know," said Margaret.

"Good night, Peg. You get a good sleep."

VII

"Mother, I talked to her. Oh, but I jollied her along. She's gone to bed now. I got the door of the dining room closed and she won't hear the boys. She'll sleep now. Here, let me heat the tea," Lizz said.

"Well may she sleep after disgracing that good boy's house," Mrs. O'Flaherty said.

"She's asleep now, and it's good she is. If she doesn't sleep, she'll make trouble," Lizz said.

"And may she never wake up," Mrs. O'Flaherty said.

"Mother, it's a sin to put curses on the head of anyone. It's tempting God," Lizz said.

"So it's tempting God when she cuts up the way she's been doing in a decent boy's household. Ah, may I never see the sight of God or me mother in Heaven if I ever speak to her again," Mrs. O'Flaherty said.

"She's a dirty, stinking stewpot, and I don't believe one word she said. But I had to kid her to get her quiet and in bed," Lizz said.

"And don't I curse the day that she was born," Mrs. O'Flaherty said.

"Here, Mother, have your tea."

Lizz poured tea.

VIII

Lizz opened the kitchen door and tiptoed down the hall. Margaret's bedroom door was open. Lizz looked in. She didn't hear any sounds of Margaret breathing. She went to the bed. It seemed empty. She felt around in the dark. The covers were thrown forward in a heap. She reached for the electric light chain and pulled it, flooding the room with light. The messy bed was empty. The room was all upset. She looked in the closet, the bathroom, went to the parlor, and the front bedroom.

"Mother! Mother!" she called excitedly.

"What is she up to now?" Mrs. O'Flaherty yelled from the kitchen.

Lizz rushed to the back of the house.

"She's gone, Mother."

"May it be for good."

"Where could she go on a night like this? Where could she go?"

"The Devil can always find playmates," Mrs. O'Flaherty said.

"Mother, can you beat it? She told me she was through drinking, and she seemed sober. She said she needed sleep," Lizz said.

"She's wise like a fox, wise in the ways of the Devil," Mrs. O'Flaherty said.

"Mother, I never heard the beat of it. For a girl like her to go out boozing in this weather. Mother, she's gone out boozing. She might get pneumonia, or killed," said Lizz.

"I'll not let her back in. This is my house, and it's time I took a hand here," Mrs. O'Flaherty said.

"Let her sleep in the snow after what she's done," Lizz said.

"I disown her!"

"Yes, Mother, do. Don't will your estate to her. Give it to me and Jim. We deserve it," Lizz said.

"I call on God to strike her dead this minute!" Mrs. O'Flaherty said.

"The stinking stewpot!" Lizz said.

"If I see her, I'll throw pepper in her eyes!" Mrs. O'Flaherty said.

"She's no good," Lizz said.

"Well, I'm going to bed. You put the children to bed. She'll be the death of me yet."

"She'll be the death of us all, Mother, if we let her," Lizz said.

"May I never set these eyes of mine on her again," Mrs. O'Flaherty said.

26

I

A man Margaret had never seen before that night turned the key in the inner hall door of the entranceway.

"Sure this is it?" he asked.

"Uh," she muttered.

"Kiddo, you're so pie-eyed you don't know yourself from hell-and-gone. But you're all right. You got the goods," the strange man said.

"Uh!" Margaret exclaimed.

He kissed her and went off. Margaret stumbled toward the stairway.

"Second floor," she mumbled.

She grasped the banister. Slowly she worked her way along it. At the second floor she fumbled in her pocketbook and held her door key in her hand.

"Home!" she muttered.

She looked at the lock. It looked strange. She bent forward and drew near it. She set her eye against it. She touched it with her left hand and slowly pushed her right, containing her key, toward it. She hit the lock with the key. She tried again. She managed to place the key in the keyhole, turned it, and the door opened. She closed the door behind her. She lunged forward and leaned against the wall. She felt along the wall to her bedroom. She wavered in her bedroom doorway. She lurched forward, the momentum of her half-fall carrying her about four feet forward in the darkness. She swayed backward and forward in a state of unbalance. She seemed to right herself. She grunted drunkenly. She took another step. She swayed again. She grunted. She swayed sideways and fell on the bed. She held her hands against the bed and stood up. She got out of her coat and let it drop to the floor. She pulled her hat off, tearing her veil, and dropped it. She fell on the bed. She lacked the co-ordination to get up. She lay on the bed, emitting drunken sounds.

II

Devils wearing green lights danced in Margaret's head. Their horns looked like toy elephant tusks sticking out behind their ears. They lifted phallic-shaped pitchforks, and they danced around in a circle. Their dance began in a slow, weaving motion and they increased their tempo, going around faster and faster, trotting, running, running ever faster, running with dizzying speed. They ran around and around in her head, around and around until her head seemed to spin as if it were a wheel. The faster her head seemed to spin, the faster the dancing devils seemed to go.

She grunted.

The dancing devils and the spinning head continued getting faster and faster and then

there were no dancing devils in her head

and there was

a room full of tables shadowed in dim lights with people scattered about them, falling off their chairs. The room was like a ship rolling and tossing on a stormy ocean, sliding to one side, slowly tipping in the opposite direction, teeter-tottering from side to side. Waiters reeled as they moved about the tables carrying bottles shaped like male sexual organs from which they poured gin. The room continued to slide. Margaret walked through the room, holding her hands over her eyes and calling out:

I can't see! I can't see!

Night seemed to spread and grow over the room. She could almost see the darkness spreading, moving slowly forward like a shadow. There was something sad about the darkness she could see moving over the room like a shadow, and it filled her with gloom. It continued to come, and it suddenly seemed to be almost like an animal creeping forward.

I can't see!

And there was nothing to see. The world was full of blackness. Faces popped in and out of the blackness but she could see no bodies, only faces which were vaguely familiar and yet without names, and they seemed in the blackness like lanterns that were hung without supports. Faces she knew and yet did not know appeared and disappeared in the thick blackness. She put a finger forward to touch a face. If she touched it, she would know the name of the face. She slowly moved her finger forward to touch a man's grinning face. She was going to touch it and know its name. She moved her finger closer. She inched her finger still closer. A hair's breadth divided her finger from the grinning face. She would touch it. It moved suddenly. She stood looking around her and the faces grinned and moved about like balls that were being thrown, and watching them made her head spin. She watched the faces, and they were propelled up and down as if they were balls being manipulated expertly by unseen jugglers. She ran about trying to touch a face and they were too fast. They moved even faster, so fast that they seemed like disks changing their colors, and they moved still faster until her head was in a whirl.

She grunted, twitched. Her body began to perspire.

The faces were gone, and there was some kind of zoo in her head, a zoo full of animals she had never seen before, animals strange in shape, with vivid hues, stripes, and patches on their hides. She did not know what kind of animals they were. They were bright in color, and they seemed to change their colors. Crawling and slimy, they defecated as they circled about her in mud and dirt. She found herself suddenly in the middle of a circle of these vivid, varicolored, crawling, slimy animals. They converged slowly on her from all sides. There was no escape. They came at a measured tempo, slowly, but steady and threatening. They came. She turned a complete about-face. The animals still came toward her. She saw their faces, ghastly faces with demonic green eyes. They were coming to get her, chew her, destroy her, kill her. She tried to run. A path opened up in the advancing animal encirclement. She ran. She ran on and on, through a shadowy world, and her race seemed endless. And still she ran, and her speed seemed so rapid that she seemed to make noises like the wind. She stopped, feeling herself to be free of the animals. She looked. They were slimy, green and purple, red and scarlet, vividly colored, with green predominating, and they had cocklike eyes and they surrounded her and were crawling toward her through slime. She looked in the opposite direction. They came. They were crawling snakelike at her. She turned to face a third side. There was nothing but darkness. She took a step. A green snake barred her path. It seemed to have come out of nothing. It seemed to have risen out of slime. Another rose slowly out of the slime, also green. The two snakes crawled patiently toward her. A third welled up and joined the others in inching toward her. She turned her face. Again a green snake rose out of slime and moved forward. She looked upward. Slime formed a ceiling over her, and green snakes covered it. The air was full of snakes, down and up, and on every side there were green snakes with purple eyes, all converging on her. She ran, and again a path opened up. She ran on and on, and she stopped to find herself still surrounded by green snakes. They came. She screamed, fell down, and the snakes began crawling over her body, and she screamed again.

III

Lizz sat suddenly upright. She heard Margaret screaming, piercing screams as if Margaret were being murdered and crying madly for help. Lizz blessed herself and asked God to be her protection. She got out of bed and put her shoes on.

She had gone to sleep with her clothes on in case she had to get up suddenly. She hastened to Margaret's room and switched on the light. Margaret lay squirming and groaning on the floor, her eyes glazed.

"Snakes. Take 'em away. Choking, choking, ugh, goddamn, take 'em away," she moaned, her words seeming to catch in her throat and to come out slowly, hoarsely, only half distinguishable.

The sight of her tortured, unconscious sister on the floor caused a deep physical revulsion, a nausea in Lizz. She turned her face away, blessed herself, turned back. Margaret writhed on the floor, her head on her coat, her dress above her knees, her garters visible. Her shirtwaist was torn. Her hair was mussed, her face smeared. She smelled of whiskey and vomit. She drooled, and a slight froth oozed from the right side of her mouth. She rolled on the floor. Suddenly she let out a piercing scream. Lizz stood for a moment as if she had been turned into stone.

"Take 'em away! Take 'em away! Take 'em away! Save me!"

"Good Jesus Mary and Joseph!" Lizz exclaimed, dropping to her knees.

She blessed herself, closed her eyes, palmed her hands together, and began:

"Hail, Mary, full of grace, the Lord is with thee . . ."

Margaret lay rolling and groaning on the floor, foaming at the mouth, trying to say something and emitting frightened, incoherent sounds that resembled terrified animal cries.

"Glory be to God!" Mrs. O'Flaherty exclaimed, appearing in her woolen nightgown, her hair straggling, her toothless shrunken gums revealed as she uttered the exclamation. Moving like a bird, she padded barefooted down the hall back to the kitchen.

"Holy Mary, Mother of God, pray for us sinners now and at the hour of our death. Amen. Hail, Mary, full of grace, the Lord is with thee . . ."

Bill in soiled B.V.D.'s, Danny in pyjamas, and Little Margaret in a flannel nightgown came to the doorway and, seeing what was happening, Danny and Little Margaret began to cry while Bill looked on in perplexity and astonishment.

Mrs. O'Flaherty came back, now wearing slippers and carrying her holy-water font.

"Get back! Don't you children look. Get back!" she ordered, giving Danny a shove.

The three children obeyed and stood huddled together in the hallway.

Mrs. O'Flaherty entered the room. She dipped her fingers in the holy-water font and sprinkled her daughter as Margaret continued to writhe on the floor, groaning and grunting and foaming at the mouth.

"Choking. Snakes crawling over me. Take 'em away," she cried and, writhing fiercely, she let out a heart-rending wail.

". . . blessed is the fruit of thy womb Jesus, Holy Mary, Mother of God . . ." Lizz prayed on.

"Be gone, Satan! Be gone, you Devil! In the name of the Father, and of the Son, and of the Holy Ghost," Mrs. O'Flaherty exclaimed, sprinkling holy water around the room and over her daughter's twisting body.

Margaret let out another piercing scream. She rolled on the floor, and her pink bloomers became visible in the entanglement of her skirt and petticoat.

"Holy Spirit, come down and save us from the Devil. God Almighty, mercifully come into this room and chase out the dirty devils that possess this poor wretch of a sinner. Chase them out of her and out of this Christian household. Hail, Mary, Mother of God, Mother like me, Mother of the Divine Protector, intercede for us, bring down the aid of your Divine Son, His Merciful Father, and the all-seeing Holy Ghost and drive the devils out of this poor sinning wretch. Father in Heaven, protect us from Satan and his horde of devils," Lizz singsonged.

"Be gone, Satan, you devil demon! Be gone, Satan, you dirty sonofabitch of a whoremaster, be gone from me decent son's home!" Mrs. O'Flaherty said, dancing a jig about her two daughters, the one praying with possessed eyes, the other writhing in a drunken delirium.

"Aunt Margaret is dying," Danny said to Bill in the hall.

"Don't let my aunty die," Little Margaret said in tears.

"She's got the d.t.'s," Bill said.

"Don't let my aunty die," Little Margaret sobbed.

"Choking me! Crawling all over me. Green snakes! Take 'em away! Take 'em away!" Margaret gasped, and then she broke off into another piercing scream.

Mrs. O'Flaherty dumped the contents of the holy-water font onto Margaret, the holy water spilling on her face and torn shirtwaist. The mother ran birdlike out of the room.

"Almighty and Powerful God of Goodness, save us. Divine Son and Crucified Saviour of the world, protect us. Bleeding and wounded Sacred Heart of Jesus, spare us from sin and evil. Holy and pure Mary, Virgin Mother, help us. Saint Joseph, protector of the Holy Family, intercede for us. Pa, help us. Louise, save us. Saint Anthony, come down and save us. Archangel Gabriel, come with your flaming sword and cut the heads off every devil that's in her," Lizz intoned, her body swaying as she prayed.

Mrs. O'Flaherty came back with a crucifix. She knelt down. She kissed the face and feet of the image of the Saviour on the cross. She held it aloft and closed her eyes.

"God Almighty, Powerful Man of Goodness, drive the devils out of her!"

Margaret suddenly went limp. She lay still and unconscious, her dress and petticoat tangled about her legs. Her face was pale, almost deathlike, and wet with holy water that had mingled with her own froth and foamlike spittle. Lizz got to her feet. She moved slowly and solemnly closer to her sister. She saw that Margaret still breathed.

Danny, Bill, and Little Margaret looked in from the doorway.

"Is she dead?" Danny asked, trembling.

"I don't want my aunty to die," Little Margaret sobbed.

"She's breathing," Bill said.

"She's alive, Mother. And the devils are gone. We drove the devils out of her," Lizz said.

"Put her in bed. Good merciful God in Heaven!" Mrs. O'Flaherty said, still on her knees and holding her crucifix aloft.

"No, Mother! I couldn't touch her after she's been possessed by devils. Leave her here and give me a badge of the Sacred Heart," Lizz said.

Mrs. O'Flaherty padded back to her own room.

Lizz knelt beside the inert, unconscious form of her drunken sister and silently prayed. Bill, Danny, and Little Margaret looked on fearfully, the two younger children quivering. Mrs. O'Flaherty returned with a badge of the Sacred Heart. Lizz got up, took the badge from Mrs. O'Flaherty and, bending down, careful not to touch her sister, she dropped the badge of the Sacred Heart onto Margaret's chest.

"We got to get out of here now and not touch her. We can't touch one that's been possessed," Lizz said.

They left the room and Lizz turned out the light and closed the door.

"Here, children, kiss this," Mrs. O'Flaherty said; she held the crucifix to each of the children and they kissed it in turn.

"Ah, Lizz, sure I knew she couldn't carry on the way she was without being possessed by the Devil," Mrs. O'Flaherty said.

"Mother, Satan always finds his own," Lizz said.

"And she even brought the Devil himself into me decent son's home," Mrs. O'Flaherty lamented.

"Mother, we must all kneel down and pray now. There's been devils in the house. We must pray so they don't come back and take hold of us or my chicks," Lizz said.

"The dirty Devil!" Mrs. O'Flaherty exclaimed.

"Mother, get a holy candle," Lizz said.

Mrs. O'Flaherty left and came back with a lighted holy candle.

Lizz set the candle on the piano stool in the parlor. She knelt before it, and her mother and children knelt beside her. Lizz blessed herself, reciting as she did so:

"In the name of the Father, and of the Son, and of the Holy Ghost!"

They blessed themselves and slowly repeated the words after her. She began the Litany of the Blessed Virgin. They prayed with her.

SECTION FOUR

1915

27

I

"Mother, I'm cured. I'm cured forever. As long as I live, I'll never touch another drop of liquor," Margaret said, drinking a cup of coffee while her mother was at the sink.

Margaret was pale and there were circles under her eyes. Her hand shook when she held the coffee cup.

"Sure, that night we thought you were going to die," Mrs. O'Flaherty said.

"I nearly did."

"It was poor Lizz that cured you," Mrs. O'Flaherty said.

"What did she do?"

"She prayed for nearly the whole night. And then, poor thing, she had to be up early, out to church, and home to take care of her man and her little ones. Jim was raving mad, too," Mrs. O'Flaherty said.

"I don't see why he should talk. He's no one to judge me. He gets drunk himself. And, Mother, I didn't have much to drink that night. I was sick, Mother," Margaret said.

"Well, he was raving mad, he was," Mrs. O'Flaherty said.

"That's what I call nerve," Margaret said.

"Ah, but I didn't know what we were going to do with you turning on the gas as fast as we could turn it off," Mrs. O'Flaherty said.

"Why, Mother, I wasn't trying to kill myself. I only wanted to make a cup of black coffee. I was nervous and I wanted to sober up. If I'd been left alone, I might have sobered up and I wouldn't have gotten sick," Margaret said.

"As true as I'm standing here, you tried to turn on the gas. Sure, you can't be making coffee by turning on the gas jet in the parlor and filling the house with gas."

"I don't remember. All I remember is that I was dying for a cup of black coffee, dying for a cup. I needed it for my nerves. And I wanted to sober up with black coffee. And that dirty little thief, Bill O'Neill, wouldn't let me get it. As long as I live, I'll never forgive him. And, Mother, he hit me in the breast. I might get cancer of the breast from the way he punched me," Margaret said.

"Ah, you were taken in hand by the Devil, and he was speaking out of your mouth. Sure, you were trying to kill us all," Mrs. O'Flaherty said.

"I swear by God that I don't remember it," Margaret said.

"It's as true as I'm standing here," Mrs. O'Flaherty said.

"I swear by God that I don't remember it," Margaret said.

"Some there is in this world that forgets easy," Mrs. O'Flaherty said curtly.

"And, Mother, I don't see why you had to call Mike Geraghty. If you got a doctor, it seems to me that you could have gotten someone else, anyone but him. I don't want him taking care of me. He may be a friend of Al's, but as a doctor he's a horse doctor. Letting him see me in such a condition. And telling him what had happened to me the night before. I was ashamed. I'll never forget that you played a dirty trick on me, bringing Mike Geraghty in on me when I didn't want him, telling him all about me. I'll never forget that," Margaret said.

"Sure, you were pale as a ghost, and sweating, and nervous, and you had to have the doctor, so I had me little grandson call him," Mrs. O'Flaherty said.

"You could have gotten another doctor. You know I don't like him. I can't stand him," Margaret said.

"And that I didn't know. He's a good man and he has a good wife," Mrs. O'Flaherty said.

"As far as I'm concerned, he can doctor horses. Mother, don't you ever dare to get him for me again if I'm sick," Margaret said.

Margaret got up from the table.

"I'm going to see if there's any mail," she said.

Mrs. O'Flaherty went on working at the sink, humming at the same time. Margaret went down to look in the mailbox.

"Peg, did you hear from him?" Mrs. O'Flaherty asked when Margaret came back to the kitchen.

"No," she said heavily.

"I can't make head or tail of him, not writing to you," Mrs. O'Flaherty said.

"I don't want to hear from him. I'm through with him for good, Mother, for good. But, Mother, it seems to me that Brother is old enough to forward his uncle's mail when I'm sick. It's a crime. There's two weeks' mail for Al that should have been forwarded. Brother can read and write, and it seems to me that he could do that much for the house when I'm sick. He's being spoiled and somebody has to take a hand with him. Not even forwarding Al's mail while I was sick," Margaret said.

"Don't be gainsaying me grandson. If you want to be gainsaying, speak of that other one here," Mrs. O'Flaherty said.

"I don't know why you are so bitter against girls. Little Margaret isn't one-fifth the trouble that Brother is," Margaret said.

The telephone rang. Margaret's face lighted up with hope as she ran to answer it.

II

"Mother, Sadie O'Flaherty just called and I asked her to come out and see me," Margaret said, returning to the kitchen after having answered the telephone.

Mrs. O'Flaherty made the sign of the cross.

"But, Mother, Sadie is such a poor thing."

"Glory be!" Mrs. O'Flaherty exclaimed.

"Mother, why are you so hard and cruel?"

"She asks me that when here I am watching after me son's home, and he out working hard on the road to pay the rent, carrying those heavy sample cases."

"Sadie's a poor, sick girl. I don't know why you're so mean about her just because I invited her out to see me. I'm nervous. I got to have somebody to talk to or I'll go crazy. No wonder I drink. I don't even have a soul to talk to," Margaret said.

"Yes, and she'll be wanting to eat me son's food," Mrs. O'Flaherty said.

"It wouldn't hurt you or your son if she did eat a little food here. It's only an act of charity, being kind to the poor thing," Margaret said.

"Charity begins at home."

"I'm sorry. I didn't want to see her, Mother, but she wanted to come out and see me, and she's such a poor thing, and there's hardly a soul in the world that she can go to," Margaret said.

"That pauper won't come to me."

"Oh, Mother, you're ridiculous. She's a good girl," Margaret said.

"Her mother was a tinker."

"She's Pa's cousin. Pa liked her family," Margaret said.

"Indeed, Pa didn't. They bled him until if he seen them on the street he wouldn't look at them," Mrs. O'Flaherty said.

"Well, I'm sorry. But I don't have a heart of stone. I wouldn't have told her to come if I knew you'd carry on like this."

"I won't see her. I'm out. And if you feed her, give her the help's butter from the icebox."

Margaret glanced at her mother in disgust. She turned on her heel and left the kitchen. Mrs. O'Flaherty immediately went to the icebox on the back porch. She took a bag of eggs, a pound of butter, and a plate of ham from it and hid these in her bedroom. She got a fresh loaf of bread from the breadbox in the pantry and hid it in one of her dresser drawers. Then she sat in her room, humming melancholy Irish tunes and darning a pair of Danny's black stockings.

III

"Sadie dear," Margaret said, opening the door.

Sadie came in and Margaret shut the door. Sadie was a small woman who looked underweight, unhealthy, and prematurely aged. She had a sallow face, hollow cheeks, dull blue eyes, and a thin neck.

They embraced. Margaret took Sadie's coat, hat, and bag and dropped them on her bed. She saw that Sadie's blue dress was shiny and shabby.

"How is your mother?" Sadie asked when they were both seated in Margaret's bedroom.

"She's got a grouch on today. Mother is the loveliest woman, Sadie, but she has her bad days and her grouches when she nags and gets mad about everything under the sun. It's best just not to pay attention to what she says when she's that way. But she's so cute when she's grouchy. She says the most terrible things to everyone and she really doesn't mean a word of it. You've got to know how to take my mother," Margaret said.

"Mary is such a dear," Sadie said.

"She's a dolly," Margaret said.

"I want to see her," Sadie said.

"You can. But wait a minute. I haven't seen you in so long, Sade, dearie. Let's talk ourselves for a little while. How are you feeling, Sade?"

"Oh, Peg, I don't know. I don't have any energy. I wish I could afford to go to Denver, but I can't. I'm not going to live long. I know I'm not. And I don't care. Peg, I don't want to live if it means going on like I have to. Peg, what's there to go on for?" Sadie said.

"You poor thing, you must brace up and pull yourself together."

"Everybody tells me I must. But what for? What for?" Sadie said nervously, shaking her head from side to side while she talked.

"Life is so hard on us girls. We sometimes have such heavy crosses to bear. Sometimes I think that some of us must have been born under an evil star," Margaret said.

"Yes, Peg. But I always say that if I only had my health, I wouldn't care about anything else. When you don't have your health, you've got nothing. You can't plan. You can't think ahead. Death walks with you every minute of the day and night."

"Sadie, you must brace up. You mustn't let yourself get to feel that way."

"But I do. I can't help it. I don't see any use in kidding myself, Peg."

"Oh, Sadie, you poor dear. I feel so sorry for you," Margaret said.

"Peg, you're about the only one I got left in the world who I can come to and lean on," Sadie said.

"I only wish I could do a lot for you, Sadie dear."

"Just to be able to talk to you, Peg, it helps me," Sadie said.

"I got such worries of my own too, Sade. I have my nerves and they never give me a minute's rest, a moment's relaxation."

"You always had bad nerves, didn't you?"

"It's because of the way I was treated when I was a little girl. I was beat so, that's why I have my nerves," Margaret said.

"Peg, I envy so much girls who didn't have greenhorn parents," Sadie said.

"Yes, Sadie, a greenhorn father and mother don't know America and the modern age. They have all this old Irish backbiting and ignorance in them," Margaret said.

"My father and mother, Lord have mercy on them, they were such dears, but they ruined my life, Peg. They ruined my health. Peg, do you know why I did things I did? They drove me to it. They had such foolish, old-fashioned ideas about girls going with boys, they did, that they drove me. I just determined and made up my mind that I didn't care what would happen, I would do things just to spite them. I went and got boys, and when I was doing it I would think of my father and mother and think of myself sinning just to spite them. I would think if they could only see me now, see what I'm doing. I didn't care about the boys. I did it because of them. I was driven. Peg, I was driven on the road to Hell by them. But I don't hold a thing against them, Lord have mercy on their souls," Sadie said with bitterness.

"I know how it is, Sadie. My family ruined my poor life," Margaret said.

"I'm ready to give up, Peg, I'm at the end of my rope. I don't care what happens to me. Let the wind cast me here or there, anywhere. I don't care. I don't! I don't! I don't!" Sadie said, shaking her head forcibly as she spoke, her mood verging on hysteria.

"Sadie, don't cry!" Margaret said sweetly and consolingly, going to her cousin. "There, now, don't take it too hard, dearie," she added.

"I don't care what becomes of me," Sadie said.

"Now, dearie, you just go ahead and have a good cry. Cry it all out of your system," Margaret said, stroking Sadie's stringy hair.

Margaret led Sadie to her bed, sat down, and laid Sadie's head against her shoulder. She supported her cousin with her left arm and continued stroking Sadie's head.

"There, there, now, Sadie dear, you have a good cry."

IV

"Peg, I'm so sorry to hear what you told me. I never thought that a man like Lorry would do such a thing to you," Sadie said.

"He did," Margaret whimpered, puffing at her cigarette.

"When I used to see you with him, I would always envy your happiness so much," Sadie said.

"I've been driven nearly crazy. I drank because of it. I'm not a drunkard. You know that, Sadie," Margaret said, her manner one that asked Sadie's agreement.

"Of course you're not."

"I'm not. It was my nerves. I did it because I was so unhappy," Margaret said.

"Isn't there any chance that he'll come back to you?" Sadie asked, trying to sound encouraging.

"I don't even know where he is," Margaret said; she relapsed into misery and her face seemed pudgy and unattractive because of the tragic expression she had assumed. She cried. Sadie went to her and caressed her.

"Don't cry, Peggy darling. I can't stand to see you unhappy," Sadie said.

"I can't help it," Margaret said.

She sank her head into Sadie's lap and wept.

V

"Mary, you're looking simply wonderful," Sadie said to Mrs. O'Flaherty, sitting down in the kitchen for a cup of coffee with Margaret.

"I don't," Mrs. O'Flaherty said.

"Mother's so cute, such a dolly. Come, Dolly, and have a cup of coffee with us," Margaret said.

"Cute be damned!" Mrs. O'Flaherty said, digging into her pocket, pulling out her rumpled package of Tip-Top tobacco and filling her pipe.

"You look so young, Mary," Sadie said.

"Sure, I'm getting gray hairs worrying about me poor son's home and them that comes into it," Mrs. O'Flaherty said, and then she took an angry puff from her pipe.

They both watched the old woman, noticing that there was scarcely a gray hair in her head.

"How old are you now, Mary?" Sadie asked.

"Eighty-five going on ninety," Mrs. O'Flaherty said.

"Why, Mary, you can't be that old," Sadie said.

"I'm eighty-seven if I'm a day," Mrs. O'Flaherty said, and Margaret winked at Sadie.

They drank their coffee and watched Mrs. O'Flaherty smoking her pipe.

"Ma used to smoke a pipe, too," Sadie said.

"Ah, your mother Nellie was a good, decent, hard-working woman, she was," Mrs. O'Flaherty said.

"Yes, she was," Sadie said.

"She worked herself into an early grave, poor Nellie did," said Mrs. O'Flaherty.

"She worked hard," Sadie said while Margaret went to the breadbox.

"Your father was Pa's first cousin. Well may he and your mother rest in peace, poor souls," Mrs. O'Flaherty said.

"Mother, haven't we any fresh bread?" Margaret called from the pantry.

"We got what's there," said Mrs. O'Flaherty.

"There's only stale bread in the house. When I don't tend to this house, nothing is done," Margaret said.

"I'll take a bite of that then, Peg," Sadie said.

"I'll make toast," Margaret said, taking the bread out and cutting slices. She lit the oven and put the slices in it.

"Sit down, Mother. Do you want toast?" Margaret asked.

"Sure, I haven't time to idle. I have too much to do," Mrs. O'Flaherty said.

She went to the pantry, brought out a cup and saucer, poured herself coffee, drew up a chair and sat down. She set her pipe beside her and put cream and sugar in her coffee.

"I can't get over how well you're looking," Sadie said to the old lady.

"Sadie, why don't you get a man and get married?" Mrs. O'Flaherty said, and Margaret, turning the toast in the oven, winced.

"Oh, Mary, I don't know. I don't think any man'll have me," Sadie said.

"Some there are that can't get a decent hard-working man for themselves, but some can. You can. Sure, you're a good girl. I got a neighbor, Jack Doolin, that poor man, and he just lost his wife. She died in the hospital. Peg, what was that that killed the poor woman?"

"Appendicitis," Margaret said, frowning and biting her lip.

"He was left with a boy and no one to take care of him. You'd make a good wife for him," Mrs. O'Flaherty said.

"Mother, why don't you stop that?" Margaret said, bringing a plate of toast to the table.

She went to the icebox on the porch and returned with a plate on which there was a small cube of butter.

"Nothing in this house, stale bread and hardly any butter."

Mrs. O'Flaherty frowned at her daughter.

"Yes, Sadie, you should get yourself a man," Mrs. O'Flaherty said.

Sadie reached for a piece of toast and buttered it. So did Margaret.

"I don't think any man wants me, Mary," Sadie said, embarrassed.

She began eating the toast rapidly, hungrily.

"You ought to get yourself a man to take care of you. He could give you milk to drink and put some flesh on your bones. A nice, decent man like Jack Doolin," Mrs. O'Flaherty said.

"Mary, I'm just an old maid," Sadie said.

"You needn't be," Mrs. O'Flaherty said.

"I don't think any man wants me. Your neighbor wouldn't, Mary," Sadie said.

"A man can always be found who wants a girl if she's decent," Mrs. O'Flaherty said, turning a pointed glance at Margaret.

"Oh, Mother, won't you please can that old Irish talk? I'm nervous," Margaret said.

"So it's old Irish to talk about decency, is it?"

"Mary, you know, my mother always used to talk about you. She used to say what a fine woman you were. She would always say that pa's cousin, Tom, got one of the finest women that walked the face of the earth," Sadie said hurriedly, to change the subject.

"She was a fine woman, and she raised a good, decent daughter, she did. You're a good girl, Sadie," Mrs. O'Flaherty said.

"Go ahead, abuse me! That's all I'm good for with my family. To be abused and milked," Margaret said while Sadie shyly reached for another piece of toast and bit into it.

"Yes, you're a good girl, Sadie," Mrs. O'Flaherty said, ignoring her daughter.

"But I'm not!" Margaret said bitterly. "Go ahead, say it! I know what's on the tip of your vile tongue, say it," Margaret went on, and Sadie seemed taken aback, shocked; she cast a pleading glance at Margaret.

"Sure, the Lord will punish one that talks back to her mother," Mrs. O'Flaherty said.

"And he'll punish a mother that ruins her daughter's life," Margaret said.

"If Nellie O'Flaherty were alive today, Lord have mercy on her soul, I know that Sadie here wouldn't be talking to her the way you do to me," Mrs. O'Flaherty said to Margaret.

"Her mother didn't abuse her like you abuse me."

"Go on, you devil!" Mrs. O'Flaherty exclaimed.

Sadie said nothing. She took another piece of toast.

"You see the goddamn nagging I have to stand, Sadie?" Margaret said.

"If I wasn't here to look after me son's house, it would go to wreck and ruin and to the Devil himself," Mrs. O'Flaherty said.

"It's my home, too, and I pay my way," Margaret said.

"Sadie, she was drunk a week or so ago, and the little children had to stay up all night, sleeping not a wink, watching her. She was here, there, all over the house, turning on the gas. When she turns on the gas to kill herself, that costs money. My son has to pay for the gas she does be wasting trying to make an end of herself," Mrs. O'Flaherty said.

"Why, that's the blackest lie, the blackest lie that was ever told," Margaret said in a high-pitched voice.

"Sadie, it's the God's truth. May I go to bed tonight and never wake up if it's not the God's truth," Mrs. O'Flaherty said.

"Sadie, how that dirty witch lies!" Margaret exclaimed.

"Please, Peg!" Sadie began, but Mrs. O'Flaherty interrupted her.

"Sadie, there's not a thing she won't do. She even wishes me dead. Well, I'll be gone some day, and then she'll rue the day she wished me gone and in the cold ground."

"You'd be better off dead!" Margaret said.

"And you'd be better off in the flames of Hell," Mrs. O'Flaherty said.

"I'm goin' there. But it's you that's driving me," Margaret screamed, rising and pointing an accusing finger at her mother.

"And you won't be there too soon. The sooner you're in Hell, the better it will be. But when you kill yourself to go to the Devil, don't waste me son's gas. Water is free. Go to the lake," Mrs. O'Flaherty said.

"Peg, I got to go," Sadie said, putting down the piece of toast she had been eating.

"Don't leave me! Please, Sadie," Margaret pleaded.

"Sadie, when you meet the likes of that one, bless yourself. The Devil is sitting there in her eyes. See him? Look, there he is in her eyes, plain as day," Mrs. O'Flaherty said.

"You'll be sorry for this. I'll never forgive you. Not as long as I live," Margaret said.

"Go on, hurrish! Hurrish! The blackguards are waiting outside for you," Mrs. O'Flaherty said.

"You witch, when you die I'll dance on your grave," Margaret said.

"Why, Peg!" Sadie said, shocked, checking her hand as she reached for the last piece of toast.

Margaret stamped out of the kitchen.

"There's no good in that one. Sadie, she has the life tormented out of us," Mrs. O'Flaherty said.

"She's nervous and doesn't mean what she says, Mary," Sadie said.

"Sure, neither did I, child. I only wanted to shame her for her own good. But the shame isn't in her," Mrs. O'Flaherty said.

"Sadie, come here, will you?" Margaret called.

"Go to her, and don't let her be turning on the gas. Quiet her. And then I'll give you a nice lunch. I hid the food on her because she's eating me out of house and home. You keep her quiet, child, and I'll give you a nice lunch," Mrs. O'Flaherty said.

Sadie finished her last piece of toast quickly and went to Margaret.

Mrs. O'Flaherty went for the food she had hidden and began to prepare a meal for Sadie, singing as she worked:

> *You made your poor old mother cry,*
> *The day that you were born.*

VI

"I'm so sorry, Sade dear. I lost my temper. She nags so. Mother is the worst nagger I ever saw," Margaret said, wiping her eyes.

"My mother was the same," Sadie said.

"All the old Irish are alike," Margaret said contemptuously.

"Peg, you must brace up. If you were in the position I am, you wouldn't think you were so bad off. I haven't even a place to stay. I'm on the street, and I haven't a job. I'm sick. Peg, you're tempting God," Sadie said, almost breaking down.

"Why, Sadie, you must stay here," Margaret said.

"There isn't room with all of you," Sadie said.

"It's my house as well as theirs. You can sleep with me, and my niece can sleep on the divan in the parlor. I'm nervous and I need you to help me. I have to have someone like you with me until I get better and my nerves permit me to go back to work," Margaret said.

"Gee, Peg, I don't know what to say. I'm at the end of my rope," Sadie said.

"You got to stay here with me, Sadie. I need you. I need you while I'm in this state. I might be able to land you something at the hotel in the checkroom or something. As soon as I put myself back on my feet, I'll see some influential men I know. I'd do it now, but I'm in no condition to," Margaret said.

"Peg, you're so good," Sadie said.

"You got to help me. I'm going out of my head, Sadie. I got to have your help in pulling myself together. Once I do, I'll be all right," Margaret said.

"Sadie, come and have a bite to eat I fixed for you," Mrs. O'Flaherty said from the doorway.

28

I

Sadie O'Flaherty was there and she was going to help take care of Aunty Margaret. Aunty Margaret was sober, but awful nervous. Even if she got drunk, it wouldn't be so bad if Sadie was there because Cousin Sadie would talk to her and help watch her. If Aunty Margaret tried turning on the gas, Sadie O'Flaherty would be there to turn it off. He and Little Margaret might be able to go to sleep at night. But Little Margaret would have to sleep on the divan in the parlor. Mother had said that she couldn't sleep with him because a boy and girl shouldn't sleep together. But if they could, maybe Little Margaret would let him, and he would know what it was like. Once when they lived on Calumet Avenue, before Little Margaret had gone to Madison, he and Little Margaret had been together in bed on a Sunday morning and Mother had been at mass and it had looked like he might find out about it. But Mother had come home from mass too soon. Since Little Margaret had come to stay with them last summer, they hadn't talked about anything like that.

Danny walked along Prairie toward Fifty-first Street on his way to school, glancing at the snow at the edge of the sidewalk. He wouldn't have to come straight home after school. Mother said he could go to Perc's house to play this afternoon. Mother said Perc was a fine boy, and his people were nice people.

"Hey, O'Neill!"

Danny turned around and saw Tommy Moriarty running to catch up with him.

"Going to school now?" Tommy asked, coming up with Danny and a little breathless from his run.

"You going to school, too?" Danny asked.

"Yuh dope, where you think I'm going, to a picnic?"

"Well, where would I be going if I ain't going to school now?" Danny said,

and immediately he remembered that Uncle Al always said he shouldn't use *ain't*
or *got*.

Well, Uncle Al hadn't heard him. So far as Uncle Al was concerned, he hadn't
said *ain't*. And it wasn't a sin to say *ain't*. It was just bad grammar and what Uncle
Al said was vulgarism in your speaking.

"Well, you like Miss McGinnis as a teacher?" Tommy asked as they walked
along, side by side.

"I like her. And I got good marks last month, that is, December. I think I'm
going to get good marks this month, too," Danny said.

"What yuh get?"

"My average was ninety," Danny said.

"I don't believe yuh," Tommy said.

"Why?" asked Danny.

"Because I don't think you're that smart," Tommy said.

"Cross my heart I did," Danny said.

"Well, then, if yuh did, you must be smarter than I thought you was. I never
got an average of ninety in school," Tommy said.

"I never did before," Danny said.

"Say, I saw your aunt last week and she couldn't hardly walk," Tommy said.

Danny didn't answer. He knew that Tommy wasn't the only kid who knew.

"I feel sorry for you. And your grandmother, she's a nice lady. She must feel
awful about your aunt," Tommy said.

There was no use trying to hide it or say it wasn't so. Tommy knew it was so.

"Your grandmother, she doesn't like it, does she?"

"No, she don't."

"It's too bad, I'm glad I ain't you," Tommy said.

She was disgracing him. If Miss McGinnis found out, he wouldn't like it. He
would hate to come to her class every day and know that she knew about Aunt
Peg.

"My old lady saw her coming out of a saloon," Tommy said.

"What did she say?"

"She told my old man it wasn't decent," Tommy said.

He guessed he better not ask Tommy not to tell other kids. Because then if
he did that, maybe Tommy would be reminded too much of it, and would tell
them. But he would be friendly with Tommy every time he could, and any time
he had candy or anything he'd give it to Tommy and make friends with him that
way. And then if he and Tommy were good friends, maybe Tommy wouldn't say
anything because they were friends.

"Bronco Billy's at the show tonight," Tommy said.

"Yeah," Danny said.

"Gee, I wish I could go," Tommy said.

"So do I," said Danny.

"Say, could you get your grandmother to give you a dime and then loan me a jit so we could go to see Bronco Billy tonight?"

"I don't know," Danny said, but he hoped he could, because if he could, then that would help to make Tommy his friend, and it might be that then Tommy wouldn't say much about Aunt Margaret being drunk.

"Sure you could. Your grandmother would give you anything you asked for. She's swell to you," Tommy said.

"I don't know. I'll try," Danny said.

"Go ahead. I'll pay yuh back, I will," Tommy said.

"I want to see Bronco Billy," Danny said.

"You can get it," Tommy said.

"I'll try," Danny said.

Tommy put his arm around Danny's shoulders and they walked along.

"You try to do that, Danny, and I'll do a favor for you some day," Tommy said.

"I'll ask her," Danny said.

"That's swell," Tommy said.

They walked on. Danny was liking Tommy better all the time. He didn't mind loaning Tommy a nickel, particularly now since he wanted to make Tommy his good friend. And he thought he'd be able to do it. He'd ask Mother, and tell her he wanted to get some candy, too, when he went to the show. He liked to eat candy in the show. If he could get fifteen cents now, he'd be able to let Tommy take a nickel and still buy candy.

"Let's see who can come closest to that lamppost ahead of us," Tommy said.

"All right."

They both packed snowballs and threw wide of the mark. Tommy hit it on the next throw. Then Danny took careful aim and smacked it.

"Even up," Tommy said, dragging on.

Danny thought again of Aunty Margaret. Gosh, he hoped she was over her drunk now. Well, it was still a long time to his birthday party. She sure ought to be over it by then. If she wasn't, he wouldn't be able to have it. He couldn't ask the kids yet because he wasn't sure about her. It would be awful to ask them and then to have to say it was off. He had to wait. And he was afraid to ask Virginia Doyle. And he wanted to ask Miss McGinnis' sister who was the prettiest girl in fifth grade. How would he ask them? What would he say?

"Know what I'd like to do?" Danny suddenly said.

"What?" asked Tommy.

"I'd like to find a quarter here on the street," Danny said.

"It's easier to find it when there isn't so much snow."

"If somebody dropped it and it was laying on the sidewalk, it'd be fun to find it," said Danny.

"Sure it would," said Tommy.

"Then we could see Bronco Billy and buy candy to eat in the show besides," Danny said.

"Hell, you know what would be more fun?"

"What?" Danny asked.

"To find a half a buck," Tommy said.

"You could see a lot of shows on that," Danny said.

"Boy, I think it's just as easy to find a dollar as it is two bits or a half a buck. It's easier, particularly now. There's no grass for silver to roll in. And if a guy drops a buck, he doesn't hear it fall. It wouldn't roll, and it would be right there on the sidewalk, sticking in your eyes," Tommy said.

"Here's Fiftieth Street. Let's turn over to Grand Boulevard," Danny said.

"All right. It don't matter which way you go, it's all the same and you got to go to school. I feel like I'm goin' to jail every day I gotta go to school. I don't like Sister Mary, the fifth-grade Sister, none too much, either," Tommy said.

"Once when I used to live back there on Calumet Avenue, I was going to the store and they gave me a five-dollar bill and I lost it," Danny said.

"You dope, you made some guy lucky by letting him find it. How'd yuh lose it?"

"I don't know. I was walking along, and I went in the store and when I had to pay the man I didn't have the money to pay him with," Danny said.

"Did yuh catch hell for losin' it?"

"They got sore at me," Danny said.

"Say, if I lost money like that goin' to the store, would my old man smack my ears off!" Tommy said.

"I never find money. When people lose money, somebody else always finds it," Danny said.

"The most I ever found was a jit."

"My brother Bill finds money lots of times but I don't," said Danny.

"He's lucky, Bill is, ain't he?"

"Uh huh!"

"Say, look, snow fight," Tommy said, pointing to kids ahead who were bombarding one another with snowballs. Tommy and Danny let out wild whoops, ran forward, and joined in the fight.

II

"You always chew pencils in school, doncha?" Perc Dineen said, walking home from school with Danny. Perc was a plump, blond-haired boy with soft features and a broad face.

"I don't know," Danny said.

"Sure you do. I was watching you in school today. You were chewing away at a pencil like it was a piece of candy," Perc said.

"Well, maybe I do. What of it?" Danny asked.

"Nothing. I was just saying that you chew your pencils," Perc said.

"I guess I do," Danny said.

"You gonna be able to stay at my house for supper?" Perc asked.

"I don't know. I gotta call up and ask," Danny said, hoping that he could because he didn't want to go home with so much fighting and yelling in the house, and with the chance that she'd be stewed again. He always liked to stay at Perc's for supper, and he would like to especially tonight.

"You can telephone when we get to my house. We got a phone that's private and you don't have to use a nickel each time. My father pays the bill for it at the end of the month," Perc said.

"We got a nickel phone," Danny said.

"I hope you can stay," Perc said.

"I'll ask. Maybe if I can, then you can get out," Danny said.

"There's a better chance for me if you do. There's no chance if you don't," Perc said, and while he talked Danny packed a snowball.

"Like Bronco Billy?" Danny asked.

"Yes. But, say, know who lives in the building next to me?" Perc asked as Danny let fly a snowball, missing the lamppost at which he'd aimed.

"Who?" Danny asked.

"Mr. Egbert Ames, the actor," Perc said.

"Gee!" Danny exclaimed.

"We can play we're playing a play like the ones he acts in at the Willard Theater," Perc said.

"We haven't got enough kids," Danny said.

"We got us two, and my brother and little sister. That'll be as much fun as going to see Bronco Billy."

"If we do, who'll be Egbert?" Danny asked.

"I'll be," Perc said.

"Why?"

"I look like I should be," Perc said.

"I don't want to be somebody else. I want to be Egbert," Danny said.

"We'll take turns," Perc said, and they walked on for a while in silence, Danny throwing snowballs at random.

"What's the matter with your brother today?" Danny asked as they turned the corner of Fiftieth and Prairie.

"He's got a cold and couldn't go to school," Perc said.

"What play'll we make believe we're playing?" Danny asked.

"*Madame X,*" Perc said.

"I'd rather have it *Graustark,*" Danny said.

"All right," Perc said.

"Did you see that one?" Danny asked.

"Yeah."

"Gee, wasn't it swell? I'd like to live in Graustark," Danny said.

"Me, too," said Perc.

"Where's Graustark?" Danny asked.

"I don't know. Some place," Perc said.

"I wonder if schools there are like they are here," Danny said.

"So do I."

"They must be. The Catholic ones."

"Why?" asked Perc.

"Because in catechism it says that the Church is one, holy, universal, and Catholic everywhere. And universal, that means everywhere. Well, if the Church is the same everywhere, the schools of the Church must be, and so the schools of the Church in Graustark must be like ours," Danny said.

"I guess you're right," Perc said.

"But they don't have nothing about the schools and kids in the play," Danny said.

"Well, here we are. Come on up and call up. Tell 'em to let you stay. If you want, I'll have my mother ask," Perc said.

"I'll ask," Danny said, suddenly afraid lest Perc's mother talk and get Aunt Peg on the phone and hear her yelling if she was drunk.

They went into the hallway of the wide-fronted, yellowstone three-story apartment building where Perc lived.

III

Danny stood with Perc by the back-porch stairway in Perc's yard. He looked out at the yard, a large, wide one, almost square. It was divided by a sidewalk which led to the alley gate, and behind it was the elevated. The yard was now covered with dirty, melting snow. Danny thought how much better it was for playing ball in than his, and how the diamond could be planned so as not to have any danger of breaking windows. Just his luck. Perc, who didn't give a darn about playing ball, had a yard perfect for games, and he had one with those damn hothouses. Such was luck.

"I wish it was April already," Danny said, thinking of the games that could be played in the yard.

"Why?"

"We could play ball."

"Who cares?"

"I do."

"It's goofy to think of playing ball in April when it's only the end of January."

"I don't see why it is."

"Sure you don't. You always get a lot of goofy ideas."

"They ain't so goofy."

"Some of them are."

"How?" Danny asked, thinking that he liked Perc, but that there was something about the way Perc sometimes acted and talked to him that made him feel like a goof.

Danny picked up a stick and waved it. Perc stuck his hands in his pockets and looked at the snow.

"Virginia Doyle is pretty, ain't she?" Perc said.

"Uh huh!" Danny exclaimed. He packed a snowball and slammed it against the back fence.

"She's smart, too. But then, girls are always smarter than fellows," Perc said.

"Yeah, except for Al, and Joe Conlan," Danny said, packing another snowball.

"They're smart, ain't they?" Perc said as Danny threw the snowball at random.

An elevated train passed.

"That's six," Perc said.

"Six what?"

"Elevated trains passed. I'm counting 'em," Perc said.

"What for?" Danny asked.

"Oh, just counting 'em," Perc said.

"You ever ride downtown on the train alone?" Danny asked.

"My mother won't let me," Perc said.

Danny threw another snowball, plumping it against the garbage can near the gate.

"I'm sorry we couldn't play acting, but then my mother was cleaning house. We can do it after supper if I can't go out. I'm glad your grandmother's letting you stay," Perc said.

Danny looked away. He had heard her yelling when he telephoned. She must be stewed again.

"Say, Dan, why are you so crazy about baseball?" Perc asked.

"You don't like it?"

"No," Perc said.

Danny picked up the stick he had waved a little while ago and waved it again. Then he shot it, javelinlike, into the snow.

"Why are you and Marty Hogan friends?" Perc asked.

"I don't know. We are. We used to be better ones in third grade."

"Does he still stick up for you?"

"Uh huh, if I need him. I ain't needed him in a long time."

"His old man's only a janitor," Perc said.

"Yeah."

"That's why he wears black waists to school. A janitor's son can't wear white waists to school because his father can't afford to buy them, and washing them makes the laundry bill too high. My mother, now, she wouldn't let me wear black waists," Perc said.

"Neither would my grandmother," Danny said.

"That makes seven trains gone by," Perc said as another elevated train rumbled past.

"Let's build a snow fort," Danny said.

"Naw. You get too wet, and there's nobody to have a snow fight with. You get wet for nothing with no fun," Perc said.

They strolled out along the sidewalk toward the alley gate. Danny flung snowballs. Perc made one, threw it, his motions like a girl's. They walked on and climbed up onto the alley fence. They sat facing the buildings, with the elevated behind them, and they dangled their legs.

"Let's see who can spit the farthest," Perc said.

"All right, you go first," Danny said.

"You go first," Perc said.

Danny hawked to get saliva in his mouth. He held his breath for a moment, and spat out, his body moving forward with the effort. He saw his spit land about four feet away in the snow.

"Now it's my turn," Perc said.

Perc prepared himself and let go, his spit landing about four inches short of Danny's.

"Eight trains gone by," Perc said, hearing one overhead.

"Want to try again?" Danny asked.

"You win," Perc said, and Danny liked that; he liked winning in everything, and he was proud that he'd out-spitted his friend.

"Gonna have your birthday party next month?" Perc asked.

"I donno. I ain't sure they'll let me. I hope so," he said, realizing that he'd used *ain't* again.

"Ain't they said you could?"

"Not for certain," Danny said, wondering would she be sober then. If they came and she was drunk and acting like a holy show he would never have it in him to go back to school.

"If you do, what girl you gonna have for your partner?" asked Perc.

"I donno."

"What one you want?"

"I ain't figured it out."

"Well, what girl you like best in our class?"

"I donno."

"Neither do I," Perc said.

"I know who Al Throckwaite likes best," Danny said.

"So do I."

"Who?" Danny asked.

"You tell me who you think it is, and I'll tell you who I think she is," Perc said.

"Virginia Doyle," Danny said.

"Yes, Virginia Doyle," Perc said.

"Think she's sweet on Al?" Danny asked.

"That's eleven trains gone by," Perc said.

"Think she is?"

"I wouldn't be surprised. All the girls in the room like Al."

"Yeah, they do," Danny said wistfully.

"So I say suppose they do."

"I guess you're right there. Gee, I wish we could have gone ice skating today," Danny said, thinking of the fun he might have been able to have at the duck pond if the gang was there.

"I'd rather roller skate."

"It's too soon for that," Danny said.

"And I like tobogganing."

"Can't now with the snow melting."

They sat. The winter day was slowly dying, and there were puffs of purple in the blue-gray sky over the apartment building they faced. A woman from the third-floor flat, right over where Perc lived, came onto her porch wearing a gingham apron. She put something into the garbage can outside her door and went back into her kitchen.

"Twelve trains gone by," Perc said.

"Yeah," Danny said.

They sat. Danny looked up at the sky. In school they had drawing and they were told about perspective. That was drawing lines on a piece of paper or the blackboard so that it looked like there wasn't only lines. It looked like it was distance, or a room, or something inside of something else because of the way you drew the lines. When you looked at the lines of the building slanting toward the sky, it seemed a little the same. It was perspective.

"Thirteen trains," Perc said.

It looked different than it was. In school he'd learned that the sky was not just over a building. It was away far and away. It was millions of miles away. If somebody was standing in the sky, and he could see you on earth, it was so far away that it would take him more years than Mother had lived for him to see you on earth. That was, all except God and the people in Heaven. They saw everything that was going on on earth just as soon as it happened. It was air that was over the building, and the sky was much farther away than it looked. It was getting darker now. The sky got more blue when it got darker.

"Fourteen trains," Perc said.

It was air that was over the buildings. It was the sky that was far away. The sky got bluer when it got dark. It was getting dark now.

"What you thinking about?" Perc asked.

"Nothin'. What you thinking about?" Danny replied.

"Nothing," Perc said.

Why did she have to get drunk? Why wouldn't she sober up and stay sober? Would she, so he could have his birthday party next month? She ought to be sobered up by then.

"It's getting dark," Perc said.

"Yep, it is," Danny said.

"That's fifteen trains gone by since I started counting 'em," Perc said.

"I see," Danny said.

God was above the sky. God could see right through the sky. That was because God was God. If God wasn't God, He couldn't see through the sky. But because God was God, He could see through the sky. Danny kept looking up at the sky. The clouds moved. They were white and they moved, like ships and islands, and they moved because God moved them. It was funny. God made everything in the world. He made whiskey. Why did He make whiskey? Did He make people drunk? No, because when they reached the age of reason, they could do what they wanted to. He made whiskey but He didn't make people drunk. He made the Devil but He didn't make sin. Why did God make people? Why did God make you? God made me to know Him, to love Him, and to serve Him in this world, and to be happy with Him for ever in the next. Was Aunt Margaret serving God? She couldn't be serving Him when she got drunk. But why did God make the sky? God made the sky, but why? So that there would be something between Heaven and earth, and you couldn't see Heaven? He didn't know. He knew God made it. When he died, if he went to Heaven, he'd know. Father Hunt had once told them that in school. That was when Father Hunt was an assistant priest at Crucifixion. Father Hunt now had his own parish somewhere on the West Side. Father Hunt had said that when you died you would learn from God everything about yourself and the earth that you didn't know now. Would he know why Aunty Peg got drunk? There were mysteries in the world and they would only be found out when you died. The catechism said that mysteries were things that a person couldn't understand.

"Seventeen trains," Perc said.

"There'll be more to count now. They're going to start coming faster, bringing people home from work," Danny said.

"Yeah," said Perc.

"This the first time you counted trains?" Danny asked.

"Yeah. You ever count 'em? That's eighteen," Perc said.

"Sure. And I once counted automobiles and wagons on Prairie Avenue," Danny said.

"What for?"

"I donno. I just counted 'em."

"I'd like to be a motorman and run an elevated train when I grow up. But when I said that, my mother said I ought to want to be something else because that would be just being a workingman, and I ought to want to be something better than a workingman," Perc said.

"I guess I'll be a ballplayer," Danny said.

"Al says he's gonna be a priest," Perc said.

"I know it," Danny said.

"Nineteen trains," Perc said.

It was getting darker. Many of the kitchens along the alley were lit up. Danny knew what the women were doing. They were cooking supper everywhere along here. Who was cooking supper at home? Was it being cooked while Aunty Peg yelled and cursed and did the things she always did when she was drunk? Here, in all the houses they had electric lights and cooked by gas. In Mama's neighborhood a lot of the houses used lamps, and the women cooked by wood stoves. People who were richer than Mama and Papa had electric lights and gas. Perc's father was well off. Uncle Al and Aunt Margaret knew about Perc's father and said he was supposed to have quite a bit of money. He was in the whiskey business. Was Aunt Peg drinking the whiskey he made and sold?

"Twenty trains," Perc said.

"Uh huh!"

"Pretty soon we can lag buttons," Perc said.

"Yeah."

"How many buttons you got?"

"About sixty," said Danny.

"Once you had a lot more, didn't yuh?"

"I lost a lot to kids on Indiana Avenue."

"It's hard to get buttons now," Perc said.

"Yeah, but when they have elections for mayor in a couple of months, there'll be a lot of them. Whenever a guy tries to get elected to something they give out buttons about it. Wilson buttons are hard to get now. Kids think they're valuable. But I had a lot when Wilson was running for President. That's when we was in second grade," Danny said.

"I can't lag buttons good. And I ain't got any now. But I'm sure my father can get me a lot when kids start lagging buttons," Perc said.

Getting darker still. A funny feeling, watching it get dark. He liked it better when it wasn't dark. He hated the night to come.

"Twenty-two," Perc said.

They sat, moody, looking around them at it getting dark, at the lighted windows all along the alley.

"Another train," Danny said.

"I gave up counting," Perc said.

"Boys!" Mrs. Dineen called from the second-story porch where Perc lived. Her voice was soft and quiet. She wasn't drunk like Aunt Peg probably was at this minute.

"Yes, Mother," Perc replied.

"Come up now," she called, and turned and went back into her kitchen.

"Let's go. We got to wash ourselves before eating," Perc said.

They climbed off the fence and walked toward the steps to go upstairs.

29

I

"You boys had better get washed for supper now," Mrs. Dineen said when Danny and Perc entered the kitchen; she was a buxom woman, evenly proportioned, with soft white skin, blue eyes, a round face, and fleshy arms.

"Yes, Mother," Perc said, and Danny noticed that they had things in the kitchen like a coffee grinder that Mother didn't have.

"Percy, you take Danny to the bathroom and see that he has a towel," Mrs. Dineen said.

"Hello!" said Emily, coming into the kitchen; she was four years old, chubby, blonde, blue-eyed and pretty.

"Hello," said Danny.

"Hello, Dan," Ferdinand, Perc's seven-year-old brother, said; he also was fair and blue-eyed, and looked like Perc.

"Come on, Dan," Perc said.

He led Danny down the hallway of the eight-room apartment to the bathroom, which was located halfway to the front of the apartment. It was larger than the bathroom at home. Perc pulled a towel from the rack and handed it to Danny.

"I'll come in and wash when you get finished," he said.

"You can wash with me," Danny said.

"You go ahead," Perc said, leaving and closing the door.

Danny sensed how Perc acted different than usual in the bathroom, giving him the towel and going out. Perc acted grown-up doing that, taking care of him like a visitor, just the same way Mrs. Dineen always acted with him when he stayed for supper. Danny looked at himself in the mirror. He urinated with care so as not to squirt on the floor. If he hit the floor, that wouldn't be right. Perc would see it when he came in. He did once and Perc told him he acted like he was brought up in a barn. There was a place for it and you didn't go into a bathroom like you went to take a leak in a prairie or beside an alley fence, Perc had said. Danny was pleased buttoning up because he hadn't missed the bowl. He took his glasses off and let water run in the basin. He rolled up his sleeves and carefully scrubbed his hands, using plenty of soap. Then he took a washrag that lay over the tub and carefully washed his face with soap and water. Washing was certainly a lot of trouble. He wiped his face, leaving dirt marks on the towel and a water line on his neck. He washed the basin out, put on his coat and glasses, and came out of the bathroom.

"Finished?" Perc asked.

"Uh huh!"

"I'll wash then," Perc said.

Perc went into the bathroom and closed the door behind him. Danny stood in the hallway, feeling out of place and alone.

"Hello," Emily said.

"Hello," Danny answered as she toddled up to him.

"My brother Ferdinand is sick with a cold and he didn't go to school today," she said, pronouncing her brother's name slowly but correctly.

"What did he do?"

"He played with me."

"What did he play?" Danny asked.

"Oh, he played. We played house," Emily said.

"We didn't," Ferdinand said, joining them.

"No?" said Danny.

"She just likes to talk. Don't believe her, Danny," Ferdinand said.

"Children, go in the front until supper's ready," Miss Muldoon, the aunt, said as she passed down the hall. She looked like her sister, Mrs. Dineen.

Emily ran ahead. Danny followed Ferdinand. The parlor was large, lit by electricity from an ornate chandelier hanging from the center of the ceiling. There was heavy, stuffed furniture, newly polished, and unscratched. There were a piano, a victrola, a long mirror on the side wall, lace curtains, and a lamp on a small table. Perc's father sat in a comfortable chair, reading a newspaper and wearing carpet slippers. He looked up when the children entered. He was a thin man of about five foot nine, a trifle shorter than his wife. He was slightly wizened, with lines by his nose and small bags under his gray eyes. His hair was dark brown.

"Hello, Danny," he said.

"Hello, Mr. Dineen," Danny said.

"Going to be with us for supper?"

"Yes, sir."

"That's fine. We always like to have you," he said cordially.

"Daddy?" said Emily.

"What now?"

"I want to sit on your lap," she said.

Danny took a chair by the side of the piano.

"Daddy wants to read his newspaper."

"Read me the funnies."

"Your mother or your aunt reads you and Ferdinand the funnies after supper," Mr. Dineen said.

"I wanna know what Skinny Shaner does today."

"You must obey, Emily. Now, your mother will read them all to you after supper," he said gently but firmly.

Emily walked, glum and silent, to a chair and sat down. Perc came in and Danny immediately felt more at ease.

"Hello, Father," Perc said.

"Hello, Son," Mr. Dineen said.

"Hello, Monkey," Perc said to Emily.

She made a face at him. He smiled. Ferdinand came over and stood beside Perc, both of them near Danny.

"Hungry?" Perc asked Danny.

"Uh huh!"

"Me, too," Perc said.

Danny slumped in his chair. There never seemed to be any fighting in Perc's home like there was in his. And everybody was always sober. Perc's aunt didn't smoke cigarettes, and he knew she didn't drink gin and whiskey. He'd never heard the grownups curse here except that once in a while Mr. Dineen said hell or damn.

"I'm hungry, too," Emily said.

"She's always hungry," Ferdinand said.

"Supper," the aunt called.

Emily took Perc's hand and walked beside him. Ferdinand was behind them, and Danny shyly made up the rear. He liked to stay for supper at Perc's, but still he never felt really right here. He didn't always know what to say or do like he did at home.

II

Mrs. Dineen had Danny take a chair at the right of Perc, who in turn sat at the right of Mr. Dineen, who was at the head of the table. Danny sat, shyly waiting, his hands folded in his lap. He wasn't sure what to do. Table manners had to be observed. Uncle Al always spoke about table manners. Well, he didn't have bad table manners because Uncle Al always watched him and told him, and Uncle Al traveled a lot and had good table manners.

Mrs. Dineen and her sister brought in a platter of steak and one of vegetables. Danny saw that there weren't any mashed potatoes, and he was sorry because he liked mashed potatoes so much.

"Thomas, you serve the little guest first," Mrs. Dineen said to her husband, sitting down opposite him.

Mr. Dineen cut a large piece of steak, and put it, canned corn, and peas on a plate. Danny watched him. He was glad it was canned corn and peas. He liked them. He didn't like a lot of vegetables.

"Here, give that to your friend," Mr. Dineen said, handing the plate to Perc. Perc passed it to Danny.

Danny waited while Mr. Dineen served everyone else, and then they all began to eat. Danny was self-conscious. He had to be careful and have good table manners here and not spill anything on the clean tablecloth.

"How is your uncle these days, Daniel?" Mr. Dineen asked.

"He's on the road now," Danny said.

"He's a nice fellow," Mr. Dineen said.

"How did it go in school today with you boys?" Perc's aunt asked.

"Oh, all right. He's becoming a scholar. He got ninety on his last report card. He's good, too, in arithmetic," Perc said, nodding his head in Danny's direction.

"Why, that's fine. Was your grandmother proud?" Mrs. Dineen said.

"Yes. And I think my uncle will be when he comes home and finds it out. But my grandmother didn't exactly know what it meant. You see, she can't read," Danny said.

Mrs. Dineen looked knowingly, a bit surprised and shocked, toward her husband and sister. The three grownups at the table nodded their heads as if to express pathos.

"What do you mean?" Perc asked.

"No, she never went to school very much in Ireland. My aunt reads the papers to her and now she sometimes has me read them to her," Danny said.

"She's a fine woman," Mrs. Dineen said.

"Everybody says she is," Danny said.

"I never knew your grandmother couldn't read," Perc said.

"Well, she can't, but I'm gonna teach her," Danny said.

"You're a good boy, a fine little man," the aunt said.

"Your father and mother weren't born in Ireland, too, were they, Daniel?"

"No, they were born in America."

"Percy, you should study harder and get ninety on your report card, too," the aunt said.

"I'm going to school soon, amn't I, Daddy?" Emily asked.

"Sure, all you kids'll go to school," Mr. Dineen said.

"Just guess who I saw today," the aunt said.

"Who?" asked the mother.

"Lily Geoghan," the aunt said.

"What's Lily doing?" asked the mother.

"She's married to a man named Jones. He's Catholic. He went into the Church for her, and he owns a hardware store on the North Side. She was dressed nice, and I could see that she's not wanting," the aunt said.

"I'm glad to hear that," the father said.

"She always was a nice girl," the mother said.

"Daddy, what's a hardware store?" asked Emily.

"That's where you buy nails, and wires, and hammers and things like that. Mr. Perkins owns a hardware store, and you go into it with me sometimes," the father said.

"Oh!" Emily exclaimed.

She put a piece of steak in her mouth, and while she was chewing it she smiled over at Perc.

"What's in the paper about the war, Tom?" asked the mother.

"Oh, it's winter and too cold for a lot of fighting. But the way I look at it is this. The Germans can't lick the whole world," the father said.

"I never liked the Germans," the aunt said.

"I got to deal a lot with them. They got thick heads, all right. But then, they had that militarism over there. It don't mean such a damn sight to us. We're out of it, and business all over is picking up because of the war," he said.

"I know where Europe is," Ferdinand said.

"Where?" asked the aunt.

"The other side of the Atlantic Ocean," Ferdinand said.

"Good. You'll be a good pupil in geography, Ferdinand," said the aunt.

They continued eating, and no one talked for a couple of minutes. Danny was eating carefully, remembering not to put too much in his mouth at one time, and also not to talk when he had food in his mouth. Uncle Al had said that only people with bad manners did that. He saw, too, that all the Dineens put their knives across their plates, instead of laying the handle on the tablecloth and the tip on the plate. He did the same. That was the way to place your knife at the table when you weren't using it. Uncle Al had taught him to do that. All of the Dineens had table manners, too.

"Have some more, Daniel?" the father asked.

"No, thank you, sir," Danny said, because Uncle Al had told him never to ask for a second helping when he was eating in somebody else's home.

"Sure, come on, give me your plate," the father said.

Perc took Danny's plate and passed it to his father, who put a second helping on it.

"Who else?" the father asked while Perc was passing back Danny's plate.

"This steak turned out good," the mother said while Perc, Ferdinand, and the aunt passed their plates.

"Uh huh!" the father exclaimed, replenishing the plates.

"Goodhue's Market is the best on Fifty-first Street. I always get good cuts there," the mother said.

"They are good," the aunt said.

"Good people," the father said, passing the plate on to the aunt.

Danny ate, silently and seriously. He liked his supper as well as he liked most suppers at home, only he'd have liked it better if they'd had mashed potatoes. There was enough to eat, too, just as there was at home. At Papa's there wasn't always enough to eat. That was because Papa was poorer.

When they had finished their main course, Mrs. Dineen and her sister carried out the plates and brought in tea and apple pie. Danny told himself that another thing to watch was not to keep his spoon in his cup of tea, because if he did, why, he might spill the tea.

"You like apple pie, Daniel?" Mrs. Dineen asked.

"Sure he does. Every kid likes apple pie. Golly, when I was a youngster, my mother used to bake the swellest apple pies and I was crazy about 'em. Oh, boy, did I like apple pies!" Mr. Dineen said.

"You still do," Mrs. Dineen said affectionately.

"Nothing to quarrel about in that statement. I most certainly still do like apple pies," the man of the house said.

Danny took two spoons of sugar and poured milk in his tea. He stirred it carefully and put his spoon on his saucer.

"And I got a wife who bakes apples pies just as good as my mother, Lord have mercy on her soul, used to bake them," Mr. Dineen said.

"That's a real compliment," Mrs. Dineen said, smiling at her sister.

Danny ate on. He was watching himself so much in order not to spill or show bad table manners that he wasn't enjoying his pie. He wanted supper to be over with.

And he was glad when it was and they got up from the table.

"Now, Percy, you and Daniel, you can go into your room and you won't be disturbed while you do your homework," Mrs. Dineen said.

III

"Aren't you gonna ask them about getting out to see Bronco Billy?" Danny asked, disappointed, when he and Perc were alone in the bedroom.

"After a while," Perc said.

"It'll be too late then," Danny said.

"I don't care so much about Bronco Billy."

"Gee, I do. I wanted to see him," Danny said.

"I didn't promise you I'd go with you."

"I just wanted to see him," Danny said.

"But I didn't promise we'd go," Perc said.

"I didn't say you did," Danny said.

"I hate these darn books and homework," Perc said.

"I don't always feel like doing it," Danny said.

"Miss McGinnis doesn't say a lot if you miss it one night," Perc said.

"No, but she takes it off your marks on your report card at the end of the month," Danny said.

"I know. But once in a month doesn't take too much off, and if you miss it once, but do it good the rest of the time, then she might forget. Why, last month even Al missed his homework in arithmetic once or twice, but he got the highest mark in the room in arithmetic, even higher than the smartest girls got. Miss McGinnis is easy. I'm glad they were short of nuns to teach and had to hire her and we got her," Perc said.

"Gee, I'm sorry we ain't gonna see Bronco Billy," Danny said.

"You won't die if you miss him once," Perc said.

"I just don't like to miss him," Danny said.

"Well, I suppose we got to get this homework done," Perc said.

"Yeah, I suppose we do," Danny said.

"Isn't it swell in vacation? No homework at all," Perc said.

"That won't happen until Easter," Danny said.

"Well, I guess we better start doing this darn homework," Perc said.

"Uh huh!" Danny exclaimed, and he was thinking of Bronco Billy, wishing that he had a horse and gun and was a cowboy. And he could see himself riding on a white horse, using his lasso, shooting his gun when he chased cattle rustlers, pulling one of them off a horse with a perfect lasso, dragging him along the ground all the way in to where the jail was.

"What'll we do first?" asked Perc.

"What you think we ought to?" asked Danny.

"I don't know. What do you think?"

"Anything you wanna start first," Danny said.

"I'll start doing whatever lesson you say first," Perc said.

"I don't know. Any one," Danny said.

"How about catechism?" Perc asked.

"It's all right," said Danny.

They opened their paper-covered catechisms.

"I don't like studying catechism. You got to learn too many questions and answers by heart," Perc said.

"Yeah," Danny exclaimed.

"She called on the boys in catechism today. She ought to call on the girls tomorrow. There's a good chance we won't be asked, and while she's asking the girls we can listen close and learn the lesson that way. It's easier," Perc said.

"That's a good idea," Danny said.

"Maybe if we study it and learn the whole lesson, we won't be asked to answer questions. Then won't we wanna kick ourselves?" Perc said.

"Uh huh!"

"I done that lots of times, studied and was never asked, and every time I felt like a fool," Perc said.

"Yeah."

"Arithmetic is hardest. I can't do it good. I always have a fuss with it. You do the arithmetic," Perc said.

Perc sat on the bed with a catechism opened before him. His face was blank. Danny ruled off a sheet of paper, put his name and grade at the top, right-hand side, and started on the problems assigned for homework. He worked through them one by one. They were easy problems in fractions. He liked it, liked the figuring, getting the answers right, and knowing they were right. He worked quickly, absorbed in what he was doing, and he didn't notice Perc, still sitting with an opened catechism before him, his eyes wandering dreamily off toward the wall.

"I'm done," Danny said proudly.

"I studied the catechism lesson. Now you learn it, and I'll copy your arithmetic homework," Perc said.

Perc took Danny's paper, ruled off a sheet for himself, wrote his name and grade more legibly than Danny had done, and copied Danny's solutions.

"I think we done enough homework now," he said when he had finished.

"I guess so," Danny said.

"Guys who go to public schools don't have to do homework at night like we do. They get a study period, I heard, during the school day, and they get their homework done then," Perc said.

"That's what we ought to get."

"Yeah, in some ways the public schools got it over the Catholic ones," Perc said.

"I guess so," Danny said.

"But, of course, they don't have any religion in the public schools."

They sat silent for several moments.

"What you wanna do?" asked Danny.

"Oh, anything," said Perc.

"Why don't you ask them to let you go to see Bronco Billy with me?" Danny said.

"They won't. It ain't no use," Perc said.

"I wish you could go and we could see him," Danny said.

"So do I, but they won't let me go. They say that only a janitor or somebody like that would let his children be on the streets at night. They watch who I play with, and don't like me playing with everybody. They like me to play with you, and they like Al a lot, too," Perc said.

"Well, I wish they'd let you go see the show with me," Danny said glumly.

IV

"What'll we play?" Danny asked, standing with the three Dineen children in the parlor.

"I'm going to play show now. When do we start playing show?" said Emily.

"Keep still until we get started," Perc told his sister.

"Can't we have a show with cowboys?" Ferdinand said.

"Let's play *Graustark*," Danny said.

"Oh, let's play something else," said Perc.

"We ought to have cowboys in our show," Ferdinand said.

"Let's play Bronco Billy," Danny said.

"I'll be Bronco Billy," said Perc.

"I want to be Bronco Billy," said Danny.

"I tell you what," said Perc.

"What?" asked Danny.

"You be Bronco Billy and I'll be Egbert, and we'll both be cowboys together," said Perc.

"But Egbert doesn't act cowboys. He's in the stock company and he plays heroes in love with ladies, and detectives and things like that," Danny said.

"Well, why can't he be a cowboy, too?" asked Perc.

"I guess you're right," said Danny.

"What am I gonna be?" asked Ferdinand.

"You're the rustler," said Perc.

"I wanna be a cowboy," said Ferdinand.

"You want to play with us or not?"

"I wanna be a cowboy," said Ferdinand.

"When we gonna play show?" Emily asked, but she was ignored.

"Answer me!" Perc said.

"What?"

"Do you wanna play with us or don't you?"

"Yeah, I wanna play," said Ferdinand.

"Then you got to be what we tell you to be," said Perc.

"What's that?"

"You steal the cattle," said Perc.

"And then what happens to me?" Ferdinand asked.

"We'll tell you when we get it figured out. Now, how do we start, Dan?"

"Let's see," Danny exclaimed, and they waited around him while he thought.

"Well, first we ought to be riding horses on the plains," said Danny.

"That's a good idea."

"Now, how will we be riding?"

"We can get brooms," said Perc.

"I got a better idea," said Danny.

"What's that?" Perc asked.

"We can each get on one side of the rocking chair and pretend we're on horses," said Danny.

"Now, you two sit there on the piano bench until you come into it," said Perc.

Danny and Perc each got astride one arm of the rocker.

"We're riding now, and I say to you, let's see. I say this," said Danny.

"All right, we're riding, and I'm Egbert and you're Bronco Billy."

"Egbert, the rustlers with Bad-Eye Joe went this way, and they took Gloria with them. . . . Emily is Gloria, and Ferdinand is Bad-Eye Joe," said Danny.

"When do we play we're shooting?" asked Ferdinand.

"Wait until you come into it," said Perc while Emily eyed the two boys intently.

"What do I say?" asked Perc.

"You say, let's see . . . You say, 'Bronco Billy, they came this way.'"

"Bronco Billy, they came this way."

"Are your guns ready?"

"Yeah."

"Let's ride."

They rocked the chair.

"There he is, Egbert. He's riding away with his gang, and they got Gloria, too."

"After 'em," Perc said.

"Now we're chasing you. And Emily, your name's Gloria and he's kidnaped you and we're chasing him and his gang to rescue you."

"What do I do?" asked Ferdinand.

"You sit there with Gloria in front of you and pretend you're riding."

"We chase them and shoot, huh?" asked Perc.

The three boys yelled bang bang bang. They made a racket, and Mrs. Dineen came into the parlor.

"Goodness, what is this?"

"We're playing show," Emily said.

"Well, children, please make a little less noise. Your father is reading the newspaper and the neighbors will complain," she said, smiling at them.

"Let's play something that makes less noise and have it a play like they have at the Willard instead of a moving picture," said Perc.

"All right, let's see, what'll we play?" said Danny.

"This time, I don't have to be a rustler, do I?" asked Ferdinand.

"We got to figure it out first," said Perc.

"Let's play more show," said Emily.

"Now, let's figure it all out first, what everybody does, and then do it," said Danny.

"All right. Come on, everybody get together here," said Perc.

The four of them sat down on the floor to make up the play they were going to act.

V

Danny left the Dineens' at about a quarter after nine. The minute he got outside, he thought how he hadn't had home and Aunt Peg's drinking on his mind all night. It had just gone right out of his mind, and stayed out. And they'd had fun playing show. Wouldn't it be fun if they could get all the gang together and play show, play like they were a stock company just like the stock company of actors that were at the Willard Theater every week? They would have enough then, and they'd have girls. In some of the plays the actors kissed the actresses, and if he could be Egbert he would kiss the girls in some of the plays, and he'd have lots of fun.

And now he had to go home. And would she be stewed? He didn't want to go home. He walked slowly along Prairie Avenue in the chilling January night. It was getting a little colder, and that meant there might be skating tomorrow. He wished Perc could skate because he liked Perc. He stood for a moment, hands on hips, seeing a street car cross Fifty-first Street ahead of him. He galloped to Fifty-first Street, pretending he was a cowboy riding a horse like Bronco Billy. He waited for a street car to pass, and then ran over the tracks. He crossed over to the other side of Prairie to look at the posters in front of the lighted theater advertising the latest Bronco Billy picture. Now he wished he'd seen it instead of having stayed at Perc's, even though he did have a good time there.

Gloomy, he turned away from the theater façade and started on again toward home. The closer he would get to home the more he would worry about her and wonder if she was stewed. Would she yell all night?

A snowball skimmed by his ear. He looked around in sudden fright. Maybe it was some big kids. Maybe a kid bigger than he was, a kid who could clean him up. He saw that it was Tommy Moriarty.

"Hey, you're a swell guy," Tommy said, running up to him.

He had clean forgotten about his promise to try and get an extra nickel and take Tommy to the show.

"I didn't go to the show," he said.

"You did, too. I just seen yuh comin' out of it," Tommy said.

"I wasn't. I was just looking at the pictures in front of it."

"Don't lie to me, yuh little punk."

"I ain't. I stayed at Perc Dineen's house for supper and then did my homework with him. I just left it a little while ago and was on my way home. I'm goin' to the show Saturday, though," Danny said.

"I called for you and you weren't home."

"I'm going to the show Saturday afternoon," Danny said.

"Are yuh kiddin' me?"

"Honest," said Danny as they walked along toward home.

"Well, I thought you was ditchin' me."

"I wasn't," Danny said.

"Then can we go Saturday afternoon?" asked Tommy.

"I think so," Danny said.

"I'll call for you," Tommy said.

"I'll wait," Danny said.

"So long. I gotta get home," Tommy said.

"So do I," Danny said.

30

I

Sadie let Danny in and followed him to the dining room where Little Margaret and his grandmother were. Little Margaret's eyes were red from crying and she sat doing nothing.

"You're home, Son," Mrs. O'Flaherty said.

"You're lucky, Danny," Little Margaret said as Sadie sat down.

"Why?"

"You missed it," Little Margaret said.

"What, is she drunk again?"

"She'll be the death of us all yet," Mrs. O'Flaherty said.

"She was fighting and making all kinds of noise," said Little Margaret.

"A boy called for you, Danny," Sadie said.

"I know. I met him just now when I was coming home," Danny said.

"Did they feed you enough, Son?" Mrs. O'Flaherty asked.

"Yes," Danny answered.

"That's good. I was in fear you wouldn't get enough to eat," Mrs. O'Flaherty said.

"I did," Danny said.

"Did the mother of that boy see that you had a clean waist on?" Mrs. O'Flaherty asked.

"She didn't say anything about it," Danny said.

"She should have. Sadie, he's the cleanest-dressed boy in school," Mrs. O'Flaherty said.

"That's nice," Sadie said, smiling wanly.

"Is there a paper here?" Danny asked.

"Yes, it's in the kitchen," Sadie said.

Danny went for it. There wouldn't be much baseball news, but there would be some about players signing contracts, and there were the funnies, and the stories about the war. He didn't want the Germans to win.

"You got to watch her, Sadie," Mrs. O'Flaherty said as he came back and sat down to read the paper.

"She's asleep now. Maybe she'll sleep it off and be all right in the morning," Sadie said.

"I don't know what the neighbors'll think what with the way she was screaming and yelling here tonight," Mrs. O'Flaherty said.

"I'm awfully sorry to see her this way. She's such a handsome girl, with such fine chances in life. It's a pity what she's doing to herself," Sadie said.

"Aunt Mildred never got drunk in Madison," Little Margaret said.

"Not that good woman, my son Ned's wife," Mrs. O'Flaherty said.

"Does Al know about it?" Sadie asked.

"That poor boy, how would he know? But when he comes home, I'll tell him. Oh, but he'll know!" Mrs. O'Flaherty said.

"When is he coming home?"

"Sure, I don't know. He's out earning an honest living for all of us, the poor boy," Mrs. O'Flaherty said. "I'll tell Al. And I'll go to the church. I'll bring the priest here. I'll lay my story bare before the parish priest, Father Mulligan. And I'll tell the nuns, too. I'll tell them. Oh, but I will!"

Danny flung aside the paper.

"Wanna play cards, Danny?" Little Margaret asked.

"All right, get 'em," he said.

Little Margaret ran to get the cards from the front of the house.

"You wouldn't go telling like that on your own daughter, Mary?" Sadie said.

"That I may be struck blind if I don't!" Mrs. O'Flaherty said.

Mrs. O'Flaherty got up. She faced Sadie, shaking her fist while Little Margaret came back with the cards. Danny shuffled them to play casino with her.

"That I may be struck dead if I don't! I'll go to the holy bishop. She won't be carrying on any more like this in my decent household. Not while I'm here to watch after it with the breath of life still in me. When I'm dead and gone she can do whatever the devils and the tinkers tell her to. But while I'm alive she won't. Not in my house."

"It's a shame. It's very sad," Sadie said.

"It's a sin," Mrs. O'Flaherty said.

"She's so different, so generous and kind when she isn't this way," Sadie said.

Mrs. O'Flaherty sat down and rocked back and forth. The room was tense and silent, and the children played casino.

II

"There she is again, the devil. Go see what's she up to, Sadie, like a good girl," Mrs. O'Flaherty said when they heard Margaret stumble out to the kitchen.

Danny and Little Margaret exchanged frightened glances. Sadie and Mrs. O'Flaherty went to the kitchen.

"Danny, is Aunty Peg a whore? She was yelling about being a whore at supper time," Little Margaret said.

"I don't know what it is. She's cashier in the hotel."

"A whore's bad, I know that. And she called herself a whore," Little Margaret said.

Mrs. O'Flaherty turned back to the children. She saw how sleepy they were.

"You little ones go to bed. I'll fix your bed, Little Margaret. And you go to bed. You both have to be up and out with the scholars in the morning," she said.

"I'm sleepy, Mother," Little Margaret said, yawning.

"I hope that one lets you sleep," Mrs. O'Flaherty said.

The children followed their grandmother to the front of the house while Sadie was in the kitchen with Margaret.

III

"Come now, Peg, please go back to sleep. All you need is a little sleep and you're going to be all right," Sadie said, trying to be persuasive.

"Hungry!" Margaret exclaimed, swaying in the center of the kitchen, her expression stupid, her face dirty, her eyes bleary and inhuman with bags under them. There was no life, no interest in her face. Her cheeks were streaked and smeared. She was wearing a flimsy pink silk nightgown through which the outline of her well-proportioned figure was clearly visible.

"Hungry!" she muttered, swaying.

"But, Peg, you just ate a little while ago," Sadie said.

Margaret stumbled to the door, went outside to the icebox in the cold, and returned carrying a plate of tomatoes and a cold, greasy pork chop. She set the plates on the table and half fell into a chair. She picked up the pork chop with her hands and began gnawing at it, smearing her lips with grease. She set it down and grabbed a tomato. She bit into it and the juice dripped onto her chin, down her neck and onto her nightgown. She dropped the half-eaten tomato on the table. She gnawed on the pork chop again.

Sadie didn't like to watch her cousin eating this way. Margaret continued, staining herself with grease and tomato juice, clumsily wiping her lips with the back of her hand. Margaret dropped the gnawed pork-chop bone on a plate.

She got to her feet clumsily. She stood in the center of the kitchen, dirty and greasy-faced, her body swaying. She stared bleary-eyed past Sadie.

"Hungry!" she muttered.

"Come now, please go to bed," Sadie coaxed.

"Hungry!" Margaret again muttered.

Sadie went out to the icebox and hurried back in, shivering and coughing, with several tomatoes and half a head of lettuce. She washed the food, sliced the tomatoes, and set them before Margaret. Margaret squinted at them. Disregarding the fork which Sadie had set before her, she ate with her hands, slobbering, staining herself further with tomato juice.

Sadie went back to sit in the dining room with Mrs. O'Flaherty because she couldn't watch her cousin eat that way.

IV

"Did you eat enough, Peg?" Sadie asked, returning to the kitchen.

Margaret sat in a stupor, her face smeared from eating.

"Peg, have you had enough to eat?" Sadie asked.

Margaret grunted.

"Peg, don't you think you ought to go to bed now?"

Margaret sat, her head dropped, her chin resting on her chest. Her eyes were glazed, almost like the eyes of a corpse. She breathed heavily and did not talk. Sadie looked at her, annoyed. She stood before her for a while, helpless. She went to the bathroom and got a washcloth and towel. She washed and dried Margaret's dirty hands. She lifted Margaret's head and, holding it up with difficulty, washed and dried her face. Margaret dropped her head again. Sadie took Margaret's arm and tried to lift her, but Margaret was a dead weight, like stone. Sadie breathed heavily, and her arms and back ached from her exertion. She didn't see how she could get Margaret to bed. Margaret sat, wheezing, and Sadie looked hopelessly at her.

"Peg, come now, darling, and go to bed," Sadie said.

Margaret sat in a drunken stupor. Mrs. O'Flaherty came into the kitchen.

"Mary, I simply can't get her to bed," Sadie said despairingly.

"The devil with her!"

"But if I could get her to bed, it'd be better for her."

"Sure, and if you did, she'd be up again in a jiffy."

"Should I let her stay here? Trying to lift her is like trying to lift stones, she's so heavy," Sadie said.

"Let her be, child! Don't strain yourself lifting her. You're a good girl, Sadie."

They looked at Margaret. There was a trickle of water sliding down from her onto the floor.

"Ah, the animal!" Mrs. O'Flaherty said while Sadie looked on in revulsion.

Margaret grunted. She got to her feet. She seemed to have no consciousness. Deadened with stupidity, she stumbled out of the kitchen, down the hall, into her bedroom.

"The beast, worse than the beasts in the field," Mrs. O'Flaherty said.

She went to the pantry, got an old cloth, and bent down to clean the mess Margaret had left on the floor.

"Let me do that, Mary," Sadie said.

"Don't trouble yourself, you angel," Mrs. O'Flaherty said, wiping the floor.

Sadie got the mop, wet it in the sink, and mopped up after Mrs. O'Flaherty. The old lady threw the rag she had used in the garbage can outside, and came back to the kitchen.

"The animal!" she said in disgust.

"It's very sad," Sadie said.

"Like the beasts in the field," Mrs. O'Flaherty said.

"I don't know why this should happen to a girl like Peg," Sadie said.

"She has no fear of the Lord in her."

"I could almost cry, thinking that my cousin, Peg O'Flaherty, should be this way," Sadie said.

"I'll never have the gumption to face me neighbors, what with the way she's cut up."

"I'm terribly sorry," Sadie said ineffectually.

"You're a good girl, Sadie. I wish you were me own daughter instead of that one," Mrs. O'Flaherty said, patting Sadie on the head.

V

"You're tired, you poor thing. You had a hard day. You go to bed, child," Mrs. O'Flaherty said to Sadie, who sat yawning and exhausted in the dining room, deep circles under her eyes.

"I can stay up to watch and see if she needs anything or does anything," Sadie said.

"Ah, I just peeked in at her. She's dead to the world, like a stone. Sure, that whiskey has made her dead to the world," Mrs. O'Flaherty said.

"Well, she might get up."

"You go to bed and watch her."

"Where'll I sleep?" Sadie asked.

"You'll have to sleep with her. It's the only place in the house."

Sadie's face dropped. She got up, walked wearily out of the room. In the hallway she wiped a tear from her eyes. She went to the bathroom and undressed there, taking off her dress, petticoat, corset, stockings, garters and bloomers. She stood in a shimmy, and the bones of her body stuck through. She had skinny legs, narrow hips, and almost flat breasts. With the powder rubbed off her face, her complexion was almost dirty-looking because of its sickly, yellowish hue. She looked sick and weak, and her eyes seemed to have receded farther into her bony face since the morning, when she had arrived at the O'Flaherty apartment. She sat down on the closed toilet seat, cried, blew her nose. She yawned, got up, carried her clothes into Margaret's room, and dropped them in a chair. She climbed over Margaret, who was spread out on the bed with her legs wide apart. She lay by the wall.

Margaret reeked of alcohol and urine. She breathed heavily and stirred restlessly. Sadie tried to take up as little room as possible, but Margaret pushed against her. Margaret made it impossible for Sadie to cover herself. Sadie lay face to the wall, curled up. Margaret stirred. Sadie tried to sleep. Margaret groaned, emitted indistinguishable sounds. Sadie was almost nauseated by the odors of which Margaret reeked. She tried to pray herself to sleep. She was so weak, so exhausted, that she couldn't sleep. She sobbed quietly. Margaret rolled over and faced the window, giving Sadie some relief. Margaret grunted again. Sadie drowsed into sleep. Sadie was suddenly jolted awake again when Margaret rolled over, curled up beside her, giving her cousin no room. Margaret flailed her arms about and landed a jolt in Sadie's back. Sadie winced.

"Peg?" Sadie said softly.

Margaret snored.

Sadie tried to move Margaret to give herself more room. Margaret was too heavy, her weight was too dead, too like stone.

Again Margaret snored. She blew her whiskey breath on Sadie. Sadie lay by the wall, sobbing, utterly exhausted. She coughed, a rasping cough which tore up from her chest. She cried. She wished she were dead. Margaret snored again.

31

I

A nun led Mrs. O'Flaherty into Sister Marguerita's office. The Superior stood up and came forward to the old lady, a smile on her broad, wrinkled face.

"How do you do, Mrs. O'Flaherty," she said, shaking hands.

"How do you do yourself, Sister," Mrs. O'Flaherty replied, her voice thick and peculiar.

"Here, sit down and be comfortable. I'm very glad to see you," Sister Marguerita said, bustling as she drew a chair up beside her desk in her crowded office.

"Thank you, Sister," Mrs. O'Flaherty said, seating herself.

Noticing that there was something wrong with Mrs. O'Flaherty, Sister Marguerita looked perplexed. The nun wrinkled her forehead quizzically.

"I hope that your visit is a pleasant one, and that your purpose is not to take your grandson out of school. He's doing well, and he's getting better marks on his report cards than he has ever done. He's a good boy. His teacher, Miss McGinnis, is well satisfied with him as a pupil, and I think he's a fine a boy as we would ever want in school. I see him and say hello to him sometimes, and he always tips his hat to me and shows a sunny disposition. Yes, Daniel's a fine boy, Mrs. O'Flaherty, and he's doing very well," Sister Marguerita said.

"Indeed he is. There isn't a lad the like of him in the school."

Sister Marguerita again looked perplexedly at the old lady. She screwed up her face, sniffed. She knew what it was.

"He's a fine boy," the nun said diplomatically.

Mrs. O'Flaherty got to her feet energetically.

"When me grandson walks in the halls here, the other boys should turn their faces to the wall," she said, gesticulating forcibly with her right arm. She flung her head back, giving additional emphasis to her statement. Then she sat down.

"How is Daniel? He isn't causing any trouble at home or becoming wild?"

"How would he be but fine, Sister? I watch over him night and day like a hawk. I don't let him even look at a girl."

"He's innocent, and we think it's good to have the boys and girls in the same rooms and to let them play. I like them to have harmless little parties together," the nun said.

"Sister, I have a son forty years old, and if he got married, I'd take him over me knee. I won't let my grandson look at a girl."

"You aren't having any trouble with the boy because of girls, I hope, Mrs. O'Flaherty?" Sister Marguerita said.

"Oh, no! Oh, no!"

"If there is anything the matter with the boy, we would like to help straighten it out. Are his eyes all right? When he was in the second grade, Sister Anastasia told him to stay out of school for a month because of his eyesight and to have himself fitted for glasses. She thought the world of him, and said that he was one of her best pupils. Are his eyes troubling him again?"

"Ah, no, Sister. Ah, the poor boy!" Mrs. O'Flaherty said, starting to cry.

"Why, Mrs. O'Flaherty, what's happened? What's the matter?" Sister Marguerita asked, leaning forward, her elbows resting on her desk.

"Sister, the poor boy! Sure, me heart is broken," Mrs. O'Flaherty said.

"What is it, Mrs. O'Flaherty?"

"Me daughter."

"What has happened to her? She came to see me once and she seemed like a lovely and intelligent girl. I knew that she performed her religious duties from the way she talked," Sister Marguerita said.

"Sister, me daughter has been drunk for weeks on end. Sure, she must have the Devil in her, and that innocent little lad having to hear her and see the way she does be carrying on in me decent son's home," Mrs. O'Flaherty said almost in a lament.

"Mrs. O'Flaherty, I don't understand it."

"Sure, Sister, only the black one in Hell himself can understand the likes of it," Mrs. O'Flaherty said.

"Of course, if the boy is being exposed to sin, if he is being placed in the occasion of sin where evil will warp him, that is very bad, and it is your duty to see that he is taken out of such circumstances," Sister Marguerita said.

"Not even his mother could take me grandson away from me. Sure, Sister, and he's the apple of me eye," Mrs. O'Flaherty said, her voice becoming thicker.

"Does the boy's mother know of this going-on?" Sister Marguerita asked.

"Ah, the poor thing, and that she does."

"It's very distressing to hear this, Mrs. O'Flaherty," the nun said.

"Sister, she took up with a Protestant married man and he's done it to her.

He taught her to drink that gin and smoke cigarettes," Mrs. O'Flaherty said bitterly.

The nun winced. She was clearly uncomfortable at being forced to listen to these revelations.

"Sister, I disown her. Drinking in front of me little grandson, and his little sister. Sister, I told her I would get you after her. I swore that I'd tell the holy nuns on her. Sister, me own flesh and blood sister is a nun, a holy nun, running an orphan asylum in Brooklyn, New York. Me own Sister, Sister Dolorosa, she that came out from the old country with me. I swore I'd tell the holy nuns on her. Sister, you do something to her, you shame her," Mrs. O'Flaherty said.

"But, Mrs. O'Flaherty, what can I do? Of course, I shall pray and ask the intercession of the Lord, but I do not think that I can do anything else," Sister Marguerita said.

"I told her. I said to her that the Devil would get her, and that I would tell the holy nuns who taught me grandson. There, and I have. Sister, sure, she's the disgrace of the neighborhood, and I'm ashamed to show me face to the neighbors on Prairie Avenue," Mrs. O'Flaherty said.

"I think that you ought to pray, Mrs. O'Flaherty," Sister Marguerita said, drawing away from Mrs. O'Flaherty because of the old lady's beery breath.

"I will. Ah, Sister, that poor innocent boy."

"What does the boy's father think of it?" Sister Marguerita asked.

"That poor man, out working on a wagon, hardly able to feed the mouths of his own flesh and blood, what can he do? Sure, him and me daughter are so poor, and me daughter, the boy's mother, has another little one on the way. And there is that devil, spending money that could be used to help the poor little ones out and put some bread in their mouths and warmth in their bones," Mrs. O'Flaherty said.

"This is very sad, Mrs. O'Flaherty. We must all ask for the help of God," Sister Marguerita said.

"Ah, Sister, you're good. You'll pray."

"Of course I will."

"Sister, I won't let her be a bad example for me little grandson. That boy has the best of care, the best of care. He doesn't want for a thing. Sister, every day he wears a clean waist to school. He's the cleanest lad in the school."

"Yes, he is sent to school looking neat."

The nun smiled grimly.

"Well, good day, Sister. You're a good and holy virgin. Good day, and take care of the little fellow," Mrs. O'Flaherty said.

The nun watched her stagger out of the office. She sat a moment in reflection, shaking her head sadly from side to side.

She called her assistant.

"Sister Lorraine, see if Daniel O'Neill in the fourth grade is in class, and if he is, have him come to me immediately," Sister Marguerita said.

II

Danny came timidly into the principal's office, wondering what she wanted to say to him. He hadn't done anything that he knew about. He hadn't had too many fights this year, and he'd been studying pretty good. The nun, seeing how pale he was, smiled, and beckoned him to her.

"Come here and sit down, Daniel," she said in a reassuring voice.

"Yes, Sister."

"Daniel, your grandmother was just here to see me."

Danny blushed with shame. He didn't want Sister Marguerita to know, and he was afraid that Mother had come to tell her about Aunty Peg.

"Does that drinking go on often in your house?" Sister Marguerita asked.

He didn't answer, his face becoming more red.

"Daniel, I'm your friend. You mustn't be afraid or ashamed to answer me. You answer my questions and tell me the truth. I am asking you for your own good so that we in school here can help you," she said.

He smiled weakly at her.

"How often are they drunk at home?"

"Well, Sister, sometimes," he said.

"Your grandmother told me your aunt has been drunk for a long time."

"Well, yes, Sister."

"How long, Daniel?"

"Oh, Sister, since last month. More than two weeks now."

"Is this the first time?"

"No, Sister. But she wasn't drinking for a while, since last summer, and she said then she wasn't going to do it any more."

"And your grandmother?"

Again no answer.

"Daniel, you needn't be ashamed with me. She was just here and she had been drinking."

"Not so much. She sometimes drinks beer, and she cries a lot when she does."

"I see. Now, Daniel, do you ever go without food because of their drinking?"

"No, Sister."

"Don't be ashamed to answer me. I ask because I want to know. We do not want a boy like you going without your meals. If at any time there is this drinking in your home and no one gets your food ready for you, I want you to come here and see me, and I will see that you get a good warm meal."

"Yes, Sister."

"It is hard on you, you poor boy. What happens at home?"

Danny blushed.

"You must tell me."

"Sister, I don't like it. And neither does my little sister."

"She lives with you?"

"Yes, Sister."

"Is she too young to start school?"

"No, Sister."

"Where does she go to school?"

"The public school."

"Why is that, do you know?"

"My aunt said she was too small to go this far to school in winter and the public school's nearer. Next year they're gonna send her here."

"You should try to persuade them to send her here. Daniel, does your uncle drink, too?"

"No, Sister. But he travels on the road selling shoes, and he's away from home a lot."

"Does he know what goes on at your home?"

"When he's home. My aunt drinks sometimes when he's home and he tries to sober her up."

"Does everybody in your home go to mass on Sunday?"

"My uncle and grandmother always do, Sister, but my aunt never does."

The nun sat for a moment as if thinking, shaking her head sadly from side to side.

"Do you try to get her to go?"

"Well, Sister, I pray that she will, lots, but that's all."

"You never miss mass?"

"No, Sister."

"You mustn't. And tell me, Daniel, and tell me the truth. Do you ever go without food because of drinking in your home?"

Danny began to cry.

"You mustn't cry. You must be a little man," she said.

Danny dabbed at his eyes with a handkerchief. A wave of self-pity flooded him.

"Yes, Sister," he said, pitying himself, and he knew that he was telling a lie on Mother because she always got his meals for him; he didn't know why he was telling this lie. He hadn't meant to. And there he'd told it, and now he couldn't let Sister Marguerita know he'd lied.

"When that happens again, you must promise to come right to me and I'll see that you are fed properly. Promise me, Daniel."

"I will, Sister."

"Do any of the boys or girls in school know of this drinking in your house?" Again Danny was silent.

"Tell me. I want to know because I might stop them from talking about it."

"Well, Sister, Tommy Moriarty does. He knows about my aunt, but I don't think he knows about my grandmother."

"I'll talk to him. Does he ever speak about it to you?"

"He did."

"I'll talk to him and tell him he mustn't tell anyone."

"Yes, Sister," Danny said, at a loss for words.

"Daniel, you must offer up prayers every day and ask God to help your aunt and grandmother so that they do not go on drinking this way. Will you do that?"

"Yes, Sister, I will."

"Will you promise me not to forget it?"

"Yes, Sister."

"Now, you be a good boy and run back to your classroom. I want to help you all I can, and promise me you'll go on studying and be one of our best pupils this year."

"Yes, Sister. Sister, I got ninety for my average in December, and eighty-seven last month," Danny said.

"I know. You've been doing good work and I'm proud of you."

"Sister?" he said shyly.

"Yes, Daniel."

"You won't tell Miss McGinnis, will you?"

"I'll tell no one."

"Thank you, Sister."

"Now, don't forget. Pray every day, and you remember that you never have to go hungry. You can always come to me if there's nobody at your home in a condition to give you a good warm meal."

"Yes, Sister."

"Now, run back to your class. And pay attention to your lesson. Ask the Lord to help you," she said.

Danny walked slowly out of the office. After he had left, Sister Marguerita told her assistant to have Tommy Moriarty sent to her.

Danny walked slowly along the corridor to go back to his classroom. He blushed. Shame welled up in him. He was sorry. He had told a lie, too, about Mother, and Sister Marguerita would think that Mother didn't feed him. He shouldn't have done that, and he had. It was just like the way he had lied in confession and couldn't ever get himself to confess that he had. He walked back to class, his head hanging. Would the kids find out now? Would he be disgraced before the whole school? What would Perc Dineen say if he found out? And

Virginia Doyle? And Hortense Audrey? And Helen Smith? And Al Throckwaite? He wished he was not in school. He wished he was in a new neighborhood where nobody knew any of these things. He wished anything but that all this went on. And now when he went home, they would both be stewed. He opened the door of the classroom and tiptoed quietly to his seat, uncomfortable as the eyes of his classmates focused on him.

III

Mrs. O'Flaherty sat crying into a half-filled glass of beer in the back room of O'Callahan's saloon. She finished her beer, rose, and went to a bell near her on the wall. She rang and returned to her chair.

"The Lord will punish her!" she exclaimed, half aloud.

"Yes, mam," the waiter said.

"Bring me another glass of beer," she said.

The waiter disappeared through the swinging doors and quickly came back with a foaming glass. The voices of men in the front could be heard. She paid the waiter and he turned to leave.

"Sir!" she said.

He about-faced. She motioned to him to come back to her table, and he complied with her summons.

"You're a good man, and I want you to take this. In the old country, it's a lot of money. It'll buy you a stick of gum," she said.

"No, thank you," he said, turning from the table when he saw that she had laid a penny on it.

"Ah, don't be bashful. Take it. You're a good man, and may the Lord bless you," she said, and suddenly the frown left his face; he smiled tolerantly, returned to the table and picked up the penny.

"Thank you, mother," he said.

"God bless you," she said.

Smiling, he started to leave again.

"Come here!" she said.

He stepped back to her table.

"Is your mother living?"

"Yes, she is," the waiter said.

"You be good to her. Are you married?"

"No, I'm not."

"Well, don't you do it. You take care of your mother. I have a son over forty years old, forty years, and if he got married on me, do you know what I'd do to him?"

"What, mother?"

"I'd put a good hot paddle to him," she said; the waiter smiled.

She took another drink of beer and once again he started away.

"Wait a minute," she said.

"Yes, mother."

"Here, you buy your mother a stick of gum, too. And you be good to her. If you run off and get married on her, she ought to paddle you good and plenty."

He took the second penny, thanked her, went back to the front. He could be heard talking, and there was sudden masculine laughter. Mrs. O'Flaherty drank her beer, wiped her eyes with the back of her hand, pulled her veil over her face, and got up.

"Mrs. O'Flaherty," said O'Callahan, a beefy, ruddy man suddenly coming upon her.

"Sir!" she said.

"Your daughter borrowed five dollars off of me a week ago. She's evidently forgotten to come back and pay me. She promised to the next day. She said you were sick and she needed the money for medicine."

"Sir, I'm not sick, and that's not me daughter. She was me hired woman. I fired her," Mrs. O'Flaherty said, and with her hat askew she staggered proudly out of the saloon.

She walked zigzag to the corner, turned it, and staggered along the street, singing half aloud. People stared at her. A group of young boys trailed her, laughing and imitating her walk.

"I know who she is," one of them said.

"Who?" another asked.

"Four-Eyed O'Neill's grandmother."

"He would have a drunken grandmother, wouldn't he?"

"Hey, lady, your hat's on crooked."

The boys laughed.

"Be about your business," she yelled at them.

She staggered on, heedless of them as they trailed after her.

32

I

"Gee, I'm glad you came down, Peg," Jack Doolin said as he and Margaret lay relaxed in his bedroom. The shades were drawn, but the late afternoon light sifted through the cracks.

"Yes," she answered softly.

"Some things are so damn hard to get over, to forget. God, these days if I can only forget for a few minutes at a time, I'm grateful."

"If I could only forget," Margaret said, sighing.

"God, it's still like a nightmare. Since she died, it's been like a nightmare. I can't make myself realize it. You see, I keep thinking of her, and suddenly I come to my senses and I know she's gone."

"I felt that way after my father and sister died. That year we had two deaths," Margaret said.

"I never expected this. She used to say she had a pain, and she thought it was just indigestion. And then that night I came home and I saw her. She knew she was going to die when she went to the hospital," he said.

"She was a lovely woman," Margaret said.

"It's tougher on the kid than on me. It's hell to be a kid and be without a mother."

"When she's a good mother like your wife was," said Margaret.

"My poor kid. It's damn tough on him, Peg."

"And he's such a lovely boy," Margaret said.

"She never regained consciousness. She kissed me goodbye before they wheeled her into the operating room and she said to me, 'Jack, be a good father to Georgie.' Well, I will be. I'll be a good father to him. But goddamn it, it was a tough jolt. You know, ever since the funeral I've been drinking like a fish. I had to. I never drank like I been drinking. I got to. I got to get it out of my head," he said.

"Oh, Jack, I know. I know. Why do you think I have drunk? Why? To forget," Margaret said.

"Well, such is life," he said grimly.

"I know how you feel," she said.

"Kiss me, Peg," he said.

He embraced her, held her body firmly against his own, planted a long kiss on her lips.

<h1 style="text-align:center">II</h1>

Margaret lay quietly beside him. He dozed, breathing a bit heavily. Asleep now. And he was talking so much about forgetting. Men forgot too easy. They didn't love. They had appetites. Satisfy their appetites, and look at them. There he was, sleeping now. Yes, he was forgetting. But would she ever forget? Could she ever forget? Here she was lying in bed with this man. He was practically a stranger. This was what Lorry had driven her to. This sin of hers with Jack Doolin, it was on the soul of Lorry Robinson. No answer to her letter. No word from him. Only just before she had come down here, she'd had Sadie call four hotels. Not registered. She didn't know where he was. Did he care where she was? Suppose he saw her now in bed with this sleeping man beside her, would he care? Would he be jealous?

Men didn't care.

She dozed off, and when she awoke again he was looking at her. There was a queer look in his eyes.

"What's the matter?" she asked.

"Nothing," he said, and she saw it in his eyes.

Now that he had gotten out of her what she could give, he didn't care. Now he was hating her. Now he was looking at her and comparing her to his wife.

She wanted to scream at him. And she lay there, quiet. She wanted to tell him that she knew what thoughts were going on in his mind. He could never understand how misery drove her into his bed. Did he think he was giving her such a good time? Did he think that he was the best she could get? Why, he was only a little cigar alongside of men she knew!

Oh, but a woman's cup sometimes filled and overflowed with bitterness.

They lay quietly, their bodies touching.

III

"We better get dressed now," he said.

He got out of bed, yawned, and began drawing on his BVD's. She looked at him when he had buttoned them. A man looked so funny in his underwear. She always wanted to laugh, seeing those BVD's on a man, seeing a man's knees. Look at him now. His body was coarse, just as his soul was. And he was too hairy. And look at his knees. He sat on a chair, put his socks on, and hooked his garters. He drew on his pants.

She got out of bed and carried her clothes to the bathroom. When she came out, dressed, he was sitting in the parlor in his shirt sleeves. There was a harassed look in his eyes. He looked utterly miserable, and sympathy for him suddenly welled within her. She walked to his chair, bent down, and brushed a kiss on his forehead.

He smiled at her, an absent-minded, weary smile.

"The thing that you got to do, Jack, is not to let your mind dwell on it all the time," she said.

"I was thinking of the kid, my poor, motherless boy."

"I know. I know how is it when one's heart is unhappy. Take my word for it, I do, Jack," she said.

"Sometimes, Peg, I wonder is there a God."

"Jack, that's the very question I've been asking myself," she said.

"If there's a God, why do such things happen? Why is my fine boy left motherless?"

"I have racked my brain, Jack, asking myself if there's a God, oh, why are people so miserable?"

He got up and walked nervously across the room, turned around, went back to his chair, and flopped in it.

"Damn it, if there's a God, why did He let it happen? He could have stopped it," Jack said.

And why did God make her so miserable, she asked herself.

"Unless He was punishing me. I wasn't good enough for her. That's why He took her away from me. The sins of the fathers are visited upon the children. That's what the Bible says. It was because of me. If I didn't carouse around, maybe it wouldn't have happened."

"Jack, now don't you be saying those things. You aren't responsible."

"But, hell, I didn't do so much hell-raising. Once in a while I tried to have a good time. No more than any man does. You know, men are made different from women. They like to go around a bit," he said.

She relapsed into brooding thoughts, and did not respond to what he had said.

"Hell, I don't know," he said, sinking his chin in his hands.

They sat in gloomy silence.

"Damn it, it would almost make a man cry to think of that wonderful kid motherless," he said reflectively.

"But you'll be a good father to him," she said.

"Damn it, but I will. I'll do everything in my power to make it up to him. But what the hell can I do?"

"Now, Jack, you'll make the best of it, and maybe you'll marry again and get another good woman," she said.

"I couldn't marry again," he said.

"Time is a great healer, Jack," she said.

"It's my fault. I wasn't good enough for her. I wasn't. I used to come home cranky, and she would be so sweet. Peg, do you know that that woman was a saint," he said.

"She was lovely," Margaret said.

"She was so pretty when I first knew her. I was married to her nine years," he said.

"Well, Jack, we have to learn to face death," she said.

"Nine years, and it seems like it was only yesterday," Jack said.

Margaret sat silent, as if reflecting.

"I remember winning five bucks on the world series in 1906 and I bought her a new pair of shoes. Goddamn it, why did it have to be her? When you think of it, there're millions and millions of people on this earth, and she is the one that has to die. I walk around, you know, Peg, like I'm in a daze, and I see other men, and I say to myself, they got their wives and mine's dead," he said.

"And I walk around and see women, and I think, they're happy and look at me," Margaret said bitterly.

"Yes, it's enough to make me ask, is there a God?" Jack said.

"The good are so often called and they die young," Margaret said.

"It seems to me that the world could be run in a better way than it is," he said.

"We all must bear our crosses and some are heavier than others," she said.

Jack took out a cigarette, lit it. He tossed her a cigarette and matches. She lit up also.

"I'm gonna see if I got any bourbon left in the house," he said, getting up.

She watched him stride out of the room. Why did she stay here talking to him? She ought to go. But she had no place to go. It didn't matter if she was here, there, anywhere. Jack's wife was to be envied. She was dead. It was all over. She had no ache in her heart. Ah, what woman had an ache in her heart like hers?

"I found this bottle. Peg, can you drink it straight?" he asked.

"Yes," she said dully.

"Well, here, want to start it off?" he said, handing her the bottle.

She took a drink. He drank.

"That's good," he said, sitting down and setting the bottle at his feet.

"One or two drinks is good when you got the blues. But I don't want to let myself get drunk," she said.

"You won't, girlie. I don't wanna get snozzled myself. I been drinking too much. I got to pull myself together. You know, it was an awful shock. It takes time to get over such a shock," he said.

Margaret looked down at the carpet.

"Next June on our wedding anniversary we was going to go away on a vacation, up to some lake resort, and I was gonna give her the chance to get away and get a little rest."

"There's no rest for an aching heart," she said.

"Goddamn it, we got to quit sittin' here like we was in a morgue. Let's drink another to buck up," he said.

He handed her the bottle and she took a long gulp.

"Say, you can put it down, can't you?" he said.

"I wouldn't drink if I wasn't so unhappy," she said.

"Who the hell would? Well, here goes," he said, also taking a big swig.

She squashed her cigarette.

"I wonder what time it is?" she asked.

"Don't go. There's time. The kid won't be back. I sent him to his aunt's tonight."

"I got lots to do," said Margaret.

"Forget it. Stick around, Peg. I don't like to be alone these days. It makes me think of her when I am. I get feeling almost creepy. I think she's gone to the store and she'll be home now, or that she's in the next room, or that she's cooking supper. And then I realize she's dead. She's out there in the cemetery. I won't see her again. It gives me a creepy feeling. I can't get used to it," he said.

And Lorry seemed to be farther away from her than if he was dead. If he was dead, he wouldn't be so far away. She wouldn't be so unhappy. She could bear the thought of him dead easier than she could the thought of him in the arms of another woman.

"Give me another drink," she said.

"Here," he said.

She drank.

IV

"What the hell are you laughing about?" he asked when she broke into another ripple of drunken laughter.

The bottle was almost empty. He took another drink. She laughed again.

"Say, what in the hell are you laughing about?"

"I'm laughing."

"What the hell do you see to laugh at?"

"I'm happy. Come and laugh and be happy with me," she said, and again she broke into laughter.

"Five minutes ago you were crying. Now you're laughing," he said.

"Tears and laughter," she said, continuing to laugh.

"Hey, for Christ sake, cut that monkey laugh out, will you?"

"Then I'll sing. Want to hear me sing? I used to have a beautiful voice," she said.

"I don't want any songs," he said.

She stood up, swayed, sang in a drunken singsong:

> *When you and I were young, Maggie,*
> *When you and I were young, Maggie.*
> *When you and I were young, Maggie.*

"Can't you stop that singing?"

"Don't you like my singing?"

"No."

"I like my singing."

"I don't like your singing."

"I like my singing. He don't like my singing."

"Oh, for Christ sake, can it. Here, have another drink."

"Have another drink. Do I want another drink? Yes, I want another drink."

She staggered to him, picked up the bottle, took a long drink.

"Leave a little for me."

"There," she said.

She sat down and looked stupidly at him.

"You know, she knew she was never gonna come back when she was taken out of here to the hospital that night."

"Everybody's gonna die."

"She knew it. She didn't want to die because of me and the kid."

"I don't believe in God," she said, getting to her feet.

"Oh, quit chattering," he said.

"Chattering like the bird. Hear the little birdies in the yard? Hear the little birdies chattering in the yard?"

"Do you always get like this when you drink?"

"The little birdies do not sing. The little birdies chatter in the yard, chatter in the yard."

Jack sat, looking at her, annoyed.

"If you had a piano, I'd play the piano. I could have been a wonderful piano player, but I didn't let myself learn. I could have been anything and I ruined my life. My life is ruined."

Jack took a drink. He went to Margaret, led her to a chair and sat her down.

"Now I'll bet you you can keep still."

She looked docilely at him. They sat for several minutes without talking.

"I kept still," she said.

"Shut up!"

"No gentleman talks that way to a lady," she said.

"Where's the lady? For Christ sake, you don't call yourself a lady?" he said, and then he laughed ironically.

"Am I a lady? I am a lady. I am an unhappy lady."

"I can't stand your damn chatter."

"You're no gentleman."

"Who asked you for your opinion?"

"If you were a gentleman you wouldn't raise your voice to me."

"I'm tired of your voice."

"You're tired of hearing my voice, are you? Who asked you to hear it?"

"Where the hell do you think you are?"

She rose, and looked around the room.

"Where am I? Where am I? Where am I?"

"Sit down!"

"Don't you insult me, Jack Doolin."

"A woman like you can't be insulted."

"Oh, is that so? Is that so? You pious hypocrite! And you're so sad about your wife. You're another damn masculine hypocrite."

"Get the hell out of my house before I throw you out."

"You got no more use for me now, so he says get out. I go in his bed and listen to him bellyache and that's all he wants. And now he says to get the hell out of his house. Jesus Christ, do you call this a house?"

Jack went to the coat rack and returned with her hat, coat, and pocketbook.

"Here, take these and get out before I lose my temper."

"I'm going out. Am I going out? Yes, I'm going out."

"Hurry up. I got to fumigate the house after you."

"He's going to fumigate his dirty mind," she said, bursting into laughter.

He shoved her.

"Take your hands off me or I'll scream until I get the police."

"Well, get out then."

"I'm going."

"Hurry up! I can't stand looking at you."

"You could when I was in bed with you, though, couldn't you? Couldn't you? Couldn't you?"

"See that door? If you ain't through it in five seconds, I'll knock you through it and you can call the damn police."

She cowered away from him.

"I'm going. I don't stay with little cigars who ain't gentlemen," she said, staggering to the door.

"And to think I had you in her bed! God Almighty!" he said.

She went to the door.

"Goodbye and screw yourself, you hypocrite," she said, slamming the door.

He rushed to the door, opened it. She was staggering upstairs to her own apartment.

"Close that door or I'll scream till the neighbors know what you are."

He closed the door. She went up to the second story, sat on the landing, and looked at her fingers.

"One finger, two, and two fingers makes four fingers, and one makes five, and five makes ten little fingers," she said to herself and started laughing.

She sat on the landing, studying her fingers.

33

I

Al let himself in the door, and as he closed it Sadie came forward.

"Hello, Al," she said.

"Why, hello, Sadie. Well, well, well, how are you?"

"Oh, I'm pretty good, Al. How are you?" she said, her tired and haggard face belying her words.

"Pretty good myself, Sadie. I had to pass through town and I dropped in as a surprise for a day or two. Where's Mother?"

"Oh, here's my son," Mrs. O'Flaherty cried, hastening down the hallway.

Al embraced her.

Then he started looking at the mail by the hall tree; there was a stack of it for him.

"Why didn't anybody forward my mail? I haven't gotten any for over two weeks," he said, annoyed.

"Al, sure, she has the life plagued out of all of us," Mrs. O'Flaherty said.

"What do you mean, Mother?" he asked, wrinkling his brow with sudden worry.

"It's Peg, Al. She's been drunk again."

"Jesus Christ!"

"She's been drunk for weeks like a pig."

"Just a minute until I put my suitcase away," he said, going into his bedroom off the hall. He set the suitcase on the bed, hung up his hat and coat, and stood for a moment by the street window, looking out at the silently falling snow.

"Al, that Protestant devil did it," Mrs. O'Flaherty said.

"What's this?" he asked, swinging around to face his mother and frowning.

"I think that she's coming out of it now, Mary," Sadie said.

"Al, the Devil has her. One night me and Lizz had to pray over her, and then we had to have Doctor Geraghty. And she was no sooner up again than she was hitting the bottle."

"How long has this been going on?"

"Al, it's been over a month. And, Al, Jack Doolin's wife is dead, and she's running around with him, drinking with him, and that poor woman not cold in the ground hardly. Al, she has no shame."

"Jesus Christ! And there isn't even anyone around here to forward my mail or anything. Goddamn it!"

"Al, sure, I was waiting for you to come home. She has the life plagued out of all of us. Glory be to God, she's been nothing but trouble. The storekeepers on Fifty-first Street stop me on the street and ask me for money she's borrowed, and I'm ashamed to show me head on the block for what she's done and the holy show she's made of herself and us all."

"She wrote me that the kids were troubling her. Goddamn them, why can't they behave?"

"Al, don't believe a word of it. It's a lie, a black lie. The little ones have been as quiet as a mouse. You wouldn't know they were in the house. She won't let them be at their books of a night even. It's a wonder we're not all dead with her."

"She wrote me that Bill hit her in the breast and she was afraid he had given her cancer of the breast."

"Ah, and that he might have."

"Mother, don't say such awful things," Al said.

"If it weren't for William, we'd be dead. He was the one that wouldn't let her turn the gas on," Mrs. O'Flaherty said.

Al paced back and forth across the room.

"And have you been staying here, Sadie?"

"Yes, I've been trying to take care of her."

"How long?"

"Over two weeks."

"And you haven't been able to sober her up, either?"

"I tried to, Al."

"Sure, she's had this poor sick girl here doing everything for her, watching her night and day."

"And she promised me that she was through drinking," Al said, hurt.

"Me eye with her promises, Al, they don't mean a word."

"She promised me on her word of honor that she'd never touch another drop," Al said.

"But, Al, I think that she'll sober up now," Sadie said.

"How has Danny been? Has he behaved?"

"The poor boy, having to see her running around in her pelt, my heart has been aching for him and his little sister."

"Well, let's hope that she doesn't drink any more."

"Al, we've done nothing but throw bottles out all week. She hides them, and then she goes out for more, borrowing money right and left to pay for them."

"And what's this about Doolin?"

"His wife died of an operation and she's after him now. Al, Al, it ain't decent."

"What do you mean?"

"I think she just helped the poor fellow out when he was so distracted," said Sadie.

"Ah, I know better. I know better. Sure, didn't she drink with him and then cut up until she told us herself that he threw her out of his house."

"Have you tried to talk to her, Sadie? Maybe she could be kidded into sobering up," Al said.

"I tried, Al. But I don't know. She'll promise to stop, and you believe her, and suddenly when your back is turned she's off again," Sadie said.

"Where is she?"

"Sleeping," Sadie said.

"Al, this poor sick girl hasn't the strength to be watching her," Mrs. O'Flaherty said.

"I'm perfectly willing to do anything I can to help Peg out," Sadie said.

"There's nothing to do but bring Father Mulligan down to her and have him shame her. He'll shame her and make her be good."

"Well, let's hope for the best," Al said disconsolately.

II

Margaret stumbled into the dining room just as the family was beginning to eat. Her face was dirty, and she kept blinking her eyes like one trying to accustom oneself to sudden light.

"Hello, Al. I didn't know you were coming home," she said.

"Well, well, well, if it isn't the slim Princess herself. Slip us a kiss," Al said, jumping up, embracing her, and giving her cheek a pinch.

"I'm hungry," she said.

"Here, sit down, Peg, and I'll fix you a plate and things," Sadie said.

Sadie went to the kitchen, returning with a plate, knife, and fork for Margaret.

"Sure, you eat, Peg, and we'll have a nice family supper," Al said.

"Ah, Al, there's been no peace in the house since you left," Mrs. O'Flaherty said, ignoring Al's signal to her.

"Sure there has, and there's going to be," Al said.

"I've been sick, Al," Margaret said.

"Well, you're going to be better now, aren't you? Come on, Peg, say yes and flash us a sunny smile," Al said.

"Al, you simply got to do something with him," Margaret said unexpectedly, pointing an accusing finger at Danny.

Danny glanced at his aunt, shocked, surprised, injured.

"Danny didn't do nothing," Little Margaret said.

"No, I didn't do nothing," Danny said timidly.

"Al, she's lying," Mrs. O'Flaherty said, again ignoring Al's signals.

"Al, I can't sleep with him in the house. And when his brother is here they're driving me out of my head with that dice game of theirs. I curse the day you ever brought that game into this house. And his brother can't come here any more. You got to choose. Either Bill O'Neill doesn't come inside these doors or I go," Margaret said, talking with a mouthful of food.

"What has my brother Bill done?" Little Margaret asked.

"You keep out of this. You're to be seen and not heard now," Al said to his niece curtly.

"Al, as true as I'm sittin' here, the children haven't done a thing," Mrs. O'Flaherty said.

"She protects them. She doesn't give two hangs in hell for me. She protects them," Margaret said.

"Come, Peg, eat your pork chop there before it gets cold," Sadie said.

"Let me alone. I'll have my say. I'm not the servant around here. I think I'm entitled to some consideration," Margaret said childishly.

"Of course you are! Of course you are," Al said.

"Then answer me! Does that dirty little thief, Bill O'Neill, come into this house or doesn't he?" Margaret challenged.

"Of course he doesn't," Al said.

"Al, she sits here and lies. She's been drunk for a month, and then she blames those poor little boys," Mrs. O'Flaherty said bitterly.

"You were drunk yourself. And it hasn't been the first time. You old hypocrite, you, rushing your can of beer and judging others. I was driven to it. I was driven to it by her and by that little bastard and his brother!"

"I didn't do anything. You can't say that and tell lies about me," Danny said in a sudden flash of spirit.

"Keep still, Danny!" Al said.

"Don't you do it, Son! Tell her! Tell him what's she done," Mrs. O'Flaherty said.

"I can't call my home my own. With my poor nerves, what did I get? All of the time nagging. Those two fighting," Margaret said, pointing to Danny and his sister. "It's enough to drive anyone to drink. I wouldn't have touched a drop if I lived in a decent house. I didn't have a nerve left in my body and I was driven to it."

"Peg, please don't go exciting yourself. Now be quiet and let's settle these difficulties amicably," Al said.

"I swear by everything that's holy that she's lying," Mrs. O'Flaherty said.

"You've already called me everything you could think of. Go ahead, call me a liar!"

"Here! Here! Let's have peace in the house," Al said.

"There can be no peace with that one around."

"Mother, for God's sake, please!"

"It's no use talking to her. She's got fight in her bones," Margaret said.

"Indeed I have, and I'll always have when there's one in me presence who don't act decent."

"Please, Mother!" Al begged excitedly, screwing up his face as he talked.

"Please and be damned! Please and be damned!" Mrs. O'Flaherty exclaimed.

"It's all right, Al, I'll leave. I'll go. I can't stand it any more. I'll go. My life is ruined. I have no peace at home. This isn't home to me. I've had every nerve in my body shattered," Margaret said.

"And it's good riddance when you leave," Mrs. O'Flaherty said.

"Jesus Christ, Mother!" Al exploded.

"Don't be cursing at me that bore you!" Mrs. O'Flaherty said to her son.

"See for yourself, Al! That's what I put up with every day of my life, every day of my life," Margaret said.

"Now, here, let's all be quiet and count to ten and be calm. There's no good comes from these recriminations," Al said.

"Indeed I won't be quiet with that one sitting at this table," Mrs. O'Flaherty said.

"I don't care. I give up. It's useless. A saint couldn't live with the mother I got. She drove Father to his grave, and she'll drive me there. She's made it a walking hell on earth, a walking hell on earth," Margaret said.

"Peg, you're just excited and nervous," Sadie said.

"Please don't fight, Aunty Margaret," Little Margaret said.

"She made me a nervous wreck," Margaret sobbed.

"Well that I done it then," Mrs. O'Flaherty said.

"She's even glad she did it. Look at the way she gloats," Margaret said.

"Oh, good Jesus Christ!" Al exclaimed, raising his hands as though to pull his hair.

"Ah, that I might have dropped your head on the floor when you were a baby and let you die. I'd be the happier woman now in me old age," Mrs. O'Flaherty said.

"Mary! Peg!" Sadie said in a worried, ineffectual tone.

Al rushed to his mother's side.

"Come out in the kitchen and help me get the tea," he said.

"Take your hands off me," Mrs. O'Flaherty said to her son as he tried to lift her out of the chair.

"He can see for himself now, Sadie, what I put up with," Margaret said.

"Please, Aunty Margaret," Danny begged.

"Shut up, you dirty little O'Neill brat!" Margaret screamed.

"Hey, Dan, nix! Nix!" Al said, standing by his mother's chair.

"Don't be talking that way to me grandson. You won't in my presence," Mrs. O'Flaherty said, glaring at her daughter.

"Sadie!" Al said, and he nodded at Margaret and gestured with his left hand, signaling Sadie to get his sister out of the room.

"Come on, Peg, you need to lay down. I'll bring the rest of your supper to you in your bedroom," Sadie said, placing her hand on Margaret's arm.

"I can't stand this any more," Margaret said, getting up.

She let Sadie lead her out of the room, and they could hear her choking sobs as she went to her bedroom.

"Crying will do her good," Mrs. O'Flaherty said.

"Mother, you shouldn't be so vindictive," Al said.

"I'm sick and tired of her," Mrs. O'Flaherty said.

"So am I. So are we all. Danny there doesn't like it, do you, Sport? Or his sister?" Al said.

Both children looked sadly at their uncle and shook their heads from side to side.

"Mother, you mustn't antagonize her when she's this way. She has to be humored a little. Don't pour oil on the blazing fire," Al said.

"The Devil take her! She's been carrying on like this long enough," Mrs. O'Flaherty said.

"Try to humor her! Try not to fly off the handle, Mother, please, for the sake of a little peace in this house," Al said.

"Humor her? I'll humor her with a stick!" She looked at Danny and said tenderly, "Son, eat your supper."

"Yes, Sport, and you, too, Little Margaret, eat your suppers," Al said in a kindly tone.

The supper was finished in a tense silence.

III

"Here, Sport, take your sister with you and go see the moving-picture show. But come straight home from it," Al said, patting Danny on the head.

"Thank you, Uncle Al," Danny said.

"Thank you, Uncle Al," Little Margaret said.

Al walked to the door with them, patted both their heads. He heard a murmuring voice from his sister's room, and his mother was out in the kitchen singing mournfully as she washed the supper dishes.

He filled a pipe and sat smoking in the parlor in the dark. He saw the boy and girl running down the street. Danny jumped over a fence in the snow, jumped back onto the sidewalk. He remembered a line from a poem of Longfellow's that he had once read:

The thoughts of youth are long, long thoughts.

The children disappeared from sight. Prairie was quiet, dark, and the darkness seemed almost like a gloomy presence, a presence bearing in itself all the sadness of a human lifetime. There were people walking along, seeming happy. He puffed. What he had always wished for in his own house was just a little peace, a warm hearth filled with love. And instead, look what his home was. A sister always drinking. The two children having to witness that, to live in it. It was a bad example for them. He himself, he had not had any too happy a childhood. He wanted both of the children to have a better childhood than his. And it would be if there wasn't so damn much fighting and drinking in the house. Oh, good Jesus Christ, couldn't anything be done to stop it? A woman should be a lady, like a flower, a beautiful and noble creature made by God to be an ornament of beauty, a home-builder, a mother, a comfort and a joy in life. And so many women were. And what was his own sister? He puffed away at his pipe. And just when business was getting good all over, and money was being made because of the war, just when he was looking ahead to his best year as a salesman, he had to come home to this. It was damn lonely living night after night in hotel rooms, and then, to come home like this!

He puffed away at his pipe.

He wanted to know what in the name of all holy Harry he could do to help Peg stop drinking and cutting up. What was it that made her do it? Was it in her blood? Her heredity? He and Ned didn't, although Ned took a sip now and then. Christ, he'd do any damn thing on earth if he could only help her stop it, and only make their home a place of peace and comfort, a sanctuary. He sat puffing at his pipe. He suddenly got up, went to his room, and took out a mouth organ. He closed the door and stood before his dresser mirror, softly playing old-time popular songs, songs which had, in his youth, become inextricably bound up with all that he had hoped for from life.

34

I

"Daniel, I had you stay after school to help me because you've studied so well and have done good work, and your deportment in school has been excellent. If you keep up this work, Virginia Doyle and Albert Throckwaite will have to be careful or you'll be getting a higher average than they get," Miss McGinnis said.

Danny smiled shyly at her. She was a young woman in her twenties, with blue eyes, a round pretty face, and a well-built figure.

"You're becoming a good pupil, Daniel," Miss McGinnis said.

"I study and do my homework," he said.

"Now, you go and clean the erasers for me," she said.

He went to the blackboard and collected the erasers, passing Virginia Doyle who, along with Albert and Hortense Audrey, had also stayed after school to help Miss McGinnis. He said nothing to Virginia. He wanted to ask her to come to his birthday party. He could have it. Aunt Peg had said so. She seemed all right, and had been very nice at noon, only a little nervous. Without his mentioning it, she had said he should invite his friends to his birthday party. She called them his little friends. He had asked Hortense Audrey and she said she'd come. But he hadn't asked Virginia. He was afraid to. And he wanted to ask Miss McGinnis if her sister Bridget McGinnis would come. Bridget McGinnis was the prettiest girl in the fifth-grade class.

He covertly glanced at Virginia Doyle. She wore a dark blue dress with little red anchors on it, and she had a narrow blue ribbon around her hair. Her hair was nice and it fell down her back. She was talking now with Hortense Audrey. He wondered what they were talking about. Hortense Audrey had a big pink ribbon on her hair, where it was tied in the back. They were talking. He didn't know why he got kind of afraid when he was with girls, and he didn't know always what to say. He guessed of all the girls in school he wanted to get Virginia Doyle to be his girl. But he didn't have much chance. It looked like she was Albert Throckwaite's girl, all right. Al was a nice kid and he liked him. He said he was going to be a priest when he grew up. His father had a lot of money. He was an awful fast runner. Whenever they played tag before school started during the noon hour, nobody could catch Al, he ran so fast. He looked and talked like a sissy, but he wasn't, and he was a good ballplayer, too. He was smart in school and he wasn't afraid to talk to girls. Danny wished he was like Albert, and that kids liked him as much as they did Albert, and that he got along with girls as well as Albert did, and that Uncle Al had as much money as Albert's old man.

But, gee, it was swell to feel that Aunt Peg had gotten over her drunk and he would have his party and not have worry on his mind. He guessed, from the way she acted at noon and the way she talked, she was planning what she was going to do at home, planning to bake a cake for his party, and things like that.

He stood in the back of the room raising chalk dust as he beat the erasers against each other. The other kids were gathered around Miss McGinnis' desk, but he couldn't hear what they were saying. Miss McGinnis was nice, and she was young and pretty. Her sister Bridget was pretty, too. She was a tall, thin girl, and she had brown hair that hung down her back, and she always looked nice with the hair ribbons she wore. He liked girls to be pretty like Bridget McGinnis and Virginia Doyle were, with long hair falling down their backs.

He went on beating the erasers. He wanted to get through so he could go up and stand around while they were talking. He just wanted to stand near Virginia Doyle and Hortense Audrey. If one wouldn't be his girl, maybe the other would. And, gee, who was he going to take for his partner at the party? That was a problem. If he took Virginia Doyle, what about Al? But then he could have Al be Bridget McGinnis' partner if he could get her to come. How was he going to ask?

He beat the erasers slowly, noticing that Al was wiping off the blackboard now with a damp cloth and the girls were sorting papers for Miss McGinnis. How would he ask? Would he go to Virginia Doyle and say I'm having a birthday party Saturday afternoon, will you come? And should he ask if she would be his partner? No, he better let that go until the party. Because maybe she might want to come, but might not want to be his partner, and if he asked her to be his partner, too, she wouldn't come. And how would he ask Miss McGinnis if she would ask her sister Bridget to come? He went on beating erasers.

"Finished, Dan?" Albert asked.

"Yeah," Danny said.

"You got a harder job than I did. This is easier than beating erasers together," Albert said.

"I don't care."

"I guess the ice skating is over for the year," Albert said.

"Yeah, but in a little while we can play ball. What do yuh say we make up a baseball team out of the kids in the class?"

"That's a swell idea. We'll talk about it," Albert said.

"Say, Al, wanna do me a favor?"

"Sure, what is it?" Al asked, and Danny experienced relief; this was a swell idea. Why hadn't he thought of it sooner?

"Wanna do me a favor and ask Virginia Doyle if she wants to come to my birthday party?"

"Sure, I'll do it for you," Al said.

"Thanks, Al," Danny said.

"Finished, Daniel?" Miss McGinnis called.

"Yes, Miss McGinnis," he said.

Now he had to ask her about her sister.

"Well, we just have about everything done, and you children can go out and play now," she said.

"I'll put them back along the board," Danny said.

He went along the blackboard, arranging the erasers at regular places. He'd ask her. And, gee, Sister Marguerita must have kept her promise because Miss McGinnis had never shown that she knew about Aunt Peg. He was lucky in not having had the kids find out. And Tommy hadn't snitched. Tommy had asked him did he tell Sister Marguerita. And he'd told Tommy no, that Sister Marguerita had found out and guessed maybe Tommy knew about it living so near to his house. And Tommy said he wouldn't be blabbing it. He'd asked Tommy to the party but Tommy was home now, sick with chicken pox.

He saw Albert talking to Virginia. They came over to him and she smiled.

"I can come to your party. Thank you for asking me," she said, smiling at him.

She had really smiled at him.

"It's my birthday party," he said.

"How old are you going to be?" she asked.

"Eleven," he said.

"I was only ten last month," she said.

"I asked all the kids to come to it," he said.

"What time is it?" she asked.

"Three o'clock," he said.

"I can come, and thank you," she said, and she smiled again.

He went up to Miss McGinnis.

"Miss McGinnis?" he said, more confident because of Virginia's smile and acceptance.

"Yes, Daniel."

"I'm having a birthday party Saturday. I'm eleven years old. I wanted to know if you would ask your sister Bridget if she could come," Danny asked.

She smiled at him, showing a set of perfect white teeth.

"Why, she'd love to. Wait until I get a pencil and write down the address," she said.

Danny gave her his address.

"Thank you, Miss McGinnis," he said.

He went back to Virginia and gave her his address, too.

The children gathered around the teacher.

"Well, now you can go and play," Miss McGinnis said.

"I like to play in winter better than in summer," Hortense said.

"Why, Hortense?"

"Because in winter you can go ice skating. We went ice skating at the duck pond all the time this winter and we had lots of fun. Didn't we?" she said, turning to Albert and Danny, and they both nodded their heads in agreement.

"I can't skate," Virginia Doyle said.

"What do you like most to do?" Miss McGinnis asked Virginia.

"I like to go home and read books. I like to read *The Lives of the Saints*," Virginia Doyle said.

"I like to read books, but I like ice skating better," Hortense Audrey said.

"What do you like to do, Daniel?" the teacher asked.

"Play ball," Danny said.

"I know what he likes to do more than play ball, Miss McGinnis," Hortense Audrey said.

"What?"

"He likes to fight," she said.

"No, I don't," Danny said, blushing.

"Yes, you do, Daniel O'Neill. I watched you. You used to be fighting all the time when school started this year," she said.

"I like to play ball," Danny said.

"Fighting isn't nice, and you shouldn't like to fight. It isn't being a little gentleman to fight all the time," Miss McGinnis said.

"I don't never like to fight," Danny said.

"I watched you," Hortense Audrey said with a twinkle in her eyes. "Last fall you had lots of fights," she added.

"Did you, Daniel?" asked Miss McGinnis.

"Well, not a lot," he said.

"How many?"

"Oh, some," he said.

"Why?"

"I don't know. I just got in some fights," he said.

"Who won them?" asked Hortense Audrey.

"I won some and lost some," Danny said.

"You haven't been fighting of late?" asked Miss McGinnis.

"No, I ain't."

"You don't want to. If I hear of you fighting, I won't like you as much," she said.

"He will. I watched him. He likes to fight," Hortense Audrey said.

"No, I don't. Honest, I don't," Danny said.

"Well, you get your coats on and I'll close up the room, children," Miss McGinnis said.

The children scrambled into the dressing room for their coats.

"You do so like to fight. I saw you fighting all the time last fall," Hortense said to him.

"No, I wasn't. I couldn't help it," he said.

The children came out of the dressing room and walked out of the classroom ahead of Miss McGinnis. Danny started running down the hall just to show off in front of his teacher and the girls. Albert and the girls tagged by Miss McGinnis' side. They came out into the rectangular schoolyard, which was half covered with soiled, melting snow, the gravel showing through in many spots. An Italian passed down the alley calling out his vegetables, and Danny laughed at the foreigner's accent.

"Soon you children won't have this yard to play in. The men will start working on the new church in April," Miss McGinnis said.

"When will it be built?" Hortense Audrey asked.

"It will be started in April," the teacher said.

"How long does it take to build a church?" Virginia Doyle asked.

"Oh, it will take two or three years. But when it's built, Father Mulligan will have one of the most beautiful churches in the whole city. And it's so nice, you children have the chance to contribute to the window that the school is donating. When you are grown men and women you can come back and look at the window you built along with the rest of those in school," Miss McGinnis said.

"And when the church is built we'll all be big and in sixth or seventh grade," Hortense Audrey said.

"Some day when I'm big and become a nun, just think, I might come here and teach. Just think, I'll teach kids like us. Won't that be fun? And I'll tell them about how the church was before the new one was built, and how we all gave some money to put a window in the new church," Virginia Doyle said, clapping her hands together girlishly as she talked.

Danny glanced at her. He wanted to ask her if she was really going to become a nun, but there was a choke in his throat. He was beginning really to hope she might be his girl, since she had smiled at him just a little while ago in the classroom. But if she was going to be a nun she could never marry him when he grew up and was a rich man.

"Well, goodbye, children," Miss McGinnis said, leaving them at the school-yard gate on Forty-ninth Street.

"Goodbye," they chorused.

"I got to go down Grand Boulevard. I'll walk to the corner with you kids," Danny said.

"Are you really going to be a nun, Virginia?" Albert asked as they drifted side by side toward the corner.

She smiled shyly, nodding her head yes, her blue eyes flashing as she did so.

Danny was glad they were walking slowly. But, gee, only half a block and he had to leave them.

"I'm gonna be a priest when I grow up," Albert said.

"Maybe you'll be a priest here and I'll be a Sister, and you'll come to my room when I'm teaching just like the priests sometimes come to see us in the classroom," Virginia Doyle said.

"That'll be fun," Albert said.

"When I'm a woman I don't know what I'm gonna be," Hortense Audrey said.

"Not a washerwoman," Danny said, trying to say something funny.

"I won't be a Four Eyes," Hortense Audrey said.

Danny laughed, trying to pretend that he was not wounded by her jibe.

"Who all's going to your party?" Hortense Audrey asked.

"You kids, and Jennie Conlan, and Joe Conlan, and Miss McGinnis' sister, and Perc Dineen, and Jimmy Keogh, and all the kids," he said.

"Well, here we are at Grand Boulevard," Al said.

"I got to go down," Danny said.

"So long, Dan," Al said.

"Goodbye," Virginia said.

"You go that way?" Hortense Audrey asked.

"Yes, I gotta go this way," Danny said, not sure whether or not she was hinting for him to walk on home with them.

"Well, so long," Danny said, and he turned and ran down Grand Boulevard, pretending he was carefree, wanting them to watch him run off like this.

Halfway down the block he stopped, caught his wind and looked back. They were not in sight. He walked slowly. He couldn't wait until his party on Saturday. It would have to be a nice one with a cake. And he was so glad Aunty Margaret was sober. Oh, he hoped God would help him out by keeping her sober. But he was pretty sure that she meant it this time. Yes, she did. She had to. She had to be sober because of the party. He couldn't have them all there at the party and have them see her drunk and hear her cursing and swearing, and see her smoking cigarettes. And, gee, he had to figure out who was going to be partners with who. Now, should he take Virginia Doyle or Hortense Audrey for his partner? He had to figure it out. He really wanted Virginia Doyle. But then he could take Hortense Audrey. She had seemed to look at him in a way he wasn't sure about. And if he took Virginia Doyle and Hortense didn't like it, then she might be sore and he couldn't get either to be his girl. He wanted a girl, too.

He drifted dreamily along, and saw ahead of him the huge statue of George Washington on horseback dominating the entrance to Washington Park. He'd like to be a hero and the father of his country like George Washington. He couldn't be like George Washington. George Washington had never told a lie. He had. He had told lies to God. He had told lies about Bill. He had told Sister Marguerita a lie about Mother. But then, suppose he was like George Washington and never told a lie and was the father of his country, and had a statue of himself put up, riding on horseback with his sword held in the air like that statue ahead of him. Girls like Virginia Doyle and Hortense Audrey would come and look at it and be proud of him. Maybe that would even be better than being a great baseball star like Eddie Collins or Ty Cobb.

He'd be a general in war and win the war for America, and they'd put up a statue for him like the one they had put up here for George Washington. Only George Washington was dead and couldn't come around to look at the statue of himself. But George Washington must be in Heaven and could look down from Heaven and see the people looking at his statue and hear them say what a great hero he was. But wouldn't it be so much better not to be dead and be a hero and the father of your country, and come around and look at your own statue and hear the people say what a great hero you were? After you got to Heaven you could still look down on it like George Washington must do.

He turned the corner of Fifty-first Street. It was getting kind of dark, and by the time he got home there wouldn't be any time to go out and play. But he didn't care. It had been more fun staying after school and beating out erasers and talking to them, and he had gotten Virginia Doyle to come to his party, and Bridget McGinnis, too. Now, if he was older and in fifth grade instead of fourth, he might want her to be his girl. He swung his books on the strap and trailed on, not seeing the street and its sights. Gee, he wished it was Saturday and the party was started. Maybe they could play post office and he would call in Virginia Doyle and kiss her. Oh, if Aunty Peg only stayed sober now and didn't spoil the party.

35

I

"Al, I'm all right now," Margaret said, with self-possession, seated at the table after supper had been eaten.

"We're going to forget it all now. You're our slim Princess, Peg," Al said.

"I was just so upset," Margaret said.

"That's all right! That's all right, Peg. Now we've forgotten it. It's all forgotten in the book of the past, and this evening begins a new chapter in the book of the future," Al said.

"Maybe Sadie and I will go to a moving picture tonight," Margaret said.

"Sure, go. It'll do you good," Al said.

"Yes, I'll go with you if you want me to, Peg," Sadie said.

"I need a day or two of rest and then I'll be able to go back to work. I telephoned the hotel this afternoon and I told them I was better and I'd be able to go to work next Monday," Margaret said.

"Ah, Peg, you're lucky to be able to go back after being off so much time," Mrs. O'Flaherty said.

"They know that I'm their best cashier. They're so nice to me. I get along very nicely with everyone, even the bus boys. The bus boys all adore me."

"Well, I'm glad you're yourself again, Peg. From now on everything is going to run smoothly and according to order in this house. Now, do you kids remember that?" Al said, looking at Danny and Little Margaret. They nodded their heads affirmatively. "Everything is going to be in its place. No fighting about who gets in the bathroom to wash first in the morning. No shouting or running in the hall. If your aunt is asleep, you aren't to be yelling like wild Indians in the yard. In that case take the children you are playing with further away. No pouting about doing your duties. You're both going to help your aunt and grandmother keep the house clean."

Again the children nodded their heads.

"Al, yes, as true as I'm alive and sitting here, I'm through. You know me, Sadie, and so do you, Al. You know that when I really say I'm through, I mean it. When I say I'm through, you could place a whole tableful of bourbon and gin before me on this table and I wouldn't touch one drop of it. That's me. I have will power, and when I say I'm through drinking, I mean it. Now I only need a day or two of rest, and then I'll be my old self again. Tomorrow I'm going to clean the house, and it is going to be spick and span for Little Brother's party. I'm so glad he's having it. I promised him he could months ago, and he would have been so disappointed. Ah, Little Brother, your aunt loves you and, Little Margaret, she loves you, too."

"They're such sweet children," Sadie said.

"I'm careful who I let him take up with. I don't let him run with every tinker and Tom, Dick, and Harry along the block," Mrs. O'Flaherty said.

"Mother loves him so, and she watches over him just like a hawk," Margaret said.

"He's behaving better, isn't he?" Al said, smiling.

"Yes, this afternoon when they came home, I was sleeping, and they were so quiet. You could have heard a pin drop in the house. I got a nice rest, and it did me good," Margaret said.

"Fine, Sport. Fine, Little Margaret," Al said.

"And Mother is such a darling dolly. Mother, you do forgive me, don't you?" Margaret said.

"Of course she does. Of course Mother does," Al said.

"I was so bad and so much trouble. I could cry to think of all the trouble I was. But I learned my lesson. I'm through now. Never again for me. No sirree!" Margaret said.

"Now, Peg, don't you go brooding or casting self-recriminations on yourself. Forget it. You want to laugh now and be happy and think of nice things, sunshine and joy. It's all over," Al said.

"And Sadie here has been so kind and considerate. She's been such a darling, such a help and comfort to me. I don't know what I would have done during these trying days without you, Sadie," Margaret said.

"Peg, I'd always do anything I could to help you," Sadie said.

"Sadie, dearie, I don't know how I can ever really repay you for your kindness and understanding, for what you've done to help me. But that's all right, Sadie, I'm sure I'll be able to get you a job next week, and then you can get a nice little place for yourself and I'll help you fix it up sweet. I'll look for it with you," Margaret said.

"Well, we're not having any more drinking in this house," Mrs. O'Flaherty said, and Al frowned at her.

"You don't have to worry. You couldn't bribe me to take a drink," Margaret said.

"It's a chapter out of the past and let's not even trouble ourselves discussing it," Al said.

"Sadie, my brother Al is so understanding," Margaret said.

"Come on, Peg, slip us a kiss, and then I'm going to walk over to see Mike," Al said, rising.

He embraced his sister and kissed her cheek chastely.

"Now, Al, you have a nice visit with Mike. Tell him I'm all right now, and I'm so sorry. Tell him that that isn't my normal self. And send my regards to his lovely wife. Oh, Sadie, Mike Geraghty has such a lovely wife," Margaret said.

"Well, goodbye. You kids be good now," Al said.

"Oh, Al, they will. They're so lovely. And Little Brother, your aunt is going to help you make your party for your little friends so nice," Margaret said as Al went to the front to put on his coat.

II

"Sadie, call the Hotel Shrifton and see if Lorry is registered," Margaret said to Sadie as soon as Al had left.

"I called yesterday and they said he wasn't in, but if you want me to I'll call again."

"Here's a slug. Call and find out. I have a hunch he's there and I got to see him. I got to. And I got to get some money. God, Sadie, why did you, why did everybody let me do those things? Why was I let borrow money right and left? I'm ashamed to walk down Fifty-first Street, I owe so much money."

"Now, Peg, you mustn't let that worry you. Here, let me call for you."

Margaret followed Sadie to the telephone and anxiously stood over her while Sadie gave the operator the number.

"I hope he is. He must be. I got to see him," Margaret said.

"Desk clerk, please," Sadie said.

"He's got to be in," Margaret said.

She lit a cigarette and waited while Sadie asked if Mr. Robinson was registered.

"Oh, God, what'll I do?" Margaret said when Sadie hung up.

"I'm sorry, Peg. They say he isn't registered," Sadie said.

Margaret went to her bedroom. Sadie followed her. Margaret stood brooding in the center of the room.

"Come now, Peg, let's see the moving-picture show."

"I will. I'm all right. I was just thinking, Sadie. I'm all right. And, Sadie, you couldn't pay me enough money to take another drink. I'm all right. I just want to think and collect my thoughts a minute. Then we'll go to the show," Margaret said.

Sadie sat on the bed, sadly watching her cousin.

III

Al lit a cigar, settled himself comfortably in a chair in Mike's office, puffed, watched clouds of smoke float to the ceiling.

"I didn't expect you'd be in town, Al."

"I came in because of the domestic situation," Al said.

"It's tough on you, Al," Mike said.

"Well, it's all cleared up now. When I left home everything was fine and dandy, Mike. I think my sister's all right now. I kidded her into bucking up," Al said.

"Al, I want to talk frankly to you. You coddle her too much."

"Mike, you know, you have to be psychological with people. You have to use a different psychology on one kind of person than you do on another. Take my mother now. She does everything to get my sister going. I don't. I kid her."

Al reflectively dumped ashes into a tray beside him.

"She's all right, you say?" Mike said.

"She told me so. And she seemed to mean it. I wouldn't have left the house if she wasn't."

"She told me that, too. I was called over, you know."

"Yes. Was she badly off?"

"Well, she was getting over the d.t.'s, that's all. She wasn't in any serious danger. Just the aftereffects of delirium tremens. I kept her in bed and gave her something to put her to sleep. The last time I saw her she was satisfactory. I'll tell you what was the matter with her, Al. When I treated her, I felt that I wasn't treating a woman. I felt that I was called in to treat a distillery," Mike said.

Al's face saddened.

"She says she has bad nerves," Al said.

"I know. She's as strong as a horse, Al. She's got a constitution like iron. Al, if you or I tried to drink the way she does when she gets going, know where we'd be? We'd be taking a nice little trip in a six-foot box."

"Well, I hope that the domestic difficulties are ironed out now."

"I hope so, Al, for your sake. How's the other branch of your family?"

"My sister, Lizz?" Al asked.

"Yeah."

"She's on the Stork Special again, Mike," Al said.

"She's knocked up again?" Mike said.

"I've tried to tell her that she has to do something to restrain her husband's impetuosity. But you can't talk to her."

"I see that all the time. They got poor families around here on the other side of the railroad tracks, and they're like rabbits, Al."

"Human beings don't practice enough self-restraint. Mike, the more I live, the more I learn that. If there was more self-restraint, more self-discipline in the world, this would be the happy world that God made it to be."

"You can't get much self-restraint that way. I get kids coming in here, and I ask them, why did you do it? Look what's happened to you now. You've risked your happiness in life. Think it does any good?"

"Social diseases, huh, Mike?"

"Yeah. The town's full of it. You can't get any sense into lots of people, Al."

"Take some of these salesmen I see on the road. They know if they drink all night they'll have a head as big as a house, feel like hell, and they'll not be able to tend to business in the morning. But do you think that deters them? Not on your life. They'll sit up all night, taking one shot after another. I'll see them the next day, and goddamn it, they start bellyaching that they're sorry they did it. They don't know why they drank so much. All right. I go on to another town. I meet them again. There they are, trying to drink out the saloon. And I meet them again and they tell me the same story."

"That makes me laugh, Al. I got one fellow whose wife is always coming to me. First she comes to me, and then she goes down to Father Kiley. Her husband, Pat Cooney, can't stay on the water wagon. So I meet Pat on the street, and I say hello to him and ask him, 'Pat, are you on the water wagon?' And he's ready with an answer. He went on a terrible spree not so long ago, and got the hell kicked out of him in a saloon. I had to put two stitches over his eyes. Well, he says to me, 'Doctor Mike, I got two enemies in the world. One is the King of England and the other is whiskey. Well, we're going to free Ireland and put the King under the ground, and I'm going to drink up all the whiskey in the world. And when that happens, ah, Doctor Mike, I'll be the most exemplary of men.'"

They laughed.

"But tell me, Al, how is business?"

"Fine, Mike. Fine. I had one of my best trips in years."

"The war, huh, Al?"

"Business has been going fine ever since the start of the year, and it's going to get better. Every town I go to I find that business men are hopeful and optimistic. The war's done it. I'm expecting this to be one of the best years I ever had," Al said.

"Al, I want to tell you something. Don't let your family be milking you of everything. Save something and invest it. Don't be a damn fool, now. It's a fine thing for you to take care of your family, and that's every man's duty. But don't be a fool. Your sister's drink cure last summer cost you a pretty penny, and I guess this one will, too, because I know how she pours money in the sewer when she does that. Now, you look out for yourself and invest some of the money you earn this year."

"I'm going to. Whatever I save, I'm going to put into railroad bonds. They're a sound investment."

"Yes, I guess they are. I'm glad you're going to do that. You got to look out for yourself, Al, you know."

"Well, things are promising for me on the business side. I believe that I'm going to have some good years now. What worries me is the domestic angle."

"I tell you, don't coddle your sister. You know, when I saw her, she tried to play on me. I didn't fall for it. If she sees you're going to fall for her line, she'll take advantage of you."

"Of course, you know the reason. It's that fellow Robinson. He seems to have dropped her cold."

"She had no right to monkey around with him."

"Her trouble, Mike, is her friends. She doesn't pick out the right kind of people to associate with. She's got a girl friend, for instance, named Myrtle Peck. Mike, she's vulgar. No refinement. No culture. Just one of those women who are out for a good time and thinks that the world's full of suckers. I don't know what it is in my sister, but she always finds that kind of person. If I could get my sister to associate with the right kind of people, people who would improve her, refined people, half the battle would be won."

"Well, there's a wild streak in her. She needs to be married to a nice fellow, but a fellow who isn't a fool and wouldn't coddle her. A dame like her, Al, needs a little bit of rough treatment. She has to be made to understand that you're not fooling with her. I tell you that because you're a friend, and I say it even if she is your sister. I tell you, Al, don't coddle her," Mike said.

"I don't coddle her. But Jesus Christ, Mike, you can't deal with her acting like a bull in a china shop."

"Al, I tell you you ought to get married and have more of a life of your own. You're over forty now. It's high time you got yourself married."

"Well, Mike, somebody has to look out for my mother and my nephew," Al said.

"And somebody has to look out for Al O'Flaherty, too. After all is said and done, Al, a man has to consider himself as well as his family. The years slip up on us. Why, it only seems like yesterday when I was in medical school. And now look, I'm middle-aged. A man has to think of himself, too, once in a while."

"Well, Mike, I'd be happy at home if I was sure my sister was settled down. I think she will now. I guess she received a jolt from that fellow. Once he's out of her life, I think she's going to be a good girl."

"She will if she isn't coddled," Mike said.

"Mike, have you been reading much lately?"

"I never get any time to read, Al."

"I met a fellow on the train, and he was telling me of an English writer named Thomas Hardy, I think that's his name. Yeah. Thomas Hardy. Said that Hardy's great stuff. So I read a book of his called *Jude the Obscure*. It's a little bit off color. Met a priest, too, and I asked him about it, and he said it was. But it's a classic, Mike. A classic you want to read. And then I read *Pickwick Papers* by Dickens when I was on the road. Gee, Mike, that's a great book. Ever read it?"

"No, I didn't. I read *Oliver Twist*."

"Pickwick is a darb, Mike, he's a darb. He's a very civilized man, and he is interested in life. He is always going around to learn. He has great curiosity. And he has friends. One of them is named Winkle. Mike, he's one of these fellows who talks big and is never able to accomplish anything. He pretends he's a sportsman and he can't shoot a gun. And he can't skate. You know the type, Mike, one of these birds who is all window and nothing in the store inside. I meet lots of them on the road, salesmen who talk in big figures, and you don't know how they earn their expense account. But, Mike, you want to read this book, *Pickwick Papers*. Pickwick is a real gentleman, and he's always getting in trouble. He gets in the funniest jams all of the time."

"Maybe I will. Say, Al, how have you been feeling?"

"Pretty good, Mike. I seem to be functioning these days like a good engine, all right."

"Your heart been causing you any trouble?"

"No, Mike."

"Just let me put a stethoscope to it."

"All right, Mike."

Al stood up, took off his coat and vest and shirt. Mike went to his case and returned with his stethoscope. Al opened his underwear. Mike listened to his heartbeats.

"All right. If you keep on taking a little care of yourself, that leakage you got won't be serious."

"I haven't felt in better shape in years, Mike," Al said, buttoning his underwear.

"Good. You take good care of yourself and that's smart."

"Yeah, Mike, a fellow who doesn't is a sucker," Al said.

He buttoned his shirt and went to a mirror to tie his tie.

"Mike, I wanted to tell you about this priest I met. Was going to Saint Paul, and we started to converse on the train. Some of the best conversation I ever had. Very smart man, fine priest and very intelligent. Mike, when it comes to gray matter in the old noodle, there isn't anyone to beat the priests. They get a thorough education. They study theology and philosophy, and philosophy is the queen of the sciences. Well, I was talking to him. Heard about an American philosopher named William James. His brother is a fine writer. Wrote a book called *Daisy Miller.* The story is laid in Rome. A wonderful book. He writes with a beautiful style. Well, Mike, I asked this priest about William James."

"I don't think I ever heard of him."

Al put on his coat and vest and sat down again. He lit a fresh cigar and Mike lit a cigarette.

"This priest, Father McKeon his name was, he told me that William James is one of the most dangerous opponents of the Church. Said he writes so beautifully and has such a wonderful style that he seduces people easy and they don't see the heresies he is writing."

"Well, Al, my philosophy is to live and be as healthy as you can, and be happy. You like to read a lot. You ought to have made a good lawyer."

"I would like to have been if I could have had the education. Well, the nephew will be a lawyer. I'm going to start training his mind soon. He's getting old enough to read *The Letters of Lord Chesterfield.* Ever read that, Mike?"

"No, Al, I haven't."

"Ah, that's a classic. It's the manual of a gentleman. He wrote these letters to his son, trying to train him, telling him how to be a gentleman. He was a gentleman, and he knew good form. Well-bred, he was. Well, I'm going to have the nephew read it. I don't want him growing up and getting all this rough stuff," Al said, and he leaned back his head, puffed, watched the smoke from his cigar.

"Is he a bit wild?" asked Mike.

"Oh, no. He's coming along. Getting good marks in school, too."

"How's the brother doing?" Mike asked, squashing his cigarette.

"I received a letter from him a couple of months ago. He was hopeful."

"He still selling shoes?"

"Yeah. He tied up with a new outfit and seems satisfied."

"That's good. Everything will be sweet for you then if this sister of yours behaves."

"I think she's going to now. She seemed herself again tonight at supper."

"Well, I hope so. And don't coddle her. It'll be a big mistake if you do."

"I don't, Mike. And I think she's going to be all right now."

"Say, let's go upstairs with the missus and have her make us a cup of tea, Al."

"All right, if it isn't any trouble," Al said.

They went upstairs to the dining room for a cup of tea.

IV

Al walked briskly along Garfield Boulevard. The night was crisp and clear and he breathed deeply, liking it, liking to breathe deeply of the good, clear air. A man needed fresh air in his lungs to live. He walked on and tipped his hat as he passed Saint Rose's church. It was a joy and a consolation to visit friends in a nice home, to see people who were enjoying a happy home life. The home was the cornerstone of life, he told himself, and, yes, it was a joy to be in a good, fine home. Mike and his wife Nora were fine people, as fine as human beings came. It was always a treat to visit them. He threw his cigar butt away and strode on.

Mike had suggested he get married. Years ago there had been Norah Keogh. Well, there was no use raking over dead ashes. She had been a lovely girl. Yes, she had lied to him and jilted him, but she had been a lovely girl, and he hoped that she was happy and contented, building a lovely home with the laughter of little ones ringing in the house. He couldn't get married with Mother and the little fellow, and now there was the girl, too. He'd be satisfied, just as he told Mike, if the domestic situation was cleared up and home was happy and peaceful. Well, he wasn't giving up hope. He had confidence in Peg. She wasn't a bad girl. She had made mistakes. What they must do at home was to make her forget. Any human being can make mistakes, and let him who is without sin cast the first stone. He had hope and confidence now, and if he let Peg know he had hope and confidence in her, then she would try to justify it. That was psychology. Psychology always helped along in such matters, and he would apply psychology with her. And kid her along. Tell her she's a slim princess and a lovely girl. That was what to do. That wasn't coddling her, either. It was using psychology, that's all. He had meant to talk to Mike more about psychology tonight. That priest had told him a lot about it on the train.

Again he breathed deeply. He looked up at the clear blue sky and then glanced around him at the boulevard. A fine snow was beginning to fall. Maybe it would get colder. Before he went away on Monday, if it got colder, he'd take Danny ice skating. When you raised a boy, you had to be a pal with him. And he must not forget to induce the boy to read *The Letters of Lord Chesterfield*.

He hoped the domestic situation was good and all was quiet on that front. Well, he'd send out a thought through the cosmos wishing it was, and try to make it that way. He'd send out a thought and maybe that would go home ahead of him and enter their minds and help make everything peaceful on the domestic front. There were many subtle ways of improving the domestic situation and one way was to send out thoughts.

He walked on home briskly, sending out thoughts which he hoped would help to assure peace when he got there.

V

"What did you wake me up for, you old whorekeeper, you goddamn toothless madam," Margaret screamed, coming out to the kitchen where Mrs. O'Flaherty sat eating.

"Get out of my sight before I call the curse of God down on you," Mrs. O'Flaherty said.

"To hell with you. Go on and start a whorehouse and do what you're best fitted to do. You'd make a better madam than you've made a mother," Margaret yelled.

Al came in unheard as Margaret yelled. He ran out to the kitchen without taking off his coat.

"Good jumping Jesus Christ! What the hell's going on here?" he asked.

"Al, she's drunk again. She ran away from Sadie at the show and just came home drunk. Look at her, Al!" Mrs. O'Flaherty said, rising, staggering herself.

Al turned to Sadie and the children who stood by her at the dining-room entrance.

"What's happened? How did they get this way?"

"I went to the show with her, and she said she was going to the ladies' room and wouldn't let me go with her. She never came back and just got home like this a little while ago. And when I came back, Mary was this way, too."

"What happened to Mother?" Al asked Danny.

"She went out and came back with a can of beer. And then she went out again," Danny said.

"Why didn't you stop her?"

"I couldn't," Danny said.

"Uncle Al, Mother called me names. She said she didn't want me living here," Little Margaret said, her eyes already red from tears; she sobbed.

"Peggy, now you dry your little eyes and let me put you to bed," Sadie said.

"Don't cry, Little Margaret. They're drunk," Danny said, himself on the verge of tears.

Al gave Danny his overcoat, suit coat, and derby to be hung up.

"Al, I want you to give her enough money to start a whorehouse. She'll make a better madam than a mother," Margaret shrieked.

"Jesus Christ! Shut up, you!" Al said to his sister, losing his temper.

"Da da, da dee! Da da de de! Da da da de! Da dadada dadada!" Mrs. O'Flaherty singsonged, jigging around her daughter with lifted skirts.

"Mother, go on into your room," Al said.

Mrs. O'Flaherty thumbed her nose at Margaret.

"Your ass looks like the face of the Devil! The Devil's already kissed your dirty ass!" Margaret shouted.

"That you may die a whore's death!" Mrs. O'Flaherty yelled at Margaret.

Al shoved his sister out of the kitchen. She shrieked, and Mrs. O'Flaherty followed, spitting at Margaret.

"Take your hands off me! Help! Murder! Police!" Margaret screamed.

"Put her in the bridewell! Give her over to the police!" Mrs. O'Flaherty said.

Al put his hand over Margaret's mouth as she attempted to shriek again. She bit it. He lost his temper, and his face reddened, flamed with anger. He swung at her with his left fist, catching her on the point of the chin. She dropped to the floor in the hallway. She lay whimpering on the floor. He looked at his hand.

"Hit her again! Kick her! Step on her!" Mrs. O'Flaherty shouted.

"Ooh, he killed me!" Margaret said in a low, melodramatic tone as Sadie bent over her and the children looked on, silent and frightened.

"Come on, you, go to your room and keep still!" Al said.

"Don't be pushing me!" Mrs. O'Flaherty yelled at her son.

"Come on, goddamn it, I stood enough of this. You get to your room and hold your tongue!" he said, and he pushed his mother into the kitchen, closed the door on her. He noticed the key in the door on his side and he locked it. Mrs. O'Flaherty pounded on the door.

"Sadie, I'm sorry this happened. Give me a hand, please, and we'll put her to bed. Good Jesus Christ!" Al said.

"He killed me," Margaret moaned, lying limp on the floor.

Al and Sadie picked her up and half carried her to her bedroom. Suddenly, at the edge of her bedroom doorway, she broke loose from them.

"You take your filthy hands off me! You just keep your hands to yourself, god-damn you! When I was a little girl, you hit me, beat me! You won't now, or I'll kill you! I'll kill you!"

Sadie stood by, helpless, almost in tears. In the kitchen Mrs. O'Flaherty shrieked for the door to be unlocked. Danny and Little Margaret sat looking at each other.

"What you gonna do about your party?"

"I don't know."

"You get out or I'll kill you!" Margaret shrieked.

"Peg, will you please shut up!" Al said, his voice low, tense but firm.

"Please, Peg," Sadie said.

"Sadie O'Flaherty, after all I done to you, turning spy on me for that damn little runt," Margaret yelled.

"I'm going. I won't stand this," Sadie said in tears.

"Sadie, please stay. Go out and watch the children and I'll make it up to you. And don't unlock the door to let my mother get out," Al said.

Sadie went out of the room and stood sobbing in the hallway.

"Get out of my room, you dirty little runt! I can't stand the sight of you with that goddamn hawk nose of yours. Why don't you get married? Won't any woman have you? Goddamn you!" Margaret yelled.

"I had enough from you," Al said.

"Help!" Margaret shrieked after Al had slapped her face.

He pushed her over to the bed, and she cried for help again.

"Shut up! Goddamn you, I told you I stood enough from you!" he said, and he again slapped her face.

"Help!" she cried.

"Sadie! Sadie, bring me a towel," Al called loudly.

"Murderer!"

"Shut up! Shut up!" he said angrily, slapping her face.

"Murderer! Murderer!" she shrieked.

"Shut up! Goddamn you, shut up!" he said, slapping and punching her.

With trembling hands, Sadie handed him the towel. He shoved it in Margaret's mouth. She tried to talk, twisted, and squirmed. Then she lay still. He took the towel out. She lay moaning on the bed.

"Oh, good God!" he exclaimed.

He walked out of the room and went to the dining room. He could hear his mother in the kitchen.

"The curse of God on you! May you never see the sight or light of God!"

He stood by the kitchen door. He clenched his fists. He relaxed. He raised his hands over his head in a gesture of helplessness.

Margaret moaned semi-audibly from her bedroom, and Sadie could be heard murmuring to her.

"May God strike every one of you! May He take you away with the black consumption for locking up your poor old mother!" Mrs. O'Flaherty shouted from the kitchen.

Al went into the dining room. He saw Danny and Little Margaret sobbing, shivering like persons stricken with cold.

"Pray for us, Sport. And you, too, Little Peggy," he said quietly in a trembling voice.

"The curse of God!"

"Murderer!"

Both mother and daughter shrieked from different parts of the apartment.

"Oh, God!" Al exclaimed, raising his hands slowly as if to implore Heaven, looking up at the ceiling, his face clenched in a grimace.

Danny and Little Margaret cried. Al sat down on a chair by the dining-room table, lowered his head, covering his eyes with his left arm. He sobbed. His body shook with each sob. Danny and Little Margaret cried hysterically. Sadie came into the dining room. Seeing them, she sat down, wearied, tears rolling down her yellowed unhealthy cheeks.

"The curse of God on you! Let me out or I'll tear the hair out of your scalps!"

Margaret staggered to the kitchen door and hammered on it.

"You foul-mouthed madam!" Margaret shrieked.

She turned, and wavered at the dining-room entrance, sneered at her brother, who continued sobbing with lowered head.

"You dirty brute!" she yelled.

Al continued to sob. Danny and Little Margaret were hysterical with fear. Sadie sat, worn and haggard. Margaret staggered back to her bedroom, went to the closet, took out a bottle of gin which she had hidden there, and gulped from it, the gin spilling on her chin, dripping onto her dress.

36

I

"Oh, they ought to be coming soon now," Danny said anxiously.

Danny went to the parlor window and looked down the street, seeing all its familiar details. The sidewalk was wet from melting snow. Georgie Doolin was riding his three-wheel bicycle. A grocery wagon passed. A group of children were in front of the moving-picture theater on the other side. He would be missing the serial today. Well, it was worth it. It'd be worth it all right if she didn't cause any trouble and disgrace him. Danny turned from the window and sat on the piano stool.

Little Margaret sat opposite him, wearing a white dress with white stockings, a blue taffeta ribbon sash and a broad ribbon of the same color on her hair.

"What girl's gonna be your partner?" she asked.

"I don't know. I ain't figured it out yet," he said.

"Who's gonna be my partner?"

"I'll figure it out when they all come and when we sit down at the table to eat," Danny said.

From the kitchen, Mrs. O'Flaherty could be heard excitedly talking to Martha, the colored washwoman who had been hired to help out because of the party. Bill came into the parlor.

"Well, Dan, how does it feel to be older?" he asked.

"I don't know. Say, Aunt Margaret was supposed to bake a cake for my party, but she went and fell off the water wagon all over again. So Sadie went out and bought one with money Uncle Al gave her to buy it with."

"What kind of presents will he get, do you think, Bill?" Little Margaret asked.

"How do I know?"

"Gee, won't it be awful if she starts yelling," Little Margaret said.

Danny didn't answer. He grew pale. He couldn't speak. If she came out and they saw her drunk and heard her curse! He didn't want to think of how awful it would be.

"Maybe she won't. She's asleep now, and maybe she won't wake up until after the party's over," Danny said.

"And maybe she'll wake up. You never know when she's going to wake up and make a lot of noise," Little Margaret said.

"You're a killjoy," Danny said.

"I wish they'd come. I want the party to start. Bill, do you like my hair ribbon? Sadie tied it for me."

"What?"

"You like my hair ribbon?"

"I didn't see it before."

"Sadie tied it nice for me. I told her I wanted to look nice for Danny's party and she tied it and told me I looked nice."

But she wouldn't look as nice as Virginia Doyle, and Hortense Audrey, and Helen Smith, who'd all be here soon.

And what about the partners? He still hadn't figured it out. He had to.

"Danny, what games we gonna play?" Little Margaret asked.

"Don't bother me. I'm figuring things out," he said.

II

"Is she all right, Sadie?" Mrs. O'Flaherty asked anxiously as Sadie came into the kitchen.

"I think so. She's quiet now. She's been sleeping, and now she's in bed, laying there, not saying much."

"I don't want her spoiling my grandson's birthday party."

"I don't think she will. She knows there's going to be a party, and she said she doesn't want to spoil it. She promised me she'll be good."

"Martha, hurry, hurrish! You fix the rest of those sandwiches for the children," Mrs. O'Flaherty said excitedly.

"Yes, mam," Martha said.

The bell rang.

"They're coming now. Hurry! Hurrish!"

"I'll go back with Peg to keep her in the room," Sadie said.

"Don't let that one out of the room," Mrs. O'Flaherty said.

III

There hadn't been any trouble from Aunt Peg so far. And the first one had come. Danny looked over at Bridget McGinnis.

Bridget sat in a corner on the divan, shy and blushing, her deep brown eyes roving about the room, avoiding the gazes the three O'Neill children were directing at her. She smoothed out her white silk dress and touched the deep red sash she was wearing, a sash that matched the broad red ribbon she wore on her long and rich, brown curly hair. Danny looked at her. He liked girls who had nice hair, hanging down their backs in curls. She had nicer hair than even Virginia Doyle or Helen Smith.

"They'll all be here soon," he said, to be saying something.

"I didn't think I'd get here so early. I thought others would be here first," Bridget McGinnis said.

She blushed and looked down at the floor.

"I like the tie you brought my brother for a birthday present," Little Margaret said.

"My sister picked it out and bought it for me yesterday," she said.

"Your sister's my teacher in school," Danny said.

"I know it. She told me you asked her to ask me to come to your party," Bridget said.

"I did," Danny said.

"They ought to be coming," Bill said.

The children fidgeted. Danny got up and went to the window. Not a sight of them yet. He wished they'd hurry up and come. Suppose they didn't come after promising to? No, they'd come.

IV

"Those brats come yet?" Margaret asked, lying in bed.

"I don't know how many have come," Sadie said.

"I wish they'd come and get their party over with and go home."

"An afternoon isn't long, after all, Peg. And you need rest and quiet."

"Rest and quiet when I'm going to have a house full of brats? Sadie, gimme some gin."

"You had enough. Now, please, Peg, try and straighten out and give it up," Sadie said.

"I want some gin."

"No, I won't give it to you. Al asked me not to."

"Al! I don't care what he asked. Gimme some gin."

"No, Peg, I won't. You got to straighten up."

"Do you want me to scream at the top of my voice?"

Sadie took a half-filled bottle of gin from the closet and poured out a shot.

"Do you want water for a chaser?"

"No. Gimme it."

Sadie handed Margaret the glass of gin. Margaret drank it down in a gulp.

"Al don't want me to drink! Al don't! You know what Al can do."

Sadie sat, silent, anxiously watching her cousin.

V

"You all came together," Little Margaret said to the group of children.

"I had to wait for Hortense," said Helen Smith, who wore a blue dress, and had no bow on her lovely long red hair.

"My mother was fixing me. She said she wanted me to look nice."

"You do, Hortense," Albert said, clean and shiny, wearing a blue serge suit, dancing pumps, and a Buster Brown collar.

"Yes," Danny said, to get in the conversation and give Hortense Audrey a compliment.

"And I forgot where I put the handkerchiefs I was bringing as a present," she said.

"Al's present was the funniest one," said Tommy Keefe.

"What do you mean?" Al asked, blanching a trifle.

"You brought him a paint box to draw with and he's the worst drawer in the room," Tommy said.

"I can learn," Danny said.

"I'll draw with them for him," Bill said, uncomfortable in a room full of younger kids. He wished a couple of fellows or a girl his own age had come.

"He's good in arithmetic," Jennie Conlan said.

Danny looked at Virginia Doyle, who was sitting beside Bridget. She was shy, blushing, silent, beautiful in her white dress and blue ribbons, with bows on her luxurious blonde hair. He was thinking. Bridget McGinnis was too big for him. Virginia would be his partner. Bridget could be Al's. And Hortense could be Joe Conlan's, and Helen Smith could be Jimmy Keogh's. Now, if Aunty Peg would only stay quiet and keep in her room.

The bell rang.

"It must be Perc," Danny said.

"He would be late," Tommy Keefe said.

Danny ran to answer the door. Pressing the buzzer in the hall, he listened at his aunt's closed door. There was murmuring conversation between her and Sadie. Well, so far nothing had happened. He ran back to the door, and the boys crowded around him.

VI

"This is a funny party," Helen Smith said.

"Why?" Perc Dineen asked.

"All the boys talk to the boys and the girls to the girls," said Helen Smith, and Danny reddened.

"Well, talk to me," Tommy Keefe said.

Danny wanted to say that they ought to play post office. But he couldn't get himself to do it. If only everything went all right now. There hadn't been any trouble yet.

Bill sat in a corner, and he smiled with yellowed teeth. He looked from the boys to the girls, all of them cleaned and scrubbed and shiny, the girls with ribbons and sashes and white stockings, huddled together, looking at one another and then at the boys. The blond-haired girl in the blue sailor dress, Jennie Conlan, she kept looking at Danny when Danny wasn't watching her. She must be sweet on him. Bill decided that afterward he was going to kid Danny.

"Are you in Danny's class?" Little Margaret asked Hortense Audrey.

"Yes," said Hortense.

"I'm in third grade. I'll be in fourth next year and I'm going to Crucifixion then instead of the public school."

"You go to the public school?" Virginia Doyle asked Little Margaret.

"Yes," Little Margaret said.

Bill still looked around, bored.

VII

"Martha, did you see the little girls? Ah, they're little dreams, the angels," Mrs. O'Flaherty said in the kitchen, watching Martha, who was stacking sandwiches on a platter.

"Yas'm," Martha said.

"Sure, they're the prettiest little dolls. I never saw such little dreams, the innocent angels," Mrs. O'Flaherty said.

"They all look like they come from good people," Martha said.

"If they didn't, they wouldn't be let in this house for my grandson's party," Mrs. O'Flaherty said proudly.

"Yas'm."

"If that one in the bedroom is only quiet," Mrs. O'Flaherty said.

"She sho' can drink, mam," Martha said.

"It's the Devil she drinks," Mrs. O'Flaherty said.

"The Devil sho' powerful, Mrs. O'Flaherty. If you let me take her to mah preacher and he prays over her, he'll drive the Devil from her," Martha said.

"You're a good Christian, Martha. But here, fix the candles on my grandson's birthday cake," Mrs. O'Flaherty said.

VIII

"Well, everybody's here now," Danny said, standing in the center of the parlor.

"Everybody you invited came?" Jennie Conlan said.

"Yes, they did," Danny said.

"I'd like to see all the presents you got," Hortense Audrey said.

"Let's," Jennie Conlan said.

"I wanna see them, too," Little Margaret said.

Danny went to the front bedroom where he had placed all the presents on the dresser. He took the boxes, and some of them tumbled on the floor. He placed them back on his uncle's dresser.

"You better come in here if you wanna see them. They're too many to carry out," he yelled.

Led by Danny, the children all rushed into the bedroom.

"Here's the paint box Al gave me," Danny said, handing out a set of water colors. Jimmy Keogh grabbed it.

He passed it on.

"And here's a tie," Danny said, handing to Perc a box with a black knit tie.

Perc read the neatly written greeting card.

> *To Daniel O'Neill, Happy Birthday.*
> *Bridget McGinnis*

"And here's handkerchiefs from Hortense Audrey," Danny said, showing handkerchiefs in a piece of tissue paper while the other presents were passed around the circle and the girls oohhed and ahed and giggled.

"Well, now he can blow his nose instead of picking it," Tommy Keefe said, looking at the handkerchiefs.

"Tommy Keefe, you're awful," Helen Smith said, laughing.

"Well, I seen him picking his nose in class," Tommy said.

"I didn't," Danny said heatedly.

"See, he wants to fight now," Hortense Audrey said.

"I don't. But I didn't," Danny said.

"Tommy, cut it out at his birthday party," Perc Dineen said while Danny stood, livid, facing Tommy, wondering if he could lick him or would he be licked, hoping he wouldn't have to fight now, here at his birthday party, telling himself that if he had to he would fight Tommy, and he would, he would. He imagined himself beating up Tommy in front of all the girls.

"Aren't we gonna see the rest of the presents? What did Virginia bring?" Hortense Audrey asked, her voice and words driving the anger out of his mind.

Blushing, he shyly took a small box and opened it. He held up shimmering white rosary beads.

"And I had 'em blessed," Virginia Doyle said.

"Aren't they pretty?" Little Margaret exclaimed.

"It's such a nice present," Jennie Conlan said, biting her lip and looking at Virginia, with a thin smile on her face.

"That's something he can use, too," Jimmy Keogh said.

"Everybody can use rosary beads," Al said.

"And here is this," Danny said, handing another box with a tie, the card in it signed by Jennie Conlan.

"That's a pretty tie," said Perc.

"Red," said Tom Cantwell, a dark-haired, pretty boy in a blue suit with a Buster Brown collar.

"You oughta get a girl with that tie, Danny," Little Margaret said.

"Maybe he doesn't want a girl," Jennie Conlan said.

"If you had a girl, what would you do with her?" asked Tommy Keefe.

"Here's this," Danny said, hastily passing a copy of *Tom Sawyer*.

"Whose is that?" asked Little Margaret.

"Perc's," Danny said.

"I read that book," Al said.

"And here's this from Tommy Keefe," Danny said, handing out a white scarf wrapped in tissue paper.

"That's to keep the soup off his pants," Tommy said, and they all laughed.

They went on examining the presents.

IX

"Did you see the little girls?" Margaret asked Sadie.

"Yes. They're little darlings. They're so sweet," Sadie said wistfully.

Margaret began to cry.

"I was a little girl, the prettiest and most innocent little girl, once. Sadie, I was a little dolly," Margaret said, continuing to cry.

"You must have been," Sadie said.

"I was the sweetest little dolly. I was such a lovely, innocent child," Margaret said.

"Yes, you were, Peg, and you're still sweet," Sadie said.

"I was as innocent as an angel. I didn't know what sin was. And now look at me," Margaret said, burying her head in the pillow.

"Peg, you mustn't disturb yourself this way," Sadie said.

Margaret looked up tearfully at Sadie.

"I got to have another shot of gin," Margaret said.

"Peg, you promised me," Sadie said.

"Gimme some gin," Margaret demanded.

Sadie obediently poured her out another shot of gin.

X

"Well, I'm willing to play post office if everybody else wants to," Danny said.

"Let's," Little Margaret said.

"Go ahead. It's your party. You start the game," Tommy said.

"All right, if everybody else wants to. But who's going to be postmaster?" asked Danny.

"I'll be postmaster," Bill said.

Danny went into his uncle's bedroom followed by Bill.

"Well, who yuh want, Dan?"

"I don't know. I wanna think," Danny said.

"That one with blonde hair in the blue sailor dress is sweet on you. I seen her looking at you all during the party, Dan," Bill said.

"I got to think," Danny said.

"You afraid to kiss a girl?"

"No, I'm thinkin'," Danny said.

"Don't give yourself rheumatism of the brain," Bill said.

"Tell Perc and Jimmy Keogh and Al Throckwaite to come in," Danny said.

"No girl?" Bill asked.

"I want them," Danny said.

Bill scratched his head.

"That ain't the way you play post office," Bill said.

"I can call them in if I wanna," Danny said.

"All right, I don't care," Bill said, closing the door.

Danny stood nervously by the bed. He heard laughter and giggling from the next room.

XI

"He wants Jimmy Keogh, Al Throckwaite, and Perc Dineen," Bill said.

Jennie Conlan looked at Bill and lowered her blue eyes in disappointment.

"Maybe he's afraid to kiss a girl," Hortense said, and she giggled, while Virginia Doyle and Bridget McGinnis, sitting side by side, blushed.

"He's afraid. But I wouldn't be," said Tommy Keefe.

"Maybe the girls wouldn't want you to kiss 'em," Helen Smith said.

"Then I'd kiss myself," Tommy Keefe said, and the girls giggled.

Perc, Jimmy, and Al went laughing into the bedroom.

XII

"What you wanna do, Dan, slap us on the wrist?" asked Jimmy Keogh.

"Guys, I got an idea."

"A bright one?" asked Perc.

"We're one, like a team, and we call in a girl and all kiss her and when a girl calls us, they gotta kiss us all," said Danny.

"Swell," said Perc.

"Bill, call in, let's see who? How about Virginia Doyle?" Danny said.

Bill closed the door.

XIII

"Virginia Doyle," he said.

Virginia's face turned red.

"You gotta go," said Hortense Audrey.

"No fun playing this game if you don't play it," Tommy Keefe said.

"Let Hortense Audrey go," Virginia Doyle said.

"I can't. They didn't call me," Hortense Audrey said.

"You go," Virginia said to Little Margaret.

"Maybe they'll step on your toe instead of kissing you," Tom Cantwell said, and there was giggling and laughter.

"You gotta go," said Hortense Audrey.

Virginia Doyle rose, walked slowly out of the parlor.

XIV

She came timidly into the bedroom, stood there with flushed cheeks, and Bill closed the door, staying inside.

The boys looked at her, none of them approaching her.

"I'm here," she said, her blue eyes lowered.

"Well, who starts the ball rolling?" Danny asked.

"You do," Perc said.

"Don't blush so, Dan. Go ahead," Bill said.

"Al, you start it," Danny said.

Al didn't move.

Danny suddenly walked to Virginia, and while she continued to lower her eyes, he brushed a kiss on her cheeks.

Virginia looked at him with fear. She retreated into a corner. She looked at the boys like a cornered animal.

"Go ahead. You guys gotta do it," Danny said.

Perc and Al approached her, kissed her hastily on the cheek.

"I guess the postmaster gotta get in here," Bill said, kissing her near the ear.

"Now we go out," Danny said, leading them out of the room.

Virginia started to go out.

"You're supposed to tell me who I call," Bill said.

"I don't wanna call anybody," she said, standing stiffly against the wall in a corner.

"You gotta play the game," Bill said.

"Can I call a girl?"

"You're supposed to call a boy."

"I want Bridget McGinnis," she said, not looking at Bill.

Bill went out. She stood there, her cheeks still flushed, her eyes still betraying fright.

Bridget came slowly into the bedroom.

"You call a boy. I'm afraid to."

"You do it. I don't like to."

"I never been kissed before," she said in shame and humiliation.

"I never been kissed," Bridget said.

"I won't call any boy."

"I don't like this game."

"I was never kissed before."

"Let's call Jennie. Maybe she'll call some boy in."

"All right."

Bridget opened the door.

"Call Jennie Conlan," she said.

Jennie Conlan came in.

"You two are bashful. Oh, look at the way you're blushing."

"You call in some boy," Bridget said.

Virginia slipped out of the room, followed by Bridget.

XV

"Danny O'Neill," Bill called.

"Come on, gang," Danny said, jumping up, followed by Perc, Jimmy, and Al.

"Hey, quit hogging the kisses," Tommy Keefe yelled.

"You'll be called," Danny said.

Virginia and Bridget sat in silence, not looking anyone in the eye.

XVI

"Bridget McGinnis," Bill called as Jennie came out and took a seat near the window.

"I was called," she said.

"You're called again. Wanted in the post office."

"You have to go, Bridget," Helen Smith said.

Bridget rose and walked shyly out of the parlor.

XVII

"Now everything is ready. We can wait for the little ones to get hungry and we have all this food for their little stomachs," Mrs. O'Flaherty said to Martha.

"Yas'm."

"If that one in the bedroom only holds her peace now. I'd be shamed if she yells and curses in front of those innocent little ones," Mrs. O'Flaherty said.

XVIII

"I think we ought to make it three more kisses," Danny said boldly.

"No, you had your kiss. That's not fair. It's not supposed to be that three boys call in one girl. One boy is supposed to do it. That's the rules of the game," Hortense Audrey said.

"We changed the rules," Danny said.

"Well, you had your kiss," Hortense Audrey said.

"We decided we want three more," Danny said.

Hortense started to run out of the bedroom, but Danny caught her. He kissed her three times, and as she tried to get away from him there was a rip.

"Now you tore my dress."

Perc looked at Danny in disgust. Danny stood speechless before Hortense Audrey.

"You tore my new dress."

"I'm awful sorry."

"You play post office like you was fighting," she said.

"Honest, I didn't mean it," he said.

"Look what you did," she said, pointing to a rent on the side in the lower part of her white dress.

"I'm awful sorry," Danny said.

"My dress is torn and it's the first time I wore it," she said.

"It's Hortense's turn now, Danny. We got to get out," Perc said.

Danny shamefacedly followed them out of the room.

"Took a long time that time," Tommy said.

Danny didn't answer.

"Joe Conlan," Bill called.

XIX

Danny came back from the bathroom. He was sorry about Hortense's dress but she wasn't mad now, and the game was going on, and it was fun. He liked kissing girls. He had kissed every girl at the party lots of times.

He heard the bedroom door open. Aunt Margaret, glassy-eyed, stepped into the hall. Sadie grabbed her arm. Martha, seeing her, rushed down the hall. Danny stood petrified.

It was all over now. He was disgraced forever.

"Please go back to your room, Aunty Margaret," he begged.

"Don't go out there, Peg," said Sadie in great anxiety.

"Right back you goes now. You ain't 'lowed out of that there room and I ain't agonna let you," Martha said firmly, taking Margaret by both arms and turning her around.

Margaret docilely allowed them to lead her back into her room. Danny saw the door close. He went back to the parlor, thinking that that had been a close shave. Gee, if she did it again. And if they saw her?

XX

"I wish they'd play something else," Virginia Doyle said to Bridget McGinnis beside her.

"I do, too," Bridget said.

"Think they will?"

"They all like this game," said Bridget.

"I don't," said Virginia.

"I wish I didn't come."

"Do we have to play it?"

"It'll look funny if we don't, and the other girls'll laugh at us," said Bridget.

"Virginia Doyle. The gang wants you," Bill called.

Virginia went to the bedroom, stood coldly by the door, and let Danny, Perc, and Al kiss her cheek.

They went out.

"Tommy Cantwell," she said to Bill.

Tommy came in.

She kissed him lightly on the cheek as if performing an onerous duty and walked out.

XXI

Margaret sat dull-eyed on the bed. Sadie watched her.

"Gin," she said.

"This is the last drink," Sadie said.

"Gin."

Sadie poured the last of the gin in a glass. She handed it to Margaret. Margaret could not hold it. The gin spilled on her kimono and the glass tumbled to the floor.

"I was innocent," she mumbled.

She sat there, seeing nothing with her dull eyes.

XXII

"Now wait till I tell you who's partners," Danny said to the laughing, giggling children.

"Go ahead, and don't take the best girl yourself," Tommy said.

"I'm telling who sits where," Danny said.

"All right. I wanna eat," Tommy Cantwell said.

"Now, let's see," Danny said.

"Shake a leg, will yuh?" said Tommy Keefe.

"Al Throckwaite and Bridget McGinnis are partners, and they sit here and here," Danny said, pointing to the two chairs on the right of the head of the table.

Al and Bridget sat down. Danny looked over the table, spread with coffee cups, little bonbons, peanuts and colored candies, plates, stacks of sandwiches, a large vanilla layer cake with burning candles, bowls of chocolate candies, and two angel food cakes set on either side of the birthday cake. Danny gazed at the chandelier. It was decorated with green and red tissue paper.

"Joe Conlan and Hortense Audrey sit next to Al and Bridget. And then Perc and Jennie Conlan."

Perc darted an angry look as he sat down beside Jennie. She turned her pretty round face to him, smiled, put her napkin in her lap.

"Jimmy Keogh and Helen Smith sit there. And Tommy Keefe and my sister over here. Bill and Susan Moore there. Tommy Cantwell and Alice there. And we sit here," he said, turning to Virginia, who gave him an expressionless look as she sat down.

"Where's the favors?" asked Hortense Audrey.

"What?" asked Danny.

"Where's the favors?"

"Oh, there ain't any," Danny said.

Perc glanced down at Danny, raised his eyebrows, then turned to Jennie Conlan and said:

"This ain't the way to run a party."

"I like it," she said.

"Now we eat," Danny said.

"You got to blow out the candles on the cake, Danny," Little Margaret said to her brother.

"Oh, yeah!"

Martha brought him the cake, held it, and he blew. They clapped as the candles went out.

Martha then brought in a large pitcher of hot chocolate and, going around the table, poured it into the cups.

"Eat your fill now, little ones," Mrs. O'Flaherty said from the dining-room doorway.

XXIII

"Watch me!" Danny said gayly to Virginia at his left.

She looked up at him but said nothing. Danny aimed a peanut at Tommy, shot it off his thumb as if shooting a marble. It splashed in Tommy's cup of cocoa.

"You ain't a good shot at all, O'Neill," Tommy yelled, throwing a piece of bread at Danny.

It hit Virginia Doyle on the side of the head.

"They're just like this when Miss McGinnis goes out of the room at school. They yell and throw erasers all over," Hortense Audrey said.

"Miss McGinnis' sister is here and will tell. Keep still, Hortense," Tommy Keefe said, throwing a peanut at Bridget.

Tommy Cantwell flung a piece of cake at Danny. It went over his head and landed near the window sill behind him.

"Watch me do better than that," Danny told Virginia.

He threw a bread crumb at Tommy Keefe and it caught Tommy on the nose.

Helen Smith threw a peanut at Perc. He frowned at her.

"You all ready foh the ice cream?" Martha called from the doorway.

They nodded their heads in agreement.

XXIV

"Let's all walk over to the duck pond," Danny said when they were putting on their hats and coats.

"Come on," said Tommy Keefe.

"Hey, kids, we're gonna walk over to the duck pond," Joe Conlan yelled.

"I have to go home," said Bridget McGinnis.

"Come on, don't break up the party. It's fun," Helen Smith said.

There was a rush, crowding, laughter, giggling, and they got their coats on and crowded down the stairs, making as much noise as they seemed able to.

XXV

"They sho' made a lot of mess in that dining room," Martha said.

"Ah, they're only children. Those little girls looked like angels," Mrs. O'Flaherty said.

"They're sweet. Did they have a good time?" Sadie asked.

"That they did. They were talking and laughing and they ate their fill."

"I'm glad. And it was lucky Peg didn't make any trouble," Sadie said.

"Is she asleep?"

"Yeah. I'll help Martha clean up now," Sadie said.

XXVI

"He's a goof," Tommy Keefe said.

"And hasn't he got nerve? Picking the prettiest girl for himself like that at his own party," Perc said.

"She don't like him, either, I'll bet," said Tommy Keefe.

"How could she? That Four Eyes!" Tommy Cantwell said.

"I'm gonna have a party after Easter. Know what I'm gonna do? But don't tell him. I'm gonna have Maggie Grady there and she's gonna be his partner," Perc said, and they laughed.

"Come on, let's race to the corner of Calumet," Danny said happily, rushing up to Perc.

"Come on," Perc said.

"Al, you start us," Danny said.

They all paused to watch.

Danny, Tommy Keefe, Tommy Cantwell, and Perc stood ready to run, their toes on a crack in the sidewalk.

"On your mark!"

"Get set!"

"Ready!"
"Go!"

Danny sprang off, running with all his might. The others didn't move. He turned, after having raced about twenty-five yards, and saw them laughing at him.

"You're fine guys," he said.

XXVII

Danny packed a snowball, as they entered the park.

"Watch me hit that tree, guys," he said, pointing at a tree about forty yards distant. He wanted the girls, and particularly Virginia Doyle, to see how well he could throw.

He wound up and threw. The snowball struck the center of the tree trunk about fifteen feet from the ground.

"You're a pretty good show-off," Perc Dineen said, but Danny didn't hear him.

Tommy caught Danny in the back of the neck with a snowball. He turned around, laughed, and flung a snowball back at Tommy. The girls watched the boys have a snow fight.

XXVIII

The duck pond was covered with a layer of melting snow. The children stood at the edge of it.

"I guess ice skating is over for this year," Hortense Audrey said.

"Let's run over it," Danny said.

"It won't hold you," Al said.

"Sure it will," Danny said.

"Go ahead and see," Tommy Cantwell said.

"Come on with me," Danny said.

He took Hortense Audrey's hand. She ran after him. They raced about fifteen feet. Her foot broke through the ice.

"OOOH!" she yelled, and at the same moment, Danny's foot also broke through. He could feel the water soaking through his high, laced boots. He took her by the hand and led her back to the group.

"Thought you were too smart," Perc yelled.

"It's your fault," Hortense Audrey said to him.

"I thought it was harder," Danny said.

"I got my dress torn and my feet wet. I gotta go home now," Hortense said.

"Let's all go," Perc said.

"You're not mad at me?" Danny asked Hortense Audrey.

"No," she laughed.

They started back out of the park. Virginia Doyle and Bridget McGinnis walked together, moving slowly so the others could get ahead.

"I don't like him," Virginia Doyle said.

"I'm gonna tell my sister how fresh he is. She won't like it. He's awful fresh. And I didn't wanna be kissed," Bridget McGinnis said.

"I didn't have fun at the party," Virginia Doyle said.

XXIX

"Virginia Doyle is your girl, ain't she, Danny?" Little Margaret said as the three O'Neill children walked home alone.

"I donno," Danny said, moodily.

"You took her for your partner and called her in the post office a lot of times," Little Margaret said.

"I like her," Danny said.

"We'll play our Steel's League tonight, Dan," Bill said.

"Virginia Doyle is pretty," Little Margaret said.

"She was the prettiest girl at the party," Danny proudly said.

He had had her for his partner and kissed her. Maybe now he would have Virginia Doyle as his girl. He'd see her at school Monday and talk to her, and maybe walk home with her. And when it was time to go roller skating, he'd skate by her house and maybe get her to go roller skating with him. He held an image of her face in his mind. He liked girls to have pretty hair. She had the prettiest hair of all the girls, too, even prettier than Bridget McGinnis'.

"I'll bet you're thinking about Virginia Doyle," Little Margaret said.

"I'm thinking who I'm going to have pitch in our Steel's League when I play Bill," Danny said.

"How was the party?" Uncle Al asked, coming up on them.

"We had a lot of fun," Danny said.

"It was a nice party, Uncle Al," Little Margaret said.

"Did Aunt Peg cause any trouble, Sport?"

"No. She came out of her room once, but nobody seen her, and we got her right back."

"Dan, I told you," Uncle Al said.

"What?"

"It's grammatically incorrect to say 'I seen her.' Say, 'I saw her.'"

"I saw her," Danny said.

"That's the Sport. And what was she doing when you left home?"

"She was asleep. She didn't yell at all today."

"I'm glad of that. And you had a fine party with all the little ladies and gentlemen enjoying themselves."

"Yes, it was a swell party," Danny said.

"That's good, Sport."

SECTION FIVE

1915

37

I

"I can't get over the little fellow," Mrs. O'Flaherty said, looking at Arty as he stood in the center of the O'Flaherty parlor. He was dressed in a white sailor suit, with white stockings, and little black pumps with a strap and button. He was combed and washed, and he glanced curiously from face to face, from his mother to his father, to his grandmother, to his uncle, to his aunt. The other O'Neill children were seated about the room.

"He's such a darling. Oh, Lizz, I always say that you have such lovely children," Margaret said.

Al got up, went to his room, and returned with two cigars.

"Here, Jim, have a cigar," he said.

"Thanks, Al, I will," Jim said, accepting it.

Al drew out his pearl-handled knife and cut off the end of his cigar. Jim bit off his end. Al lit Jim's cigar and then his own. Jim stretched his legs, puffed.

"Such a pretty baby," Margaret said.

"That one will grow up to be a fine man, Lizz," Mrs. O'Flaherty said.

Arty saw himself reflected in the wall mirror. He looked, pointed his finger at his own image. He ran to it and looked at himself in the mirror. He again pointed his finger at his image, and it threw back at him a reflection of himself pointing a finger. He laughed.

"Mither!" he exclaimed, looking inquiringly at her. She didn't notice him because she was talking with Margaret and her mother.

Arty turned again to the mirror. Little Margaret went to him.

"That's yourself in the mirror, Arty," she said.

"Look at her. Just like a little mother," Lizz said, nodding her head toward Little Margaret as the girl held her baby brother under the armpits and looked with him into the mirror.

"Baby," Arty said, pointing at his own reflection.

Wide-eyed, he gazed up at Little Margaret.

"That's you in the mirror," Little Margaret said.

She turned him around and made faces into the mirror, and he tried to touch his reflection with his hand.

II

"Mama," Catherine said, coming into the parlor from the bathroom.

"Yes, my love," Lizz said.

"I wanna show you something," she said.

"What? Your mother's busy," Lizz said.

"I wanna show you something," she said.

"Go see if she's done anything, Lizz," Mrs. O'Flaherty said.

"I done nothing. I just wanna show Mama something," Catherine said.

"Jim, you go with her," Lizz said.

"I'll be right back. Come on, Dolly," Jim said, getting up.

Catherine took his hand and led him to the bathroom.

"Papa," she said.

"Yes, Catherine," Jim said.

"See that," she said, pointing to the bathtub faucets.

"What is it?"

"Turn this one," Catherine said, pointing to the hot-water faucet.

Jim turned it.

"Feel it."

Jim let the hot water run over his hand.

"It's hot water, and it comes out just like the cold water comes out of the sink at home," Catherine said.

"Yes, it's hot water."

"Where does it come from?"

"It comes through the pipe and it's heated by a furnace in the cellar."

"We don't have that."

"No."

"I didn't know hot water comes out of the faucet."

"Some day your father will get a house for all you kids with hot water coming out of faucets."

"Papa, what's this for?" Catherine asked, pointing at the bathtub.

"That's a bathtub. You take a bath in it."

"We ain't got that. We got a different kind of tub," Catherine said.

Jim turned the hot water off and took her back into the parlor.

III

"Bill, let's play Steel's," Danny said, sitting in the parlor, bored.

"Come on. After we play another series, we got to figure the batting averages of our players again," Bill said.

"We're going to play Steel's," Danny said.

"Sure, go ahead," Al said.

IV

"Al, when do you go away?" Jim asked.

"Tomorrow. I just got in for the week end," Al said.

"Business any good?"

"Yes, it's pretty good, Jim. This is turning out to be a very good year."

"All the express companies are moving plenty of freight."

"I guess they must be," Al said.

"Yes, we're working pretty steady and hard these days."

"It's a shame that we have to get all this business because there's a war. But then I suppose it can't be helped. We didn't make it, and there you are. And, of course, those Germans think they can rule the world."

"Well, I don't know much about that, Al. After all, if there's a war, you can be sure somebody's getting something out of it besides the poor John Dub who has to shoot the guns off in the trenches."

"Sure, if they go to war over here I won't let my son go. Pa's brother was called in the Civil War and he ran off to Australia and we never heard from him in years. He ran off when they called him," Mrs. O'Flaherty said.

"We don't need to worry. I don't think we're going to go to war," Al said.

"Ah, I'd fight them if we did. I'd fight," said Mrs. O'Flaherty.

"You wouldn't care who you were fighting as long as you fought?" said Margaret.

"You bet your boots I'd fight them," Mrs. O'Flaherty said, and her children and son-in-law smiled at her.

V

"I saw hot water come out of a faucet," Catherine said to Bob.

"That's nothing," Bob said.

"I saw it. You didn't know it until I told you."

"I did so."

"How did you?"

"I came to Mother's before and saw it."

"Where does it come from?"

"It comes from God."

"It does not. Papa told me where it comes from. He said it comes from pipes," Catherine said.

VI

"Lizz, you were so good to me. I'll never forget how kind you were. I was just upset. But I'm all right now. I'm back at work and you couldn't bribe me to touch a drop of it."

"Sure, we had an awful time with her this time," Mrs. O'Flaherty said in a low voice, the three women sitting together near the window.

"I know you did. I was bad. But I was so nervous. I didn't mean to do it. I don't like the taste of it. I hate it. I was just nervous," Margaret said.

"How is Sadie O'Flaherty?" asked Lizz.

"Sadie is such a poor, sick girl. She has t.b. She won't live long, the poor thing," Margaret said.

"I wanted her to go. She had to go. I've taken care of me little grandson and he's never had whooping cough. It's because I've watched him. And I didn't want her around to give him the consumption. There she was, spitting blood. She had to go."

"I got her a job as hat-check girl in my hotel and she found a sweet little room on the North Side," said Margaret.

"Mother, she can't help it that she's sick," Lizz said.

"Me little grandson never had whooping cough. She had to go so she didn't make him sick."

"Mother gives Danny such care," Margaret said.

"I know she does. He's the apple of her eye."

"Lizz, you better watch all your children. I've been reading in the newspaper about the spread of diphtheria in the city."

"I do. Oh, I don't let them play with other children. I keep them in the yard. They got each other to play with, and I have them all wear holy medals to protect them," Lizz said.

"If any of them get sick, don't let them come near my little grandson. He never had the whooping cough because I watched over him like a hawk," Mrs. O'Flaherty said.

VII

"Lemme see your dollies?" Catherine said to Little Margaret.

"Come on."

Catherine ran ahead of Little Margaret.

"Wait till I get Arty to take with me," Little Margaret said.

"I don't want him to come," Catherine said.

"Why?"

"He breaks dolls. When I cut out paper dollies, he tears them up every time he gets his hands on them."

"Bob, you watch Little Arty," Little Margaret said.

She took Catherine by the hand and led her into Aunt Margaret's bedroom, where she slept.

"Here's my best doll," Little Margaret said, taking down a large doll with flaxen hair, blue eyes that closed when it was laid flat, and a blue dress.

"That's a pretty dolly," Catherine said.

"I call her Annabelle," said Little Margaret.

"Why do you call her that?" said Catherine.

"Because a girl I go to school with thinks she has the prettiest doll of all the girls in school and she calls her best doll Annabelle. So I call mine Annabelle. Aunty Margaret got it for me last payday," said Little Margaret.

"Can I hold it?" asked Catherine.

"Don't you drop it," said Little Margaret.

"Let's play house with it," Catherine said.

"All right. I'll be the mother and you be the nursemaid, and Annabelle is the little baby," Little Margaret said.

VIII

"What I'm worried about in the elections is that they're going to have a whispering campaign against Sweitzer because he's on our side of the fence and that'll put Thompson in," Al said.

"That's possible. Of course, I want to see Sweitzer get in because he's a Democrat and a Democrat's for the workingman. Take Wilson in the White House. He's doing things for the workingman, and he isn't getting us mixed up in that war across the waters. A workingman doesn't want to see this country mixed up in that war because after all it's him and his kids will have to be marching off with the guns. But anyway, Al, I'm glad that my kids are pretty young," Jim said.

"It won't last long enough for your kids to have to go in it," Al said.

"Of course, if anybody was to come over here and try to invade us, well, then I'd want my kids to go and defend their country and their home. It's an awful thing, these stories in the papers about what the Germans did to the Belgian women," Jim said.

"Yes, it is, Jim. But as I said, the Germans can't whip the whole world," Al said.

"I think the war is simply terrible," Margaret said, glancing over at the men.

"I'd love to see my friend from Twenty-fifth and La Salle, Mrs. Bodenheimer, now. I'd like to see her and say to her, 'Now, what about your German sausage-eaters?'" Lizz said.

"Oh, Lizz, the Germans aren't a bad people. I got nothing against them," Jim said.

"Jim, don't think I'm trying to be a buttinsky here, but after all, a man wants to use good diction. That's the way to be a wise guy. And nobody who uses good diction uses *got*. Say *have*."

"Oh, Al, got is all right to use. I hear many rich business men at the hotel use *got*," Margaret said.

"No really educated man does. It's a vulgarism," Al said.

"I never was a highbrow. I'm a workingman and I don't see where I get off at trying to talk like a highbrow. As long as I'm understood, that's enough for me," Jim said.

"Jim," Al said, shooting out his left hand in a crisp gesture. "Jim, you want to change your attitude. When you meet refined people you want to impress them, and style makes the man. You want to learn to talk with style. I'm telling you this because I know. Two words you don't want to use are *ain't* and *got*."

"I'll use any words I damn well please to use," Jim said.

"All right, if that's the way you look at it," Al said.

"It is!"

"I was only telling you for your own good," Al said.

"I'll look after my own good," Jim said.

"Now, Al, forget it. I don't want to hear any quarreling. Jim uses lovely language and he's a smart man," Margaret said.

Al said nothing. He sat puffing at his cigar.

"Jim! I want to speak to my son-in-law. Jim, is my cousin running for alderman this year?"

"Yes, Paddy is."

"Oh, Mother, didn't I tell you?" Lizz said.

"What is it?" asked Mrs. O'Flaherty.

"Paddy got Jim a job on election day this year," Lizz said.

"Good, Jim, I'm very glad to hear it," said Al.

"It's just for the day. I'm judge of elections in my precinct. I'll make a few extra dollars that way," Jim said.

"Jim, you see that my cousin, Paddy Slattery, is elected," Mrs. O'Flaherty said.

"Oh, Mother, if he wasn't, there'd be heads split in our neighborhood. Why, Mother, Paddy Slattery is the cock of the walk in our neighborhood. He's the most popular man in the whole ward. Say, all you got to do in our ward if you get in trouble with a cop is to say to him, 'Say, you, I'm a cousin of Paddy Slattery,'" Lizz said.

"Ah, Lizz, he's a fine man, a fine man," Mrs. O'Flaherty said.

"Yes, he is. He'll probably be elected, Mary. He's very popular in the ward," Jim said.

"Oh, Mother, there'd be many heads split open if he wasn't. The people wouldn't let anybody else but Cousin Paddy be alderman from our ward," Lizz said.

IX

"Denny, what are those glass houses?" Bob asked, pointing out of the dining-room window at the hothouses.

"Glass houses for flowers," Dennis said while Bill and Danny went on shaking the dice, playing Steel's.

"How do you know they are?"

"I'm telling you they are!"

"How do you know?"

"I'm telling you they are," Dennis said.

"Bill, is he right?" Bob asked.

"What?" Bill asked, looking up, annoyed.

"Denny says those glass houses are for flowers. Are they?"

"Yeah, and don't bother us. Can't you see we're doin' something?" Bill said.

X

Arty quickly drew his fingers away from the radiator and yelled.

"Oh, what's the matter with Mama's Angel Child?" Lizz said, going to him, her pregnant belly protruding very noticeably.

"Is he hurt, Lizz?" asked Mrs. O'Flaherty.

"He burned his hand on the radiator. Here, let Mama kiss his little burn," Lizz said while Arty still cried.

"Here, Lizz, I'll take him back and put something on it," Margaret said.

"Butter is good," Lizz said.

"Peg, be sure and use the help's butter," Mrs. O'Flaherty said.

Margaret carried Arty out to the rear as he howled.

"Oh, the little man is going to be brave and not cry. And he's growing to be such a big little man," Margaret said, carrying the squirming, crying baby.

"Mither!" he howled.

Margaret kissed his forehead.

She set him down on a kitchen chair and rubbed a little butter on his finger. She took him into the bathroom and turned on the light.

"Oohh!" Arty said, pointing up at the glowing electric bulb.

"What?"

"Ooh!" Arty exclaimed, pointing to the bulb again.

"Oh, you little darling. You didn't know that was electricity. You sweet little thing. Your aunty adores you, and when you grow up she's going to help you so much and you're going to be so handsome," Margaret said.

She kissed her nephew, and bandaged his hand.

Arty watched her with surprise as she turned off the light. He pointed.

"Light," she said.

"Uh?" Arty exclaimed inquisitively.

"Ah, you darling," she said, picking him up, kissing him tenderly.

She set him down and watched him run down the hall.

XI

"Oh, Mother, you should have gone to Mamie Casey's wake," Lizz said.

"And what should I be going to see them low Irish for? Who was there, Lizz?"

"Oh, Mother, everybody asked for you," Lizz said.

"A nerve they have, asking for me," Mrs. O'Flaherty said.

"Mother, they tried to four-flush, too. Would you believe it, they tried to four-flush," Lizz said.

"How was she laid out, Lizz?" asked Mrs. O'Flaherty.

"Oh, Mother, she looked beautiful. She looked like a dream in the coffin," Lizz said.

"The poor thing!" Mrs. O'Flaherty exclaimed.

XII

"I tell you, Lizz, you're looking wonderful. Your hair is combed nice and your face is washed and that black dress looks becoming on you," Al said gayly.

"Say, you, I always wash my face and comb my hair," said Lizz.

"I didn't say you didn't. Now, don't be getting belligerent. We're just having a happy family Sunday, and I was telling you how swelldingerino you looked," Al said.

"Jim, Lizz has the loveliest skin and hair. I wish I had a complexion like yours, Lizz," said Margaret.

"I tell her how fine a skin and what nice hair she's got," Jim said.

"Oh, but I don't feel good. I wish this ordeal was over. The last months are always the worst," Lizz said.

"How much longer have you got, Lizz?"

"Some time in April," Lizz said.

"Well, it's March now. Another month and you'll be through it," said Margaret.

"Ah, sure, Lizz, it's nothing. After I had mine, I'd be up the next day washing clothes," Mrs. O'Flaherty said.

"Mother, you were always stronger than me," Lizz said.

"Ah, I never minded it," Mrs. O'Flaherty said.

"My teeth ache so and my neuralgia still troubles me. Oh, I wish it was over," Lizz said.

"Lizz, I'm expecting some money. You know, I'm sure that I haven't heard from Lorry because he must be so busy with his timberlands. You know, all of the lumber men are making money these days because of the war, and I'm sure he's been so busy. I know I'll hear from him. You know, he promised me some of his timberlands when they are in shape and free. Most of them were frozen and tied up. And now I'm sure that I'll be hearing from him and he'll give me the timberlands he promised me. We'll have lots of money then and I'll be able to get your teeth fixed and do lots for you," said Margaret.

"Maybe you can send Little Margaret to a convent school," Lizz said.

"I want to give her the finest education."

"I want one of my daughters to be a real lady," Lizz said.

"She will. She'll be a lovely girl," Margaret said.

"Ah, girls don't need much education. They need to know how to cook and sew and be good for some man," said Mrs. O'Flaherty.

"Mother, that's an old-fashioned notion. Those days are gone forever. These are modern times. Girls nowadays want to be independent and live their own lives and become business women," Margaret said.

"Glory be, I don't know what the times is coming to. Ah, Lizz, I tell you, the times is left-handed nowadays," Mrs. O'Flaherty said.

XIII

"Here, Sport, you don't want that," Al said, suddenly noticing that Arty had pulled a small vase off the low mantelpiece under the mirror and was examining it.

"He won't hurt it," Lizz said.

"It's breakable. We'll get him something else," Al said, taking the vase from Arty.

Arty reached for it.

"No! No, Sport. Not that," Al said.

"No! No!" Arty exclaimed.

"Ah, he's such a little angel," said Mrs. O'Flaherty.

"He's my cherub," Lizz said.

"But Daniel was prettier when he was his age," Mrs. O'Flaherty said.

"There couldn't be a baby prettier than Arty, Mother. Look at the lovely brown eyes of the little cherub," Lizz said.

Al handed Arty a small brass dog from the mantelpiece.

"Look at that. It won't break," Al said, smiling at him.

"Doggie!" Arty exclaimed.

"Oh, Al, he likes you," Lizz said.

"Sure he does," Al said.

"Fither! Fither!" Arty said, toddling to Jim.

He held the dog up to his father.

"Doggie, Fither!" Arty exclaimed.

"Ah, he's a cute little beggar," Jim said proudly, accepting the dog which Arty handed him.

XIV

"Dennis, what's this?" Bob asked, pointing to a closed pipe end which jutted out of the dining-room wall near the lower portion of woodwork.

"I donno," said Dennis.

Bob sat down by it, scratched his head, felt it, looked at it.

Dennis ran back to the parlor.

"Sport, you mustn't run here. There's people under us, and you make noise over their heads," Al said to Dennis.

Dennis sat down shyly near his father. Jim frowned but said nothing.

XV

"Let's go back and stay in the parlor," Little Margaret said.

"All right," Catherine said.

The two girls returned to the parlor.

"We was playing house, Mama," Catherine said.

"Oh, you sweet darling. Lizz, she's so pretty. All your children are the most beautiful and the loveliest children," Margaret said.

"Sisser," Arty exclaimed, coming up to Catherine.

Little Margaret enfolded him in her arms and kissed him.

"I'm your sister, too. I'm your big sister, Arty. Don't you know your big sister?"

Arty laughed, reached to touch her face.

"What's my name?"

"Big sisser."

She kissed him.

"Oh, you're so sweet," Little Margaret said.

"Can you beat it, Peg? Just like a little mother," Lizz whispered to Margaret, and the two sisters smiled at Little Margaret as she petted and kissed Arty.

XVI

"I have to go now. Goodbye, Jim," Al said, shaking hands firmly with Jim.

"Goodbye, Al," Jim said.

"I'll be home early," Al told his mother.

"Well, we'll be here and the house'll be standing, Al, when you come home," Mrs. O'Flaherty said.

"Goodbye, Lizz," Al said.

"Goodbye, Al," Lizz said.

"We got to be going soon ourselves," Jim said.

"Oh, no, Jim, you stay for supper. I'll send the boys out for some things and you all stay. I'll fix up a nice supper in no time," said Margaret.

"Oh, no, Peg, it's too much trouble," said Lizz.

"Now, it won't be any trouble at all. You stay, Lizz," Margaret said.

"Goodbye, Sport," Al said, and he bent down and shook hands with Arty.

"Doo bye," Arty said.

"He knows his good uncle," Lizz said.

"Goodbye, Uncle Al," Little Margaret said.

"Goodbye, everybody," Al said, and he motioned to Lizz to follow him into the hall.

"Here, Lizz, take this, and take care of yourself," Al said.

He handed her a five-dollar bill.

"Al, you're so good, and thank you. I'll say some prayers for you, and God will bless you for this," Lizz said.

"Don't mention it, and say some prayers that everything goes well," Al said.

"I will, Al."

"And be careful what you say to Peg. She's just getting on her feet again, and don't say anything to aggravate her," Al said.

"Sure, why would I want to?" Lizz said.

"You just got to be careful with her," Al said.

"Aren't you gonna kiss your sister goodbye?"

Al perfunctorily kissed Lizz and went out.

XVII

Jim wandered out to the dining room and sat down by Bill and Danny.

"You kids still at the baseball game?"

"Yes, Papa," Danny said.

"Who's winning?"

"He is. His team is in first place now," Danny said.

"Papa, what's this?" Bob said, pointing to the pipe-end he had discovered.

"What?"

"This?"

"That's an end of a pipe, I guess," Jim said.

"What's it for?"

"I guess it's for an extra radiator to be attached to," Jim said.

"Oh!" Bob exclaimed.

Jim sat watching his two oldest boys playing their ball game. Bob ran into the front to see Dennis.

XVIII

"Look at the little fellow. He's asleep," Mrs. O'Flaherty said, pointing to Arty who lay asleep in the center of the carpet.

"I'll put him on the couch," Lizz said.

"Let me lift him, Lizz. You can't in your condition," Margaret said.

She tenderly lifted Arty, laid him on the couch, and went to her room. She returned with a blanket and covered him.

Margaret, Mrs. O'Flaherty, and Lizz stood looking at him. In sleep, his face was innocent and relaxed, his lips in a pout, his hair tangled in curls.

"He's the most beautiful baby," Margaret said.

"Ah, he'll be a fine man," Mrs. O'Flaherty said.

"He wasn't much trouble this winter. He only had a few colds. In fact, I didn't have so much trouble with them. Oh, but it was cold, though, some days in the cottage. But none of them got very sick, just colds," Lizz said.

"He sleeps so quietly, and he's so pretty in his sleep," Margaret said.

"He takes after Father," Lizz said.

"Ah, Peg, did you ever see as wise a little fellow before," Mrs. O'Flaherty said.

"The most beautiful child," Margaret exclaimed.

Little Arty slept peacefully.

38

I

Laughing, wet, and gay, Dennis, Bob, and Catherine worked laboriously building a snow man in the back yard while the snow silently and steadily fell. It was an unexpected late March snowfall.

"We'll call the snow man Papa," said Bob.

"We can't make him big enough to be Papa," Dennis said.

"Let's call him Santa Claus," said Catherine.

"I don't like Santa Claus," Bob said.

"Bob O'Neill, aren't you afraid to say that? If you say that, Santa Claus won't give you any toys next Christmas," Catherine said.

"I didn't get the toys from him I asked for Christmas. I don't like Santa Claus," Bob said.

"Are you kids gonna let me do all the work or ain't you gonna help me? You wanted a snow man," Dennis said, bending down and rolling a large snowball along to enlarge it further.

"Denny, what you wanna call him?" asked Catherine.

"Call what?" Dennis asked.

"The snow man," Catherine said.

"But we ain't got one yet. We got to do lots of work before we get him done," Dennis said, pointing to the mound of snow they had piled up to a height of about two feet. He lifted his snowball, carried it to the mound, and set it on top.

"I can't roll the snow," Catherine said.

"Then don't. It ain't gonna be your snow man if you don't help," Dennis said.

"I can't," Catherine said.

"Why cancha if you want him to be your snow man as well as ours?" asked Dennis.

"My hands get wet and that makes them cold," Catherine said.

"All right, then, go on in the house and play with Arty. You don't need to play with us. We don't need you."

"I won't go in," Catherine said.

"I don't care whatcha do. We're gonna make a snow man," Dennis said.

"I wanna call our snow man Papa," said Bob.

"Well, get to work," Dennis said.

He packed a snowball, set it in the snow, slowly rolled it around. Bob imitated him. Catherine picked up a handful of snow and dropped it on the mound. Dennis and Bob silently rolled their snowballs. The snow filled the air with flying whiteness that fell at a silent, steady slant, wreathing the three children. The flakes were so thick that the church across the street was only half visible, and the houses extending along the series of back yards on the left were covered with a white crust and stood only dimly outlined. The noise of a passing train echoed from the west, and then there was silence and the endless fall of snow. Dennis lifted a large snowball and, staggering under its weight, managed to carry it and set it on the mound.

"Listen, you kids," he said.

"What?" Bob asked.

Catherine, setting a small ball of snow on the mound, looked at him with her intent blue eyes.

"We got to watch now how we build it. You kids don't pile any more balls on it. Set them right here beside it and call me. If we're gonna build a snow man, we gotta make him look like a snow man, and you kids can't do it as good as I can. Then we're going to give him arms, and a face with eyes and a mouth and ears and a nose," said Dennis.

"Denny, I can go in and cop Pa's glasses that he had for reading and put them on him," said Bob.

"Swell, but let's get him done first," said Dennis.

"We'll call him Pa then," said Bob.

"Get to work," Dennis said.

They all patiently rolled balls in the snow.

II

"Ooh!" Catherine exclaimed, putting her hand to her ear after a snowball thrown from the other side of the fence had smacked her.

"What's the matter?" asked Dennis, who was bending down near her.

"Somebody hit me," she bawled.

"Aw, you're seein' things," Dennis said, and as he spoke a snowball whizzed by his nose.

"Denny! Denny!"

Dennis ran through the snow toward the fence. He saw a group of four kids, the two Connerty boys and two others. They all let fly, and a snowball hit him on the side of the head. He bent down behind the fence, packed a snowball, and threw it. A rain of snowballs pelted on them. The hostile kids swarmed over the fence.

"Wash their faces," Buddy Connerty said.

The three O'Neill children tried to run. Catherine fell down in the snow. Buddy Connerty bent over her and rubbed her face in the snow. She screamed. Two others cornered Bob, and as he yelled, he was flung into the snow and his face washed.

Dennis bolted into the house. He grabbed a hatchet from the wood basket.

"Merciful Saviour, what's the matter?" Lizz called to him.

He didn't stop to answer, but ran out brandishing the hatchet.

"I'll kill you! I'll kill you!" Dennis shouted in hysteria.

He ran toward the boys, who were now kicking over the snow man which the O'Neill children had been building so patiently.

"I'll kill you!"

"Look out, he's got a hatchet!" Buddy Connerty yelled.

The four boys cut across the snow, followed by Dennis.

"I'll kill you!"

Dennis fell down as they were scrambling over the fence. He let out a yell, got to his feet, and hurled the hatchet after them. It missed Buddy Connerty's head by inches. Lizz appeared on her doorstep.

"Denny! Denny!" she called.

"Mama, the Connertys did it. They hit me with snowballs, and washed our faces in the snow. Denny's chasing them with a hatchet. Mama, they hurt me and pushed my head in the snow," Catherine sobbed.

"Get inside the house!" Lizz said, and she looked through the snow-laden air. She could see the group of boys off a distance of some yards from her fence. Dennis was at the fence.

"I'll kill every one of you!" Dennis yelled.

"Come on out and try it. I'll fight you!" Buddy Connerty yelled at him.

"Say, you, Buddy Connerty, you dirty bum! You let my children alone. Go away, you low tramps, before I come after you with a stick!" Lizz screamed at them.

"Oh, go on in and do your wash!" one of the boys yelled.

"Say, you tramp! Go home and tell your mother she's not a lady or she wouldn't have a child like you. You low-life brat!" Lizz yelled.

The kids laughed at her. A snowball struck the side of the house.

"Denny, go get me a stick till I get them," Lizz yelled.

Dennis darted into the house past his mother. He ran to Bill's room and dragged out Bill's BB gun. He ran out of the front of the house, slamming the door after him. He tore through the snow, crying and sobbing.

"I'll kill you! I'll kill you!" he screamed.

He ran forward, carrying the BB gun. Snowballs whizzed by him. When he was fifty feet distant from the group of kids, he halted, cocked the gun, shot. He cocked it again and shot.

"Jiggers, he's got a BB gun," one of the kids said.

"Denny, come here this minute," Lizz called.

Dennis shot again.

"Ouch. He hit my leg! Ouch," Buddy Connerty yelled.

"Let's rush him," Albie Connerty said.

Dennis backed up against the O'Neill fence.

"If you come near me, I'll shoot your eyes out!" Dennis screamed.

Lizz went to the fence, though it meant getting her feet soaking wet.

"Go 'way, you tramps, and let my boy alone or I'll brain every one of you. Go 'way, you Connerty bums!" she yelled.

Mrs. Connerty, a black shawl thrown over her head, labored through the snow. Dennis, seeing her, climbed the fence, and the group of boys ran.

"And am I after hearing the Connertys called bums?" Mrs. Connerty said, standing about six yards from Lizz, the snow beginning to cover her shawl.

"Your boys were picking on my little ones. If I catch them again I'll go after them with a stick," Lizz yelled at her neighbor.

Dennis slunk into the house. Bob followed him.

"Am I after hearing the Connertys called bums? Am I after hearing attributions made against my boys?" Mrs. Connerty cried at Lizz.

"Your boys are bullies. They're bullies. They were beating up my little ones," Lizz shouted.

"And am I after hearing the name of Connerty slurred?" Mrs. Connerty yelled.

"If your tramps come near my boys again, I'll get the police after them," Lizz yelled.

"And is it shanty Irish that's calling my boys names that belong to her own ones?"

"Go on home and teach your boys some manners! They're bullies! This home is my castle, and if I catch your bullies in my yard I'll brain them with a stove poker. Go on home and see if your man's drunk again," Lizz cried.

"She talks about my man and I do be seeing her own man come rolling home, drunk as a lord," Mrs. Connerty yelled.

"Say, you, when your man dies they're going to pour him back in the whiskey distillery," Lizz yelled.

The snow came down steadily, and both women were wreathed in it.

"The O'Neills are a disgrace to this decent neighborhood," Mrs. Connerty yelled, shaking a gloved hand at her neighbor.

"Say, you, if I wasn't in the condition I'm in, I'd come out there and knock you down in the snow and step on you," Lizz yelled.

"Ah, come out and let me get my hands on that hair of yours, you black-haired pauper!" Mrs. Connerty yelled.

"Come on over here. I'll scratch your eyes out!" Lizz yelled.

"The likes of you having the nerve to be after calling the Connertys bums! The nerve of you!"

"Bums! Bums! You're all dirty bums. My cousin is the alderman of this ward and I'll get him after you. I'll get Paddy Slattery after you," Lizz yelled.

"And sure, Paddy Slattery would be running a mile to hide from seeing you, cousin or no cousin," Mrs. Connerty yelled.

"I'll get him to raise your taxes. I'll get him to drive you out of the neighborhood. Go on back of the yards with the smell of the pigs where you belong!" Lizz yelled.

"Come out here until I lay my hands on you, you black-haired divil!"

"Come over here! Sick as I am in my eighth month, I'll fix you! Come over and I'll fix you!"

"Sure, and it wouldn't be worth my while to go soiling my hands on the likes of you!"

"If you or your dirty, bullying sons do anything more to me or mine, Mrs. Connerty, I won't be responsible for what I do. I'm warning you, Mrs. Connerty! I'm warning you! Whatever happens to you, it'll be on your conscience," Lizz yelled, shaking her fist.

Both women were well covered with snow, and the snow was falling so thickly that they could not see one another clearly.

"Don't let me be hearing you slurring the name of Connerty again, Mrs. O'Neill. I warn you, don't let me be hearing it!"

"Who could slur the name of Connerty? My people owned land in Ireland. They were landowners. But the name of Connerty was nothing. Tinkers, my mother would call you," Lizz yelled.

"Blessed Mother, but you're the lyin' one. It's a miracle of God's goodness that your tongue isn't stricken dumb with the words that fall from it," Mrs. Connerty yelled.

"Say, I'll have you know I never told a lie in my life. I'm like George Washington. I never told a lie," Lizz shouted.

"Go on with you, you're dirt under the feet of decent people," Mrs. Connerty yelled.

"You'll hear from me, and you'll hear from my cousin Paddy Slattery for the insults you've heaped on me, Mrs. Connerty."

"An O'Neill is beyond insult," Mrs. Connerty yelled.

"Oh, Mrs. Connerty, and aren't you going to have tea with the booze-fighting McGahans, you wearing your dress that looks like a petticoat, trying to play the lady. The wife of a janitor, trying to play the lady," Lizz said, mimicking as she talked.

"Go on, you pauper, get back in your dirty house," Mrs. Connerty yelled.

"Say, you, go tie a tin can to yourself," Lizz yelled.

"If it wasn't beneath my place in life I'd come into your yard and stop that bad tongue of yours up," Mrs. Connerty yelled.

"Come on and try it! I dare you! You'll never get out on those fat legs of yours. Go on down to the butcher. He's looking for pork! Go on over to the stockyards and sell yourself to the butchers for sausage before the price of pork goes down!" Lizz yelled.

Mrs. Connerty and Lizz simultaneously turned their backs to each other and stuck out their rumps. Mrs. Connerty trudged back through the snow, her shawl covered with white flakes.

"Go on home and tie a can to yourself, you old biddy," Lizz yelled.

Covered with snow, her hair wet, shivering, Lizz hastened back into the house.

The children were seated by the stove with their feet in the oven.

"If I ever catch you kids with the Connertys I'll break your necks," Lizz said, shaking her fists at them.

"Mama, they hit me with snowballs and hurt me, and they knocked our snow man down," Catherine said.

"Mama, they washed my face in snow," Bob said.

"And you, out fighting with them. An O'Neill shouldn't even fight with such low Irish. Denny O'Neill, if I ever find you fighting with those Connerty boys again, I'll beat you within an inch of your life," Lizz said.

"Mama, they picked on me. I didn't do nothing to them," Dennis said.

"The nerve of that one. I could've got my death of pneumonia out there fighting with her. Oh, but if I wasn't sick, I'd've gone out there and I'd've made mush out of that fat one. Oh, but when I'm myself again, what I won't do to her!" Lizz said loudly.

She drank a cup of warm tea.

"Dennis, you take care of your brothers and Catherine. I'm going to go over to Father Corbett this minute and put an end to that one's troublemaking. I'll go to that holy priest and I'll put an end to her," Lizz said with determination.

She went to her room, put on her old coat, threw an old shawl over her head, and went out to see the parish priest.

III

"Good day, Mrs. O'Neill. Very bad weather it is," Father Corbett said, coming into the parish visiting-parlor where Lizz sat waiting for him.

It was a small room, simply furnished, with a few standard literary works and the *Lives of the Saints* in a bookcase on the side, a small table in the center, and several leather chairs in the corners. Father Corbett was a tall man in his forties, ruddy, hearty, with a smiling face, twinkling brown eyes, and sandy hair.

"Father Corbett, I throw myself on you," Lizz said.

"But, Mrs. O'Neill, what's the matter?" the priest asked in surprise, stepping back, looking at Mrs. O'Neill in her old coat, her shawl on the chair behind her, her black hair uncombed, straggling out on the side, her ungainly pregnant shape showing through her opened coat and the apron she wore over an old skirt.

"Father, I place myself in your hands. And don't believe a word you hear about me. I'm a good woman, a mother. I'm poor, but I'm one of the Lord's poor," she said.

"But don't be so excited. Sit down and tell me what's the trouble, Mrs. O'Neill. Is one of the little ones sick? Or has your husband broken his pledge?"

"Father, my husband's a good man," Lizz said.

"A fine man. And I always enjoy those frogs' legs he sends over to me from time to time," Father Corbett said.

"Father, I'm a sick woman and I'm about to become a mother again. Father, I place myself in your hands," Lizz said.

"But tell me the trouble, my good Mrs. O'Neill," Father Corbett said.

The housekeeper entered the room and said respectfully to the priest:

"Father Corbett, Mrs. Connerty is here and she's very excited and wants to see you."

"You ask her to wait in the room right across the hall," Father Corbett said.

The housekeeper bowed and went out.

"Father, she came to backbite me. Father, I'm a good woman, and she came to backbite me."

"But, Mrs. O'Neill, I don't understand this."

"Father, that one came to backbite me and turn you against me. That's why I came here to see you. I place myself in your hands, Father Corbett," Lizz said.

"What is this? Have you and Mrs. Connerty been having a neighborly spat?"

"Father, her boys beat my boys and little girl, washed their faces in the snow. And she said things to me that I wouldn't dare to repeat in the presence of a man as holy as you," Lizz said.

Father Corbett's eyes twinkled. He pushed a bell at his side, and when the housekeeper stuck her head in the door, he turned to her and said:

"Would you please ask Mrs. Connerty to come in."

"Father, I won't speak to her. I won't speak to that one. Father, she insulted me."

Father Corbett opened his mouth to say something, but at that moment Mrs. Connerty entered. Seeing Lizz, she bridled up, lifted her nose, and castigated her neighbor with a fierce look.

"So you came over to talk behind my back," Mrs. Connerty said.

"Sit down, Mrs. Connerty," Father Corbett said.

"Sure, and the Lord bless you, Father Corbett, I can't be sitting down in a room with that one. Father, she's after slurring my good name and the good name of my husband who's worked for you these last ten years," Mrs. Connerty said.

"Father Corbett, on my word of honor, I'm a mother, and I never did," Lizz said, getting to her feet.

"Please, sit down, both of you women, and don't excite yourselves," Father Corbett said.

"Father, her boys bullied my little ones," Lizz said.

"Father, she's after violating the eighth commandment and lying in your holy presence," Mrs. Connerty said, getting to her feet.

"Father Corbett believes me. He knows I wouldn't lie," Lizz said.

"Father, you know me these many years, and I never missed mass of a Sunday when I was able to carry my legs across the street. That one, Father, is a black mark on the parish."

"Father Corbett, my aunt is a holy nun, and I'm a mother. Father Corbett, she backbites me," Lizz said.

"Sit down, my good women, and please calm yourselves," Father Corbett said, embarrassed.

Lizz and Mrs. Connerty didn't move.

"Please sit down, my good women," Father Corbett repeated.

"Father, one of her boys took a gun at my boys," said Mrs. Connerty.

"What?" asked the priest, sitting up in his chair.

"It wasn't a gun. It was a BB gun, and he was protecting himself. Her boys and some tramps came into my yard and beat my little ones up and washed their faces in the snow," Lizz said.

"Father, as true as I'm sittin' here, that isn't so. My Albie, Father, serves at holy mass for you. He wouldn't do such a thing," said Mrs. Connerty.

"Father, she threatened to hit me, me in my condition," Lizz said.

"Father, she's after misrepresentin' me," Mrs. Connerty said.

"Both of you women will have to be quiet and calm yourselves," Father Corbett said firmly.

They sat, self-righteously glaring at one another.

"You two women are good women, and I'm proud to have you as my parishioners. I don't want to hear of any more fighting between you. You mustn't have such misunderstandings, and you must have more patience," Father Corbett said.

"Father, these many months she's tried my patience to the breaking point," Mrs. Connerty said.

"Father, I mind my own business and all I ask is that others do the same," said Lizz.

"Is it my business when I hear my name and the name of himself slurred on the street, and my boys set upon by one of her wild Indians with a gun?"

"I told you women now that I wanted to talk. You must both listen to me," Father Corbett said coldly.

Silent, the two women glared at each other.

"I want you both to be good neighbors, helpful to one another, like good Christians," Father Corbett said.

"Oh, but Father—"

Father Corbett raised his hand.

"I'm talking, Mrs. O'Neill. Now, I want both of you good women to let bygones be bygones and become friends," he said. The eyes of both women met, turned frigidly away. "I want you to leave this house as friends and I want you both to promise me that you won't be fighting like this and coming to me in this state of excitement again. I don't want to hear any more of it. You should be good neighbors, and you should not allow your excitement to get the better of you. You're both good women and have good husbands and fine children," Father Corbett continued.

"Father, I have nothing against no one. I only stand on me rights," Mrs. Connerty said.

"Father Corbett, I was in my house working when my children screamed, and when I came out her boys were beating them," Lizz said.

"I was at my work and I do hear her screamin' and yellin' at me boys," Mrs. Connerty said.

"Both of you women are right. You just had a misunderstanding, and your boys are fine and upstanding. Boys will be boys, and they get a little bit wild. You mustn't fight because of it. You must understand it, and know that it doesn't mean so much. I'll have the Sisters give the boys a talking-to and tell them that I said they must be good friends, and if I hear of the O'Neill children fighting with the Connerty children, I'll give them a little warming myself. It's bad to spare the rod and spoil the child. Now, I want to see you two women tell each other you're sorry, and give me your promise you'll have no more of these misunderstandings," Father Corbett said.

Neither spoke.

"Go ahead. The Lord forgives. You must forgive one another," Father Corbett said.

Both women looked down at the floor.

"Father, sure, I wasn't meaning things serious. It was just as I started a-tellin' you, I looks out of me window a little while ago and what do I see but Mrs. O'Neill comin' to you, so I came," Mrs. Connerty said.

"Father, I'm a peaceful woman," Lizz said.

"Mrs. Connerty, tell me that you forgive Mrs. O'Neill," Father Corbett said.

"Indeed, Father, and I do," Mrs. Connerty said.

"Mrs. O'Neill, tell me you forgive Mrs. Connerty."

"Yes, Father Corbett, I harbor no ill feelings," Lizz said.

"That's fine. Do you mean it?"

They both nodded their heads affirmatively.

"Do you both promise me you won't repeat this unfortunate quarrel?"

Again they nodded.

"You both live right in the shadow of the church, and what kind of an example is it when you quarrel, both of you good Catholic women raising families? You should be ashamed of yourselves and pay a little visit to the Blessed Sacrament and say a prayer in penance after losing your tempers this way. And you both are going to become good neighbors and friends. If I hear of this happening again, I'm not going to like it," Father Corbett said.

"Sure, Father, and you won't from my side of it," said Mrs. Connerty.

"Father, I'm a peace-loving woman," Lizz said.

"Are you going to become friends?"

"Yes, Father. I was just thinking that Mrs. Connerty might step in one of these days and have a cup of tea with me," Lizz said.

"And I was after having the same thought myself," said Mrs. Connerty.

"Good. Now you promised me. Don't forget. I expect to hear no more of this. And I'll have the Sisters give your boys a talking-to and tell them I have my eye on them. I can look out of the window, you know, and check up on them," he said, wagging his finger.

"Father, I'm going to raise one of my boys to be a priest," Lizz said.

"And, sure, my Albie is going to be a priest, too. He's the most religious boy, Father Corbett," Mrs. Connerty said.

"You both must set good examples. And now you women shake hands."

They shook hands and smiled.

"And you had better be getting home to start cooking supper for your husbands. They're both good men," Father Corbett said.

"Ah, Father, himself worships the very ground you walk on," Mrs. Connerty said.

"Mr. O'Neill thinks that there's no man that walks the earth finer than you, Father," Lizz said.

"Now that you are friends, good day," Father Corbett said.

They walked out of the priest's house together.

"Well, good day, Mrs. O'Neill," Mrs. Connerty said.

"Good day," Lizz said.

They turned their backs on one another and trudged home through the snow, each going to an opposite corner to cross the street.

IV

Dennis' mouth was smeared with chocolate as he returned to the kitchen where the other children still sat with their feet in the oven.

"You were eating candy," Catherine said.

"Mind your own business," Dennis said.

"I'm gonna tell Pa," Catherine said.

"Go ahead. I ain't a scaredy cat," Dennis said.

"Gimme some candy," Catherine said.

"I want some candy," Bob said.

"Go get it," Dennis said.

"Where?" asked Bob.

"It's here," Dennis said, pointing to his stomach.

"Pig!" Catherine said.

"Don't call me a pig or I'll sock you one," Dennis said.

"I want some candy," Bob said.

"Shut up and don't bawl," Dennis said.

"When Mama comes back from seeing Father Corbett, I'll tell her," Catherine said.

"See if I care," Dennis said.

Catherine glowered at Dennis.

"Snitcher!" Dennis said.

"Pig!" Catherine said.

"Who's a pig?" Dennis asked.

"You ate candy and didn't give me and Bob some," Catherine said.

"I ain't got any more left," Dennis said.

"I want some candy," Bob said.

"Pig!" Catherine said.

"Who's a pig?" Dennis asked.

"Pig!" Catherine said.

Dennis twisted her arm. She cried out.

"I'll tell Papa," she said.

"Who's a pig now?" Dennis asked.

"Nobody," Catherine said in tears.

"Don't call me a pig again," Dennis said, releasing her arm.

She ran into the dining room, flung herself on the couch and cried.

"Here comes Mama," Bob said, going to the kitchen window.

"I'm gonna tell Mama," Catherine said, returning to the kitchen.

"If you tell on me I'll kill you," Dennis said to Bob.

Bob pointed his left index finger to his chest and shook his head from side to side. Dennis went to the sink and wiped the chocolate from his face.

V

"What's happened to my baby girl?" Lizz asked on seeing Catherine in tears when she came back.

"I don't know," Dennis said, shrugging his shoulders.

"Mama, he hit me. He's a pig," Catherine said, still sobbing.

"I didn't. I didn't do nothin' to her," Dennis said.

"Dennis O'Neill!" Catherine said, looking sternly but tearfully at her brother.

"What's the matter, Dolly?" Lizz asked.

"Mama, he hit me," Catherine said.

"She's lying. Bob, did I hit her? You was here," Dennis said, pointing a finger at Bob; noticing out of the corner of his eye that his Mother was looking at Catherine, he quickly shook his head negatively as a signal and then shook a fist at Bob.

"I didn't see it. We was playing, me and Denny, and all of a sudden she started crying," Bob said.

"Bobby O'Neill, I hate you," Catherine said, again breaking into tears.

"Don't use words like that or I'll wash your mouth out with soap," Lizz said to Catherine.

"He did. His mouth was all candy, and I asked him for some. He wouldn't give me none. He's a pig. He hit me and twisted my arm. It hurt," Catherine said.

"Where did you get the candy?"

"I didn't have none," Dennis said.

"He did, too."

"Ask Bob if I did."

"You children will be the death of your mother yet. I ought to put a strap to every one of you. Now, keep quiet and let me be in peace."

Lizz went out to the kitchen.

"Smarty," Dennis said.

"I'm gonna tell Papa," Catherine said.

VI

Just after Bill came in, there was a knock on the front door. Lizz answered it, and Albie Connerty handed her a package containing half of an apple pie his mother had sent over. Lizz held him there, talking to him, telling him he was a good boy.

"Dennis ate your candy," Catherine told Bill in the dining room.

Bill got angry. He went to his bedroom and came out with an empty candy box.

"Where is he?" Bill asked.

Catherine pointed to the kitchen.

"Why'd you steal my candy?" Bill angrily asked Dennis, cornering him in the kitchen.

"Beat him good, Bill. He twisted my arm," Catherine said, standing near Bill.

"Lemme alone," Dennis whined as Bill twisted his arm behind his back.

"You little bastard, I'll teach you a lesson, taking what belongs to me," Bill said, slapping Dennis' face.

Dennis screamed.

"Shut up! Don't bawl," Bill commanded.

He punched Dennis. The boy sank to the floor. Bill stood over him with clenched fists and asked:

"Will you take it again?"

"No," Dennis whimpered.

"If you tell I socked you, I'll show you what I do with snitchers. That goes for all of you kids," Bill said.

Whining on the floor, Dennis didn't answer. Bill kicked him.

"I asked you. Hear me?"

"Yes," Dennis whimpered.

"And you, too," Bill said, pointing to Bob and Catherine.

Bill walked to the window as he heard Lizz coming back.

"What happened now? Who's yelling this time?"

They didn't answer. She saw Dennis on the floor.

"What's the matter with you?"

"Dennis fell down running. He's all right now," Bill said.

"Can't you stand up? You caused me enough trouble. I almost got my death out in the snow today because of you," she said.

"I'm all right. I just fell down," Dennis said.

Lizz sank to a chair. She was tired. She set the pie on the table beside her. She held her chin in her hands and sat there, wearied. She had pains. And her back ached. And she had to get things for Jim's supper.

"Bill, go down to the store at the corner of Wentworth and ask the man if you can get twenty-five cents' worth of hamburger on trust until payday. I got to get something for your father's supper," she said.

Bill went to get his coat. Lizz still sat in the kitchen. She sighed.

39

I

Lizz sat down by the dining-room window and looked out. The long winter was over at last. She could smell spring in the air. And the house was so quiet. Little Margaret had come to see them, and all the children had gone down the street to the park playground. She was alone and wouldn't hear the noise of the regiment for a little while on this Saturday afternoon. The long winter was over and spring could be smelled through the opened window. She breathed deeply. Yes, winters in the cottage here were hard, and it was so nice when they were over. And this one, it had been a winter of waiting, because at the end of it her time would come. Her time was coming soon. Any day now the pains would start. She thought that it would be next week. But it could come any day. She was big with the baby growing in her. Her breasts were expanded, her abdomen protuberant, swollen, and shapeless. She felt the extra weight she had to carry. Her back would ache. She would have pains. The baby would kick within her. But it didn't seem to stir as much as the others had. Would it be a boy or a girl? What would she name it if it was a boy? Should she name it after Al? After its father? Or if it was a girl, what should she name it? Mary, after the Blessed Virgin? Elizabeth, after herself? She had not spoken to Jim about naming it. And would it be a boy or a girl? She hoped that it would be a boy. Boys, once they started growing, were less trouble. And when they got to be men they could go out to work and make more money than a girl could.

She wished that her travail were over. After it was, there would be complete forgetfulness. She could remember how after she had had the others, after the pains had almost broken her back, making her scream, after it was over, the way she had gone to sleep. She longed for just that time. The time when her child would be delivered and she would be just falling asleep.

She felt so sick and so tired. Her legs bothered her, and her varicose veins had gotten larger. She had to drag herself around the house. Well, it was woman's cross. She had to bear a woman's cross and the mark of Eve on her brow.

She loved it sitting here now by the window for a few minutes. And soon her travail would be over. But then when she was on her feet after it, there would be an infant needing care. One more mouth for Jim to feed. One more child to be watched and taken care of, as if she didn't have enough already. Four of them too young to go to school. Yes, she was going to have her hands full. But anything rather than these last days of waiting, waiting for the labor to start. If it was only over. If she was only now, this minute, falling asleep after giving birth.

She sat by the window and again breathed deeply of the spring air. She felt her jaw. Her teeth were bothering her again. This morning she had started eating a sweet roll and the sugar had gotten into one of her cavities, and she had had a toothache all day. And there was no oil of cloves in the house. She'd have to wait for the children to come back.

The earth beyond the fence outside her window was muddy. Patches of soiled snow were slowly thawing and there were traces of weedy green to be seen in the soft mud. Children ran and played across the street by the picket fence of the parish ground. Little girls were seated near the curb playing jacks. She used to play jacks when she was a little girl. They had played jacks on the street down on Blue Island Avenue. She wondered what her kids were doing in the playground. She hoped they wouldn't be hurt. But her Little Margaret was a little mother and she would watch them.

There was Mrs. McCarthy going to the store. Her husband had been out of work for a long time, but he was working now. Yes, she thought she ought to name the new one Alfred after her brother if he was a boy. She had just written to Al for money and told him how much she needed it, and she had gotten a five-dollar money order. He was good, Al was, even if he was bossy.

One of the nuns walked by the fence. The nun must be going to pay a visit to church. Oh, but if she could have been a nun, living the pure and holy life of a nun. That was what she had wanted to be before she met Jim. That was what she should have been. No burdens, no children to care for, no man to cook for, just labor in the vineyard of the Master. If she had gone into the convent, she wouldn't be in the condition she was in now. Fool that she was, not having answered the call God had sent her to serve Him.

Her tooth was aching, and maybe a warm cup of tea would do it good. She walked slowly and wearily to the kitchen, poured herself a cup of tea, carried it back and set it on the window sill. She sipped it, letting the warm liquid get into the aching cavity. But it did not stop the ache. Yes, she should have answered the call God had given her to serve Him in the holy and virginal sisterhood. She sipped her tea. She could see herself wearing the habit of the Poor Clares. She would be all in black, and veiled, with rosary beads at her side rattling when she walked. Always the beads would rattle when she walked, and she could say so many rosaries to Mary every day of her life. Every day she could pray for hours, feeling herself alone in communion with her God. Now, she could steal only a few minutes here and there for prayers. And if she had been a nun, wouldn't that be a feather in Mother's cap whenever Mother saw people like the Gormans, or Jim's cousins, the O'Reilleys. But then, if she had gone into the convent, she wouldn't have known Jim. If Mother didn't know Jim, she wouldn't know his cousins, the O'Reilleys. They lived on Grand Boulevard in Crucifixion parish. If she was a nun, then whenever Mother met Mary and Martha O'Reilley, she would talk to them, talking about my daughter who is in the convent. Lizz sighed. If she had gone into the convent, she would have even had a chance to become a saint. She might have been the first saint from America to be canonized. The Lord might have worked miracles through her, might have worked through her to comfort the sick, raise the dead, give sight to the blind. Because of her, then, Mother never would have wanted, and the lives of her father and her sister, Louise, might have been spared. God might have granted her the request that they live if she'd become a holy nun, a virgin in His name. She would have prayed and God would have granted her petition to prolong their lives. But it was too late.

She took another sip of tea. It was cold. She dashed it out the window and it spilled on the fence below. She went to the kitchen and returned with a warm cup of tea. She saw herself as a black-veiled nun. How happy it would have made her. She wouldn't be feeling the way she was this minute, worn out and waiting for another one to come. Almost all of her births had been hard ones. Daniel had come the easiest. Bill's had been hard. With the twins that had died so many years ago, she had been in labor a whole day and all night, and then the next morning they had come, and they had hardly come out when they died. Oh, that God would make this one an easy birth. And if she had become a nun, she wouldn't be sitting here in this dirty house waiting for the ordeal. But if she had been a nun, none of her children would have been born, none of her lovely, beautiful chicks. Well, then, maybe Louise would have lived and married and had them all instead of her. Peg wouldn't have had them, but Louise would. But poor Peg, she was good. She was on the water wagon now and she was good. If Louise had lived and had the children she had had, and she herself had been a nun, then instead of being the mother of her little ones, she would be their aunt. It would be funny if she was the aunt of her Angel Child Arty and came in her nun's habit to see him, and looked in his brown eyes and patted his curly hair. Maybe she would have gone to New York and gone into the Order of Saint Joseph and been a nun in the same order as her own aunt. Sister was Mother Superior now. She must write to her. Her own aunt was a Mother Superior. She might have gone into the same order. And then maybe Louise would have had

Little Margaret and Little Margaret would have followed her into the convent. She had made a great mistake. And she would have been so happy if she had given her whole life to God.

She sighed again, breathed in the spring air.

She sat by the window. There was a dreamy, faraway look on her face.

II

"Good day, Mrs. O'Neill," Mrs. Connerty called from the sidewalk, standing there with a black shawl thrown over her shoulders.

"Oh, hello, Mrs. Connerty," Lizz called back, smiling.

"It's fine weather we are getting after having a bad winter," Mrs. Connerty said.

"Isn't it? I was just sitting here and resting. My children are all at the playground," Lizz said.

"I see that there's little enough snow left," Mrs. Connerty said.

"My little girl, the one that lives with my mother, is down today. She's a little mother," said Lizz.

"I seen her taking the others out," Mrs. Connerty said.

"Won't you come in and have a cup of tea, Mrs. Connerty?" Lizz called.

"I'm just after having a cup, thank you. But your time will soon be coming now, won't it?"

"Yes, I think next week," Lizz called.

"If you need anything, you call on me. Send one of the little ones in for me and I'll fly right to you, Mrs. O'Neill," Mrs. Connerty called.

"Thank you, Mrs. Connerty, you're so good," Lizz said.

"Sure, forget it. If you need me I'll come a-running. But I must be getting on to the store. Good day, Mrs. O'Neill."

"Good day, Mrs. Connerty," Lizz said, and Mrs. Connerty walked on.

Lizz sat by the window, vacantly looking out.

III

"I'm so glad you came, Mary," Lizz said to Jim's cousin, Mary O'Reilley, a sweet but plain-faced, primly-dressed woman.

"I thought that I'd come over to see you since it was a nice day," Mary said.

"My little girl who stays with my mother is down to see us and she and all of the little ones are out at the playground. I wanted to clean house, but I'm not able to. My time is coming so soon now," Lizz said.

"Oh, you poor thing," Mary O'Reilley said.

"How have you been, Mary? You look so wonderful. I paid a visit to the Blessed

Sacrament yesterday and I lit holy candles for all of you. How is Martha and Joe?"

"They're very well, Lizz," Mary O'Reilley said.

"Joe is such a wonderful man. My Jim, he looks up to Joe so much," Lizz said.

"We all do. He's so educated."

"If my sons become as fine men as Joe, I'll be a happy mother. But, Mary, I'm so sorry you came when the children are out. I'd love you to see my Little Arty," Lizz said.

"He's the youngest, isn't he?"

"But he's grown so, and he talks and walks since you were last here. He's the smartest child, and he has such lovely eyes. Would you believe it, Mary, he takes after the O'Reilleys," Lizz said.

"He does?"

"He's the spittin' image of an O'Reilley," Lizz said.

"I didn't think so when I saw him before, but then he was a baby not yet walking," Mary said.

"You'd die at the likeness. I swear but he'll look like your brother, Joe," Lizz said.

"I never would have thought it, Lizz. But how is your mother?"

"She's so healthy. Do you know, I'll bet she'll bury every one of us," Lizz said.

"She doesn't seem to remember me," Mary O'Reilley said.

"Oh, yes, she does. She speaks of you every time I see her. She thinks you're such a fine woman. Yes, she does. Indeed, she does, Mary. She thinks that the O'Reilleys are the salt of the earth."

"That's funny. Several times on Sunday when I saw her going to church, she's walked right by me without a by-your-leave."

"You don't know my mother, Mary. She's such a holy woman. She never talks to anyone on the street. And do you know why?" Lizz asked, leaning forward, pointing a fat finger at Mary.

"Why?"

"Because she's so holy. She prays. She walks along the street praying," Lizz said.

"She does?"

"Yes. She's so devout. She prays all the time. But she remembers you. She thinks the O'Reilleys are the salt of the earth."

"Lizz, are you seeing the doctor about your condition?"

"When the pains come, the doctor will be gotten. I'm all right. It's only the last days, Mary. I feel heavy and tired. And my legs ache. I can't get around much, and there are so many little ones here," Lizz said.

"You poor thing," Mary said.

"Mary, men never know what a woman goes through," Lizz said.

"I guess not," Mary said.

"Oh, Mary, you're lucky. You don't know how lucky you are. If I was in your shoes, Mary, I wouldn't change places with any woman," Lizz said.

"Martha was saying she was sorry she couldn't come with me," Mary said.

"She's so good, too. But she's probably so busy," Lizz said.

"No, Lizz, Martha and I have hardly anything to do most of the time," Mary said.

"But you take care of that lovely house and make a home for your brother, Joe, and have your niece there to take care of," Lizz said.

"We don't have much to do," Mary said.

"It was so good of you and Martha, not getting married in order to take care of your brother, Joe, and give him a home. My sister, Peg, and my brother, Al, have done the same thing for my mother," Lizz said.

"Oh, no, Lizz! We're just old maids," Mary said.

"I wish I was. Say, do I? Not that I would say a word against my Jim. He's as fine a man as walks the earth. But it's better being an old maid than have a regiment of kids like wild Indians and be in the ninth month, to boot," Lizz said.

"I know, Lizz, you poor thing. But everything will turn out for the best. When they grow up, you'll be proud of yourself for having raised such a family, and they'll take care of you," Mary said.

"Mary, you're so lucky. Think of how much time you have to pray. Why, you ought to be able to go to church every day and say the Stations of the Cross at least once. Mary, you and Martha are lucky girls. Not that you don't deserve it," Lizz said.

"You're so holy, Lizz," Mary said.

"Mary, do you know that I think I was really called to be a nun. That's why I'm so poor. I'll be poor all my life. It's my cross for not heeding the call of God. I was born to be a nun," Lizz said.

"I often think that nuns must lead such a wonderful, peaceful life. Like those Poor Clares down on Lafayette Avenue, the ones in that order who never see any outsiders, and when you go to the convent on Sunday you can hear them singing at vespers. It's so beautiful," Mary said wistfully.

"Ah, they're like the apple of our Lord's eye," Lizz said.

"But here, Lizz, I don't want to forget this. Here, you take it. You'll need it in your condition," Mary said, pulling a five-dollar bill out of her pocket and handing it to Lizz.

"Oh, Mary, you'll be needing that yourself."

"No, you take it, Lizz."

"Thank you. You're so good. You O'Reilleys are so good to me and Jim. We'll never forget you. That's why I always say a prayer for you. Do you know why Cousin Joe got to be lawyer for that brewery? Because I prayed for him. I said a novena that he would get that brewery account that made him so much money," Lizz said.

"But Joe isn't a lawyer for breweries. He's a corporation lawyer."

"I pray for him all the time," Lizz said.

"Well, Lizz, I have to be going," Mary said.

"Oh, can't you stay until the children come back? I want you to see them. Oh, but you'll fall in love with my Little Arty, Mary. He's an O'Reilley. I'll bet he'll be a fine lawyer like Joe when he grows up," Lizz said.

"I'd love to, Lizz, but I have to go. You take care of yourself and let us know if we can help you. Martha and I will send you some nice baby things for your little visitor, and tell Jim to call us up and tell us if it's a boy or a girl," Mary said.

"Yes, Mary, you're so good."

"Goodbye, Lizz. Now, take care of yourself and remember me to Jim," said Mary.

"Oh, but wait until he hears you were here. He'll be so tickled," Lizz said.

"Well, goodbye, Lizz, dear," Mary said, going to the door. Lizz followed her.

"And, Mary, if it's a boy, I think we'll name it after Cousin Joe."

"Joe will be so pleased," Mary said, turning to walk carefully down the front steps.

"And, Mary, tell Cousin Joe we asked for him," Lizz called to her.

"Yes, Lizz."

"Mary, I'll say a novena for you," Lizz yelled after her as she walked away.

"Thanks, Lizz," Mary said, waving her hand.

Lizz watched her go. She went inside and sat down again by the window, looking out at the street, watching the little girls on the opposite side as they played jacks.

IV

"You're all dry now and fixed up clean," Lizz said, buttoning up an old pair of pants on Arty. She turned to Little Margaret who stood with Dennis beside her. "Why did you let him get wet?"

"We couldn't help it. Kids sprinkled him and we couldn't help it, honest, Mama," Little Margaret said.

"Jim?" Lizz called to Jim in the kitchen. "Have you fixed up that package of frogs' legs for Father Corbett?"

"Yeah," Jim called in. "It's nice to be able to get them for nothing on my route."

Lizz took Arty by the hand and led him out to Jim.

"Our little man is going to take them over," Lizz said.

Jim looked down tenderly at Arty.

"Mama, can't I go, too?" Little Margaret asked.

"No, you got your feet wet and your shoes have to get dry," Lizz said.

She went slowly back to the front.

"Put your coats on, you kids, and go with your little brother when he takes the frogs' legs to Father Corbett," Lizz said.

"You say they're from your father when you see the priest," Jim said, squatting before Arty.

"From Fither," Arty exclaimed.

"Ha, you're going to be the smartest one of the O'Neills yet, you little beggar," Jim said.

"All right, Jim, they're ready," Lizz called.

"Denny, come here," Jim called.

"Yes, Pa," Dennis answered, coming into the kitchen.

"You carry this package until you get across the street to Father Corbett's, and then give it to Arty to hand to him. Just before you do, tell Arty to say it's from his father," Jim said.

It was dark out, and the four youngest O'Neill children trooped across the street, Dennis carrying the package and Bob and Catherine holding Arty's hands. They rang the bell at the priest's house.

"We have something for Father Corbett," Dennis said.

"I'll take it," the housekeeper said.

"We want to give it to him. My father wants my baby brother to hand it to Father Corbett. They're frog legs," said Dennis.

"Oh, yes, you're the O'Neill children. I'll call His Reverence," the housekeeper said.

They waited, and Dennis handed the package to Arty.

"You tell Father Corbett these are from your father," Dennis said, bending down to Arty.

"Hello! Hello, how are the fine young men and women?" Father Corbett said.

"Hello, Father," Dennis, Bob, and Catherine chorused.

"From Fither," Arty said, handing the priest the package of frogs' legs.

"Your father sent them to me, did he?"

"Fither," Arty said.

"Yes, Father," Dennis said.

"You children thank your father. He's a fine man. And the little fellow here, what's his name again?"

"Arty," Dennis said.

"Arty, you're a fine lad," Father Corbett said.

Arty laughed at the priest.

"You're the lad in school, Dennis, isn't that your name?" Father Corbett said.

"Yes, Father," Dennis said.

"And what's the little lady's name?" asked Father Corbett.

"Catherine," Catherine said.

"And I'm Bob," said Bob.

"And you're all good when your mother tells you to do something?" said Father Corbett.

"Yes, Father," they chorused, and Arty smiled.

"Arty good, Fither," Arty said.

Father Corbett dug into his trouser pocket under his cassock. Change rattled.

"Here, you little man," Father Corbett said, placing a half dollar in Arty's hand.

"Say thank you, Father Corbett," Catherine said to Arty.

Arty looked at the fifty-cent piece.

"Say thank you," Catherine said.

"Tank," Arty said.

"Now, be good children, and thank your father and mother for me," the priest said.

"Goodbye, Father," the three older children chorused.

"Bye-bye," Arty said, and waved.

They turned away and Father Corbett closed the door.

"We could get a lot of candy with the money Father Corbett gave Arty," Dennis said.

"How much is it?" asked Bob.

"A half dollar."

"How much is that?"

"A lot," said Dennis.

"Buy me some candy," Catherine said.

"If we do, you won't snitch?" Dennis asked.

"No," Catherine said.

"Cross your heart," Dennis said.

She crossed her heart.

"Arty don't know what it is," Dennis said, and just at that moment Arty threw the half dollar on the sidewalk.

Dennis picked it up. Dragging Arty, they ran to the candy store across the street from the cottage.

V

"Did he like the frogs' legs?" Lizz asked Dennis.

"Uh huh. He said we should thank you and Papa," Dennis said, embarrassed.

"Mither, here," Arty said.

He showed her a penny.

"That was nice of him. Did he give the rest of you a penny?" Lizz asked.

The other three each held up a penny.

"That was nice. Now your father is fixing your supper for you," Lizz said.

They took off their coats. Lizz slowly bent down and removed Arty's coat. He ran through the house laughing. He tripped. He laughed, got up, ran to the window. A horse and wagon passed.

"Horsie!" he exclaimed.

He ran his fingers up and down the window. He turned and scampered back to the dining room, up to Little Margaret who sat languidly on the couch, and handed her his penny. Her cheeks were flushed.

"Oh, you little darling," Little Margaret said, and she embraced and kissed him.

He squirmed loose and ran into the kitchen.

"Mither! Hungry!" he exclaimed.

Jim looked at him from the stove.

"Ah, you little beggar, you'll get your supper now," Jim said tenderly.

"Jim, I can't get over the way he's growing. You can see him growing before your very eyes," Lizz said.

"Lizz, before we know it they'll all be in school," Jim said.

"I hope so," Lizz said.

Arty walked over by his father and stood looking up.

"Fither!"

"Ah, you're so damn cute. You're going to be quite the lad when you grow up to be a man," Jim said.

Arty laughed.

"Tell the kids to come in to supper now, Lizz," Jim said.

40

I

"Didn't I tell you to keep Arty out to play with you and Bob?" Lizz said in sudden anger when Catherine led Arty by the hand into the dining room; outside it was a sunny morning, and the air, flowing in through the opened windows of the cottage, brought with it a sense of the young spring.

"Mama, Arty is acting funny," Catherine said.

"What did you do to him?" Lizz asked, excited.

"He's acting funny. I didn't do nothing to him. He don't run and he acts funny. He just sits down, and it's wet so he can't sit down. If he just wants to sit down, I brought him in to let him sit down in here," Catherine said.

Lizz looked at Arty. The child stood holding onto his sister's hand. Lizz saw that his face was flushed.

"And he would do this, like he was cold. I thought something was funny with him because Bob and me didn't do this like we was cold," Catherine said, imitating a person shivering.

"Is Mama's Angel Child cold?" Lizz asked, looking at Arty.

"Cold," he said in a weak voice.

"Glory be! The child must be sick," Lizz said.

She felt his cheeks, and they were warm. He shivered.

"The poor fellow must have a cold. Your big sister let him get wet when she took you all to the playground Saturday and he caught cold," Lizz said.

"I don't know. He just acted funny," Catherine said.

"You run out and play with Bob. And don't get your feet wet in any mud. It'll be bad enough to have your baby brother sick without you catching cold," Lizz said.

"He was just acting funny so I brought him in," Catherine said.

"I'll take care of him. You run out and play again, and don't go hurting or cutting yourself," Lizz said.

Catherine ran out of the house.

Lizz looked at Arty. He stood before her, stolid, with his usually pale cheeks flushed. Lizz looked at his eyes. They seemed bleared, cloudy.

"You poor child. You must have a cold. Come here, my angel precious," Lizz said.

She led him to the couch. Slowly she picked him up and set him on it. He sat quiet, looking toward his mother with a pleading expression.

Lizz was angry with Little Margaret. Why did she let Arty get wet and catch cold? But then, she was catching it in time before it could become serious.

She got a bottle of castor oil from a shelf in the kitchen. She poured a spoonful into a glass. She then mixed it with thick condensed milk and water and stirred it. She went back to Arty, and from the moment she appeared in the dining-room doorway, his eyes followed her. She sat down beside him and held up his chin.

"His Mama's going to fix him up good and he won't have any more cold, the little cherubim," Lizz said.

She held the glass to his lips. He squirmed and pushed the glass away.

"Drink, my precious. Mama is going to make her precious better," Lizz said.

She held the glass to his lips again. She could see that he was having difficulty in swallowing the liquid. When she drew the glass away, he made a face and she could see he was making a face as he tried to swallow.

"My precious must have a sore throat," she said.

She set the glass on the table and brought a spoon in from the kitchen. She brought Arty to the window, opened his mouth, and tried to look down into his throat. She thought it was red but she wasn't sure.

Again she tried to give him the castor oil in the condensed milk and water. Again he squirmed, resisted, and tried to push the glass away. She fed it to him patiently, spoon by spoon. She could see he was having difficulty in swallowing. He must have gotten a sore throat with the cold. Oh, if she had her hands on Little Margaret for letting him get wet.

When she had finished feeding him with the spoon, she set the glass and spoon on the table. She wrapped a shawl around him.

Arty sat, watching her with his bleary eyes. His cheeks were still flushed, and every so often he shivered, blowing and making lip noises to signify cold as he did so.

II

Dennis bolted into the house for his lunch.

"Denny, your little brother is sick. Why did you let him get wet Saturday at the playground?"

"I didn't. We couldn't help it. What's the matter with him?"

"He must have a cold and a little bit of a sore throat, I guess. I sent him out to play with Catherine and Bob, and he wouldn't play. The poor little fellow is sick," Lizz said.

"Hello, Arty," Dennis said.

Arty watched Dennis.

"Shake hands, kid," Dennis said, holding out his hands.

"Sake hans," Arty said as Dennis took his hand; Arty was a trifle hoarse.

"Go call your brother and sister in, and I'll give you children your dinner," Lizz said.

Lizz went to the stove. Dennis went to the back yard.

"Hey, you kids, come on in for dinner," Dennis said.

Catherine and Bob came into the kitchen. Lizz went to the dining room and took Arty by the hand. She set him up in his high chair. Lifting him was a strain. He sat watching her. She felt his face.

"I think your fever is going down," she said to him.

She kissed him and then caressed his face. Her hand casually ran down his cheek and to his neck. She looked at him with sudden puzzlement. There seemed to be a little bit of swelling.

"You poor child, you did get a cold, all right," Lizz said.

She kissed him again.

"Ma, what's the matter with Arty?" asked Bob.

"He's got a cold. Now, sit down and I'll give you your dinner," Lizz said.

III

Arty looked at his bowl of oatmeal. Tiredly and awkwardly, he lifted his spoon and dug into his oatmeal, dropping some onto the tray of his high chair as he conveyed it to his mouth. He dropped the spoon. He made a face as he swallowed.

Lizz picked the spoon from the floor, washed it at the sink, and returned to Arty.

"Eat, my precious," she said.

Arty sat there, and his breathing made a slight noise. He breathed as if he were doing so with difficulty.

Lizz stood by him and fed him. He again resisted her. She got him to eat several spoonfuls, but when she brought another spoonful to his lips, he turned his head away.

"Mama's gonna put her Angel Child to bed," she said.

She took his plate of oatmeal from the board.

She carried him to the dining room and laid him down on the couch. She went to her room and returned with a pillow and blanket. She gently set the pillow under his head and covered him with the blanket. He lay there, eyeing her.

"My baby's sick. Oh, he's so sick. But he's got his Mama to take care of him," Lizz said.

She bent down, cooed to him, kissed him.

"Kiss Mama," she said.

Making a noise as he obeyed, Arty kissed Lizz's cheek. His lips seemed chafed.

She looked at him again. When he was well he was more pale than now. And, yes, the child was not well. She could see from his eyes. She cooed to him.

"Mither!" he called in a slightly hoarse voice.

He coughed, a croupy cough.

Oh, God, she hoped it wasn't the whooping cough. It wouldn't be. God wouldn't have anything like this happen now, when any minute the pains might start coming.

"Dennis, you hurry up and finish your dinner. I want you to run down to the drugstore on Wentworth Avenue to get me some Boucher's cough medicine for your little brother," Lizz said.

Dennis, after finishing his own oatmeal, took what Arty had left in his bowl and ate it.

IV

Lizz looked down at Arty. He was sleeping, his little head rolled toward the wall. She gazed at his tangled hair. In the last six months it had gotten a little bit darker. He was going to have lovely, brown curly hair. Danny had had brown curls and Mother had used to dress him up in a white suit and he would be so cute in his white suit with his brown curls down his back. When Arty was about five, he would have curls like that and she would dress him up in a white sailor suit with white stockings, and he would have lovely curls down his back.

Ah, her poor little sick man.

She went to the back steps.

"Catherine, come here," she called.

Dirty-faced, her underdrawers hanging, one stocking ripped, Catherine ran to her mother.

"You and Bobby-boy go inside and stay there and be quiet and watch your little brother for five minutes. Your mother is going to run across the street to church to say a prayer. And you two be quiet. If you wake him up, I'll come back and spank you. He's not well," Lizz said.

"I'll be quiet," Catherine said.

"Will you be gone long, Mama?" Bob asked.

"No, only five minutes. Now you two be quiet and stay in there with him," Lizz said.

The two children came up the steps and went into parlor. They sat on the floor. Lizz threw her coat on, went across the street to say a prayer.

V

"Don't wake him up," Catherine said to Bob while Bob stood looking down at his sleeping brother.

"I'm not," said Bob.

"He's sick," Catherine said.

Bob tiptoed away, and he and Catherine sat in the parlor waiting for their mother to return.

"I know something we can play when Mama comes back," Bob said.

"What?" Catherine asked.

"Farm. We can dig in the yard and pretend we're having a farm," said Bob.

"We're going to have a farm in the yard. I heard Papa say to Mama they would grow things to eat this summer in the yard, and Mama said we'd have a farm in our back yard," Catherine said.

"We can play farm anyway, can't we?" Bob said.

"Uh huh!" Catherine said.

Arty began to cough, and it seemed to rack his body. He cried. He coughed, tossed, whimpered.

Lizz pushed open the front door.

"Did you wake him up?"

"No, he just started coughing and began crying just now," Bob said.

Lizz went to him.

"Oh, don't cry, my precious, don't cry. Your Mama is here with him," Lizz said.

She petted the feverish forehead. She gave him a spoonful of the cough medicine that Dennis had gotten at the drugstore. He lay restlessly on the couch.

VI

Lizz sat in the kitchen having a cup of tea. If Arty wasn't better when Jim came home from work, she would talk with Jim and maybe they'd call the doctor. He was a sick baby, but she was sure it was just a cold. Little Margaret had let him get wet and he had caught cold and gotten a sore throat. Little fellows like Arty were frail and they got sick easy. All the others had had colds as bad as Arty's at one time or another when they were his age. They had been as sick. Once when Bill was about Arty's age, he'd had an awful attack of bronchitis, and he got better. Arty would. God would help her now, and He would not visit her with sickness when her time was come.

She had a sudden shooting pain. Was that the beginning? Oh, she hoped not. If it was a day or two more, she would have Arty in better condition, and she'd rather have it come then. Who would take care of Arty when she was in bed? If it was an easy birth she wouldn't have to be in bed long. Well, thank God that the others weren't sick. She could hear Bob and Catherine playing in the yard. And she had watched Dennis running as he'd gone to school this afternoon. He wasn't sick. But was that pain the beginning? She would have to wait and see. Even if it was, there oughtn't to be anything serious happening before Jim got home.

Lizz got to her feet. They ached as she walked into the dining room. She looked at Arty. His eyes met hers. He was sick and his eyes were still clouded. He looked at her, hurt, sick, like a sick puppy dog.

"Mither!" he called hoarsely.

Lizz went to her room, returned with a bottle of holy water, and sprinkled him with the holy water.

He sniffled. She helped him blow his nose. She felt his cheeks and head. They were damp and feverish. His skin did not feel the same now as it did when he was well. Oh, her poor sick baby!

VII

Bill sat reading Danny's copy of the latest edition of Spalding's *Baseball Guide*. Arty was still on the couch. He coughed, and his body was racked by the cough. Now and then he emitted a low moan. He would then lie still for a brief period. Then he would stir restlessly. He would whimper.

Bill went to him.

"Sport, want a drink of water?" Bill asked, looking down at his sick brother.

Arty turned eyes of fright and pain and bewilderment on Bill.

"Aw, you'll get going again, you little fellow," Bill said.

Bill got a glass of water from the kitchen. He placed Arty in a sitting position and held the glass to his lips. Arty turned his face away.

"Dink? Dinkie, Arty?" Bill said, talking baby talk to him.

Arty opened his lips. Bill poured in water, some of it spilling down Arty's chin. Arty then turned away. He made a face as he swallowed the last drops. Bill drank the water remaining in the glass, set it on the table, and again sat down to the Spalding edition.

Lizz came in.

"How is the baby, Bill?" she asked.

"He's all right. He coughed a little and I gave him a drink of water," Bill said.

"I called up Mother. I told her Arty is sick. She thinks it must be a cold. Little Margaret, she said, has a little cold, and they kept her home from school today. But Daniel isn't sick," Lizz said.

"I wanted to go up there today, Ma, and play some more Steel's with Dan," Bill said.

"I know, but you better stay home. I'm not well, and Arty is a sick baby. I might need you. I haven't anyone else here until Pa comes that I can depend on."

Lizz looked at Arty. He seemed to beg her to help him, silently, expressively.

"Well, Bill, you better go to the store to get some things for supper. Here, get a pencil and take down the order," Lizz said.

"All right, Ma," Bill said.

41

I

Dennis sat on the couch, and a gleam from the kerosene lamp on the table revealed a slight tinge on his cheeks. He was quiet, and sat in a slightly slumped posture. He swallowed. It was funny. Now when he swallowed, his throat hurt. First he noticed it because when he swallowed his throat seemed to tickle him a little. It was not just like swallowing. Before when he swallowed, he didn't feel anything like that. He would be thirsty and want a glass of water, and he would swallow it. He would feel the water go down his throat and then he wouldn't be thirsty. And then he noticed his throat was tickling. And now when he swallowed, it hurt, like it was cut inside in his throat. He sat quietly. Mama was sitting near the dining-room stove with Arty in her arms, and Papa walked back and forth across the room. Papa needed a shave. He rubbed his hands on his whiskers. When Papa had whiskers and rubbed them against your face, they hurt, and sometimes they hurt almost as much as stickers hurt if you ran through a lot and got a sticker in your finger. It was cold. He shivered. He got up and walked slowly out to the kitchen and got a glass of water. He drank. His throat hurt. There was an ache in his back. It was kind of cold in the house. He went back to the couch. He couldn't see Mama and Papa clear. His eyes watered. He saw them almost like he was asleep and seeing them. He slouched on the couch.

"Denny, wanna draw pictures with me?" Bob asked.

"No, let me 'lone," Dennis said in protest.

II

"Here, Jim, you hold him a while. I'm so tired," Lizz said.

"Gimme the little beggar, Lizz," Jim said, reaching out his arms.

Arty, swaddled in shawls, was handed to his father. He didn't seem right. Jim went over to the light and looked at him. His cheeks were flushed. The little beggar was sick, all right.

"Lizz, I'll go out and call a doctor for him," Jim said.

"Jim, he just has grippe. He got his feet wet Saturday. Oh, but if I had my hands on that Little Margaret, letting him get his feet wet," Lizz said.

"She couldn't help it. She's just a child, and they just got a little bit wet," Jim said.

"My precious getting sick at this time," Lizz said.

"Is he any worse than he was this morning when you noticed he was sick?" Jim asked.

"No, he's pretty much the same, Jim," Lizz said.

"I don't like the feeling of his skin," Jim said.

"That's the fever. He has a little fever. It's grippe, all right," Lizz said.

"Maybe a good night's sleep will do him good and he'll pick up in the morning," Jim said.

"Time and rest are needed for grippe. And I'll keep him warm, and his bowels open," Lizz said.

"If he isn't any better in the morning, we'll telephone Doctor Geraghty to come and take a look at him," Jim said.

"My precious is going to be all right. All little children get sick. Bill had bronchitis, and whooping cough, and scarlet fever, and measles. Denny had an awful time with measles and he had tonsillitis just before we moved from La Salle Street. Part of raising a family is taking care of them when they're sick, and they all get sick," Lizz said.

"I don't like the looks of this one. He's a sick baby, all right, Lizz," Jim said.

"Of course, the little angel is sick. Oh, Jim, it would have torn your heart out to see the way he looked at me this morning when Catherine brought him in and I first noticed he wasn't himself," Lizz said.

"Yeah?"

"He gave me such a look. It would have torn your heart out," Lizz said.

"No pep in him today," Jim said.

Just then Arty coughed, saliva coming up on his lips. The cough seemed to tear through his feverish little body.

"Here, one of you kids get me a handkerchief," Jim said.

Bob jerked a dirty handkerchief out of his pocket and handed it to Jim. Jim wiped Arty's lips, noticing that Arty's breath was foul. He knitted his brows. Jim dropped the handkerchief on the floor not thinking of it, his eyes on Arty. Bob picked it up and stuck it in his pocket.

"Well, Jim, I'll put him to bed now. He needs sleep," Lizz said.

"Yeah, rest might help him to pick up," Jim said.

Lizz got matches, lit the parlor lamp, and carried it into the front bedroom while Jim followed her with Arty in his arms.

III

Dennis got off the couch, slouched across the room unnoticed. He breathed jerkily, making a slight noise with each inspiration and expiration. There were aches in his bones, and he was hot. His lips were chafed and dry. They seemed funny, and when he drank water, his throat hurt and he was still hot. He would play tricks on his throat. He would try to swallow on the right side, and it would hurt. He would try to swallow on the left side and it would hurt. He would hold back from swallowing as if he was going to fool his throat. Then he would swallow. And it would hurt. It would feel something like a knife was cutting his throat. He dropped onto the bed in the back bedroom. Slowly, he untied his shoes, dropped them. Tiredly, he pulled off his stockings. He got up. He felt as if his head was going around. There was something funny in his head. It was like the insides would go around dizzy-like, the insides of his head were going around in something that was like air and water inside of his head. He pulled off his pants, unbuttoned his waist, took it off, feebly tossed them on a chair in the corner. He crawled into bed. He lay there, his respiration slightly impeded, making noises as he breathed.

IV

"No, Lizz, I don't think it's serious," Jim said, sitting with her in the kitchen. All of the kids except Bill were in bed. He sat by the dining-room lamp, studying the official batting averages in Spalding's for the 1914 National League season.

"It was coming, Jim. I knew it was coming. We had such good luck and so little sickness with the children all winter. It was coming," Lizz said.

"Lizz, I guess you're right. Come to think of it, none of them was really sick last winter. Just a few little colds."

"Arty had never been awfully sick since he was an infant when he had an attack of bronchitis. It was coming," Lizz said.

"The poor little fellow is not himself. When I looked at him tonight and he said 'Fither' to me, he hardly seemed to whisper it. He's not himself," Jim said.

"The cold has settled in his throat and chest. I'll keep him warm tomorrow," Lizz said.

"But, Lizz, my rabbit, how are you feeling?"

"Oh, Jim, it's these last days carrying it around in me. My legs ache, and my teeth ache, and my back gets so sore. But it's soon going to be over," Lizz said.

"Too bad Arty had to get sick at just such a time," Jim said.

"Jim, we place our trust in God," Lizz said.

Jim yawned.

"You poor man, you work so hard, and now you got another mouth to feed," Lizz said.

"Don't worry about me now, Lizz, my rabbit. My back's good and strong," Jim said.

"But, Jim, if you could only get your rupture fixed," Lizz said.

"I will some day, and you'll have your teeth all tended to, and the O'Neills will even live in steam heat. We will. Lizz, they ain't gonna keep the O'Neills down," Jim said.

"Jim, do you want the newcomer to be a boy or a girl?" Lizz said.

"A boy. Say, when they grow up, we'll damn near have a baseball team of O'Neills," Jim said.

"Yes, I want it to be a boy. I prayed today in church for it to be a boy. Boys are so much easier to care of once they start growing," Lizz said.

"Well, my rabbit, we gotta hope for the best," Jim said, yawning.

Jim stood up. Arty could be heard coughing. Jim stiffened on hearing the painful coughs.

"That poor little beggar," Jim said, hastening into the front bedroom.

V

Dennis lay in a corner of the bed. He turned on his left side. He tossed, kicked his feet, and then turned on his right side. His body was covered with sweat, and his underwear was damp. His head was light. He breathed unevenly. He set his eyes on the ceiling, but could see nothing in the darkness. He swallowed, and, ooh, it hurt. He turned over again to the wall. He lay there for about five seconds. He tossed, rolled onto his back. He lay that way for about three seconds. He drew his right knee up, his right sole flat on the under-sheet. He drew his left knee up. He closed his knees. He kicked out, turned onto his left side. He turned and lay face down, breathing with noisy expirations into the pillow. He turned completely around. He touched his dry lips with his hands. He kicked off the covers and lay uncovered. A mildly chilling breeze blew over his perspiring body, and he shivered. He lay tossing and rolling in bed.

VI

A cough tore up, seemingly out of the depths of little Arty's diaphragm. Jim snored. Arty lay kicking his little legs, gasping for breath. He coughed again, saliva forming on his lips. He stirred restlessly, and suddenly he lay with his face downward. He coughed into the pillow. He stirred again. He twisted his body around to the side. Starting to cough once more, he struggled for breath. He coughed dryly. He gasped.

Arty started to cry. He emitted wailing, pitiful sounds.

"Jim, Jim, the baby," Lizz said nervously.

"Yes, he just woke me up," Jim said.

Jim climbed out of bed, went barefooted to the parlor for the lamp. He winced, hearing Arty cough. The baby called pitifully. He hadn't a match. He cursed to himself and went out to the kitchen.

"Goddamn it!" he said explosively; he had stubbed his toe on the ledge of wood in the doorway between dining room and kitchen. He held his toe for a moment. He walked out into the kitchen. He suddenly winced. A sliver of wood drove into his sole. He fumbled over the sink and found the box of matches. He pulled out several, lit one, limped to the lamp, and lit it. He limped back into the bedroom. Lizz sat in bed with Arty tossing, coughing, wailing in her arms. Catherine, at the foot of the bed, sat up, silently eying her mother and younger brother.

"Jim, hand me that bottle of holy water on the dresser," Lizz said.

Jim set the lamp on a small table which he drew from a corner and set near the bed. He dug in the litter on the top of the high dresser and pulled out a medicine bottle full of colorless liquid.

"Is this it?" he asked.

"Yes, Jim, give it here," Lizz said, reaching with her free right hand.

Jim opened the bottle and handed it to her. She put holy water on her thumb and made the sign of the cross on Arty's damp forehead. Jim stood helplessly by her, and she quickly said a prayer. She looked up at him, concerned.

"Get the Boucher's cough medicine. Maybe it will stop the poor little fellow from coughing," Lizz said.

"Where is it?"

"Over the shelf by the sink in the kitchen."

Jim limped to the parlor, lit the lamp, and limped out for the cough medicine. He returned with the bottle and a spoon.

Arty remained restless in his mother's arms. She forced down a spoonful of the medicine. He whimpered, struggled to breathe.

"We gotta get a doctor," Jim said.

"No doctor will come to us poor people at this time of the night, and you'll have to walk blocks to a telephone. The little one has stopped coughing. We'll call the doctor in the morning," Lizz said.

"I'm worried about him," Jim said.

"Mither!" Arty exclaimed in a hoarse whisper, and again he struggled to breathe.

Lizz sat holding him tenderly, and Jim stood by the bedside helplessly. Jim brought the lamp close to Arty's face. Father and mother looked at the pallid, suffering, sick little face, the filmy eyes, the tightened look, the circles under the eyes, the way the lips opened as Arty gasped.

"Oh, good Jesus Christ!" Jim said in a breaking voice.

"My poor, sick baby," Lizz said.

"Papa, you make Arty get better," Catherine said.

Arty was not coughing now. He whimpered in his mother's arms, and she swung him back and forth.

Rockabye, baby, in the tree top . . .

Lizz softly sang.

"Lizz, where's a needle?" Jim asked.

"On the dresser. Why?"

"I got a sliver in my foot. I wanna take it out," Jim said.

"You poor man. You shouldn't have walked around in your bare feet. If you wait a minute until I get the baby to sleep, I'll take it out," Lizz said.

"Don't bother, I'll do it," Jim said, searching for a needle.

"Jim, you ought to heat the water and boil the needle," Lizz said.

"It means starting a fire, and it'll take half the night."

Jim set a dirty foot up on the table by the lamp and probed for the splinter with a needle. Lizz sang to Arty as she rocked him in her arms.

VII

"Hey, keep quiet and let me sleep, will you? You been rolling around in bed and pulling the covers off me all night," Bill protested to Dennis.

Dennis said nothing. He shivered. He turned his face to the wall and lay there. He fell into an exhausted, restless, feverish sleep.

42

I

"Have Bill call up Doctor Geraghty on his way to school. The baby's a pretty sick little fellow, and I'd feel better if a doctor took a look at him," Jim said.

"I will, Jim. Oh, you poor man, having to be up most of the night with a sick child and now having to go to work," Lizz said.

"Lizz, I'm all right. You think of yourself," Jim said.

"I'm hoping that he gets better today. Grippe has to take its natural course," Lizz said.

"I don't like the way he coughs and acts. He looks to me like a damn sick little fellow," Jim said.

"I'll have Bill call the doctor," Lizz said.

Jim kissed her goodbye and, carrying his lunch, went off to work.

Lizz sat down by herself to have a cup of coffee. Soon she would have to be getting breakfast for her regiment. Every day began a new round of work.

II

Danny answered the telephone.

"Hello," he said.

"Hello, Dan, this is Bill."

"Hello, Bill, when you coming up to see me and play some more Steel's?" Danny asked.

"I don't know. I wanted to come yesterday, but I couldn't. Arty was sick and I had to stay home. Mama wanted me to call you up and tell Mother that Arty's sick."

"What's the matter with him?"

"He's got a bad cold or something, I guess. Pa and Ma were up most all of last night with him. He was coughing a lot. I just had to call Doctor Geraghty and I got to go back and tell Ma what he told me to tell her. And Ma wanted me to call you up and tell Mother he's pretty sick," Bill said.

"I'll tell her," Danny said.

"Who's it calling us up at eight o'clock in the morning?" Mrs. O'Flaherty asked, coming by Danny at the phone.

"It's Bill," Danny said.

"What yuh say, Dan?" Bill asked.

"Mother asked who it was and I was telling her it was you," Danny said.

"Here, let me speak to him," Mrs. O'Flaherty said.

She grabbed the telephone.

"Hello, William, how is your mother?" Mrs. O'Flaherty asked.

"She's all right, Mother, but she wanted me to call and let you know Arty was sick."

"How is the little fellow?" Mrs. O'Flaherty asked.

"Oh, he's sick, Mother. I guess he has an awful bad cold or grippe. Pa and Ma were up most of the night with him," Bill said.

"Your sister isn't very well. I kept her home from school," Mrs. O'Flaherty said.

"Little Margaret?"

"Yes, she has a sore throat. It's her tonsils, Peg thinks," Mrs. O'Flaherty said.

"I got to go back. Mama wanted me to call you and tell you," Bill said.

"Tell her to take care of herself and the little fellow," Mrs. O'Flaherty said.

"Yes, Mother. Goodbye," Bill said, hanging up the receiver.

III

"What did Bill say, Mother?" Margaret asked, sitting down to a cup of coffee after Danny had gone off to school.

"Sure, he said the little fellow is sick with a cold and Jim and Lizz was up the night with him," Mrs. O'Flaherty said.

"I hope he gets all right. Are they calling the doctor? Did he say?"

"He said they were calling Mike Geraghty," Mrs. O'Flaherty said.

"I hope it isn't serious. Gosh, if it is, look at all the expense. And Lizz expecting another baby. Not that I begrudge it, but my pay isn't my own since I went back to work, with all the debts I owe," Margaret said.

"Peg, sure, you don't think that the girl got something when she went down there Saturday?" Mrs. O'Flaherty asked.

"No, I think she has a little cold and a touch of tonsilitis, that's all."

Margaret went in to see Little Margaret, who was sitting up in bed, drinking a cup of tea and nibbling at a piece of toast.

"How are you, darling?"

"I'm all right, Aunty Peg. I just feel tired, and my throat's sore."

"Peg, we'll have to bundle her throat up," Mrs. O'Flaherty said.

"Yes, I'll do that and I'll call up the drugstore for a gargle for her before I go to work, Mother," Margaret said.

"Now, you stay in bed today, darling, and rest easy, and you'll be all right," Margaret added to the child.

They went out of the room.

"Peg, sure, you don't think it's the diphtheria they got?" Mrs. O'Flaherty asked.

"I don't think so. She has bad tonsils and had a sore throat around Christmas, remember? The doctor looked at it and said some time he'd have to take her tonsils out but he didn't think it was necessary yet. No, it's just that. If she isn't better in a day or two, I'll call the doctor over," Margaret said.

IV

Dennis came home from school.

"What happened to you? Were you sent home?"

"Yes, Mama," Dennis said in a weak voice.

"What did you do?"

"Sister said I was sick and should go home and go to bed," Dennis said.

"What's the matter with you? Come here in more light and let me look at you," Lizz said, drawing him out of the shadow where he was standing in the parlor.

She could see that he did not look himself. He was pale, and his eyes were watering. She felt his forehead and it was hot.

"Do you feel sick?"

"Yes, Mama," Dennis said.

"Where do you feel sick at?"

"I feel tired. I felt awful sick walking across the street from school. I felt like I might fall down," Dennis said.

"Have you got any cough?"

"No, but I got a sore throat, and I got a lump here," he said, pointing to a swollen gland on the left side of his neck.

"Good Jesus Mary and Joseph! What will be next?"

"Ma, it ain't my fault. I was sick all night," Dennis said.

"Why didn't you tell me? I wouldn't have let you go to school," Lizz said.

"I didn't know."

"Here, I'll put you to bed and give you some castor oil," Lizz said.

"Do I have to take castor oil, Ma?"

"Yes, you got to get better. Come on in the bedroom and let me undress you. You lay down and be quiet now, and I'll give you the castor oil," Lizz said.

She led him to the bedroom, and he walked listlessly. He sat down limply while she undressed him. She went to the kitchen to fix him a dose of castor oil.

V

Lizz looked at the clock. Eleven-thirty. Doctor Geraghty should be getting here. Arty was coughing in his room, and he was no better. When she attended to him, he just looked at her and hardly uttered a sound. And he was very hoarse when he talked. Oh, Blessed Virgin, what could it be? And now Dennis coming home sick. What was keeping Doctor Geraghty?

VI

"Bill, I'm glad you're home. Here's a nickel. You run down to the drugstore and telephone the doctor again. He hasn't come. I asked Mrs. Connerty to call him a little while ago and she did it for me like a good soul, but he wasn't in," Lizz said.

"Ain't Arty any better?"

"No, he's the same, and Dennis is in bed sick, too," Lizz said.

"What's the matter with him?"

"He's got a sore throat and he's weak. The Sister sent him home from school," Lizz said.

"All right, I'll go and call him, Ma," Bill said.

VII

"Aw, come on play with me, Bob," Catherine said just after Lizz had lit the kerosene lamp in the dining room.

"I don't wanna," Bob said.

"I wanna play house and I ain't got nobody to play with. You ain't sick, too, like Dennis and Arty."

"I just don't wanna play," Bob said.

He sat on the dining-room couch, his chubby body relaxed.

"You're acting funny," Catherine said.

"I don't wanna play," Bob said.

He sat there, relaxed. His eyes seemed fixed on the stove, and he did not take them from it. He scarcely moved. He continued sitting.

VIII

"Bill, I don't know what's happened to that doctor. Are you sure he is coming?"

"They told me that they would tell him and have him come as soon as he could," Bill said.

"Arty seems to be sleeping now. He was awful sick a while ago, but he's sleeping now. I'm going down to call the doctor again, and I'm going to run into the church to say a prayer. You watch the little ones. If Arty cries and coughs, try to give him a glass of water and a spoonful of Boucher's cough medicine. And if Dennis needs you, put him on the pot for me. He's a sick boy, the poor child. I'll only be gone a jiffy. I want to say a prayer for your sick brothers," Lizz said.

IX

"What's the matter with you, kid?" Bill said, noticing Bob sitting dejectedly on the couch.

"He's funny and he won't play with me," Catherine said.

"Maybe he's not a sissy and doesn't want to play with girls," Bill said.

"Well, he's funny," Catherine said.

"What's the matter, Bob?" asked Bill.

"Nothin'," Bob said.

"Don't tell me you're sick, too," Bill said.

"Lemme 'lone," Bob said in a voice which had suddenly become hoarse.

"He's funny," Catherine said.

Bob sat there. He swallowed his own saliva and made a face. His throat hurt him when he swallowed.

X

Arty was coughing again. Bill carried the parlor lamp in with him and looked at Arty. He lay there, gasping for breath. His lips were livid. His eyes were sunken. He choked for breath. He whimpered.

"Mither!" he called in a hoarse and scarcely audible whisper.

Bill left the lamp in the room and went out for a glass of water. He tried to give Arty a drink, spilling half the water on Arty and the bed. Arty fretted. Again he gasped for breath.

Bill went out of the room.

"What's the matter with Arty?" Catherine asked.

"He's sick. Don't make any noise," Bill said.

He went in to see Dennis.

"How you feel, Denny?"

Denny moaned.

"Want anything?"

"No," Dennis said hoarsely.

Bill sat down by the table. He hated being alone with the kids sick. If anything happened, what would he do? He wished Mama would come back. He noticed that Bob was lying down on the couch with his face to the wall. Bob must be sick, too.

"I don't like it with everybody sick here," Catherine said.

"What's the matter, Dolly?"

"I ain't got nobody to play with," she said.

XI

The church was quiet, deserted, and as yet unlighted. The altar light hanging in front of the Blessed Sacrament was a small gleam of red in the shadows. Lizz was alone in the church. She knelt before the altar of the Blessed Virgin. The statue before her was half lost in the shadows. The blue robe of Mary seemed less bright than usual. The color on her cheeks was diminished. There was not a sound in the church. Lizz raised her hands beseechingly to the statue of Mary. She came to Mary. She placed herself in Mary's hands. Who, if not the Mother of God, would look down on the mothers of the poor? Her trust was in Mary. No matter what happened to her, no matter what befell her family, Lizz felt that she had Mary. She felt close to the Blessed Virgin, closer to her than to any human being on earth. She said a Hail Mary, and then she knelt at the altar of the Blessed Virgin, gazing up at the statue which was not clearly visible. The candles burning a few feet in front of her cast flickering shadows. Two of these candles she had just lit in Mary's honor. She had put two pennies in the offering box beside the candle rack. They would burn as prayers all night and into the morrow, burn as prayers for her and for her little ones in these hours. She gazed enrapt at the statue of the Blessed Virgin. Mary had gone through labor and given birth. Mary had seen her Son die on the cross. Mary Herself had been a suffering mother. She was now the comfort of suffering mothers. Again Lizz said a Hail Mary. She wanted to kneel here for a long time. She wanted to feel herself close to Mary. And alone in the church, without another soul in it, without a sound, she was close to Mary. Everything in her heart, Mary knew. Mary knew of her worry. Mary knew that she was afraid. She was a child of Mary and she placed her trust in Mary's hands. If she lived or died, she was Mary's child. She beseeched Mary's help and comfort. She wiped away a tear. She prayed. Again she knelt, gazing in rapture with shining eyes at the statue while the candlelight played on it. Lizz got up reluctantly. She blessed herself. She cast a last glance at the statue. She turned and walked slowly down the aisle. She genuflected awkwardly in the rear of the church, blessed herself with holy water, and left. She walked home slowly because of the cumbersomeness of her body.

XII

"Eat your supper, boy," Jim said to Bob at the supper table.

"I ain't hungry, Pa," Bob said.

"Lizz, he's sick, too. We better get him to bed," Jim said.

"God Almighty! Jim, what have we done to have this strike us? And my little daughter at Mother's, she's sick, too. Oh, Jim, what have we done?" Lizz said.

"Lizz, I don't know."

"I'm not hungry," Bob said hoarsely.

"Jim, the children must have more than colds. Oh, God, Jim," Lizz said.

Jim went to Lizz and kissed her.

"We have to be calm now, Lizz, my rabbit," he said.

He picked up Bob and carried him to his bedroom. He undressed the boy and put him in bed alongside of Dennis.

He came back slowly to the kitchen.

"How you feeling, Bill?"

"I'm all right. Except I'm kind of tired, Pa, because I couldn't sleep much last night. Dennis was bouncing all around the bed."

"Catherine looks all right, Jim," said Lizz.

Catherine, who had been eating heartily, looked up at her father. She smiled at him. He picked her up and swung her around in the air until she giggled. He kissed her and set her back on her chair.

"Lizz, what time is he coming?" Jim asked.

"He'll be here some time after supper," Lizz said.

"It's certainly taking him a long time to come," Jim said.

XIII

Jim and Lizz went in to see Arty. There was a drop of blood on the child's lips. His eyes were sunken and inflamed. His face was now sallow in the lamplight. His expression seemed wasted. The swelling of the glands in his neck was noticeable.

"Jim, I'm afraid," Lizz said.

Jim did not answer her. He stood looking sadly at his child.

"I never had a child get this way from a cold. It might be something else," Lizz said.

"God, I hope not," Jim said.

"I'm going to rub his throat with holy oil," Lizz said.

"Before you do, I want to take a look at his throat," Jim said.

He got a spoon and washed it. He came back to the bedroom. He sat down on the bed and took the wasted little body in his arms. He put the spoon in its mouth and had Lizz hold the lamp near.

Arty cried feebly. Jim looked down his throat. He saw drops of blood and a grayish white membrane with patches of dirty gray coloring on it.

"This is bad. I wish he'd come," Jim said.

"Here, Jim, let me rub his neck with holy oil," Lizz said.

She rubbed holy oil on the baby's neck and then tied a cloth around it.

"Mither!" Arty whispered hoarsely.

He began coughing, and blood and saliva formed on his lips. Lizz gently wiped the lips. He lay restlessly, gasping for breath.

43

I

At about eight o'clock in the evening Buddy and Albie Connerty left the house to go to the store. They were walking along the sidewalk, and suddenly Albie stopped and pointed at the lighted windows of the O'Neill cottage.

"We got to go on the other side of the street," Albie said.

"Why?" Buddy asked.

"Ma told us to. She said to keep away from the O'Neills and walk on the other side of the street. There's something catching in there. She said she knows they got something like diphtheria or scarlet fever in there and we got to walk on the other side of the street," Albie said.

The two boys turned and cut across the street.

"Sister sent Denny home from school this morning because he was so sick," Buddy said.

"Ma says she knows there's something catching there. She told Father Corbett about it today, too, and he told her he'd pray for the O'Neills," Albie said.

"Is it bad?" Buddy asked.

"Ma says it is."

"I'll give you a head start to the corner and race you to Wentworth Avenue," Albie said.

"All right," said Buddy.

II

"Jim, I want the priest to pray over him," Lizz said.

"All right, Lizz. Send Bill over," Jim said.

"William, you go over to see Father Corbett and ask him if he'll come over. Tell him your little brother is deathly sick and your other brothers are in bed.

Tell him they are in bad condition with fever and swollen throats and they can't swallow and they can't breathe. Ask him to come over and say a prayer over them," Lizz said.

Bill put on his cap and sweater and went out of the house.

Lizz went to her room and dug two holy candles out of a drawer. She lit them, setting them in saucers in preparation for the priest. Jim paced back and forth across the parlor.

III

"Has your mother called the doctor, my boy?" Father Corbett asked.

"Yes, we're waiting for him," Bill said.

"How many of the little ones are sick?"

"All but me and my sister Catherine," Bill said.

"I heard about the sickness in your house. The Sister told me she had your brother go home. His throat is sore and swollen, isn't it?"

"Yes, Father," Bill said.

"Well, you tell your mother that I can't come this evening, but that I'll say some prayers here and that she should have the doctor come as soon as possible."

"Yes, Father," Bill said.

IV

"I just told the oldest O'Neill boy across the street that I couldn't come over," Father Corbett said to one of his assistants, Father Cogan.

"Yes, Father," Father Cogan said.

"Father Pat, there's diphtheria over there as sure as I'm sitting here talking to you. We can't do anything, and if we go over we might pick up the germs and give it to other little children in the neighborhood. They need a doctor more than they need the priest. We'll only risk ourselves and our parishioners. If they come back, you give them a good excuse. You be kindly to them, and give them a good excuse. There are many little ones in the neighborhood, and we don't want to risk becoming carriers and give the germs to others. There's been a lot of diphtheria going around lately, you know," Father Corbett said.

"It's sad," Father Cogan said.

"Yes, they're good, decent people, and he's a hard-working man trying to take care of a big family. I've been in this parish longer than you, Father Pat. I've seen a lot of it. They're good people here. You know, priests who have parishes like Father Mulligan and Father Gilhooley up there at Saint Patrick's, further south, they don't know what laboring in the vineyard means. Let them be pastor in a parish like this and they'll know," said Father Corbett.

V

"Why in the name of God hasn't he come?" Jim exclaimed as he paced the floor.

"Jim, I don't know. The priest wouldn't come, either," Lizz said.

"There's only one crime in this world, Lizz, to be a poor man," Jim said.

"You'd think he'd come sooner than this," Lizz said.

"We never have been able to pay him when he came before," Jim said.

"He'll come. He's my brother's best friend, and he'll come. He must be busy," Lizz said.

"If the O'Flahertys called him up, he'd be there by now," Jim said.

"He'll come, Jim," Lizz said.

"I'll go get another doctor," Jim said.

"No, Jim, we called him. He'll come. I told him what was the matter with Arty. He knows and he'll come," Lizz said.

"What did you tell him?"

"I told him about the fever, and swelling, and sore throat."

"Well, I wish to God he'd come," Jim said.

VI

Lizz knelt down in front of the holy candles which she had placed on the small bedroom table in front of a picture of the Blessed Virgin. She prayed silently, fervently. Arty lay on the bed, scarcely stirring, still gasping for breath, making a gulping noise with each attempted expiration of breath. He coughed again, more saliva forming on his lips.

VII

Bill put down his newspaper. The print seemed to dance before his eyes. He knew how he felt. Once when he had been playing ball, he'd been hit on the head. His head got funny, and he was swimming. His head went around, and he couldn't see clearly. Trees danced before his eyes, and the earth seemed to come up and act like a ship did when he saw a picture of a ship on the ocean in a nickel show. His head went that way now. He got up and went to his room to go to bed. Dennis lay gasping. Bob was asleep, but tossing restlessly as he slept.

VIII

Catherine lay beside Arty. Arty wasn't making any trouble now. He was not moving like he did last night. He wasn't kicking. He was just making noise with his mouth. She lay in bed in the darkness. Mama and Papa weren't in bed yet. She lay there. Her cheeks were hot, and there was a funny tickle in her throat every time she swallowed. Arty wasn't moving a lot. Maybe he was getting better.

IX

"It's too late now. He'll be here in the morning," Lizz said.

"If he isn't, we got to get another doctor. I'm not going to work in the morning," Jim said.

"Jim, you got to. You can't miss a day's work now and lose that time," Lizz said.

"But what about you and the kids?"

"I'll manage with them," Lizz said.

"Suppose something happens to you?"

"There's plenty of time if it does. It takes a long time, and I'll know it's coming before the pains get too close together," Lizz said.

"We'll see about it in the morning," Jim said.

"You come now and get to bed. You need your rest, you poor man," Lizz said.

"I want to sit here a while. You go to bed, Lizz. You've had a hard day of it," Jim said.

Jim and Lizz sat alone, not talking, in the darkened parlor, Jim moved his chair to the front window. He sat looking out. Moonlight splashed on the sidewalk and paving blocks, formed patches of glittering light against the shadows of the wooden houses across the street. He heard the noise of a train. A cough was heard from the boys' back bedroom. It was quiet again.

Jim finally got up and went to Lizz. He stroked her black hair.

"We got to get to bed," he said gently.

X

Standing in his long underwear, Jim looked at Arty by the lamplight. Arty lay in a semi-comatose state. His lips were livid. His eyes were expressionless, glazed and filmy. Jim noticed Catherine.

"You all right, Dolly?" Jim asked.

"Yes, Papa," she said.

"You're not asleep," he said.

"I just woke up," she said.

"Come on, Jim, we got to get to bed," Lizz said.

XI

Dennis was funny in his sleep. He would make sudden noises one right after the other when he breathed. And then he would move around and kick his feet. And then he wouldn't move. Bill was kicking, too. Bob lay looking at darkness, hearing the funny way that Dennis breathed. He kept swallowing and it kept hurting him, and he kept asking himself why it hurt his throat to swallow.

XII

"I made your father go to work. There's no use of him losing time now when we need money," Lizz said to Bill.

"Yes, Mama," Bill said, his voice weak.

"Are you all right, Bill?" Lizz asked.

"Oh, yes, Mama. I'm all right," Bill said, mopping the sweat from his brow.

"Then you better go to school, too. I don't want you losing time, either. You have to get through school and learn so you can be prepared to go out and work and help your father. Your father had no education and that's why he's a poor man. You better not lose time. I'll fix your lunch, but you come right home from school. I might need you," Lizz said.

"Is the doctor coming?"

"Yes, he'll be here this morning," Lizz said.

"Will you need someone for medicine?"

"I can get it. Or Mrs. Connerty will help me out if I need her," Lizz said.

"All right, Ma," Bill said.

"Your brother Bob is a little better this morning. Arty didn't cause any trouble last night, but he's sick, a very sick baby. He can hardly recognize his mother," Lizz said.

Bill drank coffee, making faces when he swallowed.

XIII

"Peg, the girl is worse. We'll have to get the doctor today for her," Mrs. O'Flaherty said.

"I don't like that lump in her throat. But it's a good thing, Mother, that I'm off today. I can take care of the darling. Has Lizz called again about the baby?"

"No, nary a word," said Mrs. O'Flaherty.

"I wonder if the baby is better and if the new one is coming. But she'll have Jim or one of the neighbors call us when it happens. I guess that no news is good news," Margaret said.

"Ah, my grandson is all right. He went off to school healthy as a whistle. He never had the whooping cough even," Mrs. O'Flaherty said.

"I'm glad Little Brother isn't sick. We've been lucky in raising him," Margaret said.

"Peg, go in and see the girl, and see if there's anything you can do for her," Mrs. O'Flaherty said.

XIV

"Ma, I couldn't go to school. I was falling down and had to lean against the lamppost. I had to come back," Bill said, tottering before his mother.

"You go and lay down until the doctor comes. I'm expecting him any minute now," Lizz said.

Bill staggered to his bedroom and, without undressing, fell into bed beside Dennis.

XV

Lizz sat in the kitchen with Arty in her arms. The child lay still in a semi-comatose condition. His lips and the tips of his fingernails were livid.

"Ah, my Angel Child, speak to Mama," Lizz said to him.

Arty did not react to her. The child lay, glaze-eyed, gasping for breath.

"His Mama's Angel Child is going to get better and be a big healthy man," she said, smiling at him.

Her face contorted with a sudden pain. She sat rigid, holding Arty. Then she relaxed.

"Ah, his new little brother is kicking and is going to be playing with him soon," Lizz said.

She held Arty, sitting by the kitchen. Outside, the sun flooded the street and a wagon rattled by.

XVI

Catherine and Bob stood in the doorway looking at Mama as she sat with Arty.

Mama was trying to make Arty drink milk from her breast. Arty didn't want to. Mama was trying to get him to drink her milk. Arty was making that funny noise with his mouth and Mama was trying to make him drink milk from her breast.

XVII

Dennis crawled out of bed. He leaned against the wooden frame of the bedroom door. He breathed in paroxysms. He pushed himself away from his support. He staggered into the dining room and fell down. He lay on the floor watching the ceiling go around like a merry-go-round.

XVIII

Bob gasped for breath. He stood in the doorway with Catherine beside him. She was holding his hand and watching Mama intently. Bob thought that Mama was acting funny.

"Come, my Angel Child, and drink your Mama's milk," Lizz said to him, pushing the livid lips to her swollen, drooping left breast.

Arty was so still. He didn't want to take Mama's milk. He was so still. Mama was trying to get him to take her milk. She pushed his head to her other breast. Arty couldn't drink. Didn't Mama know? It was funny. He had seen a dead rat in the yard the other day. He had poked the rat with a stick. The rat wouldn't move. Arty wasn't moving. Arty wasn't making any noise with his lips now. The rat didn't move because it was dead. Mama was trying to make Arty take her milk and Arty wouldn't move. When Arty didn't move like that it was because he was dead. Mama was acting funny. She was trying to make Arty take her milk and he didn't want it. He didn't move. Mama was acting funny. She didn't know Arty was dead.

"Arty's dead," Bob said to Catherine.

Dennis crawled to the couch, dragged himself onto it, and lay there, tossing.

"Take your Mama's milk, my Angel Child," Lizz said to the dead baby.

44

I

 Bill walked slowly and unevenly toward Wentworth Avenue. He had to get to the drugstore and call the express company to have them get Papa home, because Arty was dead. And he had to call Mother's and tell them Arty was dead. Mama got him out of bed and told him he had to go to the corner and get there and make the telephone calls. Mama had laid Arty on the dining-room couch, and she was sitting looking at him. She said call up the express company and have them send Papa home, and call up Mother and tell her Arty was dead. It was hard to walk. He was all pooped out, and his head was swimming. The sun hurt his eyes and made them blink. He walked very slowly. He leaned against a lamppost near Saint Martha's school and he looked across the street at the cindery vacant lot. He cried. His little brother was dead and everybody was sick. He had to make the telephone call. He was sick with the same thing that made Arty dead. Everybody was sick but Mama. Mama was sitting looking at Arty and Arty was dead. He shoved himself away from the lamppost. He walked on, very slowly. He had to get to the corner and make the telephone calls. Papa had to come home and do something. His throat was sore. He never had had as sore a throat as he had now. He got shivers, and he was dizzy. He tottered to the wall beside him. He stood there, looking ahead at the quarter of a block to Wentworth Avenue. A street car passed. It seemed to go by him like a boat. He went on, tottering, telling himself he had to make the telephone calls.

II

"Mother, the little one is dead," Margaret said, hanging up the telephone receiver after speaking to Bill.

"Lord bless us! When did he die?"

"This morning. Mother, it must be diphtheria," Margaret said.

"Blessed Lord in Heaven! Peg, we got to get the doctor for the girl. Peg, it's the diphtheria she's got," Mrs. O'Flaherty said.

"Mother, I felt it all along and I didn't want to let myself believe it. Mother, when I was a little girl and got diphtheria, I was the same way as she was. Oh, Mother, what'll we do? Willie-boy said all of them are sick, and he sounded so weak and hoarse over the telephone."

"Oh, me grandson. If he gets it, what'll we do, Peg? What'll we do? I protected him from catching anything since I had him. I never let him go near anyone with the whooping cough. Oh, God help us if me little grandson gets it. Get Doctor Mike, Peg! Get Doctor Mike!"

"He was well this morning when he went to school, wasn't he, Mother?" Margaret asked.

"Sure, he didn't complain and he ate a big breakfast," Mrs. O'Flaherty said.

"Oh, I hope Little Brother is all right. I'm going in to see her," Margaret said.

They both went into the bedroom and looked at Little Margaret lying on the bed, feverish, breathing with difficulty.

"How are you, little darling?"

"My throat's awful sore. I can't swallow," Little Margaret said.

"Ah, I knew it. And the little one dead," Mrs. O'Flaherty said.

Little Margaret began to cry.

"Don't cry, darling, we're going to have the doctor here any minute and he's going to make you get better," Margaret said.

III

"Ah, Doctor Mike, you're a good man. How is your wife?" Mrs. O'Flaherty said.

"She's fine, and how are you?"

"Doctor, look at my grandson," Mrs. O'Flaherty said impatiently.

"I will. Give me time to get my breath. How are you?" Doctor Mike said, turning to Danny, speaking gruffly to him.

"I'm all right," Danny said timidly.

"Look at him. Doctor, all these years I didn't let him get the whooping cough," Mrs. O'Flaherty said.

"I will, I want to look at the girl first. She's sick, isn't she?"

"Doctor, my sister's little child has just died," Margaret said.

Doctor Geraghty's face clenched momentarily.

"When did he die?"

"We just heard it a few minutes ago," Margaret said.

"I was going to go down there. They called me up but I couldn't get down. I surmised it was diphtheria and I notified the health authorities before I came here to get somebody down there. Here, let me see the girl," he said.

Mrs. O'Flaherty and Margaret followed him into the bedroom.

"Here, you stay out of here," Mrs. O'Flaherty said, pushing Danny as he followed them in.

He went into the dining room and sat down, waiting.

"How do you feel?" Doctor Geraghty asked Little Margaret.

"I got a sore throat," she said.

The doctor gave Margaret a knowing look. She turned pale.

"Here, let me sit you up and look at your throat," he said.

He opened his instrument bag. Holding her tongue down, he looked in her throat, using a flashlight. Her tonsils were swollen and the membrane of the pharynx was a dirty gray. He shook his head.

He put a thermometer in Little Margaret's mouth.

"Now, keep still and leave that in until I take it out," he said.

"Are you going down to my sister's now?" Margaret asked.

"I think the health officers will get there before I could, and they'll take care of them," Mike said.

"All of the children are sick," Margaret said.

"They'll have to remove them to the Municipal Contagious Disease Hospital," he said.

He took the thermometer out of Little Margaret's mouth and read it. Her temperature was almost 104 degrees.

He looked at Margaret and shook his head. She drew back in shock. She said nothing.

Mike walked out of the room.

"Has she got it?" Mrs. O'Flaherty asked excitedly.

"Yes, a pretty bad case."

"Look at him. See if he's got it, Doctor Mike," she said.

"Wait until I finish with the girl."

"Yes. Doctor, I always watched him so he didn't catch anything," she said.

"I know you did. I'll take a look at him in a minute," Mike said.

"Have you any alcohol?" he asked.

"Yes, come in the bathroom, Doctor," Margaret said.

He followed her to the bathroom. She gave him alcohol. He sterilized the thermometer with it.

"Doctor, is it bad?" Margaret asked.

"It's a pretty severe case. I wish you'd called me a day or two ago. Her temperature is 'way up," Mike said.

"Doctor Mike, you won't put a sign on the door, will you?" Mrs. O'Flaherty said, when the doctor and Margaret came back.

"Doctor, should I call the priest for her?" Margaret asked anxiously.

"I think we better remove her. I thought it might be this when you talked to me over the phone and I came prepared. I'm going to give her some antitoxin," Mike said.

"You'll save her, Doctor?" Margaret said.

"I'll do everything that can be done. I'll call an ambulance. It's best to send her to the Municipal Contagious Disease Hospital," he said.

"It's not like the County Hospital?"

"She'll get good care there. Don't you worry," Mike said, going back to the bedroom.

"Doctor, look at my grandson," Mrs. O'Flaherty said.

IV

Lizz sat on the floor in a trance, looking at the dead body. She touched the curly hair. She looked at the closed eyes. Suddenly she stiffened up with a pain. Her face contorted, and she felt her extended abdomen. She waited for the pain to subside. She sat in a trance, looking at the corpse.

V

"Now, we'll look at you," Mike said.

Danny was pale and sweating, and his breath came in jerks. His heart pounded.

"Don't be afraid. I won't hurt you," Mike said.

"I'm not afraid," Danny said.

"Open your mouth and let me look at it," Mike said.

Danny obeyed, and Mike looked down Danny's throat with a flashlight. He saw no redness or swelling.

"Doctor, is he all right?" Mrs. O'Flaherty asked anxiously.

"Just a minute, please, Mrs. O'Flaherty," Mike said.

"Mother, let the doctor examine him. Be patient," Margaret said.

"Leave this in your mouth now," Mike said, inserting a thermometer.

Danny sat with the thermometer in his mouth.

"He looks all right," Mike said.

"Thank God," Mrs. O'Flaherty said.

"I'm glad Little Brother is spared," Margaret said.

"I'm going to give him some antitoxin as a protective measure anyway," Mike said.

He turned back to Danny and took the thermometer out. He read it, shaking his head negatively while Mrs. O'Flaherty and Margaret waited tensely.

"His temperature is normal. He looks all right," Mike said. "Your throat doesn't hurt or you haven't had a cold, have you?"

"No," Danny said.

Mike took a throat culture of Danny.

"Come on in the bedroom and take your clothes off," he said, putting the little tube containing the culture media in his bag.

"You won't hurt the boy, will you?" Mrs. O'Flaherty said.

"No," Mike said.

VI

Danny lay on his back, naked. Mike drove the needle into Danny's backside and injected the antitoxin. Danny winced at the probe of the needle, and then relaxed, closing his eyes.

"All right," Mike said when he had finished.

Danny was sweating in fear and from shock. He sat up.

"Dress yourself. That'll make your side a little bit stiff, but it'll wear off in a couple of days," Mike said.

Danny began dressing.

"Peg, I better give you a shot," Mike said.

"Oh, Doctor, I don't need it. I had diphtheria when I was a little girl, and I had so many shots I was hardly able to walk for weeks after I got out of the County Hospital. I'm all right and I simply can't afford to be off work," she said.

"Well, that's different, Peg," Mike said.

"Doctor, you won't have to put a sign on the door?" Mrs. O'Flaherty said.

"It's the law," Mike said.

"Oh, Doctor, you can't. I can't afford to be off work, and you simply have to fix it up. And soon we're going to move. You can fix it up," said Margaret.

"If they put a sign on me door, I'll tear it off," Mrs. O'Flaherty said.

"I'll try to fix it up so you won't get one. And the ambulance will come for the girl," Mike said.

"Oh, thank you, Doctor," Margaret said.

"How's Al?" Mike asked.

"He's well. He'll be home in a couple of weeks. We're moving, too, Doctor," Margaret said.

"Where to?"

"Oh, I found a lovely place at Fifty-seventh and Indiana," Margaret said.

"It's a nice neighborhood," Mike said.

"How is your wife? Ah, she's a grand woman, Doctor Mike," Mrs. O'Flaherty said.

"She's fine, Mother. You must come over and see her one of these days," Mike said.

"That I will," Mrs. O'Flaherty said.

"How are you, Peg? Behaving?"

"Oh, yes, Doctor. I was just upset. But that's all over. I'm never going to do that again," Margaret said.

"Good. And now, don't let him go back to school for a couple of days. Keep him in, and if anything develops call me right up. But it looks like he's escaped it. I guess that it came from the other house. Was the girl there recently?"

"She was there Saturday," Margaret said.

"That's it. And the health officers will take care of the other house. I called them to look in because I was afraid I couldn't get there soon enough," Mike said.

"Oh, Doctor, you're so good," Margaret said.

VII

When Jim got home from work, he had to go out immediately in order to make all arrangements for Arty's burial. He saw the undertaker, and showed him Arty's insurance policy. There would be about forty dollars coming on it, and it would cover the cost of the funeral. Jim signed the money over to the undertaker. Then he spent over an hour locating his cousin, Mary O'Doul. She gave him the deed to the ground in which Arty would be buried. Jim's own mother had been laid to rest in the same earth. He came back to the cottage, tired and heartsick. The undertaker had come and had laid out Arty in a little gray coffin. It would be a long trip to Calvary cemetery and Jim had to go with the body right away. When the little coffin was carried out, Lizz rushed after it.

"Oh, my baby!" she sobbed.

Jim grabbed Lizz, and put his arm around her.

"My baby!" she sobbed.

"Be quiet now, Lizz, please," Jim said tenderly.

Catherine, dressed to go with her father, wearing a faded blue coat which Little Margaret had worn before her, stood silently by.

"You have to stay here with the others. The health officers will be here soon," Jim said.

"I want to go and bury my baby," Lizz sobbed.

"Lizz, please, stay here and try to control yourself," Jim said.

Lizz broke loose from him, and went hysterically down the front steps out to the hearse. Jim followed her.

"Goodbye, my Angel Child!" she sobbed as the gray coffin was inserted in the white hearse.

Jim put his arm around Lizz and led her to the cottage.

"Lizz, my rabbit, I'll come back as quick as I can. I'm taking Dolly because she's the only one who is well enough to go. I can't do it alone," Jim said.

"Oh, Jim!" she exclaimed; she put her head on his shoulder and sobbed.

Jim led her to a chair and kissed her goodbye. He stood by her for a moment, grim and speechless.

"Come with your Papa, Dolly," Jim said.

He picked up Catherine and carried her in his arms out to the waiting automobile.

Lizz went to the window. She saw the white hearse drive off, followed by the black limousine.

VIII

"Papa, do you always die when you're sick?" Catherine asked, sitting close to her father in the automobile as it sped along behind the hearse.

"Sometimes, Dolly," Jim said.

"Where's Arty now?"

"He's in Heaven, Dolly."

"Where's Heaven?" Catherine asked.

"It's up past the sky. I guess it is. Yeah, I guess it is," Jim said.

"You die sometimes when you're sick?"

"Yes, Dolly."

"My brothers are sick. Will they die?"

"No!" Jim said.

He looked out the window, saw passing store fronts as in a dream. What more? His daughter taken to the hospital from her grandmother's. God, how was she? The others home, so sick he could take only the little girl with him. And when would the new one come?

"Papa, I don't want my brothers to die," Catherine said.

"You're Papa's Dolly," Jim said. He enfolded her in his strong arms and kissed her. Tears welled up in his eyes.

IX

Lizz sat looking at a pair of Arty's rompers. She remembered the last time she had taken him to Mother's. She had washed him and he had laughed in the tub. Mother had liked him. He had looked in the mirror in Mother's parlor and he hadn't known he was looking at himself. He had wanted to know who the baby was he saw in the mirror, and he'd wanted to make friends with the baby.

He died in her arms. She was holding him and he died in her arms.

Bill came out of the bedroom, listless and gasping for breath. He slumped into a chair.

"Son, come here," she said, suddenly seeing him.

He came slowly to her.

"Sit down beside your mother," she said.

He dropped down beside her on the couch. Tenderly, she caressed his hair.

X

"Kneel down with your Papa, Dolly," Jim said.

The little coffin was lowered on ropes into the opened grave. Jim looked over the edge of the pit.

"Say goodbye to your brother, Dolly," Jim said.

"Goodbye, Arty," Catherine said.

"Goodbye, Arty," Jim repeated.

Jim blessed himself as the first shovelful of dirt thumped on the little coffin.

"Say a prayer now, Dolly," Jim said.

"What prayer, Papa?"

"Ask God to be good to your little dead brother and take care of your brothers and sister and mother," Jim said.

"God, please, take care of my brother Arty, all my brothers and my sister and my Mama and my Papa," Catherine said.

The shovelfuls of dirt were piled on the little coffin. Jim wiped his eyes with the back of his right hand. Catherine cried because her father was crying.

When the shallow grave had been filled in, Jim got up. He placed a bouquet of five white roses at the head of the sandy mound. He laid a rose on his own mother's sunken grave and knelt beside it to say prayers for the repose of her soul. His whole past seemed to well up in his mind. After she had died, he had been put in an orphan asylum. That was so many years behind him now. He prayed for his dead mother's soul. He got up and took Catherine's hand.

"Say goodbye to your little brother for the last time, Dolly," he said.

"Goodbye, Arty."

"Goodbye, my son. Goodbye, Mother," Jim said, and again the tears came.

He picked up Catherine, and slowly walked away with her on his shoulders.

XI

Big black men were coming after him. It was dark, and there were big black men coming. They were coming at him and they were going to do things to him. He couldn't move. It was black all around, and big black men were coming, and they were taking him away from Mama and Papa.

Dennis screamed.

Lizz went to the darkened bedroom.

"Mama, Denny's sick," Bob said hoarsely.

"Don't let 'em take me! Mama! Mama! Mama!"

"There now, Son, your mother's here," Lizz said, sitting down at the bedside, stroking his feverish forehead.

"Mama! Mama!" Dennis screamed.

"Your mother is with you. She won't let them hurt you. There, now, my child," Lizz said.

"Mama!"

Dennis opened his eyes and lay limp and sweating on the bed. He saw the form of his mother beside him. Her fat hand seemed cool on his forehead. Struggling to breathe, he looked at her.

"Your mother is watching you, Son," Lizz said.

"Mama!" he whispered.

XII

Jim took a small bottle of whiskey from his pocket. He glanced out the window as the car sped him home. There were blocks and blocks to go yet. What was happening at home?

He took a good stiff drink.

He looked at Catherine. She was curled up asleep beside him.

He took a smaller drink and put the bottle back in his pocket.

"Why did this have to happen to me?" he said aloud, again unable to check the tears. He let them roll down his leathery face.

He looked out the windows. Nice buildings. In these homes, the kids were happy and well-fed, and had the care of a doctor when they were sick. And in these homes, the kids were alive.

XIII

"Peg, what's that Mike did to me?" Mrs. O'Flaherty asked.

"It's nothing, just a throat culture. But you needn't worry about it. And, Mother, I wired Al about the O'Neills. He'll send them some money if they need it. Poor Al, everything falls on his and my shoulders. But, God, they need it," Margaret said.

"I wish they'd telephone. I hope the rest of them and me daughter is all right," Mrs. O'Flaherty said.

"It's so terrible, Mother. And just when Lizz is having another," Margaret said.

"And, Peg, ah, the little fellow was the cutest little one. He was such a wise little one, too," Mrs. O'Flaherty said.

"I'm going to call the hospital to find out if there's any news about Little Margaret," Margaret said.

"Ah, well, Peg, we must all bend ourselves to the will of God," Mrs. O'Flaherty said.

XIV

Jim looked at the store fronts. He saw children running up and down the street. There was a fellow of Arty's age, a little fellow with his mother. He took another drink.

"Why did it happen to me?"

XV

A blue police wagon stood in front of the O'Neill cottage. There was a crowd of the curious on the sidewalk, and two policemen were keeping them back.

"Where you going?" a cop asked as Jim broke through the crowd and started in the broken gate.

"This is my house. What's the matter here now?"

"The health officers is in there," the policeman said.

Carrying Catherine, Jim bolted up the stairs and into the house.

"Jim, the children are being taken to the hospital. It's diphtheria, all right, and all the boys have it," Lizz said.

Jim looked about the parlor bewildered, seeing two internes, a doctor, and a health officer.

"We'll have to take your children to the hospital, Mr. O'Neill. The dead child is buried now, isn't he?"

"Yes, sir. How badly are they sick?"

"That lad is pretty sick," the doctor said, pointing to Dennis who lay gasping on the couch. "And he's in bad shape," the doctor said, pointing to Bill. "This one hasn't such a bad attack yet," he said, pointing to Bob.

"Will you examine my little girl?" Jim asked.

"We were waiting to do that. We knew there was one more," the doctor said.

Jim removed her coat, and the doctor sat her in a chair to examine her.

"Jim, they're putting a sign on the door," Lizz said.

"Yeah," Jim said dully.

"We got to be quarantined."

"Mr. O'Neill, the girl will have to go, too. She has a touch of it, but she's not as bad as the others," the doctor said.

"You're taking them in the police wagon?" Jim asked, his voice still dull.

"Yes, sir!"

"They're not going to the County Hospital? That place is a butcher shop," Lizz said.

"No, it isn't, lady, but they aren't going there. They're going to the Municipal Contagious Disease Hospital at Twenty-Fifth and California Avenue and they'll have the best of care," the doctor said.

"If any of my children die there, I'll hold it against you. I'll go to the mayor," Lizz said in sudden excitement.

Jim went to Lizz.

"Please, Lizz, now, this is for the best. We got to try and save the rest," Jim said.

"Well, Mr. O'Neill, we'll have to take them now," the health officer said.

Bill slunk out of the room.

"Where you going, Son?" an interne asked.

"I wanna go to the toilet," Bill said.

He disappeared into the kitchen.

"Mr. O'Neill, we'll have to take throat cultures of you and Mrs. O'Neill," the health officer said.

"All right," Jim said lifelessly.

XVI

Bill ran down the back steps, forcing himself to his utmost. He climbed the fence and ran northward.

"There he goes," he heard someone yell.

He ran in tears. An interne and a policeman pursued him.

"Stop! Stop!" the policeman yelled.

Bill ran. They couldn't take him to jail in the paddy wagon. If he could only get away. He'd turn at this block. He knew a trick passageway. He didn't do nothing. In tears, he ran, forcing on his weak body.

Firm hands clasped him.

"You don't want to run away, Sonny," the policeman said, holding him firmly by the collar.

"I ain't done nothing," said Bill in sobs.

"Come, boy, we ain't gonna hurt you," the policeman said.

"I ain't done nothing. You can't take me in the paddy wagon," Bill screamed.

"Come, boy," the interne said.

Bill stood, resisting their efforts. They picked him up, and he kept screaming.

"I ain't gonna ride in no paddy wagon!"

XVII

"This boy is delirious and thinks that he's being arrested," the interne said as they carried Bill back into the house.

"Don't hurt him," Jim said, suddenly getting to his feet.

"We ain't hurtin' him. He's delirious and thinks he's being arrested," the interne said.

"I ain't done nothing. Goddamn you, I never took nothing!" Bill screamed.

Jim went to him.

"Bill!" he said gently.

"Don't touch me. I don't want no dicks taking me. I ain't done nothing," Bill yelled.

Bill screamed as he was put into a sheet. Then he lay limp. He was carried out to the wagon. Dennis was carried out in another sheet. Bob was helped out by an interne. Catherine walked out by herself, crying.

XVIII

The police wagon jolted slowly along. Bill lay on one side and Dennis on the other.

"Lemme 'lone! Mama! Papa!" Dennis screamed.

Bill was quiet, but restless. Bob and Catherine sat next to each other too awed and frightened to speak.

The police wagon jolted slowly along.

XIX

"Mother, that was a policeman. Jim asked him to call. He said that all of the children have been taken to the hospital and the baby's buried. He said that the two oldest boys are in very bad condition. They were in a delirium when they were taken," Margaret said.

"Glory be to God. Oh, Margaret, it's a terrible thing," Mrs. O'Flaherty said.

"My poor little nieces and nephews. Mother, they're all such lovely children," Margaret said.

"That poor man," Mrs. O'Flaherty said.

"Little Brother, your aunty is so glad you, at least, are saved," Margaret said to Danny, who listened.

"Ah, thank God for me grandson. Are you well, Son?"

"Yes, Mother, only my side hurts from what Doctor Geraghty gave me," Danny said.

"No sore throat?" Margaret asked.

"No," Danny said.

"Aren't you sorry your little brother is dead?" Aunt Margaret asked him.

"Yes. And is Bill all right?"

"He's gone to the hospital," said Margaret.

"Gee, if anything happens to Bill, I'll feel awful," Danny said.

"Peg, did he say about Lizz?" Mrs. O'Flaherty asked.

XX

Jim looked at the red sign tacked to his front door, and read the large black lettering:

DIPHTHERIA

They were quarantined as if they were lepers. The whole world was told by that red sign to stay away from them. He went inside to Lizz.

"Jim, if my newcomer is a boy, I want to name him Arthur," Lizz said.

"My rabbit, you mustn't worry now. You must save all your strength for what's to come," Jim said.

"Oh, Jim!"

"How do you feel, Lizz?"

"I'm all right. It's here, Jim," Lizz said, pointing to her heart.

"Please, don't cry, Lizz," Jim said.

"I got to cry. Oh, Jim, it's here that I'm hurt," she said, sobbing, again pointing to her heart.

Jim sat quietly beside her as she cried.

"Jim, I can't believe it. I keep feeling he's out in the kitchen or the yard. It was all so sudden," Lizz said.

Jim stroked her hair.

"Jim, sneak out and call my mother and tell her. And find out if my Daniel is all right," Lizz said.

"I'm not supposed to, but I will. If they want to do anything to me, let them. Let them now do all they damn please. Nobody came to us when it would have helped, and now they came damn quick to bury the little fellow," Jim said.

"Tell my mother. And see if our son, Daniel, is well or is he gone, too. And my little daughter," Lizz said.

"Lizz, now don't you worry yourself. You got to save your strength," Jim said.

Jim took Lizz in his arms and tenderly kissed her.

"I'll make your supper for you. You poor man, you had an awful day," Lizz said.

XXI

"Hello, Peg, this is Jim," Jim said in the telephone booth.

"Oh, Jim, I'm so sorry. How are your children? We're brokenhearted here," Margaret said.

"Arty's dead and buried," Jim said.

"Yes, we heard that. And the others?"

"They're all gone to the hospital. How are my son and daughter?"

"Little Margaret is gone to the hospital, Jim. We had Doctor Mike Geraghty. We called him this morning," Margaret said.

"He came?" Jim asked, shocked.

"Yes. He said he was going to try to get down to you but that he'd called the health officers and they'd be there ahead of him," Margaret said.

"How is my daughter? Was she very sick?"

"Yes, but I think she's going to be all right. She got anti-toxin here. She went this morning," Margaret said.

"How is my son?"

"Jim, I think he's all right. He's here and got antitoxin. The doctor doesn't think he's got it," Margaret said.

"Thank God!" Jim said.

"Here, Jim, he wants to talk to you," Margaret said.

"Hello, Papa!"

"Hello, Son," Jim said.

"Papa, is Bill all right?"

"He's in the hospital, but I think he'll be all right. All your brothers and sisters are in the hospital, Son," Jim said.

"Can I go see them?"

"Yes, in a couple of days. You take care of yourself and say a prayer for your mother and your brothers and sisters, Son," Jim said.

"Here, I want to speak to my son-in-law," Mrs. O'Flaherty said.

"Jim," Mrs. O'Flaherty said into the telephone.

"Hello, Mary."

"Jim, you poor man."

Jim didn't answer.

"How is me daughter?"

"She's broken up, Mary."

"Has her labor started yet?"

"No, but it ought to soon."

"Ah, Jim, you take care of the poor woman. Oh, Jim, Peg wired me son Al to send you some money."

"Thanks, Mary."

"God bless you and spare the rest of your family," Mrs. O'Flaherty said.

"Goodbye, Mary," Jim said.

He came out of the booth and walked quickly out of the drugstore.

XXII

"Eat your supper, Jim," Lizz said.

"I can't eat, Lizz," Jim said.

"You have to eat and get some nourishment in your body," Lizz said.

Jim poked at the hamburger steak on his plate.

"Thank God, our Daniel is well," Lizz said.

"Lizz, if I wasn't a poor man we'd have had Geraghty here sooner," Jim said bitterly.

Lizz began to cry. Jim tried to comfort her.

"Jim, do you notice how quiet the house is?" Lizz asked.

"Yes. Not a sound in it," Jim said.

"It's like a tomb. Last Saturday the girl was here and the children were talking. Do you remember? And we sent Arty over to give Father Corbett some frogs' legs?" Lizz said.

Jim said nothing. There was agony in his eyes.

"My poor little ones in that hospital," Lizz said.

"Golly, it's quiet," Jim said.

"And Arty out there in the ground," Lizz said.

"He's beside my mother," Jim said.

He poked at his hamburger.

XXIII

"Jim, they've come," Lizz said, worried.

"I'll have to get a doctor," Jim said.

"Not yet, Jim. It's too soon. Come, help me to bed," Lizz said.

Jim took her to the bedroom.

"Oh, God. And I have to give birth in the bed where my dead baby slept last night," Lizz sobbed.

"Lizz, you must try not to worry. You must save your strength," Jim said.

"Oh, God, be with me now in my hour," Lizz cried.

"Yes, Lizz. Now, you must try not to worry. You and I have been through tough going, and this is the toughest. But we got to go on. And, Lizz, we're going to win through it," Jim said with great feeling.

"Oh, God, be with me now!" Lizz intoned.

XXIV

Again Lizz moaned. Jim ran in to her.

"I can't stand it, Jim. Oh, God!" she cried; she clutched his hand, dug her fingernails into it, let out another moan.

She relaxed on the bed.

"Jim, get me a doctor now," Lizz said.

"I will, Lizz," Jim said.

XXV

There was a long row of occupied beds in the boys' ward. The beds were set about five feet apart against large windows, and now, in the night, the shades were drawn. There were several electric lights in the ward. The other end was glassed in. A nurse, wearing a mask over her nose and mouth, tripped through the ward. Then it was quiet.

Dennis O'Neill opened his eyes. There was fear and sadness in him. He could not remember what had just been happening to him. But it was something terrible. Things had been happening to him. And they were awful. He blinked. He saw a glowing electric light bulb to his left.

Mama's got electric lights like Mother, he told himself.

He lay back and fell into a restless sleep.

XXVI

The doctor came out of the room, carrying a perfectly formed but undersized, stillborn baby. He laid it on a table and covered it with a towel.

"I'm sorry, my man. I did all I could," he said.

Jim was speechless. He hung his head.

"It's hard, old man," the doctor said.

"My wife?" Jim asked, his lips trembling.

"Your wife's going to pull through."

"Do I have to bury this? Two in one day?"

"I'll take care of it, old man. I'll call an ambulance."

"And, Doctor, the fee?"

"Forget it."

"Doctor, are you sure she'll be all right?"

"Yes. You talk to her. Don't tell her it's dead for a day or two. She doesn't know. Say I took it away to be cared for because of the condition here. She was in a bad mental state and didn't know it was born dead," the doctor said.

"Yes, Doctor."

"I'll come again in the afternoon. And brace up now, old man. I'm sorry."

"Thank you, Doctor."

The doctor patted Jim's shoulder and went.

Jim looked at the wizened, inhuman little face of his son, born dead. He covered it again with the towel.

XXVII

Jim tiptoed into the bedroom with a lamp. He looked at Lizz. She lay relaxed in sleep, her face calm, except for the redness around her eyes, caused by so much crying. She was asleep, breathing evenly. He tiptoed out of the room. He blew out the kerosene lamp. He sat alone in the darkened house. The city was still. He saw the first gray streaks of dawn through the window.

SECTION SIX

1915

45

I

They were all gone and he was on the elevated and he'd be there soon himself. He'd had to go see Sister Marguerita and get his credits. He said goodbye to her and she had been nice to him and wished him well. She said she was glad he was going to a Catholic school. She had always been nice to him. He hoped the principal at the new school would be as nice. Anyway, he was glad they were moving. Ever since the party he had given on his birthday, nothing had gone right for him. Bridget McGinnis had told her sister, and Miss McGinnis hadn't seemed to like him ever since. He had hated going to school after that because she would ask him all of the hardest questions, and say things to him about the party that he didn't like. And Virginia Doyle wouldn't talk to him much after it, and soon the other girls weren't talking to him, either. Now, in the new neighborhood he might find a new girl. And the kids had kidded him at school more and more. Tommy Moriarty had told them that his aunt got drunk and they'd laughed at him. He was glad to be moving. Mother had gone up to the Sisters at Saint Patrick's and they had said he could start in the fourth grade now and they would pass him into the fifth grade next year so he wouldn't even have to finish the year out at Crucifixion. He was glad.

He looked out of the elevated window. The train drew into the Garfield Boulevard station. Fifty-eighth Street, the next stop, would be his. Bill would be out of the hospital next week and then they could get back to their Steel's League. Bill could send out cards to him that the hospital fumigated and he had just gotten one saying he'd be out soon and they'd play Steel's a lot because he wouldn't be able to play ball much for a while. Catherine and Bob were out, but Bill and Little Margaret and Dennis were still in. Mama and Papa had come up to see them Sunday. Mama was wearing black and she cried a lot, and talked about Arty. Papa had been nice to him. He felt funny about moving into a new neighborhood.

"Fifty-eighth Street. Change for Englewood!" the conductor called.

Danny hurried out of the train. He walked downstairs and came out of the station. He had to go right. He walked slowly along the street. It was a store street just like Fifty-first, except that there were no car tracks on it. There were the same kinds of stores. He wondered what it was going to be like in this neighborhood. He didn't know any kids, and you were always afraid when you came into something new like that. But he was glad. Because they didn't know him. They didn't know that the kids laughed at him at Crucifixion and said he was the kid whose aunt got drunk. And she hadn't been drunk since last winter. Maybe she wouldn't get drunk any more. He could start now as if it was all new. At the corner of Fifty-eighth and Prairie there were some kids around a fire plug. He walked on. He wondered where the nickel show around here was, or did they have one. He walked on. The Sox were doing good. Jake Fournier was playing outfield and hitting swell. When he and Bill played their Steel's again, he would have to make Jake Fournier a regular on his first team. Just beyond the alley he saw a nickel show. He read the name of it.

THE PALM

He paused to see what was there. Beverly Bayne. He liked her. Maybe they'd let him go tonight. He wondered where the kids played ball. And would he find a nice girl, as pretty as Virginia Doyle or Hortense Audrey or Helen Smith? He wasn't friends even with Perc any more. Perc had had a party a little while ago at Easter time and had made him have Maggie Grady as partner. And he'd gotten sore at Perc. Perc had kidded him coming home from school one day, and he told Perc he'd fight him. Perc had said he wouldn't. He'd told Perc that he'd make him fight him. And Perc had gone home and told his folks, and Perc's aunt had caught him on the street and bawled him out and called him a roughneck and asked him what did he mean by saying he'd make Percy fight. Well, he was glad to be moving, and it was all starting new. He turned the corner at Fifty-eighth and Indiana and crossed to the west side of the street. Next to the corner there was a large vacant lot. He guessed the kids around here played ball in the lot. He'd have to know them. Maybe he'd get on a team around here. He walked along. It was sunny, and grass was sprouting on the plots in front of the buildings. They were moving to a building at the other end of the block. He hoped he wouldn't have to do a lot of work while they were getting settled.

Two kids came along. He wondered should he ask them about playing ball and try to start making friends or not. They came nearer. They were both bigger and heavier than he was. One, the bigger, was a broad fellow, and the other was a little bit chubby and had dark hair.

"Hey!" he said as they were even with him.

"What do yuh want?" the chubby one said.

"Where do you guys around here play ball?" Danny asked.

"What you wanna know for?" the chubby one asked.

"I'm moving around here and I wondered where you played ball."

"What's it your business?"

"I thought maybe I could play with you."

"How do I know you're any good?"

"Well, I could play with you and you could find out."

"You're kinda fresh, aincha?"

"I was asking you a question."

"We don't like fresh guys around here," the chubby one said.

"Just a minute, Johnny," the bigger one said.

Danny watched them, afraid, wondering what they would try. Well, if they picked on him he'd have to try and fight back.

"What's your name?" the bigger one asked.

"Danny O'Neill."

"Where you come from?" the chubby one asked.

"Fifty-first Street."

"What school did you go to?" the bigger one asked.

"I went to Crucifixion but I'm startin' in at Saint Patrick's next week."

"What grade you gonna be in?" the chubby one asked.

"Fourth."

"I'm in fifth."

"He seems all right," the bigger one said.

"What you say your name was?" the chubby one asked.

"Danny O'Neill."

"Mine's Johnny O'Brien. And this is Studs Lonigan."

"Where you gonna live?" Studs Lonigan asked.

"Right down there at the end of the block," Danny said.

"I live near you. Walk along. I'll show you," Johnny O'Brien said.

Danny walked with them. They seemed all right and it was good luck and swell to make new friends on his first day in the new neighborhood. They walked past a series of two-story, gray-brick houses, and at the end of the row Johnny O'Brien pointed.

"That's where I live."

"I live over on Wabash," Studs said.

"Call for me, and I'll take you around. You seem like a nice kid," John O'Brien said.

"Sure I will. I don't think I can get out today. I guess I'll have to help with the moving."

"Well, when you can get out, call for me."

"Sure I will."

"So long," Johnny O'Brien said.

"So long, kid," Studs Lonigan said.

Danny went in the three-story brick apartment building where they were moving and rang the first-floor bell. Aunt Margaret let him in.

"Oh, Little Brother," Aunt Margaret said.

"Here's my grandson," Mrs. O'Flaherty said.

"You're going to like your new home," Aunt Margaret said.

"Hello, Sport. Get your coat off and give us a hand. The men are bringing in the stuff," Al said.

"Let him get his breath first," Mrs. O'Flaherty said.

"Al, you like it now?"

"Sure, of course. It's swell."

"And, Al, I'm not going to drink here. I'm going to make a nice home for all of you," Margaret said.

"Of course the Princess is. We're going to be happier here than we ever were," Al said.

"Al, we are."

"That's the ticket, sister," Al said, smiling.

"Well, we'll all pitch in and get our home in order. Brother, you go help the men carry things in, but only carry little things so you don't strain yourself," Margaret said.

Danny ran through the bare hallway and outside, to help carry things in from the moving van.

"Well, mother, you like it?" Al asked.

"Sure, it's all right. It's not as big as the other one but it'll do," Mrs. O'Flaherty said.

"But wait, Al, until you and Mother see how I fix it up for you," Margaret said.

"Yes, this is going to be a fine home."

"We'll get busy and start making it one right away, Al," Margaret said.

JAMES T. FARRELL, author of a prodigious volume of work, dedicated his career to depicting the Irish-American, urban world in which he had grown up. Best known for his Studs Lonigan trilogy, Farrell also wrote four large fiction cycles, several volumes of critical writings, and approximately 250 short stories.

CHARLES FANNING is a professor of English and history and director of the Center for Irish Studies at Southern Illinois University in Carbondale. Fanning is the author or editor of several books and articles, including Farrell's *Chicago Stories*.

The text for this edition of *No Star Is Lost*
was taken from the 1938 first edition from
the Vanguard Press.

The University of Illinois Press
is a founding member of the
Association of American University Presses.

Composed in 10/13 Janson Text
with Hoefler Text display
by Jim Proefrock
at the University of Illinois Press
Designed by Dennis Roberts
Manufactured by Sheridan Books, Inc.

University of Illinois Press
1325 South Oak Street
Champaign, IL 61820-6903
www.press.uillinois.edu